# THE
# DA VINCI
# CODE

# Also by Dan Brown
## available from Random House Large Print

Angels and Demons

# THE
# DA VINCI
# CODE  A Novel

## DAN
## BROWN

RANDOM HOUSE
LARGE PRINT

All rights reserved.
Published in the United States of America
by Random House Large Print in
association with Doubleday, New York.
Distributed by Random House, Inc., New York.

**The Library of Congress has established a Cataloging-in-Publication record for this title.**

ISBN-13: 978-0-7393-2674-9
ISBN-10: 0-7393-2674-0

www.randomlargeprint.com

10  9  8  7  6  5  4  3

This Large Print edition published in accord with the standards of the N.A.V.H.

FOR BLYTHE . . . AGAIN.
MORE THAN EVER.

# Acknowledgments

First and foremost, to my friend and editor, Jason Kaufman, for working so hard on this project and for truly understanding what this book is all about. And to the incomparable Heide Lange—tireless champion of *The Da Vinci Code,* agent extraordinaire, and trusted friend.

I cannot fully express my gratitude to the exceptional team at Doubleday, for their generosity, faith, and superb guidance. Thank you especially to Bill Thomas and Steve Rubin, who believed in this book from the start. My thanks also to the initial core of early in-house supporters, headed by Michael Palgon, Suzanne Herz, Janelle Moburg, Jackie Everly, and Adrienne Sparks, as well as to the talented people of Doubleday's sales force.

For their generous assistance in the research of the book, I would like to acknowledge the Louvre Museum, the French Ministry of Culture, Project Gutenberg, Bibliothèque Nationale, the Gnostic Society Library, the Department of Paintings Study and Documentation Service at the Louvre, Catholic World News, Royal Observatory Greenwich, London Record Society, the Muniment Collection at Westminster Abbey,

John Pike and the Federation of American Scientists, and the five members of Opus Dei (three active, two former) who recounted their stories, both positive and negative, regarding their experiences inside Opus Dei.

My gratitude also to Water Street Bookstore for tracking down so many of my research books, my father Richard Brown—mathematics teacher and author—for his assistance with the Divine Proportion and the Fibonacci Sequence, Stan Planton, Sylvie Baudeloque, Peter McGuigan, Francis McInerney, Margie Wachtel, Andre Vernet, Ken Kelleher at Anchorball Web Media, Cara Sottak, Karyn Popham, Esther Sung, Miriam Abramowitz, William Tunstall-Pedoe, and Griffin Wooden Brown.

And finally, in a novel drawing so heavily on the sacred feminine, I would be remiss if I did not mention the two extraordinary women who have touched my life. First, my mother, Connie Brown—fellow scribe, nurturer, musician, and role model. And my wife, Blythe—art historian, painter, front-line editor, and without a doubt the most astonishingly talented woman I have ever known.

# THE
# DA VINCI
# CODE

# FACT:

The Priory of Sion—
a European secret society founded in 1099—
is a real organization.
In 1975 Paris's Bibliothèque Nationale
discovered parchments known as *Les Dossiers
Secrets,* identifying numerous members of the
Priory of Sion, including Sir Isaac Newton,
Botticelli, Victor Hugo, and Leonardo da Vinci.

The Vatican prelature known as Opus Dei is a
deeply devout Catholic sect that has been the
topic of recent controversy due to reports of
brainwashing, coercion, and a dangerous
practice known as "corporal mortification."
Opus Dei has just completed construction of a
$47 million World Headquarters at 243
Lexington Avenue in New York City.

All descriptions of artwork, architecture,
documents, and secret rituals in this novel are
accurate.

# Prologue

Renowned curator Jacques Saunière staggered through the vaulted archway of the museum's Grand Gallery. He lunged for the nearest painting he could see, a Caravaggio. Grabbing the gilded frame, the seventy-six-year-old man heaved the masterpiece toward himself until it tore from the wall and Saunière collapsed backward in a heap beneath the canvas.

As he had anticipated, a thundering iron gate fell nearby, barricading the entrance to the suite. The parquet floor shook. Far off, an alarm began to ring.

The curator lay a moment, gasping for breath, taking stock. *I am still alive.* He crawled out from under the canvas and scanned the cavernous space for someplace to hide.

A voice spoke, chillingly close. "Do not move."

On his hands and knees, the curator froze, turning his head slowly.

Only fifteen feet away, outside the sealed gate,

the mountainous silhouette of his attacker stared through the iron bars. He was broad and tall, with ghost-pale skin and thinning white hair. His irises were pink with dark red pupils. The albino drew a pistol from his coat and aimed the barrel through the bars, directly at the curator. "You should not have run." His accent was not easy to place. "Now tell me where it is."

"I told you already," the curator stammered, kneeling defenseless on the floor of the gallery. "I have no idea what you are talking about!"

"You are lying." The man stared at him, perfectly immobile except for the glint in his ghostly eyes. "You and your brethren possess something that is not yours."

The curator felt a surge of adrenaline. *How could he possibly know this?*

"Tonight the rightful guardians will be restored. Tell me where it is hidden, and you will live." The man leveled his gun at the curator's head. "Is it a secret you will die for?"

Saunière could not breathe.

The man tilted his head, peering down the barrel of his gun.

Saunière held up his hands in defense. "Wait," he said slowly. "I will tell you what you need to know." The curator spoke his next words carefully. The lie he told was one he had rehearsed many times . . . each time praying he would never have to use it.

When the curator had finished speaking, his assailant smiled smugly. "Yes. This is exactly what the others told me."

Saunière recoiled. *The others?*

"I found them, too," the huge man taunted. "All three of them. They confirmed what you have just said."

*It cannot be!* The curator's true identity, along with the identities of his three *sénéchaux,* was almost as sacred as the ancient secret they protected. Saunière now realized his *sénéchaux,* following strict procedure, had told the same lie before their own deaths. It was part of the protocol.

The attacker aimed his gun again. "When you are gone, I will be the only one who knows the truth."

*The truth.* In an instant, the curator grasped the true horror of the situation. *If I die, the truth will be lost forever.* Instinctively, he tried to scramble for cover.

The gun roared, and the curator felt a searing heat as the bullet lodged in his stomach. He fell forward . . . struggling against the pain. Slowly, Saunière rolled over and stared back through the bars at his attacker.

The man was now taking dead aim at Saunière's head.

Saunière closed his eyes, his thoughts a swirling tempest of fear and regret.

The click of an empty chamber echoed through the corridor.

The curator's eyes flew open.

The man glanced down at his weapon, looking almost amused. He reached for a second clip, but then seemed to reconsider, smirking calmly at Saunière's gut. "My work here is done."

The curator looked down and saw the bullet hole in his white linen shirt. It was framed by a small circle of blood a few inches below his breastbone. *My stomach.* Almost cruelly, the bullet had missed his heart. As a veteran of *la Guerre d'Algérie,* the curator had witnessed this horribly drawn-out death before. For fifteen minutes, he would survive as his stomach acids seeped into his chest cavity, slowly poisoning him from within.

"Pain is good, monsieur," the man said.

Then he was gone.

Alone now, Jacques Saunière turned his gaze again to the iron gate. He was trapped, and the doors could not be reopened for at least twenty minutes. By the time anyone got to him, he would be dead. Even so, the fear that now gripped him was a fear far greater than that of his own death.

*I must pass on the secret.*

Staggering to his feet, he pictured his three murdered brethren. He thought of the genera-tions who had come before them . . . of the mis-sion with which they had all been entrusted.

*An unbroken chain of knowledge.*

Suddenly, now, despite all the precautions . . . despite all the fail-safes . . . Jacques Saunière was the only remaining link, the sole guardian of one of the most powerful secrets ever kept.

Shivering, he pulled himself to his feet.

*I must find some way. . . .*

He was trapped inside the Grand Gallery, and there existed only one person on earth to whom he could pass the torch. Saunière gazed up at the walls of his opulent prison. A collection of the world's most famous paintings seemed to smile down on him like old friends.

Wincing in pain, he summoned all of his faculties and strength. The desperate task before him, he knew, would require every remaining second of his life.

# CHAPTER 1

**Robert Langdon** awoke slowly.

A telephone was ringing in the darkness—a tinny, unfamiliar ring. He fumbled for the bedside lamp and turned it on. Squinting at his surroundings he saw a plush Renaissance bedroom with Louis XVI furniture, hand-frescoed walls, and a colossal mahogany four-poster bed.

*Where the hell am I?*

The jacquard bathrobe hanging on his bedpost bore the monogram: HOTEL RITZ PARIS.

Slowly, the fog began to lift.

Langdon picked up the receiver. "Hello?"

"Monsieur Langdon?" a man's voice said. "I hope I have not awoken you?"

Dazed, Langdon looked at the bedside clock. It was 12:32 A.M. He had been asleep only an hour, but he felt like the dead.

"This is the concierge, monsieur. I apologize for this intrusion, but you have a visitor. He insists it is urgent."

Langdon still felt fuzzy. *A visitor?* His eyes focused now on a crumpled flyer on his bedside table.

THE AMERICAN UNIVERSITY OF PARIS
*proudly presents*
AN EVENING WITH ROBERT LANGDON
PROFESSOR OF RELIGIOUS SYMBOLOGY,
HARVARD UNIVERSITY

Langdon groaned. Tonight's lecture—a slide show about pagan symbolism hidden in the stones of Chartres Cathedral—had probably ruffled some conservative feathers in the audience. Most likely, some religious scholar had trailed him home to pick a fight.

"I'm sorry," Langdon said, "but I'm very tired and—"

"*Mais, monsieur,*" the concierge pressed, lowering his voice to an urgent whisper. "Your guest is an important man."

Langdon had little doubt. His books on religious paintings and cult symbology had made him a reluctant celebrity in the art world, and last year Langdon's visibility had increased a hundredfold after his involvement in a widely publicized incident at the Vatican. Since then, the stream of self-important historians and art buffs arriving at his door had seemed never-ending.

"If you would be so kind," Langdon said, doing his best to remain polite, "could you take the man's name and number, and tell him I'll try to call him before I leave Paris on Tuesday? Thank you." He hung up before the concierge could protest.

Sitting up now, Langdon frowned at his bedside *Guest Relations Handbook,* whose cover boasted: SLEEP LIKE A BABY IN THE CITY OF LIGHTS. SLUMBER AT THE PARIS RITZ. He turned and gazed tiredly into the full-length mirror across the room. The man staring back at him was a stranger—tousled and weary.

*You need a vacation, Robert.*

The past year had taken a heavy toll on him, but he didn't appreciate seeing proof in the mirror. His usually sharp blue eyes looked hazy and drawn tonight. A dark stubble was shrouding his strong jaw and dimpled chin. Around his temples, the gray highlights were advancing, making their way deeper into his thicket of coarse black hair. Although his female colleagues insisted the gray only accentuated his bookish appeal, Langdon knew better.

*If* Boston Magazine *could see me now.*

Last month, much to Langdon's embarrassment, *Boston Magazine* had listed him as one of that city's top ten most intriguing people—a dubious honor that made him the brunt of endless ribbing by his Harvard colleagues. Tonight, three thousand miles from home, the accolade had resurfaced to haunt him at the lecture he had given.

"Ladies and gentlemen . . ." the hostess had announced to a full house at the American University of Paris's Pavillon Dauphine, "Our guest tonight needs no introduction. He is the author of numerous books: *The Symbology of Secret Sects, The Art of the Illuminati, The Lost Language of Ideograms,* and when I say he wrote the book on *Religious Iconology,* I mean that quite literally. Many of you use his textbooks in class."

The students in the crowd nodded enthusiastically.

"I had planned to introduce him tonight by sharing his impressive curriculum vitae. However . . ." She glanced playfully at Langdon, who was seated onstage. "An audience member has just handed me a far more, shall we say . . . *intriguing* introduction."

She held up a copy of *Boston Magazine.*

Langdon cringed. *Where the hell did she get that?*

The hostess began reading choice excerpts from the inane article, and Langdon felt himself sinking lower and lower in his chair. Thirty seconds later, the crowd was grinning, and the woman showed no signs of letting up. "And Mr. Langdon's refusal to speak publicly about his unusual role in last year's Vatican conclave certainly wins him points on our intrigue-o-meter." The hostess goaded the crowd. "Would you like to hear more?"

The crowd applauded.

*Somebody stop her,* Langdon pleaded as she dove into the article again.

"Although Professor Langdon might not be considered hunk-handsome like some of our younger awardees, this forty-something academic has more than his share of scholarly allure. His captivating presence is punctuated by an unusually low, baritone speaking voice, which his female students describe as 'chocolate for the ears.' "

The hall erupted in laughter.

Langdon forced an awkward smile. He knew what came next—some ridiculous line about "Harrison Ford in Harris tweed"—and because this evening he had figured it was finally safe again to wear his Harris tweed and Burberry turtleneck, he decided to take action.

"Thank you, Monique," Langdon said, standing prematurely and edging her away from the podium. "*Boston Magazine* clearly has a gift for fiction." He turned to the audience with an embarrassed sigh. "And if I find which one of you provided that article, I'll have the consulate deport you."

The crowd laughed.

"Well, folks, as you all know, I'm here tonight to talk about the power of symbols . . ."

The ringing of Langdon's hotel phone once again broke the silence.

Groaning in disbelief, he picked up. "Yes?"

As expected, it was the concierge. "Mr. Langdon, again my apologies. I am calling to inform you that your guest is now en route to your room. I thought I should alert you."

Langdon was wide awake now. "You sent someone to my *room*?"

"I apologize, monsieur, but a man like this . . . I cannot presume the authority to stop him."

"Who exactly *is* he?"

But the concierge was gone.

Almost immediately, a heavy fist pounded on Langdon's door.

Uncertain, Langdon slid off the bed, feeling his toes sink deep into the savonniere carpet. He donned the hotel bathrobe and moved toward the door. "Who is it?"

"Mr. Langdon? I need to speak with you." The man's English was accented—a sharp, authoritative bark. "My name is Lieutenant Jérome Collet. Direction Centrale Police Judiciaire."

Langdon paused. *The Judicial Police?* The DCPJ was the rough equivalent of the U.S. FBI.

Leaving the security chain in place, Langdon opened the door a few inches. The face staring back at him was thin and washed out. The man was exceptionally lean, dressed in an official-looking blue uniform.

"May I come in?" the agent asked.

Langdon hesitated, feeling uncertain as the

stranger's sallow eyes studied him. "What is this all about?"

"My *capitaine* requires your expertise in a private matter."

"Now?" Langdon managed. "It's after midnight."

"Am I correct that you were scheduled to meet with the curator of the Louvre this evening?"

Langdon felt a sudden surge of uneasiness. He and the revered curator Jacques Saunière had been slated to meet for drinks after Langdon's lecture tonight, but Saunière had never shown up. "Yes. How did you know that?"

"We found your name in his daily planner."

"I trust nothing is wrong?"

The agent gave a dire sigh and slid a Polaroid snapshot through the narrow opening in the door.

When Langdon saw the photo, his entire body went rigid.

"This photo was taken less than an hour ago. Inside the Louvre."

As Langdon stared at the bizarre image, his initial revulsion and shock gave way to a sudden upwelling of anger. "Who would do this!"

"We had hoped that you might help us answer that very question, considering your knowledge in symbology and your plans to meet with him."

Langdon stared at the picture, his horror now

laced with fear. The image was gruesome and profoundly strange, bringing with it an unsettling sense of déjà vu. A little over a year ago, Langdon had received a photograph of a corpse and a similar request for help. Twenty-four hours later, he had almost lost his life inside Vatican City. This photo was entirely different, and yet something about the scenario felt disquietingly familiar.

The agent checked his watch. "My *capitaine* is waiting, sir."

Langdon barely heard him. His eyes were still riveted on the picture. "This symbol here, and the way his body is so oddly . . ."

"Positioned?" the agent offered.

Langdon nodded, feeling a chill as he looked up. "I can't imagine who would do this to someone."

The agent looked grim. "You don't understand, Mr. Langdon. What you see in this photograph . . ." He paused. "Monsieur Saunière did that to himself."

# CHAPTER 2

**One mile** away, the hulking albino named Silas limped through the front gate of the luxurious brownstone residence on Rue La Bruyère. The spiked *cilice* belt that he wore around his thigh cut into his flesh, and yet his soul sang with satisfaction of service to the Lord.

*Pain is good.*

His red eyes scanned the lobby as he entered the residence. Empty. He climbed the stairs quietly, not wanting to awaken any of his fellow numeraries. His bedroom door was open; locks were forbidden here. He entered, closing the door behind him.

The room was spartan—hardwood floors, a pine dresser, a canvas mat in the corner that served as his bed. He was a visitor here this week, and yet for many years he had been blessed with a similar sanctuary in New York City.

*The Lord has provided me shelter and purpose in my life.*

Tonight, at last, Silas felt he had begun to repay his debt. Hurrying to the dresser, he found the cell phone hidden in his bottom drawer and placed a call.

"Yes?" a male voice answered.

"Teacher, I have returned."

"Speak," the voice commanded, sounding pleased to hear from him.

"All four are gone. The three *sénéchaux* . . . and the *Grand Master* himself."

There was a momentary pause, as if for prayer. "Then I assume you have the information?"

"All four concurred. Independently."

"And you believed them?"

"Their agreement was too great for coincidence."

An excited breath. "Excellent. I had feared the brotherhood's reputation for secrecy might prevail."

"The prospect of death is strong motivation."

"So, my pupil, tell me what I must know."

Silas knew the information he had gleaned from his victims would come as a shock. "Teacher, all four confirmed the existence of the *clef de voûte* . . . the legendary *keystone*."

He heard a quick intake of breath over the phone and could feel the Teacher's excitement. "The *keystone*. Exactly as we suspected."

According to lore, the brotherhood had created a map of stone—a *clef de voûte* . . . or *keystone*—an engraved tablet that revealed the final resting place of the brotherhood's greatest secret . . . information so powerful that its protection was the reason for the brotherhood's very existence.

"When we possess the keystone," the Teacher said, "we will be only one step away."

"We are closer than you think. The keystone is here in Paris."

"Paris? Incredible. It is almost too easy."

Silas relayed the earlier events of the evening . . . how all four of his victims, moments before death, had desperately tried to buy back their godless lives by telling their secret. Each had told Silas the exact same thing—that the keystone was ingeniously hidden at a precise location inside one of Paris's ancient churches—the Eglise de Saint-Sulpice.

"Inside a house of the Lord," the Teacher exclaimed. "How they mock us!"

"As they have for centuries."

The Teacher fell silent, as if letting the triumph of this moment settle over him. Finally, he spoke. "You have done a great service to God. We have waited centuries for this. You must retrieve the stone for me. Immediately. Tonight. You understand the stakes."

Silas knew the stakes were incalculable, and yet what the Teacher was now commanding seemed impossible. "But the church, it is a fortress. Especially at night. How will I enter?"

With the confident tone of a man of enormous influence, the Teacher explained what was to be done.

———

When Silas hung up the phone, his skin tingled with anticipation.

*One hour,* he told himself, grateful that the Teacher had given him time to carry out the necessary penance before entering a house of God. *I must purge my soul of today's sins.* The sins committed today had been holy in purpose. Acts of war against the enemies of God had been committed for centuries. Forgiveness was assured.

Even so, Silas knew, absolution required sacrifice.

Pulling his shades, he stripped naked and knelt in the center of his room. Looking down, he examined the spiked *cilice* belt clamped around his thigh. All true followers of The Way wore this device—a leather strap, studded with sharp metal barbs that cut into the flesh as a perpetual reminder of Christ's suffering. The pain caused by the device also helped counteract the desires of the flesh.

Although Silas already had worn his *cilice* today longer than the requisite two hours, he knew today was no ordinary day. Grasping the buckle, he cinched it one notch tighter, wincing as the barbs dug deeper into his flesh. Exhaling slowly, he savored the cleansing ritual of his pain.

*Pain is good,* Silas whispered, repeating the sacred mantra of Father Josemaría Escrivá—the Teacher of all Teachers. Although Escrivá had died in 1975, his wisdom lived on, his words still whispered by thousands of faithful servants around the globe as they knelt on the floor and performed the sacred practice known as "corporal mortification."

Silas turned his attention now to a heavy knotted rope coiled neatly on the floor beside him. *The Discipline.* The knots were caked with dried blood. Eager for the purifying effects of his own agony, Silas said a quick prayer. Then, gripping one end of the rope, he closed his eyes and swung it hard over his shoulder, feeling the knots slap against his back. He whipped it over his shoulder again, slashing at his flesh. Again and again, he lashed.

*Castigo corpus meum.*

Finally, he felt the blood begin to flow.

# CHAPTER 3

**The crisp** April air whipped through the open window of the Citroën ZX as it skimmed south past the Opera House and crossed Place Vendôme. In the passenger seat, Robert Langdon felt the city tear past him as he tried to clear his thoughts. His quick shower and shave had left him looking reasonably presentable but had done little to ease his anxiety. The frightening image of the curator's body remained locked in his mind.

*Jacques Saunière is dead.*

Langdon could not help but feel a deep sense of loss at the curator's death. Despite Saunière's reputation for being reclusive, his recognition for dedication to the arts made him an easy man to revere. His books on the secret codes hidden in the paintings of Poussin and Teniers were some of Langdon's favorite classroom texts. Tonight's meeting had been one Langdon was very much looking forward to, and he was disappointed when the curator had not shown.

Again the image of the curator's body flashed in his mind. *Jacques Saunière did that to himself?* Langdon turned and looked out the window, forcing the picture from his mind.

Outside, the city was just now winding down—street vendors wheeling carts of candied *amandes,* waiters carrying bags of garbage to the curb, a pair of late night lovers cuddling to stay warm in a breeze scented with jasmine blossom. The Citroën navigated the chaos with authority, its dissonant two-tone siren parting the traffic like a knife.

"*Le capitaine* was pleased to discover you were still in Paris tonight," the agent said, speaking for the first time since they'd left the hotel. "A fortunate coincidence."

Langdon was feeling anything but fortunate, and coincidence was a concept he did not entirely trust. As someone who had spent his life exploring the hidden interconnectivity of disparate emblems and ideologies, Langdon viewed the world as a web of profoundly intertwined histories and events. *The connections may be invisible,* he often preached to his symbology classes at Harvard, *but they are always there, buried just beneath the surface.*

"I assume," Langdon said, "that the American University of Paris told you where I was staying?"

The driver shook his head. "Interpol."

*Interpol,* Langdon thought. *Of course.* He had forgotten that the seemingly innocuous request of all European hotels to see a passport at check-in was more than a quaint formality—it was the law. On any given night, all across Europe, Interpol officials could pinpoint exactly who was sleeping where. Finding Langdon at the Ritz had probably taken all of five seconds.

As the Citroën accelerated southward across the city, the illuminated profile of the Eiffel Tower appeared, shooting skyward in the distance to the right. Seeing it, Langdon thought of Vittoria, re- calling their playful promise a year ago that every six months they would meet again at a different romantic spot on the globe. The Eiffel Tower, Langdon suspected, would have made their list. Sadly, he last kissed Vittoria in a noisy airport in Rome more than a year ago.

"Did you mount her?" the agent asked, looking over.

Langdon glanced up, certain he had misunder- stood. "I beg your pardon?"

"She is lovely, no?" The agent motioned through the windshield toward the Eiffel Tower. "Have you mounted her?"

Langdon rolled his eyes. "No, I haven't climbed the tower."

"She is the symbol of France. I think she is perfect."

Langdon nodded absently. Symbologists often remarked that France—a country renowned for machismo, womanizing, and diminutive insecure leaders like Napoleon and Pepin the Short— could not have chosen a more apt national em- blem than a thousand-foot phallus.

When they reached the intersection at Rue de Rivoli, the traffic light was red, but the Citroën didn't slow. The agent gunned the sedan across the junction and sped onto a wooded section of Rue Castiglione, which served as the northern entrance to the famed Tuileries Gardens—Paris's own version of Central Park. Most tourists mistranslated Jardins des Tuileries as relating to the thousands of tulips that bloomed here, but *Tuileries* was actually a literal reference to something far less romantic. This park had once been an enormous, polluted excavation pit from which Parisian contractors mined clay to manufacture the city's famous red roofing tiles—or *tuiles.*

As they entered the deserted park, the agent reached under the dash and turned off the blaring siren. Langdon exhaled, savoring the sudden quiet. Outside the car, the pale wash of halogen headlights skimmed over the crushed gravel parkway, the rugged whir of the tires intoning a hypnotic rhythm. Langdon had always considered the Tuileries to be sacred ground. These were the gardens in which Claude Monet had experimented with form and color, and literally inspired the birth of the Impressionist movement. Tonight, however, this place held a strange aura of foreboding.

The Citroën swerved left now, angling west down the park's central boulevard. Curling around a circular pond, the driver cut across a desolate avenue out into a wide quadrangle beyond. Langdon could now see the end of the Tuileries Gardens, marked by a giant stone archway.

Arc du Carrousel.

Despite the orgiastic rituals once held at the Arc du Carrousel, art aficionados revered this place for another reason entirely. From the esplanade at the end of the Tuileries, four of the finest art museums in the world could be seen . . . one at each point of the compass.

Out the right-hand window, south across the Seine and Quai Voltaire, Langdon could see the dramatically lit facade of the old train station—now the esteemed Musée d'Orsay. Glancing left, he could make out the top of the ultramodern Pompidou Center, which housed the Museum of Modern Art. Behind him to the west, Langdon knew the ancient obelisk of Ramses rose above the trees, marking the Musée du Jeu de Paume.

But it was straight ahead, to the east, through the archway, that Langdon could now see the monolithic Renaissance palace that had become the most famous art museum in the world.

Musée du Louvre.

Langdon felt a familiar tinge of wonder as his eyes made a futile attempt to absorb the entire mass of the edifice. Across a staggeringly expansive plaza, the imposing facade of the Louvre rose like a citadel against the Paris sky. Shaped like an enormous horseshoe, the Louvre was the longest building in Europe, stretching farther than three Eiffel Towers laid end to end. Not even the million square feet of open plaza between the museum wings could challenge the majesty of the facade's breadth. Langdon had once walked the Louvre's entire perimeter, an astonishing three-mile journey.

Despite the estimated five days it would take a visitor to properly appreciate the 65,300 pieces of art in this building, most tourists chose an abbreviated experience Langdon referred to as "Louvre Lite"—a full sprint through the museum to see the three most famous objects: the *Mona Lisa, Venus de Milo,* and *Winged Victory.* Art Buchwald had once boasted he'd seen all three masterpieces in five minutes and fifty-six seconds.

The driver pulled out a handheld walkie-talkie and spoke in rapid-fire French. *"Monsieur Langdon est arrivé. Deux minutes."*

An indecipherable confirmation came crackling back.

The agent stowed the device, turning now to Langdon. "You will meet the *capitaine* at the main entrance."

The driver ignored the signs prohibiting auto traffic on the plaza, revved the engine, and gunned the Citroën up over the curb. The Louvre's main entrance was visible now, rising boldly in the distance, encircled by seven triangular pools from which spouted illuminated fountains.

*La Pyramide.*

The new entrance to the Paris Louvre had become almost as famous as the museum itself. The controversial, neomodern glass pyramid designed by Chinese-born American architect I. M. Pei still evoked scorn from traditionalists who felt it destroyed the dignity of the Renaissance courtyard. Goethe had described architecture as frozen music, and Pei's critics described this pyramid as fingernails on a chalkboard. Progressive admirers, though, hailed Pei's seventy-one-foot-tall transparent pyramid as a dazzling synergy of ancient structure and modern method—a symbolic link between the old and new—helping usher the Louvre into the next millennium.

"Do you like our pyramid?" the agent asked.

Langdon frowned. The French, it seemed, loved to ask Americans this. It was a loaded question, of course. Admitting you liked the pyramid made you a tasteless American, and expressing dislike was an insult to the French.

"Mitterrand was a bold man," Langdon replied, splitting the difference. The late French president who had commissioned the pyramid was said to have suffered from a "Pharaoh complex." Single-handedly responsible for filling Paris with Egyptian obelisks, art, and artifacts, François

Mitterrand had an affinity for Egyptian culture that was so all-consuming that the French still referred to him as the Sphinx.

"What is the captain's name?" Langdon asked, changing topics.

"Bezu Fache," the driver said, approaching the pyramid's main entrance. "We call him *le Taureau*."

Langdon glanced over at him, wondering if every Frenchman had a mysterious animal epithet. "You call your captain *the Bull?*"

The man arched his eyebrows. "Your French is better than you admit, Monsieur Langdon."

*My French stinks,* Langdon thought, *but my zodiac iconography is pretty good.* Taurus was always the bull. Astrology was a symbolic constant all over the world.

The agent pulled the car to a stop and pointed between two fountains to a large door in the side of the pyramid. "There is the entrance. Good luck, monsieur."

"You're not coming?"

"My orders are to leave you here. I have other business to attend to."

Langdon heaved a sigh and climbed out. *It's your circus.*

The agent revved his engine and sped off.

As Langdon stood alone and watched the departing taillights, he realized he could easily reconsider, exit the courtyard, grab a taxi, and head home to bed. Something told him it was probably a lousy idea.

As he moved toward the mist of the fountains, Langdon had the uneasy sense he was crossing an imaginary threshold into another world. The dreamlike quality of the evening was settling around him again. Twenty minutes ago he had been asleep in his hotel room. Now he was standing in front of a transparent pyramid built by the Sphinx, waiting for a policeman they called the Bull.

*I'm trapped in a Salvador Dalí painting,* he thought.

Langdon strode to the main entrance—an enormous revolving door. The foyer beyond was dimly lit and deserted.

*Do I knock?*

Langdon wondered if any of Harvard's revered Egyptologists had ever knocked on the front door of a pyramid and expected an answer. He raised his hand to bang on the glass, but out of the darkness below, a figure appeared, striding up the curving staircase. The man was stocky and dark, almost Neanderthal, dressed in a dark double-breasted suit that strained to cover his wide shoulders. He advanced with unmistakable authority on squat, powerful legs. He was speaking on his cell phone but finished the call as he arrived. He motioned for Langdon to enter.

"I am Bezu Fache," he announced as Langdon pushed through the revolving door. "Captain of the Central Directorate Judicial Police." His tone was fitting—a guttural rumble . . . like a gathering storm.

Langdon held out his hand to shake. "Robert Langdon."

Fache's enormous palm wrapped around Langdon's with crushing force.

"I saw the photo," Langdon said. "Your agent said Jacques Saunière *himself* did—"

"Mr. Langdon," Fache's ebony eyes locked on. "What you see in the photo is only the beginning of what Saunière did."

# CHAPTER 4

**Captain Bezu** Fache carried himself like an angry ox, with his wide shoulders thrown back and his chin tucked hard into his chest. His dark hair was slicked back with oil, accentuating an arrow-like widow's peak that divided his jutting brow and preceded him like the prow of a battleship. As he advanced, his dark eyes seemed to scorch the earth before him, radiating a fiery clarity that forecast his reputation for unblinking severity in all matters.

Langdon followed the captain down the famous marble staircase into the sunken atrium beneath the glass pyramid. As they descended, they passed between two armed Judicial Police guards with machine guns. The message was clear: Nobody goes in or out tonight without the blessing of Captain Fache.

Descending below ground level, Langdon fought a rising trepidation. Fache's presence was anything but welcoming, and the Louvre itself had an almost sepulchral aura at this hour. The staircase, like the aisle of a dark movie theater, was illuminated by subtle tread-lighting embedded in each step. Langdon could hear his own footsteps reverberating off the glass overhead. As he glanced up, he could see the faint illuminated wisps of mist from the fountains fading away outside the transparent roof.

"Do you approve?" Fache asked, nodding upward with his broad chin.

Langdon sighed, too tired to play games. "Yes, your pyramid is magnificent."

Fache grunted. "A scar on the face of Paris."

*Strike one.* Langdon sensed his host was a hard man to please. He wondered if Fache had any idea that this pyramid, at President Mitterrand's explicit demand, had been constructed of exactly 666 panes of glass—a bizarre request that had always been a hot topic among conspiracy buffs who claimed 666 was the number of Satan.

Langdon decided not to bring it up.

As they dropped farther into the subterranean foyer, the yawning space slowly emerged from the shadows. Built fifty-seven feet beneath ground level, the Louvre's newly constructed 70,000-square-foot lobby spread out like an endless grotto. Constructed in warm ocher marble to be compatible with the honey-colored stone of the Louvre facade above, the subterranean hall was usually vibrant with sunlight and tourists. Tonight, however, the lobby was barren and dark, giving the entire space a cold and crypt-like atmosphere.

"And the museum's regular security staff?" Langdon asked.

*"En quarantaine,"* Fache replied, sounding as if Langdon were questioning the integrity of Fache's team. "Obviously, someone gained entry tonight who should not have. All Louvre night wardens are in the Sully Wing being questioned. My own agents have taken over museum security for the evening."

Langdon nodded, moving quickly to keep pace with Fache.

"How well did you know Jacques Saunière?" the captain asked.

"Actually, not at all. We'd never met."

Fache looked surprised. "Your first meeting was to be tonight?"

"Yes. We'd planned to meet at the American University reception following my lecture, but he never showed up."

Fache scribbled some notes in a little book. As they walked, Langdon caught a glimpse of the Louvre's lesser-known pyramid—*La Pyramide Inversée*—a huge inverted skylight that hung from the ceiling like a stalactite in an adjoining section of the entresol. Fache guided Langdon up a short set of stairs to the mouth of an arched tunnel, over which a sign read: DENON. The Denon Wing was the most famous of the Louvre's three main sections.

"Who requested tonight's meeting?" Fache asked suddenly. "You or he?"

The question seemed odd. "Mr. Saunière did," Langdon replied as they entered the tunnel. "His secretary contacted me a few weeks ago via e-mail. She said the curator had heard I would be lecturing in Paris this month and wanted to discuss something with me while I was here."

"Discuss what?"

"I don't know. Art, I imagine. We share similar interests."

Fache looked skeptical. "You have *no* idea what your meeting was about?"

Langdon did not. He'd been curious at the time but had not felt comfortable demanding specifics. The venerated Jacques Saunière had a renowned penchant for privacy and granted very few meetings; Langdon was grateful simply for the opportunity to meet him.

"Mr. Langdon, can you at least *guess* what our murder victim might have wanted to discuss with you on the night he was killed? It might be helpful."

The pointedness of the question made Langdon uncomfortable. "I really can't imagine. I didn't ask. I felt honored to have been contacted at all. I'm an admirer of Mr. Saunière's work. I use his texts often in my classes."

Fache made note of that fact in his book.

The two men were now halfway up the Denon Wing's entry tunnel, and Langdon could see the twin ascending escalators at the far end, both motionless.

"So you shared interests with him?" Fache asked.

"Yes. In fact, I've spent much of the last year writing the draft for a book that deals with Mr. Saunière's primary area of expertise. I was looking forward to picking his brain."

Fache glanced up. "Pardon?"

The idiom apparently didn't translate. "I was looking forward to learning his thoughts on the topic."

"I see. And what is the topic?"

Langdon hesitated, uncertain exactly how to put it. "Essentially, the manuscript is about the iconography of goddess worship—the concept of female sanctity and the art and symbols associated with it."

Fache ran a meaty hand across his hair. "And Saunière was knowledgeable about this?"

"Nobody more so."

"I see."

Langdon sensed Fache did not see at all. Jacques Saunière was considered the premiere goddess iconographer on earth. Not only did Saunière have a personal passion for relics relating to fertility, goddess cults, Wicca, and the sacred feminine, but during his twenty-year tenure as curator, Saunière had helped the Louvre amass the largest collection of goddess art on earth—labrys axes from the priestesses' oldest Greek shrine in Delphi, gold caducei wands, hundreds of Tjet ankhs resembling small standing angels, sistrum rattles used in ancient Egypt to dispel evil spirits, and an astonishing array of statues depicting Horus being nursed by the goddess Isis.

"Perhaps Jacques Saunière knew of your manuscript?" Fache offered. "And he called the meeting to offer his help on your book."

Langdon shook his head. "Actually, nobody yet knows about my manuscript. It's still in draft form, and I haven't shown it to anyone except my editor."

Fache fell silent.

Langdon did not add the *reason* he hadn't yet shown the manuscript to anyone else. The three-hundred-page draft—tentatively titled *Symbols of the Lost Sacred Feminine*—proposed some very unconventional interpretations of established religious iconography which would certainly be controversial.

Now, as Langdon approached the stationary escalators, he paused, realizing Fache was no longer beside him. Turning, Langdon saw Fache standing several yards back at a service elevator.

"We'll take the elevator," Fache said as the lift doors opened. "As I'm sure you're aware, the gallery is quite a distance on foot."

Although Langdon knew the elevator would expedite the long, two-story climb to the Denon Wing, he remained motionless.

"Is something wrong?" Fache was holding the door, looking impatient.

Langdon exhaled, turning a longing glance back up the open-air escalator. *Nothing's wrong at all,* he lied to himself, trudging back toward the elevator. As a boy, Langdon had fallen down an abandoned well shaft and almost died treading water in the narrow space for hours before being rescued. Since then, he'd suffered a haunting phobia of enclosed spaces—elevators, subways, squash courts. *The elevator is a perfectly safe machine,* Langdon continually told himself, never believing it. *It's a tiny metal box hanging in an enclosed shaft!* Holding his breath, he stepped into the lift, feeling the familiar tingle of adrenaline as the doors slid shut.

*Two floors. Ten seconds.*

"You and Mr. Saunière," Fache said as the lift began to move, "you never spoke at all? Never corresponded? Never sent each other anything in the mail?"

Another odd question. Langdon shook his head. "No. Never."

Fache cocked his head, as if making a mental note of that fact. Saying nothing, he stared dead ahead at the chrome doors.

As they ascended, Langdon tried to focus on

anything other than the four walls around him. In the reflection of the shiny elevator door, he saw the captain's tie clip—a silver crucifix with thirteen embedded pieces of black onyx. Langdon found it vaguely surprising. The symbol was known as a *crux gemmata*—a cross bearing thirteen gems—a Christian ideogram for Christ and His twelve apostles. Somehow Langdon had not expected the captain of the French police to broadcast his religion so openly. Then again, this was France; Christianity was not a religion here so much as a birthright.

"It's a *crux gemmata*," Fache said suddenly.

Startled, Langdon glanced up to find Fache's eyes on him in the reflection.

The elevator jolted to a stop, and the doors opened.

Langdon stepped quickly out into the hallway, eager for the wide-open space afforded by the famous high ceilings of the Louvre galleries. The world into which he stepped, however, was nothing like he expected.

Surprised, Langdon stopped short.

Fache glanced over. "I gather, Mr. Langdon, you have never seen the Louvre after hours?"

*I guess not,* Langdon thought, trying to get his bearings.

Usually impeccably illuminated, the Louvre galleries were startlingly dark tonight. Instead of the customary flat-white light flowing down from above, a muted red glow seemed to emanate upward from the baseboards—intermittent patches of red light spilling out onto the tile floors.

As Langdon gazed down the murky corridor, he realized he should have anticipated this scene. Virtually all major galleries employed red service lighting at night—strategically placed, low-level, noninvasive lights that enabled staff members to navigate hallways and yet kept the paintings in relative darkness to slow the fading effects of overexposure to light. Tonight, the museum possessed an almost oppressive quality. Long shadows encroached everywhere, and the usually soaring vaulted ceilings appeared as a low, black void.

"This way," Fache said, turning sharply right and setting out through a series of interconnected galleries.

Langdon followed, his vision slowly adjusting to the dark. All around, large-format oils began to materialize like photos developing before him in an enormous darkroom . . . their eyes following as he moved through the rooms. He could taste the familiar tang of museum air—an arid, deionized essence that carried a faint hint of carbon— the product of industrial, coal-filter dehumidifiers that ran around the clock to counteract the corrosive carbon dioxide exhaled by visitors.

Mounted high on the walls, the visible security

cameras sent a clear message to visitors: *We see you. Do not touch anything.*

"Any of them real?" Langdon asked, motioning to the cameras.

Fache shook his head. "Of course not."

Langdon was not surprised. Video surveillance in museums this size was cost-prohibitive and in-effective. With acres of galleries to watch over, the Louvre would require several hundred technicians simply to monitor the feeds. Most large museums now used "containment security." *Forget keeping thieves out. Keep them in.* Containment was activated after hours, and if an intruder removed a piece of artwork, compartmentalized exits would seal around that gallery, and the thief would find himself behind bars even before the police arrived.

The sound of voices echoed down the marble corridor up ahead. The noise seemed to be coming from a large recessed alcove that lay ahead on the right. A bright light spilled out into the hallway.

"Office of the curator," the captain said.

As he and Fache drew nearer the alcove, Langdon peered down a short hallway, into Saunière's luxurious study—warm wood, Old Master paintings, and an enormous antique desk on which stood a two-foot-tall model of a knight in full armor. A handful of police agents bustled about the room, talking on phones and taking notes. One of them was seated at Saunière's desk, typing into a laptop. Apparently, the curator's private office had become DCPJ's makeshift command post for the evening.

*"Messieurs,"* Fache called out, and the men turned. *"Ne nous dérangez pas sous aucun prétexte. Entendu?"*

Everyone inside the office nodded their understanding.

Langdon had hung enough NE PAS DERANGER signs on hotel room doors to catch the gist of the captain's orders. Fache and Langdon were not to be disturbed under any circumstances.

Leaving the small congregation of agents behind, Fache led Langdon farther down the darkened hallway. Thirty yards ahead loomed the gateway to the Louvre's most popular section—*la Grande Galerie*—a seemingly endless corridor that housed the Louvre's most valuable Italian masterpieces. Langdon had already discerned that *this* was where Saunière's body lay; the Grand Gallery's famous parquet floor had been unmistakable in the Polaroid.

As they approached, Langdon saw the entrance was blocked by an enormous steel grate that looked like something used by medieval castles to keep out marauding armies.

*"Containment security,"* Fache said, as they neared the grate.

Even in the darkness, the barricade looked like it could have restrained a tank. Arriving outside, Langdon peered through the bars into the dimly lit caverns of the Grand Gallery.

"After you, Mr. Langdon," Fache said.

Langdon turned. *After me, where?*

Fache motioned toward the floor at the base of the grate.

Langdon looked down. In the darkness, he hadn't noticed. The barricade was raised about two feet, providing an awkward clearance underneath.

"This area is still off limits to Louvre security," Fache said. "My team from *Police Technique et Scientifique* has just finished their investigation." He motioned to the opening. "Please slide under."

Langdon stared at the narrow crawl space at his feet and then up at the massive iron grate. *He's kidding, right?* The barricade looked like a guillotine waiting to crush intruders.

Fache grumbled something in French and checked his watch. Then he dropped to his knees and slithered his bulky frame underneath the grate. On the other side, he stood up and looked back through the bars at Langdon.

Langdon sighed. Placing his palms flat on the polished parquet, he lay on his stomach and pulled himself forward. As he slid underneath, the nape of his Harris tweed snagged on the bottom of the grate, and he cracked the back of his head on the iron.

*Very suave, Robert,* he thought, fumbling and then finally pulling himself through. As he stood up, Langdon was beginning to suspect it was going to be a very long night.

# CHAPTER 5

**Murray Hill** Place—the new Opus Dei World Headquarters and conference center—is located at 243 Lexington Avenue in New York City. With a price tag of just over $47 million, the 133,000-square-foot tower is clad in red brick and Indiana limestone. Designed by May & Pinska, the building contains over one hundred bedrooms, six dining rooms, libraries, living rooms, meeting rooms, and offices. The second, eighth, and sixteenth floors contain chapels, ornamented with millwork and marble. The seventeenth floor is entirely residential. Men enter the building through the main doors on Lexington Avenue. Women enter through a side street and are "acoustically and visually separated" from the men at all times within the building.

Earlier this evening, within the sanctuary of his penthouse apartment, Bishop Manuel Aringarosa had packed a small travel bag and dressed in a traditional black cassock. Normally, he would have wrapped a purple cincture around his waist, but tonight he would be traveling among the public, and he preferred not to draw attention to his high office. Only those with a keen eye would notice his 14-karat gold bishop's ring with purple amethyst, large diamonds, and hand-tooled mitre-crozier appliqué. Throwing the travel bag over his shoulder, he said a silent prayer and left his apartment, descending to the lobby where his driver was waiting to take him to the airport.

Now, sitting aboard a commercial airliner bound for Rome, Aringarosa gazed out the window at the dark Atlantic. The sun had already set, but Aringarosa knew his own star was on the rise. *Tonight the battle will be won,* he thought, amazed that only months ago he had felt powerless against the hands that threatened to destroy his empire.

As president-general of Opus Dei, Bishop Aringarosa had spent the last decade of his life spreading the message of "God's Work"— literally, *Opus Dei.* The congregation, founded in 1928 by the Spanish priest Josemaría Escrivá, promoted a return to conservative Catholic values and encouraged its members to make sweeping sacrifices in their own lives in order to do the Work of God.

Opus Dei's traditionalist philosophy initially had taken root in Spain before Franco's regime, but with the 1934 publication of Josemaría Escrivá's spiritual book *The Way*—999 points of meditation for doing God's Work in one's own life— Escrivá's message exploded across the world. Now, with over four million copies of *The Way* in circulation in forty-two languages, Opus Dei was a global force. Its residence halls, teaching centers, and even universities could be found in almost every major metropolis on earth. Opus Dei was the fastest-growing and most financially secure Catholic organization in the world. Unfortunately, Aringarosa had learned, in an age of religious cynicism, cults, and televangelists, Opus Dei's escalating wealth and power was a magnet for suspicion.

"Many call Opus Dei a brainwashing cult," reporters often challenged. "Others call you an ultraconservative Christian secret society. Which are you?"

"Opus Dei is neither," the bishop would patiently reply. "We are a Catholic Church. We are a congregation of Catholics who have chosen as our priority to follow Catholic doctrine as rigorously as we can in our own daily lives."

"Does God's Work necessarily include vows of chastity, tithing, and atonement for sins through self-flagellation and the *cilice?*"

"You are describing only a small portion of the Opus Dei population," Aringarosa said. "There are many levels of involvement. Thousands of Opus Dei members are married, have families, and do God's Work in their own communities. Others choose lives of asceticism within our cloistered residence halls. These choices are personal, but everyone in Opus Dei shares the goal of bettering the world by doing the Work of God. Surely this is an admirable quest."

Reason seldom worked, though. The media always gravitated toward scandal, and Opus Dei, like most large organizations, had within its membership a few misguided souls who cast a shadow over the entire group.

Two months ago, an Opus Dei group at a midwestern university had been caught drugging new recruits with mescaline in an effort to induce a euphoric state that neophytes would perceive as a religious experience. Another university student had used his barbed *cilice* belt more often than the recommended two hours a day and had given himself a near lethal infection. In Boston not long ago, a disillusioned young investment banker had signed over his entire life savings to Opus Dei before attempting suicide.

*Misguided sheep,* Aringarosa thought, his heart going out to them.

Of course the ultimate embarrassment had been the widely publicized trial of FBI spy Robert Hanssen, who, in addition to being a prominent member of Opus Dei, had turned out to be a sexual deviant, his trial uncovering evidence that he had rigged hidden video cameras in his own bedroom so his friends could watch him having sex with his wife. "Hardly the pastime of a devout Catholic," the judge had noted.

Sadly, all of these events had helped spawn the new watch group known as the Opus Dei Awareness Network (ODAN). The group's popular website—*www.odan.org*—relayed frightening stories from former Opus Dei members who warned of the dangers of joining. The media was now referring to Opus Dei as "God's Mafia" and "the Cult of Christ."

*We fear what we do not understand,* Aringarosa thought, wondering if these critics had any idea how many lives Opus Dei had enriched. The group enjoyed the full endorsement and blessing of the Vatican. *Opus Dei is a personal prelature of the Pope himself.*

Recently, however, Opus Dei had found itself threatened by a force infinitely more powerful than the media . . . an unexpected foe from which Aringarosa could not possibly hide. Five months ago, the kaleidoscope of power had been shaken, and Aringarosa was still reeling from the blow.

"They know not the war they have begun," Aringarosa whispered to himself, staring out the plane's window at the darkness of the ocean below. For an instant, his eyes refocused, lingering on the reflection of his awkward face—dark and oblong, dominated by a flat, crooked nose that had been shattered by a fist in Spain when he was a young missionary. The physical flaw barely registered now. Aringarosa's was a world of the soul, not of the flesh.

As the jet passed over the coast of Portugal, the cell phone in Aringarosa's cassock began vibrating in silent ring mode. Despite airline regulations prohibiting the use of cell phones during flights, Aringarosa knew this was a call he could not miss. Only one man possessed this number, the man who had mailed Aringarosa the phone.

Excited, the bishop answered quietly. "Yes?"

"Silas has located the keystone," the caller said. "It is in Paris. Within the Church of Saint-Sulpice."

Bishop Aringarosa smiled. "Then we are close."

"We can obtain it immediately. But we need your influence."

"Of course. Tell me what to do."

When Aringarosa switched off the phone, his heart was pounding. He gazed once again into the void of night, feeling dwarfed by the events he had put into motion.

Five hundred miles away, the albino named Silas stood over a small basin of water and dabbed the blood from his back, watching the patterns of red spinning in the water. *Purge me with hyssop and I shall be clean,* he prayed, quoting Psalms. *Wash me, and I shall be whiter than snow.*

Silas was feeling an aroused anticipation that he had not felt since his previous life. It both surprised and electrified him. For the last decade, he had been following *The Way,* cleansing himself of sins . . . rebuilding his life . . . erasing the violence in his past. Tonight, however, it had all come rushing back. The hatred he had fought so hard to bury had been summoned. He had been startled how quickly his past had resurfaced. And with it, of course, had come his skills. Rusty but serviceable.

*Jesus' message is one of peace . . . of nonviolence . . . of love.* This was the message Silas had been taught from the beginning, and the message he held in his heart. And yet *this* was the message the enemies of Christ now threatened to destroy. *Those who threaten God with force will be met with force. Immovable and steadfast.*

For two millennia, Christian soldiers had defended their faith against those who tried to displace it. Tonight, Silas had been called to battle.

Drying his wounds, he donned his ankle-length, hooded robe. It was plain, made of dark wool, accentuating the whiteness of his skin and hair. Tightening the rope-tie around his waist, he raised the hood over his head and allowed his red eyes to admire his reflection in the mirror. *The wheels are in motion.*

# CHAPTER 6

**Having squeezed** beneath the security gate, Robert Langdon now stood just inside the entrance to the Grand Gallery. He was staring into the mouth of a long, deep canyon. On either side of the gallery, stark walls rose thirty feet, evaporating into the darkness above. The reddish glow of the service lighting sifted upward, casting an unnatural smolder across a staggering collection of Da Vincis, Titians, and Caravaggios that hung suspended from ceiling cables. Still lifes, religious scenes, and landscapes accompanied portraits of nobility and politicians.

Although the Grand Gallery housed the Louvre's most famous Italian art, many visitors felt the wing's most stunning offering was actually its famous parquet floor. Laid out in a dazzling geometric design of diagonal oak slats, the floor produced an ephemeral optical illusion—a multidimensional network that gave visitors the sense they were floating through the gallery on a surface that changed with every step.

As Langdon's gaze began to trace the inlay, his eyes stopped short on an unexpected object lying on the floor just a few yards to his left, surrounded by police tape. He spun toward Fache. "Is that . . . a *Caravaggio* on the floor?"

Fache nodded without even looking.

The painting, Langdon guessed, was worth upward of two million dollars, and yet it was lying on the floor like a discarded poster. "What the devil is it doing on the floor!"

Fache glowered, clearly unmoved. "This is a crime scene, Mr. Langdon. We have touched nothing. That canvas was pulled from the wall by the curator. It was how he activated the security system."

Langdon looked back at the gate, trying to picture what had happened.

"The curator was attacked in his office, fled into the Grand Gallery, and activated the security gate by pulling that painting from the wall. The gate fell immediately, sealing off all access. This is the only door in or out of this gallery."

Langdon felt confused. "So the curator actually captured his attacker inside the Grand Gallery?"

Fache shook his head. "The security gate *separated* Saunière from his attacker. The killer was locked out there in the hallway and shot Saunière through this gate." Fache pointed toward an orange tag hanging from one of the bars on the gate under which they had just passed. "The PTS team found flashback residue from a gun. He fired through the bars. Saunière died in here alone."

Langdon pictured the photograph of Saunière's body. *They said he did that to himself.* Langdon looked out at the enormous corridor before them. "So where is his body?"

Fache straightened his cruciform tie clip and began to walk. "As you probably know, the Grand Gallery is quite long."

The exact length, if Langdon recalled correctly, was around fifteen hundred feet, the length of three Washington Monuments laid end to end. Equally breathtaking was the corridor's width, which easily could have accommodated a pair of side-by-side passenger trains. The center of the hallway was dotted by the occasional statue or colossal porcelain urn, which served as a tasteful divider and kept the flow of traffic moving down one wall and up the other.

Fache was silent now, striding briskly up the right side of the corridor with his gaze dead ahead. Langdon felt almost disrespectful to be racing past so many masterpieces without pausing for so much as a glance.

*Not that I could see anything in this lighting*, he thought.

The muted crimson lighting unfortunately conjured memories of Langdon's last experience in noninvasive lighting in the Vatican Secret Archives. This was tonight's second unsettling parallel with his near-death in Rome. He flashed on Vittoria again. She had been absent from his dreams for months. Langdon could not believe Rome had been only a year ago; it felt like decades. *Another life.* His last correspondence from Vittoria had been in December—a postcard saying she was headed to the Java Sea to continue her research in entanglement physics . . . something about using satellites to track manta ray migrations. Langdon had never harbored delusions that a woman like Vittoria Vetra could have been happy living with him on a college campus, but their encounter in Rome had unlocked in him a longing he never imagined he could feel. His life-long affinity for bachelorhood and the simple freedoms it allowed had been shaken somehow . . . replaced by an unexpected emptiness that seemed to have grown over the past year.

They continued walking briskly, yet Langdon still saw no corpse. "Jacques Saunière went this *far?*"

"Mr. Saunière suffered a bullet wound to his stomach. He died very slowly. Perhaps over fifteen or twenty minutes. He was obviously a man of great personal strength."

Langdon turned, appalled. "Security took *fifteen* minutes to get here?"

"Of course not. Louvre security responded immediately to the alarm and found the Grand Gallery sealed. Through the gate, they could hear someone moving around at the far end of the corridor, but they could not see who it was. They shouted, but they got no answer. Assuming it could only be a criminal, they followed proto- col and called in the Judicial Police. We took up positions within fifteen minutes. When we ar- rived, we raised the barricade enough to slip un- derneath, and I sent a dozen armed agents inside. They swept the length of the gallery to corner the intruder."

"And?"

"They found no one inside. Except . . ." He pointed farther down the hall. "Him."

Langdon lifted his gaze and followed Fache's outstretched finger. At first he thought Fache was pointing to a large marble statue in the middle of the hallway. As they continued, though, Langdon began to see past the statue. Thirty yards down the hall, a single spotlight on a portable pole stand shone down on the floor, creating a stark island of white light in the dark crimson gallery. In the center of the light, like an insect under a micro- scope, the corpse of the curator lay naked on the parquet floor.

"You saw the photograph," Fache said, "so this should be of no surprise."

Langdon felt a deep chill as they approached the body. Before him was one of the strangest images he had ever seen.

The pallid corpse of Jacques Saunière lay on the parquet floor exactly as it appeared in the photograph. As Langdon stood over the body and squinted in the harsh light, he reminded himself to his amazement that Saunière had spent his last minutes of life arranging his own body in this strange fashion.

Saunière looked remarkably fit for a man of his years . . . and all of his musculature was in plain view. He had stripped off every shred of clothing, placed it neatly on the floor, and laid down on his back in the center of the wide corridor, perfectly aligned with the long axis of the room. His arms and legs were sprawled outward in a wide spread eagle, like those of a child making a snow angel . . . or, perhaps more appropriately, like a man being drawn and quartered by some invisible force.

Just below Saunière's breastbone, a bloody smear marked the spot where the bullet had pierced his flesh. The wound had bled surprisingly little, leaving only a small pool of blackened blood.

Saunière's left index finger was also bloody, apparently having been dipped into the wound to create the most unsettling aspect of his own macabre deathbed; using his own blood as ink, and employing his own naked abdomen as a canvas, Saunière had drawn a simple symbol on his flesh—five straight lines that intersected to form a five-pointed star.

*The pentacle.*

The bloody star, centered on Saunière's navel, gave his corpse a distinctly ghoulish aura. The photo Langdon had seen was chilling enough, but now, witnessing the scene in person, Langdon felt a deepening uneasiness.

*He did this to himself.*

"Mr. Langdon?" Fache's dark eyes settled on him again.

"It's a pentacle," Langdon offered, his voice feeling hollow in the huge space. "One of the oldest symbols on earth. Used over four thousand years before Christ."

"And what does it mean?"

Langdon always hesitated when he got this question. Telling someone what a symbol "meant" was like telling them how a song should make them feel—it was different for all people. A white Ku Klux Klan headpiece conjured images of hatred and racism in the United States, and yet the same costume carried a meaning of religious faith in Spain.

"Symbols carry different meanings in different settings," Langdon said. "Primarily, the pentacle is a pagan religious symbol."

Fache nodded. "Devil worship."

"No," Langdon corrected, immediately realizing his choice of vocabulary should have been clearer.

Nowadays, the term *pagan* had become almost

synonymous with devil worship—a gross misconception. The word's roots actually reached
back to the Latin *paganus,* meaning country-
dwellers. "Pagans" were literally unindoctrinated
country-folk who clung to the old, rural religions
of Nature worship. In fact, so strong was the
Church's fear of those who lived in the rural *villes*
that the once innocuous word for "villager"—
*villain*—came to mean a wicked soul.

"The pentacle," Langdon clarified, "is a pre-
Christian symbol that relates to Nature worship.
The ancients envisioned their world in two
halves—masculine and feminine. Their gods and
goddesses worked to keep a balance of power.
Yin and yang. When male and female were balanced, there was harmony in the world. When
they were unbalanced, there was chaos." Langdon
motioned to Saunière's stomach. "This pentacle is
representative of the *female* half of all things—a
concept religious historians call the 'sacred feminine' or the 'divine goddess.' Saunière, of all people, would know this."

"Saunière drew a *goddess* symbol on his
stomach?"

Langdon had to admit, it seemed odd. "In its
most specific interpretation, the pentacle symbol-
izes Venus—the goddess of female sexual love and
beauty."

Fache eyed the naked man, and grunted.

"Early religion was based on the divine order of

Nature. The goddess Venus and the planet Venus were one and the same. The goddess had a place in the nighttime sky and was known by many names—Venus, the Eastern Star, Ishtar, Astarte—all of them powerful female concepts with ties to Nature and Mother Earth."

Fache looked more troubled now, as if he somehow preferred the idea of devil worship.

Langdon decided not to share the pentacle's most astonishing property—the *graphic* origin of its ties to Venus. As a young astronomy student, Langdon had been stunned to learn the planet Venus traced a *perfect* pentacle across the ecliptic sky every four years. So astonished were the ancients to observe this phenomenon, that Venus and her pentacle became symbols of perfection, beauty, and the cyclic qualities of sexual love. As a tribute to the magic of Venus, the Greeks used her four-year cycle to organize their Olympiads. Nowadays, few people realized that the four-year schedule of modern Olympic Games still followed the cycles of Venus. Even fewer people knew that the five-pointed star had almost become the official Olympic seal but was modified at the last moment—its five points exchanged for five intersecting rings to better reflect the games' spirit of inclusion and harmony.

"Mr. Langdon," Fache said abruptly. "Obviously, the pentacle must *also* relate to the devil.

Your American horror movies make that point clearly."

Langdon frowned. *Thank you, Hollywood.* The five-pointed star was now a virtual cliché in Satanic serial killer movies, usually scrawled on the wall of some Satanist's apartment along with other alleged demonic symbology. Langdon was always frustrated when he saw the symbol in this context; the pentacle's true origins were actually quite godly.

"I assure you," Langdon said, "despite what you see in the movies, the pentacle's demonic interpretation is historically inaccurate. The original feminine meaning is correct, but the symbolism of the pentacle has been distorted over the millennia. In this case, through bloodshed."

"I'm not sure I follow."

Langdon glanced at Fache's crucifix, uncertain how to phrase his next point. "The Church, sir. Symbols are very resilient, but the pentacle was altered by the early Roman Catholic Church. As part of the Vatican's campaign to eradicate pagan religions and convert the masses to Christianity, the Church launched a smear campaign against the pagan gods and goddesses, recasting their divine symbols as evil."

"Go on."

"This is very common in times of turmoil," Langdon continued. "A newly emerging power will take over the existing symbols and degrade them over time in an attempt to erase their meaning. In the battle between the pagan symbols and Christian symbols, the pagans lost; Poseidon's trident became the devil's pitchfork, the wise crone's pointed hat became the symbol of a witch, and Venus's pentacle became a sign of the devil." Langdon paused. "Unfortunately, the United States military has also perverted the pentacle; it's now our foremost symbol of war. We paint it on all our fighter jets and hang it on the shoulders of all our generals." *So much for the goddess of love and beauty.*

"Interesting." Fache nodded toward the spread-eagle corpse. "And the positioning of the body? What do you make of that?"

Langdon shrugged. "The position simply reinforces the reference to the pentacle and sacred feminine."

Fache's expression clouded. "I beg your pardon?"

"Replication. Repeating a symbol is the simplest way to strengthen its meaning. Jacques Saunière positioned himself in the shape of a five-pointed star." *If one pentacle is good, two is better.*

Fache's eyes followed the five points of Saunière's arms, legs, and head as he again ran a hand across his slick hair. "Interesting analysis." He paused. "And the *nudity?*" He grumbled as he spoke the word, sounding repulsed by the sight of an aging male body. "Why did he remove his clothing?"

*Damned good question,* Langdon thought. He'd been wondering the same thing ever since he first saw the Polaroid. His best guess was that a naked human form was yet another endorsement of Venus—the goddess of human sexuality. Although modern culture had erased much of Venus's association with the male/female physical union, a sharp etymological eye could still spot a vestige of Venus's original meaning in the word "venereal." Langdon decided not to go there.

"Mr. Fache, I obviously can't tell you why Mr. Saunière drew that symbol on himself or placed himself in this way, but I *can* tell you that a man like Jacques Saunière would consider the pentacle a sign of the female deity. The correlation between this symbol and the sacred feminine is widely known by art historians and symbologists."

"Fine. And the use of his own blood as ink?"

"Obviously he had nothing else to write with."

Fache was silent a moment. "Actually, I believe he used blood such that the police would follow certain forensic procedures."

"I'm sorry?"

"Look at his left hand."

Langdon's eyes traced the length of the curator's pale arm to his left hand but saw nothing. Uncertain, he circled the corpse and crouched down, now noting with surprise that the curator was clutching a large, felt-tipped marker.

"Saunière was holding it when we found him," Fache said, leaving Langdon and moving several yards to a portable table covered with investigation tools, cables, and assorted electronic gear. "As I told you," he said, rummaging around the table, "we have touched nothing. Are you familiar with this kind of pen?"

Langdon knelt down farther to see the pen's label.

STYLO DE LUMIERE NOIRE.

He glanced up in surprise.

The black-light pen or watermark stylus was a specialized felt-tipped marker originally designed by museums, restorers, and forgery police to place invisible marks on items. The stylus wrote in a noncorrosive, alcohol-based fluorescent ink that was visible only under black light. Nowadays, museum maintenance staffs carried these markers on their daily rounds to place invisible "tick marks" on the frames of paintings that needed restoration.

As Langdon stood up, Fache walked over to the spotlight and turned it off. The gallery plunged into sudden darkness.

Momentarily blinded, Langdon felt a rising uncertainty. Fache's silhouette appeared, illuminated in bright purple. He approached carrying a portable light source, which shrouded him in a violet haze.

"As you may know," Fache said, his eyes luminescing in the violet glow, "police use black-light illumination to search crime scenes for blood and other forensic evidence. So you can imagine our surprise . . ." Abruptly, he pointed the light down at the corpse.

Langdon looked down and jumped back in shock.

His heart pounded as he took in the bizarre sight now glowing before him on the parquet floor. Scrawled in luminescent handwriting, the curator's final words glowed purple beside his corpse. As Langdon stared at the shimmering text, he felt the fog that had surrounded this entire night growing thicker.

Langdon read the message again and looked up at Fache. "What the hell does this mean!"

Fache's eyes shone white. "*That,* monsieur, is precisely the question you are here to answer."

Not far away, inside Saunière's office, Lieutenant Collet had returned to the Louvre and was huddled over an audio console set up on the curator's enormous desk. With the exception of the eerie, robot-like doll of a medieval knight that seemed to be staring at him from the corner of Saunière's desk, Collet was comfortable. He adjusted his AKG headphones and checked the input levels on the hard-disk recording system. All systems were go. The microphones were functioning flawlessly, and the audio feed was crystal clear.

*Le moment de vérité,* he mused.

Smiling, he closed his eyes and settled in to enjoy the rest of the conversation now being taped inside the Grand Gallery.

# CHAPTER 7

**The modest** dwelling within the Church of Saint-Sulpice was located on the second floor of the church itself, to the left of the choir balcony. A two-room suite with a stone floor and minimal furnishings, it had been home to Sister Sandrine Bieil for over a decade. The nearby convent was her formal residence, if anyone asked, but she preferred the quiet of the church and had made herself quite comfortable upstairs with a bed, phone, and hot plate.

As the church's *conservatrice d'affaires*, Sister Sandrine was responsible for overseeing all non-religious aspects of church operations—general maintenance, hiring support staff and guides, securing the building after hours, and ordering supplies like communion wine and wafers.

Tonight, asleep in her small bed, she awoke to the shrill of her telephone. Tiredly, she lifted the receiver.

"*Soeur Sandrine. Eglise Saint-Sulpice.*"

"Hello, Sister," the man said in French.

Sister Sandrine sat up. *What time is it?* Although she recognized her boss's voice, in fifteen years she had never been awoken by him. The abbé was a deeply pious man who went home to bed immediately after mass.

"I apologize if I have awoken you, Sister," the abbé said, his own voice sounding groggy and on edge. "I have a favor to ask of you. I just received a call from an influential American bishop. Perhaps you know him? Manuel Aringarosa?"

"The head of Opus Dei?" *Of course I know of him. Who in the Church doesn't?* Aringarosa's conservative prelature had grown powerful in recent years. Their ascension to grace was jump-started in 1982 when Pope John Paul II unexpectedly elevated them to a "personal prelature of the Pope," officially sanctioning all of their practices. Suspiciously, Opus Dei's elevation occurred the same year the wealthy sect allegedly had transferred almost one billion dollars into the Vatican's Institute for Religious Works—commonly known as the Vatican Bank—bailing it out of an embarrassing bankruptcy. In a second maneuver that raised eyebrows, the Pope placed the founder of Opus Dei on the "fast track" for sainthood, accelerating an often century-long waiting period for canonization to a mere twenty years. Sister Sandrine could not help but feel that Opus Dei's good standing in Rome was suspect, but one did not argue with the Holy See.

"Bishop Aringarosa called to ask me a favor," the abbé told her, his voice nervous. "One of his numeraries is in Paris tonight. . . ."

As Sister Sandrine listened to the odd request, she felt a deepening confusion. "I'm sorry, you say this visiting Opus Dei numerary cannot wait until morning?"

"I'm afraid not. His plane leaves very early. He has always dreamed of seeing Saint-Sulpice."

"But the church is far more interesting by day. The sun's rays through the oculus, the graduated shadows on the gnomon, *this* is what makes Saint-Sulpice unique."

"Sister, I agree, and yet I would consider it a personal favor if you could let him in tonight. He can be there at . . . say one o'clock? That's in twenty minutes."

Sister Sandrine frowned. "Of course. It would be my pleasure."

The abbé thanked her and hung up.

Puzzled, Sister Sandrine remained a moment in the warmth of her bed, trying to shake off the cobwebs of sleep. Her sixty-year-old body did not awake as fast as it used to, although tonight's phone call had certainly roused her senses. Opus Dei had always made her uneasy. Beyond the prelature's adherence to the arcane ritual of corporal mortification, their views on women were medieval at best. She had been shocked to learn that female numeraries were forced to clean the men's residence halls for no pay while the men were at mass; women slept on hardwood floors, while the men had straw mats; and women were

forced to endure additional requirements of corporal mortification . . . all as added penance for
original sin. It seemed Eve's bite from the apple
of knowledge was a debt women were doomed
to pay for eternity. Sadly, while most of the
Catholic Church was gradually moving in the
right direction with respect to women's rights,
Opus Dei threatened to reverse the progress.
Even so, Sister Sandrine had her orders.

Swinging her legs off the bed, she stood slowly,
chilled by the cold stone on the soles of her bare
feet. As the chill rose through her flesh, she felt
an unexpected apprehension.

*Women's intuition?*

A follower of God, Sister Sandrine had learned
to find peace in the calming voices of her own
soul. Tonight, however, those voices were as
silent as the empty church around her.

# CHAPTER 8

**Langdon couldn't** tear his eyes from the glowing purple text scrawled across the parquet floor. Jacques Saunière's final communication seemed as unlikely a departing message as any Langdon could imagine.

The message read:

13-3-2-21-1-1-8-5
O, Draconian devil!
Oh, lame saint!

Although Langdon had not the slightest idea what it meant, he did understand Fache's instinct that the pentacle had something to do with devil worship.

*O, Draconian devil!*

Saunière had left a literal reference to the devil. Equally as bizarre was the series of numbers. "Part of it looks like a numeric cipher."

"Yes," Fache said. "Our cryptographers are already working on it. We believe these numbers may be the key to who killed him. Maybe a telephone exchange or some kind of social identification. Do the numbers have any symbolic meaning to you?"

Langdon looked again at the digits, sensing it would take him hours to extract any symbolic meaning. *If Saunière had even intended any.* To Langdon, the numbers looked totally random. He was accustomed to symbolic progressions that made some semblance of sense, but everything here—the pentacle, the text, the numbers—seemed disparate at the most fundamental level.

"You alleged earlier," Fache said, "that Saunière's actions here were all in an effort to send some sort of message . . . goddess worship or something in that vein? How does this message fit in?"

Langdon knew the question was rhetorical. This bizarre communiqué obviously did not fit Langdon's scenario of goddess worship at all.

*O, Draconian devil? Oh, lame saint?*

Fache said, "This text appears to be an accusation of some sort. Wouldn't you agree?"

Langdon tried to imagine the curator's final minutes trapped alone in the Grand Gallery, knowing he was about to die. It seemed logical. "An accusation against his murderer makes sense, I suppose."

"My job, of course, is to put a name to that person. Let me ask you this, Mr. Langdon. To your eye, beyond the numbers, what about this message is most strange?"

*Most strange?* A dying man had barricaded himself in the gallery, drawn a pentacle on himself, and scrawled a mysterious accusation on the floor. What about the scenario *wasn't* strange?

"The word 'Draconian'?" he ventured, offering the first thing that came to mind. Langdon was fairly certain that a reference to Draco—the ruthless seventh-century B.C. politician—was an unlikely dying thought. " 'Draconian devil' seems an odd choice of vocabulary."

*"Draconian?"* Fache's tone came with a tinge of impatience now. "Saunière's choice of vocabulary hardly seems the primary issue here."

Langdon wasn't sure what issue Fache had in mind, but he was starting to suspect that Draco and Fache would have gotten along well.

"Saunière was a Frenchman," Fache said flatly. "He lived in Paris. And yet he chose to write this message . . ."

"In English," Langdon said, now realizing the captain's meaning.

Fache nodded. *"Précisément.* Any idea why?"

Langdon knew Saunière spoke impeccable English, and yet the reason he had chosen English as the language in which to write his final words escaped Langdon. He shrugged.

Fache motioned back to the pentacle on Saunière's abdomen. "Nothing to do with devil worship? Are you still certain?"

Langdon was certain of nothing anymore. "The symbology and text don't seem to coincide. I'm sorry I can't be of more help."

"Perhaps this will clarify." Fache backed away from the body and raised the black light again, letting the beam spread out in a wider angle. "And now?"

To Langdon's amazement, a rudimentary circle glowed around the curator's body. Saunière had apparently lay down and swung the pen around himself in several long arcs, essentially inscribing himself inside a circle.

In a flash, the meaning became clear.

*"The Vitruvian Man,"* Langdon gasped. Saunière had created a life-sized replica of Leonardo da Vinci's most famous sketch.

Considered the most anatomically correct drawing of its day, Da Vinci's *The Vitruvian Man* had become a modern-day icon of culture, appearing on posters, mouse pads, and T-shirts around the world. The celebrated sketch consisted of a perfect circle in which was inscribed a nude male . . . his arms and legs outstretched in a naked spread eagle.

*Da Vinci.* Langdon felt a shiver of amazement. The clarity of Saunière's intentions could not be denied. In his final moments of life, the curator had stripped off his clothing and arranged his body in a clear image of Leonardo da Vinci's *Vitruvian Man.*

The circle had been the missing critical element. A feminine symbol of protection, the circle around the naked man's body completed Da

Vinci's intended message—male and female harmony. The question now, though, was *why* Saunière would imitate a famous drawing.

"Mr. Langdon," Fache said, "certainly a man like yourself is aware that Leonardo da Vinci had a tendency toward the darker arts."

Langdon was surprised by Fache's knowledge of Da Vinci, and it certainly went a long way toward explaining the captain's suspicions about devil worship. Da Vinci had always been an awkward subject for historians, especially in the Christian tradition. Despite the visionary's genius, he was a flamboyant homosexual and worshipper of Nature's divine order, both of which placed him in a perpetual state of sin against God. Moreover, the artist's eerie eccentricities projected an admittedly demonic aura: Da Vinci exhumed corpses to study human anatomy; he kept mysterious journals in illegible reverse handwriting; he believed he possessed the alchemic power to turn lead into gold and even cheat God by creating an elixir to postpone death; and his inventions included horrific, never-before-imagined weapons of war and torture.

*Misunderstanding breeds distrust,* Langdon thought.

Even Da Vinci's enormous output of breathtaking Christian art only furthered the artist's reputation for spiritual hypocrisy. Accepting hundreds of lucrative Vatican commissions, Da Vinci painted

Christian themes not as an expression of his own beliefs but rather as a commercial venture—a means of funding a lavish lifestyle. Unfortunately, Da Vinci was a prankster who often amused himself by quietly gnawing at the hand that fed him. He incorporated in many of his Christian paintings hidden symbolism that was anything but Christian—tributes to his own beliefs and a subtle thumbing of his nose at the Church. Langdon had even given a lecture once at the National Gallery in London entitled: "The Secret Life of Leonardo: Pagan Symbolism in Christian Art."

"I understand your concerns," Langdon now said, "but Da Vinci never really practiced any dark arts. He was an exceptionally spiritual man, albeit one in constant conflict with the Church." As Langdon said this, an odd thought popped into his mind. He glanced down at the message on the floor again. *O, Draconian devil! Oh, lame saint!*

"Yes?" Fache said.

Langdon weighed his words carefully. "I was just thinking that Saunière shared a lot of spiritual ideologies with Da Vinci, including a concern over the Church's elimination of the sacred feminine from modern religion. Maybe, by imitating a famous Da Vinci drawing, Saunière was simply echoing some of their shared frustrations with the modern Church's demonization of the goddess."

Fache's eyes hardened. "You think Saunière is

calling the Church a lame saint and a Draconian devil?"

Langdon had to admit it seemed far-fetched, and yet the pentacle seemed to endorse the idea on some level. "All I am saying is that Mr. Saunière dedicated his life to studying the history of the goddess, and nothing has done more to erase that history than the Catholic Church. It seems reasonable that Saunière might have chosen to express his disappointment in his final good-bye."

"Disappointment?" Fache demanded, sounding hostile now. "This message sounds more *enraged* than disappointed, wouldn't you say?"

Langdon was reaching the end of his patience. "Captain, you asked for my instincts as to what Saunière is trying to say here, and that's what I'm giving you."

"That this is an indictment of the Church?" Fache's jaw tightened as he spoke through clenched teeth. "Mr. Langdon, I have seen a lot of death in my work, and let me tell you something. When a man is murdered by another man, I do not believe his final thoughts are to write an obscure spiritual statement that no one will understand. I believe he is thinking of one thing only." Fache's whispery voice sliced the air. "*La vengeance*. I believe Saunière wrote this note to tell us who killed him."

Langdon stared. "But that makes no sense whatsoever."

"No?"

"No," he fired back, tired and frustrated. "You told me Saunière was attacked in his office by someone he had apparently invited in."

"Yes."

"So it seems reasonable to conclude that the curator *knew* his attacker."

Fache nodded. "Go on."

"So if Saunière *knew* the person who killed him, what kind of indictment is this?" He pointed at the floor. "Numeric codes? Lame saints? Draconian devils? Pentacles on his stomach? It's all too cryptic."

Fache frowned as if the idea had never occurred to him. "You have a point."

"Considering the circumstances," Langdon said, "I would assume that if Saunière wanted to tell you who killed him, he would have written down somebody's *name*."

As Langdon spoke those words, a smug smile crossed Fache's lips for the first time all night. *"Précisément,"* Fache said. *"Précisément."*


*I am witnessing the work of a master,* mused Lieutenant Collet as he tweaked his audio gear and listened to Fache's voice coming through the headphones. The *agent supérieur* knew it was moments like these that had lifted the captain to the pinnacle of French law enforcement.

*Fache will do what no one else dares.*

The delicate art of *cajoler* was a lost skill in modern law enforcement, one that required exceptional poise under pressure. Few men possessed the necessary sangfroid for this kind of operation, but Fache seemed born for it. His restraint and patience bordered on the robotic.

Fache's sole emotion this evening seemed to be one of intense resolve, as if this arrest were somehow personal to him. Fache's briefing of his agents an hour ago had been unusually succinct and assured. *I know who murdered Jacques Saunière,* Fache had said. *You know what to do. No mistakes tonight.*

And so far, no mistakes had been made.

Collet was not yet privy to the evidence that had cemented Fache's certainty of their suspect's guilt, but he knew better than to question the instincts of the Bull. Fache's intuition seemed almost supernatural at times. *God whispers in his ear,* one agent had insisted after a particularly impressive display of Fache's sixth sense. Collet had to admit, if there was a God, Bezu Fache would be on His A-list. The captain attended mass and confession with zealous regularity—far more than the requisite holiday attendance fulfilled by other officials in the name of good public relations. When the Pope visited Paris a few years back, Fache had used all his muscle to obtain the honor of an audience. A photo of Fache with the Pope now hung in his office. *The Papal Bull,* the agents secretly called it.

Collet found it ironic that one of Fache's rare popular public stances in recent years had been his outspoken reaction to the Catholic pedophilia scandal. *These priests should be hanged twice!* Fache had declared. *Once for their crimes against children. And once for shaming the good name of the Catholic Church.* Collet had the odd sense it was the latter that angered Fache more.

Turning now to his laptop computer, Collet attended to the other half of his responsibilities here tonight—the GPS tracking system. The image onscreen revealed a detailed floor plan of the Denon Wing, a structural schematic uploaded from the Louvre Security Office. Letting his eyes trace the maze of galleries and hallways, Collet found what he was looking for.

Deep in the heart of the Grand Gallery blinked a tiny red dot.

*La marque.*

Fache was keeping his prey on a very tight leash tonight. Wisely so. Robert Langdon had proven himself one cool customer.

# CHAPTER 9

**To ensure** his conversation with Mr. Langdon would not be interrupted, Bezu Fache had turned off his cellular phone. Unfortunately, it was an expensive model equipped with a two-way radio feature, which, contrary to his orders, was now being used by one of his agents to page him.

"*Capitaine?*" The phone crackled like a walkie-talkie.

Fache felt his teeth clench in rage. He could imagine nothing important enough that Collet would interrupt this *surveillance cachée*—especially at this critical juncture.

He gave Langdon a calm look of apology. "One moment please." He pulled the phone from his belt and pressed the radio transmission button. "*Oui?*"

"*Capitaine, un agent du Département de Cryptographie est arrivé.*"

Fache's anger stalled momentarily. *A cryptographer?* Despite the lousy timing, this was probably good news. Fache, after finding Saunière's cryptic text on the floor, had uploaded photographs of the entire crime scene to the Cryptography Department in hopes someone there could tell him what the hell Saunière was trying to say. If a code breaker had now arrived, it most likely meant someone had decrypted Saunière's message.

"I'm busy at the moment," Fache radioed back, leaving no doubt in his tone that a line had been crossed. "Ask the cryptographer to wait at the command post. I'll speak to him when I'm done."

*"Her,"* the voice corrected. "It's Agent Neveu."

Fache was becoming less amused with this call every passing moment. Sophie Neveu was one of DCPJ's biggest mistakes. A young Parisian *déchiffreuse* who had studied cryptography in England at the Royal Holloway, Sophie Neveu had been foisted on Fache two years ago as part of the ministry's attempt to incorporate more women into the police force. The ministry's on-going foray into political correctness, Fache argued, was weakening the department. Women not only lacked the physicality necessary for police work, but their mere presence posed a dangerous distraction to the men in the field. As Fache had feared, Sophie Neveu was proving far more distracting than most.

At thirty-two years old, she had a dogged determination that bordered on obstinate. Her eager espousal of Britain's new cryptologic methodology continually exasperated the veteran French cryptographers above her. And by far the most troubling to Fache was the inescapable universal truth that in an office of middle-aged men, an attractive young woman always drew eyes away from the work at hand.

The man on the radio said, "Agent Neveu insisted on speaking to you immediately, Captain. I tried to stop her, but she's on her way into the gallery."

Fache recoiled in disbelief. "Unacceptable! I made it very clear—"

For a moment, Robert Langdon thought Bezu Fache was suffering a stroke. The captain was mid-sentence when his jaw stopped moving and his eyes bulged. His blistering gaze seemed fixated on something over Langdon's shoulder. Before Langdon could turn to see what it was, he heard a woman's voice chime out behind him.

*"Excusez-moi, messieurs."*

Langdon turned to see a young woman approaching. She was moving down the corridor toward them with long, fluid strides . . . a haunting certainty to her gait. Dressed casually in a knee-length, cream-colored Irish sweater over black leggings, she was attractive and looked to be about thirty. Her thick burgundy hair fell unstyled to her shoulders, framing the warmth of her face. Unlike the waifish, cookie-cutter blondes that adorned Harvard dorm room walls, this woman was healthy with an unembellished beauty and genuineness that radiated a striking personal confidence.

To Langdon's surprise, the woman walked directly up to him and extended a polite hand. "Monsieur Langdon, I am Agent Neveu from DCPJ's Cryptology Department." Her words curved richly around her muted Anglo-Franco accent. "It is a pleasure to meet you."

Langdon took her soft palm in his and felt himself momentarily fixed in her strong gaze. Her eyes were olive-green—incisive and clear.

Fache drew a seething inhalation, clearly preparing to launch into a reprimand.

"Captain," she said, turning quickly and beating him to the punch, "please excuse the interruption, but—"

"*Ce n'est pas le moment!*" Fache sputtered.

"I tried to phone you." Sophie continued in English, as if out of courtesy to Langdon. "But your cell phone was turned off."

"I turned it off for a reason," Fache hissed. "I am speaking to Mr. Langdon."

"I've deciphered the numeric code," she said flatly.

Langdon felt a pulse of excitement. *She broke the code?*

Fache looked uncertain how to respond.

"Before I explain," Sophie said, "I have an urgent message for Mr. Langdon."

Fache's expression turned to one of deepening concern. "For Mr. Langdon?"

She nodded, turning back to Langdon. "You need to contact the U.S. Embassy, Mr. Langdon. They have a message for you from the States."

Langdon reacted with surprise, his excitement over the code giving way to a sudden ripple of concern. *A message from the States?* He tried to imagine who could be trying to reach him. Only a few of his colleagues knew he was in Paris.

Fache's broad jaw had tightened with the news. "The U.S. Embassy?" he demanded, sounding suspicious. "How would they know to find Mr. Langdon *here?*"

Sophie shrugged. "Apparently they called Mr. Langdon's hotel, and the concierge told them Mr. Langdon had been collected by a DCPJ agent."

Fache looked troubled. "And the embassy contacted DCPJ *Cryptography?*"

"No, sir," Sophie said, her voice firm. "When I called the DCPJ switchboard in an attempt to contact you, they had a message waiting for Mr. Langdon and asked me to pass it along if I got through to you."

Fache's brow furrowed in apparent confusion. He opened his mouth to speak, but Sophie had already turned back to Langdon.

"Mr. Langdon," she declared, pulling a small slip of paper from her pocket, "this is the number for your embassy's messaging service. They asked that you phone in as soon as possible." She handed him the paper with an intent gaze. "While I explain the code to Captain Fache, you need to make this call."

Langdon studied the slip. It had a Paris phone number and extension on it. "Thank you," he said, feeling worried now. "Where do I find a phone?"

Sophie began to pull a cell phone from her sweater pocket, but Fache waved her off. He now looked like Mount Vesuvius about to erupt. Without taking his eyes off Sophie, he produced his own cell phone and held it out. "This line is secure, Mr. Langdon. You may use it."

Langdon felt mystified by Fache's anger with the young woman. Feeling uneasy, he accepted the captain's phone. Fache immediately marched Sophie several steps away and began chastising her in hushed tones. Disliking the captain more and more, Langdon turned away from the odd confrontation and switched on the cell phone. Checking the slip of paper Sophie had given him, Langdon dialed the number.

The line began to ring.

One ring . . . two rings . . . three rings . . .

Finally the call connected.

Langdon expected to hear an embassy operator,

but he found himself instead listening to an answering machine. Oddly, the voice on the tape was familiar. It was that of Sophie Neveu.

*"Bonjour, vous êtes bien chez Sophie Neveu,"* the woman's voice said. *"Je suis absente pour le moment, mais . . ."*

Confused, Langdon turned back toward Sophie. "I'm sorry, Ms. Neveu? I think you may have given me—"

"No, that's the right number," Sophie interjected quickly, as if anticipating Langdon's confusion. "The embassy has an automated message system. You have to dial an access code to pick up your messages."

Langdon stared. "But—"

"It's the three-digit code on the paper I gave you."

Langdon opened his mouth to explain the bizarre error, but Sophie flashed him a silencing glare that lasted only an instant. Her green eyes sent a crystal-clear message.

*Don't ask questions. Just do it.*

Bewildered, Langdon punched in the extension on the slip of paper: 454.

Sophie's outgoing message immediately cut off, and Langdon heard an electronic voice announce in French: "You have *one* new message." Apparently, 454 was Sophie's remote access code for picking up her messages while away from home.

*I'm picking up this woman's messages?*

Langdon could hear the tape rewinding now. Finally, it stopped, and the machine engaged. Langdon listened as the message began to play. Again, the voice on the line was Sophie's.

"Mr. Langdon," the message began in a fearful whisper. "Do *not* react to this message. Just listen calmly. You are in danger right now. Follow my directions very closely."

# CHAPTER 10

**Silas sat** behind the wheel of the black Audi the Teacher had arranged for him and gazed out at the great Church of Saint-Sulpice. Lit from beneath by banks of floodlights, the church's two bell towers rose like stalwart sentinels above the building's long body. On either flank, a shadowy row of sleek buttresses jutted out like the ribs of a beautiful beast.

*The heathens used a house of God to conceal their keystone.* Again the brotherhood had confirmed their legendary reputation for illusion and deceit. Silas was looking forward to finding the keystone and giving it to the Teacher so they could recover what the brotherhood had long ago stolen from the faithful.

*How powerful that will make Opus Dei.*

Parking the Audi on the deserted Place Saint-Sulpice, Silas exhaled, telling himself to clear his mind for the task at hand. His broad back still ached from the corporal mortification he had endured earlier today, and yet the pain was inconsequential compared with the anguish of his life before Opus Dei had saved him.

Still, the memories haunted his soul.

*Release your hatred,* Silas commanded himself. *Forgive those who trespassed against you.*

Looking up at the stone towers of Saint-Sulpice, Silas fought that familiar undertow . . . that force that often dragged his mind back in time, locking him once again in the prison that had been his world as a young man. The memories of purgatory came as they always did, like a tempest to his senses . . . the reek of rotting cabbage, the stench of death, human urine and feces. The cries of hopelessness against the howling wind of the Pyrenees and the soft sobs of forgotten men.

*Andorra,* he thought, feeling his muscles tighten.

Incredibly, it was in that barren and forsaken suzerain between Spain and France, shivering in his stone cell, wanting only to die, that Silas had been saved.

He had not realized it at the time.

*The light came long after the thunder.*

His name was not Silas then, although he didn't recall the name his parents had given him. He had left home when he was seven. His drunken father, a burly dockworker, enraged by the arrival of an albino son, beat his mother regularly, blaming her for the boy's embarrassing condition. When the boy tried to defend her, he too was badly beaten.

One night, there was a horrific fight, and his mother never got up. The boy stood over his lifeless mother and felt an unbearable upwelling of guilt for permitting it to happen.

*This is my fault!*

As if some kind of demon were controlling his body, the boy walked to the kitchen and grasped a butcher knife. Hypnotically, he moved to the bedroom where his father lay on the bed in a drunken stupor. Without a word, the boy stabbed him in the back. His father cried out in pain and tried to roll over, but his son stabbed him again, over and over until the apartment fell quiet.

The boy fled home but found the streets of Marseilles equally unfriendly. His strange appearance made him an outcast among the other young runaways, and he was forced to live alone in the basement of a dilapidated factory, eating stolen fruit and raw fish from the dock. His only companions were tattered magazines he found in the trash, and he taught himself to read them. Over time, he grew strong. When he was twelve, another drifter—a girl twice his age—mocked him on the streets and attempted to steal his food. The girl found herself pummeled to within inches of her life. When the authorities pulled the boy off her, they gave him an ultimatum—leave Marseilles or go to juvenile prison.

The boy moved down the coast to Toulon. Over time, the looks of pity on the streets turned to looks of fear. The boy had grown to a powerful young man. When people passed by, he could hear them whispering to one another. *A ghost,* they would say, their eyes wide with fright as they stared at his white skin. *A ghost with the eyes of a devil!*

And he felt like a ghost . . . transparent . . . floating from seaport to seaport.

People seemed to look right through him.

At eighteen, in a port town, while attempting to steal a case of cured ham from a cargo ship, he was caught by a pair of crewmen. The two sailors who began to beat him smelled of beer, just as his father had. The memories of fear and hatred surfaced like a monster from the deep. The young man broke the first sailor's neck with his bare hands, and only the arrival of the police saved the second sailor from a similar fate.

Two months later, in shackles, he arrived at a prison in Andorra.

*You are as white as a ghost,* the inmates ridiculed as the guards marched him in, naked and cold. *Mira el espectro! Perhaps the ghost will pass right through these walls!*

Over the course of twelve years, his flesh and soul withered until he knew he had become transparent.

*I am a ghost.*

*I am weightless.*

*Yo soy un espectro . . . pálido como una fantasma . . . caminando este mundo a solas.*

One night the ghost awoke to the screams of

other inmates. He didn't know what invisible force was shaking the floor on which he slept, nor what mighty hand was trembling the mortar of his stone cell, but as he jumped to his feet, a large boulder toppled onto the very spot where he had been sleeping. Looking up to see where the stone had come from, he saw a hole in the trembling wall, and beyond it, a vision he had not seen in over ten years. The moon.

Even while the earth still shook, the ghost found himself scrambling through a narrow tunnel, staggering out into an expansive vista, and tumbling down a barren mountainside into the woods. He ran all night, always downward, delirious with hunger and exhaustion.

Skirting the edges of consciousness, he found himself at dawn in a clearing where train tracks cut a swath across the forest. Following the rails, he moved on as if dreaming. Seeing an empty freight car, he crawled in for shelter and rest. When he awoke the train was moving. *How long? How far?* A pain was growing in his gut. *Am I dying?* He slept again. This time he awoke to someone yelling, beating him, throwing him out of the freight car. Bloody, he wandered the outskirts of a small village looking in vain for food. Finally, his body too weak to take another step, he lay down by the side of the road and slipped into unconsciousness.

The light came slowly, and the ghost wondered

how long he had been dead. *A day? Three days?* It
didn't matter. His bed was soft like a cloud, and
the air around him smelled sweet with candles.
Jesus was there, staring down at him. *I am here,*
Jesus said. *The stone has been rolled aside, and you are
born again.*

He slept and awoke. Fog shrouded his thoughts.
He had never believed in heaven, and yet Jesus
was watching over him. Food appeared beside his
bed, and the ghost ate it, almost able to feel the
flesh materializing on his bones. He slept again.
When he awoke, Jesus was still smiling down,
speaking. *You are saved, my son. Blessed are those
who follow my path.*

Again, he slept.

It was a scream of anguish that startled the ghost
from his slumber. His body leapt out of bed, staggered down a hallway toward the sounds of
shouting. He entered into a kitchen and saw a
large man beating a smaller man. Without knowing why, the ghost grabbed the large man and
hurled him backward against a wall. The man
fled, leaving the ghost standing over the body of
a young man in priest's robes. The priest had a
badly shattered nose. Lifting the bloody priest, the
ghost carried him to a couch.

"Thank you, my friend," the priest said in awkward French. "The offertory money is tempting
for thieves. You speak French in your sleep. Do
you also speak Spanish?"

The ghost shook his head.

"What is your name?" he continued in broken French.

The ghost could not remember the name his parents had given him. All he heard were the taunting gibes of the prison guards.

The priest smiled. "*No hay problema.* My name is Manuel Aringarosa. I am a missionary from Madrid. I was sent here to build a church for the Obra de Dios."

"Where am I?" His voice sounded hollow.

"Oviedo. In the north of Spain."

"How did I get here?"

"Someone left you on my doorstep. You were ill. I fed you. You've been here many days."

The ghost studied his young caretaker. Years had passed since anyone had shown any kindness. "Thank you, Father."

The priest touched his bloody lip. "It is I who am thankful, my friend."

When the ghost awoke in the morning, his world felt clearer. He gazed up at the crucifix on the wall above his bed. Although it no longer spoke to him, he felt a comforting aura in its presence. Sitting up, he was surprised to find a newspaper clipping on his bedside table. The article was in French, a week old. When he read the story, he filled with fear. It told of an earthquake in the mountains that had destroyed a prison and freed many dangerous criminals.

His heart began pounding. *The priest knows who I am!* The emotion he felt was one he had not felt for some time. Shame. Guilt. It was accompanied by the fear of being caught. He jumped from his bed. *Where do I run?*

"The Book of Acts," a voice said from the door.

The ghost turned, frightened.

The young priest was smiling as he entered. His nose was awkwardly bandaged, and he was holding out an old Bible. "I found one in French for you. The chapter is marked."

Uncertain, the ghost took the Bible and looked at the chapter the priest had marked.

*Acts 16.*

The verses told of a prisoner named Silas who lay naked and beaten in his cell, singing hymns to God. When the ghost reached Verse 26, he gasped in shock.

"*. . . And suddenly, there was a great earthquake, so that the foundations of the prison were shaken, and all the doors fell open.*"

His eyes shot up at the priest.

The priest smiled warmly. "From now on, my friend, if you have no other name, I shall call you Silas."

The ghost nodded blankly. *Silas.* He had been given flesh. *My name is Silas.*

"It's time for breakfast," the priest said. "You will need your strength if you are to help me build this church."

Twenty thousand feet above the Mediterranean, Alitalia flight 1618 bounced in turbulence, causing passengers to shift nervously. Bishop Aringarosa barely noticed. His thoughts were with the future of Opus Dei. Eager to know how plans in Paris were progressing, he wished he could phone Silas. But he could not. The Teacher had seen to that.

"It is for your own safety," the Teacher had explained, speaking in English with a French accent. "I am familiar enough with electronic communications to know they can be intercepted. The results could be disastrous for you."

Aringarosa knew he was right. The Teacher seemed an exceptionally careful man. He had not revealed his own identity to Aringarosa, and yet he had proven himself a man well worth obeying. After all, he had somehow obtained very secret information. *The names of the brotherhood's four top members!* This had been one of the coups that convinced the bishop the Teacher was truly capable of delivering the astonishing prize he claimed he could unearth.

"Bishop," the Teacher had told him, "I have made all the arrangements. For my plan to succeed, you must allow Silas to answer *only* to me for several days. The two of you will not speak. I will communicate with him through secure channels."

"You will treat him with respect?"

"A man of faith deserves the highest."

"Excellent. Then I understand. Silas and I shall not speak until this is over."

"I do this to protect your identity, Silas's identity, and my investment."

"Your investment?"

"Bishop, if your own eagerness to keep abreast of progress puts you in jail, then you will be unable to pay me my fee."

The bishop smiled. "A fine point. Our desires are in accord. Godspeed."

*Twenty million euro,* the bishop thought, now gazing out the plane's window. The sum was approximately the same number of U.S. dollars. *A pittance for something so powerful.*

He felt a renewed confidence that the Teacher and Silas would not fail. Money and faith were powerful motivators.

# CHAPTER 11

*"Une plaisanterie numérique?"* Bezu Fache was livid, glaring at Sophie Neveu in disbelief. *A numeric joke?* "Your professional assessment of Saunière's code is that it is some kind of mathematical prank?"

Fache was in utter incomprehension of this woman's gall. Not only had she just barged in on Fache without permission, but she was now trying to convince him that Saunière, in his final moments of life, had been inspired to leave a mathematical gag?

"This code," Sophie explained in rapid French, "is simplistic to the point of absurdity. Jacques Saunière must have known we would see through it immediately." She pulled a scrap of paper from her sweater pocket and handed it to Fache. "Here is the decryption."

Fache looked at the card.

1-1-2-3-5-8-13-21

"This is it?" he snapped. "All you did was put the numbers in increasing order!"

Sophie actually had the nerve to give a satisfied smile. "Exactly."

Fache's tone lowered to a guttural rumble. "Agent Neveu, I have no idea where the hell you're going with this, but I suggest you get there fast." He shot an anxious glance at Langdon, who stood nearby with the phone pressed to his ear, apparently still listening to his phone message from the U.S. Embassy. From Langdon's ashen expression, Fache sensed the news was bad.

"Captain," Sophie said, her tone dangerously defiant, "the sequence of numbers you have in your hand happens to be one of the most famous mathematical progressions in history."

Fache was not aware there even existed a mathematical progression that qualified as famous, and he certainly didn't appreciate Sophie's off-handed tone.

"This is the Fibonacci sequence," she declared, nodding toward the piece of paper in Fache's hand. "A progression in which each term is equal to the sum of the two preceding terms."

Fache studied the numbers. Each term was indeed the sum of the two previous, and yet Fache could not imagine what the relevance of all this was to Saunière's death.

"Mathematician Leonardo Fibonacci created this succession of numbers in the thirteenth-century. Obviously there can be no coincidence that *all* of the numbers Saunière wrote on the floor belong to Fibonacci's famous sequence."

Fache stared at the young woman for several

moments. "Fine, if there is no coincidence, would you tell me *why* Jacques Saunière chose to do this. What is he saying? What does this *mean?*"

She shrugged. "Absolutely nothing. That's the point. It's a simplistic cryptographic joke. Like taking the words of a famous poem and shuffling them at random to see if anyone recognizes what all the words have in common."

Fache took a menacing step forward, placing his face only inches from Sophie's. "I certainly hope you have a much more satisfying explanation than *that.*"

Sophie's soft features grew surprisingly stern as she leaned in. "Captain, considering what you have at stake here tonight, I thought you might appreciate knowing that Jacques Saunière might be playing games with you. Apparently not. I'll inform the director of Cryptography you no longer need our services."

With that, she turned on her heel, and marched off the way she had come.

Stunned, Fache watched her disappear into the darkness. *Is she out of her mind?* Sophie Neveu had just redefined *le suicide professionnel.*

Fache turned to Langdon, who was still on the phone, looking more concerned than before, listening intently to his phone message. *The U.S. Embassy.* Bezu Fache despised many things . . . but few drew more wrath than the U.S. Embassy.

Fache and the ambassador locked horns regularly over shared affairs of state—their most common battleground being law enforcement for visiting Americans. Almost daily, DCPJ arrested American exchange students in possession of drugs, U.S. businessmen for soliciting underage prostitutes, American tourists for shoplifting or destruction of property. Legally, the U.S. Embassy could intervene and extradite guilty citizens back to the United States, where they received nothing more than a slap on the wrist.

And the embassy invariably did just that.

*L'émasculation de la Police Judiciaire,* Fache called it. *Paris Match* had run a cartoon recently depicting Fache as a police dog, trying to bite an American criminal, but unable to reach because it was chained to the U.S. Embassy.

*Not tonight,* Fache told himself. *There is far too much at stake.*

By the time Robert Langdon hung up the phone, he looked ill.

"Is everything all right?" Fache asked.

Weakly, Langdon shook his head.

*Bad news from home,* Fache sensed, noticing Langdon was sweating slightly as Fache took back his cell phone.

"An accident," Langdon stammered, looking at Fache with a strange expression. "A friend . . ." He hesitated. "I'll need to fly home first thing in the morning."

Fache had no doubt the shock on Langdon's

face was genuine, and yet he sensed another emotion there too, as if a distant fear were suddenly simmering in the American's eyes. "I'm sorry to hear that," Fache said, watching Langdon closely. "Would you like to sit down?" He motioned toward one of the viewing benches in the gallery.

Langdon nodded absently and took a few steps toward the bench. He paused, looking more confused with every moment. "Actually, I think I'd like to use the rest room."

Fache frowned inwardly at the delay. "The rest room. Of course. Let's take a break for a few minutes." He motioned back down the long hallway in the direction they had come from. "The rest rooms are back toward the curator's office."

Langdon hesitated, pointing in the other direction toward the far end of the Grand Gallery corridor. "I believe there's a much closer rest room at the end."

Fache realized Langdon was right. They were two thirds of the way down, and the Grand Gallery dead-ended at a pair of rest rooms. "Shall I accompany you?"

Langdon shook his head, already moving deeper into the gallery. "Not necessary. I think I'd like a few minutes alone."

Fache was not wild about the idea of Langdon wandering alone down the remaining length of corridor, but he took comfort in knowing the Grand Gallery was a dead end whose only exit was at the other end—the gate under which they had entered. Although French fire regulations required several emergency stairwells for a space this large, those stairwells had been sealed automatically when Saunière tripped the security system. Granted, that system had now been reset, unlocking the stairwells, but it didn't matter—the external doors, if opened, would set off fire alarms and were guarded outside by DCPJ agents. Langdon could not possibly leave without Fache knowing about it.

"I need to return to Mr. Saunière's office for a moment," Fache said. "Please come find me directly, Mr. Langdon. There is more we need to discuss."

Langdon gave a quiet wave as he disappeared into the darkness.

Turning, Fache marched angrily in the opposite direction. Arriving at the gate, he slid under, exited the Grand Gallery, marched down the hall, and stormed into the command center at Saunière's office.

"Who gave the approval to let Sophie Neveu into this building!" Fache bellowed.

Collet was the first to answer. "She told the guards outside she'd broken the code."

Fache looked around. "Is she gone?"

"She's not with you?"

"She left." Fache glanced out at the darkened hallway. Apparently Sophie had been in no mood to stop by and chat with the other officers on her way out.

For a moment, Fache considered radioing the guards in the entresol and telling them to stop Sophie and drag her back up here before she could leave the premises. He thought better of it. That was only his pride talking . . . wanting the last word. He'd had enough distractions tonight.

*Deal with Agent Neveu later,* he told himself, already looking forward to firing her.

Pushing Sophie from his mind, Fache stared for a moment at the miniature knight standing on Saunière's desk. Then he turned back to Collet. "Do you have him?"

Collet gave a curt nod and spun the laptop toward Fache. The red dot was clearly visible on the floor plan overlay, blinking methodically in a room marked TOILETTES PUBLIQUES.

"Good," Fache said, lighting a cigarette and stalking into the hall. "I've got a phone call to make. Be damned sure the rest room is the only place Langdon goes."

# CHAPTER 12

**Robert Langdon** felt light-headed as he trudged toward the end of the Grand Gallery. Sophie's phone message played over and over in his mind. At the end of the corridor, illuminated signs bearing the international stick-figure symbols for rest rooms guided him through a maze-like series of dividers displaying Italian drawings and hiding the rest rooms from sight.

Finding the men's room door, Langdon entered and turned on the lights.

The room was empty.

Walking to the sink, he splashed cold water on his face and tried to wake up. Harsh fluorescent lights glared off the stark tile, and the room smelled of ammonia. As he toweled off, the rest room's door creaked open behind him. He spun.

Sophie Neveu entered, her green eyes flashing fear. "Thank God you came. We don't have much time."

Langdon stood beside the sinks, staring in bewilderment at DCPJ cryptographer Sophie Neveu. Only minutes ago, Langdon had listened to her phone message, thinking the newly arrived cryptographer must be insane. And yet, the more he listened, the more he sensed Sophie Neveu was speaking in earnest. *Do not react to this message. Just listen calmly. You are in danger right now. Follow my directions very closely.* Filled with uncertainty, Langdon had decided to do exactly as Sophie advised. He told Fache that the phone message was regarding an injured friend back home. Then he had asked to use the rest room at the end of the Grand Gallery.

Sophie stood before him now, still catching her breath after doubling back to the rest room. In the fluorescent lights, Langdon was surprised to see that her strong air actually radiated from unexpectedly soft features. Only her gaze was sharp, and the juxtaposition conjured images of a multilayered Renoir portrait . . . veiled but distinct, with a boldness that somehow retained its shroud of mystery.

"I wanted to warn you, Mr. Langdon . . ." Sophie began, still catching her breath, "that you are *sous surveillance cachée.* Under a guarded observation." As she spoke, her accented English resonated off the tile walls, giving her voice a hollow quality.

"But . . . why?" Langdon demanded. Sophie had already given him an explanation on the phone, but he wanted to hear it from her lips.

"Because," she said, stepping toward him, "Fache's primary suspect in this murder is *you.*"

Langdon was braced for the words, and yet they still sounded utterly ridiculous. According to

Sophie, Langdon had been called to the Louvre tonight not as a symbologist but rather as a *suspect* and was currently the unwitting target of one of DCPJ's favorite interrogation methods—*surveillance cachée*—a deft deception in which the police calmly invited a suspect to a crime scene and interviewed him in hopes he would get nervous and mistakenly incriminate himself.

"Look in your jacket's left pocket," Sophie said. "You'll find proof they are watching you."

Langdon felt his apprehension rising. *Look in my pocket?* It sounded like some kind of cheap magic trick.

"Just look."

Bewildered, Langdon reached his hand into his tweed jacket's left pocket—one he never used. Feeling around inside, he found nothing. *What the devil did you expect?* He began wondering if Sophie might just be insane after all. Then his fingers brushed something unexpected. Small and hard. Pinching the tiny object between his fingers, Langdon pulled it out and stared in astonishment. It was a metallic, button-shaped disk, about the size of a watch battery. He had never seen it before. "What the . . . ?"

"GPS tracking dot," Sophie said. "Continuously transmits its location to a Global Positioning System satellite that DCPJ can monitor. We use them to monitor people's locations. It's accurate within two feet anywhere on the globe. They have you on an electronic leash. The agent who picked you up at the hotel slipped it inside your pocket before you left your room."

Langdon flashed back to the hotel room . . . his quick shower, getting dressed, the DCPJ agent politely holding out Langdon's tweed coat as they left the room. *It's cool outside, Mr. Langdon,* the agent had said. *Spring in Paris is not all your song boasts.* Langdon had thanked him and donned the jacket.

Sophie's olive gaze was keen. "I didn't tell you about the tracking dot earlier because I didn't want you checking your pocket in front of Fache. He can't know you've found it."

Langdon had no idea how to respond.

"They tagged you with GPS because they thought you might run." She paused. "In fact, they *hoped* you would run; it would make their case stronger."

"Why would I run!" Langdon demanded. "I'm innocent!"

"Fache feels otherwise."

Angrily, Langdon stalked toward the trash receptacle to dispose of the tracking dot.

"No!" Sophie grabbed his arm and stopped him. "Leave it in your pocket. If you throw it out, the signal will stop moving, and they'll know you found the dot. The only reason Fache left you alone is because he can monitor where you are. If he thinks you've discovered what he's doing . . ." Sophie did not finish the thought. Instead, she pried the metallic disk from Langdon's hand and slid it back into the pocket of his tweed coat. "The dot stays with you. At least for the moment."

Langdon felt lost. "How the hell could Fache actually believe I killed Jacques Saunière!"

"He has some fairly persuasive reasons to suspect you." Sophie's expression was grim. "There is a piece of evidence here that you have not yet seen. Fache has kept it carefully hidden from you."

Langdon could only stare.

"Do you recall the three lines of text that Saunière wrote on the floor?"

Langdon nodded. The numbers and words were imprinted on Langdon's mind.

Sophie's voice dropped to a whisper now. "Unfortunately, what you saw was not the entire message. There was a *fourth* line that Fache photographed and then wiped clean before you arrived."

Although Langdon knew the soluble ink of a watermark stylus could easily be wiped away, he could not imagine why Fache would erase evidence.

"The last line of the message," Sophie said, "was something Fache did not want you to know about." She paused. "At least not until he was done with you."

Sophie produced a computer printout of a photo from her sweater pocket and began unfolding it. "Fache uploaded images of the crime scene to the Cryptology Department earlier tonight in hopes we could figure out what Saunière's message was trying to say. This is a photo of the complete message." She handed the page to Langdon.

Bewildered, Langdon looked at the image. The close-up photo revealed the glowing message on the parquet floor. The final line hit Langdon like a kick in the gut.

13-3-2-21-1-1-8-5
O, Draconian devil!
Oh, lame saint!
P.S. Find Robert Langdon

# CHAPTER 13

**For several** seconds, Langdon stared in wonder at the photograph of Saunière's postscript. *P.S. Find Robert Langdon.* He felt as if the floor were tilting beneath his feet. *Saunière left a postscript with my name on it?* In his wildest dreams, Langdon could not fathom why.

"Now do you understand," Sophie said, her eyes urgent, "why Fache ordered you here tonight, and why you are his primary suspect?"

The only thing Langdon understood at the moment was why Fache had looked so smug when Langdon suggested Saunière would have accused his killer by name.

*Find Robert Langdon.*

"Why would Saunière write this?" Langdon demanded, his confusion now giving way to anger. "Why would I want to kill Jacques Saunière?"

"Fache has yet to uncover a motive, but he has been recording his entire conversation with you tonight in hopes you might reveal one."

Langdon opened his mouth, but still no words came.

"He's fitted with a miniature microphone," Sophie explained. "It's connected to a transmitter in his pocket that radios the signal back to the command post."

"This is impossible," Langdon stammered. "I have an alibi. I went directly back to my hotel after my lecture. You can ask the hotel desk."

"Fache already did. His report shows you retrieving your room key from the concierge at about ten-thirty. Unfortunately, the time of the murder was closer to eleven. You easily could have left your hotel room unseen."

"This is insanity! Fache has no evidence!"

Sophie's eyes widened as if to say: *No evidence?* "Mr. Langdon, your name is written on the floor beside the body, and Saunière's date book says you were with him at approximately the time of the murder." She paused. "Fache has more than enough evidence to take you into custody for questioning."

Langdon suddenly sensed that he needed a lawyer. "I didn't do this."

Sophie sighed. "This is not American television, Mr. Langdon. In France, the laws protect the police, not criminals. Unfortunately, in this case, there is also the media consideration. Jacques Saunière was a very prominent and well-loved figure in Paris, and his murder will be news in the morning. Fache will be under immediate pressure to make a statement, and he looks a lot better having a suspect in custody already. Whether or not you are guilty, you most certainly will be held by DCPJ until they can figure out what really happened."

Langdon felt like a caged animal. "Why are you telling me all this?"

"Because, Mr. Langdon, I believe you are innocent." Sophie looked away for a moment and then back into his eyes. "And also because it is partially *my* fault that you're in trouble."

"I'm sorry? It's *your* fault Saunière is trying to frame me?"

"Saunière wasn't trying to frame you. It was a mistake. That message on the floor was meant for me."

Langdon needed a minute to process that one. "I beg your pardon?"

"That message wasn't for the police. He wrote it for *me*. I think he was forced to do everything in such a hurry that he just didn't realize how it would look to the police." She paused. "The numbered code is meaningless. Saunière wrote it to make sure the investigation included cryptographers, ensuring that *I* would know as soon as possible what had happened to him."

Langdon felt himself losing touch fast. Whether or not Sophie Neveu had lost her mind was at this point up for grabs, but at least Langdon now understood why she was trying to help him. *P.S. Find Robert Langdon.* She apparently believed the curator had left her a cryptic postscript telling her to find Langdon. "But why do you think his message was for you?"

"*The Vitruvian Man,*" she said flatly. "That particular sketch has always been my favorite Da Vinci work. Tonight he used it to catch my attention."

"Hold on. You're saying the curator *knew* your favorite piece of art?"

She nodded. "I'm sorry. This is all coming out of order. Jacques Saunière and I . . ."

Sophie's voice caught, and Langdon heard a sudden melancholy there, a painful past, simmering just below the surface. Sophie and Jacques Saunière apparently had some kind of special relationship. Langdon studied the beautiful young woman before him, well aware that aging men in France often took young mistresses. Even so, Sophie Neveu as a "kept woman" somehow didn't seem to fit.

"We had a falling-out ten years ago," Sophie said, her voice a whisper now. "We've barely spoken since. Tonight, when Crypto got the call that he had been murdered, and I saw the images of his body and text on the floor, I realized he was trying to send me a message."

"Because of *The Vitruvian Man?*"

"Yes. And the letters P.S."

"*Post Script?*"

She shook her head. "P.S. are my initials."

"But your name is Sophie Neveu."

She looked away. "P.S. is the nickname he called me when I lived with him." She blushed. "It stood for *Princesse Sophie.*"

Langdon had no response.

"Silly, I know," she said. "But it was years ago. When I was a little girl."

"You knew him when you were a little *girl?*"

"Quite well," she said, her eyes welling now with emotion. "Jacques Saunière was my grand-father."

# CHAPTER 14

**"Where's Langdon?"** Fache demanded, exhaling the last of a cigarette as he paced back into the command post.

"Still in the men's room, sir." Lieutenant Collet had been expecting the question.

Fache grumbled, "Taking his time, I see."

The captain eyed the GPS dot over Collet's shoulder, and Collet could almost hear the wheels turning. Fache was fighting the urge to go check on Langdon. Ideally, the subject of an observation was allowed the most time and freedom possible, lulling him into a false sense of security. Langdon needed to return of his own volition. Still, it had been almost ten minutes.

*Too long.*

"Any chance Langdon is onto us?" Fache asked.

Collet shook his head. "We're still seeing small movements inside the men's room, so the GPS dot is obviously still on him. Perhaps he feels ill? If he had found the dot, he would have removed it and tried to run."

Fache checked his watch. "Fine."

Still Fache seemed preoccupied. All evening, Collet had sensed an atypical intensity in his captain. Usually detached and cool under pressure,

Fache tonight seemed emotionally engaged, as if this were somehow a personal matter for him.

*Not surprising,* Collet thought. *Fache needs this arrest desperately.* Recently the Board of Ministers and the media had become more openly critical of Fache's aggressive tactics, his clashes with powerful foreign embassies, and his gross overbudgeting on new technologies. Tonight, a high-tech, high-profile arrest of an American would go a long way to silence Fache's critics, helping him secure the job a few more years until he could retire with the lucrative pension. *God knows he needs the pension,* Collet thought. Fache's zeal for technology had hurt him both professionally and personally. Fache was rumored to have invested his entire savings in the technology craze a few years back and lost his shirt. *And Fache is a man who wears only the finest shirts.*

Tonight, there was still plenty of time. Sophie Neveu's odd interruption, though unfortunate, had been only a minor wrinkle. She was gone now, and Fache still had cards to play. He had yet to inform Langdon that his name had been scrawled on the floor by the victim. *P.S. Find Robert Langdon.* The American's reaction to that little bit of evidence would be telling indeed.

"Captain?" one of the DCPJ agents now called from across the office. "I think you better take this call." He was holding out a telephone receiver, looking concerned.

"Who is it?" Fache said.

The agent frowned. "It's the director of our Cryptology Department."

"And?"

"It's about Sophie Neveu, sir. Something is not quite right."

# CHAPTER 15

## It was time.

Silas felt strong as he stepped from the black Audi, the nighttime breeze rustling his loose-fitting robe. *The winds of change are in the air.* He knew the task before him would require more finesse than force, and he left his handgun in the car. The thirteen-round Heckler Koch USP 40 had been provided by the Teacher.

*A weapon of death has no place in a house of God.*

The plaza before the great church was deserted at this hour, the only visible souls on the far side of Place Saint-Sulpice a couple of teenage hookers showing their wares to the late night tourist traffic. Their nubile bodies sent a familiar longing to Silas's loins. His thigh flexed instinctively, causing the barbed *cilice* belt to cut painfully into his flesh.

The lust evaporated instantly. For ten years now, Silas had faithfully denied himself all sexual indulgence, even self-administered. It was *The Way.* He knew he had sacrificed much to follow Opus Dei, but he had received much more in return. A vow of celibacy and the relinquishment of all personal assets hardly seemed a sacrifice. Considering the poverty from which he had come and the sexual horrors he had endured in prison, celibacy was a welcome change.

Now, having returned to France for the first time since being arrested and shipped to prison in Andorra, Silas could feel his homeland testing him, dragging violent memories from his redeemed soul. *You have been reborn,* he reminded himself. His service to God today had required the sin of murder, and it was a sacrifice Silas knew he would have to hold silently in his heart for all eternity.

*The measure of your faith is the measure of the pain you can endure,* the Teacher had told him. Silas was no stranger to pain and felt eager to prove himself to the Teacher, the one who had assured him his actions were ordained by a higher power.

*"Hago la obra de Dios,"* Silas whispered, moving now toward the church entrance.

Pausing in the shadow of the massive doorway, he took a deep breath. It was not until this instant that he truly realized what he was about to do, and what awaited him inside.

*The keystone. It will lead us to our final goal.*

He raised his ghost-white fist and banged three times on the door.

Moments later, the bolts of the enormous wooden portal began to move.

# CHAPTER 16

**Sophie wondered** how long it would take Fache to figure out she had not left the building. Seeing that Langdon was clearly overwhelmed, Sophie questioned whether she had done the right thing by cornering him here in the men's room.

*What else was I supposed to do?*

She pictured her grandfather's body, naked and spread-eagle on the floor. There was a time when he had meant the world to her, yet tonight, Sophie was surprised to feel almost no sadness for the man. Jacques Saunière was a stranger to her now. Their relationship had evaporated in a single instant one March night when she was twenty-two. *Ten years ago.* Sophie had come home a few days early from graduate university in England and mistakenly witnessed her grandfather engaged in something Sophie was obviously not supposed to see. It was an image she barely could believe to this day.

*If I hadn't seen it with my own eyes . . .*

Too ashamed and stunned to endure her grandfather's pained attempts to explain, Sophie immediately moved out on her own, taking money she had saved, and getting a small flat with some roommates. She vowed never to speak to anyone about what she had seen. Her grandfather tried desperately to reach her, sending cards and letters, begging Sophie to meet him so he could explain. *Explain how!?* Sophie never responded except once—to forbid him ever to call her or try to meet her in public. She was afraid his explanation would be more terrifying than the incident itself.

Incredibly, Saunière had never given up on her, and Sophie now possessed a decade's worth of correspondence unopened in a dresser drawer. To her grandfather's credit, he had never once disobeyed her request and phoned her.

*Until this afternoon.*

"Sophie?" His voice had sounded startlingly old on her answering machine. "I have abided by your wishes for so long . . . and it pains me to call, but I must speak to you. Something terrible has happened."

Standing in the kitchen of her Paris flat, Sophie felt a chill to hear him again after all these years. His gentle voice brought back a flood of fond childhood memories.

"Sophie, please listen." He was speaking English to her, as he always did when she was a little girl. *Practice French at school. Practice English at home.* "You cannot be mad forever. Have you not read the letters that I've sent all these years? Do you not yet understand?" He paused. "We must speak at once. Please grant your grandfather this one wish. Call me at the Louvre. Right away. I believe you and I are in grave danger."

Sophie stared at the answering machine. *Danger?* What was he talking about?

"Princess . . ." Her grandfather's voice cracked with an emotion Sophie could not place. "I know I've kept things from you, and I know it has cost me your love. But it was for your own safety. Now you must know the truth. Please, I must tell you the truth about your family."

Sophie suddenly could hear her own heart. *My family?* Sophie's parents had died when she was only four. Their car went off a bridge into fast-moving water. Her grandmother and younger brother had also been in the car, and Sophie's entire family had been erased in an instant. She had a box of newspaper clippings to confirm it.

His words had sent an unexpected surge of longing through her bones. *My family!* In that fleeting instant, Sophie saw images from the dream that had awoken her countless times when she was a little girl: *My family is alive! They are coming home!* But, as in her dream, the pictures evaporated into oblivion.

*Your family is dead, Sophie. They are not coming home.*

"Sophie . . ." her grandfather said on the machine. "I have been waiting for years to tell you. Waiting for the right moment, but now time has run out. Call me at the Louvre. As soon as you get this. I'll wait here all night. I fear we both may be in danger. There's so much you need to know."

The message ended.

In the silence, Sophie stood trembling for what felt like minutes. As she considered her grandfather's message, only one possibility made sense, and his true intent dawned.

It was bait.

Obviously, her grandfather wanted desperately to see her. He was trying anything. Her disgust for the man deepened. Sophie wondered if maybe he had fallen terminally ill and had decided to attempt any ploy he could think of to get Sophie to visit him one last time. If so, he had chosen wisely.

*My family.*

Now, standing in the darkness of the Louvre men's room, Sophie could hear the echoes of this afternoon's phone message. *Sophie, we both may be in danger. Call me.*

She had not called him. Nor had she planned to. Now, however, her skepticism had been deeply challenged. Her grandfather lay murdered inside his own museum. And he had written a code on the floor.

A code for *her.* Of this, she was certain.

Despite not understanding the meaning of his message, Sophie was certain its cryptic nature was additional proof that the words were intended for her. Sophie's passion and aptitude for cryptography were a product of growing up with Jacques Saunière—a fanatic himself for codes, word games, and puzzles. *How many Sundays did we spend doing the cryptograms and crosswords in the newspaper?*

At the age of twelve, Sophie could finish the *Le Monde* crossword without any help, and her grandfather graduated her to crosswords in English, mathematical puzzles, and substitution ciphers. Sophie devoured them all. Eventually she turned her passion into a profession by becoming a codebreaker for the Judicial Police.

Tonight, the cryptographer in Sophie was forced to respect the efficiency with which her grandfather had used a simple code to unite two total strangers—Sophie Neveu and Robert Langdon.

The question was *why?*

Unfortunately, from the bewildered look in Langdon's eyes, Sophie sensed the American had no more idea than she did why her grandfather had thrown them together.

She pressed again. "You and my grandfather had planned to meet tonight. What about?"

Langdon looked truly perplexed. "His secretary set the meeting and didn't offer any specific reason, and I didn't ask. I assumed he'd heard I would be lecturing on the pagan iconography of

French cathedrals, was interested in the topic, and thought it would be fun to meet for drinks after the talk."

Sophie didn't buy it. The connection was flimsy. Her grandfather knew more about pagan iconography than anyone else on earth. Moreover, he was an exceptionally private man, not someone prone to chatting with random American professors unless there were an important reason.

Sophie took a deep breath and probed further. "My grandfather called me this afternoon and told me he and I were in grave danger. Does *that* mean anything to you?"

Langdon's blue eyes now clouded with concern. "No, but considering what just happened . . ."

Sophie nodded. Considering tonight's events, she would be a fool not to be frightened. Feeling drained, she walked to the small plate-glass window at the far end of the bathroom and gazed out in silence through the mesh of alarm tape embedded in the glass. They were high up—forty feet at least.

Sighing, she raised her eyes and gazed out at Paris's dazzling landscape. On her left, across the Seine, the illuminated Eiffel Tower. Straight ahead, the Arc de Triomphe. And to the right, high atop the sloping rise of Montmartre, the graceful arabesque dome of Sacré-Coeur, its polished stone glowing white like a resplendent sanctuary.

Here at the westernmost tip of the Denon Wing, the north-south thoroughfare of Place du Carrousel ran almost flush with the building with only a narrow sidewalk separating it from the Louvre's outer wall. Far below, the usual caravan of the city's nighttime delivery trucks sat idling, waiting for the signals to change, their running lights seeming to twinkle mockingly up at Sophie.

"I don't know what to say," Langdon said, coming up behind her. "Your grandfather is obviously trying to tell us something. I'm sorry I'm so little help."

Sophie turned from the window, sensing a sincere regret in Langdon's deep voice. Even with all the trouble around him, he obviously wanted to help her. *The teacher in him,* she thought, having read DCPJ's workup on their suspect. This was an academic who clearly despised not understanding.

*We have that in common,* she thought.

As a codebreaker, Sophie made her living extracting meaning from seemingly senseless data. Tonight, her best guess was that Robert Langdon, whether he knew it or not, possessed information that she desperately needed. *Princesse Sophie, Find Robert Langdon.* How much clearer could her grandfather's message be? Sophie needed more time with Langdon. Time to think. Time to sort out this mystery together. Unfortunately, time was running out.

Gazing up at Langdon, Sophie made the only play she could think of. "Bezu Fache will be taking you into custody at any minute. I can get you out of this museum. But we need to act now."

Langdon's eyes went wide. "You want me to *run?*"

"It's the smartest thing you could do. If you let Fache take you into custody now, you'll spend weeks in a French jail while DCPJ and the U.S. Embassy fight over which courts try your case. But if we get you out of here, and make it to your embassy, then your government will protect your rights while you and I prove you had nothing to do with this murder."

Langdon looked not even vaguely convinced. "Forget it! Fache has armed guards on every single exit! Even if we escape without being shot, running away only makes me look guilty. You need to tell Fache that the message on the floor was for *you,* and that my name is not there as an accusation."

"I *will* do that," Sophie said, speaking hurriedly, "but after you're safely inside the U.S. Embassy. It's only about a mile from here, and my car is parked just outside the museum. Dealing with Fache from here is too much of a gamble. Don't you see? Fache has made it his mission tonight to prove you are guilty. The only reason he post-poned your arrest was to run this observance in hopes you did something that made his case stronger."

"Exactly. Like *running!*"

The cell phone in Sophie's sweater pocket suddenly began ringing. *Fache probably.* She reached in her sweater and turned off the phone.

"Mr. Langdon," she said hurriedly, "I need to ask you one last question." *And your entire future may depend on it.* "The writing on the floor is obviously not proof of your guilt, and yet Fache told our team he is *certain* you are his man. Can you think of any other reason he might be convinced you're guilty?"

Langdon was silent for several seconds. "None whatsoever."

Sophie sighed. *Which means Fache is lying.* Why, Sophie could not begin to imagine, but that was hardly the issue at this point. The fact remained that Bezu Fache was determined to put Robert Langdon behind bars tonight, at any cost. Sophie needed Langdon for herself, and it was this dilemma that left Sophie only one logical conclusion.

*I need to get Langdon to the U.S. Embassy.*

Turning toward the window, Sophie gazed through the alarm mesh embedded in the plate glass, down the dizzying forty feet to the pavement below. A leap from this height would leave Langdon with a couple of broken legs. At best.

Nonetheless, Sophie made her decision.

Robert Langdon was about to escape the Louvre, whether he wanted to or not.

# CHAPTER 17

"**What do** you mean she's not answering?" Fache looked incredulous. "You're calling her cell phone, right? I know she's carrying it."

Collet had been trying to reach Sophie now for several minutes. "Maybe her batteries are dead. Or her ringer's off."

Fache had looked distressed ever since talking to the director of Cryptology on the phone. After hanging up, he had marched over to Collet and demanded he get Agent Neveu on the line. Now Collet had failed, and Fache was pacing like a caged lion.

"Why did Crypto call?" Collet now ventured.

Fache turned. "To tell us they found no references to Draconian devils and lame saints."

"That's all?"

"No, also to tell us that they had just identified the numerics as Fibonacci numbers, but they suspected the series was meaningless."

Collet was confused. "But they already sent Agent Neveu to tell us that."

Fache shook his head. "They didn't send Neveu."

"What?"

"According to the director, at my orders he

paged his entire team to look at the images I'd wired him. When Agent Neveu arrived, she took one look at the photos of Saunière and the code and left the office without a word. The director said he didn't question her behavior because she was understandably upset by the photos."

"Upset? She's never seen a picture of a dead body?"

Fache was silent a moment. "I was not aware of this, and it seems neither was the director until a coworker informed him, but apparently Sophie Neveu is Jacques Saunière's granddaughter."

Collet was speechless.

"The director said she never once mentioned Saunière to him, and he assumed it was because she probably didn't want preferential treatment for having a famous grandfather."

*No wonder she was upset by the pictures.* Collet could barely conceive of the unfortunate coincidence that called in a young woman to decipher a code written by a dead family member. Still, her actions made no sense. "But she obviously recognized the numbers as Fibonacci numbers because she came here and *told* us. I don't understand why she would leave the office without telling anyone she had figured it out."

Collet could think of only one scenario to explain the troubling developments: Saunière had written a numeric code on the floor in hopes Fache would involve cryptographers in the investigation, and therefore involve his own granddaughter. As for the rest of the message, was Saunière communicating in some way with his granddaughter? If so, what did the message tell her? And how did Langdon fit in?

Before Collet could ponder it any further, the silence of the deserted museum was shattered by an alarm. The bell sounded like it was coming from inside the Grand Gallery.

"*Alarme!*" one of the agents yelled, eyeing his feed from the Louvre security center. "*Grande Galerie! Toilettes Messieurs!*"

Fache wheeled to Collet. "Where's Langdon?"

"Still in the men's room!" Collet pointed to the blinking red dot on his laptop schematic. "He must have broken the window!" Collet knew Langdon wouldn't get far. Although Paris fire codes required windows above fifteen meters in public buildings be breakable in case of fire, exiting a Louvre second-story window without the help of a hook and ladder would be suicide. Furthermore, there were no trees or grass on the western end of the Denon Wing to cushion a fall. Directly beneath that rest room window, the two-lane Place du Carrousel ran within a few feet of the outer wall. "My God," Collet exclaimed, eyeing the screen. "Langdon's moving to the window ledge!"

But Fache was already in motion. Yanking his

Manurhin MR-93 revolver from his shoulder holster, the captain dashed out of the office.

Collet watched the screen in bewilderment as the blinking dot arrived at the window ledge and then did something utterly unexpected. The dot moved *outside* the perimeter of the building.

*What's going on?* he wondered. *Is Langdon out on a ledge or—*

"*Jesu!*" Collet jumped to his feet as the dot shot farther outside the wall. The signal seemed to shudder for a moment, and then the blinking dot came to an abrupt stop about ten yards outside the perimeter of the building.

Fumbling with the controls, Collet called up a Paris street map and recalibrated the GPS. Zooming in, he could now see the exact location of the signal.

It was no longer moving.

It lay at a dead stop in the middle of Place du Carrousel.

Langdon had jumped.

# CHAPTER 18

**Fache sprinted** down the Grand Gallery as Collet's radio blared over the distant sound of the alarm.

"He jumped!" Collet was yelling. "I'm showing the signal out on Place du Carrousel! Outside the bathroom window! And it's not moving at all! Jesus, I think Langdon has just committed suicide!"

Fache heard the words, but they made no sense. He kept running. The hallway seemed never-ending. As he sprinted past Saunière's body, he set his sights on the partitions at the far end of the Denon Wing. The alarm was getting louder now.

"Wait!" Collet's voice blared again over the radio. "He's moving! My God, he's alive. Langdon's moving!"

Fache kept running, cursing the length of the hallway with every step.

"Langdon's moving faster!" Collet was still yelling on the radio. "He's running down Carrousel. Wait . . . he's picking up speed. He's moving too fast!"

Arriving at the partitions, Fache snaked his way through them, saw the rest room door, and ran for it.

The walkie-talkie was barely audible now over the alarm. "He must be in a car! I think he's in a car! I can't—"

Collet's words were swallowed by the alarm as Fache finally burst into the men's room with his gun drawn. Wincing against the piercing shrill, he scanned the area.

The stalls were empty. The bathroom deserted. Fache's eyes moved immediately to the shattered window at the far end of the room. He ran to the opening and looked over the edge. Langdon was nowhere to be seen. Fache could not imagine anyone risking a stunt like this. Certainly if he had dropped that far, he would be badly injured.

The alarm cut off finally, and Collet's voice became audible again over the walkie-talkie.

"... moving south ... faster ... crossing the Seine on Pont du Carrousel!"

Fache turned to his left. The only vehicle on Pont du Carrousel was an enormous twin-bed Trailor delivery truck moving southward away from the Louvre. The truck's open-air bed was covered with a vinyl tarp, roughly resembling a giant hammock. Fache felt a shiver of apprehension. That truck, only moments ago, had probably been stopped at a red light directly beneath the rest room window.

*An insane risk,* Fache told himself. Langdon had no way of knowing what the truck was carrying beneath that tarp. What if the truck were carrying steel? Or cement? Or even garbage? A forty-foot leap? It was madness.

"The dot is turning!" Collet called. "He's turning right on Pont des Saints-Pères!"

Sure enough, the Trailor truck that had crossed the bridge was slowing down and making a right turn onto Pont des Saints-Pères. *So be it,* Fache thought. Amazed, he watched the truck disappear around the corner. Collet was already radioing the agents outside, pulling them off the Louvre perimeter and sending them to their patrol cars in pursuit, all the while broadcasting the truck's changing location like some kind of bizarre play-by-play.

*It's over,* Fache knew. His men would have the truck surrounded within minutes. Langdon was not going anywhere.

Stowing his weapon, Fache exited the rest room and radioed Collet. "Bring my car around. I want to be there when we make the arrest."

As Fache jogged back down the length of the Grand Gallery, he wondered if Langdon had even survived the fall.

Not that it mattered.

*Langdon ran. Guilty as charged.*


Only fifteen yards from the rest room, Langdon and Sophie stood in the darkness of the Grand

Gallery, their backs pressed to one of the large partitions that hid the bathrooms from the gallery. They had barely managed to hide themselves before Fache had darted past them, gun drawn, and disappeared into the bathroom.

The last sixty seconds had been a blur.

Langdon had been standing inside the men's room refusing to run from a crime he didn't commit, when Sophie began eyeing the plate-glass window and examining the alarm mesh running through it. Then she peered downward into the street, as if measuring the drop.

"With a little aim, you can get out of here," she said.

*Aim?* Uneasy, he peered out the rest room window.

Up the street, an enormous twin-bed eighteen-wheeler was headed for the stoplight beneath the window. Stretched across the truck's massive cargo bay was a blue vinyl tarp, loosely covering the truck's load. Langdon hoped Sophie was not thinking what she seemed to be thinking.

"Sophie, there's no way I'm jump—"

"Take out the tracking dot."

Bewildered, Langdon fumbled in his pocket until he found the tiny metallic disk. Sophie took it from him and strode immediately to the sink. She grabbed a thick bar of soap, placed the tracking dot on top of it, and used her thumb to push the disk down hard into the bar. As the disk sank into the soft surface, she pinched the hole closed, firmly embedding the device in the bar.

Handing the bar to Langdon, Sophie retrieved a heavy, cylindrical trash can from under the sinks. Before Langdon could protest, Sophie ran at the window, holding the can before her like a battering ram. Driving the bottom of the trash can into the center of the window, she shattered the glass.

Alarms erupted overhead at earsplitting decibel levels.

"Give me the soap!" Sophie yelled, barely audible over the alarm.

Langdon thrust the bar into her hand.

Palming the soap, she peered out the shattered window at the eighteen-wheeler idling below. The target was plenty big—an expansive, stationary tarp—and it was less than ten feet from the side of the building. As the traffic lights prepared to change, Sophie took a deep breath and lobbed the bar of soap out into the night.

The soap plummeted downward toward the truck, landing on the edge of the tarp, and sliding downward into the cargo bay just as the traffic light turned green.

"Congratulations," Sophie said, dragging him toward the door. "You just escaped from the Louvre."

Fleeing the men's room, they moved into the shadows just as Fache rushed past.

Now, with the fire alarm silenced, Langdon could hear the sounds of DCPJ sirens tearing away from the Louvre. *A police exodus.* Fache had hurried off as well, leaving the Grand Gallery deserted.

"There's an emergency stairwell about fifty meters back into the Grand Gallery," Sophie said. "Now that the guards are leaving the perimeter, we can get out of here."

Langdon decided not to say another word all evening. Sophie Neveu was clearly a hell of a lot smarter than he was.

# CHAPTER 19

**The Church** of Saint-Sulpice, it is said, has the most eccentric history of any building in Paris. Built over the ruins of an ancient temple to the Egyptian goddess Isis, the church possesses an architectural footprint matching that of Notre Dame to within inches. The sanctuary has played host to the baptisms of the Marquis de Sade and Baudelaire, as well as the marriage of Victor Hugo. The attached seminary has a well-documented history of unorthodoxy and was once the clandestine meeting hall for numerous secret societies.

Tonight, the cavernous nave of Saint-Sulpice was as silent as a tomb, the only hint of life the faint smell of incense from mass earlier that evening. Silas sensed an uneasiness in Sister Sandrine's demeanor as she led him into the sanctuary. He was not surprised by this. Silas was accustomed to people being uncomfortable with his appearance.

"You're an American," she said.

"French by birth," Silas responded. "I had my calling in Spain, and I now study in the United States."

Sister Sandrine nodded. She was a small woman

with quiet eyes. "And you have *never* seen Saint-Sulpice?"

"I realize this is almost a sin in itself."

"She is more beautiful by day."

"I am certain. Nonetheless, I am grateful that you would provide me this opportunity tonight."

"The abbé requested it. You obviously have powerful friends."

*You have no idea,* Silas thought.

As he followed Sister Sandrine down the main aisle, Silas was surprised by the austerity of the sanctuary. Unlike Notre Dame with its colorful frescoes, gilded altar-work, and warm wood, Saint-Sulpice was stark and cold, conveying an almost barren quality reminiscent of the ascetic cathedrals of Spain. The lack of decor made the interior look even more expansive, and as Silas gazed up into the soaring ribbed vault of the ceiling, he imagined he was standing beneath the hull of an enormous overturned ship.

*A fitting image,* he thought. The brotherhood's ship was about to be capsized forever. Feeling eager to get to work, Silas wished Sister Sandrine would leave him. She was a small woman whom Silas could incapacitate easily, but he had vowed not to use force unless absolutely necessary. *She is a woman of the cloth, and it is not her fault the brotherhood chose her church as a hiding place for their keystone. She should not be punished for the sins of others.*

"I am embarrassed, Sister, that you were awoken on my behalf."

"Not at all. You are in Paris a short time. You should not miss Saint-Sulpice. Are your interests in the church more architectural or historical?"

"Actually, Sister, my interests are spiritual."

She gave a pleasant laugh. "That goes without saying. I simply wondered where to begin your tour."

Silas felt his eyes focus on the altar. "A tour is unnecessary. You have been more than kind. I can show myself around."

"It is no trouble," she said. "After all, I am awake."

Silas stopped walking. They had reached the front pew now, and the altar was only fifteen yards away. He turned his massive body fully toward the small woman, and he could sense her recoil as she gazed up into his red eyes. "If it does not seem too rude, Sister, I am not accustomed to simply walking into a house of God and taking a tour. Would you mind if I took some time alone to pray before I look around?"

Sister Sandrine hesitated. "Oh, of course. I shall wait in the rear of the church for you."

Silas put a soft but heavy hand on her shoulder and peered down. "Sister, I feel guilty already for having awoken you. To ask you to stay awake is too much. Please, you should return to bed. I can enjoy your sanctuary and then let myself out."

She looked uneasy. "Are you sure you won't feel abandoned?"

"Not at all. Prayer is a solitary joy."

"As you wish."

Silas took his hand from her shoulder. "Sleep well, Sister. May the peace of the Lord be with you."

"And also with you." Sister Sandrine headed for the stairs. "Please be sure the door closes tightly on your way out."

"I will be sure of it." Silas watched her climb out of sight. Then he turned and knelt in the front pew, feeling the *cilice* cut into his leg.

*Dear God, I offer up to you this work I do today. . . .*

Crouching in the shadows of the choir balcony high above the altar, Sister Sandrine peered silently through the balustrade at the cloaked monk kneeling alone. The sudden dread in her soul made it hard to stay still. For a fleeting instant, she wondered if this mysterious visitor could be the enemy they had warned her about, and if tonight she would have to carry out the orders she had been holding all these years. She decided to stay there in the darkness and watch his every move.

# CHAPTER 20

**Emerging from** the shadows, Langdon and Sophie moved stealthily up the deserted Grand Gallery corridor toward the emergency exit stairwell.

As he moved, Langdon felt like he was trying to assemble a jigsaw puzzle in the dark. The newest aspect of this mystery was a deeply troubling one: *The captain of the Judicial Police is trying to frame me for murder.*

"Do you think," he whispered, "that maybe *Fache* wrote that message on the floor?"

Sophie didn't even turn. "Impossible."

Langdon wasn't so sure. "He seems pretty intent on making me look guilty. Maybe he thought writing my name on the floor would help his case?"

"The Fibonacci sequence? The P.S.? All the Da Vinci and goddess symbolism? That *had* to be my grandfather."

Langdon knew she was right. The symbolism of the clues meshed too perfectly—the pentacle, *The Vitruvian Man,* Da Vinci, the goddess, and even the Fibonacci sequence. *A coherent symbolic set,* as iconographers would call it. All inextricably tied.

"And his phone call to me this afternoon,"

Sophie added. "He said he had to tell me something. I'm certain his message at the Louvre was his final effort to tell me something important, something he thought you could help me understand."

Langdon frowned. *O, Draconian devil! Oh, lame saint!* He wished he could comprehend the message, both for Sophie's well-being and for his own. Things had definitely gotten worse since he first laid eyes on the cryptic words. His fake leap out the bathroom window was not going to help Langdon's popularity with Fache one bit. Somehow he doubted the captain of the French police would see the humor in chasing down and arresting a bar of soap.

"The doorway isn't much farther," Sophie said.

"Do you think there's a possibility that the *numbers* in your grandfather's message hold the key to understanding the other lines?" Langdon had once worked on a series of Baconian manuscripts that contained epigraphical ciphers in which certain lines of code were clues as to how to decipher the other lines.

"I've been thinking about the numbers all night. Sums, quotients, products. I don't see anything. Mathematically, they're arranged at random. Cryptographic gibberish."

"And yet they're all part of the Fibonacci sequence. That can't be coincidence."

"It's not. Using Fibonacci numbers was my

grandfather's way of waving another flag at me—
like writing the message in English, or arranging
himself like my favorite piece of art, or drawing a
pentacle on himself. All of it was to catch my
attention."

"The pentacle has meaning to you?"

"Yes. I didn't get a chance to tell you, but the
pentacle was a special symbol between my grandfather and me when I was growing up. We used
to play Tarot cards for fun, and my indicator card
*always* turned out to be from the suit of pentacles.
I'm sure he stacked the deck, but pentacles got to
be our little joke."

Langdon felt a chill. *They played Tarot?* The medieval Italian card game was so replete with hidden heretical symbolism that Langdon had
dedicated an entire chapter in his new manuscript
to the Tarot. The game's twenty-two cards bore
names like *The Female Pope, The Empress,* and *The
Star.* Originally, Tarot had been devised as a secret means to pass along ideologies banned by the
Church. Now, Tarot's mystical qualities were
passed on by modern fortune-tellers.

*The Tarot indicator suit for feminine divinity is pen-
tacles,* Langdon thought, realizing that if Saunière
had been stacking his granddaughter's deck for
fun, pentacles was an apropos inside joke.

They arrived at the emergency stairwell, and
Sophie carefully pulled open the door. No alarm
sounded. Only the doors to the outside were

wired. Sophie led Langdon down a tight set of switchback stairs toward the ground level, picking up speed as they went.

"Your grandfather," Langdon said, hurrying behind her, "when he told you about the pentacle, did he mention goddess worship or any resentment of the Catholic Church?"

Sophie shook her head. "I was more interested in the mathematics of it—the Divine Proportion, PHI, Fibonacci sequences, that sort of thing."

Langdon was surprised. "Your grandfather taught you about the number PHI?"

"Of course. The Divine Proportion." Her expression turned sheepish. "In fact, he used to joke that I was half divine . . . you know, because of the letters in my name."

Langdon considered it a moment and then groaned.

*s-o-PHI-e.*

Still descending, Langdon refocused on *PHI.* He was starting to realize that Saunière's clues were even more consistent than he had first imagined.

*Da Vinci . . . Fibonacci numbers . . . the pentacle.*

Incredibly, all of these things were connected by a single concept so fundamental to art history that Langdon often spent several class periods on the topic.

*PHI.*

He felt himself suddenly reeling back to

Harvard, standing in front of his "Symbolism in Art" class, writing his favorite number on the chalkboard.

1.618

Langdon turned to face his sea of eager students. "Who can tell me what this number is?"

A long-legged math major in back raised his hand. "That's the number PHI." He pronounced it *fee*.

"Nice job, Stettner," Langdon said. "Everyone, meet PHI."

"Not to be confused with PI," Stettner added, grinning. "As we mathematicians like to say: PHI is one *H* of a lot cooler than PI!"

Langdon laughed, but nobody else seemed to get the joke.

Stettner slumped.

"This number PHI," Langdon continued, "one-point-six-one-eight, is a very important number in art. Who can tell me why?"

Stettner tried to redeem himself. "Because it's so pretty?"

Everyone laughed.

"Actually," Langdon said, "Stettner's right again. PHI is generally considered the most beautiful number in the universe."

The laughter abruptly stopped, and Stettner gloated.

As Langdon loaded his slide projector, he explained that the number PHI was derived from the Fibonacci sequence—a progression famous not only because the sum of adjacent terms equaled the next term, but because the *quotients* of adjacent terms possessed the astonishing property of approaching the number 1.618—PHI!

Despite PHI's seemingly mystical mathematical origins, Langdon explained, the truly mind-boggling aspect of PHI was its role as a fundamental building block in nature. Plants, animals, and even human beings all possessed dimensional properties that adhered with eerie exactitude to the ratio of PHI to 1.

"PHI's ubiquity in nature," Langdon said, killing the lights, "clearly exceeds coincidence, and so the ancients assumed the number PHI must have been preordained by the Creator of the universe. Early scientists heralded one-point-six-one-eight as the *Divine Proportion.*"

"Hold on," said a young woman in the front row. "I'm a bio major and I've never seen this Divine Proportion in nature."

"No?" Langdon grinned. "Ever study the relationship between females and males in a honeybee community?"

"Sure. The female bees always outnumber the male bees."

"Correct. And did you know that if you divide the number of female bees by the number of male bees in any beehive in the world, you always get the same number?"

"You do?"

"Yup. PHI."

The girl gaped. "NO WAY!"

"Way!" Langdon fired back, smiling as he projected a slide of a spiral seashell. "Recognize this?"

"It's a nautilus," the bio major said. "A cephalopod mollusk that pumps gas into its chambered shell to adjust its buoyancy."

"Correct. And can you guess what the ratio is of each spiral's diameter to the next?"

The girl looked uncertain as she eyed the concentric arcs of the nautilus spiral.

Langdon nodded. "PHI. The Divine Proportion. One-point-six-one-eight to one."

The girl looked amazed.

Langdon advanced to the next slide—a close-up of a sunflower's seed head. "Sunflower seeds grow in opposing spirals. Can you guess the ratio of each rotation's diameter to the next?"

"PHI?" everyone said.

"Bingo." Langdon began racing through slides now—spiraled pinecone petals, leaf arrangement on plant stalks, insect segmentation—all displaying astonishing obedience to the Divine Proportion.

"This is amazing!" someone cried out.

"Yeah," someone else said, "but what does it have to do with *art?*"

"Aha!" Langdon said. "Glad you asked." He pulled up another slide—a pale yellow parchment displaying Leonardo da Vinci's famous male nude—*The Vitruvian Man*—named for Marcus Vitruvius, the brilliant Roman architect who praised the Divine Proportion in his text *De Architectura.*

"Nobody understood better than Da Vinci the divine structure of the human body. Da Vinci actually *exhumed* corpses to measure the exact proportions of human bone structure. He was the first to show that the human body is literally made of building blocks whose proportional ratios *always* equal PHI."

Everyone in class gave him a dubious look.

"Don't believe me?" Langdon challenged. "Next time you're in the shower, take a tape measure."

A couple of football players snickered.

"Not just you insecure jocks," Langdon prompted. "*All* of you. Guys and girls. Try it. Measure the distance from the tip of your head to the floor. Then divide that by the distance from your belly button to the floor. Guess what number you get."

"Not PHI!" one of the jocks blurted out in disbelief.

"Yes, PHI," Langdon replied. "One-point-six-one-eight. Want another example? Measure the distance from your shoulder to your fingertips, and then divide it by the distance from your elbow to your fingertips. PHI again. Another? Hip to floor divided by knee to floor. PHI again. Finger joints. Toes. Spinal divisions. PHI. PHI. PHI. My friends, each of you is a walking tribute to the Divine Proportion."

Even in the darkness, Langdon could see they were all astounded. He felt a familiar warmth inside. This is why he taught. "My friends, as you can see, the chaos of the world has an underlying order. When the ancients discovered PHI, they were certain they had stumbled across God's building block for the world, and they worshipped Nature because of that. And one can understand why. God's hand is evident in Nature, and even to this day there exist pagan, Mother Earth–revering religions. Many of us celebrate nature the way the pagans did, and don't even know it. May Day is a perfect example, the celebration of spring . . . the earth coming back to life to produce her bounty. The mysterious magic inherent in the Divine Proportion was written at the beginning of time. Man is simply playing by Nature's rules, and because *art* is man's attempt to imitate the beauty of the Creator's hand, you can imagine we might be seeing a lot of instances of the Divine Proportion in art this semester."

Over the next half hour, Langdon showed them slides of artwork by Michelangelo, Albrecht Dürer, Da Vinci, and many others, demonstrating each artist's intentional and rigorous adherence to the Divine Proportion in the layout of his compositions. Langdon unveiled PHI in the architectural dimensions of the Greek Parthenon, the pyramids of Egypt, and even the United Nations Building in New York. PHI appeared in the organizational structures of Mozart's sonatas, Beethoven's Fifth Symphony, as well as the works of Bartók, Debussy, and Schubert. The number PHI, Langdon told them, was even used by Stradivarius to calculate the exact placement of the f-holes in the construction of his famous violins.

"In closing," Langdon said, walking to the chalkboard, "we return to *symbols*." He drew five intersecting lines that formed a five-pointed star. "This symbol is one of the most powerful images you will see this term. Formally known as a pentagram—or *pentacle,* as the ancients called it— this symbol is considered both divine and magical by many cultures. Can anyone tell me why that might be?"

Stettner, the math major, raised his hand. "Because if you draw a pentagram, the lines automatically divide themselves into segments according to the Divine Proportion."

Langdon gave the kid a proud nod. "Nice job.

Yes, the ratios of line segments in a pentacle *all* equal PHI, making this symbol the *ultimate* expression of the Divine Proportion. For this reason, the five-pointed star has always been the symbol for beauty and perfection associated with the goddess and the sacred feminine."

The girls in class beamed.

"One note, folks. We've only touched on Da Vinci today, but we'll be seeing a lot more of him this semester. Leonardo was a well-documented devotee of the ancient ways of the goddess. Tomorrow, I'll show you his fresco *The Last Supper,* which is one of the most astonishing tributes to the sacred feminine you will ever see."

"You're kidding, right?" somebody said. "I thought *The Last Supper* was about Jesus!"

Langdon winked. "There are symbols hidden in places you would never imagine."

"Come on," Sophie whispered. "What's wrong? We're almost there. Hurry!"

Langdon glanced up, feeling himself return from faraway thoughts. He realized he was standing at a dead stop on the stairs, paralyzed by sudden revelation.

*O, Draconian devil! Oh, lame saint!*

Sophie was looking back at him.

*It can't be that simple,* Langdon thought.

But he knew of course that it was.

There in the bowels of the Louvre . . . with images of PHI and Da Vinci swirling through his mind, Robert Langdon suddenly and unexpectedly deciphered Saunière's code.

"O, Draconian devil!" he said. "Oh, lame saint! It's the simplest kind of code!"

Sophie was stopped on the stairs below him, staring up in confusion. *A code?* She had been pondering the words all night and had not seen a code. Especially a simple one.

"You said it yourself." Langdon's voice reverberated with excitement. "Fibonacci numbers only have meaning in their proper order. Otherwise they're mathematical gibberish."

Sophie had no idea what he was talking about. *The Fibonacci numbers?* She was certain they had been intended as nothing more than a means to get the Cryptography Department involved tonight. *They have another purpose?* She plunged her hand into her pocket and pulled out the printout, studying her grandfather's message again.

13-3-2-21-1-1-8-5
O, Draconian devil!
Oh, lame saint!

*What about the numbers?*

"The scrambled Fibonacci sequence is a clue," Langdon said, taking the printout. "The numbers are a hint as to how to decipher the rest of the message. He wrote the sequence out of order to tell us to apply the same concept to the text. O, Draconian devil? Oh, lame saint? Those lines mean nothing. They are simply *letters* written out of order."

Sophie needed only an instant to process Langdon's implication, and it seemed laughably simple. "You think this message is . . . *une ana-gramme?*" She stared at him. "Like a word jumble from a newspaper?"

Langdon could see the skepticism on Sophie's face and certainly understood. Few people realized that anagrams, despite being a trite modern amusement, had a rich history of sacred symbolism.

The mystical teachings of the Kabbala drew heavily on anagrams—rearranging the letters of Hebrew words to derive new meanings. French kings throughout the Renaissance were so convinced that anagrams held magic power that they appointed royal anagrammatists to help them make better decisions by analyzing words in important documents. The Romans actually referred to the study of anagrams as *ars magna*—"the great art."

Langdon looked up at Sophie, locking eyes

with her now. "Your grandfather's meaning was right in front of us all along, and he left us more than enough clues to see it."

Without another word, Langdon pulled a pen from his jacket pocket and rearranged the letters in each line.

O, Draconian devil!
Oh, lame saint!

was a perfect anagram of . . .

Leonardo da Vinci!
The Mona Lisa!

# CHAPTER 21

## *The Mona Lisa.*

For an instant, standing in the exit stairwell, Sophie forgot all about trying to leave the Louvre.

Her shock over the anagram was matched only by her embarrassment at not having deciphered the message herself. Sophie's expertise in complex cryptanalysis had caused her to overlook simplistic word games, and yet she knew she should have seen it. After all, she was no stranger to anagrams—especially in English.

When she was young, often her grandfather would use anagram games to hone her English spelling. Once he had written the English word "planets" and told Sophie that an astonishing sixty-two *other* English words of varying lengths could be formed using those same letters. Sophie had spent three days with an English dictionary until she found them all.

"I can't imagine," Langdon said, staring at the printout, "how your grandfather created such an intricate anagram in the minutes before he died."

Sophie knew the explanation, and the realization made her feel even worse. *I should have seen this!* She now recalled that her grandfather—a wordplay aficionado and art lover—had entertained himself as a young man by creating anagrams of famous works of art. In fact, one of his anagrams had gotten him in trouble once when Sophie was a little girl. While being interviewed by an American art magazine, Saunière had expressed his distaste for the modernist Cubist movement by noting that Picasso's masterpiece *Les Demoiselles d'Avignon* was a perfect anagram of *vile meaningless doodles*. Picasso fans were not amused.

"My grandfather probably created this *Mona Lisa* anagram long ago," Sophie said, glancing up at Langdon. *And tonight he was forced to use it as a makeshift code.* Her grandfather's voice had called out from beyond with chilling precision.

*Leonardo da Vinci!*

*The Mona Lisa!*

Why his final words to her referenced the famous painting, Sophie had no idea, but she could think of only one possibility. A disturbing one.

*Those were not his final words. . . .*

Was she supposed to visit the *Mona Lisa*? Had her grandfather left her a message there? The idea seemed perfectly plausible. After all, the famous painting hung in the Salle des Etats—a private viewing chamber accessible only from the Grand Gallery. In fact, Sophie now realized, the doors that opened into the chamber were situated only twenty meters from where her grandfather had been found dead.

*He easily could have visited the Mona Lisa before he died.*

Sophie gazed back up the emergency stairwell and felt torn. She knew she should usher Langdon from the museum immediately, and yet instinct urged her to the contrary. As Sophie recalled her first childhood visit to the Denon Wing, she realized that if her grandfather had a secret to tell her, few places on earth made a more apt rendezvous than Da Vinci's *Mona Lisa.*

"She's just a little bit farther," her grandfather had whispered, clutching Sophie's tiny hand as he led her through the deserted museum after hours.

Sophie was six years old. She felt small and insignificant as she gazed up at the enormous ceilings and down at the dizzying floor. The empty museum frightened her, although she was not about to let her grandfather know that. She set her jaw firmly and let go of his hand.

"Up ahead is the Salle des Etats," her grandfather said as they approached the Louvre's most famous room. Despite her grandfather's obvious excitement, Sophie wanted to go home. She had seen pictures of the *Mona Lisa* in books and didn't like it at all. She couldn't understand why everyone made such a fuss.

"*C'est ennuyeux,*" Sophie grumbled.

"Boring," he corrected. "French at school. English at home."

"*Le Louvre, c'est pas chez moi!*" she challenged.

He gave her a tired laugh. "Right you are. Then let's speak English just for fun."

Sophie pouted and kept walking. As they entered the Salle des Etats, her eyes scanned the narrow room and settled on the obvious spot of honor—the center of the right-hand wall, where a lone portrait hung behind a protective Plexiglas wall. Her grandfather paused in the doorway and motioned toward the painting.

"Go ahead, Sophie. Not many people get a chance to visit her alone."

Swallowing her apprehension, Sophie moved slowly across the room. After everything she'd heard about the *Mona Lisa,* she felt as if she were approaching royalty. Arriving in front of the protective Plexiglas, Sophie held her breath and looked up, taking it in all at once.

Sophie was not sure what she had expected to feel, but it most certainly was not this. No jolt of amazement. No instant of wonder. The famous face looked as it did in books. She stood in silence for what felt like forever, waiting for something to happen.

"So what do you think?" her grandfather whispered, arriving behind her. "Beautiful, yes?"

"She's too little."

Saunière smiled. "You're little and you're beautiful."

*I am not beautiful,* she thought. Sophie hated her red hair and freckles, and she was bigger than all the boys in her class. She looked back at the *Mona Lisa* and shook her head. "She's even worse than in the books. Her face is . . . *brumeux.*"

"Foggy," her grandfather tutored.

"Foggy," Sophie repeated, knowing the conversation would not continue until she repeated her new vocabulary word.

"That's called the *sfumato* style of painting," he told her, "and it's very hard to do. Leonardo da Vinci was better at it than anyone."

Sophie still didn't like the painting. "She looks like she knows something . . . like when kids at school have a secret."

Her grandfather laughed. "That's part of why she is so famous. People like to guess why she is smiling."

"Do *you* know why she's smiling?"

"Maybe." Her grandfather winked. "Someday I'll tell you all about it."

Sophie stamped her foot. "I told you I don't like secrets!"

"Princess," he smiled. "Life is filled with secrets. You can't learn them all at once."

"I'm going back up," Sophie declared, her voice hollow in the stairwell.

"To the *Mona Lisa*?" Langdon recoiled. *"Now?"*

Sophie considered the risk. "I'm not a murder suspect. I'll take my chances. I need to understand what my grandfather was trying to tell me."

"What about the embassy?"

Sophie felt guilty turning Langdon into a fugitive only to abandon him, but she saw no other option. She pointed down the stairs to a metal door. "Go through that door, and follow the illuminated exit signs. My grandfather used to bring me down here. The signs will lead you to a security turnstile. It's monodirectional and opens out." She handed Langdon her car keys. "Mine is the red SmartCar in the employee lot. Directly outside this bulkhead. Do you know how to get to the embassy?"

Langdon nodded, eyeing the keys in his hand.

"Listen," Sophie said, her voice softening. "I think my grandfather may have left me a message at the *Mona Lisa*—some kind of clue as to who killed him. Or why I'm in danger." *Or what happened to my family.* "I have to go see."

"But if he wanted to tell you why you were in danger, why wouldn't he simply write it on the floor where he died? Why this complicated word game?"

"Whatever my grandfather was trying to tell

me, I don't think he wanted anyone else to hear it. Not even the police." Clearly, her grandfather had done everything in his power to send a confidential transmission directly to *her*. He had written it in code, included her secret initials, and told her to find Robert Langdon—a wise command, considering the American symbologist had deciphered his code. "As strange as it may sound," Sophie said, "I think he wants me to get to the *Mona Lisa* before anyone else does."

"I'll come."

"No! We don't know how long the Grand Gallery will stay empty. *You* have to go."

Langdon seemed hesitant, as if his own academic curiosity were threatening to override sound judgment and drag him back into Fache's hands.

"Go. Now." Sophie gave him a grateful smile. "I'll see you at the embassy, Mr. Langdon."

Langdon looked displeased. "I'll meet you there on *one* condition," he replied, his voice stern.

She paused, startled. "What's that?"

"That you stop calling me *Mr.* Langdon."

Sophie detected the faint hint of a lopsided grin growing across Langdon's face, and she felt herself smile back. "Good luck, Robert."

When Langdon reached the landing at the bottom of the stairs, the unmistakable smell of linseed oil and plaster dust assaulted his nostrils. Ahead, an illuminated SORTIE/EXIT displayed an arrow pointing down a long corridor.

Langdon stepped into the hallway.

To the right gaped a murky restoration studio out of which peered an army of statues in various states of repair. To the left, Langdon saw a suite of studios that resembled Harvard art classrooms— rows of easels, paintings, palettes, framing tools— an art assembly line.

As he moved down the hallway, Langdon wondered if at any moment he might awake with a start in his bed in Cambridge. The entire evening had felt like a bizarre dream. *I'm about to dash out of the Louvre . . . a fugitive.*

Saunière's clever anagrammatic message was still on his mind, and Langdon wondered what Sophie would find at the *Mona Lisa* . . . if anything. She had seemed certain her grandfather meant for her to visit the famous painting one more time. As plausible an interpretation as this seemed, Langdon felt haunted now by a troubling paradox.

*P.S. Find Robert Langdon.*

Saunière had written Langdon's name on the floor, commanding Sophie to find him. But why? Merely so Langdon could help her break an anagram?

It seemed quite unlikely.

After all, Saunière had no reason to think

Langdon was especially skilled at anagrams. *We've never even met.* More important, Sophie had stated flat out that *she* should have broken the anagram on her own. It had been Sophie who spotted the Fibonacci sequence, and, no doubt, Sophie who, if given a little more time, would have deciphered the message with no help from Langdon.

*Sophie was supposed to break that anagram on her own.* Langdon was suddenly feeling more certain about this, and yet the conclusion left an obvious gaping lapse in the logic of Saunière's actions.

*Why me?* Langdon wondered, heading down the hall. *Why was Saunière's dying wish that his estranged granddaughter find me? What is it that Saunière thinks I know?*

With an unexpected jolt, Langdon stopped short. Eyes wide, he dug in his pocket and yanked out the computer printout. He stared at the last line of Saunière's message.

*P.S. Find Robert Langdon.*

He fixated on two letters.

*P.S.*

In that instant, Langdon felt Saunière's puzzling mix of symbolism fall into stark focus. Like a peal of thunder, a career's worth of symbology and history came crashing down around him. Everything Jacques Saunière had done tonight suddenly made perfect sense.

Langdon's thoughts raced as he tried to assemble the implications of what this all meant.

Wheeling, he stared back in the direction from which he had come.

*Is there time?*

He knew it didn't matter.

Without hesitation, Langdon broke into a sprint back toward the stairs.

# CHAPTER 22

**Kneeling in** the first pew, Silas pretended to pray as he scanned the layout of the sanctuary. Saint-Sulpice, like most churches, had been built in the shape of a giant Roman cross. Its long central section—the nave—led directly to the main altar, where it was transversely intersected by a shorter section, known as the transept. The intersection of nave and transept occurred directly beneath the main cupola and was considered the heart of the church . . . her most sacred and mystical point.

*Not tonight,* Silas thought. *Saint-Sulpice hides her secrets elsewhere.*

Turning his head to the right, he gazed into the south transept, toward the open area of floor beyond the end of the pews, to the object his victims had described.

*There it is.*

Embedded in the gray granite floor, a thin polished strip of brass glistened in the stone . . . a golden line slanting across the church's floor. The line bore graduated markings, like a ruler. It was a gnomon, Silas had been told, a pagan astronomical device like a sundial. Tourists, scientists, historians, and pagans from around the world came to Saint-Sulpice to gaze upon this famous line.

*The Rose Line.*

Slowly, Silas let his eyes trace the path of the brass strip as it made its way across the floor from his right to left, slanting in front of him at an awkward angle, entirely at odds with the symmetry of the church. Slicing across the main altar itself, the line looked to Silas like a slash wound across a beautiful face. The strip cleaved the communion rail in two and then crossed the entire width of the church, finally reaching the corner of the north transept, where it arrived at the base of a most unexpected structure.

A colossal Egyptian obelisk.

Here, the glistening Rose Line took a ninety-degree *vertical* turn and continued directly up the face of the obelisk itself, ascending thirty-three feet to the very tip of the pyramidical apex, where it finally ceased.

*The Rose Line,* Silas thought. *The brotherhood hid the keystone at the Rose Line.*

Earlier tonight, when Silas told the Teacher that the Priory keystone was hidden inside Saint-Sulpice, the Teacher had sounded doubtful. But when Silas added that the brothers had all given him a precise location, with relation to a brass line running through Saint-Sulpice, the Teacher had gasped with revelation. "You speak of the Rose Line!"

The Teacher quickly told Silas of Saint-Sulpice's famed architectural oddity—a strip of brass that

segmented the sanctuary on a perfect north-south
axis. It was an ancient sundial of sorts, a vestige of
the pagan temple that had once stood on this very
spot. The sun's rays, shining through the oculus
on the south wall, moved farther down the line
every day, indicating the passage of time, from
solstice to solstice.

The north-south stripe had been known as the
Rose Line. For centuries, the symbol of the Rose
had been associated with maps and guiding souls
in the proper direction. The Compass Rose—
drawn on almost every map—indicated North,
East, South, and West. Originally known as the
Wind Rose, it denoted the directions of the
thirty-two winds, blowing from the directions of
eight major winds, eight half-winds, and sixteen
quarter-winds. When diagrammed inside a circle,
these thirty-two points of the compass perfectly
resembled a traditional thirty-two petal rose
bloom. To this day, the fundamental navigational
tool was still known as a Compass Rose, its
northernmost direction still marked by an arrow-
head . . . or, more commonly, the symbol of the
fleur-de-lis.

On a globe, a Rose Line—also called a meridian or longitude—was any imaginary line drawn
from the North Pole to the South Pole. There
were, of course, an infinite number of Rose Lines
because every point on the globe could have a
longitude drawn through it connecting north and

south poles. The question for early navigators was *which* of these lines would be called *the* Rose Line—the zero longitude—the line from which all other longitudes on earth would be measured.

Today that line was in Greenwich, England.

But it had not always been.

Long before the establishment of Greenwich as the prime meridian, the zero longitude of the entire world had passed directly through Paris, and through the Church of Saint-Sulpice. The brass marker in Saint-Sulpice was a memorial to the world's first prime meridian, and although Greenwich had stripped Paris of the honor in 1888, the original Rose Line was still visible today.

"And so the legend is true," the Teacher had told Silas. "The Priory keystone has been said to lie 'beneath the Sign of the Rose.' "

Now, still on his knees in a pew, Silas glanced around the church and listened to make sure no one was there. For a moment, he thought he heard a rustling in the choir balcony. He turned and gazed up for several seconds. Nothing.

*I am alone.*

Standing now, he faced the altar and genuflected three times. Then he turned left and followed the brass line due north toward the obelisk.

At that moment, at Leonardo da Vinci International Airport in Rome, the jolt of tires hitting the runway startled Bishop Aringarosa from his slumber.

*I drifted off,* he thought, impressed he was re-laxed enough to sleep.

*"Benvenuto a Roma,"* the intercom announced.

Sitting up, Aringarosa straightened his black cassock and allowed himself a rare smile. This was one trip he had been happy to make. *I have been on the defensive for too long.* Tonight, however, the rules had changed. Only five months ago, Aringarosa had feared for the future of the Faith. Now, as if by the will of God, the solution had presented itself.

*Divine intervention.*

If all went as planned tonight in Paris, Aringarosa would soon be in possession of something that would make him the most powerful man in Christendom.

# CHAPTER 23

**Sophie arrived** breathless outside the large wooden doors of the Salle des Etats—the room that housed the *Mona Lisa*. Before entering, she gazed reluctantly farther down the hall, twenty yards or so, to the spot where her grandfather's body still lay under the spotlight.

The remorse that gripped her was powerful and sudden, a deep sadness laced with guilt. The man had reached out to her so many times over the past ten years, and yet Sophie had remained immovable—leaving his letters and packages unopened in a bottom drawer and denying his efforts to see her. *He lied to me! Kept appalling secrets! What was I supposed to do?* And so she had blocked him out. Completely.

Now her grandfather was dead, and he was talking to her from the grave.

*The Mona Lisa.*

She reached for the huge wooden doors, and pushed. The entryway yawned open. Sophie stood on the threshold a moment, scanning the large rectangular chamber beyond. It too was bathed in a soft red light. The Salle des Etats was one of this museum's rare *culs-de-sac*—a dead end and the only room off the middle of the Grand

Gallery. This door, the chamber's sole point of entry, faced a dominating fifteen-foot Botticelli on the far wall. Beneath it, centered on the parquet floor, an immense octagonal viewing divan served as a welcome respite for thousands of visitors to rest their legs while they admired the Louvre's most valuable asset.

Even before Sophie entered, though, she knew she was missing something. *A black light.* She gazed down the hall at her grandfather under the lights in the distance, surrounded by electronic gear. If he had written anything in here, he almost certainly would have written it with the watermark stylus.

Taking a deep breath, Sophie hurried down to the well-lit crime scene. Unable to look at her grandfather, she focused solely on the PTS tools. Finding a small ultraviolet penlight, she slipped it in the pocket of her sweater and hurried back up the hallway toward the open doors of the Salle des Etats.

Sophie turned the corner and stepped over the threshold. Her entrance, however, was met by an unexpected sound of muffled footsteps racing toward her from inside the chamber. *There's someone in here!* A ghostly figure emerged suddenly from out of the reddish haze. Sophie jumped back.

"There you are!" Langdon's hoarse whisper cut

the air as his silhouette slid to a stop in front of her.

Her relief was only momentary. "Robert, I told you to get out of here! If Fache—"

"Where were you?"

"I had to get the black light," she whispered, holding it up. "If my grandfather left me a message—"

"Sophie, listen." Langdon caught his breath as his blue eyes held her firmly. "The letters P.S. . . . do they mean anything else to you? Anything at all?"

Afraid their voices might echo down the hall, Sophie pulled him into the Salle des Etats and closed the enormous twin doors silently, sealing them inside. "I told you, the initials mean Princess Sophie."

"I know, but did you ever see them anywhere *else?* Did your grandfather ever use P.S. in any other way? As a monogram, or maybe on stationery or a personal item?"

The question startled her. *How would Robert know that?* Sophie had indeed seen the initials P.S. once before, in a kind of monogram. It was the day before her ninth birthday. She was secretly combing the house, searching for hidden birthday presents. Even then, she could not bear secrets kept from her. *What did Grand-père get for me this year?* She dug through cupboards and drawers.

*Did he get me the doll I wanted? Where would he hide it?*

Finding nothing in the entire house, Sophie mustered the courage to sneak into her grandfather's bedroom. The room was off-limits to her, but her grandfather was downstairs asleep on the couch.

*I'll just take a fast peek!*

Tiptoeing across the creaky wood floor to his closet, Sophie peered on the shelves behind his clothing. Nothing. Next she looked under the bed. Still nothing. Moving to his bureau, she opened the drawers and one by one began pawing carefully through them. *There must be something for me here!* As she reached the bottom drawer, she still had not found any hint of a doll. Dejected, she opened the final drawer and pulled aside some black clothes she had never seen him wear. She was about to close the drawer when her eyes caught a glint of gold in the back of the drawer. It looked like a pocket watch chain, but she knew he didn't wear one. Her heart raced as she realized what it must be.

*A necklace!*

Sophie carefully pulled the chain from the drawer. To her surprise, on the end was a brilliant gold key. Heavy and shimmering. Spellbound, she held it up. It looked like no key she had ever seen. Most keys were flat with jagged teeth, but this one had a triangular column with little pockmarks all over it. Its large golden head was in the shape of a cross, but not a normal cross. This was an even-armed one, like a plus sign. Embossed in the middle of the cross was a strange symbol— two letters intertwined with some kind of flowery design.

"P.S.," she whispered, scowling as she read the letters. *Whatever could this be?*

"Sophie?" her grandfather spoke from the doorway.

Startled, she spun, dropping the key on the floor with a loud clang. She stared down at the key, afraid to look up at her grandfather's face. "I . . . was looking for my birthday present," she said, hanging her head, knowing she had betrayed his trust.

For what seemed like an eternity, her grandfather stood silently in the doorway. Finally, he let out a long troubled breath. "Pick up the key, Sophie."

Sophie retrieved the key.

Her grandfather walked in. "Sophie, you need to respect other people's privacy." Gently, he knelt down and took the key from her. "This key is very special. If you had lost it . . ."

Her grandfather's quiet voice made Sophie feel even worse. "I'm sorry, *Grand-père.* I really am." She paused. "I thought it was a necklace for my birthday."

He gazed at her for several seconds. "I'll say this

once more, Sophie, because it's important. You need to learn to respect other people's privacy."

"Yes, *Grand-père.*"

"We'll talk about this some other time. Right now, the garden needs to be weeded."

Sophie hurried outside to do her chores.

The next morning, Sophie received no birthday present from her grandfather. She hadn't expected one, not after what she had done. But he didn't even wish her happy birthday all day. Sadly, she trudged up to bed that night. As she climbed in, though, she found a note card lying on her pillow. On the card was written a simple riddle. Even before she solved the riddle, she was smiling. *I know what this is!* Her grandfather had done this for her last Christmas morning.

*A treasure hunt!*

Eagerly, she pored over the riddle until she solved it. The solution pointed her to another part of the house, where she found another card and another riddle. She solved this one too, racing on to the next card. Running wildly, she darted back and forth across the house, from clue to clue, until at last she found a clue that directed her back to her own bedroom. Sophie dashed up the stairs, rushed into her room, and stopped in her tracks. There in the middle of the room sat a shining red bicycle with a ribbon tied to the handlebars. Sophie shrieked with delight.

"I know you asked for a doll," her grandfather

said, smiling in the corner. "I thought you might like this even better."

The next day, her grandfather taught her to ride, running beside her down the walkway. When Sophie steered out over the thick lawn and lost her balance, they both went tumbling onto the grass, rolling and laughing.

"*Grand-père,*" Sophie said, hugging him. "I'm really sorry about the key."

"I know, sweetie. You're forgiven. I can't possibly stay mad at you. Grandfathers and granddaughters always forgive each other."

Sophie knew she shouldn't ask, but she couldn't help it. "What does it open? I never saw a key like that. It was very pretty."

Her grandfather was silent a long moment, and Sophie could see he was uncertain how to answer. *Grand-père never lies.* "It opens a box," he finally said. "Where I keep many secrets."

Sophie pouted. "I hate secrets!"

"I know, but these are important secrets. And someday, you'll learn to appreciate them as much as I do."

"I saw letters on the key, and a flower."

"Yes, that's my favorite flower. It's called a fleur-de-lis. We have them in the garden. The white ones. In English we call that kind of flower a lily."

"I know those! They're *my* favorite too!"

"Then I'll make a deal with you." Her grandfather's eyebrows raised the way they always did when he was about to give her a challenge. "If you can keep my key a secret, and *never* talk about it ever again, to me or anybody, then someday I will give it to you."

Sophie couldn't believe her ears. "You *will?*"

"I promise. When the time comes, the key will be yours. It has your name on it."

Sophie scowled. "No it doesn't. It said P.S. My name isn't P.S.!"

Her grandfather lowered his voice and looked around as if to make sure no one was listening. "Okay, Sophie, if you *must* know, P.S. is a code. It's your secret initials."

Her eyes went wide. "I have secret initials?"

"Of course. Granddaughters *always* have secret initials that only their grandfathers know."

"P.S.?"

He tickled her. *"Princesse Sophie."*

She giggled. "I'm not a princess!"

He winked. "You are to me."

From that day on, they never again spoke of the key. And she became his Princess Sophie.

Inside the Salle des Etats, Sophie stood in silence and endured the sharp pang of loss.

"The initials," Langdon whispered, eyeing her strangely. "Have you seen them?"

Sophie sensed her grandfather's voice whispering in the corridors of the museum. *Never speak of this key, Sophie. To me or to anyone.* She knew she had failed him in forgiveness, and she wondered if she could break his trust again. *P.S. Find Robert Langdon.* Her grandfather wanted Langdon to help. Sophie nodded. "Yes, I saw the initials P.S. once. When I was very young."

"Where?"

Sophie hesitated. "On something very important to him."

Langdon locked eyes with her. "Sophie, this is crucial. Can you tell me if the initials appeared with a symbol? A fleur-de-lis?"

Sophie felt herself staggering backward in amazement. "But . . . how could you possibly know that!"

Langdon exhaled and lowered his voice. "I'm fairly certain your grandfather was a member of a secret society. A very old covert brotherhood."

Sophie felt a knot tighten in her stomach. She was certain of it too. For ten years she had tried to forget the incident that had confirmed that horrifying fact for her. She had witnessed something unthinkable. *Unforgivable.*

"The fleur-de-lis," Langdon said, "combined with the initials P.S., that is the brotherhood's official device. Their coat of arms. Their logo."

"How do you know this?" Sophie was praying Langdon was not going to tell her that he *himself* was a member.

"I've written about this group," he said, his voice tremulous with excitement. "Researching the symbols of secret societies is a specialty of mine. They call themselves the *Prieuré de Sion*—the Priory of Sion. They're based here in France and attract powerful members from all over Europe. In fact, they are one of the oldest surviving secret societies on earth."

Sophie had never heard of them.

Langdon was talking in rapid bursts now. "The Priory's membership has included some of history's most cultured individuals: men like Botticelli, Sir Isaac Newton, Victor Hugo." He paused, his voice brimming now with academic zeal. "And, Leonardo da Vinci."

Sophie stared. "Da Vinci was in a secret society?"

"Da Vinci presided over the Priory between 1510 and 1519 as the brotherhood's Grand Master, which might help explain your grandfather's passion for Leonardo's work. The two men share a historical fraternal bond. And it all fits perfectly with their fascination for goddess iconology, paganism, feminine deities, and contempt for the Church. The Priory has a well-documented history of reverence for the sacred feminine."

"You're telling me this group is a pagan goddess worship cult?"

"More like *the* pagan goddess worship cult. But

more important, they are known as the guardians of an ancient secret. One that made them immeasurably powerful."

Despite the total conviction in Langdon's eyes, Sophie's gut reaction was one of stark disbelief. *A secret pagan cult? Once headed by Leonardo da Vinci?* It all sounded utterly absurd. And yet, even as she dismissed it, she felt her mind reeling back ten years—to the night she had mistakenly surprised her grandfather and witnessed what she still could not accept. *Could that explain—?*

"The identities of living Priory members are kept extremely secret," Langdon said, "but the P.S. and fleur-de-lis that you saw as a child are proof. It could *only* have been related to the Priory."

Sophie realized now that Langdon knew far more about her grandfather than she had previously imagined. This American obviously had volumes to share with her, but this was not the place. "I can't afford to let them catch you, Robert. There's a lot we need to discuss. You need to go!"

Langdon heard only the faint murmur of her voice. He wasn't going anywhere. He was lost in another place now. A place where ancient secrets rose to the surface. A place where forgotten histories emerged from the shadows.

Slowly, as if moving underwater, Langdon turned his head and gazed through the reddish haze toward the *Mona Lisa.*

*The fleur-de-lis . . . the flower of Lisa . . . the Mona Lisa.*

It was all intertwined, a silent symphony echoing the deepest secrets of the Priory of Sion and Leonardo da Vinci.


A few miles away, on the riverbank beyond Les Invalides, the bewildered driver of a twin-bed Trailor truck stood at gunpoint and watched as the captain of the Judicial Police let out a guttural roar of rage and heaved a bar of soap out into the turgid waters of the Seine.

# CHAPTER 24

**Silas gazed** upward at the Saint-Sulpice obelisk, taking in the length of the massive marble shaft. His sinews felt taut with exhilaration. He glanced around the church one more time to make sure he was alone. Then he knelt at the base of the structure, not out of reverence, but out of necessity.

*The keystone is hidden beneath the Rose Line.*

*At the base of the Sulpice obelisk.*

All the brothers had concurred.

On his knees now, Silas ran his hands across the stone floor. He saw no cracks or markings to indicate a movable tile, so he began rapping softly with his knuckles on the floor. Following the brass line closer to the obelisk, he knocked on each tile adjacent to the brass line. Finally, one of them echoed strangely.

*There's a hollow area beneath the floor!*

Silas smiled. His victims had spoken the truth.

Standing, he searched the sanctuary for something with which to break the floor tile.

High above Silas, in the balcony, Sister Sandrine stifled a gasp. Her darkest fears had just been confirmed. This visitor was not who he seemed. The mysterious Opus Dei monk had come to Saint-Sulpice for another purpose.

A secret purpose.

*You are not the only one with secrets,* she thought.

Sister Sandrine Bieil was more than the keeper of this church. She was a sentry. And tonight, the ancient wheels had been set in motion. The arrival of this stranger at the base of the obelisk was a signal from the brotherhood.

*It was a silent call of distress.*

# CHAPTER 25

**The U.S.** Embassy in Paris is a compact complex on Avenue Gabriel, just north of the Champs-Elysées. The three-acre compound is considered U.S. soil, meaning all those who stand on it are subject to the same laws and protections as they would encounter standing in the United States.

The embassy's night operator was reading *Time* magazine's International Edition when the sound of her phone interrupted.

"U.S. Embassy," she answered.

"Good evening." The caller spoke English accented with French. "I need some assistance." Despite the politeness of the man's words, his tone sounded gruff and official. "I was told you had a phone message for me on your automated system. The name is Langdon. Unfortunately, I have forgotten my three-digit access code. If you could help me, I would be most grateful."

The operator paused, confused. "I'm sorry, sir. Your message must be quite old. That system was removed two years ago for security precautions. Moreover, all the access codes were *five*-digit. Who told you we had a message for you?"

"You have *no* automated phone system?"

"No, sir. Any message for you would be hand-written in our services department. What was your name again?"

But the man had hung up.


Bezu Fache felt dumbstruck as he paced the banks of the Seine. He was certain he had seen Langdon dial a local number, enter a three-digit code, and then listen to a recording. *But if Langdon didn't phone the embassy, then who the hell did he call?*

It was at that moment, eyeing his cellular phone, that Fache realized the answers were in the palm of his hand. *Langdon used my phone to place that call.*

Keying into the cell phone's menu, Fache pulled up the list of recently dialed numbers and found the call Langdon had placed.

A Paris exchange, followed by the three-digit code 454.

Redialing the phone number, Fache waited as the line began ringing.

Finally a woman's voice answered. *"Bonjour, vous êtes bien chez Sophie Neveu,"* the recording announced. *"Je suis absente pour le moment, mais . . ."*

Fache's blood was boiling as he typed the numbers 4 . . . 5 . . . 4.

# CHAPTER 26

**Despite her** monumental reputation, the *Mona Lisa* was a mere thirty-one inches by twenty-one inches—smaller even than the posters of her sold in the Louvre gift shop. She hung on the northwest wall of the Salle des Etats behind a two-inch-thick pane of protective Plexiglas. Painted on a poplar wood panel, her ethereal, mist-filled atmosphere was attributed to Da Vinci's mastery of the *sfumato* style, in which forms appear to evaporate into one another.

Since taking up residence in the Louvre, the *Mona Lisa*—or *La Jaconde* as they call her in France—had been stolen twice, most recently in 1911, when she disappeared from the Louvre's *"salle impénétrable"*—Le Salon Carré. Parisians wept in the streets and wrote newspaper articles begging the thieves for the painting's return. Two years later, the *Mona Lisa* was discovered hidden in the false bottom of a trunk in a Florence hotel room.

Langdon, now having made it clear to Sophie that he had no intention of leaving, moved with her across the Salle des Etats. The *Mona Lisa* was still twenty yards ahead when Sophie turned on the black light, and the bluish crescent of penlight fanned out on the floor in front of them. She swung the beam back and forth across the floor like a minesweeper, searching for any hint of luminescent ink.

Walking beside her, Langdon was already feeling the tingle of anticipation that accompanied his face-to-face reunions with great works of art. He strained to see beyond the cocoon of purplish light emanating from the black light in Sophie's hand. To the left, the room's octagonal viewing divan emerged, looking like a dark island on the empty sea of parquet.

Langdon could now begin to see the panel of dark glass on the wall. Behind it, he knew, in the confines of her own private cell, hung the most celebrated painting in the world.

The *Mona Lisa*'s status as the most famous piece of art in the world, Langdon knew, had nothing to do with her enigmatic smile. Nor was it due to the mysterious interpretations attributed her by many art historians and conspiracy buffs. Quite simply, the *Mona Lisa* was famous because Leonardo da Vinci claimed she was his finest accomplishment. He carried the painting with him whenever he traveled and, if asked why, would reply that he found it hard to part with his most sublime expression of female beauty.

Even so, many art historians suspected Da Vinci's reverence for the *Mona Lisa* had nothing to do with its artistic mastery. In actuality, the painting was a surprisingly ordinary *sfumato* portrait. Da Vinci's veneration for this work, many claimed, stemmed from something far deeper: a hidden message in the layers of paint. The *Mona Lisa* was, in fact, one of the world's most documented inside jokes. The painting's well-documented collage of double entendres and playful allusions had been revealed in most art history tomes, and yet, incredibly, the public at large still considered her smile a great mystery.

*No mystery at all,* Langdon thought, moving forward and watching as the faint outline of the painting began to take shape. *No mystery at all.*

Most recently Langdon had shared the *Mona Lisa*'s secret with a rather unlikely group—a dozen inmates at the Essex County Penitentiary. Langdon's jail seminar was part of a Harvard outreach program attempting to bring education into the prison system—*Culture for Convicts,* as Langdon's colleagues liked to call it.

Standing at an overhead projector in a darkened penitentiary library, Langdon had shared the *Mona Lisa*'s secret with the prisoners attending class, men whom he found surprisingly engaged—rough, but sharp. "You may notice," Langdon told them, walking up to the projected image of the *Mona Lisa* on the library wall, "that the background behind her face is uneven."

Langdon motioned to the glaring discrepancy. "Da Vinci painted the horizon line on the left significantly lower than the right."

"He screwed it up?" one of the inmates asked.

Langdon chuckled. "No. Da Vinci didn't do that too often. Actually, this is a little trick Da Vinci played. By lowering the countryside on the left, Da Vinci made Mona Lisa look much larger from the left side than from the right side. A little Da Vinci inside joke. Historically, the concepts of male and female have assigned sides—left is female, and right is male. Because Da Vinci was a big fan of feminine principles, he made Mona Lisa look more majestic from the *left* than the right."

"I heard he was a fag," said a small man with a goatee.

Langdon winced. "Historians don't generally put it quite that way, but yes, Da Vinci was a homosexual."

"Is that why he was into that whole feminine thing?"

"Actually, Da Vinci was in tune with the *balance* between male and female. He believed that a human soul could not be enlightened unless it had both male and female elements."

"You mean like chicks with dicks?" someone called.

This elicited a hearty round of laughs. Langdon considered offering an etymological sidebar about the word *hermaphrodite* and its ties to Hermes and Aphrodite, but something told him it would be lost on this crowd.

"Hey, Mr. Langford," a muscle-bound man said. "Is it true that the *Mona Lisa* is a picture of Da Vinci in drag? I heard that was true."

"It's quite possible," Langdon said. "Da Vinci was a prankster, and computerized analysis of the *Mona Lisa* and Da Vinci's self-portraits confirm some startling points of congruency in their faces. Whatever Da Vinci was up to," Langdon said, "his Mona Lisa is neither male nor female. It carries a subtle message of androgyny. It is a fusing of both."

"You sure that's not just some Harvard bullshit way of saying Mona Lisa is one ugly chick."

Now Langdon laughed. "You may be right. But actually Da Vinci left a big clue that the painting was supposed to be androgynous. Has anyone here ever heard of an Egyptian god named Amon?"

"Hell yes!" the big guy said. "God of masculine fertility!"

Langdon was stunned.

"It says so on every box of Amon condoms." The muscular man gave a wide grin. "It's got a guy with a ram's head on the front and says he's the Egyptian god of fertility."

Langdon was not familiar with the brand name, but he was glad to hear the prophylactic manufacturers had gotten their hieroglyphs right. "Well done. Amon is indeed represented as a man with a ram's head, and his promiscuity and curved horns are related to our modern sexual slang 'horny.' "

"No shit!"

"No shit," Langdon said. "And do you know who Amon's counterpart was? The Egyptian *goddess* of fertility?"

The question met with several seconds of silence.

"It was Isis," Langdon told them, grabbing a grease pen. "So we have the male god, Amon." He wrote it down. "And the female goddess, Isis, whose ancient pictogram was once called L'ISA."

Langdon finished writing and stepped back from the projector.

AMON L'ISA

"Ring any bells?" he asked.

"Mona Lisa . . . holy crap," somebody gasped.

Langdon nodded. "Gentlemen, not only does the face of Mona Lisa look androgynous, but her name is an anagram of the divine union of male and female. And *that,* my friends, is Da Vinci's little secret, and the reason for Mona Lisa's knowing smile."

"My grandfather was here," Sophie said, dropping suddenly to her knees, now only ten feet from the *Mona Lisa*. She pointed the black light tentatively to a spot on the parquet floor.

At first Langdon saw nothing. Then, as he knelt beside her, he saw a tiny droplet of dried liquid that was luminescing. *Ink?* Suddenly he recalled what black lights were actually used for. *Blood.* His senses tingled. Sophie was right. Jacques Saunière had indeed paid a visit to the *Mona Lisa* before he died.

"He wouldn't have come here without a reason," Sophie whispered, standing up. "I know he left a message for me here." Quickly striding the final few steps to the *Mona Lisa,* she illuminated the floor directly in front of the painting. She waved the light back and forth across the bare parquet.

"There's nothing here!"

At that moment, Langdon saw a faint purple glimmer on the protective glass before the *Mona Lisa.* Reaching down, he took Sophie's wrist and slowly moved the light up to the painting itself.

They both froze.

On the glass, six words glowed in purple, scrawled directly across the *Mona Lisa*'s face.

# CHAPTER 27

**Seated at** Saunière's desk, Lieutenant Collet pressed the phone to his ear in disbelief. *Did I hear Fache correctly?* "A bar of soap? But how could Langdon have known about the GPS dot?"

"Sophie Neveu," Fache replied. "She told him."

"What! Why?"

"Damned good question, but I just heard a recording that confirms she tipped him off."

Collet was speechless. *What was Neveu thinking?* Fache had proof that Sophie had interfered with a DCPJ sting operation? Sophie Neveu was not only going to be fired, she was also going to jail. "But, Captain . . . then where is Langdon *now?*"

"Have any fire alarms gone off there?"

"No, sir."

"And no one has come out under the Grand Gallery gate?"

"No. We've got a Louvre security officer on the gate. Just as you requested."

"Okay, Langdon must still be inside the Grand Gallery."

"Inside? But what is he doing?"

"Is the Louvre security guard armed?"

"Yes, sir. He's a senior warden."

"Send him in," Fache commanded. "I can't get my men back to the perimeter for a few minutes, and I don't want Langdon breaking for an exit." Fache paused. "And you'd better tell the guard Agent Neveu is probably in there with him."

"Agent Neveu left, I thought."

"Did you actually *see* her leave?"

"No, sir, but—"

"Well, nobody on the perimeter saw her leave either. They only saw her go in."

Collet was flabbergasted by Sophie Neveu's bravado. *She's still inside the building?*

"Handle it," Fache ordered. "I want Langdon and Neveu at gunpoint by the time I get back."

As the Trailor truck drove off, Captain Fache rounded up his men. Robert Langdon had proven an elusive quarry tonight, and with Agent Neveu now helping him, he might be far harder to corner than expected.

Fache decided not to take any chances.

Hedging his bets, he ordered half of his men back to the Louvre perimeter. The other half he sent to guard the only location in Paris where Robert Langdon could find safe harbor.

# CHAPTER 28

**Inside the** Salle des Etats, Langdon stared in astonishment at the six words glowing on the Plexiglas. The text seemed to hover in space, casting a jagged shadow across Mona Lisa's mysterious smile.

"The Priory," Langdon whispered. "This proves your grandfather was a member!"

Sophie looked at him in confusion. "You *understand* this?"

"It's flawless," Langdon said, nodding as his thoughts churned. "It's a proclamation of one of the Priory's most fundamental philosophies!"

Sophie looked baffled in the glow of the message scrawled across the *Mona Lisa*'s face.

SO DARK THE CON OF MAN

"Sophie," Langdon said, "the Priory's tradition of perpetuating goddess worship is based on a belief that powerful men in the early Christian church 'conned' the world by propagating lies that devalued the female and tipped the scales in favor of the masculine."

Sophie remained silent, staring at the words.

"The Priory believes that Constantine and his

male successors successfully converted the world from matriarchal paganism to patriarchal Christianity by waging a campaign of propaganda that demonized the sacred feminine, obliterating the goddess from modern religion forever."

Sophie's expression remained uncertain. "My grandfather sent me to this spot to find this. He must be trying to tell me more than *that*."

Langdon understood her meaning. *She thinks this is another code.* Whether a hidden meaning existed here or not, Langdon could not immediately say. His mind was still grappling with the bold clarity of Saunière's outward message.

*So dark the con of man,* he thought. *So dark indeed.*

Nobody could deny the enormous good the modern Church did in today's troubled world, and yet the Church had a deceitful and violent history. Their brutal crusade to "reeducate" the pagan and feminine-worshipping religions spanned three centuries, employing methods as inspired as they were horrific.

The Catholic Inquisition published the book that arguably could be called the most blood-soaked publication in human history. *Malleus Maleficarum*—or *The Witches' Hammer*—indoctrinated the world to "the dangers of freethinking women" and instructed the clergy how to locate, torture, and destroy them. Those deemed "witches" by the Church included all female scholars, priestesses, gypsies, mystics, nature lovers, herb gatherers, and any women "suspiciously attuned to the natural world." Midwives also were killed for their heretical practice of using medical knowledge to ease the pain of childbirth—a suffering, the Church claimed, that was God's rightful punishment for Eve's partaking of the Apple of Knowledge, thus giving birth to the idea of Original Sin. During three hundred years of witch hunts, the Church burned at the stake an astounding five *million* women.

The propaganda and bloodshed had worked.

Today's world was living proof.

Women, once celebrated as an essential half of spiritual enlightenment, had been banished from the temples of the world. There were no female Orthodox rabbis, Catholic priests, nor Islamic clerics. The once hallowed act of Hieros Gamos—the natural sexual union between man and woman through which each became spiritually whole—had been recast as a shameful act. Holy men who had once required sexual union with their female counterparts to commune with God now feared their natural sexual urges as the work of the devil, collaborating with his favorite accomplice . . . *woman.*

Not even the feminine association with the *left-hand* side could escape the Church's defamation. In France and Italy, the words for "left"—*gauche* and *sinistra*—came to have deeply negative over-tones, while their right-hand counterparts rang of *right*eousness, dexterity, and correctness. To this day, radical thought was considered *left* wing, ir-rational thought was *left* brain, and anything evil, *sinister.*

The days of the goddess were over. The pen-dulum had swung. Mother Earth had become a *man's* world, and the gods of destruction and war were taking their toll. The male ego had spent two millennia running unchecked by its female counterpart. The Priory of Sion believed that it was this obliteration of the sacred feminine in modern life that had caused what the Hopi Native Americans called *koyanisquatsi*—"life out of balance"—an unstable situation marked by testosterone-fueled wars, a plethora of misogynis-tic societies, and a growing disrespect for Mother Earth.

"Robert!" Sophie said, her whisper yanking him back. "Someone's coming!"

He heard the approaching footsteps out in the hallway.

"Over here!" Sophie extinguished the black light and seemed to evaporate before Langdon's eyes.

For an instant he felt totally blind. *Over where!* As his vision cleared he saw Sophie's silhouette racing toward the center of the room and ducking out of sight behind the octagonal viewing bench. He was about to dash after her when a booming voice stopped him cold.

"*Arretez!*" a man commanded from the doorway.

The Louvre security agent advanced through the entrance to the Salle des Etats, his pistol out-stretched, taking deadly aim at Langdon's chest.

Langdon felt his arms raise instinctively for the ceiling.

"*Couchez-vous!*" the guard commanded. "*Lie down!*"

Langdon was face first on the floor in a matter of seconds. The guard hurried over and kicked his legs apart, spreading Langdon out.

"*Mauvaise idée, Monsieur Langdon,*" he said, pressing the gun hard into Langdon's back. "*Mauvaise idée.*"

Face down on the parquet floor with his arms and legs spread wide, Langdon found little humor in the irony of his position. *The Vitruvian Man,* he thought. *Face down.*

# CHAPTER 29

**Inside Saint-Sulpice,** Silas carried the heavy iron votive candle holder from the altar back toward the obelisk. The shaft would do nicely as a battering ram. Eyeing the gray marble panel that covered the apparent hollow in the floor, he realized he could not possibly shatter the covering without making considerable noise.

*Iron on marble.* It would echo off the vaulted ceilings.

Would the nun hear him? She should be asleep by now. Even so, it was a chance Silas preferred not to take. Looking around for a cloth to wrap around the tip of the iron pole, he saw nothing except the altar's linen mantle, which he refused to defile. *My cloak,* he thought. Knowing he was alone in the great church, Silas untied his cloak and slipped it off his body. As he removed it, he felt a sting as the wool fibers stuck to the fresh wounds on his back.

Naked now, except for his loin swaddle, Silas wrapped his cloak over the end of the iron rod. Then, aiming at the center of the floor tile, he drove the tip into it. A muffled thud. The stone did not break. He drove the pole into it again. Again a dull thud, but this time accompanied by a crack. On the third swing, the covering finally shattered, and stone shards fell into a hollow area beneath the floor.

*A compartment!*

Quickly pulling the remaining pieces from the opening, Silas gazed into the void. His blood pounded as he knelt down before it. Raising his pale bare arm, he reached inside.

At first he felt nothing. The floor of the compartment was bare, smooth stone. Then, feeling deeper, reaching his arm in under the Rose Line, he touched something! A thick stone tablet. Getting his fingers around the edge, he gripped it and gently lifted the tablet out. As he stood and examined his find, he realized he was holding a rough-hewn stone slab with engraved words. He felt for an instant like a modern-day Moses.

As Silas read the words on the tablet, he felt surprise. He had expected the keystone to be a map, or a complex series of directions, perhaps even encoded. The keystone, however, bore the simplest of inscriptions.

Job 38:11

*A Bible verse?* Silas was stunned with the devilish simplicity. The secret location of that which they sought was revealed in a Bible verse? The brotherhood stopped at nothing to mock the righteous!

*Job. Chapter thirty-eight. Verse eleven.*

Although Silas did not recall the exact contents

of verse eleven by heart, he knew the Book of Job told the story of a man whose faith in God survived repeated tests. *Appropriate,* he thought, barely able to contain his excitement.

Looking over his shoulder, he gazed down the shimmering Rose Line and couldn't help but smile. There atop the main altar, propped open on a gilded book stand, sat an enormous leather-bound Bible.

Up in the balcony, Sister Sandrine was shaking. Moments ago, she had been about to flee and carry out her orders, when the man below suddenly removed his cloak. When she saw his alabaster-white flesh, she was overcome with a horrified bewilderment. His broad, pale back was soaked with blood-red slashes. Even from here she could see the wounds were fresh.

*This man has been mercilessly whipped!*

She also saw the bloody *cilice* around his thigh, the wound beneath it dripping. *What kind of God would want a body punished this way?* The rituals of Opus Dei, Sister Sandrine knew, were not something she would ever understand. But that was hardly her concern at this instant. *Opus Dei is searching for the keystone.* How they knew of it, Sister Sandrine could not imagine, although she knew she did not have time to think.

The bloody monk was now quietly donning his

cloak again, clutching his prize as he moved toward the altar, toward the Bible.

In breathless silence, Sister Sandrine left the balcony and raced down the hall to her quarters. Getting on her hands and knees, she reached beneath her wooden bed frame and retrieved the sealed envelope she had hidden there years ago.

Tearing it open, she found four Paris phone numbers.

Trembling, she began to dial.

Downstairs, Silas laid the stone tablet on the altar and turned his eager hands to the leather Bible. His long white fingers were sweating now as he turned the pages. Flipping through the Old Testament, he found the Book of Job. He located chapter thirty-eight. As he ran his finger down the column of text, he anticipated the words he was about to read.

*They will lead the way!*

Finding verse number eleven, Silas read the text. It was only seven words. Confused, he read it again, sensing something had gone terribly wrong. The verse simply read:

HITHERTO SHALT THOU COME, BUT NO FURTHER.

# CHAPTER 30

**Security warden** Claude Grouard simmered with rage as he stood over his prostrate captive in front of the *Mona Lisa. This bastard killed Jacques Saunière!* Saunière had been like a well-loved father to Grouard and his security team.

Grouard wanted nothing more than to pull the trigger and bury a bullet in Robert Langdon's back. As senior warden, Grouard was one of the few guards who actually carried a loaded weapon. He reminded himself, however, that killing Langdon would be a generous fate compared to the misery about to be communicated by Bezu Fache and the French prison system.

Grouard yanked his walkie-talkie off his belt and attempted to radio for backup. All he heard was static. The additional electronic security in this chamber always wrought havoc with the guards' communications. *I have to move to the doorway.* Still aiming his weapon at Langdon, Grouard began backing slowly toward the entrance. On his third step, he spied something that made him stop short.

*What the hell is that!*

An inexplicable mirage was materializing near

the center of the room. A silhouette. There was someone else in the room? A woman was moving through the darkness, walking briskly toward the far left wall. In front of her, a purplish beam of light swung back and forth across the floor, as if she were searching for something with a colored flashlight.

*"Qui est là?"* Grouard demanded, feeling his adrenaline spike for a second time in the last thirty seconds. He suddenly didn't know where to aim his gun or what direction to move.

"PTS," the woman replied calmly, still scanning the floor with her light.

*Police Technique et Scientifique.* Grouard was sweating now. *I thought all the agents were gone!* He now recognized the purple light as ultraviolet, consistent with a PTS team, and yet he could not understand why DCPJ would be looking for evidence in here.

*"Votre nom!"* Grouard yelled, instinct telling him something was amiss. *"Répondez!"*

*"C'est moi,"* the voice responded in calm French. *"Sophie Neveu."*

Somewhere in the distant recesses of Grouard's mind, the name registered. *Sophie Neveu?* That was the name of Saunière's granddaughter, wasn't it? She used to come in here as a little kid, but that was years ago. *This couldn't possibly be her!* And even if it were Sophie Neveu, that was hardly a reason to trust her; Grouard had heard the rumors of the painful falling-out between Saunière and his granddaughter.

"You know me," the woman called. "And Robert Langdon did not kill my grandfather. Believe me."

Warden Grouard was not about to take *that* on faith. *I need backup!* Trying his walkie-talkie again, he got only static. The entrance was still a good twenty yards behind him, and Grouard began backing up slowly, choosing to leave his gun trained on the man on the floor. As Grouard inched backward, he could see the woman across the room raising her UV light and scrutinizing a large painting that hung on the far side of the Salle des Etats, directly opposite the *Mona Lisa*.

Grouard gasped, realizing which painting it was.

*What in the name of God is she doing?*

Across the room, Sophie Neveu felt a cold sweat breaking across her forehead. Langdon was still spread-eagle on the floor. *Hold on, Robert. Almost there.* Knowing the guard would never actually shoot either of them, Sophie now turned her attention back to the matter at hand, scanning the entire area around one masterpiece in particular—another Da Vinci. But the UV light revealed nothing out of the ordinary. Not on the floor, on the walls, or even on the canvas itself.

*There must be something here!*

Sophie felt totally certain she had deciphered her grandfather's intentions correctly.

*What else could he possibly intend?*

The masterpiece she was examining was a five-foot-tall canvas. The bizarre scene Da Vinci had painted included an awkwardly posed Virgin Mary sitting with Baby Jesus, John the Baptist, and the Angel Uriel on a perilous outcropping of rocks. When Sophie was a little girl, no trip to the *Mona Lisa* had been complete without her grandfather dragging her across the room to see this second painting.

*Grand-père, I'm here! But I don't see it!*

Behind her, Sophie could hear the guard trying to radio again for help.

*Think!*

She pictured the message scrawled on the protective glass of the *Mona Lisa. So dark the con of man.* The painting before her had no protective glass on which to write a message, and Sophie knew her grandfather would never have defaced this masterpiece by writing on the painting itself. She paused. *At least not on the front.* Her eyes shot upward, climbing the long cables that dangled from the ceiling to support the canvas.

*Could that be it?* Grabbing the left side of the carved wood frame, she pulled it toward her. The painting was large and the backing flexed as she swung it away from the wall. Sophie slipped her head and shoulders in behind the painting and raised the black light to inspect the back.

It took only seconds to realize her instinct had been wrong. The back of the painting was pale and blank. There was no purple text here, only the mottled brown backside of aging canvas and—

*Wait.*

Sophie's eyes locked on an incongruous glint of lustrous metal lodged near the bottom edge of the frame's wooden armature. The object was small, partially wedged in the slit where the canvas met the frame. A shimmering gold chain dangled off it.

To Sophie's utter amazement, the chain was affixed to a familiar gold key. The broad, sculpted head was in the shape of a cross and bore an engraved seal she had not seen since she was nine years old. A fleur-de-lis with the initials P.S. In that instant, Sophie felt the ghost of her grandfather whispering in her ear. *When the time comes, the key will be yours.* A tightness gripped her throat as she realized that her grandfather, even in death, had kept his promise. *This key opens a box,* his voice was saying, *where I keep many secrets.*

Sophie now realized that the entire purpose of tonight's word game had been this key. Her grandfather had it with him when he was killed. Not wanting it to fall into the hands of the police, he hid it behind this painting. Then he devised an ingenious treasure hunt to ensure only Sophie would find it.

*"Au secours!"* the guard's voice yelled.

Sophie snatched the key from behind the painting and slipped it deep in her pocket along with the UV penlight. Peering out from behind the canvas, she could see the guard was still trying desperately to raise someone on the walkie-talkie. He was backing toward the entrance, still aiming the gun firmly at Langdon.

*"Au secours!"* he shouted again into his radio.

Static.

*He can't transmit,* Sophie realized, recalling that tourists with cell phones often got frustrated in here when they tried to call home to brag about seeing the *Mona Lisa.* The extra surveillance wiring in the walls made it virtually impossible to get a carrier unless you stepped out into the hall. The guard was backing quickly toward the exit now, and Sophie knew she had to act immediately.

Gazing up at the large painting behind which she was partially ensconced, Sophie realized that Leonardo da Vinci, for the second time tonight, was there to help.

*Another few meters,* Grouard told himself, keeping his gun leveled.

*"Arrêtez! Ou je la détruis!"* the woman's voice echoed across the room.

Grouard glanced over and stopped in his tracks. *"Mon dieu, non!"*

Through the reddish haze, he could see that the woman had actually lifted the large painting off its cables and propped it on the floor in front of her. At five feet tall, the canvas almost entirely hid her body. Grouard's first thought was to wonder why the painting's trip wires hadn't set off alarms, but of course the artwork cable sensors had yet to be reset tonight. *What is she doing!*

When he saw it, his blood went cold.

The canvas started to bulge in the middle, the fragile outlines of the Virgin Mary, Baby Jesus, and John the Baptist beginning to distort.

*"Non!"* Grouard screamed, frozen in horror as he watched the priceless Da Vinci stretching. The woman was pushing her knee into the center of the canvas from behind! *"NON!"*

Grouard wheeled and aimed his gun at her but instantly realized it was an empty threat. The canvas was only fabric, but it was utterly impenetrable— a six-million-dollar piece of body armor.

*I can't put a bullet through a Da Vinci!*

"Set down your gun and radio," the woman said in calm French, "or I'll put my knee through this painting. I think you know how my grandfather would feel about that."

Grouard felt dizzy. "Please . . . no. That's *Madonna of the Rocks*!" He dropped his gun and radio, raising his hands over his head.

"Thank you," the woman said. "Now do exactly as I tell you, and everything will work out fine."

Moments later, Langdon's pulse was still thundering as he ran beside Sophie down the emergency stairwell toward the ground level. Neither of them had said a word since leaving the trembling Louvre guard lying in the Salle des Etats. The guard's pistol was now clutched tightly in Langdon's hands, and he couldn't wait to get rid of it. The weapon felt heavy and dangerously foreign.

Taking the stairs two at a time, Langdon wondered if Sophie had any idea how valuable a painting she had almost ruined. Her choice in art seemed eerily pertinent to tonight's adventure. The Da Vinci she had grabbed, much like the *Mona Lisa,* was notorious among art historians for its plethora of hidden pagan symbolism.

"You chose a valuable hostage," he said as they ran.

*"Madonna of the Rocks,"* she replied. "But I didn't choose it, my grandfather did. He left me a little something behind the painting."

Langdon shot her a startled look. "What!? But

how did you know which painting? Why *Madonna of the Rocks?*"

"So dark the con of man." She flashed a triumphant smile. "I missed the first two anagrams, Robert. I wasn't about to miss the third."

# CHAPTER 31

**"They're dead!"** Sister Sandrine stammered into the telephone in her Saint-Sulpice residence. She was leaving a message on an answering machine. "Please pick up! They're all dead!"

The first three phone numbers on the list had produced terrifying results—a hysterical widow, a detective working late at a murder scene, and a somber priest consoling a bereaved family. All three contacts were dead. And now, as she called the fourth and final number—the number she was not supposed to call unless the first three could not be reached—she got an answering machine. The outgoing message offered no name but simply asked the caller to leave a message.

"The floor panel has been broken!" she pleaded as she left the message. "The other three are dead!"

Sister Sandrine did not know the identities of the four men she protected, but the private phone numbers stashed beneath her bed were for use on only one condition.

*If that floor panel is ever broken,* the faceless messenger had told her, *it means the upper echelon has been breached. One of us has been mortally threatened and been forced to tell a desperate lie. Call the numbers. Warn the others. Do not fail us in this.*

It was a silent alarm. Foolproof in its simplicity. The plan had amazed her when she first heard it. If the identity of one brother was compromised, he could tell a lie that would start in motion a mechanism to warn the others. Tonight, however, it seemed that more than one had been compromised.

"Please answer," she whispered in fear. "Where are you?"

"Hang up the phone," a deep voice said from the doorway.

Turning in terror, she saw the massive monk. He was clutching the heavy iron candle stand. Shaking, she set the phone back in the cradle.

"They are dead," the monk said. "All four of them. And they have played me for a fool. Tell me where the keystone is."

"I don't know!" Sister Sandrine said truthfully. "That secret is guarded by others." *Others who are dead!*

The man advanced, his white fists gripping the iron stand. "You are a sister of the Church, and yet you serve *them*?"

"Jesus had but one true message," Sister Sandrine said defiantly. "I cannot see that message in Opus Dei."

A sudden explosion of rage erupted behind the

monk's eyes. He lunged, lashing out with the candle stand like a club. As Sister Sandrine fell, her last feeling was an overwhelming sense of foreboding.

*All four are dead.*

*The precious truth is lost forever.*

# CHAPTER 32

**The security** alarm on the west end of the
Denon Wing sent the pigeons in the nearby
Tuileries Gardens scattering as Langdon and
Sophie dashed out of the bulkhead into the Paris
night. As they ran across the plaza to Sophie's car,
Langdon could hear police sirens wailing in the
distance.

"That's it there," Sophie called, pointing to a
red snub-nosed two-seater parked on the plaza.

*She's kidding, right?* The vehicle was easily the
smallest car Langdon had ever seen.

"SmartCar," she said. "A hundred kilometers to
the liter."

Langdon had barely thrown himself into the
passenger seat before Sophie gunned the
SmartCar up and over a curb onto a gravel divider. He gripped the dash as the car shot out
across a sidewalk and bounced back down over
into the small rotary at Carrousel du Louvre.

For an instant, Sophie seemed to consider taking the shortcut across the rotary by plowing
straight ahead, through the median's perimeter
hedge, and bisecting the large circle of grass in the
center.

"No!" Langdon shouted, knowing the hedges

around Carrousel du Louvre were there to hide the perilous chasm in the center—*La Pyramide Inversée*—the upside-down pyramid skylight he had seen earlier from inside the museum. It was large enough to swallow their SmartCar in a single gulp. Fortunately, Sophie decided on the more conventional route, jamming the wheel hard to the right, circling properly until she exited, cut left, and swung into the northbound lane, accelerating toward Rue de Rivoli.

The two-tone police sirens blared louder behind them, and Langdon could see the lights now in his side view mirror. The SmartCar engine whined in protest as Sophie urged it faster away from the Louvre. Fifty yards ahead, the traffic light at Rivoli turned red. Sophie cursed under her breath and kept racing toward it. Langdon felt his muscles tighten.

"Sophie?"

Slowing only slightly as they reached the intersection, Sophie flicked her headlights and stole a quick glance both ways before flooring the accelerator again and carving a sharp left turn through the empty intersection onto Rivoli. Accelerating west for a quarter of a mile, Sophie banked to the right around a wide rotary. Soon they were shooting out the other side onto the wide avenue of Champs-Elysées.

As they straightened out, Langdon turned in his seat, craning his neck to look out the rear window toward the Louvre. The police did not seem to be chasing them. The sea of blue lights was assembling at the museum.

His heartbeat finally slowing, Langdon turned back around. "That was interesting."

Sophie didn't seem to hear. Her eyes remained fixed ahead down the long thoroughfare of Champs-Elysées, the two-mile stretch of posh storefronts that was often called the Fifth Avenue of Paris. The embassy was only about a mile away, and Langdon settled into his seat.

*So dark the con of man.*

Sophie's quick thinking had been impressive.

*Madonna of the Rocks.*

Sophie had said her grandfather left her something behind the painting. *A final message?* Langdon could not help but marvel over Saunière's brilliant hiding place; *Madonna of the Rocks* was yet another fitting link in the evening's chain of interconnected symbolism. Saunière, it seemed, at every turn, was reinforcing his fondness for the dark and mischievous side of Leonardo da Vinci.

Da Vinci's original commission for *Madonna of the Rocks* had come from an organization known as the Confraternity of the Immaculate Conception, which needed a painting for the centerpiece of an altar triptych in their church of San Francesco in Milan. The nuns gave Leonardo specific dimensions, and the desired theme for the painting—the Virgin Mary, baby John the Baptist, Uriel, and Baby Jesus sheltering in a cave. Although Da Vinci did as they requested, when he delivered the work, the group reacted with horror. He had filled the painting with explosive and disturbing details.

The painting showed a blue-robed Virgin Mary sitting with her arm around an infant child, presumably Baby Jesus. Opposite Mary sat Uriel, also with an infant, presumably baby John the Baptist. Oddly, though, rather than the usual Jesus-blessing-John scenario, it was baby *John* who was blessing Jesus . . . and Jesus was submitting to his authority! More troubling still, Mary was holding one hand high above the head of infant John and making a decidedly threatening gesture—her fingers looking like eagle's talons, gripping an invisible head. Finally, the most obvious and frightening image: Just below Mary's curled fingers, Uriel was making a cutting gesture with his hand—as if slicing the neck of the invisible head gripped by Mary's claw-like hand.

Langdon's students were always amused to learn that Da Vinci eventually mollified the confraternity by painting them a second, "watered-down" version of *Madonna of the Rocks* in which everyone was arranged in a more orthodox manner. The second version now hung in London's National Gallery under the name *Virgin of the Rocks,* although Langdon still preferred the Louvre's more intriguing original.

As Sophie gunned the car up Champs-Elysées, Langdon said, "The painting. What was behind it?"

Her eyes remained on the road. "I'll show you once we're safely inside the embassy."

"You'll *show* it to me?" Langdon was surprised. "He left you a physical object?"

Sophie gave a curt nod. "Embossed with a fleur-de-lis and the initials P.S."

Langdon couldn't believe his ears.

*We're going to make it,* Sophie thought as she swung the SmartCar's wheel to the right, cutting sharply past the luxurious Hôtel de Crillon into Paris's tree-lined diplomatic neighborhood. The embassy was less than a mile away now. She was finally feeling like she could breathe normally again.

Even as she drove, Sophie's mind remained locked on the key in her pocket, her memories of seeing it many years ago, the gold head shaped as an equal-armed cross, the triangular shaft, the indentations, the embossed flowery seal, and the letters P.S.

Although the key barely had entered Sophie's thoughts through the years, her work in the intelligence community had taught her plenty about security, and now the key's peculiar tooling no longer looked so mystifying. *A laser-tooled varying matrix. Impossible to duplicate.* Rather than teeth that moved tumblers, this key's complex series of laser-burned pockmarks was examined by an electric eye. If the eye determined that the hexagonal pockmarks were correctly spaced, arranged, and rotated, then the lock would open.

Sophie could not begin to imagine what a key like this opened, but she sensed Robert would be able to tell her. After all, he had described the key's embossed seal without ever seeing it. The cruciform on top implied the key belonged to some kind of Christian organization, and yet Sophie knew of no churches that used laser-tooled varying matrix keys.

*Besides, my grandfather was no Christian. . . .*

Sophie had witnessed proof of that ten years ago. Ironically, it had been another *key*—a far more normal one—that had revealed his true nature to her.

The afternoon had been warm when she landed at Charles de Gaulle Airport and hailed a taxi home. *Grand-père will be so surprised to see me,* she thought. Returning from graduate school in Britain for spring break a few days early, Sophie couldn't wait to see him and tell him all about the encryption methods she was studying.

When she arrived at their Paris home, however, her grandfather was not there. Disappointed, she knew he had not been expecting her and was probably working at the Louvre. *But it's Saturday afternoon,* she realized. He seldom worked on weekends. On weekends, he usually—

Grinning, Sophie ran out to the garage. Sure enough, his car was gone. It was the weekend. Jacques Saunière despised city driving and owned a car for one destination only—his vacation château in Normandy, north of Paris. Sophie, after months in the congestion of London, was eager for the smells of nature and to start her vacation right away. It was still early evening, and she decided to leave immediately and surprise him. Borrowing a friend's car, Sophie drove north, winding into the deserted moon-swept hills near Creully. She arrived just after ten o'clock, turning down the long private driveway toward her grandfather's retreat. The access road was over a mile long, and she was halfway down it before she could start to see the house through the trees—a mammoth, old stone château nestled in the woods on the side of a hill.

Sophie had half expected to find her grandfather asleep at this hour and was excited to see the house twinkling with lights. Her delight turned to surprise, however, when she arrived to find the driveway filled with parked cars—Mercedeses, BMWs, Audis, and a Rolls-Royce.

Sophie stared a moment and then burst out laughing. *My grand-père, the famous recluse!* Jacques Saunière, it seemed, was far less reclusive than he liked to pretend. Clearly he was hosting a party while Sophie was away at school, and from the looks of the automobiles, some of Paris's most influential people were in attendance.

Eager to surprise him, she hurried to the front door. When she got there, though, she found it locked. She knocked. Nobody answered. Puzzled, she walked around and tried the back door. It too was locked. No answer.

Confused, she stood a moment and listened. The only sound she heard was the cool Normandy air letting out a low moan as it swirled through the valley.

No music.

No voices.

Nothing.

In the silence of the woods, Sophie hurried to the side of the house and clambered up on a woodpile, pressing her face to the living room window. What she saw inside made no sense at all.

"Nobody's here!"

The entire first floor looked deserted.

*Where are all the people?*

Heart racing, Sophie ran to the woodshed and got the spare key her grandfather kept hidden under the kindling box. She ran to the front door and let herself in. As she stepped into the deserted foyer, the control panel for the security system started blinking red—a warning that the entrant had ten seconds to type the proper code before the security alarms went off.

*He has the alarm on during a party?*

Sophie quickly typed the code and deactivated the system.

Entering, she found the entire house uninhab-
ited. Upstairs too. As she descended again to the
deserted living room, she stood a moment in the
silence, wondering what could possibly be happening.

It was then that Sophie heard it.

Muffled voices. And they seemed to be coming
from underneath her. Sophie could not imagine.
Crouching, she put her ear to the floor and listened. Yes, the sound was definitely coming from
below. The voices seemed to be singing, or . . .
*chanting?* She was frightened. Almost more eerie
than the sound itself was the realization that this
house did not even have a basement.

*At least none I've ever seen.*

Turning now and scanning the living room,
Sophie's eyes fell to the only object in the entire
house that seemed out of place—her grandfather's
favorite antique, a sprawling Aubusson tapestry. It
usually hung on the east wall beside the fireplace,
but tonight it had been pulled aside on its brass
rod, exposing the wall behind it.

Walking toward the bare wooden wall, Sophie
sensed the chanting getting louder. Hesitant, she
leaned her ear against the wood. The voices were
clearer now. People were definitely chanting . . .
intoning words Sophie could not discern.

*The space behind this wall is hollow!*

Feeling around the edge of the panels, Sophie
found a recessed fingerhold. It was discreetly

crafted. *A sliding door.* Heart pounding, she placed her finger in the slot and pulled it. With noiseless precision, the heavy wall slid sideways. From out of the darkness beyond, the voices echoed up.

Sophie slipped through the door and found herself on a rough-hewn stone staircase that spiraled downward. She'd been coming to this house since she was a child and yet had no idea this staircase even existed!

As she descended, the air grew cooler. The voices clearer. She heard men and women now. Her line of sight was limited by the spiral of the staircase, but the last step was now rounding into view. Beyond it, she could see a small patch of the basement floor—stone, illuminated by the flickering orange blaze of firelight.

Holding her breath, Sophie inched down another few steps and crouched down to look. It took her several seconds to process what she was seeing.

The room was a grotto—a coarse chamber that appeared to have been hollowed from the granite of the hillside. The only light came from torches on the walls. In the glow of the flames, thirty or so people stood in a circle in the center of the room.

*I'm dreaming,* Sophie told herself. *A dream. What else could this be?*

Everyone in the room was wearing a mask.

The women were dressed in white gossamer gowns and golden shoes. Their masks were white, and in their hands they carried golden orbs. The men wore long black tunics, and their masks were black. They looked like pieces in a giant chess set. Everyone in the circle rocked back and forth and chanted in reverence to something on the floor before them . . . something Sophie could not see.

The chanting grew steady again. Accelerating. Thundering now. Faster. The participants took a step inward and knelt. In that instant, Sophie could finally see what they all were witnessing. Even as she staggered back in horror, she felt the image searing itself into her memory forever. Overtaken by nausea, Sophie spun, clutching at the stone walls as she clambered back up the stairs. Pulling the door closed, she fled the deserted house, and drove in a tearful stupor back to Paris.

That night, with her life shattered by disillusionment and betrayal, she packed her belongings and left her home. On the dining room table, she left a note.

I WAS THERE. DON'T TRY TO FIND ME.

Beside the note, she laid the old spare key from the château's woodshed.

———

"Sophie!" Langdon's voice intruded. "Stop! *Stop!*"

Emerging from the memory, Sophie slammed on the brakes, skidding to a halt. "What? What happened?!"

Langdon pointed down the long street before them.

When she saw it, Sophie's blood went cold. A hundred yards ahead, the intersection was blocked by a couple of DCPJ police cars, parked askew, their purpose obvious. *They've sealed off Avenue Gabriel!*

Langdon gave a grim sigh. "I take it the embassy is off-limits this evening?"

Down the street, the two DCPJ officers who stood beside their cars were now staring in their direction, apparently curious about the headlights that had halted so abruptly up the street from them.

*Okay, Sophie, turn around very slowly.*

Putting the SmartCar in reverse, she performed a composed three-point turn and reversed her direction. As she drove away, she heard the sound of squealing tires behind them. Sirens blared to life.

Cursing, Sophie slammed down the accelerator.

# CHAPTER 33

**Sophie's SmartCar** tore through the diplomatic quarter, weaving past embassies and consulates, finally racing out a side street and taking a right turn back onto the massive thoroughfare of Champs-Elysées.

Langdon sat white-knuckled in the passenger seat, twisted backward, scanning behind them for any signs of the police. He suddenly wished he had not decided to run. *You didn't,* he reminded himself. Sophie had made the decision for him when she threw the GPS dot out the bathroom window. Now, as they sped away from the embassy, serpentining through sparse traffic on Champs-Elysées, Langdon felt his options deteriorating. Although Sophie seemed to have lost the police, at least for the moment, Langdon doubted their luck would hold for long.

Behind the wheel Sophie was fishing in her sweater pocket. She removed a small metal object and held it out for him. "Robert, you'd better have a look at this. This is what my grandfather left me behind *Madonna of the Rocks.*"

Feeling a shiver of anticipation, Langdon took the object and examined it. It was heavy and shaped like a cruciform. His first instinct was that he was holding a funeral *pieu*—a miniature version of a memorial spike designed to be stuck into the ground at a gravesite. But then he noted the shaft protruding from the cruciform was prismatic and triangular. The shaft was also pockmarked with hundreds of tiny hexagons that appeared to be finely tooled and scattered at random.

"It's a laser-cut key," Sophie told him. "Those hexagons are read by an electric eye."

*A key?* Langdon had never seen anything like it.

"Look at the other side," she said, changing lanes and sailing through an intersection.

When Langdon turned the key, he felt his jaw drop. There, intricately embossed on the center of the cross, was a stylized fleur-de-lis with the initials P.S.! "Sophie," he said, "this is the seal I told you about! The official device of the Priory of Sion."

She nodded. "As I told you, I saw the key a long time ago. He told me never to speak of it again."

Langdon's eyes were still riveted on the embossed key. Its high-tech tooling and age-old symbolism exuded an eerie fusion of ancient and modern worlds.

"He told me the key opened a box where he kept many secrets."

Langdon felt a chill to imagine what kind of secrets a man like Jacques Saunière might keep. What an ancient brotherhood was doing with a futuristic key, Langdon had no idea. The Priory existed for the sole purpose of protecting a secret. A secret of incredible power. *Could this key have something to do with it?* The thought was overwhelming. "Do you know what it opens?"

Sophie looked disappointed. "I was hoping *you* knew."

Langdon remained silent as he turned the cruciform in his hand, examining it.

"It looks Christian," Sophie pressed.

Langdon was not so sure about that. The head of this key was not the traditional long-stemmed Christian cross but rather was a *square* cross—with four arms of equal length—which predated Christianity by fifteen hundred years. This kind of cross carried none of the Christian connotations of crucifixion associated with the longer-stemmed Latin Cross, originated by Romans as a torture device. Langdon was always surprised how few Christians who gazed upon "the crucifix" realized their symbol's violent history was reflected in its very name: "cross" and "crucifix" came from the Latin verb *cruciare*—to torture.

"Sophie," he said, "all I can tell you is that equal-armed crosses like this one are considered *peaceful* crosses. Their square configurations make them impractical for use in crucifixion, and their balanced vertical and horizontal elements convey a natural union of male and female, making them symbolically consistent with Priory philosophy."

She gave him a weary look. "You have no idea, do you?"

Langdon frowned. "Not a clue."

"Okay, we have to get off the road." Sophie checked her rearview mirror. "We need a safe place to figure out what that key opens."

Langdon thought longingly of his comfortable room at the Ritz. Obviously, that was not an option. "How about my hosts at the American University of Paris?"

"Too obvious. Fache will check with them."

"You must know people. You live here."

"Fache will run my phone and e-mail records, talk to my coworkers. My contacts are compromised, and finding a hotel is no good because they all require identification."

Langdon wondered again if he might have been better off taking his chances letting Fache arrest him at the Louvre. "Let's call the embassy. I can explain the situation and have the embassy send someone to meet us somewhere."

"Meet us?" Sophie turned and stared at him as if he were crazy. "Robert, you're dreaming. Your embassy has no jurisdiction except on their own property. Sending someone to retrieve us would be considered aiding a fugitive of the French government. It won't happen. If you walk into your embassy and request temporary asylum, that's one thing, but asking them to take action against French law enforcement in the field?" She shook her head. "Call your embassy right now, and they are going to tell you to avoid further damage and turn yourself over to Fache. Then they'll promise to pursue diplomatic channels to get you a fair trial." She gazed up the line of elegant storefronts on Champs-Elysées. "How much cash do you have?"

Langdon checked his wallet. "A hundred dollars. A few euro. Why?"

"Credit cards?"

"Of course."

As Sophie accelerated, Langdon sensed she was formulating a plan. Dead ahead, at the end of Champs-Elysées, stood the Arc de Triomphe— Napoleon's 164-foot-tall tribute to his own military potency—encircled by France's largest rotary, a nine-lane behemoth.

Sophie's eyes were on the rearview mirror again as they approached the rotary. "We lost them for the time being," she said, "but we won't last another five minutes if we stay in this car."

*So steal a different one,* Langdon mused, *now that we're criminals.* "What are you going to do?"

Sophie gunned the SmartCar into the rotary. "Trust me."

Langdon made no response. Trust had not gotten him very far this evening. Pulling back the sleeve of his jacket, he checked his watch—a vintage, collector's-edition Mickey Mouse wristwatch that had been a gift from his parents on his tenth birthday. Although its juvenile dial often drew odd looks, Langdon had never owned any other watch; Disney animations had been his first introduction to the magic of form and color, and Mickey now served as Langdon's daily reminder to stay young at heart. At the moment, however, Mickey's arms were skewed at an awkward angle, indicating an equally awkward hour.

2:51 A.M.

"Interesting watch," Sophie said, glancing at his wrist and maneuvering the SmartCar around the wide, counterclockwise rotary.

"Long story," he said, pulling his sleeve back down.

"I imagine it would have to be." She gave him a quick smile and exited the rotary, heading due north, away from the city center. Barely making two green lights, she reached the third intersection and took a hard right onto Boulevard Malesherbes. They'd left the rich, tree-lined streets of the diplomatic neighborhood and plunged into a darker industrial neighborhood. Sophie took a quick left, and a moment later, Langdon realized where they were.

Gare Saint-Lazare.

Ahead of them, the glass-roofed train terminal resembled the awkward offspring of an airplane hangar and a greenhouse. European train stations never slept. Even at this hour, a half-dozen taxis idled near the main entrance. Vendors manned carts of sandwiches and mineral water while grungy kids in backpacks emerged from the station rubbing their eyes, looking around as if trying to remember what city they were in now. Up ahead on the street, a couple of city policemen stood on the curb giving directions to some confused tourists.

Sophie pulled her SmartCar in behind the line of taxis and parked in a red zone despite plenty of legal parking across the street. Before Langdon could ask what was going on, she was out of the car. She hurried to the window of the taxi in front of them and began speaking to the driver.

As Langdon got out of the SmartCar, he saw Sophie hand the taxi driver a big wad of cash. The taxi driver nodded and then, to Langdon's bewilderment, sped off without them.

"What happened?" Langdon demanded, joining Sophie on the curb as the taxi disappeared.

Sophie was already heading for the train station entrance. "Come on. We're buying two tickets on the next train out of Paris."

Langdon hurried along beside her. What had begun as a one-mile dash to the U.S. Embassy had now become a full-fledged evacuation from Paris. Langdon was liking this idea less and less.

# CHAPTER 34

**The driver** who collected Bishop Aringarosa from Leonardo da Vinci International Airport pulled up in a small, unimpressive black Fiat sedan. Aringarosa recalled a day when all Vatican transports were big luxury cars that sported grille-plate medallions and flags emblazoned with the seal of the Holy See. *Those days are gone.* Vatican cars were now less ostentatious and almost always unmarked. The Vatican claimed this was to cut costs to better serve their dioceses, but Aringarosa suspected it was more of a security measure. The world had gone mad, and in many parts of Europe, advertising your love of Jesus Christ was like painting a bull's-eye on the roof of your car.

Bundling his black cassock around himself, Aringarosa climbed into the back seat and settled in for the long drive to Castel Gandolfo. It would be the same ride he had taken five months ago.

*Last year's trip to Rome,* he sighed. *The longest night of my life.*

Five months ago, the Vatican had phoned to request Aringarosa's immediate presence in Rome. They offered no explanation. *Your tickets are at the airport.* The Holy See worked hard to retain a veil of mystery, even for its highest clergy.

The mysterious summons, Aringarosa suspected, was probably a photo opportunity for the Pope and other Vatican officials to piggyback on Opus Dei's recent public success—the completion of their World Headquarters in New York City. *Architectural Digest* had called Opus Dei's building "a shining beacon of Catholicism sublimely integrated with the modern landscape," and lately the Vatican seemed to be drawn to anything and everything that included the word "modern."

Aringarosa had no choice but to accept the invitation, albeit reluctantly. Not a fan of the current papal administration, Aringarosa, like most conservative clergy, had watched with grave concern as the new Pope settled into his first year in office. An unprecedented liberal, His Holiness had secured the papacy through one of the most controversial and unusual conclaves in Vatican history. Now, rather than being humbled by his unexpected rise to power, the Holy Father had wasted no time flexing all the muscle associated with the highest office in Christendom. Drawing on an unsettling tide of liberal support within the College of Cardinals, the Pope was now declaring his papal mission to be "rejuvenation of Vatican doctrine and updating Catholicism into the third millennium."

The translation, Aringarosa feared, was that the man was actually arrogant enough to think he

could rewrite God's laws and win back the hearts
of those who felt the demands of true Catholicism had become too inconvenient in a modern
world.

Aringarosa had been using all of his political
sway—substantial considering the size of the
Opus Dei constituency and their bankroll—to
persuade the Pope and his advisers that softening
the Church's laws was not only faithless and cow-
ardly, but political suicide. He reminded them
that previous tempering of Church law—the
Vatican II fiasco—had left a devastating legacy:
Church attendance was now lower than ever, do-
nations were drying up, and there were not even
enough Catholic priests to preside over their
churches.

*People need structure and direction from the Church,*
Aringarosa insisted, *not coddling and indulgence!*

On that night, months ago, as the Fiat had left
the airport, Aringarosa was surprised to find
himself heading not toward Vatican City but
rather eastward up a sinuous mountain road.
"Where are we going?" he had demanded of his
driver.

"Alban Hills," the man replied. "Your meeting
is at Castel Gandolfo."

*The Pope's summer residence?* Aringarosa had
never been, nor had he ever desired to see it. In
addition to being the Pope's summer vacation

home, the sixteenth-century citadel housed the Specula Vaticana—the Vatican Observatory— one of the most advanced astronomical observatories in Europe. Aringarosa had never been comfortable with the Vatican's historical need to dabble in science. What was the rationale for fusing science and faith? Unbiased science could not possibly be performed by a man who possessed faith in God. Nor did faith have any need for physical confirmation of its beliefs.

*Nonetheless, there it is,* he thought as Castel Gandolfo came into view, rising against a star-filled November sky. From the access road, Gandolfo resembled a great stone monster pondering a suicidal leap. Perched at the very edge of a cliff, the castle leaned out over the cradle of Italian civilization—the valley where the Curiazi and Orazi clans fought long before the founding of Rome.

Even in silhouette, Gandolfo was a sight to behold—an impressive example of tiered, defensive architecture, echoing the potency of this dramatic cliffside setting. Sadly, Aringarosa now saw, the Vatican had ruined the building by constructing two huge aluminum telescope domes atop the roof, leaving this once dignified edifice looking like a proud warrior wearing a couple of party hats.

When Aringarosa got out of the car, a young

Jesuit priest hurried out and greeted him. "Bishop, welcome. I am Father Mangano. An astronomer here."

*Good for you.* Aringarosa grumbled his hello and followed his host into the castle's foyer—a wide-open space whose decor was a graceless blend of Renaissance art and astronomy images. Following his escort up the wide travertine marble staircase, Aringarosa saw signs for conference centers, science lecture halls, and tourist information services. It amazed him to think the Vatican was failing at every turn to provide coherent, stringent guidelines for spiritual growth and yet somehow still found time to give astrophysics lectures to tourists.

"Tell me," Aringarosa said to the young priest, "when did the tail start wagging the dog?"

The priest gave him an odd look. "Sir?"

Aringarosa waved it off, deciding not to launch into that particular offensive again this evening. *The Vatican has gone mad.* Like a lazy parent who found it easier to acquiesce to the whims of a spoiled child than to stand firm and teach values, the Church just kept softening at every turn, trying to reinvent itself to accommodate a culture gone astray.

The top floor's corridor was wide, lushly appointed, and led in only one direction—toward a huge set of oak doors with a brass sign.

## BIBLIOTECA ASTRONOMICA

Aringarosa had heard of this place—the Vatican's Astronomy Library—rumored to contain more than twenty-five thousand volumes, including rare works of Copernicus, Galileo, Kepler, Newton, and Secchi. Allegedly, it was also the place in which the Pope's highest officers held private meetings . . . those meetings they preferred not to hold within the walls of Vatican City.

Approaching the door, Bishop Aringarosa would never have imagined the shocking news he was about to receive inside, or the deadly chain of events it would put into motion. It was not until an hour later, as he staggered from the meeting, that the devastating implications settled in. *Six months from now!* he had thought. *God help us!*

Now, seated in the Fiat, Bishop Aringarosa realized his fists were clenched just thinking about that first meeting. He released his grip and forced a slow inhalation, relaxing his muscles.

*Everything will be fine,* he told himself as the Fiat wound higher into the mountains. Still, he wished his cell phone would ring. *Why hasn't the*

*Teacher called me? Silas should have the keystone by now.*

Trying to ease his nerves, the bishop meditated on the purple amethyst in his ring. Feeling the textures of the mitre-crozier appliqué and the facets of the diamonds, he reminded himself that this ring was a symbol of power far less than that which he would soon attain.

# CHAPTER 35

**The inside** of Gare Saint-Lazare looked like every other train station in Europe, a gaping indoor-outdoor cavern dotted with the usual suspects—homeless men holding cardboard signs, collections of bleary-eyed college kids sleeping on backpacks and zoning out to their portable MP3 players, and clusters of blue-clad baggage porters smoking cigarettes.

Sophie raised her eyes to the enormous departure board overhead. The black and white tabs reshuffled, ruffling downward as the information refreshed. When the update was finished, Langdon eyed the offerings. The topmost listing read:

LYON—RAPIDE—3:06

"I wish it left sooner," Sophie said, "but Lyon will have to do."

*Sooner?* Langdon checked his watch 2:59 A.M. The train left in seven minutes and they didn't even have tickets yet.

Sophie guided Langdon toward the ticket window and said, "Buy us two tickets with your credit card."

"I thought credit card usage could be traced by—"

"Exactly."

Langdon decided to stop trying to keep ahead of Sophie Neveu. Using his Visa card, he purchased two coach tickets to Lyon and handed them to Sophie.

Sophie guided him out toward the tracks, where a familiar tone chimed overhead and a P.A. announcer gave the final boarding call for Lyon. Sixteen separate tracks spread out before them. In the distance to the right, at quay three, the train to Lyon was belching and wheezing in preparation for departure, but Sophie already had her arm through Langdon's and was guiding him in the exact opposite direction. They hurried through a side lobby, past an all-night café, and finally out a side door onto a quiet street on the west side of the station.

A lone taxi sat idling by the doorway.

The driver saw Sophie and flicked his lights.

Sophie jumped in the back seat. Langdon got in after her.

As the taxi pulled away from station, Sophie took out their newly purchased train tickets and tore them up.

Langdon sighed. *Seventy dollars well spent.*

It was not until their taxi had settled into a monotonous northbound hum on Rue de Clichy that Langdon felt they'd actually escaped. Out the window to his right, he could see Montmartre and the beautiful dome of Sacré-Coeur. The image was interrupted by the flash of police lights sailing past them in the opposite direction.

Langdon and Sophie ducked down as the sirens faded.

Sophie had told the cab driver simply to head out of the city, and from her firmly set jaw, Langdon sensed she was trying to figure out their next move.

Langdon examined the cruciform key again, holding it to the window, bringing it close to his eyes in an effort to find any markings on it that might indicate where the key had been made. In the intermittent glow of passing streetlights, he saw no markings except the Priory seal.

"It doesn't make sense," he finally said.

"Which part?"

"That your grandfather would go to so much trouble to give you a key that you wouldn't know what to do with."

"I agree."

"Are you sure he didn't write anything else on the back of the painting?"

"I searched the whole area. This is all there was. This key, wedged behind the painting. I saw the Priory seal, stuck the key in my pocket, then we left."

Langdon frowned, peering now at the blunt end of the triangular shaft. Nothing. Squinting, he brought the key close to his eyes and examined the rim of the head. Nothing there either. "I think this key was cleaned recently."

"Why?"

"It smells like rubbing alcohol."

She turned. "I'm sorry?"

"It smells like somebody polished it with a cleaner." Langdon held the key to his nose and sniffed. "It's stronger on the other side." He flipped it over. "Yes, it's alcohol-based, like it's been buffed with a cleaner or—" Langdon stopped.

"What?"

He angled the key to the light and looked at the smooth surface on the broad arm of the cross. It seemed to shimmer in places . . . like it was wet. "How well did you look at the back of this key before you put it in your pocket?"

"What? Not well. I was in a hurry."

Langdon turned to her. "Do you still have the black light?"

Sophie reached in her pocket and produced the UV penlight. Langdon took it and switched it on, shining the beam on the back of the key.

The back luminesced instantly. There was writing there. In penmanship that was hurried but legible.

"Well," Langdon said, smiling. "I guess we know what the alcohol smell was."

Sophie stared in amazement at the purple writing on the back of the key.

24 Rue Haxo

*An address! My grandfather wrote down an address!*

"Where is this?" Langdon asked.

Sophie had no idea. Facing front again, she leaned forward and excitedly asked the driver, *"Connaissez-vous la Rue Haxo?"*

The driver thought a moment and then nodded. He told Sophie it was out near the tennis stadium on the western outskirts of Paris. She asked him to take them there immediately.

"Fastest route is through Bois de Boulogne," the driver told her in French. "Is that okay?"

Sophie frowned. She could think of far less scandalous routes, but tonight she was not going to be picky. "Oui." *We can shock the visiting American.*

Sophie looked back at the key and wondered what they would possibly find at 24 Rue Haxo. *A church? Some kind of Priory headquarters?*

Her mind filled again with images of the secret ritual she had witnessed in the basement grotto ten years ago, and she heaved a long sigh. "Robert, I have a lot of things to tell you." She paused, locking eyes with him as the taxi raced westward. "But first I want you to tell me everything you know about this Priory of Sion."

# CHAPTER 36

**Outside the** Salle des Etats, Bezu Fache was fuming as Louvre warden Grouard explained how Sophie and Langdon had disarmed him. *Why didn't you just shoot the blessed painting!*

"Captain?" Lieutenant Collet loped toward them from the direction of the command post. "Captain, I just heard. They located Agent Neveu's car."

"Did she make the embassy?"

"No. Train station. Bought two tickets. Train just left."

Fache waved off warden Grouard and led Collet to a nearby alcove, addressing him in hushed tones. "What was the destination?"

"Lyon."

"Probably a decoy." Fache exhaled, formulating a plan. "Okay, alert the next station, have the train stopped and searched, just in case. Leave her car where it is and put plainclothes on watch in case they try to come back to it. Send men to search the streets around the station in case they fled on foot. Are buses running from the station?"

"Not at this hour, sir. Only the taxi queue."

"Good. Question the drivers. See if they saw

anything. Then contact the taxi company dispatcher with descriptions. I'm calling Interpol."

Collet looked surprised. "You're putting this on the *wire?*"

Fache regretted the potential embarrassment, but he saw no other choice.

*Close the net fast, and close it tight.*

The first hour was critical. Fugitives were predictable the first hour after escape. They always needed the same thing. *Travel. Lodging. Cash.* The Holy Trinity. Interpol had the power to make all three disappear in the blink of an eye. By broadcast-faxing photos of Langdon and Sophie to Paris travel authorities, hotels, and banks, Interpol would leave no options—no way to leave the city, no place to hide, and no way to withdraw cash without being recognized. Usually, fugitives panicked on the street and did something stupid. Stole a car. Robbed a store. Used a bank card in desperation. Whatever mistake they committed, they quickly made their whereabouts known to local authorities.

"Only *Langdon,* right?" Collet said. "You're not flagging Sophie Neveu. She's our own agent."

"Of course I'm flagging her!" Fache snapped. "What good is flagging Langdon if she can do all his dirty work? I plan to run Neveu's employment file—friends, family, personal contacts— anyone she might turn to for help. I don't know what she thinks she's doing out there, but it's going to cost her one hell of a lot more than her job!"

"Do you want me on the phones or in the field?"

"Field. Get over to the train station and coordinate the team. You've got the reins, but don't make a move without talking to me."

"Yes, sir." Collet ran out.

Fache felt rigid as he stood in the alcove. Outside the window, the glass pyramid shone, its reflection rippling in the windswept pools. *They slipped through my fingers.* He told himself to relax.

Even a trained field agent would be lucky to withstand the pressure that Interpol was about to apply.

*A female cryptologist and a schoolteacher?*

They wouldn't last till dawn.

# CHAPTER 37

**The heavily** forested park known as the Bois de Boulogne was called many things, but the Parisian cognoscenti knew it as "the Garden of Earthly Delights." The epithet, despite sounding flattering, was quite to the contrary. Anyone who had seen the lurid Bosch painting of the same name understood the jab; the painting, like the forest, was dark and twisted, a purgatory for freaks and fetishists. At night, the forest's winding lanes were lined with hundreds of glistening bodies for hire, earthly delights to satisfy one's deepest unspoken desires—male, female, and everything in between.

As Langdon gathered his thoughts to tell Sophie about the Priory of Sion, their taxi passed through the wooded entrance to the park and began heading west on the cobblestone crossfare. Langdon was having trouble concentrating as a scattering of the park's nocturnal residents were already emerging from the shadows and flaunting their wares in the glare of the headlights. Ahead, two topless teenage girls shot smoldering gazes into the taxi. Beyond them, a well-oiled black man in a G-string turned and flexed his buttocks. Beside him, a gorgeous blond woman lifted her miniskirt to reveal that she was not, in fact, a woman.

*Heaven help me!* Langdon turned his gaze back inside the cab and took a deep breath.

"Tell me about the Priory of Sion," Sophie said.

Langdon nodded, unable to imagine a less congruous a backdrop for the legend he was about to tell. He wondered where to begin. The brotherhood's history spanned more than a millennium . . . an astonishing chronicle of secrets, blackmail, betrayal, and even brutal torture at the hands of an angry Pope.

"The Priory of Sion," he began, "was founded in Jerusalem in 1099 by a French king named Godefroi de Bouillon, immediately after he had conquered the city."

Sophie nodded, her eyes riveted on him.

"King Godefroi was allegedly the possessor of a powerful secret—a secret that had been in his family since the time of Christ. Fearing his secret might be lost when he died, he founded a secret brotherhood—the Priory of Sion—and charged them with protecting his secret by quietly passing it on from generation to generation. During their years in Jerusalem, the Priory learned of a stash of hidden documents buried beneath the ruins of Herod's temple, which had been built atop the earlier ruins of Solomon's Temple. These documents, they believed, corroborated Godefroi's powerful secret and were so explosive in nature that the Church would stop at nothing to get them."

Sophie looked uncertain.

"The Priory vowed that no matter how long it took, these documents must be recovered from the rubble beneath the temple and protected forever, so the truth would never die. In order to retrieve the documents from within the ruins, the Priory created a military arm—a group of nine knights called the Order of the Poor Knights of Christ and the Temple of Solomon." Langdon paused. "More commonly known as the Knights Templar."

Sophie glanced up with a surprised look of recognition.

Langdon had lectured often enough on the Knights Templar to know that almost everyone on earth had heard of them, at least abstractedly. For academics, the Templars' history was a precarious world where fact, lore, and misinformation had become so intertwined that extracting a pristine truth was almost impossible. Nowadays, Langdon hesitated even to mention the Knights Templar while lecturing because it invariably led to a barrage of convoluted inquiries into assorted conspiracy theories.

Sophie already looked troubled. "You're saying the Knights Templar were founded by the Priory of Sion to retrieve a collection of secret documents? I thought the Templars were created to protect the Holy Land."

"A common misconception. The idea of protection of pilgrims was the *guise* under which the Templars ran their mission. Their true goal in the Holy Land was to retrieve the documents from beneath the ruins of the temple."

"And did they find them?"

Langdon grinned. "Nobody knows for sure, but the one thing on which all academics agree is this: The Knights discovered *something* down there in the ruins . . . something that made them wealthy and powerful beyond anyone's wildest imagination."

Langdon quickly gave Sophie the standard academic sketch of the accepted Knights Templar history, explaining how the Knights were in the Holy Land during the Second Crusade and told King Baldwin II that they were there to protect Christian pilgrims on the roadways. Although unpaid and sworn to poverty, the Knights told the king they required basic shelter and requested his permission to take up residence in the stables under the ruins of the temple. King Baldwin granted the soldiers' request, and the Knights took up their meager residence inside the devastated shrine.

The odd choice of lodging, Langdon explained, had been anything but random. The Knights believed the documents the Priory sought were buried deep under the ruins—beneath the Holy of Holies, a sacred chamber where God Himself was believed to reside. Literally, the very center of the Jewish faith. For almost a decade, the nine Knights lived in the ruins, excavating in total secrecy through solid rock.

Sophie looked over. "And you said they discovered something?"

"They certainly did," Langdon said, explaining how it had taken nine years, but the Knights had finally found what they had been searching for. They took the treasure from the temple and traveled to Europe, where their influence seemed to solidify overnight.

Nobody was certain whether the Knights had blackmailed the Vatican or whether the Church simply tried to buy the Knights' silence, but Pope Innocent II immediately issued an unprecedented papal bull that afforded the Knights Templar limitless power and declared them "a law unto themselves"—an autonomous army independent of all interference from kings and prelates, both religious and political.

With their new carte blanche from the Vatican, the Knights Templar expanded at a staggering rate, both in numbers and political force, amassing vast estates in over a dozen countries. They began extending credit to bankrupt royals and charging interest in return, thereby establishing modern banking and broadening their wealth and influence still further.

By the 1300s, the Vatican sanction had helped the Knights amass so much power that Pope Clement V decided that something had to be done. Working in concert with France's King Philippe IV, the Pope devised an ingeniously planned sting operation to quash the Templars and seize their treasure, thus taking control of the secrets held over the Vatican. In a military maneuver worthy of the CIA, Pope Clement issued secret sealed orders to be opened simultaneously by his soldiers all across Europe on Friday, October 13 of 1307.

At dawn on the thirteenth, the documents were unsealed and their appalling contents revealed. Clement's letter claimed that God had visited him in a vision and warned him that the Knights Templar were heretics guilty of devil worship, homosexuality, defiling the cross, sodomy, and other blasphemous behavior. Pope Clement had been asked by God to cleanse the earth by rounding up all the Knights and torturing them until they confessed their crimes against God. Clement's Machiavellian operation came off with clockwork precision. On that day, countless Knights were captured, tortured mercilessly, and finally burned at the stake as heretics. Echoes of the tragedy still resonated in modern culture; to this day, Friday the thirteenth was considered unlucky.

Sophie looked confused. "The Knights Templar

were obliterated? I thought fraternities of Templars still exist today?"

"They do, under a variety of names. Despite Clement's false charges and best efforts to eradicate them, the Knights had powerful allies, and some managed to escape the Vatican purges. The Templars' potent treasure trove of documents, which had apparently been their source of power, was Clement's true objective, but it slipped through his fingers. The documents had long since been entrusted to the Templars' shadowy architects, the Priory of Sion, whose veil of secrecy had kept them safely out of range of the Vatican's onslaught. As the Vatican closed in, the Priory smuggled their documents from a Paris preceptory by night onto Templar ships in La Rochelle."

"Where did the documents go?"

Langdon shrugged. "That mystery's answer is known only to the Priory of Sion. Because the documents remain the source of constant investigation and speculation even today, they are believed to have been moved and rehidden several times. Current speculation places the documents somewhere in the United Kingdom."

Sophie looked uneasy.

"For a thousand years," Langdon continued, "legends of this secret have been passed on. The entire collection of documents, its power, and the secret it reveals have become known by a single name—Sangreal. Hundreds of books have been written about it, and few mysteries have caused as much interest among historians as the Sangreal."

"The Sangreal? Does the word have anything to do with the French word *sang* or Spanish *sangre*—meaning 'blood'?"

Langdon nodded. Blood was the backbone of the Sangreal, and yet not in the way Sophie probably imagined. "The legend is complicated, but the important thing to remember is that the Priory guards the proof, and is purportedly awaiting the right moment in history to reveal the truth."

"What truth? What secret could possibly be that powerful?"

Langdon took a deep breath and gazed out at the underbelly of Paris leering in the shadows. "Sophie, the word *Sangreal* is an ancient word. It has evolved over the years into another term . . . a more modern name." He paused. "When I tell you its modern name, you'll realize you already know a lot about it. In fact, almost everyone on earth has heard the story of the Sangreal."

Sophie looked skeptical. "I've never heard of it."

"Sure you have." Langdon smiled. "You're just used to hearing it called by the name 'Holy Grail.' "

# CHAPTER 38

**Sophie scrutinized** Langdon in the back of the taxi. *He's joking.* "The Holy Grail?"

Langdon nodded, his expression serious. "Holy Grail is the literal meaning of Sangreal. The phrase derives from the French *Sangraal*, which evolved to Sangreal, and was eventually split into two words, *San Greal*."

*Holy Grail.* Sophie was surprised she had not spotted the linguistic ties immediately. Even so, Langdon's claim still made no sense to her. "I thought the Holy Grail was a *cup*. You just told me the Sangreal is a collection of documents that reveals some dark secret."

"Yes, but the Sangreal documents are only *half* of the Holy Grail treasure. They are buried with the Grail itself . . . and reveal its true meaning. The documents gave the Knights Templar so much power because the pages revealed the true nature of the Grail."

*The true nature of the Grail?* Sophie felt even more lost now. The Holy Grail, she had thought, was the cup that Jesus drank from at the Last Supper and with which Joseph of Arimathea later caught His blood at the crucifixion. "The Holy

Grail is the Cup of Christ," she said. "How much simpler could it be?"

"Sophie," Langdon whispered, leaning toward her now, "according to the Priory of Sion, the Holy Grail is not a cup at all. They claim the Grail legend—that of a *chalice*—is actually an ingeniously conceived allegory. That is, that the Grail story uses the *chalice* as a metaphor for something else, something far more powerful." He paused. "Something that fits perfectly with everything your grandfather has been trying to tell us tonight, including all his symbologic references to the sacred feminine."

Still unsure, Sophie sensed in Langdon's patient smile that he empathized with her confusion, and yet his eyes remained earnest. "But if the Holy Grail is not a cup," she asked, "what is it?"

Langdon had known this question was coming, and yet he still felt uncertain exactly how to tell her. If he did not present the answer in the proper historical background, Sophie would be left with a vacant air of bewilderment—the exact expression Langdon had seen on his own editor's face a few months ago after Langdon handed him a draft of the manuscript he was working on.

"This manuscript claims *what?*" his editor had choked, setting down his wineglass and staring across his half-eaten power lunch. "You can't be serious."

"Serious enough to have spent a year researching it."

Prominent New York editor Jonas Faukman tugged nervously at his goatee. Faukman no doubt had heard some wild book ideas in his illustrious career, but this one seemed to have left the man flabbergasted.

"Robert," Faukman finally said, "don't get me wrong. I love your work, and we've had a great run together. But if I agree to publish an idea like this, I'll have people picketing outside my office for months. Besides, it will kill your reputation. You're a Harvard historian, for God's sake, not a pop schlockmeister looking for a quick buck. Where could you possibly find enough credible evidence to support a theory like this?"

With a quiet smile Langdon pulled a piece of paper from the pocket of his tweed coat and handed it to Faukman. The page listed a bibliography of over fifty titles—books by well-known historians, some contemporary, some centuries old—many of them academic bestsellers. All the book titles suggested the same premise Langdon had just proposed. As Faukman read down the list, he looked like a man who had just discovered the earth was actually flat. "I *know* some of these authors. They're . . . real historians!"

Langdon grinned. "As you can see, Jonas, this is not only *my* theory. It's been around for a long time. I'm simply building on it. No book has yet explored the legend of the Holy Grail from a symbologic angle. The iconographic evidence I'm finding to support the theory is, well, staggeringly persuasive."

Faukman was still staring at the list. "My God, one of these books was written by Sir Leigh Teabing—a British Royal Historian."

"Teabing has spent much of his life studying the Holy Grail. I've met with him. He was actually a big part of my inspiration. He's a believer, Jonas, along with all of the others on that list."

"You're telling me all of these historians actually believe . . ." Faukman swallowed, apparently unable to say the words.

Langdon grinned again. "The Holy Grail is arguably the most sought-after treasure in human history. The Grail has spawned legends, wars, and lifelong quests. Does it make sense that it is merely a cup? If so, then certainly *other* relics should generate similar or greater interest—the Crown of Thorns, the True Cross of the Crucifixion, the Titulus—and yet, they do not. Throughout history, the Holy Grail has been the most special." Langdon grinned. "Now you know why."

Faukman was still shaking his head. "But with all these books written about it, why isn't this theory more widely known?"

"These books can't possibly compete with centuries of established history, especially when that history is endorsed by the ultimate bestseller of all time."

Faukman's eyes went wide. "Don't tell me *Harry Potter* is actually about the Holy Grail."

"I was referring to the Bible."

Faukman cringed. "I knew that."

*"Laissez-le!"* Sophie's shouts cut the air inside the taxi. "Put it down!"

Langdon jumped as Sophie leaned forward over the seat and yelled at the taxi driver. Langdon could see the driver was clutching his radio mouthpiece and speaking into it.

Sophie turned now and plunged her hand into the pocket of Langdon's tweed jacket. Before Langdon knew what had happened, she had yanked out the pistol, swung it around, and was pressing it to the back of the driver's head. The driver instantly dropped his radio, raising his one free hand overhead.

"Sophie!" Langdon choked. "What the hell—"

*"Arrêtez!"* Sophie commanded the driver.

Trembling, the driver obeyed, stopping the car and putting it in park.

It was then that Langdon heard the metallic voice of the taxi company's dispatcher coming from the dashboard. *". . . qui s'appelle Agent Sophie Neveu . . ."* the radio crackled. *"Et un Américain, Robert Langdon . . ."*

Langdon's muscles turned rigid. *They found us already?*

"*Descendez*," Sophie demanded.

The trembling driver kept his arms over his head as he got out of his taxi and took several steps backward.

Sophie had rolled down her window and now aimed the gun outside at the bewildered cabbie. "Robert," she said quietly, "take the wheel. You're driving."

Langdon was not about to argue with a woman wielding a gun. He climbed out of the car and jumped back in behind the wheel. The driver was yelling curses, his arms still raised over his head.

"Robert," Sophie said from the back seat, "I trust you've seen enough of our magic forest?"

He nodded. *Plenty.*

"Good. Drive us out of here."

Langdon looked down at the car's controls and hesitated. *Shit.* He groped for the stick shift and clutch. "Sophie? Maybe you—"

"Go!" she yelled.

Outside, several hookers were walking over to see what was going on. One woman was placing a call on her cell phone. Langdon depressed the clutch and jostled the stick into what he hoped was first gear. He touched the accelerator, testing the gas.

Langdon popped the clutch. The tires howled as the taxi leapt forward, fishtailing wildly and sending the gathering crowd diving for cover. The woman with the cell phone leapt into the woods, only narrowly avoiding being run down.

*"Doucement!"* Sophie said, as the car lurched down the road. "What are you doing?"

"I tried to warn you," he shouted over the sound of gnashing gears. "I drive an automatic!"

# CHAPTER 39

**Although the** spartan room in the brown-stone on Rue La Bruyère had witnessed a lot of suffering, Silas doubted anything could match the anguish now gripping his pale body. *I was deceived. Everything is lost.*

Silas had been tricked. The brothers had lied, choosing death instead of revealing their true secret. Silas did not have the strength to call the Teacher. Not only had Silas killed the only four people who knew where the keystone was hidden, he had killed a nun inside Saint-Sulpice. *She was working against God! She scorned the work of Opus Dei!*

A crime of impulse, the woman's death complicated matters greatly. Bishop Aringarosa had placed the phone call that got Silas into Saint-Sulpice; what would the abbé think when he discovered the nun was dead? Although Silas had placed her back in her bed, the wound on her head was obvious. Silas had attempted to replace the broken tiles in the floor, but that damage too was obvious. They would know someone had been there.

Silas had planned to hide within Opus Dei

when his task here was complete. *Bishop Aringarosa will protect me.* Silas could imagine no more blissful existence than a life of meditation and prayer deep within the walls of Opus Dei's headquarters in New York City. He would never again set foot outside. Everything he needed was within that sanctuary. *Nobody will miss me.* Unfortunately, Silas knew, a prominent man like Bishop Aringarosa could not disappear so easily.

*I have endangered the bishop.* Silas gazed blankly at the floor and pondered taking his own life. After all, it had been Aringarosa who gave Silas life in the first place . . . in that small rectory in Spain, educating him, giving him purpose.

"My friend," Aringarosa had told him, "you were born an albino. Do not let others shame you for this. Do you not understand how special this makes you? Were you not aware that Noah himself was an albino?"

"Noah of the Ark?" Silas had never heard this.

Aringarosa was smiling. "Indeed, Noah of the Ark. An albino. Like you, he had skin white like an angel. Consider this. Noah saved all of life on the planet. You are destined for great things, Silas. The Lord has freed you for a reason. You have your calling. The Lord needs your help to do His work."

Over time, Silas learned to see himself in a new light. *I am pure. White. Beautiful. Like an angel.*

At the moment, though, in his room at the residence hall, it was his father's disappointed voice that whispered to him from the past.

*Tu es un désastre. Un spectre.*

Kneeling on the wooden floor, Silas prayed for forgiveness. Then, stripping off his robe, he reached again for the Discipline.

# CHAPTER 40

**Struggling with** the gear shift, Langdon managed to maneuver the hijacked taxi to the far side of the Bois de Boulogne while stalling only twice. Unfortunately, the inherent humor in the situation was overshadowed by the taxi dispatcher repeatedly hailing their cab over the radio.

*"Voiture cinq-six-trois. Où êtes-vous? Répondez!"*

When Langdon reached the exit of the park, he swallowed his machismo and jammed on the brakes. "You'd better drive."

Sophie looked relieved as she jumped behind the wheel. Within seconds she had the car humming smoothly westward along Allée de Longchamp, leaving the Garden of Earthly Delights behind.

"Which way is Rue Haxo?" Langdon asked, watching Sophie edge the speedometer over a hundred kilometers an hour.

Sophie's eyes remained focused on the road. "The cab driver said it's adjacent to the Roland Garros tennis stadium. I know that area."

Langdon pulled the heavy key from his pocket again, feeling the weight in his palm. He sensed it was an object of enormous consequence. Quite possibly the key to his own freedom.

Earlier, while telling Sophie about the Knights Templar, Langdon had realized that this key, in addition to having the Priory seal embossed on it, possessed a more subtle tie to the Priory of Sion. The equal-armed cruciform was symbolic of balance and harmony but also of the Knights Templar. Everyone had seen the paintings of Knights Templar wearing white tunics emblazoned with red equal-armed crosses. Granted, the arms of the Templar cross were slightly flared at the ends, but they were still of equal length.

*A square cross. Just like the one on this key.*

Langdon felt his imagination starting to run wild as he fantasized about what they might find. *The Holy Grail.* He almost laughed out loud at the absurdity of it. The Grail was believed to be somewhere in England, buried in a hidden chamber beneath one of the many Templar churches, where it had been hidden since at least 1500.

*The era of Grand Master Da Vinci.*

The Priory, in order to keep their powerful documents safe, had been forced to move them many times in the early centuries. Historians now suspected as many as six different Grail relocations since its arrival in Europe from Jerusalem. The last Grail "sighting" had been in 1447 when numerous eyewitnesses described a fire that had broken out and almost engulfed the documents before they were carried to safety in four huge chests that each required six men to carry. After that, nobody claimed to see the Grail ever again. All that remained were occasional whisperings that it was hidden in Great Britain, the land of King Arthur and the Knights of the Round Table.

Wherever it was, two important facts remained:

*Leonardo knew where the Grail resided during his lifetime.*

*That hiding place had probably not changed to this day.*

For this reason, Grail enthusiasts still pored over Da Vinci's art and diaries in hopes of unearthing a hidden clue as to the Grail's current location. Some claimed the mountainous backdrop in *Madonna of the Rocks* matched the topography of a series of cave-ridden hills in Scotland. Others insisted that the suspicious placement of disciples in *The Last Supper* was some kind of code. Still others claimed that X rays of the *Mona Lisa* revealed she originally had been painted wearing a lapis lazuli pendant of Isis—a detail Da Vinci purportedly later decided to paint over. Langdon had never seen any evidence of the pendant, nor could he imagine how it could possibly reveal the Holy Grail, and yet Grail aficionados still discussed it ad nauseum on Internet bulletin boards and worldwide-web chat rooms.

*Everyone loves a conspiracy.*

And the conspiracies kept coming. Most recently, of course, had been the earthshaking discovery that Da Vinci's famed *Adoration of the Magi* was hiding a dark secret beneath its layers of paint. Italian art diagnostician Maurizio Seracini had unveiled the unsettling truth, which the *New York Times Magazine* carried prominently in a story titled "The Leonardo Cover-Up."

Seracini had revealed beyond any doubt that while the *Adoration*'s gray-green sketched underdrawing was indeed Da Vinci's work, the painting itself was not. The truth was that some anonymous painter had filled in Da Vinci's sketch like a paint-by-numbers years after Da Vinci's death. Far more troubling, however, was what lay *beneath* the impostor's paint. Photographs taken with infrared reflectography and X ray suggested that this rogue painter, while filling in Da Vinci's sketched study, had made suspicious departures from the underdrawing . . . as if to subvert Da Vinci's true intention. Whatever the true nature of the underdrawing, it had yet to be made public. Even so, embarrassed officials at Florence's Uffizi Gallery immediately banished the painting to a warehouse across the street. Visitors at the gallery's Leonardo Room now found a misleading and unapologetic plaque where the *Adoration* once hung.

---

**THIS WORK IS UNDERGOING DIAGNOSTIC TESTS IN PREPARATION FOR RESTORATION.**

---

In the bizarre underworld of modern Grail seekers, Leonardo da Vinci remained the quest's great enigma. His artwork seemed bursting to tell a secret, and yet whatever it was remained hidden, perhaps beneath a layer of paint, perhaps enciphered in plain view, or perhaps nowhere at all. Maybe Da Vinci's plethora of tantalizing clues was nothing but an empty promise left behind to frustrate the curious and bring a smirk to the face of his knowing Mona Lisa.

"Is it possible," Sophie asked, drawing Langdon back, "that the key you're holding unlocks the hiding place of the Holy Grail?"

Langdon's laugh sounded forced, even to him. "I really can't imagine. Besides, the Grail is believed to be hidden in the United Kingdom somewhere, not France." He gave her the quick history.

"But the Grail seems the only rational conclusion," she insisted. "We have an extremely secure key, stamped with the Priory of Sion seal, delivered to us by a member of the Priory of Sion—a brotherhood which, you just told me, are guardians of the Holy Grail."

Langdon knew her contention was logical, and yet intuitively he could not possibly accept it. Rumors existed that the Priory had vowed someday to bring the Grail back to France to a final resting place, but certainly no historical evidence existed to suggest that this indeed had happened.

Even if the Priory had managed to bring the Grail back to France, the address 24 Rue Haxo near a tennis stadium hardly sounded like a noble final resting place. "Sophie, I really don't see how this key could have anything to do with the Grail."

"Because the Grail is supposed to be in England?"

"Not only that. The location of the Holy Grail is one of the best kept secrets in history. Priory members wait decades proving themselves trust-worthy before being elevated to the highest ech-elons of the fraternity and learning where the Grail is. That secret is protected by an intricate system of compartmentalized knowledge, and al-though the Priory brotherhood is very large, only *four* members at any given time know where the Grail is hidden—the Grand Master and his three *sénéchaux*. The probability of your grandfather being one of those four top people is very slim."

*My grandfather was one of them*, Sophie thought, pressing down on the accelerator. She had an im-age stamped in her memory that confirmed her grandfather's status within the brotherhood be-yond any doubt.

"And even if your grandfather *were* in the up-per echelon, he would never be allowed to reveal anything to anyone outside the brotherhood. It is inconceivable that he would bring you into the inner circle."

*I've already been there,* Sophie thought, picturing the ritual in the basement. She wondered if this were the moment to tell Langdon what she had witnessed that night in the Normandy château. For ten years now, simple shame had kept her from telling a soul. Just thinking about it, she shuddered. Sirens howled somewhere in the distance, and she felt a thickening shroud of fatigue settling over her.

"There!" Langdon said, feeling excited to see the huge complex of the Roland Garros tennis stadium looming ahead.

Sophie snaked her way toward the stadium. After several passes, they located the intersection of Rue Haxo and turned onto it, driving in the direction of the lower numbers. The road became more industrial, lined with businesses.

*We need number twenty-four,* Langdon told himself, realizing he was secretly scanning the horizon for the spires of a church. *Don't be ridiculous. A forgotten Templar church in this neighborhood?*

"There it is," Sophie exclaimed, pointing.

Langdon's eyes followed to the structure ahead. *What in the world?*

The building was modern. A squat citadel with a giant, neon equal-armed cross emblazoned atop its facade. Beneath the cross were the words:

## DEPOSITORY BANK OF ZURICH

Langdon was thankful not to have shared his Templar church hopes with Sophie. A career hazard of symbologists was a tendency to extract hidden meaning from situations that had none. In this case, Langdon had entirely forgotten that the peaceful, equal-armed cross had been adopted as the perfect symbol for the flag of neutral Switzerland.

At least the mystery was solved.

Sophie and Langdon were holding the key to a Swiss bank deposit box.

# CHAPTER 41

**Outside Castel** Gandolfo, an updraft of mountain air gushed over the top of the cliff and across the high bluff, sending a chill through Bishop Aringarosa as he stepped from the Fiat. *I should have worn more than this cassock,* he thought, fighting the reflex to shiver. The last thing he needed to appear tonight was weak or fearful.

The castle was dark save the windows at the very top of the building, which glowed ominously. *The library,* Aringarosa thought. *They are awake and waiting.* He ducked his head against the wind and continued on without so much as a glance toward the observatory domes.

The priest who greeted him at the door looked sleepy. He was the same priest who had greeted Aringarosa five months ago, albeit tonight he did so with much less hospitality. "We were worried about you, Bishop," the priest said, checking his watch and looking more perturbed than worried.

"My apologies. Airlines are so unreliable these days."

The priest mumbled something inaudible and then said, "They are waiting upstairs. I will escort you up."

The library was a vast square room with dark

wood from floor to ceiling. On all sides, towering bookcases burgeoned with volumes. The floor was amber marble with black basalt trim, a handsome reminder that this building had once been a palace.

"Welcome, Bishop," a man's voice said from across the room.

Aringarosa tried to see who had spoken, but the lights were ridiculously low—much lower than they had been on his first visit, when everything was ablaze. *The night of stark awakening.* Tonight, these men sat in the shadows, as if they were somehow ashamed of what was about to transpire.

Aringarosa entered slowly, regally even. He could see the shapes of three men at a long table on the far side of the room. The silhouette of the man in the middle was immediately recognizable—the obese Secretariat Vaticana, overlord of all legal matters within Vatican City. The other two were high-ranking Italian cardinals.

Aringarosa crossed the library toward them. "My humble apologies for the hour. We're on different time zones. You must be tired."

"Not at all," the secretariat said, his hands folded on his enormous belly. "We are grateful you have come so far. The least we can do is be awake to meet you. Can we offer you some coffee or refreshments?"

"I'd prefer we don't pretend this is a social visit. I have another plane to catch. Shall we get to business?"

"Of course," the secretariat said. "You have acted more quickly than we imagined."

"Have I?"

"You still have a month."

"You made your concerns known five months ago," Aringarosa said. "Why should I wait?"

"Indeed. We are very pleased with your expediency."

Aringarosa's eyes traveled the length of the long table to a large black briefcase. "Is that what I requested?"

"It is." The secretariat sounded uneasy. "Although, I must admit, we are concerned with the request. It seems quite . . ."

"Dangerous," one of the cardinals finished. "Are you certain we cannot wire it to you somewhere? The sum is exorbitant."

*Freedom is expensive.* "I have no concerns for my own safety. God is with me."

The men actually looked doubtful.

"The funds are exactly as I requested?"

The secretariat nodded. "Large-denomination bearer bonds drawn on the Vatican Bank. Negotiable as cash anywhere in the world."

Aringarosa walked to the end of the table and opened the briefcase. Inside were two thick stacks of bonds, each embossed with the Vatican seal and the title *PORTATORE*, making the bonds re-deemable to whoever was holding them.

The secretariat looked tense. "I must say, Bishop, all of us would feel less apprehensive if these funds were in *cash.*"

*I could not lift that much cash,* Aringarosa thought, closing the case. "Bonds are negotiable as cash. You said so yourself."

The cardinals exchanged uneasy looks, and fi-nally one said, "Yes, but these bonds are traceable directly to the Vatican Bank."

Aringarosa smiled inwardly. That was precisely the reason the Teacher suggested Aringarosa get the money in Vatican Bank bonds. It served as in-surance. *We are all in this together now.* "This is a perfectly legal transaction," Aringarosa defended. "Opus Dei is a personal prelature of Vatican City, and His Holiness can disperse monies however he sees fit. No law has been broken here."

"True, and yet . . ." The secretariat leaned for-ward and his chair creaked under the burden. "We have no knowledge of what you intend to do with these funds, and if it is in any way illegal . . ."

"Considering what you are asking of me," Aringarosa countered, "what I do with this money is not your concern."

There was a long silence.

*They know I'm right,* Aringarosa thought. "Now, I imagine you have something for me to sign?"

They all jumped, eagerly pushing the paper toward him, as if they wished he would simply leave.

Aringarosa eyed the sheet before him. It bore the papal seal. "This is identical to the copy you sent me?"

"Exactly."

Aringarosa was surprised how little emotion he felt as he signed the document. The three men present, however, seemed to sigh in relief.

"Thank you, Bishop," the secretariat said. "Your service to the Church will never be forgotten."

Aringarosa picked up the briefcase, sensing promise and authority in its weight. The four men looked at one another for a moment as if there were something more to say, but apparently there was not. Aringarosa turned and headed for the door.

"Bishop?" one of the cardinals called out as Aringarosa reached the threshold.

Aringarosa paused, turning. "Yes?"

"Where will you go from here?"

Aringarosa sensed the query was more spiritual than geographical, and yet he had no intention of discussing morality at this hour. "Paris," he said, and walked out the door.

CHAPTER **42**

**The Depository** Bank of Zurich was a twenty-four-hour *Geldschrank* bank offering the full modern array of anonymous services in the tradition of the Swiss numbered account. Maintaining offices in Zurich, Kuala Lumpur, New York, and Paris, the bank had expanded its services in recent years to offer anonymous computer source code escrow services and faceless digitized backup.

The bread and butter of its operation was by far its oldest and simplest offering—the *anonyme Lager*—blind drop services, otherwise known as anonymous safe-deposit boxes. Clients wishing to store anything from stock certificates to valuable paintings could deposit their belongings anonymously, through a series of high-tech veils of privacy, withdrawing items at any time, also in total anonymity.

As Sophie pulled the taxi to a stop in front of their destination, Langdon gazed out at the building's uncompromising architecture and sensed the Depository Bank of Zurich was a firm with little sense of humor. The building was a windowless rectangle that seemed to be forged entirely of dull steel. Resembling an enormous metal brick, the edifice sat back from the road with a fifteen-foot-tall, neon, equilateral cross glowing over its facade.

Switzerland's reputation for secrecy in banking had become one of the country's most lucrative exports. Facilities like this had become controversial in the art community because they provided a perfect place for art thieves to hide stolen goods, for years if necessary, until the heat was off. Because deposits were protected from police inspection by privacy laws and were attached to numbered accounts rather than people's names, thieves could rest easily knowing their stolen goods were safe and could never be traced to them.

Sophie stopped the taxi at an imposing gate that blocked the bank's driveway—a cement-lined ramp that descended beneath the building. A video camera overhead was aimed directly at them, and Langdon had the feeling that this camera, unlike those at the Louvre, was authentic.

Sophie rolled down the window and surveyed the electronic podium on the driver's side. An LCD screen provided directions in seven languages. Topping the list was English.

INSERT KEY.

Sophie took the gold laser-pocked key from her pocket and turned her attention back to the podium. Below the screen was a triangular hole.

"Something tells me it will fit," Langdon said.

Sophie aligned the key's triangular shaft with the hole and inserted it, sliding it in until the entire shaft had disappeared. This key apparently required no turning. Instantly, the gate began to swing open. Sophie took her foot off the brake and coasted down to a second gate and podium. Behind her, the first gate closed, trapping them like a ship in a lock.

Langdon disliked the constricted sensation. *Let's hope this second gate works too.*

This second podium bore familiar directions.

INSERT KEY.

When Sophie inserted the key, the second gate immediately opened. Moments later they were winding down the ramp into the belly of the structure.

The private garage was small and dim, with spaces for about a dozen cars. At the far end, Langdon spied the building's main entrance. A red carpet stretched across the cement floor, welcoming visitors to a huge door that appeared to be forged of solid metal.

*Talk about mixed messages*, Langdon thought. *Welcome and keep out.*

Sophie pulled the taxi into a parking space near the entrance and killed the engine. "You'd better leave the gun here."

*With pleasure*, Langdon thought, sliding the pistol under the seat.

Sophie and Langdon got out and walked up the red carpet toward the slab of steel. The door had no handle, but on the wall beside it was another triangular keyhole. No directions were posted this time.

"Keeps out the slow learners," Langdon said.

Sophie laughed, looking nervous. "Here we go." She stuck the key in the hole, and the door swung inward with a low hum. Exchanging glances, Sophie and Langdon entered. The door shut with a thud behind them.

The foyer of the Depository Bank of Zurich employed as imposing a decor as any Langdon had ever seen. Where most banks were content with the usual polished marble and granite, this one had opted for wall-to-wall metal and rivets.

*Who's their decorator?* Langdon wondered. *Allied Steel?*

Sophie looked equally intimidated as her eyes scanned the lobby.

The gray metal was everywhere—the floor, walls, counters, doors, even the lobby chairs appeared to be fashioned of molded iron. Nonetheless, the effect was impressive. The message was clear: You are walking into a vault.

A large man behind the counter glanced up as they entered. He turned off the small television he was watching and greeted them with a pleasant smile. Despite his enormous muscles and visible sidearm, his diction chimed with the polished courtesy of a Swiss bellhop.

"*Bonsoir,*" he said. "How may I help you?"

The dual-language greeting was the newest hospitality trick of the European host. It presumed nothing and opened the door for the guest to reply in whichever language was more comfortable.

Sophie replied with neither. She simply laid the gold key on the counter in front of the man.

The man glanced down and immediately stood straighter. "Of course. Your elevator is at the end of the hall. I will alert someone that you are on your way."

Sophie nodded and took her key back. "Which floor?"

The man gave her an odd look. "Your key instructs the elevator which floor."

She smiled. "Ah, yes."

The guard watched as the two newcomers made their way to the elevators, inserted their key, boarded the lift, and disappeared. As soon as the door had closed, he grabbed the phone. He was not calling to alert anyone of their arrival; there was no need for that. A vault greeter already had been alerted automatically when the client's key was inserted outside in the entry gate.

Instead, the guard was calling the bank's night manager. As the line rang, the guard switched the television back on and stared at it. The news story he had been watching was just ending. It didn't matter. He got another look at the two faces on the television.

The manager answered. "*Oui?*"

"We have a situation down here."

"What's happening?" the manager demanded.

"The French police are tracking two fugitives tonight."

"So?"

"Both of them just walked into our bank."

The manager cursed quietly. "Okay. I'll contact Monsieur Vernet immediately."

The guard then hung up and placed a second call. This one to Interpol.

Langdon was surprised to feel the elevator dropping rather than climbing. He had no idea how many floors they had descended beneath the Depository Bank of Zurich before the door finally opened. He didn't care. He was happy to be out of the elevator.

Displaying impressive alacrity, a host was already standing there to greet them. He was elderly and pleasant, wearing a neatly pressed flannel suit that made him look oddly out of place—an old-world banker in a high-tech world.

"*Bonsoir,*" the man said. "Good evening. Would you be so kind as to follow me, *s'il vous plaît?*" Without waiting for a response, he spun on his heel and strode briskly down a narrow metal corridor.

Langdon walked with Sophie down a series of corridors, past several large rooms filled with blinking mainframe computers.

"*Voici,*" their host said, arriving at a steel door and opening it for them. "Here you are."

Langdon and Sophie stepped into another world. The small room before them looked like a lavish sitting room at a fine hotel. Gone were the metal and rivets, replaced with oriental carpets, dark oak furniture, and cushioned chairs. On the broad desk in the middle of the room, two crystal glasses sat beside an opened bottle of Perrier, its bubbles still fizzing. A pewter pot of coffee steamed beside it.

*Clockwork*, Langdon thought. *Leave it to the Swiss.*

The man gave a perceptive smile. "I sense this is your first visit to us?"

Sophie hesitated and then nodded.

"Understood. Keys are often passed on as inheritance, and our first-time users are invariably uncertain of the protocol." He motioned to the table of drinks. "This room is yours as long as you care to use it."

"You say keys are sometimes inherited?" Sophie asked.

"Indeed. Your key is like a Swiss numbered account, which are often willed through generations. On our gold accounts, the shortest safety-deposit box lease is fifty years. Paid in advance. So we see plenty of family turnover."

Langdon stared. "Did you say fifty *years*?"

"At a minimum," their host replied. "Of course, you can purchase much longer leases, but barring further arrangements, if there is no activity on an account for fifty years, the contents of that safe-deposit box are automatically destroyed. Shall I run through the process of accessing your box?"

Sophie nodded. "Please."

Their host swept an arm across the luxurious salon. "This is your private viewing room. Once I leave the room, you may spend all the time you need in here to review and modify the contents of your safe-deposit box, which arrives . . . over here." He walked them to the far wall where a wide conveyor belt entered the room in a graceful curve, vaguely resembling a baggage claim carousel. "You insert your key in that slot there. . . ." The man pointed to a large electronic podium facing the conveyor belt. The podium had a familiar triangular hole. "Once the computer confirms the markings on your key, you enter your account number, and your safe-deposit box will be retrieved robotically from the vault below for your inspection. When you are finished with your box, you place it back on the conveyor belt, insert your key again, and the process is reversed. Because everything is automated, your privacy is guaranteed, even from the staff of this bank. If you need anything at all, simply press the call button on the table in the center of the room."

Sophie was about to ask a question when a telephone rang. The man looked puzzled and embarrassed. "Excuse me, please." He walked over to the phone, which was sitting on the table beside the coffee and Perrier.

"*Oui?*" he answered.

His brow furrowed as he listened to the caller. "*Oui . . . oui . . . d'accord.*" He hung up, and gave them an uneasy smile. "I'm sorry, I must leave you now. Make yourselves at home." He moved quickly toward the door.

"Excuse me," Sophie called. "Could you clarify something before you go? You mentioned that we enter an *account* number?"

The man paused at the door, looking pale. "But of course. Like most Swiss banks, our safe-deposit boxes are attached to a *number*, not a name. You have a key and a personal account number known only to you. Your key is only half of your identification. Your personal account number is the

other half. Otherwise, if you lost your key, anyone could use it."

Sophie hesitated. "And if my benefactor gave
me no account number?"

The banker's heart pounded. *Then you obviously
have no business here!* He gave them a calm smile.
"I will ask someone to help you. He will be in
shortly."

Leaving, the banker closed the door behind him
and twisted a heavy lock, sealing them inside.

Across town, Collet was standing in the Gare du
Nord train terminal when his phone rang.

It was Fache. "Interpol got a tip," he said. "Forget the train. Langdon and Neveu just walked
into the Paris branch of the Depository Bank of
Zurich. I want your men over there right away."

"Any leads yet on what Saunière was trying to
tell Agent Neveu and Robert Langdon?"

Fache's tone was cold. "If you arrest them,
Lieutenant Collet, then I can ask them
personally."

Collet took the hint. "Twenty-four Rue Haxo.
Right away, Captain." He hung up and radioed
his men.

# CHAPTER 43

**André Vernet**—president of the Paris branch of the Depository Bank of Zurich—lived in a lavish flat above the bank. Despite his plush accommodations, he had always dreamed of owning a riverside apartment on L'Ile Saint-Louis, where he could rub shoulders with the true *cognoscenti*, rather than here, where he simply met the filthy rich.

*When I retire,* Vernet told himself, *I will fill my cellar with rare Bordeaux, adorn my salon with a Fragonard and perhaps a Boucher, and spend my days hunting for antique furniture and rare books in the Quartier Latin.*

Tonight, Vernet had been awake only six and a half minutes. Even so, as he hurried through the bank's underground corridor, he looked as if his personal tailor and hairdresser had polished him to a fine sheen. Impeccably dressed in a silk suit, Vernet sprayed some breath spray in his mouth and tightened his tie as he walked. No stranger to being awoken to attend to his international clients arriving from different time zones, Vernet modeled his sleep habits after the Maasai warriors— the African tribe famous for their ability to rise from the deepest sleep to a state of total battle readiness in a matter of seconds.

*Battle ready,* Vernet thought, fearing the comparison might be uncharacteristically apt tonight. The arrival of a gold key client always required an extra flurry of attention, but the arrival of a gold key client who was *wanted* by the Judicial Police would be an extremely delicate matter. The bank had enough battles with law enforcement over the privacy rights of their clients without proof that some of them were criminals.

*Five minutes,* Vernet told himself. *I need these people out of my bank before the police arrive.*

If he moved quickly, this impending disaster could be deftly sidestepped. Vernet could tell the police that the fugitives in question had indeed walked into his bank as reported, but because they were not clients and had no account number, they were turned away. He wished the damned watchman had not called Interpol. Discretion was apparently not part of the vocabulary of a 15-euro-per-hour watchman.

Stopping at the doorway, he took a deep breath and loosened his muscles. Then, forcing a balmy smile, he unlocked the door and swirled into the room like a warm breeze.

"Good evening," he said, his eyes finding his clients. "I am André Vernet. How can I be of serv—" The rest of the sentence lodged some-

where beneath his Adam's apple. The woman before him was as unexpected a visitor as Vernet
had ever had.


"I'm sorry, do we know each other?" Sophie
asked. She did not recognize the banker, but he
for a moment looked as if he'd seen a ghost.

"No . . . ," the bank president fumbled. "I
don't . . . believe so. Our services are anonymous." He exhaled and forced a calm smile. "My
assistant tells me you have a gold key but no account number? Might I ask how you came by this
key?"

"My grandfather gave it to me," Sophie replied,
watching the man closely. His uneasiness seemed
more evident now.

"Really? Your grandfather gave you the key but
failed to give you the account number?"

"I don't think he had time," Sophie said. "He
was murdered tonight."

Her words sent the man staggering backward.
"Jacques Saunière is dead?" he demanded, his
eyes filling with horror. "But . . . how?!"

Now it was Sophie who reeled, numb with
shock. "You *knew* my grandfather?"

Banker André Vernet looked equally astounded, steadying himself by leaning on an end
table. "Jacques and I were dear friends. When did
this happen?"

"Earlier this evening. Inside the Louvre."

Vernet walked to a deep leather chair and sank into it. "I need to ask you both a very important question." He glanced up at Langdon and then back to Sophie. "Did either of you have anything to do with his death?"

"No!" Sophie declared. "Absolutely not."

Vernet's face was grim, and he paused, pondering. "Your pictures are being circulated by Interpol. This is how I recognized you. You're wanted for a murder."

Sophie slumped. *Fache ran an Interpol broadcast already?* It seemed the captain was more motivated than Sophie had anticipated. She quickly told Vernet who Langdon was and what had happened inside the Louvre tonight.

Vernet looked amazed. "And as your grandfather was dying, he left you a message telling you to find Mr. Langdon?"

"Yes. And this key." Sophie laid the gold key on the coffee table in front of Vernet, placing the Priory seal face down.

Vernet glanced at the key but made no move to touch it. "He left you only this key? Nothing else? No slip of paper?"

Sophie knew she had been in a hurry inside the Louvre, but she was certain she had seen nothing else behind *Madonna of the Rocks*. "No. Just the key."

Vernet gave a helpless sigh. "I'm afraid every

key is electronically paired with a ten-digit account number that functions as a password.
Without that number, your key is worthless."

*Ten digits.* Sophie reluctantly calculated the
cryptographic odds. *Over ten billion possible choices.*
Even if she could bring in DCPJ's most powerful
parallel processing computers, she still would
need weeks to break the code. "Certainly, monsieur, considering the circumstances, you can
help us."

"I'm sorry. I truly can do nothing. Clients select
their own account numbers via a secure terminal,
meaning account numbers are known only to the
client and computer. This is one way we ensure
anonymity. And the safety of our employees."

Sophie understood. Convenience stores did the
same thing. EMPLOYEES DO NOT HAVE KEYS TO
THE SAFE. This bank obviously did not want to
risk someone stealing a key and then holding an
employee hostage for the account number.

Sophie sat down beside Langdon, glanced down
at the key and then up at Vernet. "Do you have
any idea what my grandfather is storing in your
bank?"

"None whatsoever. That is the definition of a
*Geldschrank* bank."

"Monsieur Vernet," she pressed, "our time
tonight is short. I am going to be very direct if I
may." She reached out to the gold key and flipped
it over, watching the man's eyes as she revealed

the Priory of Sion seal. "Does the symbol on this key mean anything to you?"

Vernet glanced down at the fleur-de-lis seal and made no reaction. "No, but many of our clients emboss corporate logos or initials onto their keys."

Sophie sighed, still watching him carefully. "This seal is the symbol of a secret society known as the Priory of Sion."

Vernet again showed no reaction. "I know nothing of this. Your grandfather was a friend, but we spoke mostly of business." The man adjusted his tie, looking nervous now.

"Monsieur Vernet," Sophie pressed, her tone firm. "My grandfather called me tonight and told me he and I were in grave danger. He said he had to give me something. He gave me a key to your bank. Now he is dead. Anything you can tell us would be helpful."

Vernet broke a sweat. "We need to get out of the building. I'm afraid the police will arrive shortly. My watchman felt obliged to call Interpol."

Sophie had feared as much. She took one last shot. "My grandfather said he needed to tell me the truth about my family. Does that mean anything to you?"

"Mademoiselle, your family died in a car accident when you were young. I'm sorry. I know your grandfather loved you very much. He mentioned to me several times how much it pained him that you two had fallen out of touch."

Sophie was uncertain how to respond.

Langdon asked, "Do the contents of this account have anything to do with the Sangreal?"

Vernet gave him an odd look. "I have no idea what that is." Just then, Vernet's cell phone rang, and he snatched it off his belt. *"Oui?"* He listened a moment, his expression one of surprise and growing concern. *"La police? Si rapidement?"* He cursed, gave some quick directions in French, and said he would be up to the lobby in a minute.

Hanging up the phone, he turned back to Sophie. "The police have responded far more quickly than usual. They are arriving as we speak."

Sophie had no intention of leaving empty-handed. "Tell them we came and went already. If they want to search the bank, demand a search warrant. That will take them time."

"Listen," Vernet said, "Jacques was a friend, and my bank does not need this kind of press, so for those two reasons, I have no intention of allowing this arrest to be made on my premises. Give me a minute and I will see what I can do to help you leave the bank undetected. Beyond that, I cannot get involved." He stood up and hurried for the door. "Stay here. I'll make arrangements and be right back."

"But the safe-deposit box," Sophie declared. "We can't just leave."

"There's nothing I can do," Vernet said, hurrying out the door. "I'm sorry."

Sophie stared after him a moment, wondering if maybe the account number was buried in one of the countless letters and packages her grandfather had sent her over the years and which she had left unopened.

Langdon stood suddenly, and Sophie sensed an unexpected glimmer of contentment in his eyes.

"Robert? You're smiling."

"Your grandfather was a genius."

"I'm sorry?"

"Ten digits?"

Sophie had no idea what he was talking about.

"The account number," he said, a familiar lopsided grin now crossing his face. "I'm pretty sure he left it for us after all."

"Where?"

Langdon produced the printout of the crime scene photo and spread it out on the coffee table. Sophie needed only to read the first line to know Langdon was correct.

13-3-2-21-1-1-8-5
O, Draconian devil!
Oh, lame saint!
P.S. Find Robert Langdon

# CHAPTER 44

**"Ten digits,"** Sophie said, her cryptologic senses tingling as she studied the printout.

$$13-3-2-21-1-1-8-5$$

*Grand-père wrote his account number on the Louvre floor!*

When Sophie had first seen the scrambled Fibonacci sequence on the parquet, she had assumed its sole purpose was to encourage DCPJ to call in their cryptographers and get Sophie *involved.* Later, she realized the numbers were also a clue as to how to decipher the other lines—*a sequence out of order . . . a numeric anagram.* Now, utterly amazed, she saw the numbers had a more important meaning still. They were almost certainly the final key to 'opening her grandfather's mysterious safe-deposit box.

"He was the master of double-entendres," Sophie said, turning to Langdon. "He loved anything with multiple layers of meaning. Codes within codes."

Langdon was already moving toward the electronic podium near the conveyor belt. Sophie grabbed the computer printout and followed.

The podium had a keypad similar to that of a bank ATM terminal. The screen displayed the bank's cruciform logo. Beside the keypad was a triangular hole. Sophie wasted no time inserting the shaft of her key into the hole.

The screen refreshed instantly.

```
ACCOUNT NUMBER:

_ _ _ _ _ _ _ _ _ _
```

The cursor blinked. Waiting.

*Ten digits.* Sophie read the numbers off the printout, and Langdon typed them in.

```
ACCOUNT NUMBER:
1332211185
```

When he had typed the last digit, the screen refreshed again. A message in several languages appeared. English was on top.

```
CAUTION:
Before you strike the enter
key, please check the accuracy
of your account number.
For your own security, if the
computer does not recognize
your account number, this
system will automatically
shut down.
```

*"Fonction terminer,"* Sophie said, frowning. "Looks like we only get one try." Standard ATM machines allowed users *three* attempts to type a PIN before confiscating their bank card. This was obviously no ordinary cash machine.

"The number looks right," Langdon confirmed, carefully checking what they had typed and comparing it to the printout. He motioned to the ENTER key. "Fire away."

Sophie extended her index finger toward the keypad, but hesitated, an odd thought now hitting her.

"Go ahead," Langdon urged. "Vernet will be back soon."

"No." She pulled her hand away. "This isn't the right account number."

"Of course it is! Ten digits. What else would it be?"

"It's too random."

*Too random?* Langdon could not have disagreed more. Every bank advised its customers to choose PINs at random so nobody could guess them. Certainly clients *here* would be advised to choose their account numbers at random.

Sophie deleted everything she had just typed in and looked up at Langdon, her gaze self-assured. "It's far too coincidental that this supposedly *random* account number could be rearranged to form the Fibonacci sequence."

Langdon realized she had a point. Earlier,

Sophie had rearranged this account number into the Fibonacci sequence. What were the odds of being able to do that?

Sophie was at the keypad again, entering a different number, as if from memory. "Moreover, with my grandfather's love of symbolism and codes, it seems to follow that he would have chosen an account number that had meaning to him, something he could easily remember." She finished typing the entry and gave a sly smile. "Something that appeared random . . . but was *not*."

Langdon looked at the screen.

```
ACCOUNT NUMBER:
  1123581321
```

It took him an instant, but when Langdon spotted it, he knew she was right.

*The Fibonacci sequence.*

*1-1-2-3-5-8-13-21*

When the Fibonacci sequence was melded into a single ten-digit number, it became virtually unrecognizable. *Easy to remember, and yet seemingly random.* A brilliant ten-digit code that Saunière would never forget. Furthermore, it perfectly explained why the scrambled numbers on the Louvre floor could be rearranged to form the famous progression.

Sophie reached down and pressed the ENTER key.

Nothing happened.

At least nothing they could detect.


At that moment, beneath them, in the bank's cavernous subterranean vault, a robotic claw sprang to life. Sliding on a double-axis transport system attached to the ceiling, the claw headed off in search of the proper coordinates. On the cement floor below, hundreds of identical plastic crates lay aligned on an enormous grid . . . like rows of small coffins in an underground crypt.

Whirring to a stop over the correct spot on the floor, the claw dropped down, an electric eye confirming the bar code on the box. Then, with computer precision, the claw grasped the heavy handle and hoisted the crate vertically. New gears engaged, and the claw transported the box to the far side of the vault, coming to a stop over a stationary conveyor belt.

Gently now, the retrieval arm set down the crate and retracted.

Once the arm was clear, the conveyor belt whirred to life. . . .


Upstairs, Sophie and Langdon exhaled in relief to see the conveyor belt move. Standing beside the belt, they felt like weary travelers at baggage claim awaiting a mysterious piece of luggage whose contents were unknown.

The conveyor belt entered the room on their right through a narrow slit beneath a retractable door. The metal door slid up, and a huge plastic box appeared, emerging from the depths on the inclined conveyor belt. The box was black, heavy molded plastic, and far larger than she imagined. It looked like an air-freight pet transport crate without any airholes.

The box coasted to a stop directly in front of them.

Langdon and Sophie stood there, silent, staring at the mysterious container.

Like everything else about this bank, this crate was industrial—metal clasps, a bar code sticker on top, and molded heavy-duty handle. Sophie thought it looked like a giant toolbox.

Wasting no time, Sophie unhooked the two buckles facing her. Then she glanced over at Langdon. Together, they raised the heavy lid and let it fall back.

Stepping forward, they peered down into the crate.

At first glance, Sophie thought the crate was empty. Then she saw something. Sitting at the bottom of the crate. A lone item.

The polished wooden box was about the size of a shoebox and had ornate hinges. The wood was a lustrous deep purple with a strong grain. *Rosewood,* Sophie realized. Her grandfather's favorite. The lid bore a beautiful inlaid design of a rose. She and Langdon exchanged puzzled looks. Sophie leaned in and grabbed the box, lifting it out.

*My God, it's heavy!*

She carried it gingerly to a large receiving table and set it down. Langdon stood beside her, both of them staring at the small treasure chest her grandfather apparently had sent them to retrieve.

Langdon stared in wonderment at the lid's hand-carved inlay—a five-petal rose. He had seen this type of rose many times. "The five-petal rose," he whispered, "is a Priory symbol for the Holy Grail."

Sophie turned and looked at him. Langdon could see what she was thinking, and he was thinking it too. The dimensions of the box, the apparent weight of its contents, and a Priory symbol for the Grail all seemed to imply one unfathomable conclusion. *The Cup of Christ is in this wooden box.* Langdon again told himself it was impossible.

"It's a perfect size," Sophie whispered, "to hold . . . a chalice."

*It can't be a chalice.*

Sophie pulled the box toward her across the table, preparing to open it. As she moved it, though, something unexpected happened. The box let out an odd gurgling sound.

Langdon did a double take. *There's liquid inside?*

Sophie looked equally confused. "Did you just hear . . . ?"

Langdon nodded, lost. "Liquid."

Reaching forward, Sophie slowly unhooked the clasp and raised the lid.

The object inside was unlike anything Langdon had ever seen. One thing was immediately clear to both of them, however. This was definitely *not* the Cup of Christ.

# CHAPTER 45

**"The police** are blocking the street," André Vernet said, walking into the waiting room. "Getting you out will be difficult." As he closed the door behind him, Vernet saw the heavy-duty plastic case on the conveyor belt and halted in his tracks. *My God! They accessed Saunière's account?*

Sophie and Langdon were at the table, huddling over what looked to be a large wooden jewelry box. Sophie immediately closed the lid and looked up. "We had the account number after all," she said.

Vernet was speechless. This changed everything. He respectfully diverted his eyes from the box and tried to figure out his next move. *I have to get them out of the bank!* But with the police already having set up a roadblock, Vernet could imagine only one way to do that. "Mademoiselle Neveu, if I can get you safely out of the bank, will you be taking the item with you or returning it to the vault before you leave?"

Sophie glanced at Langdon and then back to Vernet. "We need to take it."

Vernet nodded. "Very well. Then whatever the item is, I suggest you wrap it in your jacket as we move through the hallways. I would prefer nobody else see it."

As Langdon shed his jacket, Vernet hurried over to the conveyor belt, closed the now empty crate, and typed a series of simple commands. The conveyor belt began moving again, carrying the plastic container back down to the vault. Pulling the gold key from the podium, he handed it to Sophie.

"This way please. Hurry."

When they reached the rear loading dock, Vernet could see the flash of police lights filtering through the underground garage. He frowned. They were probably blocking the ramp. *Am I really going to try to pull this off?* He was sweating now.

Vernet motioned to one of the bank's small armored trucks. *Transport sûr* was another service offered by the Depository Bank of Zurich. "Get in the cargo hold," he said, heaving open the massive rear door and motioning to the glistening steel compartment. "I'll be right back."

As Sophie and Langdon climbed in, Vernet hurried across the loading dock to the dock overseer's office, let himself in, collected the keys for the truck, and found a driver's uniform jacket and cap. Shedding his own suit coat and tie, he began to put on the driver's jacket. Reconsidering, he donned a shoulder holster beneath the uniform. On his way out, he grabbed a driver's pistol from the rack, put in a clip, and stuffed it in the holster, buttoning his uniform over it. Returning to the truck, Vernet pulled the driver's cap down low and peered in at Sophie and Langdon, who were standing inside the empty steel box.

"You'll want this on," Vernet said, reaching inside and flicking a wall switch to illuminate the lone courtesy bulb on the hold's ceiling. "And you'd better sit down. Not a sound on our way out the gate."

Sophie and Langdon sat down on the metal floor. Langdon cradled the treasure wadded in his tweed jacket. Swinging the heavy doors closed, Vernet locked them inside. Then he got in behind the wheel and revved the engine.

As the armored truck lumbered toward the top of the ramp, Vernet could feel the sweat already collecting beneath his driver's cap. He could see there were far more police lights in front than he had imagined. As the truck powered up the ramp, the interior gate swung inward to let him pass. Vernet advanced and waited while the gate behind him closed before pulling forward and tripping the next sensor. The second gate opened, and the exit beckoned.

*Except for the police car blocking the top of the ramp.*
Vernet dabbed his brow and pulled forward.

A lanky officer stepped out and waved him to a stop a few meters from the roadblock. Four patrol cars were parked out front.

Vernet stopped. Pulling his driver's cap down farther, he effected as rough a facade as his cultured upbringing would allow. Not budging from behind the wheel, he opened the door and gazed down at the agent, whose face was stern and sallow.

"*Qu'est-ce qui se passe?*" Vernet asked, his tone rough.

"*Je suis Jérome Collet,*" the agent said. "*Lieutenant Police Judiciaire.*" He motioned to the truck's cargo hold. "*Qu'est-ce qu'il y a là dedans?*"

"Hell if I know," Vernet replied in crude French. "I'm only a driver."

Collet looked unimpressed. "We're looking for two criminals."

Vernet laughed. "Then you came to the right spot. Some of these bastards I drive for have so much money they must be criminals."

The agent held up a passport picture of Robert Langdon. "Was this man in your bank tonight?"

Vernet shrugged. "No clue. I'm a dock rat. They don't let us anywhere near the clients. You need to go in and ask the front desk."

"Your bank is demanding a search warrant before we can enter."

Vernet put on a disgusted look. "Administrators. Don't get me started."

"Open your truck, please." Collet motioned toward the cargo hold.

Vernet stared at the agent and forced an obnoxious laugh. "Open the truck? You think I have keys? You think they trust us? You should see the crap wages I get paid."

The agent's head tilted to one side, his skepticism evident. "You're telling me you don't have keys to your own truck?"

Vernet shook his head. "Not the cargo area. Ignition only. These trucks get sealed by overseers on the loading dock. Then the truck sits in dock while someone drives the cargo keys to the drop-off. Once we get the call that the cargo keys are with the recipient, then I get the okay to drive. Not a second before. I never know what the hell I'm lugging."

"When was *this* truck sealed?"

"Must have been hours ago. I'm driving all the way up to St. Thurial tonight. Cargo keys are already up there."

The agent made no response, his eyes probing as if trying to read Vernet's mind.

A drop of sweat was preparing to slide down Vernet's nose. "You mind?" he said, wiping his nose with his sleeve and motioning to the police car blocking his way. "I'm on a tight schedule."

"Do all the drivers wear Rolexes?" the agent asked, pointing to Vernet's wrist.

Vernet glanced down and saw the glistening band of his absurdly expensive watch peeking out from beneath the sleeve of his jacket. *Merde.* "This piece of shit? Bought it for twenty euro from a Taiwanese street vendor in St. Germain des Prés. I'll sell it to you for forty."

The agent paused and finally stepped aside. "No thanks. Have a safe trip."

Vernet did not breathe again until the truck was a good fifty meters down the street. And now he had another problem. His cargo. *Where do I take them?*

# CHAPTER 46

**Silas lay** prone on the canvas mat in his room, allowing the lash wounds on his back to clot in the air. Tonight's second session with the Discipline had left him dizzy and weak. He had yet to remove the *cilice* belt, and he could feel the blood trickling down his inner thigh. Still, he could not justify removing the strap.

*I have failed the Church.*

*Far worse, I have failed the bishop.*

Tonight was supposed to be Bishop Aringarosa's salvation. Five months ago, the bishop had returned from a meeting at the Vatican Observatory, where he had learned something that left him deeply changed. Depressed for weeks, Aringarosa had finally shared the news with Silas.

"But this is impossible!" Silas had cried out. "I cannot accept it!"

"It is true," Aringarosa said. "Unthinkable, but true. In only six months."

The bishop's words terrified Silas. He prayed for deliverance, and even in those dark days, his trust in God and The Way never wavered. It was only a month later that the clouds parted miraculously and the light of possibility shone through.

*Divine intervention,* Aringarosa had called it.

The bishop had seemed hopeful for the first time. "Silas," he whispered, "God has bestowed upon us an opportunity to protect The Way. Our battle, like all battles, will take sacrifice. Will you be a soldier of God?"

Silas fell to his knees before Bishop Aringarosa—the man who had given him a new life—and he said, "I am a lamb of God. Shepherd me as your heart commands."

When Aringarosa described the opportunity that had presented itself, Silas knew it could only be the hand of God at work. *Miraculous fate!* Aringarosa put Silas in contact with the man who had proposed the plan—a man who called himself the Teacher. Although the Teacher and Silas never met face-to-face, each time they spoke by phone, Silas was awed, both by the profundity of the Teacher's faith and by the scope of his power. The Teacher seemed to be a man who knew all, a man with eyes and ears in all places. How the Teacher gathered his information, Silas did not know, but Aringarosa had placed enormous trust in the Teacher, and he had told Silas to do the same. "Do as the Teacher commands you," the bishop told Silas. "And we will be victorious."

*Victorious.* Silas now gazed at the bare floor and feared victory had eluded them. The Teacher had been tricked. The keystone was a devious dead end. And with the deception, all hope had vanished.

Silas wished he could call Bishop Aringarosa and warn him, but the Teacher had removed all their lines of direct communication tonight. *For our safety.*

Finally, overcoming enormous trepidation, Silas crawled to his feet and found his robe, which lay on the floor. He dug his cell phone from the pocket. Hanging his head in shame, he dialed.

"Teacher," he whispered, "all is lost." Silas truthfully told the man how he had been tricked.

"You lose your faith too quickly," the Teacher replied. "I have just received news. Most unexpected and welcome. The secret lives. Jacques Saunière transferred information before he died. I will call you soon. Our work tonight is not yet done."

# CHAPTER 47

**Riding inside** the dimly lit cargo hold of the armored truck was like being transported inside a cell for solitary confinement. Langdon fought the all too familiar anxiety that haunted him in confined spaces. *Vernet said he would take us a safe distance out of the city. Where? How far?*

Langdon's legs had gotten stiff from sitting cross-legged on the metal floor, and he shifted his position, wincing to feel the blood pouring back into his lower body. In his arms, he still clutched the bizarre treasure they had extricated from the bank.

"I think we're on the highway now," Sophie whispered.

Langdon sensed the same thing. The truck, after an unnerving pause atop the bank ramp, had moved on, snaking left and right for a minute or two, and was now accelerating to what felt like top speed. Beneath them, the bulletproof tires hummed on smooth pavement. Forcing his attention to the rosewood box in his arms, Langdon laid the precious bundle on the floor, unwrapped his jacket, and extracted the box, pulling it toward him. Sophie shifted her position so they were sitting side by side. Langdon suddenly felt like they were two kids huddled over a Christmas present.

In contrast to the warm colors of the rosewood box, the inlaid rose had been crafted of a pale wood, probably ash, which shone clearly in the dim light. *The Rose.* Entire armies and religions had been built on this symbol, as had secret societies. *The Rosicrucians. The Knights of the Rosy Cross.*

"Go ahead," Sophie said. "Open it."

Langdon took a deep breath. Reaching for the lid, he stole one more admiring glance at the intricate woodwork and then, unhooking the clasp, he opened the lid, revealing the object within.

Langdon had harbored several fantasies about what they might find inside this box, but clearly he had been wrong on every account. Nestled snugly inside the box's heavily padded interior of crimson silk lay an object Langdon could not even begin to comprehend.

Crafted of polished white marble, it was a stone cylinder approximately the dimensions of a tennis ball can. More complicated than a simple column of stone, however, the cylinder appeared to have been assembled in many pieces. Six doughnut-sized disks of marble had been stacked and affixed to one another within a delicate brass framework. It looked like some kind of tubular, multiwheeled kaleidoscope. Each end of the cylinder was affixed with an end cap, also marble, making it impossible to see inside. Having heard liquid within, Langdon assumed the cylinder was hollow.

As mystifying as the construction of the cylinder was, however, it was the engravings around the tube's circumference that drew Langdon's primary focus. Each of the six disks had been carefully carved with the same unlikely series of letters—the entire alphabet. The lettered cylinder reminded Langdon of one of his childhood toys—a rod threaded with lettered tumblers that could be rotated to spell different words.

"Amazing, isn't it?" Sophie whispered.

Langdon glanced up. "I don't know. What the hell is it?"

Now there was a glint in Sophie's eye. "My grandfather used to craft these as a hobby. They were invented by Leonardo da Vinci."

Even in the diffuse light, Sophie could see Langdon's surprise.

"Da Vinci?" he muttered, looking again at the canister.

"Yes. It's called a *cryptex*. According to my grandfather, the blueprints come from one of Da Vinci's secret diaries."

"What is it for?"

Considering tonight's events, Sophie knew the answer might have some interesting implications. "It's a vault," she said. "For storing secret information."

Langdon's eyes widened further.

Sophie explained that creating models of Da Vinci's inventions was one of her grandfather's best-loved hobbies. A talented craftsman who spent hours in his wood and metal shop, Jacques Saunière enjoyed imitating master craftsmen—Fabergé, assorted cloisonné artisans, and the less artistic, but far more practical, Leonardo da Vinci.

Even a cursory glance through Da Vinci's journals revealed why the luminary was as notorious for his lack of follow-through as he was famous for his brilliance. Da Vinci had drawn up blueprints for hundreds of inventions he had never built. One of Jacques Saunière's favorite pastimes was bringing Da Vinci's more obscure brainstorms to life—timepieces, water pumps, cryptexes, and even a fully articulated model of a medieval French knight, which now stood proudly on the desk in his office. Designed by Da Vinci in 1495 as an outgrowth of his earliest anatomy and kinesiology studies, the internal mechanism of the robot knight possessed accurate joints and tendons, and was designed to sit up, wave its arms, and move its head via a flexible neck while opening and closing an anatomically correct jaw. This armor-clad knight, Sophie had always believed, was the most beautiful object her grandfather had ever built . . . that was, until she had seen the cryptex in this rosewood box.

"He made me one of these when I was little,"

Sophie said. "But I've never seen one so ornate and large."

Langdon's eyes had never left the box. "I've never heard of a cryptex."

Sophie was not surprised. Most of Leonardo's unbuilt inventions had never been studied or even named. The term *cryptex* possibly had been her grandfather's creation, an apt title for this device that used the science of *cryptology* to protect information written on the contained scroll or *codex*.

Da Vinci had been a cryptology pioneer, Sophie knew, although he was seldom given credit. Sophie's university instructors, while presenting computer encryption methods for securing data, praised modern cryptologists like Zimmerman and Schneier but failed to mention that it was Leonardo who had invented one of the first rudimentary forms of public key encryption centuries ago. Sophie's grandfather, of course, had been the one to tell her all about that.

As their armored truck roared down the highway, Sophie explained to Langdon that the cryptex had been Da Vinci's solution to the dilemma of sending secure messages over long distances. In an era without telephones or e-mail, anyone wanting to convey private information to someone far away had no option but to write it down and then trust a messenger to carry the letter.

Unfortunately, if a messenger suspected the letter might contain valuable information, he could make far more money selling the information to adversaries than he could delivering the letter properly.

Many great minds in history had invented cryptologic solutions to the challenge of data protection: Julius Caesar devised a code-writing scheme called the Caesar Box; Mary, Queen of Scots created a transposition cipher and sent secret communiqués from prison; and the brilliant Arab scientist Abu Yusuf Ismail al-Kindi protected his secrets with an ingeniously conceived polyalphabetic substitution cipher.

Da Vinci, however, eschewed mathematics and cryptology for a *mechanical* solution. The cryptex. A portable container that could safeguard letters, maps, diagrams, anything at all. Once information was sealed inside the cryptex, only the individual with the proper password could access it.

"We require a password," Sophie said, pointing out the lettered dials. "A cryptex works much like a bicycle's combination lock. If you align the dials in the proper position, the lock slides open. This cryptex has five lettered dials. When you rotate them to their proper sequence, the tumblers inside align, and the entire cylinder slides apart."

"And inside?"

"Once the cylinder slides apart, you have access to a hollow central compartment, which can hold a scroll of paper on which is the information you want to keep private."

Langdon looked incredulous. "And you say your grandfather built these for you when you were younger?"

"Some smaller ones, yes. A couple times for my birthday, he gave me a cryptex and told me a riddle. The answer to the riddle was the password to the cryptex, and once I figured it out, I could open it up and find my birthday card."

"A lot of work for a card."

"No, the cards always contained another riddle or clue. My grandfather loved creating elaborate treasure hunts around our house, a string of clues that eventually led to my real gift. Each treasure hunt was a test of character and merit, to ensure I earned my rewards. And the tests were never simple."

Langdon eyed the device again, still looking skeptical. "But why not just pry it apart? Or smash it? The metal looks delicate, and marble is a soft rock."

Sophie smiled. "Because Da Vinci is too smart for that. He designed the cryptex so that if you try to force it open in any way, the information self-destructs. Watch." Sophie reached into the box and carefully lifted out the cylinder. "Any information to be inserted is first written on a papyrus scroll."

"Not vellum?"

Sophie shook her head. "Papyrus. I know sheep's vellum was more durable and more common in those days, but it had to be papyrus. The thinner the better."

"Okay."

"Before the papyrus was inserted into the cryptex's compartment, it was rolled around a delicate glass vial." She tipped the cryptex, and the liquid inside gurgled. "A vial of liquid."

"Liquid *what?*"

Sophie smiled. "Vinegar."

Langdon hesitated a moment and then began nodding. "Brilliant."

*Vinegar and papyrus,* Sophie thought. If someone attempted to force open the cryptex, the glass vial would break, and the vinegar would quickly dissolve the papyrus. By the time anyone extracted the secret message, it would be a glob of meaningless pulp.

"As you can see," Sophie told him, "the only way to access the information inside is to know the proper five-letter password. And with five dials, each with twenty-six letters, that's twenty-six to the fifth power." She quickly estimated the permutations. "Approximately twelve million possibilities."

"If you say so," Langdon said, looking like he had approximately twelve million questions running through his head. "What information do you think is inside?"

"Whatever it is, my grandfather obviously wanted very badly to keep it secret." She paused, closing the box lid and eyeing the five-petal Rose inlaid on it. Something was bothering her. "Did you say earlier that the Rose is a symbol for the Grail?"

"Exactly. In Priory symbolism, the Rose and the Grail are synonymous."

Sophie furrowed her brow. "That's strange, because my grandfather always told me the Rose meant *secrecy*. He used to hang a rose on his office door at home when he was having a confidential phone call and didn't want me to disturb him. He encouraged me to do the same." *Sweetie,* her grandfather said, *rather than lock each other out, we can each hang a rose—la fleur des secrets—on our door when we need privacy. This way we learn to respect and trust each other. Hanging a rose is an ancient Roman custom.*

"*Sub rosa,*" Langdon said. "The Romans hung a rose over meetings to indicate the meeting was confidential. Attendees understood that whatever was said *under the rose*—or *sub rosa*—had to remain a secret."

Langdon quickly explained that the Rose's overtone of secrecy was not the only reason the Priory used it as a symbol for the Grail. *Rosa rugosa,* one of the oldest species of rose, had five petals and pentagonal symmetry, just like the guiding star of Venus, giving the Rose strong iconographic ties to *womanhood*. In addition, the Rose had close ties to the concept of "true direction" and navigating one's way. The Compass Rose helped travelers navigate, as did Rose Lines, the longitudinal lines on maps. For this reason, the Rose was a symbol that spoke of the Grail on many levels—secrecy, womanhood, and guidance—the feminine chalice and guiding star that led to secret truth.

As Langdon finished his explanation, his expression seemed to tighten suddenly.

"Robert? Are you okay?"

His eyes were riveted to the rosewood box. *"Sub . . . rosa,"* he choked, a fearful bewilderment sweeping across his face. "It can't be."

"What?"

Langdon slowly raised his eyes. "Under the sign of the Rose," he whispered. "This cryptex . . . I think I know what it is."

# CHAPTER 48

**Langdon could** scarcely believe his own supposition, and yet, considering *who* had given this stone cylinder to them, *how* he had given it to them, and now, the inlaid Rose on the container, Langdon could formulate only one conclusion.

*I am holding the Priory keystone.*

The legend was specific.

*The keystone is an encoded stone that lies beneath the sign of the Rose.*

"Robert?" Sophie was watching him. "What's going on?"

Langdon needed a moment to gather his thoughts. "Did your grandfather ever speak to you of something called *la clef de voûte?*"

"The key to the vault?" Sophie translated.

"No, that's the literal translation. *Clef de voûte* is a common architectural term. *Voûte* refers not to a bank vault, but to a *vault* in an archway. Like a *vaulted* ceiling."

"But vaulted ceilings don't have keys."

"Actually they do. Every stone archway requires a central, wedge-shaped stone at the top which locks the pieces together and carries all the weight. This stone is, in an architectural sense, the key to the vault. In English we call it a *keystone.*"

Langdon watched her eyes for any spark of recognition.

Sophie shrugged, glancing down at the cryptex. "But this obviously is not a keystone."

Langdon didn't know where to begin. Keystones as a masonry technique for building stone archways had been one of the best-kept secrets of the early Masonic brotherhood. *The Royal Arch Degree. Architecture. Keystones.* It was all interconnected. The secret knowledge of how to use a wedged keystone to build a vaulted archway was part of the wisdom that had made the Masons such wealthy craftsmen, and it was a secret they guarded carefully. Keystones had always had a tradition of secrecy. And yet, the stone cylinder in the rosewood box was obviously something quite different. The Priory keystone— if this was indeed what they were holding—was not at all what Langdon had imagined.

"The Priory keystone is not my specialty," Langdon admitted. "My interest in the Holy Grail is primarily symbologic, so I tend to ignore the plethora of lore regarding how to actually find it."

Sophie's eyebrows arched. "*Find* the Holy Grail?"

Langdon gave an uneasy nod, speaking his next words carefully. "Sophie, according to Priory lore, the keystone is an encoded map . . . a map that reveals the hiding place of the Holy Grail."

Sophie's face went blank. "And you think this is it?"

Langdon didn't know what to say. Even to him it sounded unbelievable, and yet the keystone was the only logical conclusion he could muster. *An encrypted stone, hidden beneath the sign of the Rose.*

The idea that the cryptex had been designed by Leonardo da Vinci—former Grand Master of the Priory of Sion—shone as another tantalizing indicator that this was indeed the Priory keystone. *A former Grand Master's blueprint . . . brought to life centuries later by another Priory member.* The bond was too palpable to dismiss.

For the last decade, historians had been searching for the keystone in French churches. Grail seekers, familiar with the Priory's history of cryptic double-talk, had concluded *la clef de voûte* was a literal keystone—an architectural wedge—an engraved, encrypted stone, inserted into a vaulted archway in a church. *Beneath the sign of the Rose.* In architecture, there was no shortage of roses. *Rose windows. Rosette reliefs.* And, of course, an abundance of *cinquefoils*—the five-petaled decorative flowers often found at the top of archways, directly over the keystone. The hiding place seemed diabolically simple. The map to the Holy Grail was incorporated high in an archway of some forgotten church, mocking the blind churchgoers who wandered beneath it.

"This cryptex *can't* be the keystone," Sophie ar-

gued. "It's not old enough. I'm certain my grandfather made this. It can't be part of any ancient
Grail legend."

"Actually," Langdon replied, feeling a tingle of
excitement ripple through him, "the keystone is
believed to have been created by the Priory
sometime in the past couple of decades."

Sophie's eyes flashed disbelief. "But if this cryptex reveals the hiding place of the Holy Grail,
why would my grandfather give it to *me?* I have
no idea how to open it or what to do with it. I
don't even know what the Holy Grail *is!*"

Langdon realized to his surprise that she was
right. He had not yet had a chance to explain to
Sophie the true nature of the Holy Grail. That
story would have to wait. At the moment, they
were focused on the keystone.

*If that is indeed what this is. . . .*

Against the hum of the bulletproof wheels beneath them, Langdon quickly explained to
Sophie everything he had heard about the keystone. Allegedly, for centuries, the Priory's biggest
secret—the location of the Holy Grail—was
never written down. For security's sake, it was
verbally transferred to each new rising *sénéchal* at
a clandestine ceremony. However, at some point
during the last century, whisperings began to surface that the Priory policy had changed. Perhaps
it was on account of new electronic eavesdropping capabilities, but the Priory vowed never

again even to *speak* the location of the sacred hiding place.

"But then how could they pass on the secret?" Sophie asked.

"That's where the keystone comes in," Langdon explained. "When one of the top four members died, the remaining three would choose from the lower echelons the next candidate to ascend as *sénéchal*. Rather than *telling* the new *sénéchal* where the Grail was hidden, they gave him a test through which he could prove he was worthy."

Sophie looked unsettled by this, and Langdon suddenly recalled her mentioning how her grandfather used to make treasure hunts for her—*preuves de mérite*. Admittedly, the keystone was a similar concept. Then again, tests like this were extremely common in secret societies. The best known was the Masons', wherein members ascended to higher degrees by proving they could keep a secret and by performing rituals and various tests of merit over many years. The tasks became progressively harder until they culminated in a successful candidate's induction as thirty-second-degree Mason.

"So the keystone is a *preuve de mérite*," Sophie said. "If a rising Priory *sénéchal* can open it, he proves himself worthy of the information it holds."

Langdon nodded. "I forgot you'd had experience with this sort of thing."

"Not only with my grandfather. In cryptology, that's called a 'self-authorizing language.' That is, if you're smart enough to read it, you're permitted to know what is being said."

Langdon hesitated a moment. "Sophie, you realize that if this is indeed the keystone, your grandfather's access to it implies he was exceptionally powerful within the Priory of Sion. He would have to have been one of the highest four members."

Sophie sighed. "He was powerful in a secret society. I'm certain of it. I can only assume it was the Priory."

Langdon did a double take. "You *knew* he was in a secret society?"

"I saw some things I wasn't supposed to see ten years ago. We haven't spoken since." She paused. "My grandfather was not only a ranking top member of the group . . . I believe he was *the* top member."

Langdon could not believe what she had just said. "Grand Master? But . . . there's no way you could know that!"

"I'd rather not talk about it." Sophie looked away, her expression as determined as it was pained.

Langdon sat in stunned silence. *Jacques Saunière? Grand Master?* Despite the astonishing repercussions if it were true, Langdon had the eerie sensation it almost made perfect sense. After all, previous Priory Grand Masters had *also* been distinguished public figures with artistic souls. Proof of that fact had been uncovered years ago in Paris's Bibliothèque Nationale in papers that became known as *Les Dossiers Secrets*.

Every Priory historian and Grail buff had read the *Dossiers*. Cataloged under Number 4° lm¹ 249, the *Dossiers Secrets* had been authenticated by many specialists and incontrovertibly confirmed what historians had suspected for a long time: Priory Grand Masters included Leonardo da Vinci, Botticelli, Sir Isaac Newton, Victor Hugo, and, more recently, Jean Cocteau, the famous Parisian artist.

*Why not Jacques Saunière?*

Langdon's incredulity intensified with the realization that he had been slated to *meet* Saunière tonight. *The Priory Grand Master called a meeting with me. Why? To make artistic small talk?* It suddenly seemed unlikely. After all, if Langdon's instincts were correct, the Grand Master of the Priory of Sion had just transferred the brotherhood's legendary keystone to his granddaughter and simultaneously commanded her to find Robert Langdon.

*Inconceivable!*

Langdon's imagination could conjure no set of circumstances that would explain Saunière's behavior. Even if Saunière feared his own death, there were three *sénéchaux* who also possessed the secret and therefore guaranteed the Priory's security. Why would Saunière take such an enormous risk giving his granddaughter the keystone, especially when the two of them didn't get along? And why involve Langdon . . . a total stranger?

*A piece of this puzzle is missing,* Langdon thought.

The answers were apparently going to have to wait. The sound of the slowing engine caused them both to look up. Gravel crunched beneath the tires. *Why is he pulling over already?* Langdon wondered. Vernet had told them he would take them well outside the city to safety. The truck decelerated to a crawl and made its way over unexpectedly rough terrain. Sophie shot Langdon an uneasy look, hastily closing the cryptex box and latching it. Langdon slipped his jacket back on.

When the truck came to a stop, the engine remained idling as the locks on the rear doors began to turn. When the doors swung open, Langdon was surprised to see they were parked in a wooded area, well off the road. Vernet stepped into view, a strained look in his eye. In his hand, he held a pistol.

"I'm sorry about this," he said. "I really have no choice."

# CHAPTER 49

**André Vernet** looked awkward with a pistol, but his eyes shone with a determination that Langdon sensed would be unwise to test.

"I'm afraid I must insist," Vernet said, training the weapon on the two of them in the back of the idling truck. "Set the box down."

Sophie clutched the box to her chest. "You said you and my grandfather were friends."

"I have a duty to protect your grandfather's assets," Vernet replied. "And that is exactly what I am doing. Now set the box on the floor."

"My grandfather entrusted this to me!" Sophie declared.

"Do it," Vernet commanded, raising the gun.

Sophie set the box at her feet.

Langdon watched the gun barrel swing now in his direction.

"Mr. Langdon," Vernet said, "you will bring the box over to me. And be aware that I'm asking you because *you* I would not hesitate to shoot."

Langdon stared at the banker in disbelief. "Why are you doing this?"

"Why do you imagine?" Vernet snapped, his

accented English terse now. "To protect my client's assets."

"*We* are your clients now," Sophie said.

Vernet's visage turned ice-cold, an eerie transformation. "Mademoiselle Neveu, I don't know *how* you got that key and account number tonight, but it seems obvious that foul play was involved. Had I known the extent of your crimes, I would never have helped you leave the bank."

"I told you," Sophie said, "we had nothing to do with my grandfather's death!"

Vernet looked at Langdon. "And yet the radio claims you are wanted not only for the murder of Jacques Saunière but for those of three *other* men as well?"

"What!" Langdon was thunderstruck. *Three more murders?* The coincidental number hit him harder than the fact that he was the prime suspect. It seemed too unlikely to be a coincidence. *The three sénéchaux?* Langdon's eyes dropped to the rosewood box. *If the sénéchaux were murdered, Saunière had no options. He had to transfer the keystone to someone.*

"The police can sort that out when I turn you in," Vernet said. "I have gotten my bank involved too far already."

Sophie glared at Vernet. "You obviously have no intention of turning us in. You would have driven us back to the bank. And instead you bring us out here and hold us at gunpoint?"

"Your grandfather hired me for one reason—to keep his possessions both safe and private. Whatever this box contains, I have no intention of letting it become a piece of cataloged evidence in a police investigation. Mr. Langdon, bring me the box."

Sophie shook her head. "Don't do it."

A gunshot roared, and a bullet tore into the wall above him. The reverberation shook the back of the truck as a spent shell clinked onto the cargo floor.

*Shit!* Langdon froze.

Vernet spoke more confidently now. "Mr. Langdon, pick up the box."

Langdon lifted the box.

"Now bring it over to me." Vernet was taking dead aim, standing on the ground behind the rear bumper, his gun outstretched into the cargo hold now.

Box in hand, Langdon moved across the hold toward the open door.

*I've got to do something!* Langdon thought. *I'm about to hand over the Priory keystone!* As Langdon moved toward the doorway, his position of higher ground became more pronounced, and he began wondering if he could somehow use it to his advantage. Vernet's gun, though raised, was at Langdon's knee level. *A well-placed kick perhaps?* Unfortunately, as Langdon neared, Vernet seemed to sense the dangerous dynamic developing, and he took several steps back, repositioning himself six feet away. Well out of reach.

Vernet commanded, "Place the box beside the door."

Seeing no options, Langdon knelt down and set the rosewood box at the edge of the cargo hold, directly in front of the open doors.

"Now stand up."

Langdon began to stand up but paused, spying the small, spent pistol shell on the floor beside the truck's precision-crafted doorsill.

"Stand up, and step away from the box."

Langdon paused a moment longer, eyeing the metal threshold. Then he stood. As he did, he discreetly brushed the shell over the edge onto the narrow ledge that was the door's lower sill. Fully upright now, Langdon stepped backward.

"Return to the back wall and turn around."

Langdon obeyed.

Vernet could feel his own heart pounding. Aiming the gun with his right hand, he reached now with his left for the wooden box. He discovered that it was far too heavy. *I need two hands.* Turning his eyes back to his captives, he calculated the risk. Both were a good fifteen feet away, at the far end of the cargo hold, facing away from him. Vernet made up his mind. Quickly, he laid down the gun on the bumper, lifted the box with two hands, and set it on the ground, immediately grabbing the gun again and aiming it back into the hold. Neither of his prisoners had moved.

*Perfect.* Now all that remained was to close and lock the door. Leaving the box on the ground for the moment, he grabbed the metal door and began to heave it closed. As the door swung past him, Vernet reached up to grab the single bolt that needed to be slid into place. The door closed with a thud, and Vernet quickly grabbed the bolt, pulling it to the left. The bolt slid a few inches and crunched to an unexpected halt, not lining up with its sleeve. *What's going on?* Vernet pulled again, but the bolt wouldn't lock. The mechanism was not properly aligned. *The door isn't fully closed!* Feeling a surge of panic, Vernet shoved hard against the outside of the door, but it refused to budge. *Something is blocking it!* Vernet turned to throw full shoulder into the door, but this time the door exploded outward, striking Vernet in the face and sending him reeling backward onto the ground, his nose shattering in pain. The gun flew as Vernet reached for his face and felt the warm blood running from his nose.

Robert Langdon hit the ground somewhere nearby, and Vernet tried to get up, but he couldn't see. His vision blurred and he fell backward again. Sophie Neveu was shouting. Moments later, Vernet felt a cloud of dirt and exhaust billowing over him. He heard the crunching of tires on gravel and sat up just in time to see the truck's wide wheelbase fail to navigate a turn. There was a crash as the front bumper clipped a tree. The engine roared, and the tree bent. Finally, it was the bumper that gave, tearing half off. The armored car lurched away, its front bumper dragging. When the truck reached the paved access road, a shower of sparks lit up the night, trailing the truck as it sped away.

Vernet turned his eyes back to the ground where the truck had been parked. Even in the faint moonlight he could see there was nothing there.

The wooden box was gone.

# CHAPTER 50

**The unmarked** Fiat sedan departing Castel Gandolfo snaked downward through the Alban Hills into the valley below. In the back seat, Bishop Aringarosa smiled, feeling the weight of the bearer bonds in the briefcase on his lap and wondering how long it would be before he and the Teacher could make the exchange.

*Twenty million euro.*

The sum would buy Aringarosa power far more valuable than that.

As his car sped back toward Rome, Aringarosa again found himself wondering why the Teacher had not yet contacted him. Pulling his cell phone from his cassock pocket, he checked the carrier signal. Extremely faint.

"Cell service is intermittent up here," the driver said, glancing at him in the rearview mirror. "In about five minutes, we'll be out of the mountains, and service improves."

"Thank you." Aringarosa felt a sudden surge of concern. *No service in the mountains?* Maybe the Teacher had been trying to reach him all this time. Maybe something had gone terribly wrong.

Quickly, Aringarosa checked the phone's voice mail. Nothing. Then again, he realized, the

Teacher never would have left a recorded message; he was a man who took enormous care with his communications. Nobody understood better than the Teacher the perils of speaking openly in this modern world. Electronic eavesdropping had played a major role in how he had gathered his astonishing array of secret knowledge.

*For this reason, he takes extra precautions.*

Unfortunately, the Teacher's protocols for caution included a refusal to give Aringarosa any kind of contact number. *I alone will initiate contact,* the Teacher had informed him. *So keep your phone close.* Now that Aringarosa realized his phone might not have been working properly, he feared what the Teacher might think if he had been repeatedly phoning with no answer.

*He'll think something is wrong.*

*Or that I failed to get the bonds.*

The bishop broke a light sweat.

*Or worse . . . that I took the money and ran!*

# CHAPTER 51

**Even at** a modest sixty kilometers an hour, the dangling front bumper of the armored truck grated against the deserted suburban road with a grinding roar, spraying sparks up onto the hood.

*We've got to get off the road,* Langdon thought.

He could barely even see where they were headed. The truck's lone working headlight had been knocked off-center and was casting a skewed sidelong beam into the woods beside the country highway. Apparently the *armor* in this "armored truck" referred only to the cargo hold and not the front end.

Sophie sat in the passenger seat, staring blankly at the rosewood box on her lap.

"Are you okay?" Langdon asked.

Sophie looked shaken. "Do you believe him?"

"About the three additional murders? Absolutely. It answers a lot of questions—the issue of your grandfather's desperation to pass on the keystone, as well as the intensity with which Fache is hunting me."

"No, I meant about Vernet trying to protect his bank."

Langdon glanced over. "As opposed to?"

"Taking the keystone for himself."

Langdon had not even considered it. "How would he even know what this box contains?"

"His bank stored it. He knew my grandfather. Maybe he knew things. He might have decided he wanted the Grail for himself."

Langdon shook his head. Vernet hardly seemed the type. "In my experience, there are only two reasons people seek the Grail. Either they are naive and believe they are searching for the long-lost Cup of Christ . . ."

"Or?"

"Or they know the truth and are threatened by it. Many groups throughout history have sought to destroy the Grail."

The silence between them accentuated the sound of the scraping bumper. They had driven a few kilometers now, and as Langdon watched the cascade of sparks coming off the front of the truck, he wondered if it was dangerous. Either way, if they passed another car, it would certainly draw attention. Langdon made up his mind.

"I'm going to see if I can bend this bumper back."

Pulling onto the shoulder, he brought the truck to a stop.

Silence at last.

As Langdon walked toward the front of the truck, he felt surprisingly alert. Staring into the barrel of yet another gun tonight had given him a second wind. He took a deep breath of nighttime air and tried to get his wits about him. Accompanying the gravity of being a hunted man, Langdon was starting to feel the ponderous weight of responsibility, the prospect that he and Sophie might actually be holding an encrypted set of directions to one of the most enduring mysteries of all time.

As if this burden were not great enough, Langdon now realized that any possibility of finding a way to return the keystone to the Priory had just evaporated. News of the three additional murders had dire implications. *The Priory has been infiltrated. They are compromised.* The brotherhood was obviously being watched, or there was a mole within the ranks. It seemed to explain why Saunière might have transferred the keystone to Sophie and Langdon—people *outside* the brotherhood, people he knew were not compromised. *We can't very well give the keystone back to the brotherhood.* Even if Langdon had any idea how to find a Priory member, chances were good that whoever stepped forward to take the keystone could be the enemy himself. For the moment, at least, it seemed the keystone was in Sophie and Langdon's hands, whether they wanted it or not.

The truck's front end looked worse than Langdon had imagined. The left headlight was gone, and the right one looked like an eyeball dangling from its socket. Langdon straightened it, and it dislodged again. The only good news was that the front bumper had been torn almost clean off. Langdon gave it a hard kick and sensed he might be able to break it off entirely.

As he repeatedly kicked the twisted metal, Langdon recalled his earlier conversation with Sophie. *My grandfather left me a phone message,* Sophie had told him. *He said he needed to tell me the truth about my family.* At the time it had meant nothing, but now, knowing the Priory of Sion was involved, Langdon felt a startling new possibility emerge.

The bumper broke off suddenly with a crash. Langdon paused to catch his breath. At least the truck would no longer look like a Fourth of July sparkler. He grabbed the bumper and began dragging it out of sight into the woods, wondering where they should go next. They had no idea how to open the cryptex, or why Saunière had given it to them. Unfortunately, their survival tonight seemed to depend on getting answers to those very questions.

*We need help,* Langdon decided. *Professional help.*

In the world of the Holy Grail and the Priory of Sion, that meant only one man. The challenge, of course, would be selling the idea to Sophie.

Inside the armored car, while Sophie waited for Langdon to return, she could feel the weight of the rosewood box on her lap and resented it. *Why did my grandfather give this to me?* She had not the slightest idea what to do with it.

*Think, Sophie! Use your head. Grand-père is trying to tell you something!*

Opening the box, she eyed the cryptex's dials. *A proof of merit.* She could feel her grandfather's hand at work. *The keystone is a map that can be followed only by the worthy.* It sounded like her grandfather to the core.

Lifting the cryptex out of the box, Sophie ran her fingers over the dials. *Five letters.* She rotated the dials one by one. The mechanism moved smoothly. She aligned the disks such that her chosen letters lined up between the cryptex's two brass alignment arrows on either end of the cylinder. The dials now spelled a five-letter word that Sophie knew was absurdly obvious.

G-R-A-I-L.

Gently, she held the two ends of the cylinder and pulled, applying pressure slowly. The cryptex didn't budge. She heard the vinegar inside gurgle and stopped pulling. Then she tried again.

V-I-N-C-I

Again, no movement.

V-O-U-T-E

Nothing. The cryptex remained locked solid.

Frowning, she replaced it in the rosewood box and closed the lid. Looking outside at Langdon,

Sophie felt grateful he was with her tonight. *P.S. Find Robert Langdon.* Her grandfather's rationale for including him was now clear. Sophie was not equipped to understand her grandfather's intentions, and so he had assigned Robert Langdon as her guide. A tutor to oversee her education. Unfortunately for Langdon, he had turned out to be far more than a tutor tonight. He had become the target of Bezu Fache . . . and some unseen force intent on possessing the Holy Grail.

*Whatever the Grail turns out to be.*

Sophie wondered if finding out was worth her life.

As the armored truck accelerated again, Langdon was pleased how much more smoothly it drove. "Do you know how to get to Versailles?"

Sophie eyed him. "Sightseeing?"

"No, I have a plan. There's a religious historian I know who lives near Versailles. I can't remember exactly where, but we can look it up. I've been to his estate a few times. His name is Leigh Teabing. He's a former British Royal Historian."

"And he lives in Paris?"

"Teabing's life passion is the Grail. When whisperings of the Priory keystone surfaced about fifteen years ago, he moved to France to search churches in hopes of finding it. He's written some books on the keystone and the Grail. He may be able to help us figure out how to open it and what to do with it."

Sophie's eyes were wary. "Can you trust him?"

"Trust him to what? Not steal the information?"

"And not to turn us in."

"I don't intend to tell him we're wanted by the police. I'm hoping he'll take us in until we can sort all this out."

"Robert, has it occurred to you that every television in France is probably getting ready to broadcast our pictures? Bezu Fache always uses the media to his advantage. He'll make it impossible for us to move around without being recognized."

*Terrific,* Langdon thought. *My French TV debut will be on "Paris's Most Wanted."* At least Jonas Faukman would be pleased; every time Langdon made the news, his book sales jumped.

"Is this man a good enough friend?" Sophie asked.

Langdon doubted Teabing was someone who watched television, especially at this hour, but still the question deserved consideration. Instinct told Langdon that Teabing would be totally trustworthy. An ideal safe harbor. Considering the circumstances, Teabing would probably trip over himself to help them as much as possible. Not only did he owe Langdon a favor, but Teabing was a Grail researcher, and Sophie claimed her grandfather was the actual *Grand Master* of the Priory of Sion. If Teabing heard *that,* he would salivate at the thought of helping them figure this out.

"Teabing could be a powerful ally," Langdon said. *Depending on how much you want to tell him.*

"Fache probably will be offering a monetary reward."

Langdon laughed. "Believe me, money is the last thing this guy needs." Leigh Teabing was wealthy in the way small countries were wealthy. A descendant of Britain's First Duke of Lancaster, Teabing had gotten his money the old-fashioned way—he'd inherited it. His estate outside of Paris was a seventeenth-century palace with two private lakes.

Langdon had first met Teabing several years ago through the British Broadcasting Corporation. Teabing had approached the BBC with a proposal for a historical documentary in which he would expose the explosive history of the Holy Grail to a mainstream television audience. The BBC producers loved Teabing's hot premise, his research, and his credentials, but they had concerns that the concept was so shocking and hard to swallow that the network might end up tarnishing its reputation for quality journalism. At Teabing's suggestion, the BBC solved its credibility fears by soliciting three cameos from respected historians from around the world, all of whom corroborated the stunning nature of the Holy Grail secret with their own research.

Langdon had been among those chosen.

The BBC had flown Langdon to Teabing's Paris estate for the filming. He sat before cameras in Teabing's opulent drawing room and shared his story, admitting his initial skepticism on hearing of the alternate Holy Grail story, then describing how years of research had persuaded him that the story was true. Finally, Langdon offered some of his own research—a series of symbologic connections that strongly supported the seemingly controversial claims.

When the program aired in Britain, despite its ensemble cast and well-documented evidence, the premise rubbed so hard against the grain of popular Christian thought that it instantly confronted a firestorm of hostility. It never aired in the States, but the repercussions echoed across the Atlantic. Shortly afterward, Langdon received a postcard from an old friend—the Catholic Bishop of Philadelphia. The card simply read: *Et tu, Robert?*

"Robert," Sophie asked, "you're *certain* we can trust this man?"

"Absolutely. We're colleagues, he doesn't need money, and I happen to know he despises the

French authorities. The French government taxes him at absurd rates because he bought a historic landmark. He'll be in no hurry to cooperate with Fache."

Sophie stared out at the dark roadway. "If we go to him, how much do you want to tell him?"

Langdon looked unconcerned. "Believe me, Leigh Teabing knows more about the Priory of Sion and the Holy Grail than anyone on earth."

Sophie eyed him. "More than my grandfather?"

"I meant more than anyone *outside* the brotherhood."

"How do you know Teabing isn't a member of the brotherhood?"

"Teabing has spent his life trying to broadcast the truth about the Holy Grail. The Priory's oath is to keep its true nature hidden."

"Sounds to me like a conflict of interest."

Langdon understood her concerns. Saunière had given the cryptex directly to Sophie, and although she didn't know what it contained or what she was supposed to do with it, she was hesitant to involve a total stranger. Considering the information potentially enclosed, the instinct was probably a good one. "We don't need to tell Teabing about the keystone immediately. Or at all, even. His house will give us a place to hide and think, and maybe when we talk to him about the Grail, you'll start to have an idea why your grandfather gave this to you."

"*Us,*" Sophie reminded.

Langdon felt a humble pride and wondered yet again why Saunière had included him.

"Do you know more or less where Mr. Teabing lives?" Sophie asked.

"His estate is called Château Villette."

Sophie turned with an incredulous look. "*The* Château Villette?"

"That's the one."

"Nice friends."

"You know the estate?"

"I've passed it. It's in the castle district. Twenty minutes from here."

Langdon frowned. "That far?"

"Yes, which will give you enough time to tell me what the Holy Grail *really* is."

Langdon paused. "I'll tell you at Teabing's. He and I specialize in different areas of the legend, so between the two of us, you'll get the full story." Langdon smiled. "Besides, the Grail has been Teabing's life, and hearing the story of the Holy Grail from Leigh Teabing will be like hearing the theory of relativity from Einstein himself."

"Let's hope Leigh doesn't mind late-night visitors."

"For the record, it's *Sir* Leigh." Langdon had made that mistake only once. "Teabing is quite a character. He was knighted by the Queen several years back after composing an extensive history on the House of York."

Sophie looked over. "You're kidding, right? We're going to visit a *knight?*"

Langdon gave an awkward smile. "We're on a Grail quest, Sophie. Who better to help us than a knight?"

# CHAPTER 52

**The sprawling** 185-acre estate of Château Villette was located twenty-five minutes northwest of Paris in the environs of Versailles. Designed by François Mansart in 1668 for the Count of Aufflay, it was one of Paris's most significant historical châteaux. Complete with two rectangular lakes and gardens designed by Le Nôtre, Château Villette was more of a modest castle than a mansion. The estate fondly had become known as *la Petite Versailles*.

Langdon brought the armored truck to a shuddering stop at the foot of the mile-long driveway. Beyond the imposing security gate, Sir Leigh Teabing's residence rose on a meadow in the distance. The sign on the gate was in English: PRIVATE PROPERTY. NO TRESPASSING.

As if to proclaim his home a British Isle unto itself, Teabing had not only posted his signs in English, but he had installed his gate's intercom entry system on the *right-hand* side of the truck—the passenger's side everywhere in Europe except England.

Sophie gave the misplaced intercom an odd look. "And if someone arrives without a passenger?"

"Don't ask." Langdon had already been through that with Teabing. "He prefers things the way they are at home."

Sophie rolled down her window. "Robert, you'd better do the talking."

Langdon shifted his position, leaning out across Sophie to press the intercom button. As he did, an alluring whiff of Sophie's perfume filled his nostrils, and he realized how close they were. He waited there, awkwardly prone, while a telephone began ringing over the small speaker.

Finally, the intercom crackled and an irritated French accent spoke. "Château Villette. Who is calling?"

"This is Robert Langdon," Langdon called out, sprawled across Sophie's lap. "I'm a friend of Sir Leigh Teabing. I need his help."

"My master is sleeping. As was I. What is your business with him?"

"It is a private matter. One of great interest to him."

"Then I'm sure he will be pleased to receive you in the morning."

Langdon shifted his weight. "It's quite important."

"As is Sir Leigh's sleep. If you are a friend, then you are aware he is in poor health."

Sir Leigh Teabing had suffered from polio as a child and now wore leg braces and walked with crutches, but Langdon had found him such a lively and colorful man on his last visit that it hardly seemed an infirmity. "If you would, please tell him I have uncovered new information about the Grail. Information that cannot wait until morning."

There was a long pause.

Langdon and Sophie waited, the truck idling loudly.

A full minute passed.

Finally, someone spoke. "My good man, I daresay you are still on Harvard Standard Time." The voice was crisp and light.

Langdon grinned, recognizing the thick British accent. "Leigh, my apologies for waking you at this obscene hour."

"My manservant tells me that not only are you in Paris, but you speak of the Grail."

"I thought that might get you out of bed."

"And so it has."

"Any chance you'd open the gate for an old friend?"

"Those who seek the truth are more than friends. They are brothers."

Langdon rolled his eyes at Sophie, well accustomed to Teabing's predilection for dramatic antics.

"Indeed I will open the gate," Teabing proclaimed, "but first I must confirm your heart is true. A test of your honor. You will answer three questions."

Langdon groaned, whispering at Sophie. "Bear with me here. As I mentioned, he's something of a character."

"Your first question," Teabing declared, his tone Herculean. "Shall I serve you coffee, or tea?"

Langdon knew Teabing's feelings about the American phenomenon of coffee. "Tea," he replied. "Earl Grey."

"Excellent. Your second question. Milk or sugar?"

Langdon hesitated.

*"Milk,"* Sophie whispered in his ear. "I think the British take milk."

"Milk," Langdon said.

Silence.

"Sugar?"

Teabing made no reply.

*Wait!* Langdon now recalled the bitter beverage he had been served on his last visit and realized this question was a trick. *"Lemon!"* he declared. "Earl Grey with *lemon.*"

"Indeed." Teabing sounded deeply amused now. "And finally, I must make the most grave of inquiries." Teabing paused and then spoke in a solemn tone. "In which year did a Harvard sculler last outrow an Oxford man at Henley?"

Langdon had no idea, but he could imagine only one reason the question had been asked. "Surely such a travesty has never occurred."

The gate clicked open. "Your heart is true, my friend. You may pass."

# CHAPTER 53

**"*Monsieur Vernet!*"** The night manager of the Depository Bank of Zurich felt relieved to hear the bank president's voice on the phone. "Where did you go, sir? The police are here, everyone is waiting for you!"

"I have a little problem," the bank president said, sounding distressed. "I need your help right away."

*You have more than a little problem,* the manager thought. The police had entirely surrounded the bank and were threatening to have the DCPJ captain himself show up with the warrant the bank had demanded. "How can I help you, sir?"

"Armored truck number three. I need to find it."

Puzzled, the manager checked his delivery schedule. "It's here. Downstairs at the loading dock."

"Actually, no. The truck was stolen by the two individuals the police are tracking."

"What? How did they drive out?"

"I can't go into the specifics on the phone, but we have a situation here that could potentially be extremely unfortunate for the bank."

"What do you need me to do, sir?"

"I'd like you to activate the truck's emergency transponder."

The night manager's eyes moved to the LoJack control box across the room. Like many armored cars, each of the bank's trucks had been equipped with a radio-controlled homing device, which could be activated remotely from the bank. The manager had only used the emergency system once, after a hijacking, and it had worked flawlessly—locating the truck and transmitting the coordinates to the authorities automatically. Tonight, however, the manager had the impression the president was hoping for a bit more prudence. "Sir, you are aware that if I activate the LoJack system, the transponder will simultaneously inform the authorities that we have a problem."

Vernet was silent for several seconds. "Yes, I know. Do it anyway. Truck number three. I'll hold. I need the exact location of that truck the instant you have it."

"Right away, sir."

Thirty seconds later, forty kilometers away, hidden in the undercarriage of the armored truck, a tiny transponder blinked to life.

# CHAPTER 54

**As Langdon** and Sophie drove the armored truck up the winding, poplar-lined driveway toward the house, Sophie could already feel her muscles relaxing. It was a relief to be off the road, and she could think of few safer places to get their feet under them than this private, gated estate owned by a good-natured foreigner.

They turned into the sweeping circular driveway, and Château Villette came into view on their right. Three stories tall and at least sixty meters long, the edifice had gray stone facing illuminated by outside spotlights. The coarse facade stood in stark juxtaposition to the immaculately landscaped gardens and glassy pond.

The inside lights were just now coming on.

Rather than driving to the front door, Langdon pulled into a parking area nestled in the evergreens. "No reason to risk being spotted from the road," he said. "Or having Leigh wonder why we arrived in a wrecked armored truck."

Sophie nodded. "What do we do with the cryptex? We probably shouldn't leave it out here, but if Leigh sees it, he'll certainly want to know what it is."

"Not to worry," Langdon said, removing his

jacket as he stepped out of the car. He wrapped the tweed coat around the box and held the bundle in his arms like a baby.

Sophie looked dubious. "Subtle."

"Teabing never answers his own door; he prefers to make an entrance. I'll find somewhere inside to stash this before he joins us." Langdon paused. "Actually, I should probably warn you before you meet him. Sir Leigh has a sense of humor that people often find a bit . . . strange."

Sophie doubted anything tonight would strike her as strange anymore.

The pathway to the main entrance was hand-laid cobblestone. It curved to a door of carved oak and cherry with a brass knocker the size of a grapefruit. Before Sophie could grasp the knocker, the door swung open from within.

A prim and elegant butler stood before them, making final adjustments on the white tie and tuxedo he had apparently just donned. He looked to be about fifty, with refined features and an austere expression that left little doubt he was unamused by their presence here.

"Sir Leigh will be down presently," he declared, his accent thick French. "He is dressing. He prefers not to greet visitors while wearing only a nightshirt. May I take your coat?" He scowled at the bunched-up tweed in Langdon's arms.

"Thank you, I'm fine."

"Of course you are. Right this way, please."

The butler guided them through a lush marble foyer into an exquisitely adorned drawing room, softly lit by tassel-draped Victorian lamps. The air inside smelled antediluvian, regal somehow, with traces of pipe tobacco, tea leaves, cooking sherry, and the earthen aroma of stone architecture. Against the far wall, flanked between two glistening suits of chain mail armor, was a rough-hewn fireplace large enough to roast an ox. Walking to the hearth, the butler knelt and touched a match to a pre-laid arrangement of oak logs and kindling. A fire quickly crackled to life.

The man stood, straightening his jacket. "His master requests that you make yourselves at home." With that, he departed, leaving Langdon and Sophie alone.

Sophie wondered which of the fireside antiques she was supposed to sit on—the Renaissance velvet divan, the rustic eagle-claw rocker, or the pair of stone pews that looked like they'd been lifted from some Byzantine temple.

Langdon unwrapped the cryptex from his coat, walked to the velvet divan, and slid the wooden box deep underneath it, well out of sight. Then, shaking out his jacket, he put it back on, smoothed the lapels, and smiled at Sophie as he sat down directly over the stashed treasure.

*The divan it is,* Sophie thought, taking a seat beside him.

As she stared into the growing fire, enjoying the warmth, Sophie had the sensation that her grandfather would have loved this room. The dark wood paneling was bedecked with Old Master paintings, one of which Sophie recognized as a Poussin, her grandfather's second-favorite painter. On the mantel above the fireplace, an alabaster bust of Isis watched over the room.

Beneath the Egyptian goddess, inside the fireplace, two stone gargoyles served as andirons, their mouths gaping to reveal their menacing hollow throats. Gargoyles had always terrified Sophie as a child; that was, until her grandfather cured her of the fear by taking her atop Notre Dame Cathedral in a rainstorm. "Princess, look at these silly creatures," he had told her, pointing to the gargoyle rainspouts with their mouths gushing water. "Do you hear that funny sound in their throats?" Sophie nodded, having to smile at the burping sound of the water gurgling through their throats. "They're *gargling*," her grandfather told her. "*Gargariser!* And that's where they get the silly name 'gargoyles.' " Sophie had never again been afraid.

The fond memory caused Sophie a pang of sadness as the harsh reality of the murder gripped her again. *Grand-père is gone.* She pictured the cryptex under the divan and wondered if Leigh Teabing would have any idea how to open it. *Or if we even should ask him.* Sophie's grandfather's final words had instructed her to find Robert Langdon. He had said nothing about involving anyone else. *We needed somewhere to hide,* Sophie said, deciding to trust Robert's judgment.

"Sir Robert!" a voice bellowed somewhere behind them. "I see you travel with a maiden."

Langdon stood up. Sophie jumped to her feet as well. The voice had come from the top of a curled staircase that snaked up to the shadows of the second floor. At the top of the stairs, a form moved in the shadows, only his silhouette visible.

"Good evening," Langdon called up. "Sir Leigh, may I present Sophie Neveu."

"An honor." Teabing moved into the light.

"Thank you for having us," Sophie said, now seeing the man wore metal leg braces and used crutches. He was coming down one stair at a time. "I realize it's quite late."

"It is so late, my dear, it's early." He laughed. *"Vous n'êtes pas Américaine?"*

Sophie shook her head. *"Parisienne."*

"Your English is superb."

"Thank you. I studied at the Royal Holloway."

"So then, that explains it." Teabing hobbled lower through the shadows. "Perhaps Robert told you I schooled just down the road at Oxford." Teabing fixed Langdon with a devilish smile. "Of course, I also applied to Harvard as my safety school."

Their host arrived at the bottom of the stairs, appearing to Sophie no more like a knight than Sir Elton John. Portly and ruby-faced, Sir Leigh Teabing had bushy red hair and jovial hazel eyes that seemed to twinkle as he spoke. He wore pleated pants and a roomy silk shirt under a paisley vest. Despite the aluminum braces on his legs, he carried himself with a resilient, vertical dignity that seemed more a by-product of noble ancestry than any kind of conscious effort.

Teabing arrived and extended a hand to Langdon. "Robert, you've lost weight."

Langdon grinned. "And you've found some."

Teabing laughed heartily, patting his rotund belly. "Touché. My only carnal pleasures these days seem to be culinary." Turning now to Sophie, he gently took her hand, bowing his head slightly, breathing lightly on her fingers, and diverting his eyes. "M'lady."

Sophie glanced at Langdon, uncertain whether she'd stepped back in time or into a nuthouse.

The butler who had answered the door now entered carrying a tea service, which he arranged on a table in front of the fireplace.

"This is Rémy Legaludec," Teabing said, "my manservant."

The slender butler gave a stiff nod and disappeared yet again.

"Rémy is *Lyonais*," Teabing whispered, as if it

were an unfortunate disease. "But he does sauces quite nicely."

Langdon looked amused. "I would have thought you'd import an English staff?"

"Good heavens, no! I would not wish a British chef on anyone except the French tax collectors." He glanced over at Sophie. "*Pardonnez-moi,* Mademoiselle Neveu. Please be assured that my distaste for the French extends only to politics and the soccer pitch. Your government steals my money, and your football squad recently humiliated us."

Sophie offered an easy smile.

Teabing eyed her a moment and then looked at Langdon. "Something has happened. You both look shaken."

Langdon nodded. "We've had an interesting night, Leigh."

"No doubt. You arrive on my doorstep unannounced in the middle of the night speaking of the Grail. Tell me, is this indeed about the Grail, or did you simply say that because you know it is the lone topic for which I would rouse myself in the middle of the night?"

*A little of both,* Sophie thought, picturing the cryptex hidden beneath the couch.

"Leigh," Langdon said, "we'd like to talk to you about the Priory of Sion."

Teabing's bushy eyebrows arched with intrigue. "The keepers. So this is indeed about the Grail.

You say you come with information? Something new, Robert?"

"Perhaps. We're not quite sure. We might have a better idea if we could get some information from you first."

Teabing wagged his finger. "Ever the wily American. A game of quid pro quo. Very well. I am at your service. What is it I can tell you?"

Langdon sighed. "I was hoping you would be kind enough to explain to Ms. Neveu the true nature of the Holy Grail."

Teabing looked stunned. "She doesn't *know?*"

Langdon shook his head.

The smile that grew on Teabing's face was almost obscene. "Robert, you've brought me a *virgin?*"

Langdon winced, glancing at Sophie. "*Virgin* is the term Grail enthusiasts use to describe anyone who has never heard the true Grail story."

Teabing turned eagerly to Sophie. "How much do you know, my dear?"

Sophie quickly outlined what Langdon had explained earlier—the Priory of Sion, the Knights Templar, the Sangreal documents, and the Holy Grail, which many claimed was not a cup . . . but rather something far more powerful.

"That's *all?*" Teabing fired Langdon a scandalous look. "Robert, I thought you were a gentleman. You've robbed her of the climax!"

"I know, I thought perhaps you and I

could . . ." Langdon apparently decided the unseemly metaphor had gone far enough.

Teabing already had Sophie locked in his twinkling gaze. "You are a Grail virgin, my dear. And trust me, you will never forget your first time."

# CHAPTER 55

**Seated on** the divan beside Langdon, Sophie drank her tea and ate a scone, feeling the welcome effects of caffeine and food. Sir Leigh Teabing was beaming as he awkwardly paced before the open fire, his leg braces clicking on the stone hearth.

"The Holy Grail," Teabing said, his voice sermonic. "Most people ask me only *where* it is. I fear that is a question I may never answer." He turned and looked directly at Sophie. "However . . . the far more relevant question is this: *What* is the Holy Grail?"

Sophie sensed a rising air of academic anticipation now in both of her male companions.

"To fully understand the Grail," Teabing continued, "we must first understand the Bible. How well do you know the New Testament?"

Sophie shrugged. "Not at all, really. I was raised by a man who worshipped Leonardo da Vinci."

Teabing looked both startled and pleased. "An enlightened soul. Superb! Then you must be aware that Leonardo was one of the keepers of the secret of the Holy Grail. And he hid clues in his art."

"Robert told me as much, yes."

"And Da Vinci's views on the New Testament?"

"I have no idea."

Teabing's eyes turned mirthful as he motioned to the bookshelf across the room. "Robert, would you mind? On the bottom shelf. *La Storia di Leonardo.*"

Langdon went across the room, found a large art book, and brought it back, setting it down on the table between them. Twisting the book to face Sophie, Teabing flipped open the heavy cover and pointed inside the rear cover to a series of quotations. "From Da Vinci's notebook on polemics and speculation," Teabing said, indicating one quote in particular. "I think you'll find this relevant to our discussion."

Sophie read the words.

> *Many have made a trade of delusions*
> *and false miracles, deceiving the stupid multitude.*
> —LEONARDO DA VINCI

"Here's another," Teabing said, pointing to a different quote.

> *Blinding ignorance does mislead us.*
> *O! Wretched mortals, open your eyes!*
> —LEONARDO DA VINCI

Sophie felt a little chill. "Da Vinci is talking about the Bible?"

Teabing nodded. "Leonardo's feelings about the Bible relate directly to the Holy Grail. In fact, Da Vinci painted the true Grail, which I will show you momentarily, but first we must speak of the Bible." Teabing smiled. "And everything you need to know about the Bible can be summed up by the great canon doctor Martyn Percy." Teabing cleared his throat and declared, "The Bible did not arrive by fax from heaven."

"I beg your pardon?"

"The Bible is a product of *man,* my dear. Not of God. The Bible did not fall magically from the clouds. Man created it as a historical record of tumultuous times, and it has evolved through countless translations, additions, and revisions. History has never had a definitive version of the book."

"Okay."

"Jesus Christ was a historical figure of staggering influence, perhaps the most enigmatic and inspirational leader the world has ever seen. As the prophesied Messiah, Jesus toppled kings, inspired millions, and founded new philosophies. As a descendant of the lines of King Solomon and King David, Jesus possessed a rightful claim to the throne of the King of the Jews. Understandably, His life was recorded by thousands of followers across the land." Teabing paused to sip his tea and then placed the cup back on the mantel. "More than *eighty* gospels were considered for the New Testament, and yet only a relative few were chosen for inclusion—Matthew, Mark, Luke, and John among them.

"Who chose which gospels to include?" Sophie asked.

"Aha!" Teabing burst in with enthusiasm. "The fundamental irony of Christianity! The Bible, as we know it today, was collated by the pagan Roman emperor Constantine the Great."

"I thought Constantine was a Christian," Sophie said.

"Hardly," Teabing scoffed. "He was a lifelong pagan who was baptized on his deathbed, too weak to protest. In Constantine's day, Rome's official religion was sun worship—the cult of *Sol Invictus,* or the Invincible Sun—and Constantine was its head priest. Unfortunately for him, a growing religious turmoil was gripping Rome. Three centuries after the crucifixion of Jesus Christ, Christ's followers had multiplied exponentially. Christians and pagans began warring, and the conflict grew to such proportions that it threatened to rend Rome in two. Constantine decided something had to be done. In 325 A.D., he decided to unify Rome under a single religion. Christianity."

Sophie was surprised. "Why would a pagan emperor choose *Christianity* as the official religion?"

Teabing chuckled. "Constantine was a very good businessman. He could see that Christianity was on the rise, and he simply backed the winning horse. Historians still marvel at the brilliance with which Constantine converted the sun-worshipping pagans to Christianity. By fusing pagan symbols, dates, and rituals into the growing Christian tradition, he created a kind of hybrid religion that was acceptable to both parties."

"Transmogrification," Langdon said. "The vestiges of pagan religion in Christian symbology are undeniable. Egyptian sun disks became the halos of Catholic saints. Pictograms of Isis nursing her miraculously conceived son Horus became the blueprint for our modern images of the Virgin Mary nursing Baby Jesus. And virtually all the elements of the Catholic ritual—the miter, the altar, the doxology, and communion, the act of "God-eating"—were taken directly from earlier pagan mystery religions."

Teabing groaned. "Don't get a symbologist started on Christian icons. Nothing in Christianity is original. The pre-Christian God Mithras—called *the Son of God* and *the Light of the World*—was born on December 25, died, was buried in a rock tomb, and then resurrected in three days. By the way, December 25 is also the birthday of Osiris, Adonis, and Dionysus. The newborn Krishna was presented with gold, frankincense, and myrrh. Even Christianity's weekly holy day was stolen from the pagans."

"What do you mean?"

"Originally," Langdon said, "Christianity honored the Jewish Sabbath of Saturday, but Constantine shifted it to coincide with the pagan's veneration day of the sun." He paused, grinning. "To this day, most churchgoers attend services on Sunday morning with no idea that they are there on account of the pagan sun god's weekly tribute—*Sun*day."

Sophie's head was spinning. "And all of this relates to the Grail?"

"Indeed," Teabing said. "Stay with me. During this fusion of religions, Constantine needed to strengthen the new Christian tradition, and held a famous ecumenical gathering known as the Council of Nicaea."

Sophie had heard of it only insofar as its being the birthplace of the Nicene Creed.

"At this gathering," Teabing said, "many aspects of Christianity were debated and voted upon— the date of Easter, the role of the bishops, the administration of sacraments, and, of course, the *divinity* of Jesus."

"I don't follow. His divinity?"

"My dear," Teabing declared, "until *that* moment in history, Jesus was viewed by His followers as a mortal prophet . . . a great and powerful man, but a *man* nonetheless. A mortal."

"Not the Son of God?"

"Right," Teabing said. "Jesus' establishment as 'the Son of God' was officially proposed and voted on by the Council of Nicaea."

"Hold on. You're saying Jesus' divinity was the result of a *vote?*"

"A relatively close vote at that," Teabing added. "Nonetheless, establishing Christ's divinity was critical to the further unification of the Roman empire and to the new Vatican power base. By officially endorsing Jesus as the Son of God, Constantine turned Jesus into a deity who existed beyond the scope of the human world, an entity whose power was unchallengeable. This not only precluded further pagan challenges to Christianity, but now the followers of Christ were able to redeem themselves *only* via the established sacred channel—the Roman Catholic Church."

Sophie glanced at Langdon, and he gave her a soft nod of concurrence.

"It was all about power," Teabing continued. "Christ as Messiah was critical to the functioning of Church and state. Many scholars claim that the early Church literally *stole* Jesus from His original followers, hijacking His human message, shrouding it in an impenetrable cloak of divinity, and using it to expand their own power. I've written several books on the topic."

"And I assume devout Christians send you hate mail on a daily basis?"

"Why would they?" Teabing countered. "The vast majority of educated Christians know the history of their faith. Jesus was indeed a great and powerful man. Constantine's underhanded political maneuvers don't diminish the majesty of Christ's life. Nobody is saying Christ was a fraud, or denying that He walked the earth and inspired millions to better lives. All we are saying is that Constantine took advantage of Christ's substantial influence and importance. And in doing so, he shaped the face of Christianity as we know it today."

Sophie glanced at the art book before her, eager to move on and see the Da Vinci painting of the Holy Grail.

"The twist is this," Teabing said, talking faster now. "Because Constantine upgraded Jesus' status almost four centuries *after* Jesus' death, thousands of documents already existed chronicling His life as a *mortal* man. To rewrite the history books, Constantine knew he would need a bold stroke. From this sprang the most profound moment in Christian history." Teabing paused, eyeing Sophie. "Constantine commissioned and financed a new Bible, which omitted those gospels that spoke of Christ's *human* traits and embellished those gospels that made Him godlike. The earlier gospels were outlawed, gathered up, and burned."

"An interesting note," Langdon added. "Anyone who chose the forbidden gospels over Constantine's version was deemed a heretic. The word *heretic* derives from that moment in history. The Latin word *haereticus* means 'choice.' Those who 'chose' the original history of Christ were the world's first *heretics*."

"Fortunately for historians," Teabing said, "some of the gospels that Constantine attempted to eradicate managed to survive. The Dead Sea Scrolls were found in the 1950s hidden in a cave near Qumran in the Judean desert. And, of course, the Coptic Scrolls in 1945 at Nag Hammadi. In addition to telling the true Grail story, these documents speak of Christ's ministry in very human terms. Of course, the Vatican, in keeping with their tradition of misinformation, tried very hard to suppress the release of these scrolls. And why wouldn't they? The scrolls highlight glaring historical discrepancies and fabrications, clearly confirming that the modern Bible was compiled and edited by men who possessed a political agenda—to promote the divinity of the man Jesus Christ and use His influence to solidify their own power base."

"And yet," Langdon countered, "it's important to remember that the modern Church's desire to suppress these documents comes from a sincere belief in their established view of Christ. The Vatican is made up of deeply pious men who truly believe these contrary documents could only be false testimony."

Teabing chuckled as he eased himself into a chair opposite Sophie. "As you can see, our professor has a far softer heart for Rome than I do. Nonetheless, he is correct about the modern clergy believing these opposing documents are false testimony. That's understandable. Constantine's Bible has been their truth for ages. Nobody is more indoctrinated than the indoctrinator."

"What he means," Langdon said, "is that we worship the gods of our fathers."

"What I mean," Teabing countered, "is that almost everything our fathers taught us about Christ is *false*. As are the stories about the Holy Grail."

Sophie looked again at the Da Vinci quote before her. *Blinding ignorance does mislead us. O! Wretched mortals, open your eyes!*

Teabing reached for the book and flipped toward the center. "And finally, before I show you Da Vinci's paintings of the Holy Grail, I'd like you to take a quick look at this." He opened the book to a colorful graphic that spanned both full pages. "I assume you recognize this fresco?"

*He's kidding, right?* Sophie was staring at the

most famous fresco of all time—*The Last Supper*—Da Vinci's legendary painting from the wall of Santa Maria delle Grazie near Milan. The decaying fresco portrayed Jesus and His disciples at the moment that Jesus announced one of them would betray Him. "I know the fresco, yes."

"Then perhaps you would indulge me this little game? Close your eyes if you would."

Uncertain, Sophie closed her eyes.

"Where is Jesus sitting?" Teabing asked.

"In the center."

"Good. And what food are He and His disciples breaking and eating?"

"Bread." *Obviously.*

"Superb. And what drink?"

"Wine. They drank wine."

"Great. And one final question. How many wineglasses are on the table?"

Sophie paused, realizing it was the trick question. *And after dinner, Jesus took the cup of wine, sharing it with His disciples.* "One cup," she said. "The chalice." *The Cup of Christ. The Holy Grail.* "Jesus passed a single chalice of wine, just as modern Christians do at communion."

Teabing sighed. "Open your eyes."

She did. Teabing was grinning smugly. Sophie looked down at the painting, seeing to her astonishment that *everyone* at the table had a glass of wine, including Christ. Thirteen cups. Moreover, the cups were tiny, stemless, and made of glass.

There was no chalice in the painting. No Holy Grail.

Teabing's eyes twinkled. "A bit strange, don't you think, considering that both the Bible and our standard Grail legend celebrate this moment as the definitive arrival of the Holy Grail. Oddly, Da Vinci appears to have forgotten to paint the Cup of Christ."

"Surely art scholars must have noted that."

"You will be shocked to learn what anomalies Da Vinci included here that most scholars either do not see or simply choose to ignore. This fresco, in fact, is the entire key to the Holy Grail mystery. Da Vinci lays it all out in the open in *The Last Supper*."

Sophie scanned the work eagerly. "Does this fresco tell us *what* the Grail really is?"

"Not *what* it is," Teabing whispered. "But rather *who* it is. The Holy Grail is not a thing. It is, in fact . . . a *person*."

# CHAPTER 56

**Sophie stared** at Teabing a long moment and then turned to Langdon. "The Holy Grail is a person?"

Langdon nodded. "A woman, in fact." From the blank look on Sophie's face, Langdon could tell they had already lost her. He recalled having a similar reaction the first time he heard the statement. It was not until he understood the *symbology* behind the Grail that the feminine connection became clear.

Teabing apparently had a similar thought. "Robert, perhaps this is the moment for the symbologist to clarify?" He went to a nearby end table, found a piece of paper, and laid it in front of Langdon.

Langdon pulled a pen from his pocket. "Sophie, are you familiar with the modern icons for male and female?" He drew the common male symbol ♂ and female symbol ♀.

"Of course," she said.

"These," he said quietly, "are not the original symbols for male and female. Many people incorrectly assume the male symbol is derived from a shield and spear, while the female symbol represents a mirror reflecting beauty. In fact, the symbols originated as ancient astronomical symbols for the planet-god Mars and planet-goddess Venus. The original symbols are far simpler." Langdon drew another icon on the paper.

"This symbol is the original icon for *male*," he told her. "A rudimentary phallus."

"Quite to the point," Sophie said.

"As it were," Teabing added.

Langdon went on. "This icon is formally known as the *blade*, and it represents aggression and manhood. In fact, this exact phallus symbol is still used today on modern military uniforms to denote rank."

"Indeed." Teabing grinned. "The more penises you have, the higher your rank. Boys will be boys."

Langdon winced. "Moving on, the female symbol, as you might imagine, is the exact opposite." He drew another symbol on the page. "This is called the *chalice*."

Sophie glanced up, looking surprised.

Langdon could see she had made the connection. "The chalice," he said, "resembles a cup or vessel, and more important, it resembles the shape of a woman's womb. This symbol communicates femininity, womanhood, and fertility." Langdon looked directly at her now. "Sophie, legend tells us the Holy Grail is a chalice—a cup. But the Grail's description as a *chalice* is actually an allegory to protect the true nature of the Holy Grail. That is to say, the legend uses the chalice as a *metaphor* for something far more important."

"A woman," Sophie said.

"Exactly." Langdon smiled. "The Grail is literally the ancient symbol for womanhood, and the *Holy* Grail represents the sacred feminine and the goddess, which of course has now been lost, virtually eliminated by the Church. The power of the female and her ability to produce life was once very sacred, but it posed a threat to the rise of the predominantly male Church, and so the sacred feminine was demonized and called unclean. It was *man,* not God, who created the concept of 'original sin,' whereby Eve tasted of the apple and caused the downfall of the human race. Woman, once the sacred giver of life, was now the enemy."

"I should add," Teabing chimed, "that this concept of woman as life-bringer was the foundation of ancient religion. Childbirth was mystical and powerful. Sadly, Christian philosophy decided to embezzle the female's creative power by ignoring biological truth and making *man* the Creator. Genesis tells us that Eve was created from Adam's rib. Woman became an offshoot of man. And a sinful one at that. Genesis was the beginning of the end for the goddess."

"The Grail," Langdon said, "is symbolic of the lost goddess. When Christianity came along, the old pagan religions did not die easily. Legends of chivalric quests for the lost Grail were in fact stories of forbidden quests to find the lost sacred feminine. Knights who claimed to be "searching for the chalice" were speaking in code as a way to protect themselves from a Church that had subjugated women, banished the Goddess, burned nonbelievers, and forbidden the pagan reverence for the sacred feminine."

Sophie shook her head. "I'm sorry, when you said the Holy Grail was a person, I thought you meant it was an actual person."

"It is," Langdon said.

"And not just *any* person," Teabing blurted, clambering excitedly to his feet. "A woman who carried with her a secret so powerful that, if revealed, it threatened to devastate the very foundation of Christianity!"

Sophie looked overwhelmed. "Is this woman well known in history?"

"Quite." Teabing collected his crutches and motioned down the hall. "And if we adjourn to the study, my friends, it would be my honor to show you Da Vinci's painting of her."

———

Two rooms away, in the kitchen, manservant Rémy Legaludec stood in silence before a television. The news station was broadcasting photos of a man and woman . . . the same two individuals to whom Rémy had just served tea.

# CHAPTER 57

**Standing at** the roadblock outside the Depository Bank of Zurich, Lieutenant Collet wondered what was taking Fache so long to come up with the search warrant. The bankers were obviously hiding something. They claimed Langdon and Neveu had arrived earlier and were turned away from the bank because they did not have proper account identification.

*So why won't they let us inside for a look?*

Finally, Collet's cellular phone rang. It was the command post at the Louvre. "Do we have a search warrant yet?" Collet demanded.

"Forget about the bank, Lieutenant," the agent told him. "We just got a tip. We have the exact location where Langdon and Neveu are hiding."

Collet sat down hard on the hood of his car. "You're kidding."

"I have an address in the suburbs. Somewhere near Versailles."

"Does Captain Fache know?"

"Not yet. He's busy on an important call."

"I'm on my way. Have him call as soon as he's free." Collet took down the address and jumped in his car. As he peeled away from the bank, Collet realized he had forgotten to ask *who* had tipped DCPJ off to Langdon's location. Not that it mattered. Collet had been blessed with a chance to redeem his skepticism and earlier blunders. He was about to make the most high-profile arrest of his career.

Collet radioed the five cars accompanying him. "No sirens, men. Langdon can't know we're coming."

Forty kilometers away, a black Audi pulled off a rural road and parked in the shadows on the edge of a field. Silas got out and peered through the rungs of the wrought-iron fence that encircled the vast compound before him. He gazed up the long moonlit slope to the château in the distance.

The downstairs lights were all ablaze. *Odd for this hour,* Silas thought, smiling. The information the Teacher had given him was obviously accurate. *I will not leave this house without the keystone,* he vowed. *I will not fail the bishop and the Teacher.*

Checking the thirteen-round clip in his Heckler Koch, Silas pushed it through the bars and let it fall onto the mossy ground inside the compound. Then, gripping the top of the fence, he heaved himself up and over, dropping to the ground on the other side. Ignoring the slash of pain from his *cilice,* Silas retrieved his gun and began the long trek up the grassy slope.

# CHAPTER 58

**Teabing's "study"** was like no study Sophie had ever seen. Six or seven times larger than even the most luxurious of office spaces, the knight's *cabinet de travail* resembled an ungainly hybrid of science laboratory, archival library, and indoor flea market. Lit by three overhead chandeliers, the boundless tile floor was dotted with clustered islands of worktables buried beneath books, artwork, artifacts, and a surprising amount of electronic gear—computers, projectors, microscopes, copy machines, and flatbed scanners.

"I converted the ballroom," Teabing said, looking sheepish as he shuffled into the room. "I have little occasion to dance."

Sophie felt as if the entire night had become some kind of twilight zone where nothing was as she expected. "This is all for your work?"

"Learning the truth has become my life's love," Teabing said. "And the Sangreal is my favorite mistress."

*The Holy Grail is a woman,* Sophie thought, her mind a collage of interrelated ideas that seemed to make no sense. "You said you have a *picture* of this woman who you claim is the Holy Grail."

"Yes, but it is not I who *claim* she is the Grail. Christ Himself made that claim."

"Which one is the painting?" Sophie asked, scanning the walls.

"Hmmm . . ." Teabing made a show of seeming to have forgotten. "The Holy Grail. The Sangreal. The Chalice." He wheeled suddenly and pointed to the far wall. On it hung an eight-foot-long print of *The Last Supper*, the same exact image Sophie had just been looking at. "There she is!"

Sophie was certain she had missed something. "That's the same painting you just showed me."

He winked. "I know, but the enlargement is so much more exciting. Don't you think?"

Sophie turned to Langdon for help. "I'm lost."

Langdon smiled. "As it turns out, the Holy Grail *does* indeed make an appearance in *The Last Supper*. Leonardo included her prominently."

"Hold on," Sophie said. "You told me the Holy Grail is a *woman*. *The Last Supper* is a painting of thirteen men."

"Is it?" Teabing arched his eyebrows. "Take a closer look."

Uncertain, Sophie made her way closer to the painting, scanning the thirteen figures—Jesus Christ in the middle, six disciples on His left, and six on His right. "They're all men," she confirmed.

"Oh?" Teabing said. "How about the one

seated in the place of honor, at the right hand of the Lord?"

Sophie examined the figure to Jesus' immediate right, focusing in. As she studied the person's face and body, a wave of astonishment rose within her. The individual had flowing red hair, delicate folded hands, and the hint of a bosom. It was, without a doubt . . . female.

"That's a woman!" Sophie exclaimed.

Teabing was laughing. "Surprise, surprise. Believe me, it's no mistake. Leonardo was skilled at painting the difference between the sexes."

Sophie could not take her eyes from the woman beside Christ. *The Last Supper is supposed to be thirteen men. Who is this woman?* Although Sophie had seen this classic image many times, she had not once noticed this glaring discrepancy.

"Everyone misses it," Teabing said. "Our preconceived notions of this scene are so powerful that our mind blocks out the incongruity and overrides our eyes."

"It's known as *skitoma*," Langdon added. "The brain does it sometimes with powerful symbols."

"Another reason you might have missed the woman," Teabing said, "is that many of the photographs in art books were taken before 1954, when the details were still hidden beneath layers of grime and several restorative repaintings done by clumsy hands in the eighteenth century. Now, at last, the fresco has been cleaned down to Da

Vinci's original layer of paint." He motioned to the photograph. "*Et voilà!*"

Sophie moved closer to the image. The woman to Jesus' right was young and pious-looking, with a demure face, beautiful red hair, and hands folded quietly. *This is the woman who singlehandedly could crumble the Church?*

"Who is she?" Sophie asked.

"That, my dear," Teabing replied, "is Mary Magdalene."

Sophie turned. "The prostitute?"

Teabing drew a short breath, as if the word had injured him personally. "Magdalene was no such thing. That unfortunate misconception is the legacy of a smear campaign launched by the early Church. The Church needed to defame Mary Magdalene in order to cover up her dangerous secret—her role as the Holy Grail."

"Her *role?*"

"As I mentioned," Teabing clarified, "the early Church needed to convince the world that the mortal prophet Jesus was a *divine* being. Therefore, any gospels that described *earthly* aspects of Jesus' life had to be omitted from the Bible. Unfortunately for the early editors, one particularly troubling earthly theme kept recurring in the gospels. Mary Magdalene." He paused. "More specifically, her marriage to Jesus Christ."

"I beg your pardon?" Sophie's eyes moved to Langdon and then back to Teabing.

"It's a matter of historical record," Teabing said, "and Da Vinci was certainly aware of that fact. *The Last Supper* practically shouts at the viewer that Jesus and Magdalene were a pair."

Sophie glanced back to the fresco.

"Notice that Jesus and Magdalene are clothed as mirror images of one another." Teabing pointed to the two individuals in the center of the fresco.

Sophie was mesmerized. Sure enough, their clothes were inverse colors. Jesus wore a red robe and blue cloak; Mary Magdalene wore a blue robe and red cloak. *Yin and yang.*

"Venturing into the more bizarre," Teabing said, "note that Jesus and His bride appear to be joined at the hip and are leaning away from one another as if to create this clearly delineated negative space between them."

Even before Teabing traced the contour for her, Sophie saw it—the indisputable ⋁ shape at the focal point of the painting. It was the same symbol Langdon had drawn earlier for the Grail, the chalice, and the female womb.

"Finally," Teabing said, "if you view Jesus and Magdalene as compositional elements rather than as people, you will see another obvious shape leap out at you." He paused. "A *letter* of the alphabet."

Sophie saw it at once. To say the letter leapt out at her was an understatement. The letter was suddenly all Sophie could see. Glaring in the center of the painting was the unquestionable outline of an enormous, flawlessly formed letter M.

"A bit too perfect for coincidence, wouldn't you say?" Teabing asked.

Sophie was amazed. "Why is it there?"

Teabing shrugged. "Conspiracy theorists will tell you it stands for *Matrimonio* or *Mary Magdalene*. To be honest, nobody is certain. The only certainty is that the hidden M is no mistake. Countless Grail-related works contain the hidden letter M— whether as watermarks, underpaintings, or compositional allusions. The most blatant M, of course, is emblazoned on the altar at Our Lady of Paris in London, which was designed by a former Grand Master of the Priory of Sion, Jean Cocteau."

Sophie weighed the information. "I'll admit, the hidden M's are intriguing, although I assume nobody is claiming they are proof of Jesus' marriage to Magdalene."

"No, no," Teabing said, going to a nearby table of books. "As I said earlier, the marriage of Jesus and Mary Magdalene is part of the historical record." He began pawing through his book collection. "Moreover, Jesus as a married man makes infinitely more sense than our standard biblical view of Jesus as a bachelor."

"Why?" Sophie asked.

"Because Jesus was a Jew," Langdon said, taking

over while Teabing searched for his book, "and the social decorum during that time virtually forbid a Jewish man to be unmarried. According to Jewish custom, celibacy was condemned, and the obligation for a Jewish father was to find a suitable wife for his son. If Jesus were not married, at least one of the Bible's gospels would have mentioned it and offered some explanation for His unnatural state of bachelorhood."

Teabing located a huge book and pulled it toward him across the table. The leather-bound edition was poster-sized, like a huge atlas. The cover read: *The Gnostic Gospels.* Teabing heaved it open, and Langdon and Sophie joined him. Sophie could see it contained photographs of what appeared to be magnified passages of ancient documents—tattered papyrus with handwritten text. She did not recognize the ancient language, but the facing pages bore typed translations.

"These are photocopies of the Nag Hammadi and Dead Sea scrolls, which I mentioned earlier," Teabing said. "The earliest Christian records. Troublingly, they do not match up with the gospels in the Bible." Flipping toward the middle of the book, Teabing pointed to a passage. "The Gospel of Philip is always a good place to start."

Sophie read the passage:

*And the companion of the Saviour is Mary Magdalene. Christ loved her more than all the dis-*

*ciples and used to kiss her often on her mouth. The rest of the disciples were offended by it and expressed disapproval. They said to him, "Why do you love her more than all of us?"*

The words surprised Sophie, and yet they hardly seemed conclusive. "It says nothing of marriage."

*"Au contraire."* Teabing smiled, pointing to the first line. "As any Aramaic scholar will tell you, the word *companion*, in those days, literally meant *spouse.*"

Langdon concurred with a nod.

Sophie read the first line again. *And the companion of the Saviour is Mary Magdalene.*

Teabing flipped through the book and pointed out several other passages that, to Sophie's surprise, clearly suggested Magdalene and Jesus had a romantic relationship. As she read the passages, Sophie recalled an angry priest who had banged on her grandfather's door when she was a schoolgirl.

"Is this the home of Jacques Saunière?" the priest had demanded, glaring down at young Sophie when she pulled open the door. "I want to talk to him about this editorial he wrote." The priest held up a newspaper.

Sophie summoned her grandfather, and the two men disappeared into his study and closed the door. *My grandfather wrote something in the paper?*

Sophie immediately ran to the kitchen and flipped through that morning's paper. She found her grandfather's name on an article on the second page. She read it. Sophie didn't understand all of what was said, but it sounded like the French government, under pressure from priests, had agreed to ban an American movie called *The Last Temptation of Christ,* which was about Jesus having sex with a lady called Mary Magdalene. Her grandfather's article said the Church was arrogant and wrong to ban it.

*No wonder the priest is mad,* Sophie thought.

"It's pornography! Sacrilege!" the priest yelled, emerging from the study and storming to the front door. "How can you possibly endorse that! This American Martin Scorsese is a blasphemer, and the Church will permit him no pulpit in France!" The priest slammed the door on his way out.

When her grandfather came into the kitchen, he saw Sophie with the paper and frowned. "You're quick."

Sophie said, "You think Jesus Christ had a girlfriend?"

"No, dear, I said the Church should not be allowed to tell us what notions we can and can't entertain."

"Did Jesus have a girlfriend?"

Her grandfather was silent for several moments. "Would it be so bad if He did?"

Sophie considered it and then shrugged. "I wouldn't mind."

Sir Leigh Teabing was still talking. "I shan't bore you with the countless references to Jesus and Magdalene's union. That has been explored ad nauseum by modern historians. I would, however, like to point out the following." He motioned to another passage. "This is from the Gospel of Mary Magdalene."

Sophie had not known a gospel existed in Magdalene's words. She read the text:

*And Peter said, "Did the Saviour really speak with a woman without our knowledge? Are we to turn about and all listen to her? Did he prefer her to us?"*

*And Levi answered, "Peter, you have always been hot-tempered. Now I see you contending against the woman like an adversary. If the Saviour made her worthy, who are you indeed to reject her? Surely the Saviour knows her very well. That is why he loved her more than us."*

"The woman they are speaking of," Teabing explained, "is Mary Magdalene. Peter is jealous of her."

"Because Jesus preferred Mary?"

"Not only that. The stakes were far greater than mere affection. At this point in the gospels, Jesus suspects He will soon be captured and crucified. So He gives Mary Magdalene instructions on how to carry on His Church after He is gone. As a result, Peter expresses his discontent over playing second fiddle to a woman. I daresay Peter was something of a sexist."

Sophie was trying to keep up. "This is *Saint* Peter. The rock on which Jesus built His Church."

"The same, except for one catch. According to these unaltered gospels, it was not *Peter* to whom Christ gave directions with which to establish the Christian Church. It was *Mary Magdalene.*"

Sophie looked at him. "You're saying the Christian Church was to be carried on by a *woman?*"

"That was the plan. Jesus was the original feminist. He intended for the future of His Church to be in the hands of Mary Magdalene."

"And Peter had a problem with that," Langdon said, pointing to *The Last Supper.* "That's Peter there. You can see that Da Vinci was well aware of how Peter felt about Mary Magdalene."

Again, Sophie was speechless. In the painting, Peter was leaning menacingly toward Mary Magdalene and slicing his blade-like hand across her neck. The same threatening gesture as in *Madonna of the Rocks*!

"And here too," Langdon said, pointing now to the crowd of disciples near Peter. "A bit ominous, no?"

Sophie squinted and saw a hand emerging from the crowd of disciples. "Is that hand wielding a *dagger?*"

"Yes. Stranger still, if you count the arms, you'll see that this hand belongs to . . . no one at all. It's disembodied. Anonymous."

Sophie was starting to feel overwhelmed. "I'm sorry, I still don't understand how all of this makes Mary Magdalene the Holy Grail."

"Aha!" Teabing exclaimed again. "Therein lies the rub!" He turned once more to the table and pulled out a large chart, spreading it out for her. It was an elaborate genealogy. "Few people realize that Mary Magdalene, in addition to being Christ's right hand, was a powerful woman already."

Sophie could now see the title of the family tree.

### THE TRIBE OF BENJAMIN

"Mary Magdalene is here," Teabing said, pointing near the top of the genealogy.

Sophie was surprised. "She was of the House of Benjamin?"

"Indeed," Teabing said. "Mary Magdalene was of royal descent."

"But I was under the impression Magdalene was poor."

Teabing shook his head. "Magdalene was recast as a whore in order to erase evidence of her powerful family ties."

Sophie found herself again glancing at Langdon, who again nodded. She turned back to Teabing. "But why would the early Church *care* if Magdalene had royal blood?"

The Briton smiled. "My dear child, it was not Mary Magdalene's royal blood that concerned the Church so much as it was her consorting with Christ, who *also* had royal blood. As you know, the Book of Matthew tells us that Jesus was of the House of David. A descendant of King Solomon—King of the Jews. By marrying into the powerful House of Benjamin, Jesus fused two royal bloodlines, creating a potent political union with the potential of making a legitimate claim to the throne and restoring the line of kings as it was under Solomon."

Sophie sensed he was at last coming to his point.

Teabing looked excited now. "The legend of the Holy Grail is a legend about royal blood. When Grail legend speaks of 'the chalice that held the blood of Christ' . . . it speaks, in fact, of Mary Magdalene—the female womb that carried Jesus' royal bloodline."

The words seemed to echo across the ballroom

and back before they fully registered in Sophie's mind. *Mary Magdalene carried the royal bloodline of Jesus Christ?* "But how could Christ have a bloodline unless . . . ?" She paused and looked at Langdon.

Langdon smiled softly. "Unless they had a child."

Sophie stood transfixed.

"Behold," Teabing proclaimed, "the greatest cover-up in human history. Not only was Jesus Christ married, but He was a father. My dear, Mary Magdalene was the Holy Vessel. She was the chalice that bore the royal bloodline of Jesus Christ. She was the womb that bore the lineage, and the vine from which the sacred fruit sprang forth!"

Sophie felt the hairs stand up on her arms. "But how could a secret *that* big be kept quiet all of these years?"

"Heavens!" Teabing said. "It has been anything but *quiet!* The royal bloodline of Jesus Christ is the source of the most enduring legend of all time—the Holy Grail. Magdalene's story has been shouted from the rooftops for centuries in all kinds of metaphors and languages. Her story is everywhere once you open your eyes."

"And the Sangreal documents?" Sophie said. "They allegedly contain proof that Jesus had a royal bloodline?"

"They do."

"So the entire Holy Grail legend is all about royal blood?"

"Quite literally," Teabing said. "The word *Sangreal* derives from *San Greal*—or Holy Grail. But in its most ancient form, the word *Sangreal* was divided in a different spot." Teabing wrote on a piece of scrap paper and handed it to her.

She read what he had written.

Sang Real

Instantly, Sophie recognized the translation. *Sang Real* literally meant *Royal Blood*.

# CHAPTER 59

**The male** receptionist in the lobby of the Opus Dei headquarters on Lexington Avenue in New York City was surprised to hear Bishop Aringarosa's voice on the line. "Good evening, sir."

"Have I had any messages?" the bishop demanded, sounding unusually anxious.

"Yes, sir. I'm very glad you called in. I couldn't reach you in your apartment. You had an urgent phone message about half an hour ago."

"Yes?" He sounded relieved by the news. "Did the caller leave a name?"

"No, sir, just a number." The operator relayed the number.

"Prefix thirty-three? That's France, am I right?"

"Yes, sir. Paris. The caller said it was critical you contact him immediately."

"Thank you. I have been waiting for that call." Aringarosa quickly severed the connection.

As the receptionist hung up the receiver, he wondered why Aringarosa's phone connection sounded so crackly. The bishop's daily schedule showed him in New York this weekend, and yet he sounded a world away. The receptionist shrugged it off. Bishop Aringarosa had been acting very strangely the last few months.

*My cellular phone must not have been receiving,* Aringarosa thought as the Fiat approached the exit for Rome's Ciampino Charter Airport. *The Teacher was trying to reach me.* Despite Aringarosa's concern at having missed the call, he felt encouraged that the Teacher felt confident enough to call Opus Dei headquarters directly.

*Things must have gone well in Paris tonight.*

As Aringarosa began dialing the number, he felt excited to know he would soon be in Paris. *I'll be on the ground before dawn.* Aringarosa had a chartered turbo prop awaiting him here for the short flight to France. Commercial carriers were not an option at this hour, especially considering the contents of his briefcase.

The line began to ring.

A female voice answered. *"Direction Centrale Police Judiciaire."*

Aringarosa felt himself hesitate. This was unexpected. "Ah, yes . . . I was asked to call this number?"

*"Qui êtes-vous?"* the woman said. "Your name?"

Aringarosa was uncertain if he should reveal it. *The French Judicial Police?*

"Your *name,* monsieur?" the woman pressed.

"Bishop Manuel Aringarosa."

*"Un moment."* There was a click on the line.

After a long wait, another man came on, his tone gruff and concerned. "Bishop, I am glad I finally reached you. You and I have much to discuss."

# CHAPTER 60

**Sangreal . . .** *Sang Real . . . San Greal . . . Royal Blood . . . Holy Grail.*

It was all intertwined.

*The Holy Grail is Mary Magdalene . . . the mother of the royal bloodline of Jesus Christ.* Sophie felt a new wave of disorientation as she stood in the silence of the ballroom and stared at Robert Langdon. The more pieces Langdon and Teabing laid on the table tonight, the more unpredictable this puzzle became.

"As you can see, my dear," Teabing said, hobbling toward a bookshelf, "Leonardo is not the only one who has been trying to tell the world the truth about the Holy Grail. The royal bloodline of Jesus Christ has been chronicled in exhaustive detail by scores of historians." He ran a finger down a row of several dozen books.

Sophie tilted her head and scanned the list of titles:

THE TEMPLAR REVELATION:
*Secret Guardians of the True Identity of Christ*

THE WOMAN WITH THE ALABASTER JAR:
*Mary Magdalene and the Holy Grail*

THE GODDESS IN THE GOSPELS
*Reclaiming the Sacred Feminine*

"Here is perhaps the best-known tome," Teabing said, pulling a tattered hardcover from the stack and handing it to her.

The cover read:

HOLY BLOOD, HOLY GRAIL
*The Acclaimed International Bestseller*

Sophie glanced up. "An international bestseller? I've never heard of it."

"You were young. This caused quite a stir back in the nineteen eighties. To my taste, the authors made some dubious leaps of faith in their analysis, but their fundamental premise is sound, and to their credit, they finally brought the idea of Christ's bloodline into the mainstream."

"What was the Church's reaction to the book?"

"Outrage, of course. But that was to be expected. After all, this was a secret the Vatican had tried to bury in the fourth century. That's part of what the Crusades were about. Gathering and destroying information. The threat Mary Magdalene posed to the men of the early Church was potentially ruinous. Not only was she the woman to whom Jesus had assigned the task of founding the Church, but she also had physical proof that the Church's newly proclaimed *deity* had spawned a mortal bloodline. The Church, in order to defend itself against the Magdalene's power, perpetuated her image as a whore and buried evidence of Christ's marriage to her, thereby defusing any potential claims that Christ had a surviving bloodline and was a mortal prophet."

Sophie glanced at Langdon, who nodded. "Sophie, the historical evidence supporting this is substantial."

"I admit," Teabing said, "the assertions are dire, but you must understand the Church's powerful motivations to conduct such a cover-up. They could never have survived public knowledge of a bloodline. A child of Jesus would undermine the critical notion of Christ's divinity and therefore the Christian Church, which declared itself the sole vessel through which humanity could access the divine and gain entrance to the kingdom of heaven."

"The five-petal rose," Sophie said, pointing suddenly to the spine of one of Teabing's books. *The same exact design inlaid on the rosewood box.*

Teabing glanced at Langdon and grinned. "She has a good eye." He turned back to Sophie. "That is the Priory symbol for the Grail. Mary Magdalene. Because her name was forbidden by the Church, Mary Magdalene became secretly known by many pseudonyms—the Chalice, the Holy Grail, and the Rose." He paused. "The Rose has ties to the five-pointed pentacle of

Venus and the guiding Compass Rose. By the way, the word *rose* is identical in English, French, German, and many other languages."

"Rose," Langdon added, "is also an anagram of Eros, the Greek god of sexual love."

Sophie gave him a surprised look as Teabing plowed on.

"The Rose has always been the premiere symbol of female sexuality. In primitive goddess cults, the five petals represented the five stations of female life—birth, menstruation, motherhood, menopause, and death. And in modern times, the flowering rose's ties to womanhood are considered more visual." He glanced at Robert. "Perhaps the symbologist could explain?"

Robert hesitated. A moment too long.

"Oh, heavens!" Teabing huffed. "You Americans are such prudes." He looked back at Sophie. "What Robert is fumbling with is the fact that the blossoming flower resembles the female genitalia, the sublime blossom from which all mankind enters the world. And if you've ever seen any paintings by Georgia O'Keeffe, you'll know exactly what I mean."

"The point here," Langdon said, motioning back to the bookshelf, "is that all of these books substantiate the same historical claim."

"That Jesus was a father." Sophie was still uncertain.

"Yes," Teabing said. "And that Mary Magdalene was the womb that carried His royal lineage. The Priory of Sion, to this day, still worships Mary Magdalene as the Goddess, the Holy Grail, the Rose, and the Divine Mother."

Sophie again flashed on the ritual in the basement.

"According to the Priory," Teabing continued, "Mary Magdalene was pregnant at the time of the crucifixion. For the safety of Christ's unborn child, she had no choice but to flee the Holy Land. With the help of Jesus' trusted uncle, Joseph of Arimathea, Mary Magdalene secretly traveled to France, then known as Gaul. There she found safe refuge in the Jewish community. It was here in France that she gave birth to a daughter. Her name was Sarah."

Sophie glanced up. "They actually know the child's *name?*"

"Far more than that. Magdalene's and Sarah's lives were scrutinously chronicled by their Jewish protectors. Remember that Magdalene's child belonged to the lineage of Jewish kings—David and Solomon. For this reason, the Jews in France considered Magdalene sacred royalty and revered her as the progenitor of the royal line of kings. Countless scholars of that era chronicled Mary Magdalene's days in France, including the birth of Sarah and the subsequent family tree."

Sophie was startled. "There exists a *family tree* of Jesus Christ?"

"Indeed. And it is purportedly one of the cornerstones of the Sangreal documents. A complete genealogy of the early descendants of Christ."

"But what good is a documented genealogy of Christ's bloodline?" Sophie asked. "It's not proof. Historians could not possibly confirm its authenticity."

Teabing chuckled. "No more so than they can confirm the authenticity of the Bible."

"Meaning?"

"Meaning that history is always written by the winners. When two cultures clash, the loser is obliterated, and the winner writes the history books—books which glorify their own cause and disparage the conquered foe. As Napoleon once said, 'What is history, but a fable agreed upon?' " He smiled. "By its very nature, history is always a one-sided account."

Sophie had never thought of it that way.

"The Sangreal documents simply tell the *other* side of the Christ story. In the end, which side of the story you believe becomes a matter of faith and personal exploration, but at least the information has survived. The Sangreal documents include tens of thousands of pages of information. Eyewitness accounts of the Sangreal treasure describe it as being carried in four enormous trunks. In those trunks are reputed to be the *Purist Documents*—thousands of pages of unaltered, pre-Constantine documents, written by the early followers of Jesus, revering Him as a wholly human teacher and prophet. Also rumored to be part of the treasure is the legendary *"Q" Document*—a manuscript that even the Vatican admits they believe exists. Allegedly, it is a book of Jesus' teachings, possibly written in His own hand."

"Writings by Christ Himself?"

"Of course," Teabing said. "Why wouldn't Jesus have kept a chronicle of His ministry? Most people did in those days. Another explosive document believed to be in the treasure is a manuscript called *The Magdalene Diaries*—Mary Magdalene's personal account of her relationship with Christ, His crucifixion, and her time in France."

Sophie was silent for a long moment. "And these four chests of documents were the treasure that the Knights Templar found under Solomon's Temple?"

"Exactly. The documents that made the Knights so powerful. The documents that have been the object of countless Grail quests throughout history."

"But you said the Holy Grail was *Mary Magdalene*. If people are searching for documents, why would you call it a search for the Holy Grail?"

Teabing eyed her, his expression softening. "Because the hiding place of the Holy Grail includes a sarcophagus."

Outside, the wind howled in the trees.

Teabing spoke more quietly now. "The quest for the Holy Grail is literally the quest to kneel before the bones of Mary Magdalene. A journey to pray at the feet of the outcast one, the lost sacred feminine."

Sophie felt an unexpected wonder. "The hiding place of the Holy Grail is actually . . . a *tomb*?"

Teabing's hazel eyes got misty. "It is. A tomb containing the body of Mary Magdalene and the documents that tell the true story of her life. At its heart, the quest for the Holy Grail has always been a quest for the Magdalene—the wronged Queen, entombed with proof of her family's rightful claim to power."

Sophie waited a moment as Teabing gathered himself. So much about her grandfather was still not making sense. "Members of the Priory," she finally said, "all these years have answered the charge of protecting the Sangreal documents and the tomb of Mary Magdalene?"

"Yes, but the brotherhood had another, more important duty as well—to protect the *bloodline* itself. Christ's lineage was in perpetual danger. The early Church feared that if the lineage were permitted to grow, the secret of Jesus and Magdalene would eventually surface and challenge the fundamental Catholic doctrine—that of a divine Messiah who did not consort with women or engage in sexual union." He paused. "Nonetheless,

Christ's line grew quietly under cover in France until making a bold move in the fifth century, when it intermarried with French royal blood and created a lineage known as the Merovingian bloodline."

This news surprised Sophie. Merovingian was a term learned by every student in France. "The Merovingians founded Paris."

"Yes. That's one of the reasons the Grail legend is so rich in France. Many of the Vatican's Grail quests here were in fact stealth missions to erase members of the royal bloodline. Have you heard of King Dagobert?"

Sophie vaguely recalled the name from a grisly tale in history class. "Dagobert was a Merovingian king, wasn't he? Stabbed in the eye while sleeping?"

"Exactly. Assassinated by the Vatican in collusion with Pepin d'Heristal. Late seventh century. With Dagobert's murder, the Merovingian bloodline was almost exterminated. Fortunately, Dagobert's son, Sigisbert, secretly escaped the attack and carried on the lineage, which later included Godefroi de Bouillon—founder of the Priory of Sion."

"The same man," Langdon said, "who ordered the Knights Templar to recover the Sangreal documents from beneath Solomon's Temple and thus provide the Merovingians proof of their hereditary ties to Jesus Christ."

Teabing nodded, heaving a ponderous sigh. "The modern Priory of Sion has a momentous duty. Theirs is a threefold charge. The brotherhood must protect the Sangreal documents. They must protect the tomb of Mary Magdalene. And, of course, they must nurture and protect the bloodline of Christ—those few members of the royal Merovingian bloodline who have survived into modern times."

The words hung in the huge space, and Sophie felt an odd vibration, as if her bones were reverberating with some new kind of truth. *Descendants of Jesus who survived into modern times.* Her grandfather's voice again was whispering in her ear. *Princess, I must tell you the truth about your family.*

A chill raked her flesh.

*Royal blood.*

She could not imagine.

*Princess Sophie.*

"Sir Leigh?" The manservant's words crackled through the intercom on the wall, and Sophie jumped. "If you could join me in the kitchen a moment?"

Teabing scowled at the ill-timed intrusion. He went over to the intercom and pressed the button. "Rémy, as you know, I am busy with my guests. If we need anything else from the kitchen tonight, we will help ourselves. Thank you and good night."

"A word with you before I retire, sir. If you would."

Teabing grunted and pressed the button. "Make it quick, Rémy."

"It is a household matter, sir, hardly fare for guests to endure."

Teabing looked incredulous. "And it cannot wait until morning?"

"No, sir. My question won't take a minute."

Teabing rolled his eyes and looked at Langdon and Sophie. "Sometimes I wonder who is serving whom?" He pressed the button again. "I'll be right there, Rémy. Can I bring you anything when I come?"

"Only freedom from oppression, sir."

"Rémy, you realize your *steak au poivre* is the only reason you still work for me."

"So you tell me, sir. So you tell me."

# CHAPTER 61

*Princess Sophie.*

Sophie felt hollow as she listened to the clicking of Teabing's crutches fade down the hallway. Numb, she turned and faced Langdon in the deserted ballroom. He was already shaking his head as if reading her mind.

"No, Sophie," he whispered, his eyes reassuring. "The same thought crossed my mind when I realized your grandfather was in the Priory, and you said he wanted to tell you a secret about your family. But it's impossible." Langdon paused. "Saunière is not a Merovingian name."

Sophie wasn't sure whether to feel relieved or disappointed. Earlier, Langdon had asked an unusual passing question about Sophie's mother's maiden name. Chauvel. The question now made sense. "And Chauvel?" she asked, anxious.

Again he shook his head. "I'm sorry. I know that would have answered some questions for you. Only two direct lines of Merovingians remain. Their family names are Plantard and Saint-Clair. Both families live in hiding, probably protected by the Priory."

Sophie repeated the names silently in her mind and then shook her head. There was no one in her family named Plantard or Saint-Clair. A weary undertow was pulling at her now. She realized she was no closer than she had been at the Louvre to understanding what truth her grandfather had wanted to reveal to her. Sophie wished her grandfather had never mentioned her family this afternoon. He had torn open old wounds that felt as painful now as ever. *They are dead, Sophie. They are not coming back.* She thought of her mother singing her to sleep at night, of her father giving her rides on his shoulders, and of her grandmother and younger brother smiling at her with their fervent green eyes. All that was stolen. And all she had left was her grandfather.

*And now he is gone too. I am alone.*

Sophie turned quietly back to *The Last Supper* and gazed at Mary Magdalene's long red hair and quiet eyes. There was something in the woman's expression that echoed the loss of a loved one. Sophie could feel it too.

"Robert?" she said softly.

He stepped closer.

"I know Leigh said the Grail story is all around us, but tonight is the first time I've ever heard any of this."

Langdon looked as if he wanted to put a comforting hand on her shoulder, but he refrained. "You've heard her story before, Sophie. Everyone has. We just don't realize it when we hear it."

"I don't understand."

"The Grail story is everywhere, but it is hidden. When the Church outlawed speaking of the shunned Mary Magdalene, her story and importance had to be passed on through more discreet channels . . . channels that supported metaphor and symbolism."

"Of course. The arts."

Langdon motioned to *The Last Supper.* "A perfect example. Some of today's most enduring art, literature, and music secretly tell the history of Mary Magdalene and Jesus."

Langdon quickly told her about works by Da Vinci, Botticelli, Poussin, Bernini, Mozart, and Victor Hugo that all whispered of the quest to restore the banished sacred feminine. Enduring legends like Sir Gawain and the Green Knight, King Arthur, and Sleeping Beauty were Grail allegories. Victor Hugo's *Hunchback of Notre Dame* and Mozart's *Magic Flute* were filled with Masonic symbolism and Grail secrets.

"Once you open your eyes to the Holy Grail," Langdon said, "you see her everywhere. Paintings. Music. Books. Even in cartoons, theme parks, and popular movies."

Langdon held up his Mickey Mouse watch and told her that Walt Disney had made it his quiet life's work to pass on the Grail story to future generations. Throughout his entire life, Disney had been hailed as "the Modern-Day Leonardo da Vinci." Both men were generations ahead of their times, uniquely gifted artists, members of secret societies, and, most notably, avid pranksters. Like Leonardo, Walt Disney loved infusing hidden messages and symbolism in his art. For the trained symbologist, watching an early Disney movie was like being barraged by an avalanche of allusion and metaphor.

Most of Disney's hidden messages dealt with religion, pagan myth, and stories of the subjugated goddess. It was no mistake that Disney retold tales like *Cinderella, Sleeping Beauty,* and *Snow White*— all of which dealt with the incarceration of the sacred feminine. Nor did one need a background in symbolism to understand that Snow White—a princess who fell from grace after partaking of a poisoned apple—was a clear allusion to the downfall of Eve in the Garden of Eden. Or that *Sleeping Beauty*'s Princess Aurora—code-named "Rose" and hidden deep in the forest to protect her from the clutches of the evil witch—was the Grail story for children.

Despite its corporate image, Disney still had a savvy, playful element among its employees, and their artists still amused themselves by inserting hidden symbolism in Disney products. Langdon would never forget one of his students bringing in a DVD of *The Lion King* and pausing the film to reveal a freeze-frame in which the word SEX was clearly visible, spelled out by floating dust particles over Simba's head. Although Langdon suspected this was more of a cartoonist's sophomoric prank than any kind of enlightened allusion to pagan human sexuality, he had learned not to underestimate Disney's grasp of symbolism. *The Little Mermaid* was a spellbinding tapestry of spiritual symbols so specifically goddess-related that they could not be coincidence.

When Langdon had first seen *The Little Mermaid,* he had actually gasped aloud when he noticed that the painting in Ariel's underwater home was none other than seventeenth-century artist Georges de la Tour's *The Penitent Magdalene*—a famous homage to the banished Mary Magdalene—fitting decor considering the movie turned out to be a ninety-minute collage of blatant symbolic references to the lost sanctity of Isis, Eve, Pisces the fish goddess, and, repeatedly, Mary Magdalene. The Little Mermaid's name, Ariel, possessed powerful ties to the sacred feminine and, in the Book of Isaiah, was synonymous with "the Holy City besieged." Of course, the Little Mermaid's flowing red hair was certainly no coincidence either.

The clicking of Teabing's crutches approached in the hallway, his pace unusually brisk. When their host entered the study, his expression was stern.

"You'd better explain yourself, Robert," he said coldly. "You have not been honest with me."

# CHAPTER 62

**"I'm being** framed, Leigh," Langdon said, trying to stay calm. *You know me. I wouldn't kill anyone.*

Teabing's tone did not soften. "Robert, you're on television, for Christ's sake. Did you know you were wanted by the authorities?"

"Yes."

"Then you abused my trust. I'm astonished you would put me at risk by coming here and asking me to ramble on about the Grail so you could hide out in my home."

"I didn't kill anyone."

"Jacques Saunière is dead, and the police say you did it." Teabing looked saddened. "Such a contributor to the arts . . ."

"Sir?" The manservant had appeared now, standing behind Teabing in the study doorway, his arms crossed. "Shall I show them out?"

"Allow me." Teabing hobbled across the study, unlocked a set of wide glass doors, and swung them open onto a side lawn. "Please find your car, and leave."

Sophie did not move. "We have information about the *clef de voûte. The Priory keystone.*"

Teabing stared at her for several seconds and

scoffed derisively. "A desperate ploy. Robert knows how I've sought it."

"She's telling the truth," Langdon said. "That's why we came to you tonight. To talk to you about the keystone."

The manservant intervened now. "Leave, or I shall call the authorities."

"Leigh," Langdon whispered, "we know where it is."

Teabing's balance seemed to falter a bit.

Rémy now marched stiffly across the room. "Leave at once! Or I will forcibly—"

"Rémy!" Teabing spun, snapping at his servant. "Excuse us for a moment."

The servant's jaw dropped. "Sir? I must protest. These people are—"

"I'll handle this." Teabing pointed to the hallway.

After a moment of stunned silence, Rémy skulked out like a banished dog.

In the cool night breeze coming through the open doors, Teabing turned back to Sophie and Langdon, his expression still wary. "This better be good. What do you know of the keystone?"


In the thick brush outside Teabing's study, Silas clutched his pistol and gazed through the glass doors. Only moments ago, he had circled the house and seen Langdon and the woman talking in the large study. Before he could move in, a man on crutches entered, yelled at Langdon, threw open the doors, and demanded his guests leave. *Then the woman mentioned the keystone, and everything changed.* Shouts turned to whispers. Moods softened. And the glass doors were quickly closed.

Now, as he huddled in the shadows, Silas peered through the glass. *The keystone is somewhere inside the house.* Silas could feel it.

Staying in the shadows, he inched closer to the glass, eager to hear what was being said. He would give them five minutes. If they did not reveal where they had placed the keystone, Silas would have to enter and persuade them with force.

Inside the study, Langdon could sense their host's bewilderment.

"Grand Master?" Teabing choked, eyeing Sophie. "Jacques Saunière?"

Sophie nodded, seeing the shock in his eyes.

"But you could not possibly know that!"

"Jacques Saunière was my grandfather."

Teabing staggered back on his crutches, shooting a glance at Langdon, who nodded. Teabing turned back to Sophie. "Miss Neveu, I am speechless. If this is true, then I am truly sorry for your loss. I should admit, for my research, I have kept lists of men in Paris whom I thought might be good candidates for involvement in the Priory. Jacques Saunière was on that list along with many others. But Grand Master, you say? It's hard to fathom." Teabing was silent a moment and then shook his head. "But it still makes no sense. Even if your grandfather *were* the Priory Grand Master and created the keystone himself, he would *never* tell you how to find it. The keystone reveals the pathway to the brotherhood's ultimate treasure. Granddaughter or not, you are not eligible to receive such knowledge."

"Mr. Saunière was dying when he passed on the information," Langdon said. "He had limited options."

"He didn't *need* options," Teabing argued. "There exist three *sénéchaux* who also know the secret. That is the beauty of their system. One will rise to Grand Master and they will induct a new *sénéchal* and share the secret of the keystone."

"I guess you didn't see the entire news broadcast," Sophie said. "In addition to my grandfather, *three* other prominent Parisians were murdered today. All in similar ways. All looked like they had been interrogated."

Teabing's jaw fell. "And you think they were . . ."

"The *sénéchaux,*" Langdon said.

"But how? A murderer could not possibly learn the identities of *all* four top members of the

Priory of Sion! Look at *me,* I have been researching them for decades, and I can't even name *one*
Priory member. It seems inconceivable that all
three *sénéchaux* and the Grand Master could be
discovered and killed in one day."

"I doubt the information was gathered in a single day," Sophie said. "It sounds like a well-
planned *décapiter.* It's a technique we use to fight
organized crime syndicates. If DCPJ wants to
move on a certain group, they will silently listen
and watch for months, identify all the main players, and then move in and take them all at the
same moment. Decapitation. With no leadership,
the group falls into chaos and divulges other
information. It's possible someone patiently
watched the Priory and then attacked, hoping the
top people would reveal the location of the
keystone."

Teabing looked unconvinced. "But the brothers would never talk. They are sworn to secrecy.
Even in the face of death."

"Exactly," Langdon said. "Meaning, if they
never divulged the secret, *and* they were
killed . . ."

Teabing gasped. "Then the location of the keystone would be lost forever!"

"And with it," Langdon said, "the location of
the Holy Grail."

Teabing's body seemed to sway with the weight

of Langdon's words. Then, as if too tired to stand another moment, he flopped in a chair and stared out the window.

Sophie walked over, her voice soft. "Considering my grandfather's predicament, it seems possible that in total desperation he tried to pass the secret on to someone outside the brotherhood. Someone he thought he could trust. Someone in his family."

Teabing was pale. "But someone capable of such an attack . . . of discovering so much about the brotherhood . . ." He paused, radiating a new fear. "It could only be one force. This kind of infiltration could only have come from the Priory's oldest enemy."

Langdon glanced up. "The Church."

"Who else? Rome has been seeking the Grail for centuries."

Sophie was skeptical. "You think the *Church* killed my grandfather?"

Teabing replied, "It would not be the first time in history the Church has killed to protect itself. The documents that accompany the Holy Grail are explosive, and the Church has wanted to destroy them for years."

Langdon was having trouble buying Teabing's premise that the Church would blatantly murder people to obtain these documents. Having met the new Pope and many of the cardinals, Langdon knew they were deeply spiritual men who would never condone assassination. *Regardless of the stakes.*

Sophie seemed to be having similar thoughts. "Isn't it possible that these Priory members were murdered by someone *outside* the Church? Someone who didn't understand what the Grail really is? The Cup of Christ, after all, would be quite an enticing treasure. Certainly treasure hunters have killed for less."

"In my experience," Teabing said, "men go to far greater lengths to avoid what they fear than to obtain what they desire. I sense a desperation in this assault on the Priory."

"Leigh," Langdon said, "the argument is paradoxical. Why would members of the Catholic clergy *murder* Priory members in an effort to find and destroy documents they believe are false testimony anyway?"

Teabing chuckled. "The ivory towers of Harvard have made you soft, Robert. Yes, the clergy in Rome are blessed with potent faith, and because of this, their beliefs can weather any storm, including documents that contradict everything they hold dear. But what about the rest of the world? What about those who are not blessed with absolute certainty? What about those who look at the cruelty in the world and say, where is God today? Those who look at Church scandals and ask, who *are* these men who claim to speak the truth about Christ and yet lie to cover up the sexual abuse of children by their own priests?" Teabing paused. "What happens to *those* people, Robert, if persuasive scientific evidence comes out that the Church's version of the Christ story is inaccurate, and that the greatest story ever told is, in fact, the greatest story ever *sold.*"

Langdon did not respond.

"I'll tell you what happens if the documents get out," Teabing said. "The Vatican faces a crisis of faith unprecedented in its two-millennia history."

After a long silence, Sophie said, "But if it *is* the Church who is responsible for this attack, why would they act now? After all these years? The Priory keeps the Sangreal documents hidden. They pose no immediate threat to the Church."

Teabing heaved an ominous sigh and glanced at Langdon. "Robert, I assume you are familiar with the Priory's final charge?"

Langdon felt his breath catch at the thought. "I am."

"Miss Neveu," Teabing said, "the Church and the Priory have had a tacit understanding for years. That is, the Church does not attack the Priory, and the Priory keeps the Sangreal documents hidden." He paused. "However, part of the Priory history has always included a plan to unveil the secret. With the arrival of a specific date in history, the brotherhood plans to break the silence and carry out its ultimate triumph by unveiling the Sangreal documents to the world and shouting the true story of Jesus Christ from the mountaintops."

Sophie stared at Teabing in silence. Finally, she too sat down. "And you think that date is approaching? And the Church knows it?"

"A speculation," Teabing said, "but it would certainly provide the Church motivation for an all-out attack to find the documents before it was too late."

Langdon had the uneasy feeling that Teabing was making good sense. "Do you think the Church would actually be capable of uncovering hard evidence of the Priory's date?"

"Why not—if we're assuming the Church was able to uncover the identities of the Priory members, then certainly they could have learned of their plans. And even if they don't have the exact date, their superstitions may be getting the best of them."

"Superstitions?" Sophie asked.

"In terms of prophecy," Teabing said, "we are currently in an epoch of enormous change. The millennium has recently passed, and with it has ended the two-thousand-year-long astrological Age of Pisces—the fish, which is also the sign of Jesus. As any astrological symbologist will tell you, the Piscean ideal believes that man must be *told* what to do by higher powers because man is incapable of thinking for himself. Hence it has been a time of fervent religion. Now, however, we are entering the Age of Aquarius—the water bearer—whose ideals claim that man will learn the *truth* and be able to think for himself. The ideological shift is enormous, and it is occurring right now."

Langdon felt a shiver. Astrological prophecy never held much interest or credibility for him, but he knew there were those in the Church who followed it very closely. "The Church calls this transitional period the End of Days."

Sophie looked skeptical. "As in the end of the world? The Apocalypse?"

"No." Langdon replied. "That's a common misconception. Many religions speak of the End of Days. It refers not to the end of the world, but rather the end of our current age—Pisces, which began at the time of Christ's birth, spanned two thousand years, and waned with the passing of the millennium. Now that we've passed into the Age of Aquarius, the End of Days has arrived."

"Many Grail historians," Teabing added, "believe that *if* the Priory is indeed planning to release this truth, *this* point in history would be a symbolically apt time. Most Priory academics, myself included, anticipated the brotherhood's release would coincide precisely with the millennium. Obviously, it did not. Admittedly, the Roman calendar does not mesh perfectly with astrological markers, so there is some gray area in the prediction. Whether the Church now has inside information that an exact date is looming, or whether they are just getting nervous on account of astrological prophecy, I don't know. Anyway, it's immaterial. Either scenario explains how the Church might be motivated to launch a preemptive attack against the Priory." Teabing frowned. "And believe me, if the Church finds the Holy Grail, they will destroy it. The documents and the relics of the blessed Mary Magdalene as well." His eyes grew heavy. "Then, my dear, with the Sangreal documents gone, all evidence will be lost. The Church will have won their age-old war to rewrite history. The past will be erased forever."

Slowly, Sophie pulled the cruciform key from her sweater pocket and held it out to Teabing.

Teabing took the key and studied it. "My goodness. The Priory seal. Where did you get this?"

"My grandfather gave it to me tonight before he died."

Teabing ran his fingers across the cruciform. "A key to a church?"

She drew a deep breath. "This key provides access to the keystone."

Teabing's head snapped up, his face wild with disbelief. "Impossible! What church did I miss? I've searched every church in France!"

"It's not in a church," Sophie said. "It's in a Swiss depository bank."

Teabing's look of excitement waned. "The keystone is in a bank?"

"A vault," Langdon offered.

"A *bank* vault?" Teabing shook his head violently. "That's impossible. The keystone is supposed to be hidden beneath the sign of the Rose."

"It is," Langdon said. "It was stored in a rosewood box inlaid with a five-petal Rose."

Teabing looked thunderstruck. "You've *seen* the keystone?"

Sophie nodded. "We visited the bank."

Teabing came over to them, his eyes wild with fear. "My friends, we must do something. The keystone is in danger! We have a duty to protect it. What if there are other keys? Perhaps stolen from the murdered *sénéchaux*? If the Church can gain access to the bank as you have—"

"Then they will be too late," Sophie said. "We removed the keystone."

"What! You removed the keystone from its hiding place?"

"Don't worry," Langdon said. "The keystone is well hidden."

"*Extremely* well hidden, I hope!"

"Actually," Langdon said, unable to hide his grin, "that depends on how often you dust under your couch."

The wind outside Château Villette had picked up, and Silas's robe danced in the breeze as he crouched near the window. Although he had been unable to hear much of the conversation, the word *keystone* had sifted through the glass on numerous occasions.

*It is inside.*

The Teacher's words were fresh in his mind. *Enter Château Villette. Take the keystone. Hurt no one.*

Now, Langdon and the others had adjourned suddenly to another room, extinguishing the study lights as they went. Feeling like a panther stalking prey, Silas crept to the glass doors. Finding them unlocked, he slipped inside and closed the doors silently behind him. He could hear muffled voices from another room. Silas pulled the pistol from his pocket, turned off the safety, and inched down the hallway.

# CHAPTER 63

**Lieutenant Collet** stood alone at the foot of Leigh Teabing's driveway and gazed up at the massive house. *Isolated. Dark. Good ground cover.* Collet watched his half-dozen agents spreading silently out along the length of the fence. They could be over it and have the house surrounded in a matter of minutes. Langdon could not have chosen a more ideal spot for Collet's men to make a surprise assault.

Collet was about to call Fache himself when at last his phone rang.

Fache sounded not nearly as pleased with the developments as Collet would have imagined. "Why didn't someone tell me we had a lead on Langdon?"

"You were on a phone call and—"

"Where exactly are you, Lieutenant Collet?"

Collet gave him the address. "The estate belongs to a British national named Teabing. Langdon drove a fair distance to get here, and the vehicle is inside the security gate, with no signs of forced entry, so chances are good that Langdon knows the occupant."

"I'm coming out," Fache said. "Don't make a move. I'll handle this personally."

Collet's jaw dropped. "But Captain, you're twenty minutes away! We should act immediately. I have him staked out. I'm with eight men total. Four of us have field rifles and the others have sidearms."

"Wait for me."

"Captain, what if Langdon has a hostage in there? What if he sees us and decides to leave on foot? We need to move *now!* My men are in position and ready to go."

"Lieutenant Collet, you will wait for me to arrive before taking action. That is an order." Fache hung up.

Stunned, Lieutenant Collet switched off his phone. *Why the hell is Fache asking me to wait?* Collet knew the answer. Fache, though famous for his instinct, was notorious for his pride. *Fache wants credit for the arrest.* After putting the American's face all over the television, Fache wanted to be sure his own face got equal time. Collet's job was simply to hold down the fort until the boss showed up to save the day.

As he stood there, Collet flashed on a second possible explanation for this delay. *Damage control.* In law enforcement, hesitating to arrest a fugitive only occurred when uncertainty had arisen regarding the suspect's guilt. *Is Fache having second thoughts that Langdon is the right man?* The thought was frightening. Captain Fache had gone out on a limb tonight to arrest Robert Langdon—*surveil-*

*lance cachée,* Interpol, and now television. Not even the great Bezu Fache would survive the political fallout if he had mistakenly splashed a prominent American's face all over French television, claiming he was a murderer. If Fache now realized he'd made a mistake, then it made perfect sense that he would tell Collet not to make a move. The last thing Fache needed was for Collet to storm an innocent Brit's private estate and take Langdon at gunpoint.

Moreover, Collet realized, if Langdon were innocent, it explained one of this case's strangest paradoxes: Why had Sophie Neveu, the *granddaughter* of the victim, helped the alleged killer escape? Unless Sophie knew Langdon was falsely charged. Fache had posited all kinds of explanations tonight to explain Sophie's odd behavior, including that Sophie, as Saunière's sole heir, had persuaded her secret lover Robert Langdon to kill off Saunière for the inheritance money. Saunière, if he had suspected this, might have left the police the message *P.S. Find Robert Langdon.* Collet was fairly certain something else was going on here. Sophie Neveu seemed far too solid of character to be mixed up in something that sordid.

"Lieutenant?" One of the field agents came running over. "We found a car."

Collet followed the agent about fifty yards past the driveway. The agent pointed to a wide shoulder on the opposite side of the road. There, parked in the brush, almost out of sight, was a black Audi. It had rental plates. Collet felt the hood. Still warm. Hot even.

"That must be how Langdon got here," Collet said. "Call the rental company. Find out if it's stolen."

"Yes, sir."

Another agent waved Collet back over in the direction of the fence. "Lieutenant, have a look at this." He handed Collet a pair of night vision binoculars. "The grove of trees near the top of the driveway."

Collet aimed the binoculars up the hill and adjusted the image intensifier dials. Slowly, the greenish shapes came into focus. He located the curve of the driveway and slowly followed it up, reaching the grove of trees. All he could do was stare. There, shrouded in the greenery, was an armored truck. A truck identical to the one Collet had permitted to leave the Depository Bank of Zurich earlier tonight. He prayed this was some kind of bizarre coincidence, but he knew it could not be.

"It seems obvious," the agent said, "that this truck is how Langdon and Neveu got away from the bank."

Collet was speechless. He thought of the armored truck driver he had stopped at the roadblock. The Rolex. His impatience to leave. *I never checked the cargo hold.*

Incredulous, Collet realized that someone in the bank had actually lied to DCPJ about Langdon and Sophie's whereabouts and then helped them escape. *But who? And why?* Collet wondered if maybe *this* were the reason Fache had told him not to take action yet. Maybe Fache realized there were more people involved tonight than just Langdon and Sophie. *And if Langdon and Neveu arrived in the armored truck, then who drove the Audi?*

Hundreds of miles to the south, a chartered Beechcraft Baron 58 raced northward over the Tyrrhenian Sea. Despite calm skies, Bishop Aringarosa clutched an airsickness bag, certain he could be ill at any moment. His conversation with Paris had not at all been what he had imagined.

Alone in the small cabin, Aringarosa twisted the gold ring on his finger and tried to ease his overwhelming sense of fear and desperation. *Everything in Paris has gone terribly wrong.* Closing his eyes, Aringarosa said a prayer that Bezu Fache would have the means to fix it.

# CHAPTER 64

**Teabing sat** on the divan, cradling the wooden box on his lap and admiring the lid's intricate inlaid Rose. *Tonight has become the strangest and most magical night of my life.*

"Lift the lid," Sophie whispered, standing over him, beside Langdon.

Teabing smiled. *Do not rush me.* Having spent over a decade searching for this keystone, he wanted to savor every millisecond of this moment. He ran a palm across the wooden lid, feeling the texture of the inlaid flower.

"The Rose," he whispered. *The Rose is Magdalene is the Holy Grail. The Rose is the compass that guides the way.* Teabing felt foolish. For years he had traveled to cathedrals and churches all over France, paying for special access, examining hundreds of archways beneath rose windows, searching for an encrypted keystone. *La clef de voûte—a stone key beneath the sign of the Rose.*

Teabing slowly unlatched the lid and raised it.

As his eyes finally gazed upon the contents, he knew in an instant it could only be the keystone. He was staring at a stone cylinder, crafted of interconnecting lettered dials. The device seemed surprisingly familiar to him.

"Designed from Da Vinci's diaries," Sophie said. "My grandfather made them as a hobby."

*Of course,* Teabing realized. He had seen the sketches and blueprints. *The key to finding the Holy Grail lies inside this stone.* Teabing lifted the heavy cryptex from the box, holding it gently. Although he had no idea how to open the cylinder, he sensed his own destiny lay inside. In moments of failure, Teabing had questioned whether his life's quest would ever be rewarded. Now those doubts were gone forever. He could hear the ancient words . . . the foundation of the Grail legend:

*Vous ne trouvez pas le Saint-Graal, c'est le Saint-Graal qui vous trouve.*

*You do not find the Grail, the Grail finds you.*

And tonight, incredibly, the key to finding the Holy Grail had walked right through his front door.

While Sophie and Teabing sat with the cryptex and talked about the vinegar, the dials, and what the password might be, Langdon carried the rosewood box across the room to a well-lit table to get a better look at it. Something Teabing had just said was now running through Langdon's mind.

*The key to the Grail is hidden beneath the sign of the Rose.*

Langdon held the wooden box up to the light

and examined the inlaid symbol of the Rose. Although his familiarity with art did not include woodworking or inlaid furniture, he had just re-called the famous tiled ceiling of the Spanish monastery outside of Madrid, where, three cen-turies after its construction, the ceiling tiles began to fall out, revealing sacred texts scrawled by monks on the plaster beneath.

Langdon looked again at the Rose.

*Beneath the Rose.*

*Sub Rosa.*

*Secret.*

A bump in the hallway behind him made Langdon turn. He saw nothing but shadows. Teabing's manservant most likely had passed through. Langdon turned back to the box. He ran his finger over the smooth edge of the inlay, won-dering if he could pry the Rose out, but the craftsmanship was perfect. He doubted even a ra-zor blade could fit in between the inlaid Rose and the carefully carved depression into which it was seated.

Opening the box, he examined the inside of the lid. It was smooth. As he shifted its position, though, the light caught what appeared to be a small hole on the underside of the lid, positioned in the exact center. Langdon closed the lid and examined the inlaid symbol from the top. No hole.

*It doesn't pass through.*

Setting the box on the table, he looked around the room and spied a stack of papers with a paper clip on it. Borrowing the clip, he returned to the box, opened it, and studied the hole again. Carefully, he unbent the paper clip and inserted one end into the hole. He gave a gentle push. It took almost no effort. He heard something clatter quietly onto the table. Langdon closed the lid to look. It was a small piece of wood, like a puzzle piece. The wooden Rose had popped out of the lid and fallen onto the desk.

Speechless, Langdon stared at the bare spot on the lid where the Rose had been. There, engraved in the wood, written in an immaculate hand, were four lines of text in a language he had never seen.

*The characters look vaguely Semitic,* Langdon thought to himself, *and yet I don't recognize the language!*

A sudden movement behind him caught his attention. Out of nowhere, a crushing blow to the head knocked Langdon to his knees.

As he fell, he thought for a moment he saw a pale ghost hovering over him, clutching a gun. Then everything went black.

# CHAPTER 65

**Sophie Neveu,** despite working in law enforcement, had never found herself at gunpoint until tonight. Almost inconceivably, the gun into which she was now staring was clutched in the pale hand of an enormous albino with long white hair. He looked at her with red eyes that radiated a frightening, disembodied quality. Dressed in a wool robe with a rope tie, he resembled a medieval cleric. Sophie could not imagine who he was, and yet she was feeling a sudden newfound respect for Teabing's suspicions that the Church was behind this.

"You know what I have come for," the monk said, his voice hollow.

Sophie and Teabing were seated on the divan, arms raised as their attacker had commanded. Langdon lay groaning on the floor. The monk's eyes fell immediately to the keystone on Teabing's lap.

Teabing's tone was defiant. "You will not be able to open it."

"My Teacher is very wise," the monk replied, inching closer, the gun shifting between Teabing and Sophie.

Sophie wondered where Teabing's manservant was. *Didn't he hear Robert fall?*

"Who is your teacher?" Teabing asked. "Perhaps we can make a financial arrangement."

"The Grail is priceless." He moved closer.

"You're bleeding," Teabing noted calmly, nodding to the monk's right ankle where a trickle of blood had run down his leg. "And you're limping."

"As do you," the monk replied, motioning to the metal crutches propped beside Teabing. "Now, hand me the keystone."

"You know of the keystone?" Teabing said, sounding surprised.

"Never mind what I know. Stand up slowly, and give it to me."

"Standing is difficult for me."

"Precisely. I would prefer nobody attempt any quick moves."

Teabing slipped his right hand through one of his crutches and grasped the keystone in his left. Lurching to his feet, he stood erect, palming the heavy cylinder in his left hand, and leaning unsteadily on his crutch with his right.

The monk closed to within a few feet, keeping the gun aimed directly at Teabing's head. Sophie watched, feeling helpless as the monk reached out to take the cylinder.

"You will not succeed," Teabing said. "Only the worthy can unlock this stone."

———

*God alone judges the worthy,* Silas thought.

"It's quite heavy," the man on crutches said, his arm wavering now. "If you don't take it soon, I'm afraid I shall drop it!" He swayed perilously.

Silas stepped quickly forward to take the stone, and as he did, the man on crutches lost his balance. The crutch slid out from under him, and he began to topple sideways to his right. *No!* Silas lunged to save the stone, lowering his weapon in the process. But the keystone was moving away from him now. As the man fell to his right, his left hand swung backward, and the cylinder tumbled from his palm onto the couch. At the same instant, the metal crutch that had been sliding out from under the man seemed to accelerate, cutting a wide arc through the air toward Silas's leg.

Splinters of pain tore up Silas's body as the crutch made perfect contact with his *cilice,* crushing the barbs into his already raw flesh. Buckling, Silas crumpled to his knees, causing the belt to cut deeper still. The pistol discharged with a deafening roar, the bullet burying itself harmlessly in the floorboards as Silas fell. Before he could raise the gun and fire again, the woman's foot caught him square beneath the jaw.

At the bottom of the driveway, Collet heard the gunshot. The muffled pop sent panic through his veins. With Fache on the way, Collet had already relinquished any hopes of claiming personal credit for finding Langdon tonight. But Collet would be damned if Fache's ego landed him in front of a Ministerial Review Board for negligent police procedure.

*A weapon was discharged inside a private home! And you waited at the bottom of the driveway?*

Collet knew the opportunity for a stealth approach had long since passed. He also knew if he stood idly by for another second, his entire career would be history by morning. Eyeing the estate's iron gate, he made his decision.

"Tie on, and pull it down."

In the distant recesses of his groggy mind, Robert Langdon had heard the gunshot. He'd also heard a scream of pain. His own? A jackhammer was boring a hole into the back of his cranium. Somewhere nearby, people were talking.

"Where the devil were you?" Teabing was yelling.

The manservant hurried in. "What happened? Oh my God! Who is that? I'll call the police!"

"Bloody hell! Don't call the police. Make yourself useful and get us something with which to restrain this monster."

"And some ice!" Sophie called after him.

Langdon drifted out again. More voices. Movement. Now he was seated on the divan. Sophie was holding an ice pack to his head. His skull ached. As Langdon's vision finally began to clear, he found himself staring at a body on the floor. *Am I hallucinating?* The massive body of an albino monk lay bound and gagged with duct tape. His chin was split open, and the robe over his right thigh was soaked with blood. He too appeared to be just now coming to.

Langdon turned to Sophie. "Who is that? What . . . happened?"

Teabing hobbled over. "You were rescued by a knight brandishing an Excalibur made by Acme Orthopedic."

*Huh?* Langdon tried to sit up.

Sophie's touch was shaken but tender. "Just give yourself a minute, Robert."

"I fear," Teabing said, "that I've just demonstrated for your lady friend the unfortunate benefit of my condition. It seems everyone underestimates you."

From his seat on the divan, Langdon gazed down at the monk and tried to imagine what had happened.

"He was wearing a *cilice,*" Teabing explained.

"A what?"

Teabing pointed to a bloody strip of barbed leather that lay on the floor. "A Discipline belt. He wore it on his thigh. I took careful aim."

Langdon rubbed his head. He knew of Discipline belts. "But how . . . did you know?"

Teabing grinned. "Christianity is my field of study, Robert, and there are certain sects who wear their hearts on their sleeves." He pointed his crutch at the blood soaking through the monk's cloak. "As it were."

"Opus Dei," Langdon whispered, recalling recent media coverage of several prominent Boston businessmen who were members of Opus Dei. Apprehensive coworkers had falsely and publicly accused the men of wearing Discipline belts beneath their three-piece suits. In fact, the three men did no such thing. Like many members of Opus Dei, these businessmen were at the "supernumerary" stage and practiced no corporal mortification at all. They were devout Catholics, caring fathers to their children, and deeply dedicated members of the community. Not surprisingly, the media spotlighted their spiritual commitment only briefly before moving on to the shock value of the sect's more stringent "numerary" members . . . members like the monk now lying on the floor before Langdon.

Teabing was looking closely at the bloody belt. "But why would Opus Dei be trying to find the Holy Grail?"

Langdon was too groggy to consider it.

"Robert," Sophie said, walking to the wooden

box. "What's this?" She was holding the small Rose inlay he had removed from the lid.

"It covered an engraving on the box. I think the text might tell us how to open the keystone."

Before Sophie and Teabing could respond, a sea of blue police lights and sirens erupted at the bottom of the hill and began snaking up the half-mile driveway.

Teabing frowned. "My friends, it seems we have a decision to make. And we'd better make it fast."

# CHAPTER 66

**Collet and** his agents burst through the front door of Sir Leigh Teabing's estate with their guns drawn. Fanning out, they began searching all the rooms on the first level. They found a bullet hole in the drawing room floor, signs of a struggle, a small amount of blood, a strange, barbed leather belt, and a partially used roll of duct tape. The entire level seemed deserted.

Just as Collet was about to divide his men to search the basement and grounds behind the house, he heard voices on the level above them.

"They're upstairs!"

Rushing up the wide staircase, Collet and his men moved room by room through the huge home, securing darkened bedrooms and hallways as they closed in on the sounds of voices. The sound seemed to be coming from the last bedroom on an exceptionally long hallway. The agents inched down the corridor, sealing off alternate exits.

As they neared the final bedroom, Collet could see the door was wide open. The voices had stopped suddenly, and had been replaced by an odd rumbling, like an engine.

Sidearm raised, Collet gave the signal. Reaching silently around the door frame, he found the light switch and flicked it on. Spinning into the room with men pouring in after him, Collet shouted and aimed his weapon at . . . nothing.

An empty guest bedroom. Pristine.

The rumbling sounds of an automobile engine poured from a black electronic panel on the wall beside the bed. Collet had seen these elsewhere in the house. Some kind of intercom system. He raced over. The panel had about a dozen labeled buttons:

STUDY . . . KITCHEN . . . LAUNDRY . . . CELLAR . . .

*So where the hell do I hear a car?*

MASTER BEDROOM . . . SUN ROOM . . . BARN . . . LIBRARY . . .

*Barn!* Collet was downstairs in seconds, running toward the back door, grabbing one of his agents on the way. The men crossed the rear lawn and arrived breathless at the front of a weathered gray barn. Even before they entered, Collet could hear the fading sounds of a car engine. He drew his weapon, rushed in, and flicked on the lights.

The right side of the barn was a rudimentary workshop—lawnmowers, automotive tools, gardening supplies. A familiar intercom panel hung on the wall nearby. One of its buttons was flipped down, transmitting.

GUEST BEDROOM II.

Collet wheeled, anger brimming. *They lured us upstairs with the intercom!* Searching the other side of the barn, he found a long line of horse stalls. No horses. Apparently the owner preferred a different kind of horsepower; the stalls had been converted into an impressive automotive parking facility. The collection was astonishing—a black Ferrari, a pristine Rolls-Royce, an antique Astin Martin sports coupe, a vintage Porsche 356.

The last stall was empty.

Collet ran over and saw oil stains on the stall floor. *They can't get off the compound.* The driveway and gate were barricaded with two patrol cars to prevent this very situation.

"Sir?" The agent pointed down the length of the stalls.

The barn's rear slider was wide open, giving way to a dark, muddy slope of rugged fields that stretched out into the night behind the barn. Collet ran to the door, trying to see out into the darkness. All he could make out was the faint shadow of a forest in the distance. No headlights. This wooded valley was probably crisscrossed by dozens of unmapped fire roads and hunting trails, but Collet was confident his quarry would never make the woods. "Get some men spread out down there. They're probably already stuck somewhere nearby. These fancy sports cars can't handle terrain."

"Um, sir?" The agent pointed to a nearby pegboard on which hung several sets of keys. The labels above the keys bore familiar names.

DAIMLER . . . ROLLS-ROYCE . . . ASTIN MARTIN . . . PORSCHE . . .

The last peg was empty.

When Collet read the label above the empty peg, he knew he was in trouble.

# CHAPTER 67

**The Range** Rover was Java Black Pearl, four-wheel drive, standard transmission, with high-strength polypropylene lamps, rear light cluster fittings, and the steering wheel on the right.

Langdon was pleased he was not driving.

Teabing's manservant Rémy, on orders from his master, was doing an impressive job of maneuvering the vehicle across the moonlit fields behind Château Villette. With no headlights, he had crossed an open knoll and was now descending a long slope, moving farther away from the estate. He seemed to be heading toward a jagged silhouette of wooded land in the distance.

Langdon, cradling the keystone, turned in the passenger seat and eyed Teabing and Sophie in the back seat.

"How's your head, Robert?" Sophie asked, sounding concerned.

Langdon forced a pained smile. "Better, thanks." It was killing him.

Beside her, Teabing glanced over his shoulder at the bound and gagged monk lying in the cramped luggage area behind the back seat. Teabing had the monk's gun on his lap and looked like an old photo of a British safari chap posing over his kill.

"So glad you popped in this evening, Robert," Teabing said, grinning as if he were having fun for the first time in years.

"Sorry to get you involved in this, Leigh."

"Oh, please, I've waited my entire life to be involved." Teabing looked past Langdon out the windshield at the shadow of a long hedgerow. He tapped Rémy on the shoulder from behind. "Remember, no brake lights. Use the emergency brake if you need it. I want to get into the woods a bit. No reason to risk them seeing us from the house."

Rémy coasted to a crawl and guided the Range Rover through an opening in the hedge. As the vehicle lurched onto an overgrown pathway, almost immediately the trees overhead blotted out the moonlight.

*I can't see a thing,* Langdon thought, straining to distinguish any shapes at all in front of them. It was pitch black. Branches rubbed against the left side of the vehicle, and Rémy corrected in the other direction. Keeping the wheel more or less straight now, he inched ahead about thirty yards.

"You're doing beautifully, Rémy," Teabing said. "That should be far enough. Robert, if you could press that little blue button just below the vent there. See it?"

Langdon found the button and pressed it.

A muted yellow glow fanned out across the path in front of them, revealing thick underbrush on either side of the pathway. *Fog lights,* Langdon realized. They gave off just enough light to keep them on the path, and yet they were deep enough into the woods now that the lights would not give them away.

"Well, Rémy," Teabing chimed happily. "The lights are on. Our lives are in your hands."

"Where are we going?" Sophie asked.

"This trail continues about three kilometers into the forest," Teabing said. "Cutting across the estate and then arching north. Provided we don't hit any standing water or fallen trees, we shall emerge unscathed on the shoulder of highway five."

*Unscathed.* Langdon's head begged to differ. He turned his eyes down to his own lap, where the keystone was safely stowed in its wooden box. The inlaid Rose on the lid was back in place, and although his head felt muddled, Langdon was eager to remove the inlay again and examine the engraving beneath more closely. He unlatched the lid and began to raise it when Teabing laid a hand on his shoulder from behind.

"Patience, Robert," Teabing said. "It's bumpy and dark. God save us if we break anything. If you didn't recognize the language in the light, you won't do any better in the dark. Let's focus on getting away in one piece, shall we? There will be time for that very soon."

Langdon knew Teabing was right. With a nod, he relatched the box.

The monk in back was moaning now, struggling against his trusses. Suddenly, he began kicking wildly.

Teabing spun around and aimed the pistol over the seat. "I can't imagine your complaint, sir. You trespassed in my home and planted a nasty welt on the skull of a dear friend. I would be well within my rights to shoot you right now and leave you to rot in the woods."

The monk fell silent.

"Are you sure we should have brought him?" Langdon asked.

"Bloody well positive!" Teabing exclaimed. "You're wanted for murder, Robert. This scoundrel is your ticket to freedom. The police apparently want you badly enough to have tailed you to my home."

"My fault," Sophie said. "The armored car probably had a transmitter."

"Not the point," Teabing said. "I'm not surprised the *police* found you, but I *am* surprised that this Opus Dei character found you. From all you've told me, I can't imagine how this man could have tailed you to my home unless he had a contact either within the Judicial Police or within the Zurich Depository."

Langdon considered it. Bezu Fache certainly seemed intent on finding a scapegoat for tonight's murders. And Vernet had turned on them rather suddenly, although considering Langdon was being charged with four murders, the banker's change of heart seemed understandable.

"This monk is not working alone, Robert," Teabing said, "and until you learn *who* is behind all this, you both are in danger. The good news, my friend, is that you are now in the position of power. This monster behind me holds that information, and whoever is pulling his strings has got to be quite nervous right now."

Rémy was picking up speed, getting comfortable with the trail. They splashed through some water, climbed a small rise, and began descending again.

"Robert, could you be so kind as to hand me that phone?" Teabing pointed to the car phone on the dash. Langdon handed it back, and Teabing dialed a number. He waited for a very long time before someone answered. "Richard? Did I wake you? Of course, I did. Silly question. I'm sorry. I have a small problem. I'm feeling a bit off. Rémy and I need to pop up to the Isles for my treatments. Well, right away, actually. Sorry for the short notice. Can you have Elizabeth ready in about twenty minutes? I know, do the best you can. See you shortly." He hung up.

"Elizabeth?" Langdon said.

"My plane. She cost me a Queen's ransom."

Langdon turned full around and looked at him.

"What?" Teabing demanded. "You two can't expect to stay in France with the entire Judicial Police after you. London will be much safer."

Sophie had turned to Teabing as well. "You think we should leave the country?"

"My friends, I am far more influential in the civilized world than here in France. Furthermore, the Grail is believed to be in Great Britain. If we unlock the keystone, I am certain we will discover a map that indicates we have moved in the proper direction."

"You're running a big risk," Sophie said, "by helping us. You won't make any friends with the French police."

Teabing gave a wave of disgust. "I am finished with France. I moved here to find the keystone. That work is now done. I shan't care if I ever again see Château Villette."

Sophie sounded uncertain. "How will we get through airport security?"

Teabing chuckled. "I fly from Le Bourget—an executive airfield not far from here. French doctors make me nervous, so every fortnight, I fly north to take my treatments in England. I pay for certain special privileges at both ends. Once we're airborne, you can make a decision as to whether or not you'd like someone from the U.S. Embassy to meet us."

Langdon suddenly didn't want anything to do

with the embassy. All he could think of was the keystone, the inscription, and whether it would all lead to the Grail. He wondered if Teabing was right about Britain. Admittedly most modern legends placed the Grail somewhere in the United Kingdom. Even King Arthur's mythical, Grail-rich Isle of Avalon was now believed to be none other than Glastonbury, England. Wherever the Grail lay, Langdon never imagined he would actually be looking for it. *The Sangreal documents. The true history of Jesus Christ. The tomb of Mary Magdalene.* He suddenly felt as if he were living in some kind of limbo tonight . . . a bubble where the real world could not reach him.

"Sir?" Rémy said. "Are you truly thinking of returning to England for good?"

"Rémy, you needn't worry," Teabing assured. "Just because I am returning to the Queen's realm does not mean I intend to subject my palate to bangers and mash for the rest of my days. I expect you will join me there permanently. I'm planning to buy a splendid villa in Devonshire, and we'll have all your things shipped up immediately. An adventure, Rémy. I say, an adventure!"

Langdon had to smile. As Teabing railed on about his plans for a triumphant return to Britain, Langdon felt himself caught up in the man's infectious enthusiasm.

Gazing absently out the window, Langdon

watched the woods passing by, ghostly pale in the yellow blush of the fog lights. The side mirror was tipped inward, brushed askew by branches, and Langdon saw the reflection of Sophie sitting quietly in the back seat. He watched her for a long while and felt an unexpected upwelling of contentment. Despite his troubles tonight, Langdon was thankful to have landed in such good company.

After several minutes, as if suddenly sensing his eyes on her, Sophie leaned forward and put her hands on his shoulders, giving him a quick rub. "You okay?"

"Yeah," Langdon said. "Somehow."

Sophie sat back in her seat, and Langdon saw a quiet smile cross her lips. He realized that he too was now grinning.

Wedged in the back of the Range Rover, Silas could barely breathe. His arms were wrenched backward and heavily lashed to his ankles with kitchen twine and duct tape. Every bump in the road sent pain shooting through his twisted shoulders. At least his captors had removed the *cilice*. Unable to inhale through the strip of tape over his mouth, he could only breathe through his nostrils, which were slowly clogging up due to the dusty rear cargo area into which he had been crammed. He began coughing.

"I think he's choking," the French driver said, sounding concerned.

The British man who had struck Silas with his crutch now turned and peered over the seat, frowning coldly at Silas. "Fortunately for you, we British judge man's civility not by his compassion for his friends, but by his compassion for his enemies." The Brit reached down and grabbed the duct tape on Silas's mouth. In one fast motion, he tore it off.

Silas felt as if his lips had just caught fire, but the air pouring into his lungs was sent from God.

"Whom do you work for?" the British man demanded.

"I do the work of God," Silas spat back through the pain in his jaw where the woman had kicked him.

"You belong to Opus Dei," the man said. It was not a question.

"You know nothing of who I am."

"Why does Opus Dei want the keystone?"

Silas had no intention of answering. The keystone was the link to the Holy Grail, and the Holy Grail was the key to protecting the faith.

*I do the work of God. The Way is in peril.*

Now, in the Range Rover, struggling against his bonds, Silas feared he had failed the Teacher and the bishop forever. He had no way even to contact them and tell them the terrible turn of events. *My captors have the keystone! They will reach the Grail before we do!* In the stifling darkness, Silas prayed. He let the pain of his body fuel his supplications.

*A miracle, Lord. I need a miracle.* Silas had no way of knowing that hours from now, he would get one.

"Robert?" Sophie was still watching him. "A funny look just crossed your face."

Langdon glanced back at her, realizing his jaw was firmly set and his heart was racing. An incredible notion had just occurred to him. *Could it really be that simple an explanation?* "I need to use your cell phone, Sophie."

"Now?"

"I think I just figured something out."

"What?"

"I'll tell you in a minute. I need your phone."

Sophie looked wary. "I doubt Fache is tracing, but keep it under a minute just in case." She gave him her phone.

"How do I dial the States?"

"You need to reverse the charges. My service doesn't cover transatlantic."

Langdon dialed zero, knowing that the next sixty seconds might answer a question that had been puzzling him all night.

# CHAPTER 68

**New York** editor Jonas Faukman had just climbed into bed for the night when the telephone rang. *A little late for callers,* he grumbled, picking up the receiver.

An operator's voice asked him, "Will you accept charges for a collect call from Robert Langdon?"

Puzzled, Jonas turned on the light. "Uh . . . sure, okay."

The line clicked. "Jonas?"

"Robert? You wake me up *and* you charge me for it?"

"Jonas, forgive me," Langdon said. "I'll keep this very short. I really need to know. The manuscript I gave you. Have you—"

"Robert, I'm sorry, I know I said I'd send the edits out to you this week, but I'm swamped. Next Monday. I promise."

"I'm not worried about the edits. I need to know if you sent any copies out for blurbs without telling me?"

Faukman hesitated. Langdon's newest manuscript—an exploration of the history of goddess worship—included several sections about Mary Magdalene that were going to raise some eyebrows. Although the material was well documented and had been covered by others, Faukman had no intention of printing Advance Reading Copies of Langdon's book without at least a few endorsements from serious historians and art luminaries. Jonas had chosen ten big names in the art world and sent them all sections of the manuscript along with a polite letter asking if they would be willing to write a short endorsement for the jacket. In Faukman's experience, most people jumped at the opportunity to see their name in print.

"Jonas?" Langdon pressed. "You sent out my manuscript, didn't you?"

Faukman frowned, sensing Langdon was not happy about it. "The manuscript was clean, Robert, and I wanted to surprise you with some terrific blurbs."

A pause. "Did you send one to the curator of the Paris Louvre?"

"What do you think? Your manuscript referenced his Louvre collection several times, his books are in your bibliography, and the guy has some serious clout for foreign sales. Saunière was a no-brainer."

The silence on the other end lasted a long time. "When did you send it?"

"About a month ago. I also mentioned you would be in Paris soon and suggested you two chat. Did he ever call you to meet?" Faukman paused, rubbing his eyes. "Hold on, aren't you supposed to *be* in Paris this week?"

"I *am* in Paris."

Faukman sat upright. "You called me collect from *Paris?*"

"Take it out of my royalties, Jonas. Did you ever hear back from Saunière? Did he like the manuscript?"

"I don't know. I haven't yet heard from him."

"Well, don't hold your breath. I've got to run, but this explains a lot. Thanks."

"Robert—"

But Langdon was gone.

Faukman hung up the phone, shaking his head in disbelief. *Authors,* he thought. *Even the sane ones are nuts.*

Inside the Range Rover, Leigh Teabing let out a guffaw. "Robert, you're saying you wrote a manuscript that delves into a secret society, and your editor *sent* a copy to that secret society?"

Langdon slumped. "Evidently."

"A cruel coincidence, my friend."

*Coincidence has nothing to do with it,* Langdon knew. Asking Jacques Saunière to endorse a manuscript on goddess worship was as obvious as asking Tiger Woods to endorse a book on golf. Moreover, it was virtually guaranteed that any book on goddess worship would have to mention the Priory of Sion.

"Here's the million-dollar question," Teabing said, still chuckling. "Was your position on the Priory favorable or unfavorable?"

Langdon could hear Teabing's true meaning loud and clear. Many historians questioned why the Priory was still keeping the Sangreal documents hidden. Some felt the information should have been shared with the world long ago. "I took no position on the Priory's actions."

"You mean lack thereof."

Langdon shrugged. Teabing was apparently on the side of making the documents public. "I simply provided history on the brotherhood and described them as a modern goddess worship society, keepers of the Grail, and guardians of ancient documents."

Sophie looked at him. "Did you mention the keystone?"

Langdon winced. He had. Numerous times. "I talked about the supposed keystone as an example of the lengths to which the Priory would go to protect the Sangreal documents."

Sophie looked amazed. "I guess that explains *P.S. Find Robert Langdon.*"

Langdon sensed it was actually something *else* in the manuscript that had piqued Saunière's interest, but that topic was something he would discuss with Sophie when they were alone.

"So," Sophie said, "you lied to Captain Fache."

"What?" Langdon demanded.

"You told him you had never corresponded with my grandfather."

"I didn't! My editor sent him a manuscript."

"Think about it, Robert. If Captain Fache didn't find the envelope in which your editor sent the manuscript, he would have to conclude that *you* sent it." She paused. "Or worse, that you hand-delivered it and lied about it."

When the Range Rover arrived at Le Bourget Airfield, Rémy drove to a small hangar at the far end of the airstrip. As they approached, a tousled man in wrinkled khakis hurried from the hangar, waved, and slid open the enormous corrugated metal door to reveal a sleek white jet within.

Langdon stared at the glistening fuselage. "*That's* Elizabeth?"

Teabing grinned. "Beats the bloody Chunnel."

The man in khakis hurried toward them, squinting into the headlights. "Almost ready, sir," he called in a British accent. "My apologies for the delay, but you took me by surprise and—" He stopped short as the group unloaded. He looked at Sophie and Langdon, and then Teabing.

Teabing said, "My associates and I have urgent business in London. We've no time to waste. Please prepare to depart immediately." As he spoke, Teabing took the pistol out of the vehicle and handed it to Langdon.

The pilot's eyes bulged at the sight of the weapon. He walked over to Teabing and whispered, "Sir, my humble apologies, but my diplomatic flight allowance provides only for you and your manservant. I cannot take your guests."

"Richard," Teabing said, smiling warmly, "two thousand pounds sterling and that loaded gun say you *can* take my guests." He motioned to the Range Rover. "And the unfortunate fellow in the back."

# CHAPTER 69

**The Hawker** 731's twin Garrett TFE-731 engines thundered, powering the plane skyward with gut-wrenching force. Outside the window, Le Bourget Airfield dropped away with startling speed.

*I'm fleeing the country,* Sophie thought, her body forced back into the leather seat. Until this moment, she had believed her game of cat and mouse with Fache would be somehow justifiable to the Ministry of Defense. *I was attempting to protect an innocent man. I was trying to fulfill my grandfather's dying wishes.* That window of opportunity, Sophie knew, had just closed. She was leaving the country, without documentation, accompanying a wanted man, and transporting a bound hostage. If a "line of reason" had ever existed, she had just crossed it. *At almost the speed of sound.*

Sophie was seated with Langdon and Teabing near the front of the cabin—the *Fan Jet Executive Elite Design*, according to the gold medallion on the door. Their plush swivel chairs were bolted to tracks on the floor and could be repositioned and locked around a rectangular hardwood table. A mini-boardroom. The dignified surroundings, however, did little to camouflage the less than dignified state of affairs in the rear of the plane where, in a separate seating area near the rest room, Teabing's manservant Rémy sat with the pistol in hand, begrudgingly carrying out Teabing's orders to stand guard over the bloody monk who lay trussed at his feet like a piece of luggage.

"Before we turn our attention to the keystone," Teabing said, "I was wondering if you would permit me a few words." He sounded apprehensive, like a father about to give the birds-and-the-bees lecture to his children. "My friends, I realize I am but a guest on this journey, and I am honored as such. And yet, as someone who has spent his life in search of the Grail, I feel it is my duty to warn you that you are about to step onto a path from which there is no return, regardless of the dangers involved." He turned to Sophie. "Miss Neveu, your grandfather gave you this cryptex in hopes you would keep the secret of the Holy Grail alive."

"Yes."

"Understandably, you feel obliged to follow the trail wherever it leads."

Sophie nodded, although she felt a second motivation still burning within her. *The truth about my family.* Despite Langdon's assurances that the keystone had nothing to do with her past, Sophie still sensed something deeply personal entwined within this mystery, as if this cryptex, forged by her grandfather's own hands, were trying to speak to her and offer some kind of resolution to the emptiness that had haunted her all these years.

"Your grandfather and three others died tonight," Teabing continued, "and they did so to keep this keystone away from the Church. Opus Dei came within inches tonight of possessing it. You understand, I hope, that this puts you in a position of exceptional responsibility. You have been handed a torch. A two-thousand-year-old flame that cannot be allowed to go out. This torch cannot fall into the wrong hands." He paused, glancing at the rosewood box. "I realize you have been given no choice in this matter, Miss Neveu, but considering what is at stake here, you must either fully embrace this responsibility . . . or you must pass that responsibility to someone else."

"My grandfather gave the cryptex to me. I'm sure he thought I could handle the responsibility."

Teabing looked encouraged but unconvinced. "Good. A strong will is necessary. And yet, I am curious if you understand that successfully unlocking the keystone will bring with it a far greater trial."

"How so?"

"My dear, imagine that you are suddenly holding a map that reveals the location of the Holy Grail. In that moment, you will be in possession of a truth capable of altering history forever. You will be the keeper of a truth that man has sought for centuries. You will be faced with the responsibility of revealing that truth to the world. The individual who does so will be revered by many and despised by many. The question is whether you will have the necessary strength to carry out that task."

Sophie paused. "I'm not sure that is *my* decision to make."

Teabing's eyebrows arched. "No? If not the possessor of the keystone, then who?"

"The brotherhood who has successfully protected the secret for so long."

"The Priory?" Teabing looked skeptical. "But how? The brotherhood was shattered tonight. *Decapitated,* as you so aptly put it. Whether they were infiltrated by some kind of eavesdropping or by a spy within their ranks, we will never know, but the fact remains that someone got to them and uncovered the identities of their four top members. I would not trust anyone who stepped forward from the brotherhood at this point."

"So what do you suggest?" Langdon asked.

"Robert, you know as well as I do that the Priory has not protected the truth all these years to have it gather dust until eternity. They have been waiting for the right moment in history to share their secret. A time when the world is ready to handle the truth."

"And you believe that moment has arrived?" Langdon asked.

"Absolutely. It could not be more obvious. All the historical signs are in place, and if the Priory did not intend to make their secret known very soon, why has the Church now attacked?"

Sophie argued, "The monk has not yet told us his purpose."

"The monk's purpose is the Church's purpose," Teabing replied, "to destroy the documents that reveal the great deception. The Church came closer tonight than they have ever come, and the Priory has put its trust in you, Miss Neveu. The task of saving the Holy Grail clearly includes carrying out the Priory's final wishes of sharing the truth with the world."

Langdon intervened. "Leigh, asking Sophie to make that decision is quite a load to drop on someone who only an hour ago learned the Sangreal documents exist."

Teabing sighed. "I apologize if I am pressing, Miss Neveu. Clearly I have always believed these documents should be made public, but in the end the decision belongs to you. I simply feel it is important that you begin to think about what happens should we succeed in opening the keystone."

"Gentlemen," Sophie said, her voice firm. "To quote your words, 'You do not find the Grail, the Grail finds you.' I am going to trust that the Grail has found me for a reason, and when the time comes, I will know what to do."

Both of them looked startled.

"So then," she said, motioning to the rosewood box. "Let's move on."

# CHAPTER 70

**Standing in** the drawing room of Château Villette, Lieutenant Collet watched the dying fire and felt despondent. Captain Fache had arrived moments earlier and was now in the next room, yelling into the phone, trying to coordinate the failed attempt to locate the missing Range Rover.

*It could be anywhere by now,* Collet thought.

Having disobeyed Fache's direct orders and lost Langdon for a second time, Collet was grateful that PTS had located a bullet hole in the floor, which at least corroborated Collet's claims that a shot had been fired. Still, Fache's mood was sour, and Collet sensed there would be dire repercussions when the dust settled.

Unfortunately, the clues they were turning up here seemed to shed no light at all on what was going on or who was involved. The black Audi outside had been rented in a false name with false credit card numbers, and the prints in the car matched nothing in the Interpol database.

Another agent hurried into the living room, his eyes urgent. "Where's Captain Fache?"

Collet barely looked up from the burning embers. "He's on the phone."

"I'm off the phone," Fache snapped, stalking into the room. "What have you got?"

The second agent said, "Sir, Central just heard from André Vernet at the Depository Bank of Zurich. He wants to talk to you privately. He is changing his story."

"Oh?" Fache said.

Now Collet looked up.

"Vernet is admitting that Langdon and Neveu spent time inside his bank tonight."

"We figured that out," Fache said. "Why did Vernet lie about it?"

"He said he'll talk only to you, but he's agreed to cooperate fully."

"In exchange for what?"

"For our keeping his bank's name out of the news and also for helping him recover some stolen property. It sounds like Langdon and Neveu stole something from Saunière's account."

"What?" Collet blurted. "How?"

Fache never flinched, his eyes riveted on the second agent. "What did they steal?"

"Vernet didn't elaborate, but he sounds like he's willing to do anything to get it back."

Collet tried to imagine how this could happen. Maybe Langdon and Neveu had held a bank employee at gunpoint? Maybe they forced Vernet to open Saunière's account and facilitate an escape in the armored truck. As feasible as it was, Collet was having trouble believing Sophie Neveu could be involved in anything like that.

From the kitchen, another agent yelled to Fache. "Captain? I'm going through Mr. Teabing's speed dial numbers, and I'm on the phone with Le Bourget Airfield. I've got some bad news."

Thirty seconds later, Fache was packing up and preparing to leave Château Villette. He had just learned that Teabing kept a private jet nearby at Le Bourget Airfield and that the plane had taken off about a half hour ago.

The Bourget representative on the phone had claimed not to know who was on the plane or where it was headed. The takeoff had been unscheduled, and no flight plan had been logged. Highly illegal, even for a small airfield. Fache was certain that by applying the right pressure, he could get the answers he was looking for.

"Lieutenant Collet," Fache barked, heading for the door. "I have no choice but to leave you in charge of the PTS investigation here. Try to do something right for a change."

# CHAPTER 71

**As the** Hawker leveled off, with its nose aimed for England, Langdon carefully lifted the rosewood box from his lap, where he had been protecting it during takeoff. Now, as he set the box on the table, he could sense Sophie and Teabing leaning forward with anticipation.

Unlatching the lid and opening the box, Langdon turned his attention not to the lettered dials of the cryptex, but rather to the tiny hole on the underside of the box lid. Using the tip of a pen, he carefully removed the inlaid Rose on top and revealed the text beneath it. *Sub Rosa,* he mused, hoping a fresh look at the text would bring clarity. Focusing all his energies, Langdon studied the strange text.

After several seconds, he began to feel the initial frustration resurfacing. "Leigh, I just can't seem to place it."

From where Sophie was seated across the table, she could not yet see the text, but Langdon's inability to immediately identify the language surprised her. *My grandfather spoke a language so obscure that even a symbologist can't identify it?* She quickly realized she should not find this surprising. This would not be the first secret Jacques Saunière had kept from his granddaughter.

Opposite Sophie, Leigh Teabing felt ready to burst. Eager for his chance to see the text, he quivered with excitement, leaning in, trying to see around Langdon, who was still hunched over the box.

"I don't know," Langdon whispered intently. "My first guess is a Semitic, but now I'm not so sure. Most primary Semitics include *nekkudot*. This has none."

"Probably ancient," Teabing offered.

*"Nekkudot?"* Sophie inquired.

Teabing never took his eyes from the box. "Most modern Semitic alphabets have no vowels and use *nekkudot*—tiny dots and dashes written either below or within the consonants—to indicate what vowel sound accompanies them. Historically speaking, *nekkudot* are a relatively modern addition to language."

Langdon was still hovering over the script. "A Sephardic transliteration, perhaps . . . ?"

Teabing could bear it no longer. "Perhaps if I just . . ." Reaching over, he edged the box away from Langdon and pulled it toward himself. No doubt Langdon had a solid familiarity with the standard ancients—Greek, Latin, the Romances—but from the fleeting glance Teabing had of *this* language, he thought it looked more specialized, possibly a Rashi script or a STA"M with crowns.

Taking a deep breath, Teabing feasted his eyes upon the engraving. He said nothing for a very long time. With each passing second, Teabing felt his confidence deflating. "I'm astonished," he said. "This language looks like nothing I've ever seen!"

Langdon slumped.

"Might I see it?" Sophie asked.

Teabing pretended not to hear her. "Robert, you said earlier that you thought you'd *seen* something like this before?"

Langdon looked vexed. "I thought so. I'm not sure. The script looks familiar somehow."

"Leigh?" Sophie repeated, clearly not appreciating being left out of the discussion. "Might I have a look at the box my grandfather made?"

"Of course, dear," Teabing said, pushing it over to her. He hadn't meant to sound belittling, and yet Sophie Neveu was light-years out of her league. If a British Royal Historian and a Harvard symbologist could not even identify the language—

"Aah," Sophie said, seconds after examining the box. "I should have guessed."

Teabing and Langdon turned in unison, staring at her.

"Guessed *what?*" Teabing demanded.

Sophie shrugged. "Guessed that *this* would be the language my grandfather would have used."

"You're saying you can *read* this text?" Teabing exclaimed.

"Quite easily," Sophie chimed, obviously enjoying herself now. "My grandfather taught me this language when I was only six years old. I'm fluent." She leaned across the table and fixed Teabing with an admonishing glare. "And frankly, sir, considering your allegiance to the Crown, I'm a little surprised you didn't recognize it."

In a flash, Langdon knew.

*No wonder the script looks so damned familiar!*

Several years ago, Langdon had attended an event at Harvard's Fogg Museum. Harvard dropout Bill Gates had returned to his alma mater to lend to the museum one of his priceless acquisitions—eighteen sheets of paper he had recently purchased at auction from the Armand Hammer Estate.

His winning bid—a cool $30.8 million.

The author of the pages—Leonardo da Vinci.

The eighteen folios—now known as Leonardo's *Codex Leicester* after their famous owner, the Earl of Leicester—were all that remained of one of Leonardo's most fascinating notebooks: essays and drawings outlining Da Vinci's progressive theories on astronomy, geology, archaeology, and hydrology.

Langdon would never forget his reaction after waiting in line and finally viewing the priceless parchment. Utter letdown. The pages were unintelligible. Despite being beautifully preserved and written in an impeccably neat penmanship—crimson ink on cream paper—the codex looked like gibberish. At first Langdon thought he could not read them because Da Vinci wrote his notebooks in an archaic Italian. But after studying them more closely, he realized he could not identify a single Italian word, or even one letter.

"Try this, sir," whispered the female docent at the display case. She motioned to a hand mirror affixed to the display on a chain. Langdon picked it up and examined the text in the mirror's surface.

Instantly it was clear.

Langdon had been so eager to peruse some of the great thinker's ideas that he had forgotten one of the man's numerous artistic talents was an ability to write in a mirrored script that was virtually illegible to anyone other than himself. Historians still debated whether Da Vinci wrote this way simply to amuse himself or to keep people from peering over his shoulder and stealing his ideas, but the point was moot. Da Vinci did as he pleased.

Sophie smiled inwardly to see that Robert understood her meaning. "I can read the first few words," she said. "It's English."

Teabing was still sputtering. "What's going on?"

"Reverse text," Langdon said. "We need a mirror."

"No we don't," Sophie said. "I bet this veneer is thin enough." She lifted the rosewood box up to a canister light on the wall and began examining the underside of the lid. Her grandfather couldn't actually write in reverse, so he always cheated by writing *normally* and then flipping the paper over and tracing the reversed impression. Sophie's guess was that he had wood-burned *normal* text into a block of wood and then run the back of the block through a sander until the wood was paper thin and the wood-burning could be seen *through* the wood. Then he'd simply flipped the piece over, and laid it in.

As Sophie moved the lid closer to the light, she

saw she was right. The bright beam sifted through the thin layer of wood, and the script appeared in reverse on the underside of the lid.

Instantly legible.

"English," Teabing croaked, hanging his head in shame. "My native tongue."

At the rear of the plane, Rémy Legaludec strained to hear beyond the rumbling engines, but the conversation up front was inaudible. Rémy did not like the way the night was progressing. Not at all. He looked down at the bound monk at his feet. The man lay perfectly still now, as if in a trance of acceptance, or perhaps, in silent prayer for deliverance.

# CHAPTER 72

**Fifteen thousand** feet in the air, Robert Langdon felt the physical world fade away as all of his thoughts converged on Saunière's mirror-image poem, which was illuminated through the lid of the box.

*an ancient word of wisdom frees this scroll*

*and helps us keep her scatter'd family whole*

*a headstone praised by templars is the key*

*and atbash will reveal the truth to thee*

Sophie quickly found some paper and copied it down longhand. When she was done, the three of them took turns reading the text. It was like some kind of archaeological crossword . . . a riddle that promised to reveal how to open the cryptex. Langdon read the verse slowly.

*An ancient word of wisdom frees this scroll . . . and helps us keep her scatter'd family whole . . . a head-stone praised by templars is the key . . . and atbash will reveal the truth to thee.*

Before Langdon could even ponder what ancient password the verse was trying to reveal, he felt something far more fundamental resonate within him—the meter of the poem. *Iambic pentameter.*

Langdon had come across this meter often over the years while researching secret societies across Europe, including just last year in the Vatican Secret Archives. For centuries, iambic pentameter had been a preferred poetic meter of outspoken literati across the globe, from the ancient Greek writer Archilochus to Shakespeare, Milton, Chaucer, and Voltaire—bold souls who chose to write their social commentaries in a meter that many of the day believed had mystical properties. The roots of iambic pentameter were deeply pagan.

*Iambs. Two syllables with opposite emphasis. Stressed and unstressed. Yin yang. A balanced pair. Arranged in strings of five. Pentameter. Five for the pentacle of Venus and the sacred feminine.*

"It's pentameter!" Teabing blurted, turning to Langdon. "And the verse is in English! *La lingua pura!*"

Langdon nodded. The Priory, like many European secret societies at odds with the Church, had considered English the only European *pure* language for centuries. Unlike French, Spanish, and Italian, which were rooted in Latin—

*the tongue of the Vatican*—English was linguistically removed from Rome's propaganda machine, and therefore became a sacred, secret tongue for those brotherhoods educated enough to learn it.

"This poem," Teabing gushed, "references not only the Grail, but the Knights Templar and the scattered family of Mary Magdalene! What more could we ask for?"

"The password," Sophie said, looking again at the poem. "It sounds like we need some kind of ancient word of wisdom?"

"Abracadabra?" Teabing ventured, his eyes twinkling.

*A word of five letters,* Langdon thought, pondering the staggering number of ancient words that might be considered *words of wisdom*—selections from mystic chants, astrological prophecies, secret society inductions, Wicca incantations, Egyptian magic spells, pagan mantras—the list was endless.

"The password," Sophie said, "appears to have something to do with the Templars." She read the text aloud. "'A headstone praised by Templars is the key.'"

"Leigh," Langdon said, "you're the Templar specialist. Any ideas?"

Teabing was silent for several seconds and then sighed. "Well, a headstone is obviously a grave marker of some sort. It's possible the poem is referencing a gravestone the Templars praised at the tomb of Magdalene, but that doesn't help us much because we have no idea where her tomb is."

"The last line," Sophie said, "says that *Atbash* will reveal the truth. I've heard that word. Atbash."

"I'm not surprised," Langdon replied. "You probably heard it in Cryptology 101. The Atbash Cipher is one of the oldest codes known to man."

*Of course!* Sophie thought. *The famous Hebrew encoding system.*

The Atbash Cipher had indeed been part of Sophie's early cryptology training. The cipher dated back to 500 B.C. and was now used as a classroom example of a basic rotational substitution scheme. A common form of Jewish cryptogram, the Atbash Cipher was a simple substitution code based on the twenty-two-letter Hebrew alphabet. In Atbash, the first letter was substituted by the last letter, the second letter by the next to last letter, and so on.

"Atbash is sublimely appropriate," Teabing said. "Text encrypted with Atbash is found throughout the Kabbala, the Dead Sea Scrolls, and even the Old Testament. Jewish scholars and mystics are *still* finding hidden meanings using Atbash. The Priory certainly would include the Atbash Cipher as part of their teachings."

"The only problem," Langdon said, "is that we don't have anything on which to apply the cipher."

Teabing sighed. "There must be a code word on the headstone. We must find this headstone praised by Templars."

Sophie sensed from the grim look on Langdon's face that finding the Templar headstone would be no small feat.

*Atbash is the key,* Sophie thought. *But we don't have a door.*

It was three minutes later that Teabing heaved a frustrated sigh and shook his head. "My friends, I'm stymied. Let me ponder this while I get us some nibblies and check on Rémy and our guest." He stood up and headed for the back of the plane.

Sophie felt tired as she watched him go.

Outside the window, the blackness of the predawn was absolute. Sophie felt as if she were being hurtled through space with no idea where she would land. Having grown up solving her grandfather's riddles, she had the uneasy sense right now that this poem before them contained information they still had not seen.

*There is more there,* she told herself. *Ingeniously hidden . . . but present nonetheless.*

Also plaguing her thoughts was a fear that what they eventually found inside this cryptex would not be as simple as "a map to the Holy Grail." Despite Teabing's and Langdon's confidence that the truth lay just within the marble cylinder, Sophie had solved enough of her grandfather's treasure hunts to know that Jacques Saunière did not give up his secrets easily.

# CHAPTER 73

**Bourget** Airfield's night shift air traffic controller had been dozing before a blank radar screen when the captain of the Judicial Police practically broke down his door.

"Teabing's jet," Bezu Fache blared, marching into the small tower, "where did it go?"

The controller's initial response was a babbling, lame attempt to protect the privacy of their British client—one of the airfield's most respected customers. It failed miserably.

"Okay," Fache said, "I am placing you under arrest for permitting a private plane to take off without registering a flight plan." Fache motioned to another officer, who approached with handcuffs, and the traffic controller felt a surge of terror. He thought of the newspaper articles debating whether the nation's police captain was a hero or a menace. That question had just been answered.

"Wait!" the controller heard himself whimper at the sight of the handcuffs. "I can tell you this much. Sir Leigh Teabing makes frequent trips to London for medical treatments. He has a hangar at Biggin Hill Executive Airport in Kent. On the outskirts of London."

Fache waved off the man with the cuffs. "Is Biggin Hill his destination tonight?"

"I don't know," the controller said honestly. "The plane left on its usual tack, and his last radar contact suggested the United Kingdom. Biggin Hill is an extremely likely guess."

"Did he have others onboard?"

"I swear, sir, there is no way for me to know that. Our clients can drive directly to their hangars, and load as they please. Who is onboard is the responsibility of the customs officials at the receiving airport."

Fache checked his watch and gazed out at the scattering of jets parked in front of the terminal. "If they're going to Biggin Hill, how long until they land?"

The controller fumbled through his records. "It's a short flight. His plane could be on the ground by . . . around six-thirty. Fifteen minutes from now."

Fache frowned and turned to one of his men. "Get a transport up here. I'm going to London. And get me the Kent local police. Not British MI5. I want this quiet. Kent *local*. Tell them I want Teabing's plane to be permitted to land. Then I want it surrounded on the tarmac. Nobody deplanes until I get there."

# CHAPTER 74

**"You're quiet,"** Langdon said, gazing across the Hawker's cabin at Sophie.

"Just tired," she replied. "And the poem. I don't know."

Langdon was feeling the same way. The hum of the engines and the gentle rocking of the plane were hypnotic, and his head still throbbed where he'd been hit by the monk. Teabing was still in the back of the plane, and Langdon decided to take advantage of the moment alone with Sophie to tell her something that had been on his mind. "I think I know part of the reason why your grandfather conspired to put us together. I think there's something he wanted me to explain to you."

"The history of the Holy Grail and Mary Magdalene isn't enough?"

Langdon felt uncertain how to proceed. "The rift between you. The reason you haven't spoken to him in ten years. I think maybe he was hoping I could somehow make that right by explaining what drove you apart."

Sophie squirmed in her seat. "I haven't told you what drove us apart."

Langdon eyed her carefully. "You witnessed a sex rite. Didn't you?"

Sophie recoiled. "How do you know that?"

"Sophie, you told me you witnessed something that convinced you your grandfather was in a secret society. And whatever you saw upset you enough that you haven't spoken to him since. I know a fair amount about secret societies. It doesn't take the brains of Da Vinci to guess what you saw."

Sophie stared.

"Was it in the spring?" Langdon asked. "Sometime around the equinox? Mid-March?"

Sophie looked out the window. "I was on spring break from university. I came home a few days early."

"You want to tell me about it?"

"I'd rather not." She turned suddenly back to Langdon, her eyes welling with emotion. "I don't know what I saw."

"Were both men and women present?"

After a beat, she nodded.

"Dressed in white and black?"

She wiped her eyes and then nodded, seeming to open up a little. "The women were in white gossamer gowns . . . with golden shoes. They held golden orbs. The men wore black tunics and black shoes."

Langdon strained to hide his emotion, and yet he could not believe what he was hearing. Sophie

Neveu had unwittingly witnessed a two-thousand-year-old sacred ceremony. "Masks?" he asked, keeping his voice calm. "Androgynous masks?"

"Yes. Everyone. Identical masks. White on the women. Black on the men."

Langdon had read descriptions of this ceremony and understood its mystic roots. "It's called Hieros Gamos," he said softly. "It dates back more than two thousand years. Egyptian priests and priestesses performed it regularly to celebrate the reproductive power of the female." He paused, leaning toward her. "And if you witnessed Hieros Gamos without being properly prepared to understand its meaning, I imagine it would be pretty shocking."

Sophie said nothing.

"Hieros Gamos is Greek," he continued. "It means *sacred marriage.*"

"The ritual I saw was no marriage."

"Marriage as in *union,* Sophie."

"You mean as in sex."

"No."

"No?" she said, her olive eyes testing him.

Langdon backpedaled. "Well . . . yes, in a manner of speaking, but not as we understand it today." He explained that although what she saw probably *looked* like a sex ritual, Hieros Gamos had nothing to do with eroticism. It was a spiritual act. Historically, intercourse was the act

through which male and female experienced
God. The ancients believed that the male was
spiritually incomplete until he had carnal knowledge of the sacred feminine. Physical union with
the female remained the sole means through
which man could become spiritually complete
and ultimately achieve *gnosis*—knowledge of the
divine. Since the days of Isis, sex rites had been
considered man's only bridge from earth to
heaven. "By communing with woman," Langdon
said, "man could achieve a climactic instant when
his mind went totally blank and he could see
God."

Sophie looked skeptical. "Orgasm as prayer?"

Langdon gave a noncommittal shrug, although
Sophie was essentially correct. Physiologically
speaking, the male climax was accompanied by a
split second entirely devoid of thought. A brief
mental vacuum. A moment of clarity during
which God could be glimpsed. Meditation gurus
achieved similar states of thoughtlessness without
sex and often described Nirvana as a never-
ending spiritual orgasm.

"Sophie," Langdon said quietly, "it's important
to remember that the ancients' view of sex was
entirely opposite from ours today. Sex begot new
life—the ultimate miracle—and miracles could be
performed only by a god. The ability of the
woman to produce life from her womb made her
sacred. A god. Intercourse was the revered union

of the two halves of the human spirit—male and female—through which the male could find spiritual wholeness and communion with God. What you saw was not about sex, it was about spirituality. The Hieros Gamos ritual is not a perversion. It's a deeply sacrosanct ceremony."

His words seemed to strike a nerve. Sophie had been remarkably poised all evening, but now, for the first time, Langdon saw the aura of composure beginning to crack. Tears materialized in her eyes again, and she dabbed them away with her sleeve.

He gave her a moment. Admittedly, the concept of sex as a pathway to God was mind-boggling at first. Langdon's Jewish students always looked flabbergasted when he first told them that the early Jewish tradition involved ritualistic sex. *In the Temple, no less.* Early Jews believed that the Holy of Holies in Solomon's Temple housed not only God but also His powerful female equal, Shekinah. Men seeking spiritual wholeness came to the Temple to visit priestesses—or *hierodules*—with whom they made love and experienced the divine through physical union. The Jewish tetragrammaton YHWH—the sacred name of God—in fact derived from Jehovah, an androgynous physical union between the masculine *Jah* and the pre-Hebraic name for Eve, *Havah*.

"For the early Church," Langdon explained in a

soft voice, "mankind's use of sex to commune directly with God posed a serious threat to the
Catholic power base. It left the Church out of the
loop, undermining their self-proclaimed status as
the *sole* conduit to God. For obvious reasons, they
worked hard to demonize sex and recast it as a
disgusting and sinful act. Other major religions
did the same."

Sophie was silent, but Langdon sensed she was
starting to understand her grandfather better.
Ironically, Langdon had made this same point in a
class lecture earlier this semester. "Is it surprising
we feel conflicted about sex?" he asked his students. "Our ancient heritage and our very physi-
ologies tell us sex is natural—a cherished route to
spiritual fulfillment—and yet modern religion
decries it as shameful, teaching us to fear our sexual desire as the hand of the devil."

Langdon decided not to shock his students with
the fact that more than a dozen secret societies
around the world—many of them quite
influential—still practiced sex rites and kept the
ancient traditions alive. Tom Cruise's character in
the film *Eyes Wide Shut* discovered this the hard
way when he sneaked into a private gathering of
ultraelite Manhattanites only to find himself witnessing Hieros Gamos. Sadly, the filmmakers had
gotten most of the specifics wrong, but the basic
gist was there—a secret society communing to
celebrate the magic of sexual union.

"Professor Langdon?" A male student in back raised his hand, sounding hopeful. "Are you saying that instead of going to chapel, we should have more sex?"

Langdon chuckled, not about to take the bait. From what he'd heard about Harvard parties, these kids were having more than enough sex. "Gentlemen," he said, knowing he was on tender ground, "might I offer a suggestion for all of you. Without being so bold as to condone premarital sex, and without being so naive as to think you're all chaste angels, I will give you this bit of advice about your sex lives."

All the men in the audience leaned forward, listening intently.

"The next time you find yourself with a woman, look in your heart and see if you cannot approach sex as a mystical, spiritual act. Challenge yourself to find that spark of divinity that man can only achieve through union with the sacred feminine."

The women smiled knowingly, nodding.

The men exchanged dubious giggles and off-color jokes.

Langdon sighed. College men were still boys.

Sophie's forehead felt cold as she pressed it against the plane's window and stared blankly into the void, trying to process what Langdon had just told her. She felt a new regret well within her. *Ten years.* She pictured the stacks of unopened letters her grandfather had sent her. *I will tell Robert everything.* Without turning from the window, Sophie began to speak. Quietly. Fearfully.

As she began to recount what had happened that night, she felt herself drifting back . . . alighting in the woods outside her grandfather's Normandy château . . . searching the deserted house in confusion . . . hearing the voices below her . . . and then finding the hidden door. She inched down the stone staircase, one step at a time, into that basement grotto. She could taste the earthy air. Cool and light. It was March. In the shadows of her hiding place on the staircase, she watched as the strangers swayed and chanted by flickering orange candles.

*I'm dreaming,* Sophie told herself. *This is a dream. What else could this be?*

The women and men were staggered, black, white, black, white. The women's beautiful gossamer gowns billowed as they raised in their right hands golden orbs and called out in unison, *"I was with you in the beginning, in the dawn of all that is holy, I bore you from the womb before the start of day."*

The women lowered their orbs, and everyone rocked back and forth as if in a trance. They were revering something in the center of the circle.

*What are they looking at?*

The voices accelerated now. Louder. Faster.

*"The woman whom you behold is love!"* The women called, raising their orbs again.

The men responded, *"She has her dwelling in eternity!"*

The chanting grew steady again. Accelerating. Thundering now. Faster. The participants stepped inward and knelt.

In that instant, Sophie could finally see what they were all watching.

On a low, ornate altar in the center of the circle lay a man. He was naked, positioned on his back, and wearing a black mask. Sophie instantly recognized his body and the birthmark on his shoulder. She almost cried out. *Grand-père!* This image alone would have shocked Sophie beyond belief, and yet there was more.

Straddling her grandfather was a naked woman wearing a white mask, her luxuriant silver hair flowing out behind it. Her body was plump, far from perfect, and she was gyrating in rhythm to the chanting—making love to Sophie's grandfather.

Sophie wanted to turn and run, but she couldn't. The stone walls of the grotto imprisoned her as the chanting rose to a fever pitch. The circle of participants seemed almost to be singing now, the noise rising in crescendo to a frenzy. With a sudden roar, the entire room seemed to erupt in climax. Sophie could not breathe. She suddenly realized she was quietly sobbing. She turned and staggered silently up the stairs, out of the house, and drove trembling back to Paris.

# CHAPTER 75

**The chartered** turboprop was just passing over the twinkling lights of Monaco when Aringarosa hung up on Fache for the second time. He reached for the airsickness bag again but felt too drained even to be sick.

*Just let it be over!*

Fache's newest update seemed unfathomable, and yet almost nothing tonight made sense anymore. *What is going on?* Everything had spiraled wildly out of control. *What have I gotten Silas into? What have I gotten myself into!*

On shaky legs, Aringarosa walked to the cockpit. "I need to change destinations."

The pilot glanced over his shoulder and laughed. "You're joking, right?"

"No. I have to get to London immediately."

"Father, this is a charter flight, not a taxi."

"I will pay you extra, of course. How much? London is only one hour farther north and requires almost no change of direction, so—"

"It's not a question of money, Father, there are other issues."

"Ten thousand euro. Right now."

The pilot turned, his eyes wide with shock.

"How much? What kind of priest carries that kind of cash?"

Aringarosa walked back to his black briefcase, opened it, and removed one of the bearer bonds. He handed it to the pilot.

"What is this?" the pilot demanded.

"A ten-thousand-euro bearer bond drawn on the Vatican Bank."

The pilot looked dubious.

"It's the same as cash."

"Only cash is cash," the pilot said, handing the bond back.

Aringarosa felt weak as he steadied himself against the cockpit door. "This is a matter of life or death. You must help me. I need to get to London."

The pilot eyed the bishop's gold ring. "Real diamonds?"

Aringarosa looked at the ring. "I could not possibly part with this."

The pilot shrugged, turning and focusing back out the windshield.

Aringarosa felt a deepening sadness. He looked at the ring. Everything it represented was about to be lost to the bishop anyway. After a long moment, he slid the ring from his finger and placed it gently on the instrument panel.

Aringarosa slunk out of the cockpit and sat back down. Fifteen seconds later, he could feel the pilot banking a few more degrees to the north.

Even so, Aringarosa's moment of glory was in shambles.

It had all begun as a holy cause. A brilliantly crafted scheme. Now, like a house of cards, it was collapsing in on itself . . . and the end was nowhere in sight.

# CHAPTER 76

**Langdon could** see Sophie was still shaken from recounting her experience of Hieros Gamos. For his part, Langdon was amazed to have heard it. Not only had Sophie witnessed the full-blown ritual, but her own grandfather had been the celebrant . . . the Grand Master of the Priory of Sion. It was heady company. *Da Vinci, Botticelli, Isaac Newton, Victor Hugo, Jean Cocteau . . . Jacques Saunière.*

"I don't know what else I can tell you," Langdon said softly.

Sophie's eyes were a deep green now, tearful. "He raised me like his own daughter."

Langdon now recognized the emotion that had been growing in her eyes as they spoke. It was remorse. Distant and deep. Sophie Neveu had shunned her grandfather and was now seeing him in an entirely different light.

Outside, the dawn was coming fast, its crimson aura gathering off the starboard. The earth was still black beneath them.

"Victuals, my dears?" Teabing rejoined them with a flourish, presenting several cans of Coke and a box of old crackers. He apologized profusely for the limited fare as he doled out the goods. "Our friend the monk isn't talking yet," he chimed, "but give him time." He bit into a cracker and eyed the poem. "So, my lovely, any headway?" He looked at Sophie. "What is your grandfather trying to tell us here? Where the devil is this headstone? This headstone praised by Templars."

Sophie shook her head and remained silent.

While Teabing again dug into the verse, Langdon popped a Coke and turned to the window, his thoughts awash with images of secret rituals and unbroken codes. *A headstone praised by Templars is the key.* He took a long sip from the can. *A headstone praised by Templars.* The cola was warm.

The dissolving veil of night seemed to evaporate quickly, and as Langdon watched the transformation, he saw a shimmering ocean stretch out beneath them. *The English Channel.* It wouldn't be long now.

Langdon willed the light of day to bring with it a second kind of illumination, but the lighter it became outside, the further he felt from the truth. He heard the rhythms of iambic pentameter and chanting, Hieros Gamos and sacred rites, resonating with the rumble of the jet.

*A headstone praised by Templars.*

The plane was over land again when a flash of enlightenment struck him. Langdon set down his empty can of Coke hard. "You won't believe this," he said, turning to the others. "The Templar headstone—I figured it out."

Teabing's eyes turned to saucers. "You *know* where the headstone is?"

Langdon smiled. "Not *where* it is. *What* it is."

Sophie leaned in to hear.

"I think the headstone references a literal *stone head*," Langdon explained, savoring the familiar excitement of academic breakthrough. "Not a grave marker."

"A stone head?" Teabing demanded.

Sophie looked equally confused.

"Leigh," Langdon said, turning, "during the Inquisition, the Church accused the Knights Templar of all kinds of heresies, right?"

"Correct. They fabricated all kinds of charges. Sodomy, urination on the cross, devil worship, quite a list."

"And on that list was the worship of *false idols,* right? Specifically, the Church accused the Templars of secretly performing rituals in which they prayed to a carved stone head . . . the pagan god—"

"Baphomet!" Teabing blurted. "My heavens, Robert, you're right! A headstone praised by Templars!"

Langdon quickly explained to Sophie that Baphomet was a pagan fertility god associated with the creative force of reproduction. Baphomet's head was represented as that of a ram or goat, a common symbol of procreation and fecundity. The Templars honored Baphomet by encircling a stone replica of his head and chanting prayers.

"Baphomet," Teabing tittered. "The ceremony honored the creative magic of sexual union, but Pope Clement convinced everyone that Baphomet's head was in fact that of the devil. The Pope used the head of Baphomet as the linchpin in his case against the Templars."

Langdon concurred. The modern belief in a *horned* devil known as Satan could be traced back to Baphomet and the Church's attempts to recast the horned fertility god as a symbol of evil. The Church had obviously succeeded, although not entirely. Traditional American Thanksgiving tables still bore pagan, horned fertility symbols. The cornucopia or "horn of plenty" was a tribute to Baphomet's fertility and dated back to Zeus being suckled by a goat whose horn broke off and magically filled with fruit. Baphomet also appeared in group photographs when some joker raised two fingers behind a friend's head in the V-symbol of horns; certainly few of the pranksters realized their mocking gesture was in fact advertising their victim's robust sperm count.

"Yes, yes," Teabing was saying excitedly. "Baphomet *must* be what the poem is referring to. A headstone praised by Templars."

"Okay," Sophie said, "but if Baphomet is the

headstone praised by Templars, then we have a new dilemma." She pointed to the dials on the cryptex. "Baphomet has eight letters. We only have room for five."

Teabing grinned broadly. "My dear, this is where the Atbash Cipher comes into play."

# CHAPTER 77

**Langdon was** impressed. Teabing had just finished writing out the entire twenty-two-letter Hebrew alphabet—*alef-beit*—from memory. Granted, he'd used Roman equivalents rather than Hebrew characters, but even so, he was now reading through them with flawless pronunciation.

A B G D H V Z Ch T Y K L M N S O P
Tz Q R Sh Th

"*Alef, Beit, Gimel, Dalet, Hei, Vav, Zayin, Chet, Tet, Yud, Kaf, Lamed, Mem, Nun, Samech, Ayin, Pei, Tzadik, Kuf, Reish, Shin, and Tav.*" Teabing dramatically mopped his brow and plowed on. "In formal Hebrew spelling, the vowel sounds are not written. Therefore, when we write the word *Baphomet* using the Hebrew alphabet, it will lose its three vowels in translation, leaving us—"

"Five letters," Sophie blurted.

Teabing nodded and began writing again. "Okay, here is the proper spelling of Baphomet in Hebrew letters. I'll sketch in the missing vowels for clarity's sake.

B a P V o M e Th

"Remember, of course," he added, "that Hebrew is normally written in the opposite direction, but we can just as easily use Atbash this way. Next, all we have to do is create our substitution scheme by rewriting the entire alphabet in reverse order opposite the original alphabet."

"There's an easier way," Sophie said, taking the pen from Teabing. "It works for all reflectional substitution ciphers, including the Atbash. A little trick I learned at the Royal Holloway." Sophie wrote the first half of the alphabet from left to right, and then, beneath it, wrote the second half, right to left. "Cryptanalysts call it the fold-over. Half as complicated. Twice as clean."

| A | B | G | D | H | V | Z | Ch | T | Y | K |
|----|----|---|---|----|---|---|----|---|---|---|
| Th | Sh | R | Q | Tz | P | O | S | N | M | L |

Teabing eyed her handiwork and chuckled. "Right you are. Glad to see those boys at the Holloway are doing their job."

Looking at Sophie's substitution matrix, Langdon felt a rising thrill that he imagined must have rivaled the thrill felt by early scholars when they first used the Atbash Cipher to decrypt the now famous *Mystery of Sheshach*. For years, religious scholars had been baffled by biblical references to a city called *Sheshach*. The city did not appear on any map nor in any other documents, and yet it was mentioned repeatedly in the Book of Jeremiah—the king of Sheshach, the city of Sheshach, the people of Sheshach. Finally, a scholar applied the Atbash Cipher to the word, and his results were mind-numbing. The cipher revealed that Sheshach was in fact a *code word* for another very well-known city. The decryption process was simple.

*Sheshach*, in Hebrew, was spelled: Sh-Sh-K.

Sh-Sh-K, when placed in the substitution matrix, became B-B-L.

B-B-L, in Hebrew, spelled *Babel*.

The mysterious city of Sheshach was revealed as the city of Babel, and a frenzy of biblical examination ensued. Within weeks, several more Atbash code words were uncovered in the Old Testament, unveiling myriad hidden meanings that scholars had no idea were there.

"We're getting close," Langdon whispered, unable to control his excitement.

"Inches, Robert," Teabing said. He glanced over at Sophie and smiled. "You ready?"

She nodded.

"Okay, Baphomet in Hebrew without the vowels reads: *B-P-V-M-Th*. Now we simply apply your Atbash substitution matrix to translate the letters into our five-letter password."

Langdon's heart pounded. *B-P-V-M-Th*. The sun was pouring through the windows now. He looked at Sophie's substitution matrix and slowly began to make the conversion. *B is Sh . . . P is V . . .*

Teabing was grinning like a schoolboy at Christmas. "And the Atbash Cipher reveals . . ." He stopped short. "Good God!" His face went white.

Langdon's head snapped up.

"What's wrong?" Sophie demanded.

"You won't believe this." Teabing glanced at Sophie. "Especially you."

"What do you mean?" she said.

"This is . . . ingenious," he whispered. "Utterly ingenious!" Teabing wrote again on the paper. "Drumroll, please. Here is your password." He showed them what he had written.

Sh – V – P – Y – A

Sophie scowled. "What is it?"

Langdon didn't recognize it either.

Teabing's voice seemed to tremble with awe. "This, my friend, is actually an ancient word of wisdom."

Langdon read the letters again. *An ancient word of wisdom frees this scroll.* An instant later he got it. He had never seen this coming. "An ancient word of wisdom!"

Teabing was laughing. "Quite literally!"

Sophie looked at the word and then at the dial. Immediately she realized Langdon and Teabing had failed to see a serious glitch. "Hold on! This can't be the password," she argued. "The cryptex doesn't have an Sh on the dial. It uses a traditional Roman alphabet."

"*Read* the word," Langdon urged. "Keep in mind two things. In Hebrew, the symbol for the sound Sh can also be pronounced as S, depending on the accent. Just as the letter P can be pronounced F."

*SVFYA?* she thought, puzzled.

"Genius!" Teabing added. "The letter Vav is often a placeholder for the vowel sound O!"

Sophie again looked at the letters, attempting to sound them out.

"*S . . . o . . . f . . . y . . . a.*"

She heard the sound of her voice, and could not believe what she had just said. "Sophia? This spells Sophia?"

Langdon was nodding enthusiastically. "Yes! *Sophia* literally means *wisdom* in Greek. The root of your name, Sophie, is literally a 'word of wisdom.' "

Sophie suddenly missed her grandfather immensely. *He encrypted the Priory keystone with my name.* A knot caught in her throat. It all seemed so perfect. But as she turned her gaze to the five lettered dials on the cryptex, she realized a problem still existed. "But wait . . . the word Sophia has *six* letters."

Teabing's smile never faded. "Look at the poem again. Your grandfather wrote, 'An *ancient* word of wisdom.' "

"Yes?"

Teabing winked. "In ancient Greek, wisdom is spelled S–O–F–I–A."

# CHAPTER 78

**Sophie felt** a wild excitement as she cradled the cryptex and began dialing in the letters. *An ancient word of wisdom frees this scroll.* Langdon and Teabing seemed to have stopped breathing as they looked on.

S . . . O . . . F . . .

"Carefully," Teabing urged. "Ever so carefully."

. . . I . . . A.

Sophie aligned the final dial. "Okay," she whispered, glancing up at the others. "I'm going to pull it apart."

"Remember the vinegar," Langdon whispered with fearful exhilaration. "Be careful."

Sophie knew that if this cryptex were like those she had opened in her youth, all she would need to do is grip the cylinder at both ends, just beyond the dials, and pull, applying slow, steady pressure in opposite directions. If the dials were properly aligned with the password, then one of the ends would slide off, much like a lens cap, and she could reach inside and remove the rolled papyrus document, which would be wrapped around the vial of vinegar. However, if the password they had entered were *incorrect,* Sophie's outward force on the ends would be transferred to a hinged lever inside, which would pivot downward into the cavity and apply pressure to the glass vial, eventually shattering it if she pulled too hard.

*Pull gently,* she told herself.

Teabing and Langdon both leaned in as Sophie wrapped her palms around the ends of the cylinder. In the excitement of deciphering the code word, Sophie had almost forgotten what they expected to find inside. *This is the Priory keystone.* According to Teabing, it contained a map to the Holy Grail, unveiling the tomb of Mary Magdalene and the Sangreal treasure . . . the ultimate treasure trove of secret truth.

Now gripping the stone tube, Sophie double-checked that all of the letters were properly aligned with the indicator. Then, slowly, she pulled. Nothing happened. She applied a little more force. Suddenly, the stone slid apart like a well-crafted telescope. The heavy end piece detached in her hand. Langdon and Teabing almost jumped to their feet. Sophie's heart rate climbed as she set the end cap on the table and tipped the cylinder to peer inside.

*A scroll!*

Peering down the hollow of the rolled paper, Sophie could see it had been wrapped around a cylindrical object—the vial of vinegar, she assumed. Strangely, though, the paper around the vinegar was not the customary delicate papyrus but rather, vellum. *That's odd,* she thought, *vinegar can't dissolve a lambskin vellum.* She looked again down the hollow of the scroll and realized the object in the center was not a vial of vinegar after all. It was something else entirely.

"What's wrong?" Teabing asked. "Pull out the scroll."

Frowning, Sophie grabbed the rolled vellum and the object around which it was wrapped, pulling them both out of the container.

"That's not papyrus," Teabing said. "It's too heavy."

"I know. It's padding."

"For what? The vial of vinegar?"

"No." Sophie unrolled the scroll and revealed what was wrapped inside. "For *this.*"

When Langdon saw the object inside the sheet of vellum, his heart sank.

"God help us," Teabing said, slumping. "Your grandfather was a pitiless architect."

Langdon stared in amazement. *I see Saunière has no intention of making this easy.*

On the table sat a second cryptex. Smaller. Made of black onyx. It had been nested within the first. Saunière's passion for dualism. *Two cryptexes.* Everything in pairs. *Double entendres. Male female. Black nested within white.* Langdon felt the web of symbolism stretching onward. *White gives birth to black.*

*Every man sprang from woman.*
*White—female.*
*Black—male.*

Reaching over, Langdon lifted the smaller cryptex. It looked identical to the first, except half the size and black. He heard the familiar gurgle. Apparently, the vial of vinegar they had heard earlier was inside this smaller cryptex.

"Well, Robert," Teabing said, sliding the page of vellum over to him. "You'll be pleased to hear that at least we're flying in the right direction."

Langdon examined the thick vellum sheet. Written in ornate penmanship was another four-line verse. Again, in iambic pentameter. The verse was cryptic, but Langdon needed to read only as far as the first line to realize that Teabing's plan to come to Britain was going to pay off.

IN LONDON LIES A KNIGHT A POPE INTERRED.

The remainder of the poem clearly implied that the password for opening the second cryptex could be found by visiting this knight's tomb, somewhere in the city.

Langdon turned excitedly to Teabing. "Do you have any idea what knight this poem is referring to?"

Teabing grinned. "Not the foggiest. But I know in precisely which crypt we should look."

At that moment, fifteen miles ahead of them, six Kent police cars streaked down rain-soaked streets toward Biggin Hill Executive Airport.

# CHAPTER 79

**Lieutenant Collet** helped himself to a Perrier from Teabing's refrigerator and strode back out through the drawing room. Rather than accompanying Fache to London where the action was, he was now baby-sitting the PTS team that had spread out through Château Villette.

So far, the evidence they had uncovered was unhelpful: a single bullet buried in the floor; a paper with several symbols scrawled on it along with the words *blade* and *chalice;* and a bloody spiked belt that PTS had told Collet was associated with the conservative Catholic group Opus Dei, which had caused a stir recently when a news program exposed their aggressive recruiting practices in Paris.

Collet sighed. *Good luck making sense of this unlikely mélange.*

Moving down a lavish hallway, Collet entered the vast ballroom study, where the chief PTS examiner was busy dusting for fingerprints. He was a corpulent man in suspenders.

"Anything?" Collet asked, entering.

The examiner shook his head. "Nothing new. Multiple sets matching those in the rest of the house."

"How about the prints on the *cilice* belt?"

"Interpol is still working. I uploaded everything we found."

Collet motioned to two sealed evidence bags on the desk. "And this?"

The man shrugged. "Force of habit. I bag anything peculiar."

Collet walked over. *Peculiar?*

"This Brit's a strange one," the examiner said. "Have a look at this." He sifted through the evidence bags and selected one, handing it to Collet.

The photo showed the main entrance of a Gothic cathedral—the traditional, recessed archway, narrowing through multiple, ribbed layers to a small doorway.

Collet studied the photo and turned. "This is peculiar?"

"Turn it over."

On the back, Collet found notations scrawled in English, describing a cathedral's long hollow nave as a secret pagan tribute to a woman's womb. This was strange. The notation describing the cathedral's *doorway,* however, was what startled him. "Hold on! He thinks a cathedral's entrance represents a woman's . . ."

The examiner nodded. "Complete with receding labial ridges and a nice little cinquefoil clitoris above the doorway." He sighed. "Kind of makes you want to go back to church."

Collet picked up the second evidence bag.

Through the plastic, he could see a large glossy photograph of what appeared to be an old document. The heading at the top read:

*Les Dossiers Secrets—Number 4° lm¹ 249*

"What's this?" Collet asked.

"No idea. He's got copies of it all over the place, so I bagged it."

Collet studied the document.

## PRIEURE DE SION—LES NAUTONIERS/ GRAND MASTERS

| | |
|---|---|
| JEAN DE GISORS | *1188–1220* |
| MARIE DE SAINT-CLAIR | *1220–1266* |
| GUILLAUME DE GISORS | *1266–1307* |
| EDOUARD DE BAR | *1307–1336* |
| JEANNE DE BAR | *1336–1351* |
| JEAN DE SAINT-CLAIR | *1351–1366* |
| BLANCE D'EVREUX | *1366–1398* |
| NICOLAS FLAMEL | *1398–1418* |
| RENE D'ANJOU | *1418–1480* |
| IOLANDE DE BAR | *1480–1483* |
| SANDRO BOTTICELLI | *1483–1510* |
| LEONARDO DA VINCI | *1510–1519* |
| CONNETABLE DE BOURBON | *1519–1527* |
| FERDINAND DE GONZAQUE | *1527–1575* |
| LOUIS DE NEVERS | *1575–1595* |
| ROBERT FLUDD | *1595–1637* |
| J. VALENTIN ANDREA | *1637–1654* |
| ROBERT BOYLE | *1654–1691* |

| | |
|---|---|
| ISAAC NEWTON | *1691–1727* |
| CHARLES RADCLYFFE | *1727–1746* |
| CHARLES DE LORRAINE | *1746–1780* |
| MAXIMILIAN DE LORRAINE | *1780–1801* |
| CHARLES NODIER | *1801–1844* |
| VICTOR HUGO | *1844–1885* |
| CLAUDE DEBUSSY | *1885–1918* |
| JEAN COCTEAU | *1918–1963* |

*Prieuré de Sion?* Collet wondered.

"Lieutenant?" Another agent stuck his head in. "The switchboard has an urgent call for Captain Fache, but they can't reach him. Will you take it?"

Collet returned to the kitchen and took the call.

It was André Vernet.

The banker's refined accent did little to mask the tension in his voice. "I thought Captain Fache said he would call me, but I have not yet heard from him."

"The captain is quite busy," Collet replied. "May I help you?"

"I was assured I would be kept abreast of your progress tonight."

For a moment, Collet thought he recognized the timbre of the man's voice, but he couldn't quite place it. "Monsieur Vernet, I am currently in charge of the Paris investigation. My name is Lieutenant Collet."

There was a long pause on the line. "Lieutenant, I have another call coming in. Please excuse me. I will call you later." He hung up.

For several seconds, Collet held the receiver. Then it dawned on him. *I knew I recognized that voice!* The revelation made him gasp.

*The armored car driver.*

*With the fake Rolex.*

Collet now understood why the banker had hung up so quickly. Vernet had remembered the name Lieutenant Collet—the officer he blatantly lied to earlier tonight.

Collet pondered the implications of this bizarre development. *Vernet is involved.* Instinctively, he knew he should call Fache. Emotionally, he knew this lucky break was going to be his moment to shine.

He immediately called Interpol and requested every shred of information they could find on the Depository Bank of Zurich and its president, André Vernet.

# CHAPTER 80

**"Seat belts,** please," Teabing's pilot announced as the Hawker 731 descended into a gloomy morning drizzle. "We'll be landing in five minutes."

Teabing felt a joyous sense of homecoming when he saw the misty hills of Kent spreading wide beneath the descending plane. England was less than an hour from Paris, and yet a world away. This morning, the damp, spring green of his homeland looked particularly welcoming. *My time in France is over. I am returning to England victorious. The keystone has been found.* The question remained, of course, as to *where* the keystone would ultimately lead. *Somewhere in the United Kingdom.* Where exactly, Teabing had no idea, but he was already tasting the glory.

As Langdon and Sophie looked on, Teabing got up and went to the far side of the cabin, then slid aside a wall panel to reveal a discreetly hidden wall safe. He dialed in the combination, opened the safe, and extracted two passports. "Documentation for Rémy and myself." He then removed a thick stack of fifty-pound notes. "And documentation for you two."

Sophie looked leery. "A bribe?"

"Creative diplomacy. Executive airfields make certain allowances. A British customs official will greet us at my hangar and ask to board the plane. Rather than permitting him to come on, I'll tell him I'm traveling with a French celebrity who prefers that nobody knows she is in England— press considerations, you know—and I'll offer the official this generous tip as gratitude for his discretion."

Langdon looked amazed. "And the official will *accept?*"

"Not from *anyone*, they won't, but these people all know me. I'm not an arms dealer, for heaven's sake. I was knighted." Teabing smiled. "Membership has its privileges."

Rémy approached up the aisle now, the Heckler Koch pistol cradled in his hand. "Sir, my agenda?"

Teabing glanced at his servant. "I'm going to have you stay onboard with our guest until we return. We can't very well drag him all over London with us."

Sophie looked wary. "Leigh, I was serious about the French police finding your plane before we return."

Teabing laughed. "Yes, imagine their surprise if they board and find Rémy."

Sophie looked surprised by his cavalier attitude. "Leigh, you transported a bound hostage across international borders. This is serious."

"So are my lawyers." He scowled toward the monk in the rear of the plane. "That animal broke into my home and almost killed me. That is a fact, and Rémy will corroborate."

"But you tied him up and flew him to London!" Langdon said.

Teabing held up his right hand and feigned a courtroom oath. "Your honor, forgive an eccentric old knight his foolish prejudice for the British court system. I realize I should have called the French authorities, but I'm a snob and do not trust those *laissez-faire* French to prosecute properly. This man almost murdered me. Yes, I made a rash decision forcing my manservant to help me bring him to England, but I was under great stress. Mea culpa. Mea culpa."

Langdon looked incredulous. "Coming from you, Leigh, that just might fly."

"Sir?" the pilot called back. "The tower just radioed. They've got some kind of maintenance problem out near your hangar, and they're asking me to bring the plane directly to the terminal instead."

Teabing had been flying to Biggin Hill for over a decade, and this was a first. "Did they mention what the problem is?"

"The controller was vague. Something about a gas leak at the pumping station? They asked me to park in front of the terminal and keep everyone onboard until further notice. Safety precaution.

We're not supposed to deplane until we get the all clear from airport authorities."

Teabing was skeptical. *Must be one hell of a gas leak.* The pumping station was a good half mile from his hangar.

Rémy also looked concerned. "Sir, this sounds highly irregular."

Teabing turned to Sophie and Langdon. "My friends, I have an unpleasant suspicion that we are about to be met by a welcoming committee."

Langdon gave a bleak sigh. "I guess Fache still thinks I'm his man."

"Either that," Sophie said, "or he is too deep into this to admit his error."

Teabing was not listening. Regardless of Fache's mind-set, action needed to be taken fast. *Don't lose sight of the ultimate goal. The Grail. We're so close.* Below them, the landing gear descended with a clunk.

"Leigh," Langdon said, sounding deeply remorseful, "I should turn myself in and sort this out legally. Leave you all out of it."

"Oh, heavens, Robert!" Teabing waved it off. "Do you really think they're going to let the rest of us go? I just transported you illegally. Miss Neveu assisted in your escape from the Louvre, and we have a man tied up in the back of the plane. Really now! We're all in this together."

"Maybe a different airport?" Sophie said.

Teabing shook his head. "If we pull up now, by

the time we get clearance anywhere else, our welcoming party will include army tanks."

Sophie slumped.

Teabing sensed that if they were to have any chance of postponing confrontation with the British authorities long enough to find the Grail, bold action had to be taken. "Give me a minute," he said, hobbling toward the cockpit.

"What are you doing?" Langdon asked.

"Sales meeting," Teabing said, wondering how much it would cost him to persuade his pilot to perform one highly irregular maneuver.

# CHAPTER 81

**The Hawker** *is on final approach.*

Simon Edwards—Executive Services Officer at Biggin Hill Airport—paced the control tower, squinting nervously at the rain-drenched runway. He never appreciated being awoken early on a Saturday morning, but it was particularly distasteful that he had been called in to oversee the arrest of one of his most lucrative clients. Sir Leigh Teabing paid Biggin Hill not only for a private hangar but a "per landing fee" for his frequent arrivals and departures. Usually, the airfield had advance warning of his schedule and was able to follow a strict protocol for his arrival. Teabing liked things just so. The custom-built Jaguar stretch limousine that he kept in his hangar was to be fully gassed, polished, and the day's *London Times* laid out on the back seat. A customs official was to be waiting for the plane at the hangar to expedite the mandatory documentation and luggage check. Occasionally, customs agents accepted large tips from Teabing in exchange for turning a blind eye to the transport of harmless organics—mostly luxury foods—French escargots, a particularly ripe unprocessed Roquefort, certain fruits. Many customs laws were absurd, anyway, and if Biggin Hill didn't accommodate its clients, certainly competing airfields would. Teabing was provided with what he wanted here at Biggin Hill, and the employees reaped the benefits.

Edwards's nerves felt frayed now as he watched the jet coming in. He wondered if Teabing's penchant for spreading the wealth had gotten him in trouble somehow; the French authorities seemed very intent on containing him. Edwards had not yet been told what the charges were, but they were obviously serious. At the French authorities' request, Kent police had ordered the Biggin Hill air traffic controller to radio the Hawker's pilot and order him directly to the terminal rather than to the client's hangar. The pilot had agreed, apparently believing the far-fetched story of a gas leak.

Though the British police did not generally carry weapons, the gravity of the situation had brought out an armed response team. Now, eight policemen with handguns stood just inside the terminal building, awaiting the moment when the plane's engines powered down. The instant this happened, a runway attendant would place safety wedges under the tires so the plane could no longer move. Then the police would step into view and hold the occupants at bay until the French police arrived to handle the situation.

The Hawker was low in the sky now, skimming

the treetops to their right. Simon Edwards went downstairs to watch the landing from tarmac level. The Kent police were poised, just out of sight, and the maintenance man waited with his wedges. Out on the runway, the Hawker's nose tipped up, and the tires touched down in a puff of smoke. The plane settled in for deceleration, streaking from right to left in front of the terminal, its white hull glistening in the wet weather. But rather than braking and turning into the terminal, the jet coasted calmly past the access lane and continued on toward Teabing's hangar in the distance.

All the police spun and stared at Edwards. "I thought you said the pilot agreed to come to the terminal!"

Edwards was bewildered. "He *did*!"

Seconds later, Edwards found himself wedged in a police car racing across the tarmac toward the distant hangar. The convoy of police was still a good five hundred yards away as Teabing's Hawker taxied calmly into the private hangar and disappeared. When the cars finally arrived and skidded to a stop outside the gaping hangar door, the police poured out, guns drawn.

Edwards jumped out too.

The noise was deafening.

The Hawker's engines were still roaring as the jet finished its usual rotation inside the hangar, positioning itself nose-out in preparation for later departure. As the plane completed its 180-degree turn and rolled toward the front of the hangar, Edwards could see the pilot's face, which understandably looked surprised and fearful to see the barricade of police cars.

The pilot brought the plane to a final stop, and powered down the engines. The police streamed in, taking up positions around the jet. Edwards joined the Kent chief inspector, who moved warily toward the hatch. After several seconds, the fuselage door popped open.

Leigh Teabing appeared in the doorway as the plane's electronic stairs smoothly dropped down. As he gazed out at the sea of weapons aimed at him, he propped himself on his crutches and scratched his head. "Simon, did I win the policemen's lottery while I was away?" He sounded more bewildered than concerned.

Simon Edwards stepped forward, swallowing the frog in his throat. "Good morning, sir. I apologize for the confusion. We've had a gas leak and your pilot said he was coming to the terminal."

"Yes, yes, well, I told him to come here instead. I'm late for an appointment. I pay for this hangar, and this rubbish about avoiding a gas leak sounded overcautious."

"I'm afraid your arrival has taken us a bit off guard, sir."

"I know. I'm off my schedule, I am. Between you and me, the new medication gives me the tinkles. Thought I'd come over for a tune-up."

The policemen all exchanged looks. Edwards winced. "Very good, sir."

"Sir," the Kent chief inspector said, stepping forward. "I need to ask you to stay onboard for another half hour or so."

Teabing looked unamused as he hobbled down the stairs. "I'm afraid that is impossible. I have a medical appointment." He reached the tarmac. "I cannot afford to miss it."

The chief inspector repositioned himself to block Teabing's progress away from the plane. "I am here at the orders of the French Judicial Police. They claim you are transporting fugitives from the law on this plane."

Teabing stared at the chief inspector a long moment, and then burst out laughing. "Is this one of those hidden camera programs? Jolly good!"

The chief inspector never flinched. "This is serious, sir. The French police claim you also may have a hostage onboard."

Teabing's manservant Rémy appeared in the doorway at the top of the stairs. "I *feel* like a hostage working for Sir Leigh, but he assures me I am free to go." Rémy checked his watch. "Master, we really are running late." He nodded toward the Jaguar stretch limousine in the far corner of the hangar. The enormous automobile was ebony with smoked glass and whitewall tires. "I'll bring the car." Rémy started down the stairs.

"I'm afraid we cannot let you leave," the chief inspector said. "Please return to your aircraft. Both of you. Representatives from the French police will be landing shortly."

Teabing looked now toward Simon Edwards. "Simon, for heaven's sake, this is ridiculous! We don't have anyone else on board. Just the usual—Rémy, our pilot, and myself. Perhaps you could act as an intermediary? Go have a look onboard, and verify that the plane is empty."

Edwards knew he was trapped. "Yes, sir. I can have a look."

"The devil you will!" the Kent chief inspector declared, apparently knowing enough about executive airfields to suspect Simon Edwards might well lie about the plane's occupants in an effort to keep Teabing's business at Biggin Hill. "I will look myself."

Teabing shook his head. "No you won't, Inspector. This is private property and until you have a search warrant, you will stay off my plane. I am offering you a reasonable option here. Mr. Edwards can perform the inspection."

"No deal."

Teabing's demeanor turned frosty. "Inspector, I'm afraid I don't have time to indulge in your games. I'm late, and I'm leaving. If it is that important to you to stop me, you'll just have to shoot me." With that, Teabing and Rémy walked around the chief inspector and headed across the hangar toward the parked limousine.

The Kent chief inspector felt only distaste for Leigh Teabing as the man hobbled around him in defiance. Men of privilege always felt like they were above the law.

*They are not.* The chief inspector turned and aimed at Teabing's back. "Stop! I will fire!"

"Go ahead," Teabing said without breaking stride or glancing back. "My lawyers will fricassee your testicles for breakfast. And if you dare board my plane without a warrant, your spleen will follow."

No stranger to power plays, the chief inspector was unimpressed. Technically, Teabing was correct and the police needed a warrant to board his jet, but because the flight had originated in France, and because the powerful Bezu Fache had given his authority, the Kent chief inspector felt certain his career would be far better served by finding out what it was on this plane that Teabing seemed so intent on hiding.

"Stop them," the inspector ordered. "I'm searching the plane."

His men raced over, guns leveled, and physically blocked Teabing and his servant from reaching the limousine.

Now Teabing turned. "Inspector, this is your last warning. Do not even think of boarding that plane. You will regret it."

Ignoring the threat, the chief inspector gripped his sidearm and marched up the plane's gangway. Arriving at the hatch, he peered inside. After a moment, he stepped into the cabin. *What the devil?*

With the exception of the frightened-looking pilot in the cockpit, the aircraft was empty. Entirely devoid of human life. Quickly checking the bathroom, the chairs, and the luggage areas, the inspector found no traces of anyone hiding . . . much less multiple individuals.

*What the hell was Bezu Fache thinking?* It seemed Leigh Teabing had been telling the truth.

The Kent chief inspector stood alone in the deserted cabin and swallowed hard. *Shit.* His face flushed, he stepped back onto the gangway, gazing across the hangar at Leigh Teabing and his servant, who were now under gunpoint near the limousine. "Let them go," the inspector ordered. "We received a bad tip."

Teabing's eyes were menacing even across the hangar. "You can expect a call from my lawyers. And for future reference, the French police cannot be trusted."

With that, Teabing's manservant opened the door at the rear of the stretch limousine and helped his crippled master into the back seat.

Then the servant walked the length of the car, climbed in behind the wheel, and gunned the engine. Policemen scattered as the Jaguar peeled out of the hangar.

"Well played, my good man," Teabing chimed from the rear seat as the limousine accelerated out of the airport. He turned his eyes now to the dimly lit front recesses of the spacious interior. "Everyone comfy?"

Langdon gave a weak nod. He and Sophie were still crouched on the floor beside the bound and gagged albino.

Moments earlier, as the Hawker taxied into the deserted hangar, Rémy had popped the hatch as the plane jolted to a stop halfway through its turn. With the police closing in fast, Langdon and Sophie dragged the monk down the gangway to ground level and out of sight behind the limousine. Then the jet engines had roared again, rotating the plane and completing its turn as the police cars came skidding into the hangar.

Now, as the limousine raced toward Kent, Langdon and Sophie clambered toward the rear of the limo's long interior, leaving the monk bound on the floor. They settled onto the long seat facing Teabing. The Brit gave them both a roguish smile and opened the cabinet on the

limo's bar. "Could I offer you a drink? Some nibblies? Crisps? Nuts? Seltzer?"

Sophie and Langdon both shook their heads.

Teabing grinned and closed the bar. "So then,
about this knight's tomb . . ."

# CHAPTER 82

**"Fleet Street?"** Langdon asked, eyeing Teabing in the back of the limo. *There's a crypt on Fleet Street?* So far, Leigh was being playfully cagey about where he thought they would find the "knight's tomb," which, according to the poem, would provide the password for opening the smaller cryptex.

Teabing grinned and turned to Sophie. "Miss Neveu, give the Harvard boy one more shot at the verse, will you?"

Sophie fished in her pocket and pulled out the black cryptex, which was wrapped in the vellum. Everyone had decided to leave the rosewood box and larger cryptex behind in the plane's strong-box, carrying with them only what they needed, the far more portable and discreet black cryptex. Sophie unwrapped the vellum and handed the sheet to Langdon.

Although Langdon had read the poem several times onboard the jet, he had been unable to extract any specific location. Now, as he read the words again, he processed them slowly and carefully, hoping the pentametric rhythms would reveal a clearer meaning now that he was on the ground.

In London lies a knight a Pope interred.
His labor's fruit a Holy wrath incurred.
You seek the orb that ought be on his tomb.
It speaks of Rosy flesh and seeded womb.

The language seemed simple enough. There was a knight buried in London. A knight who labored at something that angered the Church. A knight whose tomb was missing an orb that *should* be present. The poem's final reference—*Rosy flesh and seeded womb*—was a clear allusion to Mary Magdalene, the Rose who bore the seed of Jesus.

Despite the apparent straightforwardness of the verse, Langdon still had no idea *who* this knight was or where he was buried. Moreover, once they located the tomb, it sounded as if they would be searching for something that was absent. *The orb that ought be on his tomb?*

"No thoughts?" Teabing clucked in disappointment, although Langdon sensed the Royal Historian was enjoying being one up. "Miss Neveu?"

She shook her head.

"What would you two do without me?" Teabing said. "Very well, I will walk you through it. It's quite simple really. The first line is the key. Would you read it please?"

Langdon read aloud. "'In London lies a knight a Pope interred.'"

"Precisely. A knight a *Pope* interred." He eyed Langdon. "What does that mean to you?"

Langdon shrugged. "A knight buried by a Pope? A knight whose funeral was presided over by a Pope?"

Teabing laughed loudly. "Oh, that's rich. Always the optimist, Robert. Look at the second line. This knight obviously did something that incurred the Holy wrath of the Church. Think again. Consider the dynamic between the Church and the Knights Templar. A knight a Pope interred?"

"A knight a Pope *killed?*" Sophie asked.

Teabing smiled and patted her knee. "Well done, my dear. A knight a Pope *buried*. Or killed."

Langdon thought of the notorious Templar round-up in 1307—unlucky Friday the thirteenth—when Pope Clement killed and interred hundreds of Knights Templar. "But there must be endless graves of 'knights killed by Popes.'"

"Aha, not so!" Teabing said. "Many of them were burned at the stake and tossed unceremoniously into the Tiber River. But this poem refers to a *tomb*. A tomb in London. And there are few knights buried in London." He paused, eyeing Langdon as if waiting for light to dawn. Finally he huffed. "Robert, for heaven's sake! The church built in London by the Priory's military arm—the Knights Templar themselves!"

"The Temple Church?" Langdon drew a startled breath. "It has a crypt?"

"Ten of the most frightening tombs you will ever see."

Langdon had never actually visited the Temple Church, although he'd come across numerous references in his Priory research. Once the epicenter of all Templar/Priory activities in the United Kingdom, the Temple Church had been so named in honor of Solomon's Temple, from which the Knights Templar had extracted their own title, as well as the Sangreal documents that gave them all their influence in Rome. Tales abounded of knights performing strange, secretive rituals within the Temple Church's unusual sanctuary. "The Temple Church is on Fleet Street?"

"Actually, it's just off Fleet Street on Inner Temple Lane." Teabing looked mischievous. "I wanted to see you sweat a little more before I gave it away."

"Thanks."

"Neither of you has ever been there?"

Sophie and Langdon shook their heads.

"I'm not surprised," Teabing said. "The church is hidden now behind much larger buildings. Few people even know it's there. Eerie old place. The architecture is pagan to the core."

Sophie looked surprised. "Pagan?"

"Pantheonically pagan!" Teabing exclaimed.

"The church is *round*. The Templars ignored the traditional Christian cruciform layout and built a perfectly circular church in honor of the sun." His eyebrows did a devilish dance. "A not so subtle howdy-do to the boys in Rome. They might as well have resurrected Stonehenge in downtown London."

Sophie eyed Teabing. "What about the rest of the poem?"

The historian's mirthful air faded. "I'm not sure. It's puzzling. We will need to examine each of the ten tombs carefully. With luck, one of them will have a conspicuously absent orb."

Langdon realized how close they really were. If the missing orb revealed the password, they would be able to open the second cryptex. He had a hard time imagining what they might find inside.

Langdon eyed the poem again. It was like some kind of primordial crossword puzzle. *A five-letter word that speaks of the Grail?* On the plane, they had already tried all the obvious passwords— GRAIL, GRAAL, GREAL, VENUS, MARIA, JESUS, SARAH—but the cylinder had not budged. *Far too obvious.* Apparently there existed some other five-letter reference to the Rose's seeded womb. The fact that the word was eluding a specialist like Leigh Teabing signified to Langdon that it was no ordinary Grail reference.

"Sir Leigh?" Rémy called over his shoulder. He

was watching them in the rearview mirror through the open divider. "You said Fleet Street is near Blackfriars Bridge?"

"Yes, take Victoria Embankment."

"I'm sorry. I'm not sure where that is. We usually go only to the hospital."

Teabing rolled his eyes at Langdon and Sophie and grumbled, "I swear, sometimes it's like babysitting a child. One moment please. Help yourself to a drink and savory snacks." He left them, clambering awkwardly toward the open divider to talk to Rémy.

Sophie turned to Langdon now, her voice quiet. "Robert, nobody knows you and I are in England."

Langdon realized she was right. The Kent police would tell Fache the plane was empty, and Fache would have to assume they were still in France. *We are invisible.* Leigh's little stunt had just bought them a lot of time.

"Fache will not give up easily," Sophie said. "He has too much riding on this arrest now."

Langdon had been trying not to think about Fache. Sophie had promised she would do everything in her power to exonerate Langdon once this was over, but Langdon was starting to fear it might not matter. *Fache could easily be part of this plot.* Although Langdon could not imagine the Judicial Police tangled up in the Holy Grail, he sensed too much coincidence tonight to disregard

Fache as a possible accomplice. *Fache is religious, and he is intent on pinning these murders on me.* Then again, Sophie had argued that Fache might simply be overzealous to make the arrest. After all, the evidence against Langdon was substantial. In addition to Langdon's name scrawled on the Louvre floor and in Saunière's date book, Langdon now appeared to have lied about his manuscript and then run away. *At Sophie's suggestion.*

"Robert, I'm sorry you're so deeply involved," Sophie said, placing her hand on his knee. "But I'm very glad you're here."

The comment sounded more pragmatic than romantic, and yet Langdon felt an unexpected flicker of attraction between them. He gave her a tired smile. "I'm a lot more fun when I've slept."

Sophie was silent for several seconds. "My grandfather asked me to trust you. I'm glad I listened to him for once."

"Your grandfather didn't even know me."

"Even so, I can't help but think you've done everything he would have wanted. You helped me find the keystone, explained the Sangreal, told me about the ritual in the basement." She paused. "Somehow I feel closer to my grandfather tonight than I have in years. I know he would be happy about that."

In the distance, now, the skyline of London began to materialize through the dawn drizzle.

Once dominated by Big Ben and Tower Bridge, the horizon now bowed to the Millennium Eye—a colossal, ultramodern Ferris wheel that climbed five hundred feet and afforded breathtaking views of the city. Langdon had attempted to board it once, but the "viewing capsules" reminded him of sealed sarcophagi, and he opted to keep his feet on the ground and enjoy the view from the airy banks of the Thames.

Langdon felt a squeeze on his knee, pulling him back, and Sophie's green eyes were on him. He realized she had been speaking to him. "What do *you* think we should do with the Sangreal documents if we ever find them?" she whispered.

"What I think is immaterial," Langdon said. "Your grandfather gave the cryptex to you, and you should do with it what your instinct tells you he would want done."

"I'm asking for your opinion. You obviously wrote something in that manuscript that made my grandfather trust your judgment. He scheduled a private meeting with you. That's rare."

"Maybe he wanted to tell me I have it all wrong."

"Why would he tell me to find you unless he liked your ideas? In your manuscript, did you support the idea that the Sangreal documents should be revealed or stay buried?"

"Neither. I made no judgment either way. The

manuscript deals with the symbology of the sacred feminine—tracing her iconography throughout history. I certainly didn't presume to know where the Grail is hidden or whether it should ever be revealed."

"And yet you're writing a book about it, so you obviously feel the information should be shared."

"There's an enormous difference between hypothetically discussing an alternate history of Christ, and . . ." He paused.

"And what?"

"And presenting to the world thousands of ancient documents as scientific evidence that the New Testament is false testimony."

"But you told me the New Testament is based on fabrications."

Langdon smiled. "Sophie, *every* faith in the world is based on fabrication. That is the definition of *faith*—acceptance of that which we imagine to be true, that which we cannot prove. Every religion describes God through metaphor, allegory, and exaggeration, from the early Egyptians through modern Sunday school. Metaphors are a way to help our minds process the unprocessible. The problems arise when we begin to believe literally in our own metaphors."

"So you are in favor of the Sangreal documents staying buried forever?"

"I'm a historian. I'm opposed to the destruction of documents, and I would love to see religious scholars have more information to ponder the exceptional life of Jesus Christ."

"You're arguing both sides of my question."

"Am I? The Bible represents a fundamental guidepost for millions of people on the planet, in much the same way the Koran, Torah, and Pali Canon offer guidance to people of other religions. If you and I could dig up documentation that contradicted the holy stories of Islamic belief, Judaic belief, Buddhist belief, pagan belief, should we do that? Should we wave a flag and tell the Buddhists that we have proof the Buddha did not come from a lotus blossom? Or that Jesus was not born of a *literal* virgin birth? Those who truly understand their faiths understand the stories are metaphorical."

Sophie looked skeptical. "My friends who are devout Christians definitely believe that Christ *literally* walked on water, *literally* turned water into wine, and was born of a *literal* virgin birth."

"My point exactly," Langdon said. "Religious allegory has become a part of the fabric of reality. And living in that reality helps millions of people cope and be better people."

"But it appears their reality is false."

Langdon chuckled. "No more false than that of a mathematical cryptographer who believes in the imaginary number '$i$' because it helps her break codes."

Sophie frowned. "That's not fair."

A moment passed.

"What was your question again?" Langdon asked.

"I can't remember."

He smiled. "Works every time."

# CHAPTER 83

**Langdon's** Mickey Mouse wristwatch read almost seven-thirty when he emerged from the Jaguar limousine onto Inner Temple Lane with Sophie and Teabing. The threesome wound through a maze of buildings to a small courtyard outside the Temple Church. The rough-hewn stone shimmered in the rain, and doves cooed in the architecture overhead.

London's ancient Temple Church was constructed entirely of Caen stone. A dramatic, circular edifice with a daunting facade, a central turret, and a protruding nave off one side, the church looked more like a military stronghold than a place of worship. Consecrated on the tenth of February in 1185 by Heraclius, Patriarch of Jerusalem, the Temple Church survived eight centuries of political turmoil, the Great Fire of London, and the First World War, only to be heavily damaged by Luftwaffe incendiary bombs in 1940. After the war, it was restored to its original, stark grandeur.

*The simplicity of the circle,* Langdon thought, admiring the building for the first time. The architecture was coarse and simple, more reminiscent of Rome's rugged Castel Sant'Angelo than the refined Pantheon. The boxy annex jutting out to the right was an unfortunate eyesore, although it did little to shroud the original pagan shape of the primary structure.

"It's early on a Saturday," Teabing said, hobbling toward the entrance, "so I'm assuming we won't have services to deal with."

The church's entryway was a recessed stone niche inside which stood a large wooden door. To the left of the door, looking entirely out of place, hung a bulletin board covered with concert schedules and religious service announcements.

Teabing frowned as he read the board. "They don't open to sightseers for another couple of hours." He moved to the door and tried it. The door didn't budge. Putting his ear to the wood, he listened. After a moment, he pulled back, a scheming look on his face as he pointed to the bulletin board. "Robert, check the service schedule, will you? Who is presiding this week?"

Inside the church, an altar boy was almost finished vacuuming the communion kneelers when he heard a knocking on the sanctuary door. He ignored it. Father Harvey Knowles had his own keys and was not due for another couple of hours. The knocking was probably a curious tourist or indigent. The altar boy kept vacuuming, but the knocking continued. *Can't you read?* The sign on the door clearly stated that the church did not open until nine-thirty on Saturday. The altar boy remained with his chores.

Suddenly, the knocking turned to a forceful banging, as if someone were hitting the door with a metal rod. The young man switched off his vacuum cleaner and marched angrily toward the door. Unlatching it from within, he swung it open. Three people stood in the entryway. *Tourists,* he grumbled. "We open at nine-thirty."

The heavyset man, apparently the leader, stepped forward using metal crutches. "I am Sir Leigh Teabing," he said, his accent a highbrow, Saxonesque British. "As you are no doubt aware, I am escorting Mr. and Mrs. Christopher Wren the Fourth." He stepped aside, flourishing his arm toward the attractive couple behind them. The woman was soft-featured, with lush burgundy hair. The man was tall, dark-haired, and looked vaguely familiar.

The altar boy had no idea how to respond. Sir Christopher Wren was the Temple Church's most famous benefactor. He had made possible all the restorations following damage caused by the Great Fire. He had also been dead since the early eighteenth century. "Um . . . an honor to meet you?"

The man on crutches frowned. "Good thing you're not in sales, young man, you're not very convincing. Where is Father Knowles?"

"It's Saturday. He's not due in until later."

The crippled man's scowl deepened. "There's gratitude. He assured us he would be here, but it looks like we'll do it without him. It won't take long."

The altar boy remained blocking the doorway. "I'm sorry, *what* won't take long?"

The visitor's eyes sharpened now, and he leaned forward whispering as if to save everyone some embarrassment. "Young man, apparently you are new here. Every year Sir Christopher Wren's descendants bring a pinch of the old man's ashes to scatter in the Temple sanctuary. It is part of his last will and testament. Nobody is particularly happy about making the trip, but what can we do?"

The altar boy had been here a couple of years but had never heard of this custom. "It would be better if you waited until nine-thirty. The church isn't open yet, and I'm not finished hoovering."

The man on crutches glared angrily. "Young man, the only reason there's anything left of this building for you to hoover is on account of the gentleman in that woman's pocket."

"I'm sorry?"

"Mrs. Wren," the man on crutches said, "would you be so kind as to show this impertinent young man the reliquary of ashes?"

The woman hesitated a moment and then, as if awaking from a trance, reached in her sweater pocket and pulled out a small cylinder wrapped in protective fabric.

"There, you see?" the man on crutches snapped. "Now, you can either grant his dying wish and let us sprinkle his ashes in the sanctuary, or I tell Father Knowles how we've been treated."

The altar boy hesitated, well acquainted with Father Knowles' deep observance of church tradition . . . and, more importantly, with his foul temper when anything cast this time-honored shrine in anything but favorable light. Maybe Father Knowles had simply forgotten these family members were coming. If so, then there was far more risk in turning them away than in letting them in. *After all, they said it would only take a minute. What harm could it do?*

When the altar boy stepped aside to let the three people pass, he could have sworn Mr. and Mrs. Wren looked just as bewildered by all of this as he was. Uncertain, the boy returned to his chores, watching them out of the corner of his eye.

Langdon had to smile as the threesome moved deeper into the church. "Leigh," he whispered, "you lie entirely too well."

Teabing's eyes twinkled. "Oxford Theatre Club. They still talk of my Julius Caesar. I'm certain nobody has ever performed the first scene of Act Three with more dedication."

Langdon glanced over. "I thought Caesar was *dead* in that scene."

Teabing smirked. "Yes, but my toga tore open when I fell, and I had to lie on stage for half an hour with my todger hanging out. Even so, I never moved a muscle. I was brilliant, I tell you."

Langdon cringed. *Sorry I missed it.*

As the group moved through the rectangular annex toward the archway leading into the main church, Langdon was surprised by the barren austerity. Although the altar layout resembled that of a linear Christian chapel, the furnishings were stark and cold, bearing none of the traditional ornamentation. "Bleak," he whispered.

Teabing chuckled. "Church of England. Anglicans drink their religion straight. Nothing to distract from their misery."

Sophie motioned through the vast opening that gave way to the circular section of the church. "It looks like a fortress in there," she whispered.

Langdon agreed. Even from here, the walls looked unusually robust.

"The Knights Templar were warriors," Teabing reminded, the sound of his aluminum crutches echoing in this reverberant space. "A religio-military society. Their churches were their strongholds and their banks."

"Banks?" Sophie asked, glancing at Leigh.

"Heavens, yes. The Templars *invented* the concept of modern banking. For European nobility, traveling with gold was perilous, so the Templars allowed nobles to deposit gold in their nearest Temple Church and then draw it from any *other* Temple Church across Europe. All they needed was proper documentation." He winked. "And a small commission. They were the original ATMs." Teabing pointed toward a stained-glass window where the breaking sun was refracting through a white-clad knight riding a rose-colored horse. "Alanus Marcel," Teabing said, "Master of the Temple in the early twelve hundreds. He and his successors actually held the Parliamentary chair of Primus Baro Angiae."

Langdon was surprised. "First Baron of the Realm?"

Teabing nodded. "The Master of the Temple, some claim, held more influence than the king himself." As they arrived outside the circular chamber, Teabing shot a glance over his shoulder at the altar boy, who was vacuuming in the distance. "You know," Teabing whispered to Sophie, "the Holy Grail is said to once have been stored in this church overnight while the Templars moved it from one hiding place to another. Can you imagine the four chests of Sangreal documents sitting right here with Mary Magdalene's sarcophagus? It gives me gooseflesh."

Langdon was feeling gooseflesh too as they

stepped into the circular chamber. His eye traced the curvature of the chamber's pale stone perimeter, taking in the carvings of gargoyles, demons, monsters, and pained human faces, all staring inward. Beneath the carvings, a single stone pew curled around the entire circumference of the room.

"Theater in the round," Langdon whispered.

Teabing raised a crutch, pointing toward the far left of the room and then to the far right. Langdon had already seen them.

*Ten stone knights.*

*Five on the left. Five on the right.*

Lying prone on the floor, the carved, life-sized figures rested in peaceful poses. The knights were depicted wearing full armor, shields, and swords, and the tombs gave Langdon the uneasy sensation that someone had snuck in and poured plaster over the knights while they were sleeping. All of the figures were deeply weathered, and yet each was clearly unique—different armory pieces, distinct leg and arm positions, facial features, and markings on their shields.

*In London lies a knight a Pope interred.*

Langdon felt shaky as he inched deeper into the circular room.

This had to be the place.

# CHAPTER 84

**In a** rubbish-strewn alley very close to Temple Church, Rémy Legaludec pulled the Jaguar limousine to a stop behind a row of industrial waste bins. Killing the engine, he checked the area. Deserted. He got out of the car, walked toward the rear, and climbed back into the limousine's main cabin where the monk was.

Sensing Rémy's presence, the monk in the back emerged from a prayer-like trance, his red eyes looking more curious than fearful. All evening Rémy had been impressed with this trussed man's ability to stay calm. After some initial struggles in the Range Rover, the monk seemed to have accepted his plight and given over his fate to a higher power.

Loosening his bow tie, Rémy unbuttoned his high, starched, wing-tipped collar and felt as if he could breathe for the first time in years. He went to the limousine's wet bar, where he poured himself a Smirnoff vodka. He drank it in a single swallow and followed it with a second.

*Soon I will be a man of leisure.*

Searching the bar, Rémy found a standard service wine-opener and flicked open the sharp blade. The knife was usually employed to slice the lead foil from corks on fine bottles of wine, but it would serve a far more dramatic purpose this morning. Rémy turned and faced Silas, holding up the glimmering blade.

Now those red eyes flashed fear.

Rémy smiled and moved toward the back of the limousine. The monk recoiled, struggling against his bonds.

"Be still," Rémy whispered, raising the blade.

Silas could not believe that God had forsaken him. Even the physical pain of being bound Silas had turned into a spiritual exercise, asking the throb of his blood-starved muscles to remind him of the pain Christ endured. *I have been praying all night for liberation.* Now, as the knife descended, Silas clenched his eyes shut.

A slash of pain tore through his shoulder blades. He cried out, unable to believe he was going to die here in the back of this limousine, unable to defend himself. *I was doing God's work. The Teacher said he would protect me.*

Silas felt the biting warmth spreading across his back and shoulders and could picture his own blood, spilling out over his flesh. A piercing pain cut through his thighs now, and he felt the onset of that familiar undertow of disorientation—the body's defense mechanism against the pain.

As the biting heat tore through all of his muscles now, Silas clenched his eyes tighter, determined that the final image of his life would not be of his own killer. Instead he pictured a younger Bishop Aringarosa, standing before the small church in Spain . . . the church that he and Silas had built with their own hands. *The beginning of my life.*

Silas felt as if his body were on fire.

"Take a drink," the tuxedoed man whispered, his accent French. "It will help with your circulation."

Silas's eyes flew open in surprise. A blurry image was leaning over him, offering a glass of liquid. A mound of shredded duct tape lay on the floor beside the bloodless knife.

"Drink this," he repeated. "The pain you feel is the blood rushing into your muscles."

Silas felt the fiery throb transforming now to a prickling sting. The vodka tasted terrible, but he drank it, feeling grateful. Fate had dealt Silas a healthy share of bad luck tonight, but God had solved it all with one miraculous twist.

*God has not forsaken me.*

Silas knew what Bishop Aringarosa would call it.

*Divine intervention.*

"I had wanted to free you earlier," the servant apologized, "but it was impossible. With the police arriving at Château Villette, and then at Biggin Hill airport, this was the first possible moment. You understand, don't you, Silas?"

Silas recoiled, startled. "You know my name?"

The servant smiled.

Silas sat up now, rubbing his stiff muscles, his emotions a torrent of incredulity, appreciation, and confusion. "Are you . . . the Teacher?"

Rémy shook his head, laughing at the proposition. "I wish I had that kind of power. No, I am not the Teacher. Like you, I serve him. But the Teacher speaks highly of you. My name is Rémy."

Silas was amazed. "I don't understand. If you work for the Teacher, why did Langdon bring the keystone to *your* home?"

"Not my home. The home of the world's foremost Grail historian, Sir Leigh Teabing."

"But *you* live there. The odds . . ."

Rémy smiled, seeming to have no trouble with the apparent coincidence of Langdon's chosen refuge. "It was all utterly predictable. Robert Langdon was in possession of the keystone, and he needed help. What more logical place to run than to the home of Leigh Teabing? That I happen to live there is why the Teacher approached me in the first place." He paused. "How do you think the Teacher knows so much about the Grail?"

Now it dawned, and Silas was stunned. The Teacher had recruited a servant who had access to all of Sir Leigh Teabing's research. It was brilliant.

"There is much I have to tell you," Rémy said, handing Silas the loaded Heckler Koch pistol. Then he reached through the open partition and retrieved a small, palm-sized revolver from the glove box. "But first, you and I have a job to do."

Captain Fache descended from his transport plane at Biggin Hill and listened in disbelief to the Kent chief inspector's account of what had happened in Teabing's hangar.

"I searched the plane myself," the inspector insisted, "and there was no one inside." His tone turned haughty. "And I should add that if Sir Leigh Teabing presses charges against me, I will—"

"Did you interrogate the pilot?"

"Of course not. He is French, and our jurisdiction requires—"

"Take me to the plane."

Arriving at the hangar, Fache needed only sixty seconds to locate an anomalous smear of blood on the pavement near where the limousine had been parked. Fache walked up to the plane and rapped loudly on the fuselage.

"This is the captain of the French Judicial Police. Open the door!"

The terrified pilot opened the hatch and lowered the stairs.

Fache ascended. Three minutes later, with the help of his sidearm, he had a full confession, including a description of the bound albino monk. In addition, he learned that the pilot saw Langdon and Sophie leave something behind in Teabing's safe, a wooden box of some sort. Although the pilot denied knowing what was in the box, he admitted it had been the focus of Langdon's full attention during the flight to London.

"Open the safe," Fache demanded.

The pilot looked terrified. "I don't know the combination!"

"That's too bad. I was going to offer to let you keep your pilot's license."

The pilot wrung his hands. "I know some men in maintenance here. Maybe they could drill it?"

"You have half an hour."

The pilot leapt for his radio.

Fache strode to the back of the plane and poured himself a hard drink. It was early, but he had not yet slept, so this hardly counted as drinking before noon. Sitting in a plush bucket seat, he closed his eyes, trying to sort out what was going on. *The Kent police's blunder could cost me dearly.* Everyone was now on the lookout for a black Jaguar limousine.

Fache's phone rang, and he wished for a moment's peace. *"Allo?"*

"I'm en route to London." It was Bishop Aringarosa. "I'll be arriving in an hour."

Fache sat up. "I thought you were going to Paris."

"I am deeply concerned. I have changed my plans."

"You should not have."

"Do you have Silas?"

"No. His captors eluded the local police before I landed."

Aringarosa's anger rang sharply. "You assured me you would stop that plane!"

Fache lowered his voice. "Bishop, considering your situation, I recommend you not test my patience today. I will find Silas and the others as soon as possible. Where are you landing?"

"One moment." Aringarosa covered the receiver and then came back. "The pilot is trying to get clearance at Heathrow. I'm his only passenger, but our redirect was unscheduled."

"Tell him to come to Biggin Hill Executive Airport in Kent. I'll get him clearance. If I'm not here when you land, I'll have a car waiting for you."

"Thank you."

"As I expressed when we first spoke, Bishop, you would do well to remember that you are not the only man on the verge of losing everything."

# CHAPTER 85

**You seek** *the orb that ought be on his tomb.*

Each of the carved knights within the Temple Church lay on his back with his head resting on a rectangular stone pillow. Sophie felt a chill. The poem's reference to an "orb" conjured images of the night in her grandfather's basement.

*Hieros Gamos. The orbs.*

Sophie wondered if the ritual had been performed in this very sanctuary. The circular room seemed custom-built for such a pagan rite. A stone pew encircled a bare expanse of floor in the middle. *A theater in the round,* as Robert had called it. She imagined this chamber at night, filled with masked people, chanting by torchlight, all witnessing a "sacred communion" in the center of the room.

Forcing the image from her mind, she advanced with Langdon and Teabing toward the first group of knights. Despite Teabing's insistence that their investigation should be conducted meticulously, Sophie felt eager and pushed ahead of them, making a cursory walk-through of the five knights on the left.

Scrutinizing these first tombs, Sophie noted the similarities and differences between them. Every knight was on his back, but three of the knights had their legs extended straight out while two had their legs crossed. The oddity seemed to have no relevance to the missing orb. Examining their clothing, Sophie noted that two of the knights wore tunics over their armor, while the other three wore ankle-length robes. Again, utterly unhelpful. Sophie turned her attention to the only other obvious difference—their hand positions. Two knights clutched swords, two prayed, and one had his arms at his side. After a long moment looking at the hands, Sophie shrugged, having seen no hint anywhere of a conspicuously absent orb.

Feeling the weight of the cryptex in her sweater pocket, she glanced back at Langdon and Teabing. The men were moving slowly, still only at the third knight, apparently having no luck either. In no mood to wait, she turned away from them toward the second group of knights. As she crossed the open space, she quietly recited the poem she had read so many times now that it was committed to memory.

> In London lies a knight a Pope interred.
> His labor's fruit a Holy wrath incurred.
> You seek the orb that ought be on his tomb.
> It speaks of Rosy flesh and seeded womb.

When Sophie arrived at the second group of knights, she found that this second group was

similar to the first. All lay with varied body positions, wearing armor and swords.

That was, all except the tenth and final tomb.

Hurrying over to it, she stared down.

*No pillow. No armor. No tunic. No sword.*

"Robert? Leigh?" she called, her voice echoing
around the chamber. "There's something missing
over here."

Both men looked up and immediately began to
cross the room toward her.

"An orb?" Teabing called excitedly. His
crutches clicked out a rapid staccato as he hurried
across the room. "Are we missing an orb?"

"Not exactly," Sophie said, frowning at the
tenth tomb. "We seem to be missing an entire
knight."

Arriving beside her both men gazed down in
confusion at the tenth tomb. Rather than a knight
lying in the open air, this tomb was a sealed stone
casket. The casket was trapezoidal, tapered at the
feet, widening toward the top, with a peaked lid.

"Why isn't this knight shown?" Langdon asked.

"Fascinating," Teabing said, stroking his chin.
"I had forgotten about this oddity. It's been years
since I was here."

"This coffin," Sophie said, "looks like it was
carved at the same time and by the same sculptor
as the other nine tombs. So why is this knight in
a casket rather than in the open?"

Teabing shook his head. "One of this church's

mysteries. To the best of my knowledge, nobody has ever found any explanation for it."

"Hello?" the altar boy said, arriving with a perturbed look on his face. "Forgive me if this seems rude, but you told me you wanted to spread ashes, and yet you seem to be sightseeing."

Teabing scowled at the boy and turned to Langdon. "Mr. Wren, apparently your family's philanthropy does not buy you the time it used to, so perhaps we should take out the ashes and get on with it." Teabing turned to Sophie. "Mrs. Wren?"

Sophie played along, pulling the vellum-wrapped cryptex from her pocket.

"Now then," Teabing snapped at the boy, "if you would give us some privacy?"

The altar boy did not move. He was eyeing Langdon closely now. "You look familiar."

Teabing huffed. "Perhaps that is because Mr. Wren comes here every year!"

*Or perhaps,* Sophie now feared, *because he saw Langdon on television at the Vatican last year.*

"I have never met Mr. Wren," the altar boy declared.

"You're mistaken," Langdon said politely. "I believe you and I met in passing last year. Father Knowles failed to formally introduce us, but I recognized your face as we came in. Now, I realize this is an intrusion, but if you could afford me a few more minutes, I have traveled a great dis-

tance to scatter ashes amonst these tombs."
Langdon spoke his lines with Teabing-esque be-
lievability.

The altar boy's expression turned even more
skeptical. "These are not *tombs*."

"I'm sorry?" Langdon said.

"Of course they are tombs," Teabing declared.
"What are you talking about?"

The altar boy shook his head. "Tombs contain
bodies. These are effigies. Stone tributes to real
men. There are no bodies beneath these figures."

"This is a crypt!" Teabing said.

"Only in outdated history books. This was believed to be a crypt but was revealed as nothing
of the sort during the 1950 renovation." He
turned back to Langdon. "And I imagine Mr.
Wren would *know* that. Considering it was his
family that uncovered that fact."

An uneasy silence fell.

It was broken by the sound of a door slamming
out in the annex.

"That must be Father Knowles," Teabing said.
"Perhaps you should go see?"

The altar boy looked doubtful but stalked back
toward the annex, leaving Langdon, Sophie, and
Teabing to eye one another gloomily.

"Leigh," Langdon whispered. "No bodies?
What is he talking about?"

Teabing looked distraught. "I don't know. I always thought . . . certainly, this *must* be the place.

I can't imagine he knows what he is talking about. It makes no sense!"

"Can I see the poem again?" Langdon said.

Sophie pulled the cryptex from her pocket and carefully handed it to him.

Langdon unwrapped the vellum, holding the cryptex in his hand while he examined the poem. "Yes, the poem definitely references a *tomb*. Not an effigy."

"Could the poem be wrong?" Teabing asked. "Could Jacques Saunière have made the same mistake I just did?"

Langdon considered it and shook his head. "Leigh, you said it yourself. This church was built by Templars, the military arm of the Priory. Something tells me the Grand Master of the Priory would have a pretty good idea if there were knights buried here."

Teabing looked flabbergasted. "But this place is perfect." He wheeled back toward the knights. "We must be missing something!"

Entering the annex, the altar boy was surprised to find it deserted. "Father Knowles?" *I know I heard the door,* he thought, moving forward until he could see the entryway.

A thin man in a tuxedo stood near the doorway, scratching his head and looking lost. The altar boy gave an irritated huff, realizing he had forgotten to relock the door when he let the others in. Now some pathetic sod had wandered in off the street, looking for directions to some wedding from the looks of it. "I'm sorry," he called out, passing a large pillar, "we're closed."

A flurry of cloth ruffled behind him, and before the altar boy could turn, his head snapped backward, a powerful hand clamping hard over his mouth from behind, muffling his scream. The hand over the boy's mouth was snow-white, and he smelled alcohol.

The prim man in the tuxedo calmly produced a very small revolver, which he aimed directly at the boy's forehead.

The altar boy felt his groin grow hot and realized he had wet himself.

"Listen carefully," the tuxedoed man whispered. "You will exit this church silently, and you will run. You will not stop. Is that clear?"

The boy nodded as best he could with the hand over his mouth.

"If you call the police . . ." The tuxedoed man pressed the gun to his skin. "I will find you."

The next thing the boy knew, he was sprinting across the outside courtyard with no plans of stopping until his legs gave out.

# CHAPTER 86

**Like a** ghost, Silas drifted silently behind his target. Sophie Neveu sensed him too late. Before she could turn, Silas pressed the gun barrel into her spine and wrapped a powerful arm across her chest, pulling her back against his hulking body. She yelled in surprise. Teabing and Langdon both turned now, their expressions astonished and fearful.

"What . . . ?" Teabing choked out. "What did you do to Rémy!"

"Your only concern," Silas said calmly, "is that I leave here with the keystone." This recovery mission, as Rémy had described it, was to be clean and simple: *Enter the church, take the keystone, and walk out; no killing, no struggle.*

Holding Sophie firm, Silas dropped his hand from her chest, down to her waist, slipping it inside her deep sweater pockets, searching. He could smell the soft fragrance of her hair through his own alcohol-laced breath. "Where is it?" he whispered. *The keystone was in her sweater pocket earlier. So where is it now?*

"It's over here," Langdon's deep voice resonated from across the room.

Silas turned to see Langdon holding the black cryptex before him, waving it back and forth like a matador tempting a dumb animal.

"Set it down," Silas demanded.

"Let Sophie and Leigh leave the church," Langdon replied. "You and I can settle this."

Silas pushed Sophie away from him and aimed the gun at Langdon, moving toward him.

"Not a step closer," Langdon said. "Not until they leave the building."

"You are in no position to make demands."

"I disagree." Langdon raised the cryptex high over his head. "I will not hesitate to smash this on the floor and break the vial inside."

Although Silas sneered outwardly at the threat, he felt a flash of fear. This was unexpected. He aimed the gun at Langdon's head and kept his voice as steady as his hand. "You would never break the keystone. You want to find the Grail as much as I do."

"You're wrong. You want it much more. You've proven you're willing to kill for it."

Forty feet away, peering out from the annex pews near the archway, Rémy Legaludec felt a rising alarm. The maneuver had not gone as planned, and even from here, he could see Silas was uncertain how to handle the situation. At the

Teacher's orders, Rémy had forbidden Silas to fire his gun.

"Let them go," Langdon again demanded, holding the cryptex high over his head and staring into Silas's gun.

The monk's red eyes filled with anger and frustration, and Rémy tightened with fear that Silas might actually shoot Langdon while he was holding the cryptex. *The cryptex cannot fall!*

The cryptex was to be Rémy's ticket to freedom and wealth. A little over a year ago, he was simply a fifty-five-year-old manservant living within the walls of Château Villette, catering to the whims of the insufferable cripple Sir Leigh Teabing. Then he was approached with an extraordinary proposition. Rémy's association with Sir Leigh Teabing—the preeminent Grail historian on earth—was going to bring Rémy everything he had ever dreamed of in life. Since then, every moment he had spent inside Château Villette had been leading him to this very instant.

*I am so close,* Rémy told himself, gazing into the sanctuary of the Temple Church and the keystone in Robert Langdon's hand. If Langdon dropped it, all would be lost.

*Am I willing to show my face?* It was something the Teacher had strictly forbidden. Rémy was the only one who knew the Teacher's identity.

"Are you certain you want *Silas* to carry out

this task?" Rémy had asked the Teacher less than half an hour ago, upon getting orders to steal the keystone. "I myself am capable."

The Teacher was resolute. "Silas served us well with the four Priory members. He will recover the keystone. *You* must remain anonymous. If others see you, they will need to be eliminated, and there has been enough killing already. Do not reveal your face."

*My face will change,* Rémy thought. *With what you've promised to pay me, I will become an entirely new man.* Surgery could even change his fingerprints, the Teacher had told him. Soon he would be free—another unrecognizable, beautiful face soaking up the sun on the beach. "Understood," Rémy said. "I will assist Silas from the shadows."

"For your own knowledge, Rémy," the Teacher had told him, "the tomb in question is not in the Temple Church. So have no fear. They are looking in the wrong place."

Rémy was stunned. "And you know where the tomb is?"

"Of course. Later, I will tell you. For the moment, you must act quickly. If the others figure out the true location of the tomb and leave the church before you take the cryptex, we could lose the Grail forever."

Rémy didn't give a damn about the Grail, except that the Teacher refused to pay him until it was found. Rémy felt giddy every time he thought of the money he soon would have. *One third of twenty million euro. Plenty to disappear forever.* Rémy had pictured the beach towns on the Côte d'Azur, where he planned to live out his days basking in the sun and letting others serve him for a change.

Now, however, here in the Temple Church, with Langdon threatening to break the keystone, Rémy's future was at risk. Unable to bear the thought of coming this close only to lose it all, Rémy made the decision to take bold action. The gun in his hand was a concealable, small-caliber, J-frame Medusa, but it would be plenty deadly at close range.

Stepping from the shadows, Rémy marched into the circular chamber and aimed the gun directly at Teabing's head. "Old man, I've been waiting a long time to do this."

Sir Leigh Teabing's heart practically stalled to see Rémy aiming a gun at him. *What is he doing!* Teabing recognized the tiny Medusa revolver as his own, the one he kept locked in the limousine glove box for safety.

"Rémy?" Teabing sputtered in shock. "What is going on?"

Langdon and Sophie looked equally dumbstruck.

Rémy circled behind Teabing and rammed the

pistol barrel into his back, high and on the left, directly behind his heart.

Teabing felt his muscles seize with terror. "Rémy, I don't—"

"I'll make it simple," Rémy snapped, eyeing Langdon over Teabing's shoulder. "Set down the keystone, or I pull the trigger."

Langdon seemed momentarily paralyzed. "The keystone is worthless to you," he stammered. "You cannot possibly open it."

"Arrogant fools," Rémy sneered. "Have you not noticed that I have been listening tonight as you discussed these poems? Everything I heard, I have shared with others. Others who know more than you. You are not even looking in the right place. The tomb you seek is in another location entirely!"

Teabing felt panicked. *What is he saying!*

"Why do you want the Grail?" Langdon demanded. "To destroy it? Before the End of Days?"

Rémy called to the monk. "Silas, take the keystone from Mr. Langdon."

As the monk advanced, Langdon stepped back, raising the keystone high, looking fully prepared to hurl it at the floor.

"I would rather break it," Langdon said, "than see it in the wrong hands."

Teabing now felt a wave of horror. He could

see his life's work evaporating before his eyes. All his dreams about to be shattered.

"Robert, no!" Teabing exclaimed. "Don't! That's the Grail you're holding! Rémy would *never* shoot me. We've known each other for ten—"

Rémy aimed at the ceiling and fired the Medusa. The blast was enormous for such a small weapon, the gunshot echoing like thunder inside the stone chamber.

Everyone froze.

"I am not playing games," Rémy said. "The next one is in his back. Hand the keystone to Silas."

Langdon reluctantly held out the cryptex. Silas stepped forward and took it, his red eyes gleaming with the self-satisfaction of vengeance. Slipping the keystone in the pocket of his robe, Silas backed off, still holding Langdon and Sophie at gunpoint.

Teabing felt Rémy's arm clamp hard around his neck as the servant began backing out of the building, dragging Teabing with him, the gun still pressed in his back.

"Let him go," Langdon demanded.

"We're taking Mr. Teabing for a drive," Rémy said, still backing up. "If you call the police, he will die. If you do anything to interfere, he will die. Is that clear?"

"Take me," Langdon demanded, his voice cracking with emotion. "Let Leigh go."

Rémy laughed. "I don't think so. He and I have such a nice history. Besides, he still might prove useful."

Silas was backing up now, keeping Langdon and Sophie at gunpoint as Rémy pulled Leigh toward the exit, his crutches dragging behind him.

Sophie's voice was unwavering. "Who are you working for?"

The question brought a smirk to the departing Rémy's face. "You would be surprised, Mademoiselle Neveu."

# CHAPTER 87

**The fireplace** in Château Villette's drawing room was cold, but Collet paced before it nonetheless as he read the faxes from Interpol.

Not at all what he expected.

André Vernet, according to official records, was a model citizen. No police record—not even a parking ticket. Educated at prep school and the Sorbonne, he had a *cum laude* degree in international finance. Interpol said Vernet's name appeared in the newspapers from time to time, but always in a positive light. Apparently the man had helped design the security parameters that kept the Depository Bank of Zurich a leader in the ultramodern world of electronic security. Vernet's credit card records showed a penchant for art books, expensive wine, and classical CD's—mostly Brahms—which he apparently enjoyed on an exceptionally high-end stereo system he had purchased several years ago.

*Zero,* Collet sighed.

The only red flag tonight from Interpol had been a set of fingerprints that apparently belonged to Teabing's servant. The chief PTS examiner was reading the report in a comfortable chair across the room.

Collet looked over. "Anything?"

The examiner shrugged. "Prints belong to Rémy Legaludec. Wanted for petty crime. Nothing serious. Looks like he got kicked out of university for rewiring phone jacks to get free service . . . later did some petty theft. Breaking and entering. Skipped out on a hospital bill once for an emergency tracheotomy." He glanced up, chuckling. "Peanut allergy."

Collet nodded, recalling a police investigation into a restaurant that had failed to notate on its menu that the chili recipe contained peanut oil. An unsuspecting patron had died of anaphylactic shock at the table after a single bite.

"Legaludec is probably a live-in here to avoid getting picked up." The examiner looked amused. "His lucky night."

Collet sighed. "All right, you better forward this info to Captain Fache."

The examiner headed off just as another PTS agent burst into the living room. "Lieutenant! We found something in the barn."

From the anxious look on the agent's face, Collet could only guess. "A body."

"No, sir. Something more . . ." He hesitated. "Unexpected."

Rubbing his eyes, Collet followed the agent out to the barn. As they entered the musty, cavernous space, the agent motioned toward the center of the room, where a wooden ladder now ascended high into the rafters, propped against the ledge of a hayloft suspended high above them.

"That ladder wasn't there earlier," Collet said.

"No, sir. I set that up. We were dusting for prints near the Rolls when I saw the ladder lying on the floor. I wouldn't have given it a second thought except the rungs were worn and muddy. This ladder gets regular use. The height of the hayloft matched the ladder, so I raised it and climbed up to have a look."

Collet's eyes climbed the ladder's steep incline to the soaring hayloft. *Someone goes up there regularly?* From down here, the loft appeared to be a deserted platform, and yet admittedly most of it was invisible from this line of sight.

A senior PTS agent appeared at the top of the ladder, looking down. "You'll definitely want to see this, Lieutenant," he said, waving Collet up with a latex-gloved hand.

Nodding tiredly, Collet walked over to the base of the old ladder and grasped the bottom rungs. The ladder was an antique tapered design and narrowed as Collet ascended. As he neared the top, Collet almost lost his footing on a thin rung. The barn below him spun. Alert now, he moved on, finally reaching the top. The agent above him reached out, offering his wrist. Collet grabbed it and made the awkward transition onto the platform.

"It's over there," the PTS agent said, pointing

deep into the immaculately clean loft. "Only one set of prints up here. We'll have an ID shortly."

Collet squinted through the dim light toward the far wall. *What the hell?* Nestled against the far wall sat an elaborate computer workstation—two tower CPUs, a flat-screen video monitor with speakers, an array of hard drives, and a multi-channel audio console that appeared to have its own filtered power supply.

*Why in the world would anyone work all the way up here?* Collet moved toward the gear. "Have you examined the system?"

"It's a listening post."

Collet spun. "Surveillance?"

The agent nodded. "Very advanced surveillance." He motioned to a long project table strewn with electronic parts, manuals, tools, wires, soldering irons, and other electronic components. "Someone clearly knows what he's doing. A lot of this gear is as sophisticated as our own equipment. Miniature microphones, photo-electric recharging cells, high-capacity RAM chips. He's even got some of those new nano drives."

Collet was impressed.

"Here's a complete system," the agent said, handing Collet an assembly not much larger than a pocket calculator. Dangling off the contraption was a foot-long wire with a stamp-sized piece of wafer-thin foil stuck on the end. "The base is a high-capacity hard disk audio recording system with rechargeable battery. That strip of foil at the end of the wire is a combination microphone and photoelectric recharging cell."

Collet knew them well. These foil-like, photo-cell microphones had been an enormous break-through a few years back. Now, a hard disk recorder could be affixed behind a lamp, for ex-ample, with its foil microphone molded into the contour of the base and dyed to match. As long as the microphone was positioned such that it re-ceived a few hours of sunlight per day, the photo cells would keep recharging the system. Bugs like this one could listen indefinitely.

"Reception method?" Collet asked.

The agent signaled to an insulated wire that ran out of the back of the computer, up the wall, through a hole in the barn roof. "Simple radio wave. Small antenna on the roof."

Collet knew these recording systems were gen-erally placed in offices, were voice-activated to save hard disk space, and recorded snippets of conversation during the day, transmitting com-pressed audio files at night to avoid detection. After transmitting, the hard drive erased itself and prepared to do it all over again the next day.

Collet's gaze moved now to a shelf on which were stacked several hundred audio cassettes, all labeled with dates and numbers. *Someone has been very busy.* He turned back to the agent. "Do you have any idea what target is being bugged?"

"Well, Lieutenant," the agent said, walking to the computer and launching a piece of software. "It's the strangest thing. . . ."

# CHAPTER 88

**Langdon felt** utterly spent as he and Sophie hurdled a turnstile at the Temple tube station and dashed deep into the grimy labyrinth of tunnels and platforms. The guilt ripped through him.

*I involved Leigh, and now he's in enormous danger.*

Rémy's involvement had been a shock, and yet it made sense. Whoever was pursuing the Grail had recruited someone on the inside. *They went to Teabing's for the same reason I did.* Throughout history, those who held knowledge of the Grail had always been magnets for thieves and scholars alike. The fact that Teabing had been a target all along should have made Langdon feel less guilty about involving him. It did not. *We need to find Leigh and help him. Immediately.*

Langdon followed Sophie to the westbound District and Circle Line platform, where she hurried to a pay phone to call the police, despite Rémy's warning to the contrary. Langdon sat on a grungy bench nearby, feeling remorseful.

"The best way to help Leigh," Sophie reiterated as she dialed, "is to involve the London authorities immediately. Trust me."

Langdon had not initially agreed with this idea, but as they had hatched their plan, Sophie's logic began to make sense. Teabing was safe at the moment. Even if Rémy and the others knew where the knight's tomb was located, they still might need Teabing's help deciphering the orb reference. What worried Langdon was what would happen *after* the Grail map had been found. *Leigh will become a huge liability.*

If Langdon were to have any chance of helping Leigh, or of ever seeing the keystone again, it was essential that he find the tomb first. *Unfortunately, Rémy has a big head start.*

Slowing Rémy down had become Sophie's task.

Finding the right tomb had become Langdon's.

Sophie would make Rémy and Silas fugitives of the London police, forcing them into hiding or, better yet, catching them. Langdon's plan was less certain—to take the tube to nearby King's College, which was renowned for its electronic theological database. *The ultimate research tool,* Langdon had heard. *Instant answers to any religious historical question.* He wondered what the database would have to say about "a knight a Pope interred."

He stood up and paced, wishing the train would hurry.

At the pay phone, Sophie's call finally connected to the London police.

"Snow Hill Division," the dispatcher said. "How may I direct your call?"

"I'm reporting a kidnapping." Sophie knew to be concise.

"Name please?"

Sophie paused. "Agent Sophie Neveu with the French Judicial Police."

The title had the desired effect. "Right away, ma'am. Let me get a detective on the line for you."

As the call went through, Sophie began wondering if the police would even believe her description of Teabing's captors. *A man in a tuxedo.* How much easier to identify could a suspect be? Even if Rémy changed clothes, he was partnered with an albino monk. *Impossible to miss.* Moreover, they had a hostage and could not take public transportation. She wondered how many Jaguar stretch limos there could be in London.

Sophie's connection to the detective seemed to be taking forever. *Come on!* She could hear the line clicking and buzzing, as if she was being transferred.

Fifteen seconds passed.

Finally a man came on the line. "Agent Neveu?"

Stunned, Sophie registered the gruff tone immediately.

"Agent Neveu," Bezu Fache demanded. "Where the hell are you?"

Sophie was speechless. Captain Fache had apparently requested the London police dispatcher alert him if Sophie called in.

"Listen," Fache said, speaking to her in terse French. "I made a terrible mistake tonight. Robert Langdon is innocent. All charges against him have been dropped. Even so, both of you are in danger. You need to come in."

Sophie's jaw fell slack. She had no idea how to respond. Fache was not a man who apologized for anything.

"You did not tell me," Fache continued, "that Jacques Saunière was your grandfather. I fully intend to overlook your insubordination last night on account of the emotional stress you must be under. At the moment, however, you and Langdon need to go to the nearest London police headquarters for refuge."

*He knows I'm in London? What else does Fache know?* Sophie heard what sounded like drilling or machinery in the background. She also heard an odd clicking on the line. "Are you tracing this call, Captain?"

Fache's voice was firm now. "You and I need to cooperate, Agent Neveu. We both have a lot to lose here. This is damage control. I made errors in judgment last night, and if those errors result in the deaths of an American professor and a DCPJ cryptologist, my career will be over. I've been trying to pull you back into safety for the last several hours."

A warm wind was now pushing through the station as a train approached with a low rumble.

Sophie had every intention of being on it. Langdon apparently had the same idea; he was gathering himself together and moving toward her now.

"The man you want is Rémy Legaludec," Sophie said. "He is Teabing's servant. He just kidnapped Teabing inside the Temple Church and—"

"Agent Neveu!" Fache bellowed as the train thundered into the station. "This is not something to discuss on an open line. You and Langdon will come in now. For your own well-being! That is a direct order!"

Sophie hung up and dashed with Langdon onto the train.

# CHAPTER 89

**The immaculate** cabin of Teabing's Hawker was now covered with steel shavings and smelled of compressed air and propane. Bezu Fache had sent everyone away and sat alone with his drink and the heavy wooden box found in Teabing's safe.

Running his finger across the inlaid Rose, he lifted the ornate lid. Inside he found a stone cylinder with lettered dials. The five dials were arranged to spell SOFIA. Fache stared at the word a long moment and then lifted the cylinder from its padded resting place and examined every inch. Then, pulling slowly on the ends, Fache slid off one of the end caps. The cylinder was empty.

Fache set it back in the box and gazed absently out the jet's window at the hangar, pondering his brief conversation with Sophie, as well as the information he'd received from PTS in Château Villette. The sound of his phone shook him from his daydream.

It was the DCPJ switchboard. The dispatcher was apologetic. The president of the Depository Bank of Zurich had been calling repeatedly, and although he had been told several times that the captain was in London on business, he just kept calling. Begrudgingly Fache told the operator to forward the call.

"Monsieur Vernet," Fache said, before the man could even speak, "I am sorry I did not call you earlier. I have been busy. As promised, the name of your bank has not appeared in the media. So what precisely is your concern?"

Vernet's voice was anxious as he told Fache how Langdon and Sophie had extracted a small wooden box from the bank and then persuaded Vernet to help them escape. "Then when I heard on the radio that they were criminals," Vernet said, "I pulled over and demanded the box back, but they attacked me and stole the truck."

"You are concerned for a wooden box," Fache said, eyeing the Rose inlay on the cover and again gently opening the lid to reveal the white cylinder. "Can you tell me what was in the box?"

"The contents are immaterial," Vernet fired back. "I am concerned with the reputation of my bank. We have never had a robbery. *Ever.* It will ruin us if I cannot recover this property on behalf of my client."

"You said Agent Neveu and Robert Langdon had a password and a key. What makes you say they stole the box?"

"They *murdered* people tonight. Including Sophie Neveu's grandfather. The key and password were obviously ill-gotten."

"Mr. Vernet, my men have done some checking into your background and your interests. You are obviously a man of great culture and refinement. I would imagine you are a man of honor, as well. As am I. That said, I give you my word as commanding officer of the *Police Judiciaire* that your box, along with your bank's reputation, are in the safest of hands."

# CHAPTER 90

**High in** the hayloft at Château Villette, Collet stared at the computer monitor in amazement. "This system is eavesdropping on *all* these locations?"

"Yes," the agent said. "It looks like data has been collected for over a year now."

Collet read the list again, speechless.

> COLBERT SOSTAQUE—Chairman of the Conseil
> Constitutionnel
> JEAN CHAFFÉE—Curator, Musée du Jeu de
> Paume
> EDOUARD DESROCHERS—Senior Archivist,
> Mitterand Library
> JACQUES SAUNIÈRE—Curator, Musée du Louvre
> MICHEL BRETON—Head of DAS (French
> Intelligence)

The agent pointed to the screen. "Number four is of obvious concern."

Collet nodded blankly. He had noticed it immediately. *Jacques Saunière was being bugged.* He looked at the rest of the list again. *How could anyone possibly manage to bug these prominent people?* "Have you heard any of the audio files?"

"A few. Here's one of the most recent." The agent clicked a few computer keys. The speakers crackled to life. *"Capitaine, un agent du Département de Cryptographie est arrivé."*

Collet could not believe his ears. "That's me! That's my voice!" He recalled sitting at Saunière's desk and radioing Fache in the Grand Gallery to alert him of Sophie Neveu's arrival.

The agent nodded. "A lot of our Louvre investigation tonight would have been audible if someone had been interested."

"Have you sent anyone in to sweep for the bug?"

"No need. I know exactly where it is." The agent went to a pile of old notes and blueprints on the worktable. He selected a page and handed it to Collet. "Look familiar?"

Collet was amazed. He was holding a photocopy of an ancient schematic diagram, which depicted a rudimentary machine. He was unable to read the handwritten Italian labels, and yet he knew what he was looking at. A model for a fully articulated medieval French knight.

*The knight sitting on Saunière's desk!*

Collet's eyes moved to the margins, where someone had scribbled notes on the photocopy in red felt-tipped marker. The notes were in French and appeared to be ideas outlining how best to insert a listening device into the knight.

# CHAPTER 91

**Silas sat** in the passenger seat of the parked Jaguar limousine near the Temple Church. His hands felt damp on the keystone as he waited for Rémy to finish tying and gagging Teabing in back with the rope they had found in the trunk.

Finally, Rémy climbed out of the rear of the limo, walked around, and slid into the driver's seat beside Silas.

"Secure?" Silas asked.

Rémy chuckled, shaking off the rain and glancing over his shoulder through the open partition at the crumpled form of Leigh Teabing, who was barely visible in the shadows in the rear. "He's not going anywhere."

Silas could hear Teabing's muffled cries and realized Rémy had used some of the old duct tape to gag him.

*"Ferme ta gueule!"* Rémy shouted over his shoulder at Teabing. Reaching to a control panel on the elaborate dash, Rémy pressed a button. An opaque partition raised behind them, sealing off the back. Teabing disappeared, and his voice was silenced. Rémy glanced at Silas. "I've been listening to his miserable whimpering long enough."

Minutes later, as the Jaguar stretch limo powered through the streets, Silas's cell phone rang. *The Teacher.* He answered excitedly. "Hello?"

"Silas," the Teacher's familiar French accent said, "I am relieved to hear your voice. This means you are safe."

Silas was equally comforted to hear the Teacher. It had been hours, and the operation had veered wildly off course. Now, at last, it seemed to be back on track. "I have the keystone."

"This is superb news," the Teacher told him. "Is Rémy with you?"

Silas was surprised to hear the Teacher use Rémy's name. "Yes. Rémy freed me."

"As I ordered him to do. I am only sorry you had to endure captivity for so long."

"Physical discomfort has no meaning. The important thing is that the keystone is ours."

"Yes. I need it delivered to me at once. Time is of the essence."

Silas was eager to meet the Teacher face-to-face at last. "Yes, sir, I would be honored."

"Silas, I would like *Rémy* to bring it to me."

*Rémy?* Silas was crestfallen. After everything Silas had done for the Teacher, he had believed *he* would be the one to hand over the prize. *The Teacher favors Rémy?*

"I sense your disappointment," the Teacher said, "which tells me you do not understand my meaning." He lowered his voice to a whisper.

"You must believe that I would much prefer to receive the keystone from *you*—a man of God rather than a criminal—but Rémy must be dealt with. He disobeyed my orders and made a grave mistake that has put our entire mission at risk."

Silas felt a chill and glanced over at Rémy. Kidnapping Teabing had not been part of the plan, and deciding what to do with him posed a new problem.

"You and I are men of God," the Teacher whispered. "We cannot be deterred from our goal." There was an ominous pause on the line. "For this reason alone, I will ask Rémy to bring me the keystone. Do you understand?"

Silas sensed anger in the Teacher's voice and was surprised the man was not more understanding. *Showing his face could not be avoided*, Silas thought. *Rémy did what he had to do. He saved the keystone.* "I understand," Silas managed.

"Good. For your own safety, you need to get off the street immediately. The police will be looking for the limousine soon, and I do not want you caught. Opus Dei has a residence in London, no?"

"Of course."

"And you are welcome there?"

"As a brother."

"Then go there and stay out of sight. I will call you the moment I am in possession of the keystone and have attended to my current problem."

"You are in London?"

"Do as I say, and everything will be fine."

"Yes, sir."

The Teacher heaved a sigh, as if what he now had to do was profoundly regrettable. "It's time I speak to Rémy."

Silas handed Rémy the phone, sensing it might be the last call Rémy Legaludec ever took.

As Rémy took the phone, he knew this poor, twisted monk had no idea what fate awaited him now that he had served his purpose.

*The Teacher used you, Silas.*

*And your bishop is a pawn.*

Rémy still marveled at the Teacher's powers of persuasion. Bishop Aringarosa had trusted everything. He had been blinded by his own desperation. *Aringarosa was far too eager to believe.* Although Rémy did not particularly like the Teacher, he felt pride at having gained the man's trust and helped him so substantially. *I have earned my payday.*

"Listen carefully," the Teacher said. "Take Silas to the Opus Dei residence hall and drop him off a few streets away. Then drive to St. James's Park. It is adjacent to Parliament and Big Ben. You can park the limousine on Horse Guards Parade. We'll talk there."

With that, the connection went dead.

# CHAPTER 92

**King's College,** established by King George IV in 1829, houses its Department of Theology and Religious Studies adjacent to Parliament on property granted by the Crown. King's College Religion Department boasts not only 150 years' experience in teaching and research, but the 1982 establishment of the Research Institute in Systematic Theology, which possesses one of the most complete and electronically advanced religious research libraries in the world.

Langdon still felt shaky as he and Sophie came in from the rain and entered the library. The primary research room was as Teabing had described it—a dramatic octagonal chamber dominated by an enormous round table around which King Arthur and his knights might have been comfortable were it not for the presence of twelve flat-screen computer workstations. On the far side of the room, a reference librarian was just pouring a pot of tea and settling in for her day of work.

"Lovely morning," she said in a cheerful British accent, leaving the tea and walking over. "May I help you?"

"Thank you, yes," Langdon replied. "My name is—"

"Robert Langdon." She gave a pleasant smile. "I know who you are."

For an instant, he feared Fache had put him on English television as well, but the librarian's smile suggested otherwise. Langdon still had not gotten used to these moments of unexpected celebrity. Then again, if anyone on earth were going to recognize his face, it would be a librarian in a Religious Studies reference facility.

"Pamela Gettum," the librarian said, offering her hand. She had a genial, erudite face and a pleasingly fluid voice. The horn-rimmed glasses hanging around her neck were thick.

"A pleasure," Langdon said. "This is my friend Sophie Neveu."

The two women greeted one another, and Gettum turned immediately back to Langdon. "I didn't know you were coming."

"Neither did we. If it's not too much trouble, we could really use your help finding some information."

Gettum shifted, looking uncertain. "Normally our services are by petition and appointment only, unless of course you're the guest of someone at the college?"

Langdon shook his head. "I'm afraid we've come unannounced. A friend of mine speaks very highly of you. Sir Leigh Teabing?" Langdon felt a pang of gloom as he said the name. "The British Royal Historian."

Gettum brightened now, laughing. "Heavens, yes. What a character. Fanatical! Every time he comes in, it's always the same search strings. Grail. Grail. Grail. I swear that man will die before he gives up on that quest." She winked. "Time and money afford one such lovely luxuries, wouldn't you say? A regular Don Quixote, that one."

"Is there any chance you can help us?" Sophie asked. "It's quite important."

Gettum glanced around the deserted library and then winked at them both. "Well, I can't very well claim I'm too busy, now can I? As long as you sign in, I can't imagine anyone being too upset. What did you have in mind?"

"We're trying to find a tomb in London."

Gettum looked dubious. "We've got about twenty thousand of them. Can you be a little more specific?"

"It's the tomb of a *knight*. We don't have a name."

"A knight. That tightens the net substantially. Much less common."

"We don't have much information about the knight we're looking for," Sophie said, "but this is what we know." She produced a slip of paper on which she had written only the first two lines of the poem.

Hesitant to show the entire poem to an outsider, Langdon and Sophie had decided to share just the first two lines, those that identified the knight. *Compartmentalized cryptography,* Sophie had called it. When an intelligence agency intercepted a code containing sensitive data, cryptographers each worked on a discrete section of the code. This way, when they broke it, no single cryptographer possessed the entire deciphered message.

In this case, the precaution was probably excessive; even if this librarian saw the entire poem, identified the knight's tomb, and knew what orb was missing, the information was useless without the cryptex.

Gettum sensed an urgency in the eyes of this famed American scholar, almost as if his finding this tomb quickly were a matter of critical importance. The green-eyed woman accompanying him also seemed anxious.

Puzzled, Gettum put on her glasses and examined the paper they had just handed her.

> In London lies a knight a Pope interred.
> His labor's fruit a Holy wrath incurred.

She glanced at her guests. "What is this? Some kind of Harvard scavenger hunt?"

Langdon's laugh sounded forced. "Yeah, something like that."

Gettum paused, feeling she was not getting the whole story. Nonetheless, she felt intrigued and found herself pondering the verse carefully. "According to this rhyme, a knight did something that incurred displeasure with God, and yet a Pope was kind enough to bury him in London."

Langdon nodded. "Does it ring any bells?"

Gettum moved toward one of the workstations. "Not offhand, but let's see what we can pull up in the database."

Over the past two decades, King's College Research Institute in Systematic Theology had used optical character recognition software in unison with linguistic translation devices to digitize and catalog an enormous collection of texts—encyclopedias of religion, religious biographies, sacred scriptures in dozens of languages, histories, Vatican letters, diaries of clerics, anything at all that qualified as writings on human spirituality. Because the massive collection was now in the form of bits and bytes rather than physical pages, the data was infinitely more accessible.

Settling into one of the workstations, Gettum eyed the slip of paper and began typing. "To begin, we'll run a straight Boolean with a few obvious keywords and see what happens."

"Thank you."

Gettum typed in a few words:

LONDON, KNIGHT, POPE

As she clicked the SEARCH button, she could feel the hum of the massive mainframe downstairs scanning data at a rate of 500 MB/sec. "I'm asking the system to show us any documents whose complete text contains all three of these keywords. We'll get more hits than we want, but it's a good place to start."

The screen was already showing the first of the hits now.

*Painting the Pope. The Collected Portraits of Sir Joshua Reynolds.* London University Press.

Gettum shook her head. "Obviously not what you're looking for."

She scrolled to the next hit.

*The London Writings of Alexander Pope* by G. Wilson Knight.

Again she shook her head.

As the system churned on, the hits came up more quickly than usual. Dozens of texts appeared, many of them referencing the eighteenth-century British writer Alexander Pope, whose counterreligious, mock-epic poetry apparently contained plenty of references to knights and London.

Gettum shot a quick glance to the numeric field at the bottom of the screen. This computer, by calculating the current number of hits and multiplying by the percentage of the database left to search, provided a rough guess of how much information would be found. This particular search looked like it was going to return an obscenely large amount of data.

Estimated number of total hits:
2,692

"We need to refine the parameters further," Gettum said, stopping the search. "Is this all the information you have regarding the tomb? There's nothing else to go on?"

Langdon glanced at Sophie Neveu, looking uncertain.

*This is no scavenger hunt,* Gettum sensed. She had heard the whisperings of Robert Langdon's experience in Rome last year. This American had been granted access to the most secure library on earth—the Vatican Secret Archives. She wondered what kinds of secrets Langdon might have learned inside and if his current desperate hunt for a mysterious London tomb might relate to information he had gained within the Vatican. Gettum had been a librarian long enough to know the most common reason people came to London to look for knights. *The Grail.*

Gettum smiled and adjusted her glasses. "You are friends with Leigh Teabing, you are in England, and you are looking for a knight." She folded her hands. "I can only assume you are on a Grail quest."

Langdon and Sophie exchanged startled looks.

Gettum laughed. "My friends, this library is a base camp for Grail seekers. Leigh Teabing among them. I wish I had a shilling for every time I'd run searches for the Rose, Mary Magdalene, Sangreal, Merovingian, Priory of Sion, et cetera, et cetera. Everyone loves a conspiracy." She took off her glasses and eyed them. "I need more information."

In the silence, Gettum sensed her guests' desire for discretion was quickly being outweighed by their eagerness for a fast result.

"Here," Sophie Neveu blurted. "This is everything we know." Borrowing a pen from Langdon, she wrote two more lines on the slip of paper and handed it to Gettum.

You seek the orb that ought be on his tomb.
  It speaks of Rosy flesh and seeded womb.

Gettum gave an inward smile. *The Grail indeed,* she thought, noting the references to the Rose and her seeded womb. "I can help you," she said, looking up from the slip of paper. "Might I ask where this verse came from? And why you are seeking an orb?"

"You might ask," Langdon said, with a friendly smile, "but it's a long story and we have very little time."

"Sounds like a polite way of saying 'mind your own business.' "

"We would be forever in your debt, Pamela," Langdon said, "if you could find out who this knight is and where he is buried."

"Very well," Gettum said, typing again. "I'll play along. If this is a Grail-related issue, we should cross-reference against Grail keywords. I'll add a proximity parameter and remove the title weighting. That will limit our hits only to those instances of textual keywords that occur *near* a Grail-related word."

*Search for:*
KNIGHT, LONDON, POPE, TOMB

*Within 100 word proximity of:*
GRAIL, ROSE, SANGREAL, CHALICE

"How long will this take?" Sophie asked.

"A few hundred terabytes with multiple cross-referencing fields?" Gettum's eyes glimmered as she clicked the SEARCH key. "A mere fifteen minutes."

Langdon and Sophie said nothing, but Gettum sensed this sounded like an eternity to them.

"Tea?" Gettum asked, standing and walking toward the pot she had made earlier. "Leigh always loves my tea."

# CHAPTER 93

**London's Opus** Dei Centre is a modest brick building at 5 Orme Court, overlooking the North Walk at Kensington Gardens. Silas had never been here, but he felt a rising sense of refuge and asylum as he approached the building on foot. Despite the rain, Rémy had dropped him off a short distance away in order to keep the limousine off the main streets. Silas didn't mind the walk. The rain was cleansing.

At Rémy's suggestion, Silas had wiped down his gun and disposed of it through a sewer grate. He was glad to get rid of it. He felt lighter. His legs still ached from being bound all that time, but Silas had endured far greater pain. He wondered, though, about Teabing, whom Rémy had left bound in the back of the limousine. The Briton certainly had to be feeling the pain by now.

"What will you do with him?" Silas had asked Rémy as they drove over here.

Rémy had shrugged. "That is a decision for the Teacher." There was an odd finality in his tone.

Now, as Silas approached the Opus Dei building, the rain began to fall harder, soaking his heavy robe, stinging the wounds of the day before. He was ready to leave behind the sins of the last twenty-four hours and purge his soul. His work was done.

Moving across a small courtyard to the front door, Silas was not surprised to find the door unlocked. He opened it and stepped into the minimalist foyer. A muted electronic chime sounded upstairs as Silas stepped onto the carpet. The bell was a common feature in these halls where the residents spent most of the day in their rooms in prayer. Silas could hear movement above on the creaky wood floors.

A man in a cloak came downstairs. "May I help you?" He had kind eyes that seemed not even to register Silas's startling physical appearance.

"Thank you. My name is Silas. I am an Opus Dei numerary."

"American?"

Silas nodded. "I am in town only for the day. Might I rest here?"

"You need not even ask. There are two empty rooms on the third floor. Shall I bring you some tea and bread?"

"Thank you." Silas was famished.

Silas went upstairs to a modest room with a window, where he took off his wet robe and knelt down to pray in his undergarments. He heard his host come up and lay a tray outside his door. Silas finished his prayers, ate his food, and lay down to sleep.

———

Three stories below, a phone was ringing. The Opus Dei numerary who had welcomed Silas answered the line.

"This is the London police," the caller said. "We are trying to find an albino monk. We've had a tip-off that he might be there. Have you seen him?"

The numerary was startled. "Yes, he is here. Is something wrong?"

"He is there *now?*"

"Yes, upstairs praying. What is going on?"

"Leave him precisely where he is," the officer commanded. "Don't say a word to anyone. I'm sending officers over right away."

# CHAPTER 94

**St. James's** Park is a sea of green in the middle of London, a public park bordering the palaces of Westminster, Buckingham, and St. James's. Once enclosed by King Henry VIII and stocked with deer for the hunt, St. James's Park is now open to the public. On sunny afternoons, Londoners picnic beneath the willows and feed the pond's resident pelicans, whose ancestors were a gift to Charles II from the Russian ambassador.

The Teacher saw no pelicans today. The stormy weather had brought instead seagulls from the ocean. The lawns were covered with them—hundreds of white bodies all facing the same direction, patiently riding out the damp wind. Despite the morning fog, the park afforded splendid views of the Houses of Parliament and Big Ben. Gazing across the sloping lawns, past the duck pond and the delicate silhouettes of the weeping willows, the Teacher could see the spires of the building that housed the knight's tomb—the real reason he had told Rémy to come to this spot.

As the Teacher approached the front passenger

door of the parked limousine, Rémy leaned across and opened the door. The Teacher paused outside, taking a pull from the flask of cognac he was carrying. Then, dabbing his mouth, he slid in beside Rémy and closed the door.

Rémy held up the keystone like a trophy. "It was almost lost."

"You have done well," the Teacher said.

"*We* have done well," Rémy replied, laying the keystone in the Teacher's eager hands.

The Teacher admired it a long moment, smiling. "And the gun? You wiped it down?"

"Back in the glove box where I found it."

"Excellent." The Teacher took another drink of cognac and handed the flask to Rémy. "Let's toast our success. The end is near."

Rémy accepted the bottle gratefully. The cognac tasted salty, but Rémy didn't care. He and the Teacher were truly partners now. He could feel himself ascending to a higher station in life. *I will never be a servant again.* As Rémy gazed down the embankment at the duck pond below, Château Villette seemed miles away.

Taking another swig from the flask, Rémy could feel the cognac warming his blood. The warmth in Rémy's throat, however, mutated quickly to an uncomfortable heat. Loosening his bow tie, Rémy tasted an unpleasant grittiness and handed the flask back to the Teacher. "I've probably had enough," he managed, weakly.

Taking the flask, the Teacher said, "Rémy, as you are aware, you are the only one who knows my face. I placed enormous trust in you."

"Yes," he said, feeling feverish as he loosened his tie further. "And your identity shall go with me to the grave."

The Teacher was silent a long moment. "I believe you." Pocketing the flask and the keystone, the Teacher reached for the glove box and pulled out the tiny Medusa revolver. For an instant, Rémy felt a surge of fear, but the Teacher simply slipped it in his trousers pocket.

*What is he doing?* Rémy felt himself sweating suddenly.

"I know I promised you freedom," the Teacher said, his voice now sounding regretful. "But considering your circumstances, this is the best I can do."

The swelling in Rémy's throat came on like an earthquake, and he lurched against the steering column, grabbing his throat and tasting vomit in his narrowing esophagus. He let out a muted croak of a scream, not even loud enough to be heard outside the car. The saltiness in the cognac now registered.

*I'm being murdered!*

Incredulous, Rémy turned to see the Teacher

sitting calmly beside him, staring straight ahead out the windshield. Rémy's eyesight blurred, and he gasped for breath. *I made everything possible for him! How could he do this!* Whether the Teacher had intended to kill Rémy all along or whether it had been Rémy's actions in the Temple Church that had made the Teacher lose faith, Rémy would never know. Terror and rage coursed through him now. Rémy tried to lunge for the Teacher, but his stiffening body could barely move. *I trusted you with everything!*

Rémy tried to lift his clenched fists to blow the horn, but instead he slipped sideways, rolling onto the seat, lying on his side beside the Teacher, clutching at his throat. The rain fell harder now. Rémy could no longer see, but he could sense his oxygen-deprived brain straining to cling to his last faint shreds of lucidity. As his world slowly went black, Rémy Legaludec could have sworn he heard the sounds of the soft Riviera surf.

The Teacher stepped from the limousine, pleased to see that nobody was looking in his direction. *I had no choice,* he told himself, surprised how little remorse he felt for what he had just done. *Rémy sealed his own fate.* The Teacher had feared all along that Rémy might need to be eliminated when the mission was complete, but by brazenly showing himself in the Temple Church, Rémy had accelerated the necessity dramatically. Robert Langdon's unexpected visit to Château Villette had brought the Teacher both a fortuitous windfall and an intricate dilemma. Langdon had delivered the keystone directly to the heart of the operation, which was a pleasant surprise, and yet he had brought the police on his tail. Rémy's prints were all over Château Villette, as well as in the barn's listening post, where Rémy had carried out the surveillance. The Teacher was grateful he had taken so much care in preventing any ties between Rémy's activities and his own. Nobody could implicate the Teacher unless Rémy talked, and that was no longer a concern.

*One more loose end to tie up here,* the Teacher thought, moving now toward the rear door of the limousine. *The police will have no idea what happened . . . and no living witness left to tell them.* Glancing around to ensure nobody was watching, he pulled open the door and climbed into the spacious rear compartment.

Minutes later, the Teacher was crossing St. James's Park. *Only two people now remain. Langdon and Neveu.* They were more complicated. But manageable. At the moment, however, the Teacher had the cryptex to attend to.

Gazing triumphantly across the park, he could see his destination. *In London lies a knight a Pope interred.* As soon as the Teacher had heard the poem, he had known the answer. Even so, that the others had not figured it out was not surprising. *I have an unfair advantage.* Having listened to Saunière's conversations for months now, the Teacher had heard the Grand Master mention this famous knight on occasion, expressing esteem almost matching that he held for Da Vinci. The poem's reference to the knight was brutally simple once one saw it—a credit to Saunière's wit—and yet how this tomb would reveal the final password was still a mystery.

*You seek the orb that ought be on his tomb.*

The Teacher vaguely recalled photos of the famous tomb and, in particular, its most distinguishing feature. *A magnificent orb.* The huge sphere mounted atop the tomb was almost as large as the tomb itself. The presence of the orb seemed both encouraging and troubling to the Teacher. On one hand, it felt like a signpost, and yet, according to the poem, the missing piece of the puzzle was an orb that *ought* to be on his tomb . . . not one that was already there. He was counting on his closer inspection of the tomb to unveil the answer.

The rain was getting heavier now, and he tucked the cryptex deep in his right-hand pocket to protect it from the dampness. He kept the tiny Medusa revolver in his left, out of sight. Within minutes, he was stepping into the quiet sanctuary of London's grandest nine-hundred-year-old building.

Just as the Teacher was stepping out of the rain, Bishop Aringarosa was stepping into it. On the rainy tarmac at Biggin Hill Executive Airport, Aringarosa emerged from his cramped plane, bundling his cassock against the cold damp. He had hoped to be greeted by Captain Fache. Instead a young British police officer approached with an umbrella.

"Bishop Aringarosa? Captain Fache had to leave. He asked me to look after you. He suggested I take you to Scotland Yard. He thought it would be safest."

*Safest?* Aringarosa looked down at the heavy briefcase of Vatican bonds clutched in his hand. He had almost forgotten. "Yes, thank you."

Aringarosa climbed into the police car, wondering where Silas could be. Minutes later, the police scanner crackled with the answer.

*5 Orme Court.*

Aringarosa recognized the address instantly.

*The Opus Dei Centre in London.*

He spun to the driver. "Take me there at once!"

# CHAPTER 95

**Langdon's eyes** had not left the computer screen since the search began.

*Five minutes. Only two hits. Both irrelevant.*

He was starting to get worried.

Pamela Gettum was in the adjoining room, preparing hot drinks. Langdon and Sophie had inquired unwisely if there might be some *coffee* brewing alongside the tea Gettum had offered, and from the sound of the microwave beeps in the next room, Langdon suspected their request was about to be rewarded with instant Nescafé.

Finally, the computer pinged happily.

"Sounds like you got another," Gettum called from the next room. "What's the title?"

Langdon eyed the screen.

```
     Grail Allegory in
     Medieval Literature:
  A Treatise on Sir Gawain
     and the Green Knight.
```

"Allegory of the Green Knight," he called back.

"No good," Gettum said. "Not many mythological green giants buried in London."

Langdon and Sophie sat patiently in front of the

screen and waited through two more dubious re-
turns. When the computer pinged again, though,
the offering was unexpected.

DIE OPERN VON RICHARD WAGNER

"The operas of Wagner?" Sophie asked.

Gettum peeked back in the doorway, holding a
packet of instant coffee. "That seems like a strange
match. Was Wagner a knight?"

"No," Langdon said, feeling a sudden intrigue.
"But he was a well-known Freemason." *Along
with Mozart, Beethoven, Shakespeare, Gershwin,
Houdini, and Disney.* Volumes had been written
about the ties between the Masons and the
Knights Templar, the Priory of Sion, and the
Holy Grail. "I want to look at this one. How do
I see the full text?"

"You don't want the full text," Gettum called.
"Click on the hypertext title. The computer will
display your keyword hits along with mono prel-
ogs and triple postlogs for context."

Langdon had no idea what she had just said, but
he clicked anyway.

A new window popped up.

```
. . . mythological knight named
       Parsifal who . . .
. . . metaphorical Grail quest
       that arguably . . .
```

```
  . . . the London Philharmonic
       in 1855 . . .
  Rebecca Pope's opera
anthology "Diva's . . .
  . . . Wagner's tomb in
Bayreuth, Germany . . .
```

"Wrong Pope," Langdon said, disappointed. Even so, he was amazed by the system's ease of use. The keywords with context were enough to remind him that Wagner's opera *Parsifal* was a tribute to Mary Magdalene and the bloodline of Jesus Christ, told through the story of a young knight on a quest for truth.

"Just be patient," Gettum urged. "It's a numbers game. Let the machine run."

Over the next few minutes, the computer returned several more Grail references, including a text about *troubadours*—France's famous wandering minstrels. Langdon knew it was no coincidence that the word *minstrel* and *minister* shared an etymological root. The troubadours were the traveling servants or "ministers" of the Church of Mary Magdalene, using music to disseminate the story of the sacred feminine among the common folk. To this day, the troubadours sang songs extolling the virtues of "our Lady"—a mysterious and beautiful woman to whom they pledged themselves forever.

Eagerly, he checked the hypertext but found nothing.

The computer pinged again.

KNIGHTS, KNAVES, POPES, AND PENTACLES:
THE HISTORY OF THE HOLY GRAIL
THROUGH TAROT

"Not surprising," Langdon said to Sophie. "Some of our keywords have the same names as individual cards." He reached for the mouse to click on a hyperlink. "I'm not sure if your grandfather ever mentioned it when you played Tarot with him, Sophie, but this game is a 'flash-card catechism' into the story of the Lost Bride and her subjugation by the evil Church."

Sophie eyed him, looking incredulous. "I had no idea."

"That's the point. By teaching through a metaphorical game, the followers of the Grail disguised their message from the watchful eye of the Church." Langdon often wondered how many modern card players had any clue that their four suits—spades, hearts, clubs, diamonds—were Grail-related symbols that came directly from Tarot's four suits of swords, cups, scepters, and pentacles.

*Spades were Swords—The blade. Male.*

*Hearts were Cups—The chalice. Feminine.*

*Clubs were Scepters—The Royal Line. The flowering staff.*

*Diamonds were Pentacles—The goddess. The sacred feminine.*

Four minutes later, as Langdon began feeling fearful they would not find what they had come for, the computer produced another hit.

*The Gravity of Genius:*
Biography of a Modern Knight.

"*Gravity of Genius?*" Langdon called out to Gettum. "Bio of a modern knight?"

Gettum stuck her head around the corner. "How modern? Please don't tell me it's your Sir Rudy Giuliani. Personally, I found that one a bit off the mark."

Langdon had his own qualms about the newly knighted Sir Mick Jagger, but this hardly seemed the moment to debate the politics of modern British knighthood. "Let's have a look." Langdon summoned up the hypertext keywords.

```
      . . . honorable knight,
   Sir Isaac Newton . . .
        . . . in London in
        1727 and . . .
          . . . his tomb in
   Westminster Abbey . . .
   . . . Alexander Pope, friend
        and colleague . . .
```

"I guess 'modern' is a relative term," Sophie called to Gettum. "It's an old book. About Sir Isaac Newton."

Gettum shook her head in the doorway. "No good. Newton was buried in Westminster Abbey, the seat of English Protestantism. There's no way a Catholic Pope was present. Cream and sugar?"

Sophie nodded.

Gettum waited. "Robert?"

Langdon's heart was hammering. He pulled his eyes from the screen and stood up. "Sir Isaac Newton is our knight."

Sophie remained seated. "What are you talking about?"

"Newton is buried in London," Langdon said. "His labors produced new sciences that incurred the wrath of the Church. And he was a Grand Master of the Priory of Sion. What more could we want?"

"What more?" Sophie pointed to the poem. "How about a knight a Pope interred? You heard Ms. Gettum. Newton was not buried by a Catholic Pope."

Langdon reached for the mouse. "Who said anything about a *Catholic* Pope?" He clicked on the "Pope" hyperlink, and the complete sentence appeared.

```
    Sir Isaac Newton's burial,
attended by kings and nobles, was
```

```
presided over by Alexander Pope,
friend and colleague, who gave a
stirring eulogy before sprinkling
          dirt on the tomb.
```

Langdon looked at Sophie. "We had the correct Pope on our second hit. Alexander." He paused. "A. Pope."

*In London lies a knight A. Pope interred.*

Sophie stood up, looking stunned.

Jacques Saunière, the master of double-entendres, had proven once again that he was a frighteningly clever man.

# CHAPTER 96

**Silas awoke** with a start.

He had no idea what had awoken him or how long he had been asleep. *Was I dreaming?* Sitting up now on his straw mat, he listened to the quiet breathing of the Opus Dei residence hall, the stillness textured only by the soft murmurs of someone praying aloud in a room below him. These were familiar sounds and should have comforted him.

And yet he felt a sudden and unexpected wariness.

Standing, wearing only his undergarments, Silas walked to the window. *Was I followed?* The courtyard below was deserted, exactly as he had seen it when he entered. He listened. Silence. *So why am I uneasy?* Long ago Silas had learned to trust his intuition. Intuition had kept him alive as a child on the streets of Marseilles long before prison . . . long before he was born again by the hand of Bishop Aringarosa. Peering out the window, he now saw the faint outline of a car through the hedge. On the car's roof was a police siren. A floorboard creaked in the hallway. A door latch moved.

Silas reacted on instinct, surging across the

room and sliding to a stop just behind the door as it crashed open. The first police officer stormed through, swinging his gun left then right at what appeared an empty room. Before he realized where Silas was, Silas had thrown his shoulder into the door, crushing a second officer as he came through. As the first officer wheeled to shoot, Silas dove for his legs. The gun went off, the bullet sailing above Silas's head, just as he connected with the officer's shins, driving his legs out from under him, and sending the man down, his head hitting the floor. The second officer staggered to his feet in the doorway, and Silas drove a knee into his groin, then went clambering over the writhing body into the hall.

Almost naked, Silas hurled his pale body down the staircase. He knew he had been betrayed, but by whom? When he reached the foyer, more officers were surging through the front door. Silas turned the other way and dashed deeper into the residence hall. *The women's entrance. Every Opus Dei building has one.* Winding down narrow hallways, Silas snaked through a kitchen, past terrified workers, who left to avoid the naked albino as he knocked over bowls and silverware, bursting into a dark hallway near the boiler room. He now saw the door he sought, an exit light gleaming at the end.

Running full speed through the door out into the rain, Silas leapt off the low landing, not seeing the officer coming the other way until it was too late. The two men collided, Silas's broad, naked shoulder grinding into the man's sternum with crushing force. He drove the officer backward onto the pavement, landing hard on top of him. The officer's gun clattered away. Silas could hear men running down the hall shouting. Rolling, he grabbed the loose gun just as the officers emerged. A shot rang out on the stairs, and Silas felt a searing pain below his ribs. Filled with rage, he opened fire at all three officers, their blood spraying.

A dark shadow loomed behind, coming out of nowhere. The angry hands that grabbed at his bare shoulders felt as if they were infused with the power of the devil himself. The man roared in his ear. *SILAS, NO!*

Silas spun and fired. Their eyes met. Silas was already screaming in horror as Bishop Aringarosa fell.

# CHAPTER 97

**More than** three thousand people are entombed or enshrined within Westminster Abbey. The colossal stone interior burgeons with the remains of kings, statesmen, scientists, poets, and musicians. Their tombs, packed into every last niche and alcove, range in grandeur from the most regal of mausoleums—that of Queen Elizabeth I, whose canopied sarcophagus inhabits its own private, apsidal chapel—down to the most modest etched floor tiles whose inscriptions have worn away with centuries of foot traffic, leaving it to one's imagination whose relics might lie below the tile in the undercroft.

Designed in the style of the great cathedrals of Amiens, Chartres, and Canterbury, Westminster Abbey is considered neither cathedral nor parish church. It bears the classification of *royal peculiar,* subject only to the Sovereign. Since hosting the coronation of William the Conqueror on Christmas Day in 1066, the dazzling sanctuary has witnessed an endless procession of royal ceremonies and affairs of state—from the canonization of Edward the Confessor, to the marriage of Prince Andrew and Sarah Ferguson, to the funerals of Henry V, Queen Elizabeth I, and Lady Diana.

Even so, Robert Langdon currently felt no interest in any of the abbey's ancient history, save one event—the funeral of the British knight Sir Isaac Newton.

*In London lies a knight a Pope interred.*

Hurrying through the grand portico on the north transept, Langdon and Sophie were met by guards who politely ushered them through the abbey's newest addition—a large walk-through metal detector—now present in most historic buildings in London. They both passed through without setting off the alarm and continued to the abbey entrance.

Stepping across the threshold into Westminster Abbey, Langdon felt the outside world evaporate with a sudden hush. No rumble of traffic. No hiss of rain. Just a deafening silence, which seemed to reverberate back and forth as if the building were whispering to itself.

Langdon's and Sophie's eyes, like those of almost every visitor, shifted immediately skyward, where the abbey's great abyss seemed to explode overhead. Gray stone columns ascended like redwoods into the shadows, arching gracefully over dizzying expanses, and then shooting back down to the stone floor. Before them, the wide alley of the north transept stretched out like a deep canyon, flanked by sheer cliffs of stained glass. On sunny days, the abbey floor was a prismatic patchwork of light. Today, the rain and darkness gave this massive hollow a wraithlike aura . . . more like that of the crypt it truly was.

"It's practically empty," Sophie whispered.

Langdon felt disappointed. He had hoped for a lot more people. *A more public place.* Their earlier experience in the deserted Temple Church was not one Langdon wanted to repeat. He had been anticipating a certain feeling of security in the popular tourist destination, but Langdon's recollections of bustling throngs in a well-lit abbey had been formed during the peak summer tourist season. Today was a rainy April morning. Rather than crowds and shimmering stained glass, all Langdon saw was acres of desolate floor and shadowy, empty alcoves.

"We passed through metal detectors," Sophie reminded, apparently sensing Langdon's apprehension. "If anyone is in here, they can't be armed."

Langdon nodded but still felt circumspect. He had wanted to bring the London police with them, but Sophie's fears of who might be involved put a damper on any contact with the authorities. *We need to recover the cryptex,* Sophie had insisted. *It is the key to everything.*

She was right, of course.

*The key to getting Leigh back alive.*
*The key to finding the Holy Grail.*
*The key to learning who is behind this.*

Unfortunately, their only chance to recover the keystone seemed to be here and now . . . at the tomb of Isaac Newton. Whoever held the cryptex would have to pay a visit to the tomb to decipher the final clue, and if they had not already come and gone, Sophie and Langdon intended to intercept them.

Striding toward the left wall to get out of the open, they moved into an obscure side aisle behind a row of pilasters. Langdon couldn't shake the image of Leigh Teabing being held captive, probably tied up in the back of his own limousine. Whoever had ordered the top Priory members killed would not hesitate to eliminate others who stood in the way. It seemed a cruel irony that Teabing—a modern British knight—was a hostage in the search for his own countryman, Sir Isaac Newton.

"Which way is it?" Sophie asked, looking around.

*The tomb.* Langdon had no idea. "We should find a docent and ask."

Langdon knew better than to wander aimlessly in here. Westminster Abbey was a tangled warren of mausoleums, perimeter chambers, and walk-in burial niches. Like the Louvre's Grand Gallery, it had a lone point of entry—the door through which they had just passed—easy to find your way in, but impossible to find your way out. *A literal tourist trap,* one of Langdon's befuddled colleagues had called it. Keeping architectural tradition, the abbey was laid out in the shape of a giant crucifix. Unlike most churches, however, it had its entrance on the *side,* rather than the standard rear of the church via the narthex at the bottom of the nave. Moreover, the abbey had a series of sprawling cloisters attached. One false step through the wrong archway, and a visitor was lost in a labyrinth of outdoor passageways surrounded by high walls.

"Docents wear crimson robes," Langdon said, approaching the center of the church. Peering obliquely across the towering gilded altar to the far end of the south transept, Langdon saw several people crawling on their hands and knees. This prostrate pilgrimage was a common occurrence in Poets' Corner, although it was far less holy than it appeared. *Tourists doing grave rubbings.*

"I don't see any docents," Sophie said. "Maybe we can find the tomb on our own?"

Without a word, Langdon led her another few steps to the center of the abbey and pointed to the right.

Sophie drew a startled breath as she looked down the length of the abbey's nave, the full magnitude of the building now visible. "Aah," she said. "Let's find a docent."

———

At that moment, a hundred yards down the nave, out of sight behind the choir screen, the stately tomb of Sir Isaac Newton had a lone visitor. The Teacher had been scrutinizing the monument for ten minutes now.

Newton's tomb consisted of a massive black-marble sarcophagus on which reclined the sculpted form of Sir Isaac Newton, wearing classical costume, and leaning proudly against a stack of his own books—*Divinity, Chronology, Opticks,* and *Philosophiae Naturalis Principia Mathematica.* At Newton's feet stood two winged boys holding a scroll. Behind Newton's recumbent body rose an austere pyramid. Although the pyramid itself seemed an oddity, it was the giant shape mounted halfway *up* the pyramid that most intrigued the Teacher.

*An orb.*

The Teacher pondered Saunière's beguiling riddle. *You seek the orb that ought be on his tomb.* The massive orb protruding from the face of the pyramid was carved in basso-relievo and depicted all kinds of heavenly bodies—constellations, signs of the zodiac, comets, stars, and planets. Above it, the image of the Goddess of Astronomy beneath a field of stars.

*Countless orbs.*

The Teacher had been convinced that once he

found the tomb, discerning the missing orb would be easy. Now he was not so sure. He was gazing at a complicated map of the heavens. Was there a missing planet? Had some astronomical orb been omitted from a constellation? He had no idea. Even so, the Teacher could not help but suspect that the solution would be ingeniously clean and simple—"a knight a pope interred." *What orb am I looking for?* Certainly, an advanced knowledge of astrophysics was not a prerequisite for finding the Holy Grail, was it?

*It speaks of Rosy flesh and seeded womb.*

The Teacher's concentration was broken by several approaching tourists. He slipped the cryptex back in his pocket and watched warily as the visitors went to a nearby table, left a donation in the cup, and restocked on the complimentary grave-rubbing supplies set out by the abbey. Armed with fresh charcoal pencils and large sheets of heavy paper, they headed off toward the front of the abbey, probably to the popular Poets' Corner to pay their respects to Chaucer, Tennyson, and Dickens by rubbing furiously on their graves.

Alone again, he stepped closer to the tomb, scanning it from bottom to top. He began with the clawed feet beneath the sarcophagus, moved upward past Newton, past his books on science, past the two boys with their mathematical scroll, up the face of the pyramid to the giant orb with its constellations, and finally up to the niche's star-filled canopy.

*What orb ought to be here . . . and yet is missing?* He touched the cryptex in his pocket as if he could somehow divine the answer from Saunière's crafted marble. *Only five letters separate me from the Grail.*

Pacing now near the corner of the choir screen, he took a deep breath and glanced up the long nave toward the main altar in the distance. His gaze dropped from the gilded altar down to the bright crimson robe of an abbey docent who was being waved over by two very familiar individuals.

Langdon and Neveu.

Calmly, the Teacher moved two steps back behind the choir screen. *That was fast.* He had anticipated Langdon and Sophie would eventually decipher the poem's meaning and come to Newton's tomb, but this was sooner than he had imagined. Taking a deep breath, the Teacher considered his options. He had grown accustomed to dealing with surprises.

*I am holding the cryptex.*

Reaching down to his pocket, he touched the second object that gave him his confidence: the Medusa revolver. As expected, the abbey's metal detectors had blared as the Teacher passed through with the concealed gun. Also as expected, the guards had backed off at once when the Teacher glared indignantly and flashed his identification card. Official rank always commanded the proper respect.

Although initially the Teacher had hoped to solve the cryptex alone and avoid any further complications, he now sensed that the arrival of Langdon and Neveu was actually a welcome development. Considering the lack of success he was having with the "orb" reference, he might be able to use their expertise. After all, if Langdon had deciphered the poem to find the tomb, there was a reasonable chance he also knew something about the orb. And if Langdon knew the password, then it was just a matter of applying the right pressure.

*Not here, of course.*

*Somewhere private.*

The Teacher recalled a small announcement sign he had seen on his way into the abbey. Immediately he knew the perfect place to lure them.

The only question now . . . what to use as bait.

# CHAPTER 98

**Langdon and** Sophie moved slowly down the north aisle, keeping to the shadows behind the ample pillars that separated it from the open nave. Despite having traveled more than halfway down the nave, they still had no clear view of Newton's tomb. The sarcophagus was recessed in a niche, obscured from this oblique angle.

"At least there's nobody over there," Sophie whispered.

Langdon nodded, relieved. The entire section of the nave near Newton's tomb was deserted. "I'll go over," he whispered. "You should stay hidden just in case someone—"

Sophie had already stepped from the shadows and was headed across the open floor.

"—is watching," Langdon sighed, hurrying to join her.

Crossing the massive nave on a diagonal, Langdon and Sophie remained silent as the elaborate sepulchre revealed itself in tantalizing increments . . . a black-marble sarcophagus . . . a reclining statue of Newton . . . two winged boys . . . a huge pyramid . . . and . . . *an enormous orb.*

"Did you know about that?" Sophie said, sounding startled.

Langdon shook his head, also surprised.

"Those look like constellations carved on it," Sophie said.

As they approached the niche, Langdon felt a slow sinking sensation. Newton's tomb was *covered* with orbs—stars, comets, planets. *You seek the orb that ought be on his tomb?* It could turn out to be like trying to find a missing blade of grass on a golf course.

"Astronomical bodies," Sophie said, looking concerned. "And a lot of them."

Langdon frowned. The only link between the planets and the Grail that Langdon could imagine was the pentacle of Venus, and he had already tried the password "Venus" en route to the Temple Church.

Sophie moved directly to the sarcophagus, but Langdon hung back a few feet, keeping an eye on the abbey around them.

*"Divinity,"* Sophie said, tilting her head and reading the titles of the books on which Newton was leaning. *"Chronology. Opticks. Philosophiae Naturalis Principia Mathematica?"* She turned to him. "Ring any bells?"

Langdon stepped closer, considering it. *"Principia Mathematica,* as I remember, has something to do with the gravitation pull of planets . . . which admittedly are orbs, but it seems a little far-fetched."

"How about the signs of the zodiac?" Sophie asked, pointing to the constellations on the orb. "You were talking about Pisces and Aquarius earlier, weren't you?"

*The End of Days,* Langdon thought. "The end of Pisces and the beginning of Aquarius was allegedly the historical marker at which the Priory planned to release the Sangreal documents to the world." *But the millennium came and went without incident, leaving historians uncertain when the truth was coming.*

"It seems possible," Sophie said, "that the Priory's plans to reveal the truth might be related to the last line of the poem."

*It speaks of Rosy flesh and seeded womb.* Langdon felt a shiver of potential. He had not considered the line that way before.

"You told me earlier," she said, "that the timing of the Priory's plans to unveil the truth about 'the Rose' and her fertile womb was linked directly to the position of planets—orbs."

Langdon nodded, feeling the first faint wisps of possibility materializing. Even so, his intuition told him astronomy was not the key. The Grand Master's previous solutions had all possessed an eloquent, symbolic significance—the *Mona Lisa, Madonna of the Rocks,* SOFIA. This eloquence was definitely lacking in the concept of planetary orbs and the zodiac. Thus far, Jacques Saunière had proven himself a meticulous code writer, and Langdon had to believe that his final password—those five letters that unlocked the Priory's ultimate secret—would prove to be not only symbolically fitting but also crystal clear. If this solution were anything like the others, it would be painfully obvious once it dawned.

"Look!" Sophie gasped, jarring his thoughts as she grabbed his arm. From the fear in her touch Langdon sensed someone must be approaching, but when he turned to her, she was staring aghast at the top of the black marble sarcophagus. "Someone was here," she whispered, pointing to a spot on the sarcophagus near Newton's outstretched right foot.

Langdon did not understand her concern. A careless tourist had left a charcoal, grave-rubbing pencil on the sarcophagus lid near Newton's foot. *It's nothing*. Langdon reached out to pick it up, but as he leaned toward the sarcophagus, the light shifted on the polished black–marble slab, and Langdon froze. Suddenly, he saw why Sophie was afraid.

Scrawled on the sarcophagus lid, at Newton's feet, shimmered a barely visible charcoal-pencil message:

I have Teabing.
Go through Chapter House,
out south exit, to public garden.

Langdon read the words twice, his heart pounding wildly.

Sophie turned and scanned the nave.

Despite the pall of trepidation that settled over him upon seeing the words, Langdon told himself this was good news. *Leigh is still alive.* There was another implication here too. "They don't know the password either," he whispered.

Sophie nodded. Otherwise why make their presence known?

"They may want to trade Leigh for the password."

"Or it's a trap."

Langdon shook his head. "I don't think so. The garden is *outside* the abbey walls. A very public place." Langdon had once visited the abbey's famous College Garden—a small fruit orchard and herb garden—left over from the days when monks grew natural pharmacological remedies here. Boasting the oldest living fruit trees in Great Britain, College Garden was a popular spot for tourists to visit without having to enter the abbey. "I think sending us outside is a show of faith. So we feel safe."

Sophie looked dubious. "You mean outside, where there are no metal detectors?"

Langdon scowled. She had a point.

Gazing back at the orb-filled tomb, Langdon wished he had some idea about the cryptex password . . . something with which to negotiate. *I*

*got Leigh involved in this, and I'll do whatever it takes
if there is a chance to help him.*

"The note says to go through the Chapter
House to the south exit," Sophie said. "Maybe
from the exit we would have a view of the garden? That way we could assess the situation before we walked out there and exposed ourselves
to any danger?"

The idea was a good one. Langdon vaguely recalled the Chapter House as a huge octagonal hall
where the original British Parliament convened in
the days before the modern Parliament building
existed. It had been years since he had been there,
but he remembered it being out through the cloister somewhere. Taking several steps back from the
tomb, Langdon peered around the choir screen to
his right, across the nave to the side opposite that
which they had descended.

A gaping vaulted passageway stood nearby, with
a large sign.

---

**THIS WAY TO:**
CLOISTERS
DEANERY
COLLEGE HALL
MUSEUM
PYX CHAMBER
ST. FAITH'S CHAPEL
CHAPTER HOUSE

---

Langdon and Sophie were jogging as they passed beneath the sign, moving too quickly to notice the small announcement apologizing that certain areas were closed for renovations.

They emerged immediately into a high-walled, open-roof courtyard through which morning rain was falling. Above them, the wind howled across the opening with a low drone, like someone blowing over the mouth of a bottle. Entering the narrow, low-hanging walkways that bordered the courtyard perimeter, Langdon felt the familiar uneasiness he always felt in enclosed spaces. These walkways were called *cloisters,* and Langdon noted with uneasiness that these particular *cloisters* lived up to their Latin ties to the word *claustrophobic.*

Focusing his mind straight ahead toward the end of the tunnel, Langdon followed the signs for the Chapter House. The rain was spitting now, and the walkway was cold and damp with gusts of rain that blew through the lone pillared wall that was the cloister's only source of light. Another couple scurried past them the other way, hurrying to get out of the worsening weather. The cloisters looked deserted now, admittedly the abbey's least enticing section in the wind and rain.

Forty yards down the east cloister, an archway materialized on their left, giving way to another hallway. Although this was the entrance they were looking for, the opening was cordoned off by a swag and an official-looking sign.

---

## CLOSED FOR RENOVATION
### PYX CHAMBER
### ST. FAITH'S CHAPEL
### CHAPTER HOUSE

---

The long, deserted corridor beyond the swag was littered with scaffolding and drop cloths. Immediately beyond the swag, Langdon could see the entrances to the Pyx Chamber and St. Faith's Chapel on the right and left. The entrance to the Chapter House, however, was much farther away, at the far end of the long hallway. Even from here, Langdon could see that its heavy wooden door was wide open, and the spacious octagonal interior was bathed in a grayish natural light from the room's enormous windows that looked out on College Garden. *Go through Chapter House, out south exit, to public garden.*

"We just left the east cloister," Langdon said, "so the south exit to the garden must be through there and to the right."

Sophie was already stepping over the swag and moving forward.

As they hurried down the dark corridor, the sounds of the wind and rain from the open cloister faded behind them. The Chapter House was a kind of satellite structure—a freestanding annex at the end of the long hallway to ensure the privacy of the Parliament proceedings housed there.

"It looks huge," Sophie whispered as they approached.

Langdon had forgotten just how large this room was. Even from outside the entrance, he could gaze across the vast expanse of floor to the breathtaking windows on the far side of the octagon, which rose five stories to a vaulted ceiling. They would certainly have a clear view of the garden from in here.

Crossing the threshold, both Langdon and Sophie found themselves having to squint. After the gloomy cloisters, the Chapter House felt like a solarium. They were a good ten feet into the room, searching the south wall, when they realized the door they had been promised was not there.

They were standing in an enormous dead end.

The creaking of a heavy door behind them made them turn, just as the door closed with a resounding thud and the latch fell into place. The lone man who had been standing behind the door looked calm as he aimed a small revolver at them. He was portly and was propped on a pair of aluminum crutches.

For a moment Langdon thought he must be dreaming.

It was Leigh Teabing.

# CHAPTER 99

**Sir Leigh** Teabing felt rueful as he gazed out over the barrel of his Medusa revolver at Robert Langdon and Sophie Neveu. "My friends," he said, "since the moment you walked into my home last night, I have done everything in my power to keep you out of harm's way. But your persistence has now put me in a difficult position."

He could see the expressions of shock and betrayal on Sophie's and Langdon's faces, and yet he was confident that soon they would both understand the chain of events that had guided the three of them to this unlikely crossroads.

*There is so much I have to tell you both . . . so much you do not yet understand.*

"Please believe," Teabing said, "I never had any intention of your being involved. You came to my home. *You* came searching for *me*."

"Leigh?" Langdon finally managed. "What the hell are you doing? We thought you were in trouble. We came here to help you!"

"As I trusted you would," he said. "We have much to discuss."

Langdon and Sophie seemed unable to tear

their stunned gazes from the revolver aimed at them.

"It is simply to ensure your full attention," Teabing said. "If I had wanted to harm you, you would be dead by now. When you walked into my home last night, I risked everything to spare your lives. I am a man of honor, and I vowed in my deepest conscience only to sacrifice those who had betrayed the Sangreal."

"What are you talking about?" Langdon said. "Betrayed the Sangreal?"

"I discovered a terrible truth," Teabing said, sighing. "I learned *why* the Sangreal documents were never revealed to the world. I learned that the Priory had decided not to release the truth after all. That's why the millennium passed without any revelation, why nothing happened as we entered the End of Days."

Langdon drew a breath, about to protest.

"The Priory," Teabing continued, "was given a sacred charge to share the truth. To release the Sangreal documents when the End of Days arrived. For centuries, men like Da Vinci, Botticelli, and Newton risked everything to protect the documents and carry out that charge. And now, at the ultimate moment of truth, Jacques Saunière changed his mind. The man honored with the greatest responsibility in Christian history eschewed his duty. He decided the time was not right." Teabing turned to Sophie.

"He failed the Grail. He failed the Priory. And he failed the memory of all the generations that had worked to make that moment possible."

"You?" Sophie declared, glancing up now, her green eyes boring into him with rage and realization. "*You* are the one responsible for my grandfather's murder?"

Teabing scoffed. "Your grandfather and his *sénéchaux* were traitors to the Grail."

Sophie felt a fury rising from deep within. *He's lying!*

Teabing's voice was relentless. "Your grandfather sold out to the Church. It is obvious they pressured him to keep the truth quiet."

Sophie shook her head. "The Church had no influence on my grandfather!"

Teabing laughed coldly. "My dear, the Church has two thousand years of experience pressuring those who threaten to unveil its lies. Since the days of Constantine, the Church has successfully hidden the truth about Mary Magdalene and Jesus. We should not be surprised that *now*, once again, they have found a way to keep the world in the dark. The Church may no longer employ crusaders to slaughter nonbelievers, but their influence is no less persuasive. No less insidious." He paused, as if to punctuate his next point. "Miss Neveu, for some time now your grandfather has wanted to tell you the truth about your family."

Sophie was stunned. "How could you know that?"

"My methods are immaterial. The important thing for you to grasp right now is this." He took a deep breath. "The deaths of your mother, father, grandmother, and brother were *not* accidental."

The words sent Sophie's emotions reeling. She opened her mouth to speak but was unable.

Langdon shook his head. "What are you saying?"

"Robert, it explains everything. All the pieces fit. History repeats itself. The Church has a precedent of murder when it comes to silencing the Sangreal. With the End of Days imminent, killing the Grand Master's loved ones sent a very clear message. Be quiet, or you and Sophie are next."

"It was a car accident," Sophie stammered, feeling the childhood pain welling inside her. "An *accident!*"

"Bedtime stories to protect your innocence," Teabing said. "Consider that only two family members went untouched—the Priory's Grand Master and his lone granddaughter—the perfect pair to provide the Church with control over the brotherhood. I can only imagine the terror the Church wielded over your grandfather these past years, threatening to kill *you* if he dared release the Sangreal secret, threatening to finish the job they started unless Saunière influenced the Priory to reconsider its ancient vow."

"Leigh," Langdon argued, now visibly riled, "certainly you have no proof that the Church had anything to do with those deaths, or that it influenced the Priory's decision to remain silent."

"Proof?" Teabing fired back. "You want proof the Priory was influenced? The new millennium has arrived, and yet the world remains ignorant! Is that not proof enough?"

In the echoes of Teabing's words, Sophie heard another voice speaking. *Sophie, I must tell you the truth about your family*. She realized she was trembling. Could *this* possibly be that truth her grandfather had wanted to tell her? That her family had been *murdered?* What did she truly know about the crash that took her family? Only sketchy details. Even the stories in the newspaper had been vague. An accident? Bedtime stories? Sophie flashed suddenly on her grandfather's overprotectiveness, how he never liked to leave her alone when she was young. Even when Sophie was grown and away at university, she had the sense her grandfather was watching over. She wondered if there had been Priory members in the shadows throughout her entire life, looking after her.

"You suspected he was being manipulated," Langdon said, glaring with disbelief at Teabing. "So you *murdered* him?"

"I did not pull the trigger," Teabing said.

"Saunière was dead years ago, when the Church stole his family from him. He was compromised. Now he is free of that pain, released from the shame caused by his inability to carry out his sacred duty. Consider the alternative. Something had to be done. Shall the world be ignorant forever? Shall the Church be allowed to cement its lies into our history books for all eternity? Shall the Church be permitted to influence indefinitely with murder and extortion? No, something needed to be done! And now we are poised to carry out Saunière's legacy and right a terrible wrong." He paused. "The three of us. Together."

Sophie felt only incredulity. "How could you *possibly* believe that we would help you?"

"Because, my dear, *you* are the reason the Priory failed to release the documents. Your grandfather's love for you prevented him from challenging the Church. His fear of reprisal against his only remaining family crippled him. He never had a chance to explain the truth because you rejected him, tying his hands, making him wait. Now you owe the world the truth. You owe it to the memory of your grandfather."

Robert Langdon had given up trying to get his bearings. Despite the torrent of questions running through his mind, he knew only one thing mattered now—getting Sophie out of here alive. All the guilt Langdon had mistakenly felt earlier for involving Teabing had now been transferred to Sophie.

*I took her to Château Villette. I am responsible.*

Langdon could not fathom that Leigh Teabing would be capable of killing them in cold blood here in the Chapter House, and yet Teabing certainly had been involved in killing others during his misguided quest. Langdon had the uneasy feeling that gunshots in this secluded, thick-walled chamber would go unheard, especially in this rain. *And Leigh just admitted his guilt to us.*

Langdon glanced at Sophie, who looked shaken. *The Church murdered Sophie's family to silence the Priory?* Langdon felt certain the modern Church did not murder people. There had to be some other explanation.

"Let Sophie leave," Langdon declared, staring at Leigh. "You and I should discuss this alone."

Teabing gave an unnatural laugh. "I'm afraid that is one show of faith I cannot afford. I can, however, offer you *this.*" He propped himself fully on his crutches, gracelessly keeping the gun aimed at Sophie, and removed the keystone from his pocket. He swayed a bit as he held it out for Langdon. "A token of trust, Robert."

Robert felt wary and didn't move. *Leigh is giving the keystone back to us?*

"Take it," Teabing said, thrusting it awkwardly toward Langdon.

Langdon could imagine only one reason Teabing would give it back. "You opened it already. You removed the map."

Teabing was shaking his head. "Robert, if I had solved the keystone, I would have disappeared to find the Grail myself and kept you uninvolved. No, I do not know the answer. And I can admit that freely. A true knight learns humility in the face of the Grail. He learns to obey the signs placed before him. When I saw you enter the abbey, I understood. You were here for a reason. To help. I am not looking for singular glory here. I serve a far greater master than my own pride. The Truth. Mankind deserves to know that truth. The Grail found us all, and now she is begging to be revealed. We must work together."

Despite Teabing's pleas for cooperation and trust, his gun remained trained on Sophie as Langdon stepped forward and accepted the cold marble cylinder. The vinegar inside gurgled as Langdon grasped it and stepped backward. The dials were still in random order, and the cryptex remained locked.

Langdon eyed Teabing. "How do you know I won't smash it right now?"

Teabing's laugh was an eerie chortle. "I should have realized your threat to break it in the Temple Church was an empty one. Robert Langdon would never break the keystone. You are an historian, Robert. You are holding the key to two thousand years of history—the lost key to the Sangreal. You can feel the souls of all the knights burned at the stake to protect her secret. Would you have them die in vain? No, you will vindicate them. You will join the ranks of the great men you admire—Da Vinci, Botticelli, Newton—each of whom would have been honored to be in your shoes right now. The contents of the keystone are crying out to us. Longing to be set free. The time has come. Destiny has led us to this moment."

"I cannot help you, Leigh. I have no idea how to open this. I only saw Newton's tomb for a moment. And even if I knew the password . . ." Langdon paused, realizing he had said too much.

"You would not tell me?" Teabing sighed. "I am disappointed and surprised, Robert, that you do not appreciate the extent to which you are in my debt. My task would have been far simpler had Rémy and I eliminated you both when you walked into Château Villette. Instead I risked everything to take the nobler course."

"This is *noble?*" Langdon demanded, eyeing the gun.

"Saunière's fault," Teabing said. "He and his *sénéchaux* lied to Silas. Otherwise, I would have obtained the keystone without complication. How was I to imagine the Grand Master would go to such ends to deceive me and bequeath the keystone to an estranged granddaughter?"

Teabing looked at Sophie with disdain. "Someone so unqualified to hold this knowledge that she required a symbologist baby-sitter." Teabing glanced back at Langdon. "Fortunately, Robert, your involvement turned out to be my saving grace. Rather than the keystone remaining locked in the depository bank forever, you extracted it and walked into my home."

*Where else would I run?* Langdon thought. *The community of Grail historians is small, and Teabing and I have a history together.*

Teabing now looked smug. "When I learned Saunière left you a dying message, I had a pretty good idea you were holding valuable Priory information. Whether it was the keystone itself, or information on where to find it, I was not sure. But with the police on your heels, I had a sneaking suspicion you might arrive on my doorstep."

Langdon glared. "And if we had not?"

"I was formulating a plan to extend you a helping hand. One way or another, the keystone was coming to Château Villette. The fact that you delivered it into my waiting hands only serves as proof that my cause is just."

"What!" Langdon was appalled.

"Silas was supposed to break in and steal the keystone from you in Château Villette—thus removing you from the equation without hurting you, and exonerating me from any suspicion of complicity. However, when I saw the intricacy of

Saunière's codes, I decided to include you both in my quest a bit longer. I could have Silas steal the keystone later, once I knew enough to carry on alone."

"The Temple Church," Sophie said, her tone awash with betrayal.

*Light begins to dawn,* Teabing thought. The Temple Church was the perfect location to steal the keystone from Robert and Sophie, and its apparent relevance to the poem made it a plausible decoy. Rémy's orders had been clear—stay out of sight while Silas recovers the keystone. Unfortunately, Langdon's threat to smash the keystone on the chapel floor had caused Rémy to panic. *If only Rémy had not revealed himself,* Teabing thought ruefully, recalling his own mock kidnapping. *Rémy was the sole link to me, and he showed his face!*

Fortunately, Silas remained unaware of Teabing's true identity and was easily fooled into taking him from the church and then watching naively as Rémy pretended to tie their hostage in the back of the limousine. With the soundproof divider raised, Teabing was able to phone Silas in the front seat, use the fake French accent of the Teacher, and direct Silas to go straight to Opus Dei. A simple anonymous tip to the police was all it would take to remove Silas from the picture.

*One loose end tied up.*

The other loose end was harder. *Rémy.*

Teabing struggled deeply with the decision, but in the end Rémy had proven himself a liability. *Every Grail quest requires sacrifice.* The cleanest solution had been staring Teabing in the face from the limousine's wet bar—a flask, some cognac, and a can of peanuts. The powder at the bottom of the can would be more than enough to trigger Rémy's deadly allergy. When Rémy parked the limo on Horse Guards Parade, Teabing climbed out of the back, walked to the side passenger door, and sat in the front next to Rémy. Minutes later, Teabing got out of the car, climbed into the rear again, cleaned up the evidence, and finally emerged to carry out the final phase of his mission.

Westminster Abbey had been a short walk, and although Teabing's leg braces, crutches, and gun had set off the metal detector, the rent-a-cops never knew what to do. *Do we ask him to remove his braces and crawl through? Do we frisk his deformed body?* Teabing presented the flustered guards a far easier solution—an embossed card identifying him as Knight of the Realm. The poor fellows practically tripped over one another ushering him in.

Now, eyeing the bewildered Langdon and Neveu, Teabing resisted the urge to reveal how he had brilliantly implicated Opus Dei in the plot that would soon bring about the demise of the entire Church. That would have to wait. Right now there was work to do.

"*Mes amis,*" Teabing declared in flawless French, *"vous ne trouvez pas le Saint-Graal, c'est le Saint-Graal qui vous trouve."* He smiled. "Our paths together could not be more clear. The Grail has found us."

Silence.

He spoke to them in a whisper now. "Listen. Can you hear it? The Grail is speaking to us across the centuries. She is begging to be saved from the Priory's folly. I implore you both to recognize this opportunity. There could not possibly be three more capable people assembled at this moment to break the final code and open the cryptex." Teabing paused, his eyes alight. "We need to swear an oath together. A pledge of faith to one another. A knight's allegiance to uncover the truth and make it known."

Sophie stared deep into Teabing's eyes and spoke in a steely tone. "I will never swear an oath with my grandfather's murderer. Except an oath that I will see you go to prison."

Teabing's heart turned grave, then resolute. "I am sorry you feel that way, mademoiselle." He turned and aimed the gun at Langdon. "And you, Robert? Are you with me, or against me?"

# CHAPTER 100

**Bishop Manuel** Aringarosa's body had endured many kinds of pain, and yet the searing heat of the bullet wound in his chest felt profoundly foreign to him. Deep and grave. Not a wound of the flesh . . . but closer to the soul.

He opened his eyes, trying to see, but the rain on his face blurred his vision. *Where am I?* He could feel powerful arms holding him, carrying his limp body like a rag doll, his black cassock flapping.

Lifting a weary arm, he mopped his eyes and saw the man holding him was Silas. The great albino was struggling down a misty sidewalk, shouting for a hospital, his voice a heartrending wail of agony. His red eyes were focused dead ahead, tears streaming down his pale, blood-spattered face.

"My son," Aringarosa whispered, "you're hurt."

Silas glanced down, his visage contorted in anguish. "I am so very sorry, Father." He seemed almost too pained to speak.

"No, Silas," Aringarosa replied. "It is I who am sorry. This is my fault." *The Teacher promised me there would be no killing, and I told you to obey him fully.* "I was too eager. Too fearful. You and I were deceived." *The Teacher was never going to de-liver us the Holy Grail.*

Cradled in the arms of the man he had taken in all those years ago, Bishop Aringarosa felt himself reel back in time. To Spain. To his modest beginnings, building a small Catholic church in Oviedo with Silas. And later, to New York City, where he had proclaimed the glory of God with the towering Opus Dei Center on Lexington Avenue.

Five months ago, Aringarosa had received devastating news. His life's work was in jeopardy. He recalled, with vivid detail, the meeting inside Castel Gandolfo that had changed his life . . . the news that had set this entire calamity into motion.

Aringarosa had entered Gandolfo's Astronomy Library with his head held high, fully expecting to be lauded by throngs of welcoming hands, all eager to pat him on the back for his superior work representing Catholicism in America.

But only three people were present.

The Vatican secretariat. Obese. Dour.

Two high-ranking Italian cardinals. Sanctimonious. Smug.

"Secretariat?" Aringarosa said, puzzled.

The rotund overseer of legal affairs shook Aringarosa's hand and motioned to the chair opposite him. "Please, make yourself comfortable."

Aringarosa sat, sensing something was wrong.

"I am not skilled in small talk, Bishop," the secretariat said, "so let me be direct about the reason for your visit."

"Please. Speak openly." Aringarosa glanced at the two cardinals, who seemed to be measuring him with self-righteous anticipation.

"As you are well aware," the secretariat said, "His Holiness and others in Rome have been concerned lately with the political fallout from Opus Dei's more controversial practices."

Aringarosa felt himself bristle instantly. He already had been through this on numerous occasions with the new pontiff, who, to Aringarosa's great dismay, had turned out to be a distressingly fervent voice for liberal change in the Church.

"I want to assure you," the secretariat added quickly, "that His Holiness does not seek to change anything about the way you run your ministry."

*I should hope not!* "Then why am I here?"

The enormous man sighed. "Bishop, I am not sure how to say this delicately, so I will state it directly. Two days ago, the Secretariat Council voted unanimously to revoke the Vatican's sanction of Opus Dei."

Aringarosa was certain he had heard incorrectly. "I beg your pardon?"

"Plainly stated, six months from today, Opus Dei will no longer be considered a prelature of the Vatican. You will be a church unto yourself.

The Holy See will be disassociating itself from you. His Holiness agrees and we are already drawing up the legal papers."

"But . . . that is impossible!"

"On the contrary, it is quite possible. And necessary. His Holiness has become uneasy with your aggressive recruiting policies and your practices of corporal mortification." He paused. "Also your policies regarding women. Quite frankly, Opus Dei has become a liability and an embarrassment."

Bishop Aringarosa was stupefied. "An *embarrassment?*"

"Certainly you cannot be surprised it has come to this."

"Opus Dei is the only Catholic organization whose numbers are growing! We now have over eleven hundred priests!"

"True. A troubling issue for us all."

Aringarosa shot to his feet. "Ask His Holiness if Opus Dei was an embarrassment in 1982 when we helped the Vatican Bank!"

"The Vatican will always be grateful for that," the secretariat said, his tone appeasing, "and yet there are those who still believe your financial munificence in 1982 is the only reason you were granted prelature status in the first place."

"That is not true!" The insinuation offended Aringarosa deeply.

"Whatever the case, we plan to act in good

faith. We are drawing up severance terms that will include a reimbursement of those monies. It will be paid in five installments."

"You are buying me off?" Aringarosa demanded. "Paying me to go quietly? When Opus Dei is the only remaining voice of reason!"

One of the cardinals glanced up. "I'm sorry, did you say *reason?*"

Aringarosa leaned across the table, sharpening his tone to a point. "Do you really wonder why Catholics are leaving the Church? Look around you, Cardinal. People have lost respect. The rigors of faith are gone. The doctrine has become a buffet line. Abstinence, confession, communion, baptism, mass—take your pick—choose whatever combination pleases you and ignore the rest. What kind of spiritual guidance is the Church offering?"

"Third-century laws," the second cardinal said, "cannot be applied to the modern followers of Christ. The rules are not workable in today's society."

"Well, they seem to be working for Opus Dei!"

"Bishop Aringarosa," the secretariat said, his voice conclusive. "Out of respect for your organization's relationship with the previous Pope, His Holiness will be giving Opus Dei six months to *voluntarily* break away from the Vatican. I suggest you cite your differences of opinion with the Holy

See and establish yourself as your own Christian organization."

"I refuse!" Aringarosa declared. "And I'll tell him that in person!"

"I'm afraid His Holiness no longer cares to meet with you."

Aringarosa stood up. "He would not *dare* abolish a personal prelature established by a previous Pope!"

"I'm sorry." The secretariat's eyes did not flinch. "The Lord giveth and the Lord taketh away."

Aringarosa had staggered from that meeting in bewilderment and panic. Returning to New York, he stared out at the skyline in disillusionment for days, overwhelmed with sadness for the future of Christianity.

It was several weeks later that he received the phone call that changed all that. The caller sounded French and identified himself as *the Teacher*—a title common in the prelature. He said he knew of the Vatican's plans to pull support from Opus Dei.

*How could he know that?* Aringarosa wondered. He had hoped only a handful of Vatican power brokers knew of Opus Dei's impending annulment. Apparently the word was out. When it came to containing gossip, no walls in the world were as porous as those surrounding Vatican City.

"I have ears everywhere, Bishop," the Teacher whispered, "and with these ears I have gained certain knowledge. With your help, I can uncover the hiding place of a sacred relic that will bring you enormous power . . . enough power to make the Vatican bow before you. Enough power to save the Faith." He paused. "Not just for Opus Dei. But for all of us."

*The Lord taketh away . . . and the Lord giveth.* Aringarosa felt a glorious ray of hope. "Tell me your plan."

Bishop Aringarosa was unconscious when the doors of St. Mary's Hospital hissed open. Silas lurched into the entryway delirious with exhaustion. Dropping to his knees on the tile floor, he cried out for help. Everyone in the reception area gaped in wonderment at the half-naked albino offering forth a bleeding clergyman.

The doctor who helped Silas heave the delirious bishop onto a gurney looked gloomy as he felt Aringarosa's pulse. "He's lost a lot of blood. I am not hopeful."

Aringarosa's eyes flickered, and he returned for a moment, his gaze locating Silas. "My child . . ."

Silas's soul thundered with remorse and rage. "Father, if it takes my lifetime, I will find the one who deceived us, and I will kill him."

Aringarosa shook his head, looking sad as they

prepared to wheel him away. "Silas . . . if you have learned nothing from me, please . . . learn this." He took Silas's hand and gave it a firm squeeze. "Forgiveness is God's greatest gift."

"But Father . . ."

Aringarosa closed his eyes. "Silas, you must pray."

# CHAPTER 101

**Robert Langdon** stood beneath the lofty cupola of the deserted Chapter House and stared into the barrel of Leigh Teabing's gun.

*Robert, are you with me, or against me?* The Royal Historian's words echoed in the silence of Langdon's mind.

There was no viable response, Langdon knew. Answer *yes,* and he would be selling out Sophie. Answer *no,* and Teabing would have no choice but to kill them both.

Langdon's years in the classroom had not imbued him with any skills relevant to handling confrontations at gunpoint, but the classroom *had* taught him something about answering paradoxical questions. *When a question has no correct answer, there is only one honest response.*

The gray area between yes and no.

*Silence.*

Staring at the cryptex in his hands, Langdon chose simply to walk away.

Without ever lifting his eyes, he stepped backward, out into the room's vast empty spaces. *Neutral ground.* He hoped his focus on the cryptex signaled Teabing that collaboration might be an option, and that his silence signaled Sophie he had not abandoned her.

*All the while buying time to think.*

The act of thinking, Langdon suspected, was exactly what Teabing wanted him to do. *That's why he handed me the cryptex. So I could feel the weight of my decision.* The British historian hoped the touch of the Grand Master's cryptex would make Langdon fully grasp the magnitude of its contents, coaxing his academic curiosity to over-whelm all else, forcing him to realize that failure to unlock the keystone would mean the loss of history itself.

With Sophie at gunpoint across the room, Langdon feared that discovering the cryptex's elu-sive password would be his only remaining hope of bartering her release. *If I can free the map, Teabing will negotiate.* Forcing his mind to this critical task, Langdon moved slowly toward the far windows . . . allowing his mind to fill with the nu-merous astronomical images on Newton's tomb.

You seek the orb that ought be on his tomb.
It speaks of Rosy flesh and seeded womb.

Turning his back to the others, he walked toward the towering windows, searching for any inspiration in their stained-glass mosaics. There was none.

*Place yourself in Saunière's mind,* he urged, gazing outward now into College Garden. *What would he believe is the orb that ought be on Newton's tomb?* Images of stars, comets, and planets twinkled in the falling rain, but Langdon ignored them. Saunière was not a man of science. He was a man of humanity, of art, of history. *The sacred feminine . . . the chalice . . . the Rose . . . the banished Mary Magdalene . . . the decline of the goddess . . . the Holy Grail.*

Legend had always portrayed the Grail as a cruel mistress, dancing in the shadows just out of sight, whispering in your ear, luring you one more step and then evaporating into the mist.

Gazing out at the rustling trees of College Garden, Langdon sensed her playful presence. The signs were everywhere. Like a taunting silhouette emerging from the fog, the branches of Britain's oldest apple tree burgeoned with five-petaled blossoms, all glistening like Venus. The goddess was in the garden now. She was dancing in the rain, singing songs of the ages, peeking out from behind the bud-filled branches as if to remind Langdon that the fruit of knowledge was growing just beyond his reach.

Across the room, Sir Leigh Teabing watched with confidence as Langdon gazed out the window as if under a spell.

*Exactly as I hoped,* Teabing thought. *He will come around.*

For some time now, Teabing had suspected Langdon might hold the key to the Grail. It was no coincidence that Teabing launched his plan into action on the same night Langdon was scheduled to meet Jacques Saunière. Listening in on the curator, Teabing was certain the man's eagerness to meet privately with Langdon could mean only one thing. *Langdon's mysterious manuscript has touched a nerve with the Priory. Langdon has stumbled onto a truth, and Saunière fears its release.* Teabing felt certain the Grand Master was summoning Langdon to silence him.

*The Truth has been silenced long enough!*

Teabing knew he had to act quickly. Silas's attack would accomplish two goals. It would prevent Saunière from persuading Langdon to keep quiet, and it would ensure that once the keystone was in Teabing's hands, Langdon would be in Paris for recruitment should Teabing need him.

Arranging the fatal meeting between Saunière and Silas had been almost too easy. *I had inside information about Saunière's deepest fears.* Yesterday afternoon, Silas had phoned the curator and posed as a distraught priest. "Monsieur Saunière, forgive me, I must speak to you at once. I should never breach the sanctity of the confessional, but in this case, I feel I must. I just took confession from a man who claimed to have murdered members of your family."

Saunière's response was startled but wary. "My family died in an accident. The police report was conclusive."

"Yes, a *car* accident," Silas said, baiting the hook. "The man I spoke to said he forced their car off the road into a river."

Saunière fell silent.

"Monsieur Saunière, I would never have phoned you directly except this man made a comment which makes me now fear for *your* safety." He paused. "The man also mentioned your granddaughter, Sophie."

The mention of Sophie's name had been the catalyst. The curator leapt into action. He ordered Silas to come see him immediately in the safest location Saunière knew—his Louvre office. Then he phoned Sophie to warn her she might be in danger. Drinks with Robert Langdon were instantly abandoned.

Now, with Langdon separated from Sophie on the far side of the room, Teabing sensed he had successfully alienated the two companions from one another. Sophie Neveu remained defiant, but Langdon clearly saw the larger picture. He was trying to figure out the password. *He understands the importance of finding the Grail and releasing her from bondage.*

"He won't open it for you," Sophie said coldly. "Even if he can."

Teabing was glancing at Langdon as he held the gun on Sophie. He was fairly certain now he was going to have to use the weapon. Although the idea troubled him, he knew he would not hesitate if it came to that. *I have given her every opportunity to do the right thing. The Grail is bigger than any one of us.*

At that moment, Langdon turned from the window. "The tomb . . ." he said suddenly, facing them with a faint glimmer of hope in his eyes. "I know where to look on Newton's tomb. Yes, I think I can find the password!"

Teabing's heart soared. "Where, Robert? Tell me!"

Sophie sounded horrified. "Robert, no! You're not going to help him, *are* you?"

Langdon approached with a resolute stride, holding the cryptex before him. "No," he said, his eyes hardening as he turned to Leigh. "Not until he lets you go."

Teabing's optimism darkened. "We are so close, Robert. Don't you dare start playing games with me!"

"No games," Langdon said. "Let her go. Then I'll take you to Newton's tomb. We'll open the cryptex together."

"I'm not going anywhere," Sophie declared,

her eyes narrowing with rage. "That cryptex was given to me by my grandfather. It is not *yours* to open."

Langdon wheeled, looking fearful. "Sophie, please! You're in danger. I'm trying to help you!"

"How? By unveiling the secret my grandfather died trying to protect? He trusted you, Robert. *I* trusted you!"

Langdon's blue eyes showed panic now, and Teabing could not help but smile to see the two of them working against one another. Langdon's attempts to be gallant were more pathetic than anything. *On the verge of unveiling one of history's greatest secrets, and he troubles himself with a woman who has proven herself unworthy of the quest.*

"Sophie," Langdon pleaded. "Please . . . you must leave."

She shook her head. "Not unless you either hand me the cryptex or smash it on the floor."

"What?" Langdon gasped.

"Robert, my grandfather would prefer his secret lost forever than see it in the hands of his murderer." Sophie's eyes looked as if they would well with tears, but they did not. She stared directly back at Teabing. "Shoot me if you have to. I am not leaving my grandfather's legacy in your hands."

*Very well.* Teabing aimed the weapon.

"No!" Langdon shouted, raising his arm and

suspending the cryptex precariously over the hard stone floor. "Leigh, if you even think about it, I will drop this."

Teabing laughed. "That bluff worked on Rémy. Not on me. I know you better than that."

"Do you, Leigh?"

*Yes I do. Your poker face needs work, my friend. It took me several seconds, but I can see now that you are lying. You have no idea where on Newton's tomb the answer lies.* "Truly, Robert? You know where on the tomb to look?"

"I do."

The falter in Langdon's eyes was fleeting but Leigh caught it. There was a lie there. A desperate, pathetic ploy to save Sophie. Teabing felt a profound disappointment in Robert Langdon.

*I am a lone knight, surrounded by unworthy souls. And I will have to decipher the keystone on my own.*

Langdon and Neveu were nothing but a threat to Teabing now . . . and to the Grail. As painful as the solution was going to be, he knew he could carry it out with a clean conscience. The only challenge would be to persuade Langdon to set down the keystone so Teabing could safely end this charade.

"A show of faith," Teabing said, lowering the gun from Sophie. "Set down the keystone, and we'll talk."

Langdon knew his lie had failed.

He could see the dark resolve in Teabing's face and knew the moment was upon them. *When I set this down, he will kill us both.* Even without looking at Sophie, he could hear her heart beseeching him in silent desperation. *Robert, this man is not worthy of the Grail. Please do not place it in his hands. No matter what the cost.*

Langdon had already made his decision several minutes ago, while standing alone at the window overlooking College Garden.

*Protect Sophie.*

*Protect the Grail.*

Langdon had almost shouted out in desperation. *But I cannot see how!*

The stark moments of disillusionment had brought with them a clarity unlike any he had ever felt. *The Truth is right before your eyes, Robert.* He knew not from where the epiphany came. *The Grail is not mocking you, she is calling out to a worthy soul.*

Now, bowing down like a subject several yards in front of Leigh Teabing, Langdon lowered the cryptex to within inches of the stone floor.

"Yes, Robert," Teabing whispered, aiming the gun at him. "Set it down."

Langdon's eyes moved heavenward, up into the gaping void of the Chapter House cupola. Crouching lower, Langdon lowered his gaze to Teabing's gun, aimed directly at him.

"I'm sorry, Leigh."

In one fluid motion, Langdon leapt up, swinging his arm skyward, launching the cryptex straight up toward the dome above.

Leigh Teabing did not feel his finger pull the trigger, but the Medusa discharged with a thundering crash. Langdon's crouched form was now vertical, almost airborne, and the bullet exploded in the floor near Langdon's feet. Half of Teabing's brain attempted to adjust his aim and fire again in rage, but the more powerful half dragged his eyes upward into the cupola.

*The keystone!*

Time seemed to freeze, morphing into a slow-motion dream as Teabing's entire world became the airborne keystone. He watched it rise to the apex of its climb . . . hovering for a moment in the void . . . and then tumbling downward, end over end, back toward the stone floor.

All of Teabing's hopes and dreams were plummeting toward earth. *It cannot strike the floor! I can reach it!* Teabing's body reacted on instinct. He released the gun and heaved himself forward, dropping his crutches as he reached out with his soft, manicured hands. Stretching his arms and fingers, he snatched the keystone from midair.

Falling forward with the keystone victoriously clutched in his hand, Teabing knew he was falling too fast. With nothing to break his fall, his out-stretched arms hit first, and the cryptex collided hard with the floor.

There was a sickening crunch of glass within.

For a full second, Teabing did not breathe. Lying there outstretched on the cold floor, staring the length of his outstretched arms at the marble cylinder in his bare palms, he implored the glass vial inside to hold. Then the acrid tang of vinegar cut the air, and Teabing felt the cool liquid flowing out through the dials onto his palm.

Wild panic gripped him. *NO!* The vinegar was streaming now, and Teabing pictured the papyrus dissolving within. *Robert, you fool! The secret is lost!*

Teabing felt himself sobbing uncontrollably. *The Grail is gone. Everything destroyed.* Shuddering in disbelief over Langdon's actions, Teabing tried to force the cylinder apart, longing to catch a fleeting glimpse of history before it dissolved forever. To his shock, as he pulled the ends of the keystone, the cylinder separated.

He gasped and peered inside. It was empty except for shards of wet glass. No dissolving papyrus. Teabing rolled over and looked up at Langdon. Sophie stood beside him, aiming the gun down at Teabing.

Bewildered, Teabing looked back at the keystone and saw it. The dials were no longer at random. They spelled a five-letter word: APPLE.

"The orb from which Eve partook," Langdon said coolly, "incurring the Holy wrath of God. Original sin. The symbol of the fall of the sacred feminine."

Teabing felt the truth come crashing down on him in excruciating austerity. The orb that ought be on Newton's tomb could be none other than the Rosy apple that fell from heaven, struck Newton on the head, and inspired his life's work. *His labor's fruit! The Rosy flesh with a seeded womb!*

"Robert," Teabing stammered, overwhelmed. "You opened it. Where . . . is the map?"

Without blinking, Langdon reached into the breast pocket of his tweed coat and carefully extracted a delicate rolled papyrus. Only a few yards from where Teabing lay, Langdon unrolled the scroll and looked at it. After a long moment, a knowing smile crossed Langdon's face.

*He knows!* Teabing's heart craved that knowledge. His life's dream was right in front of him. "Tell me!" Teabing demanded. "Please! Oh God, please! It's not too late!"

As the sound of heavy footsteps thundered down the hall toward the Chapter House, Langdon quietly rolled the papyrus and slipped it back in his pocket.

"No!" Teabing cried out, trying in vain to stand.

When the doors burst open, Bezu Fache entered like a bull into a ring, his feral eyes scanning, finding his target—Leigh Teabing—helpless on the floor. Exhaling in relief, Fache holstered his Manurhin sidearm and turned to Sophie. "Agent Neveu, I am relieved you and Mr. Langdon are safe. You should have come in when I asked."

The British police entered on Fache's heels, seizing the anguished prisoner and placing him in handcuffs.

Sophie seemed stunned to see Fache. "How did you find us?"

Fache pointed to Teabing. "He made the mistake of showing his ID when he entered the abbey. The guards heard a police broadcast about our search for him."

"It's in Langdon's pocket!" Teabing was screaming like a madman. "The map to the Holy Grail!"

As they hoisted Teabing and carried him out, he threw back his head and howled. "Robert! Tell me where it's hidden!"

As Teabing passed, Langdon looked him in the eye. "Only the worthy find the Grail, Leigh. You taught me that."

# CHAPTER 102

**The mist** had settled low on Kensington Gardens as Silas limped into a quiet hollow out of sight. Kneeling on the wet grass, he could feel a warm stream of blood flowing from the bullet wound below his ribs. Still, he stared straight ahead.

The fog made it look like heaven here.

Raising his bloody hands to pray, he watched the raindrops caress his fingers, turning them white again. As the droplets fell harder across his back and shoulders, he could feel his body disappearing bit by bit into the mist.

*I am a ghost.*

A breeze rustled past him, carrying the damp, earthy scent of new life. With every living cell in his broken body, Silas prayed. He prayed for forgiveness. He prayed for mercy. And, above all, he prayed for his mentor . . . Bishop Aringarosa . . . that the Lord would not take him before his time.

*He has so much work left to do.*

The fog was swirling around him now, and Silas felt so light that he was sure the wisps would carry him away. Closing his eyes, he said a final prayer.

From somewhere in the mist, the voice of Manuel Aringarosa whispered to him.

*Our Lord is a good and merciful God.*

Silas's pain at last began to fade, and he knew the bishop was right.

# CHAPTER 103

**It was** late afternoon when the London sun broke through and the city began to dry. Bezu Fache felt weary as he emerged from the interrogation room and hailed a cab. Sir Leigh Teabing had vociferously proclaimed his innocence, and yet from his incoherent rantings about the Holy Grail, secret documents, and mysterious brotherhoods, Fache suspected the wily historian was setting the stage for his lawyers to plead an insanity defense.

*Sure,* Fache thought. *Insane.* Teabing had displayed ingenious precision in formulating a plan that protected his innocence at every turn. He had exploited both the Vatican and Opus Dei, two groups that turned out to be completely innocent. His dirty work had been carried out unknowingly by a fanatical monk and a desperate bishop. More clever still, Teabing had situated his electronic listening post in the *one* place a man with polio could not possibly reach. The actual surveillance had been carried out by his manservant, Rémy—the lone person privy to Teabing's true identity—now conveniently dead of an allergic reaction.

*Hardly the handiwork of someone lacking mental faculties,* Fache thought.

The information coming from Collet out of Château Villette suggested that Teabing's cunning ran so deep that Fache himself might even learn from it. To successfully hide bugs in some of Paris's most powerful offices, the British historian had turned to the Greeks. *Trojan horses.* Some of Teabing's intended targets received lavish gifts of artwork, others unwittingly bid at auctions in which Teabing had placed specific lots. In Saunière's case, the curator had received a dinner invitation to Château Villette to discuss the possibility of Teabing's funding a new Da Vinci Wing at the Louvre. Saunière's invitation had contained an innocuous postscript expressing fascination with a robotic knight that Saunière was rumored to have built. *Bring him to dinner,* Teabing had suggested. Saunière apparently had done just that and left the knight unattended long enough for Rémy Legaludec to make one inconspicuous addition.

Now, sitting in the back of the cab, Fache closed his eyes. *One more thing to attend to before I return to Paris.*

The St. Mary's Hospital recovery room was sunny.

"You've impressed us all," the nurse said, smiling down at him. "Nothing short of miraculous."

Bishop Aringarosa gave a weak smile. "I have always been blessed."

The nurse finished puttering, leaving the bishop alone. The sunlight felt welcome and warm on his face. Last night had been the darkest night of his life.

Despondently, he thought of Silas, whose body had been found in the park.

*Please forgive me, my son.*

Aringarosa had longed for Silas to be part of his glorious plan. Last night, however, Aringarosa had received a call from Bezu Fache, questioning the bishop about his apparent connection to a nun who had been murdered in Saint-Sulpice. Aringarosa realized the evening had taken a horrifying turn. News of the four additional murders transformed his horror to anguish. *Silas, what have you done!* Unable to reach the Teacher, the bishop knew he had been cut loose. *Used.* The only way to stop the horrific chain of events he had helped put in motion was to confess everything to Fache, and from that moment on, Aringarosa and Fache had been racing to catch up with Silas before the Teacher persuaded him to kill again.

Feeling bone weary, Aringarosa closed his eyes and listened to the television coverage of the arrest of a prominent British knight, Sir Leigh Teabing. *The Teacher laid bare for all to see.* Teabing had caught wind of the Vatican's plans to disassociate itself from Opus Dei. He had chosen

Aringarosa as the perfect pawn in his plan. *After all, who more likely to leap blindly after the Holy Grail than a man like myself with everything to lose? The Grail would have brought enormous power to anyone who possessed it.*

Leigh Teabing had protected his identity shrewdly—feigning a French accent and a pious heart, and demanding as payment the one thing he did not need—money. Aringarosa had been far too eager to be suspicious. The price tag of twenty million euro was paltry when compared with the prize of obtaining the Grail, and with the Vatican's separation payment to Opus Dei, the finances had worked nicely. *The blind see what they want to see.* Teabing's ultimate insult, of course, had been to demand payment in Vatican bonds, such that if anything went wrong, the investigation would lead to Rome.

"I am glad to see you're well, My Lord."

Aringarosa recognized the gruff voice in the doorway, but the face was unexpected—stern, powerful features, slicked-back hair, and a broad neck that strained against his dark suit. "Captain Fache?" Aringarosa asked. The compassion and concern the captain had shown for Aringarosa's plight last night had conjured images of a far gentler physique.

The captain approached the bed and hoisted a familiar, heavy black briefcase onto a chair. "I believe this belongs to you."

Aringarosa looked at the briefcase filled with bonds and immediately looked away, feeling only shame. "Yes . . . thank you." He paused while working his fingers across the seam of his bed-sheet, then continued. "Captain, I have been giving this deep thought, and I need to ask a favor of you."

"Of course."

"The families of those in Paris who Silas . . ." He paused, swallowing the emotion. "I realize no sum could possibly serve as sufficient restitution, and yet, if you could be kind enough to divide the contents of this briefcase among them . . . the families of the deceased."

Fache's dark eyes studied him a long moment. "A virtuous gesture, My Lord. I will see to it your wishes are carried out."

A heavy silence fell between them.

On the television, a lean French police officer was giving a press conference in front of a sprawling mansion. Fache saw who it was and turned his attention to the screen.

"Lieutenant Collet," a BBC reporter said, her voice accusing. "Last night, your captain publicly charged two innocent people with murder. Will Robert Langdon and Sophie Neveu be seeking accountability from your department? Will this cost Captain Fache his job?"

Lieutenant Collet's smile was tired but calm. "It is my experience that Captain Bezu Fache seldom makes mistakes. I have not yet spoken to him on this matter, but knowing how he operates, I suspect his public manhunt for Agent Neveu and Mr. Langdon was part of a ruse to lure out the real killer."

The reporters exchanged surprised looks.

Collet continued. "Whether or not Mr. Langdon and Agent Neveu were willing participants in the sting, I do not know. Captain Fache tends to keep his more creative methods to himself. All I can confirm at this point is that the captain has successfully arrested the man responsible, and that Mr. Langdon and Agent Neveu are both innocent and safe."

Fache had a faint smile on his lips as he turned back to Aringarosa. "A good man, that Collet."

Several moments passed. Finally, Fache ran his hand over his forehead, slicking back his hair as he gazed down at Aringarosa. "My Lord, before I return to Paris, there is one final matter I'd like to discuss—your impromptu flight to London. You bribed a pilot to change course. In doing so, you broke a number of international laws."

Aringarosa slumped. "I was desperate."

"Yes. As was the pilot when my men interrogated him." Fache reached in his pocket and produced a purple amethyst ring with a familiar hand-tooled mitre-crozier appliqué.

Aringarosa felt tears welling as he accepted the ring and slipped it back on his finger. "You've been so kind." He held out his hand and clasped Fache's. "Thank you."

Fache waved off the gesture, walking to the window and gazing out at the city, his thoughts obviously far away. When he turned, there was an uncertainty about him. "My Lord, where do you go from here?"

Aringarosa had been asked the exact same question as he left Castel Gandolfo the night before. "I suspect my path is as uncertain as yours."

"Yes." Fache paused. "I suspect I will be retiring early."

Aringarosa smiled. "A little faith can do wonders, Captain. A little faith."

# CHAPTER 104

**Rosslyn Chapel**—often called the Cathedral of Codes—stands seven miles south of Edinburgh, Scotland, on the site of an ancient Mithraic temple. Built by the Knights Templar in 1446, the chapel is engraved with a mind-boggling array of symbols from the Jewish, Christian, Egyptian, Masonic, and pagan traditions.

The chapel's geographic coordinates fall precisely on the north-south meridian that runs through Glastonbury. This longitudinal Rose Line is the traditional marker of King Arthur's Isle of Avalon and is considered the central pillar of Britain's sacred geometry. It is from this hallowed Rose Line that Rosslyn—originally spelled Roslin—takes its name.

Rosslyn's rugged spires were casting long evening shadows as Robert Langdon and Sophie Neveu pulled their rental car into the grassy parking area at the foot of the bluff on which the chapel stood. Their short flight from London to Edinburgh had been restful, although neither of them had slept for the anticipation of what lay ahead. Gazing up at the stark edifice framed against a cloud-swept sky, Langdon felt like Alice falling headlong into the rabbit hole. *This must be a dream.* And yet he knew the text of Saunière's final message could not have been more specific.

The Holy Grail 'neath ancient Roslin waits.

Langdon had fantasized that Saunière's "Grail map" would be a diagram—a drawing with an X-marks-the-spot—and yet the Priory's final secret had been unveiled in the same way Saunière had spoken to them from the beginning. *Simple verse.* Four explicit lines that pointed without a doubt to this very spot. In addition to identifying Rosslyn by name, the verse made reference to several of the chapel's renowned architectural features.

Despite the clarity of Saunière's final revelation, Langdon had been left feeling more off balance than enlightened. To him, Rosslyn Chapel seemed far too obvious a location. For centuries, this stone chapel had echoed with whispers of the Holy Grail's presence. The whispers had turned to shouts in recent decades when ground-penetrating radar revealed the presence of an astonishing structure *beneath* the chapel—a massive subterranean chamber. Not only did this deep vault dwarf the chapel atop it, but it appeared to have no entrance or exit. Archaeologists petitioned to begin blasting through the bedrock to reach the mysterious chamber, but the Rosslyn Trust expressly forbade any excavation of the sacred site. Of course, this only fueled the fires of speculation. What was the Rosslyn Trust trying to hide?

Rosslyn had now become a pilgrimage site for mystery seekers. Some claimed they were drawn here by the powerful magnetic field that emanated inexplicably from these coordinates, some claimed they came to search the hillside for a hidden entrance to the vault, but most admitted they had come simply to wander the grounds and absorb the lore of the Holy Grail.

Although Langdon had never been to Rosslyn before now, he always chuckled when he heard the chapel described as the current home of the Holy Grail. Admittedly, Rosslyn *once* might have been home to the Grail, long ago . . . but certainly no longer. Far too much attention had been drawn to Rosslyn in past decades, and sooner or later someone would find a way to break into the vault.

True Grail academics agreed that Rosslyn was a decoy—one of the devious dead ends the Priory crafted so convincingly. Tonight, however, with the Priory's keystone offering a verse that pointed directly to this spot, Langdon no longer felt so smug. A perplexing question had been running through his mind all day:

*Why would Saunière go to such effort to guide us to so obvious a location?*

There seemed only one logical answer.

*There is something about Rosslyn we have yet to understand.*

"Robert?" Sophie was standing outside the car, looking back at him. "Are you coming?" She was holding the rosewood box, which Captain Fache had returned to them. Inside, both cryptexes had been reassembled and nested as they had been found. The papyrus verse was locked safely at its core—minus the shattered vial of vinegar.

Making their way up the long gravel path, Langdon and Sophie passed the famous west wall of the chapel. Casual visitors assumed this oddly protruding wall was a section of the chapel that had not been finished. The truth, Langdon recalled, was far more intriguing.

*The west wall of Solomon's Temple.*

The Knights Templar had designed Rosslyn Chapel as an exact architectural blueprint of Solomon's Temple in Jerusalem—complete with a west wall, a narrow rectangular sanctuary, and a subterranean vault like the Holy of Holies, in which the original nine knights had first unearthed their priceless treasure. Langdon had to admit, there existed an intriguing symmetry in the idea of the Templars building a modern Grail repository that echoed the Grail's original hiding place.

Rosslyn Chapel's entrance was more modest

than Langdon expected. The small wooden door had two iron hinges and a simple, oak sign.

## ROSLIN

This ancient spelling, Langdon explained to Sophie, derived from the Rose Line meridian on which the chapel sat; or, as Grail academics preferred to believe, from the "Line of Rose"—the ancestral lineage of Mary Magdalene.

The chapel would be closing soon, and as Langdon pulled open the door, a warm puff of air escaped, as if the ancient edifice were heaving a weary sigh at the end of a long day. Her entry arches burgeoned with carved cinquefoils.

*Roses. The womb of the goddess.*

Entering with Sophie, Langdon felt his eyes reaching across the famous sanctuary and taking it all in. Although he had read accounts of Rosslyn's arrestingly intricate stonework, seeing it in person was an overwhelming encounter.

*Symbology heaven,* one of Langdon's colleagues had called it.

Every surface in the chapel had been carved with symbols—Christian cruciforms, Jewish stars, Masonic seals, Templar crosses, cornucopias, pyramids, astrological signs, plants, vegetables, pentacles, and roses. The Knights Templar had been master stonemasons, erecting Templar churches all over Europe, but Rosslyn was considered their most sublime labor of love and veneration. The master masons had left no stone uncarved. Rosslyn Chapel was a shrine to all faiths . . . to all traditions . . . and, above all, to nature and the goddess.

The sanctuary was empty except for a handful of visitors listening to a young man giving the day's last tour. He was leading them in a single-file line along a well-known route on the floor—an invisible pathway linking six key architectural points within the sanctuary. Generations of visitors had walked these straight lines, connecting the points, and their countless footsteps had engraved an enormous symbol on the floor.

*The Star of David,* Langdon thought. *No coincidence there.* Also known as Solomon's Seal, this hexagram had once been the secret symbol of the stargazing priests and was later adopted by the Israelite kings—David and Solomon.

The docent had seen Langdon and Sophie enter, and although it was closing time, offered a pleasant smile and motioned for them to feel free to look around.

Langdon nodded his thanks and began to move deeper into the sanctuary. Sophie, however, stood riveted in the entryway, a puzzled look on her face.

"What is it?" Langdon asked.

Sophie stared out at the chapel. "I think . . . I've been here."

Langdon was surprised. "But you said you hadn't even *heard* of Rosslyn."

"I hadn't . . ." She scanned the sanctuary, looking uncertain. "My grandfather must have brought me here when I was very young. I don't know. It feels familiar." As her eyes scanned the room, she began nodding with more certainty. "Yes." She pointed to the front of the sanctuary. "Those two pillars . . . I've seen them."

Langdon looked at the pair of intricately sculpted columns at the far end of the sanctuary. Their white lacework carvings seemed to smolder with a ruddy glow as the last of the day's sunlight streamed in through the west window. The pillars—positioned where the altar would normally stand—were an oddly matched pair. The pillar on the left was carved with simple, vertical lines, while the pillar on the right was embellished with an ornate, flowering spiral.

Sophie was already moving toward them. Langdon hurried after her, and as they reached the pillars, Sophie was nodding with incredulity. "Yes, I'm positive I have seen these!"

"I don't doubt you've seen them," Langdon said, "but it wasn't necessarily *here*."

She turned. "What do you mean?"

"These two pillars are the most duplicated architectural structures in history. Replicas exist all over the world."

"Replicas of Rosslyn?" She looked skeptical.

"No. Of the pillars. Do you remember earlier that I mentioned Rosslyn *itself* is a copy of Solomon's Temple? Those two pillars are exact replicas of the two pillars that stood at the head of Solomon's Temple." Langdon pointed to the pillar on the left. "That's called *Boaz*—or the Mason's Pillar. The other is called *Jachin*—or the Apprentice Pillar." He paused. "In fact, virtually every Masonic temple in the world has two pillars like these."

Langdon had already explained to her about the Templars' powerful historic ties to the modern Masonic secret societies, whose primary degrees— Apprentice Freemason, Fellowcraft Freemason, and Master Mason—harked back to early Templar days. Sophie's grandfather's final verse made direct reference to the Master Masons who adorned Rosslyn with their carved artistic offerings. It also noted Rosslyn's central ceiling, which was covered with carvings of stars and planets.

"I've never been in a Masonic temple," Sophie said, still eyeing the pillars. "I am almost positive I saw these *here*." She turned back into the chapel, as if looking for something else to jog her memory.

The rest of the visitors were now leaving, and

the young docent made his way across the chapel to them with a pleasant smile. He was a handsome young man in his late twenties, with a Scottish brogue and strawberry blond hair. "I'm about to close up for the day. May I help you find anything?"

*How about the Holy Grail?* Langdon wanted to say.

"The code," Sophie blurted, in sudden revelation. "There's a code here!"

The docent looked pleased by her enthusiasm. "Yes there is, ma'am."

"It's on the ceiling," she said, turning to the right-hand wall. "Somewhere over . . . there."

He smiled. "Not your first visit to Rosslyn, I see."

*The code,* Langdon thought. He had forgotten that little bit of lore. Among Rosslyn's numerous mysteries was a vaulted archway from which hundreds of stone blocks protruded, jutting down to form a bizarre multifaceted surface. Each block was carved with a symbol, seemingly at random, creating a cipher of unfathomable proportion. Some people believed the code revealed the entrance to the vault beneath the chapel. Others believed it told the true Grail legend. Not that it mattered—cryptographers had been trying for centuries to decipher its meaning. To this day the Rosslyn Trust offered a generous reward to anyone who could unveil the secret meaning, but the code remained a mystery.

"I'd be happy to show . . ."

The docent's voice trailed off.

*My first code,* Sophie thought, moving alone, in a trance, toward the encoded archway. Having handed the rosewood box to Langdon, she could feel herself momentarily forgetting all about the Holy Grail, the Priory of Sion, and all the mysteries of the past day. When she arrived beneath the encoded ceiling and saw the symbols above her, the memories came flooding back. She was recalling her first visit here, and strangely, the memories conjured an unexpected sadness.

She was a little girl . . . a year or so after her family's death. Her grandfather had brought her to Scotland on a short vacation. They had come to see Rosslyn Chapel before going back to Paris. It was late evening, and the chapel was closed. But they were still inside.

"Can we go home, *Grand-père?*" Sophie begged, feeling tired.

"Soon, dear, very soon." His voice was melancholy. "I have one last thing I need to do here. How about if you wait in the car?"

"You're doing another big person thing?"

He nodded. "I'll be fast. I promise."

"Can I do the archway code again? That was fun."

"I don't know. I have to step outside. You won't be frightened in here alone?"

"Of course not!" she said with a huff. "It's not even dark yet!"

He smiled. "Very well then." He led her over to the elaborate archway he had shown her earlier.

Sophie immediately plopped down on the stone floor, lying on her back and staring up at the collage of puzzle pieces overhead. "I'm going to break this code before you get back!"

"It's a race then." He bent over, kissed her forehead, and walked to the nearby side door. "I'll be right outside. I'll leave the door open. If you need me, just call." He exited into the soft evening light.

Sophie lay there on the floor, gazing up at the code. Her eyes felt sleepy. After a few minutes, the symbols got fuzzy. And then they disappeared.

When Sophie awoke, the floor felt cold.

*"Grand-père?"*

There was no answer. Standing up, she brushed herself off. The side door was still open. The evening was getting darker. She walked outside and could see her grandfather standing on the porch of a nearby stone house directly behind the church. Her grandfather was talking quietly to a person barely visible inside the screened door.

"*Grand-père?*" she called.

Her grandfather turned and waved, motioning for her to wait just a moment. Then, slowly, he said some final words to the person inside and blew a kiss toward the screened door. He came to her with tearful eyes.

"Why are you crying, *Grand-père?*"

He picked her up and held her close. "Oh, Sophie, you and I have said good-bye to a lot of people this year. It's hard."

Sophie thought of the accident, of saying good-bye to her mother and father, her grandmother and baby brother. "Were you saying good-bye to *another* person?"

"To a dear friend whom I love very much," he replied, his voice heavy with emotion. "And I fear I will not see her again for a very long time."

Standing with the docent, Langdon had been scanning the chapel walls and feeling a rising wariness that a dead end might be looming. Sophie had wandered off to look at the code and left Langdon holding the rosewood box, which contained a Grail map that now appeared to be no help at all. Although Saunière's poem clearly indicated Rosslyn, Langdon was not sure what to do now that they had arrived. The poem made reference to a "blade and chalice," which Langdon saw nowhere.

The Holy Grail 'neath ancient Roslin waits.
The blade and chalice guarding o'er Her gates.

Again Langdon sensed there remained some facet of this mystery yet to reveal itself.

"I hate to pry," the docent said, eyeing the rosewood box in Langdon's hands. "But this box . . . might I ask where you got it?"

Langdon gave a weary laugh. "That's an exceptionally long story."

The young man hesitated, his eyes on the box again. "It's the strangest thing—my grandmother has a box *exactly* like that—a jewelry box. Identical polished rosewood, same inlaid rose, even the hinges look the same."

Langdon knew the young man must be mistaken. If ever a box had been one of a kind, it was *this* one—the box custom-made for the Priory keystone. "The two boxes may be similar but—"

The side door closed loudly, drawing both of their gazes. Sophie had exited without a word and was now wandering down the bluff toward a fieldstone house nearby. Langdon stared after her. *Where is she going?* She had been acting strangely ever since they entered the building. He turned to the docent. "Do you know what that house is?"

He nodded, also looking puzzled that Sophie was going down there. "That's the chapel rectory. The chapel curator lives there. She also happens to be the head of the Rosslyn Trust." He paused. "And my grandmother."

"Your grandmother heads the Rosslyn Trust?"

The young man nodded. "I live with her in the rectory and help keep up the chapel and give tours." He shrugged. "I've lived here my whole life. My grandmother raised me in that house."

Concerned for Sophie, Langdon moved across the chapel toward the door to call out to her. He was only halfway there when he stopped short. Something the young man said just registered.

*My grandmother raised me.*

Langdon looked out at Sophie on the bluff, then down at the rosewood box in his hand. *Impossible.* Slowly, Langdon turned back to the young man. "You said your grandmother has a box like this one?"

"Almost identical."

"Where did she get it?"

"My grandfather made it for her. He died when I was a baby, but my grandmother still talks about him. She says he was a genius with his hands. He made all kinds of things."

Langdon glimpsed an unimaginable web of connections emerging. "You said your grandmother raised you. Do you mind my asking what happened to your parents?"

The young man looked surprised. "They died when I was young." He paused. "The same day as my grandfather."

Langdon's heart pounded. "In a car accident?"

The docent recoiled, a look of bewilderment in his olive-green eyes. "Yes. In a car accident. My entire family died that day. I lost my grandfather, my parents, and . . ." He hesitated, glancing down at the floor.

"And your sister," Langdon said.

Out on the bluff, the fieldstone house was exactly as Sophie remembered it. Night was falling now, and the house exuded a warm and inviting aura. The smell of bread wafted through the opened screened door, and a golden light shone in the windows. As Sophie approached, she could hear the quiet sounds of sobbing from within.

Through the screened door, Sophie saw an elderly woman in the hallway. Her back was to the door, but Sophie could see she was crying. The woman had long, luxuriant, silver hair that conjured an unexpected wisp of memory. Feeling herself drawn closer, Sophie stepped onto the porch stairs. The woman was clutching a framed photograph of a man and touching her fingertips to his face with loving sadness.

It was a face Sophie knew well.

*Grand-père.*

The woman had obviously heard the sad news of his death last night.

A board squeaked beneath Sophie's feet, and the

woman turned slowly, her sad eyes finding Sophie's. Sophie wanted to run, but she stood transfixed. The woman's fervent gaze never wavered as she set down the photo and approached the screened door. An eternity seemed to pass as the two women stared at one another through the thin mesh. Then, like the slowly gathering swell of an ocean wave, the woman's visage transformed from one of uncertainty . . . to disbelief . . . to hope . . . and finally, to cresting joy.

Throwing open the door, she came out, reaching with soft hands, cradling Sophie's thunderstruck face. "Oh, dear child . . . look at you!"

Although Sophie did not recognize her, she knew who this woman was. She tried to speak but found she could not even breathe.

"Sophie," the woman sobbed, kissing her forehead.

Sophie's words were a choked whisper. "But . . . *Grand-père* said you were . . ."

"I know." The woman placed her tender hands on Sophie's shoulders and gazed at her with familiar eyes. "Your grandfather and I were forced to say so many things. We did what we thought was right. I'm so sorry. It was for your own safety, princess."

Sophie heard her final word, and immediately thought of her grandfather, who had called her princess for so many years. The sound of his voice seemed to echo now in the ancient stones of

Rosslyn, settling through the earth and reverberating in the unknown hollows below.

The woman threw her arms around Sophie, the
tears flowing faster. "Your grandfather wanted so
badly to tell you everything. But things were difficult between you two. He tried so hard. There's
so much to explain. So very much to explain."
She kissed Sophie's forehead once again, then
whispered in her ear. "No more secrets, princess.
It's time you learn the truth about our family."

Sophie and her grandmother were seated on the
porch stairs in a tearful hug when the young docent dashed across the lawn, his eyes shining with
hope and disbelief.

"Sophie?"

Through her tears, Sophie nodded, standing.
She did not know the young man's face, but as
they embraced, she could feel the power of the
blood coursing through his veins . . . the blood
she now understood they shared.

When Langdon walked across the lawn to join
them, Sophie could not imagine that only yesterday she had felt so alone in the world. And now,
somehow, in this foreign place, in the company of
three people she barely knew, she felt at last that
she was home.

# CHAPTER 105

**Night had** fallen over Rosslyn.

Robert Langdon stood alone on the porch of the fieldstone house enjoying the sounds of laughter and reunion drifting through the screened door behind him. The mug of potent Brazilian coffee in his hand had granted him a hazy reprieve from his mounting exhaustion, and yet he sensed the reprieve would be fleeting. The fatigue in his body went to the core.

"You slipped out quietly," a voice behind him said.

He turned. Sophie's grandmother emerged, her silver hair shimmering in the night. Her name, for the last twenty-eight years at least, was Marie Chauvel.

Langdon gave a tired smile. "I thought I'd give your family some time together." Through the window, he could see Sophie talking with her brother.

Marie came over and stood beside him. "Mr. Langdon, when I first heard of Jacques's murder, I was terrified for Sophie's safety. Seeing her standing in my doorway tonight was the greatest relief of my life. I cannot thank you enough."

Langdon had no idea how to respond. Although he had offered to give Sophie and her grandmother time to talk in private, Marie had asked him to stay and listen. *My husband obviously trusted you, Mr. Langdon, so I do as well.*

And so Langdon had remained, standing beside Sophie and listening in mute astonishment while Marie told the story of Sophie's late parents. Incredibly, both had been from Merovingian families—direct descendants of Mary Magdalene and Jesus Christ. Sophie's parents and ancestors, for protection, had changed their family names of Plantard and Saint-Clair. Their children represented the most direct surviving royal bloodline and therefore were carefully guarded by the Priory. When Sophie's parents were killed in a car accident whose cause could not be determined, the Priory feared the identity of the royal line had been discovered.

"Your grandfather and I," Marie had explained in a voice choked with pain, "had to make a grave decision the instant we received the phone call. Your parents' car had just been found in the river." She dabbed at the tears in her eyes. "All six of us—including you two grandchildren—were supposed to be traveling together in that car that very night. Fortunately we changed our plans at the last moment, and your parents were alone. Hearing of the accident, Jacques and I had no way to know what had really happened . . . or if this was truly an *accident.*" Marie looked at

Sophie. "We knew we had to protect our grand-children, and we did what we thought was best. Jacques reported to the police that your brother and I had been in the car . . . our two bodies apparently washed off in the current. Then your brother and I went underground with the Priory. Jacques, being a man of prominence, did not have the luxury of disappearing. It only made sense that Sophie, being the eldest, would stay in Paris to be taught and raised by Jacques, close to the heart and protection of the Priory." Her voice fell to a whisper. "Separating the family was the hardest thing we ever had to do. Jacques and I saw each other only very infrequently, and always in the most secret of settings . . . under the protection of the Priory. There are certain ceremonies to which the brotherhood always stays faithful."

Langdon had sensed the story went far deeper, but he also sensed it was not for him to hear. So he had stepped outside. Now, gazing up at the spires of Rosslyn, Langdon could not escape the hollow gnaw of Rosslyn's unsolved mystery. *Is the Grail really here at Rosslyn? And if so, where are the blade and chalice that Saunière mentioned in his poem?*

"I'll take that," Marie said, motioning to Langdon's hand.

"Oh, thank you." Langdon held out his empty coffee cup.

She stared at him. "I was referring to your *other* hand, Mr. Langdon."

Langdon looked down and realized he was holding Saunière's papyrus. He had taken it from the cryptex once again in hopes of seeing something he had missed earlier. "Of course, I'm sorry."

Marie looked amused as she took the paper. "I know of a man at a bank in Paris who is probably very eager to see the return of this rosewood box. André Vernet was a dear friend of Jacques, and Jacques trusted him explicitly. André would have done anything to honor Jacques's requests for the care of this box."

*Including shooting me,* Langdon recalled, deciding not to mention that he had probably broken the poor man's nose. Thinking of Paris, Langdon flashed on the three *sénéchaux* who had been killed the night before. "And the Priory? What happens now?"

"The wheels are already in motion, Mr. Langdon. The brotherhood has endured for centuries, and it will endure this. There are always those waiting to move up and rebuild."

All evening Langdon had suspected that Sophie's grandmother was closely tied to the operations of the Priory. After all, the Priory had always had women members. Four Grand Masters had been women. The *sénéchaux* were traditionally men—the guardians—and yet women held far more honored status within the Priory and could ascend to the highest post from virtually any rank.

Langdon thought of Leigh Teabing and Westminster Abbey. It seemed a lifetime ago. "Was the Church pressuring your husband not to release the Sangreal documents at the End of Days?"

"Heavens no. The End of Days is a legend of paranoid minds. There is nothing in the Priory doctrine that identifies a date at which the Grail should be unveiled. In fact the Priory has always maintained that the Grail should *never* be unveiled."

"Never?" Langdon was stunned.

"It is the mystery and wonderment that serve our souls, not the Grail itself. The beauty of the Grail lies in her ethereal nature." Marie Chauvel gazed up at Rosslyn now. "For some, the Grail is a chalice that will bring them everlasting life. For others, it is the quest for lost documents and secret history. And for most, I suspect the Holy Grail is simply a grand idea . . . a glorious unattainable treasure that somehow, even in today's world of chaos, inspires us."

"But if the Sangreal documents remain hidden, the story of Mary Magdalene will be lost forever," Langdon said.

"Will it? Look around you. Her story is being told in art, music, and books. More so every day.

The pendulum is swinging. We are starting to sense the dangers of our history . . . and of our destructive paths. We are beginning to sense the need to restore the sacred feminine." She paused. "You mentioned you are writing a manuscript about the symbols of the sacred feminine, are you not?"

"I am."

She smiled. "Finish it, Mr. Langdon. Sing her song. The world needs modern troubadours."

Langdon fell silent, feeling the weight of her message upon him. Across the open spaces, a new moon was rising above the tree line. Turning his eyes toward Rosslyn, Langdon felt a boyish craving to know her secrets. *Don't ask,* he told himself. *This is not the moment.* He glanced at the papyrus in Marie's hand, and then back at Rosslyn.

"Ask the question, Mr. Langdon," Marie said, looking amused. "You have earned the right."

Langdon felt himself flush.

"You want to know if the Grail is here at Rosslyn."

"Can you tell me?"

She sighed in mock exasperation. "Why is it that men simply *cannot* let the Grail rest?" She laughed, obviously enjoying herself. "Why do you think it's here?"

Langdon motioned to the papyrus in her hand. "Your husband's poem speaks specifically of Rosslyn, except it also mentions a blade and chalice watching over the Grail. I didn't see any symbols of the blade and chalice up there."

"The blade and chalice?" Marie asked. "What exactly do they look like?"

Langdon sensed she was toying with him, but he played along, quickly describing the symbols.

A look of vague recollection crossed her face. "Ah, yes, of course. The blade represents all that is masculine. I believe it is drawn like this, no?" Using her index finger, she traced a shape on her palm.

"Yes," Langdon said. Marie had drawn the less common "closed" form of the blade, although Langdon had seen the symbol portrayed both ways.

"And the inverse," she said, drawing again on her palm, "is the chalice, which represents the feminine."

"Correct," Langdon said.

"And you are saying that in all the hundreds of symbols we have here in Rosslyn Chapel, these two shapes appear nowhere?"

"I didn't see them."

"And if I show them to you, will you get some sleep?"

Before Langdon could answer, Marie Chauvel had stepped off the porch and was heading toward the chapel. Langdon hurried after her. Entering the ancient building, Marie turned on the lights and pointed to the center of the sanctuary floor. "There you are, Mr. Langdon. The blade and chalice."

Langdon stared at the scuffed stone floor. It was blank. "There's nothing here. . . ."

Marie sighed and began to walk along the famous path worn into the chapel floor, the same path Langdon had seen the visitors walking earlier this evening. As his eyes adjusted to see the giant symbol, he still felt lost. "But that's the Star of Dav—"

Langdon stopped short, mute with amazement as it dawned on him.

*The blade and chalice.*
*Fused as one.*

*The Star of David . . . the perfect union of male and female . . . Solomon's Seal . . . marking the Holy of Holies, where the male and female deities—Yahweh and Shekinah—were thought to dwell.*

Langdon needed a minute to find his words. "The verse *does* point here to Rosslyn. Completely. Perfectly."

Marie smiled. "Apparently."

The implications chilled him. "So the Holy Grail is in the vault beneath us?"

She laughed. "Only in spirit. One of the Priory's most ancient charges was one day to return the Grail to her homeland of France where she could rest for eternity. For centuries, she was dragged across the countryside to keep her safe. Most undignified. Jacques's charge when he became Grand Master was to restore her honor by returning her to France and building her a resting place fit for a queen."

"And he succeeded?"

Now her face grew serious. "Mr. Langdon, considering what you've done for me tonight, and as curator of the Rosslyn Trust, I can tell you for certain that the Grail is no longer here."

Langdon decided to press. "But the keystone is supposed to point to the place where the Holy Grail is hidden *now*. Why does it point to Rosslyn?"

"Maybe you're misreading its meaning. Remember, the Grail can be deceptive. As could my late husband."

"But how much clearer could he be?" he asked. "We are standing over an underground vault marked by the blade and chalice, underneath a ceiling of stars, surrounded by the art of Master Masons. Everything speaks of Rosslyn."

"Very well, let me see this mysterious verse." She unrolled the papyrus and read the poem aloud in a deliberate tone.

The Holy Grail 'neath ancient Roslin waits.
The blade and chalice guarding o'er Her gates.
Adorned in masters' loving art, She lies.
She rests at last beneath the starry skies.

When she finished, she was still for several seconds, until a knowing smile crossed her lips. "Aah, Jacques."

Langdon watched her expectantly. "You *understand* this?"

"As you have witnessed on the chapel floor, Mr. Langdon, there are many ways to see simple things."

Langdon strained to understand. Everything about Jacques Saunière seemed to have double meanings, and yet Langdon could see no further.

Marie gave a tired yawn. "Mr. Langdon, I will make a confession to you. I have never officially been privy to the present location of the Grail. But, of course, I *was* married to a person of enormous influence . . . and my women's intuition is strong." Langdon started to speak but Marie continued. "I am sorry that after all your hard work, you will be leaving Rosslyn without any real answers. And yet, something tells me you will eventually find what you seek. One day it will dawn on you." She smiled. "And when it does, I trust that you, of all people, can keep a secret."

There was a sound of someone arriving in the doorway. "Both of you disappeared," Sophie said, entering.

"I was just leaving," her grandmother replied, walking over to Sophie at the door. "Good night, princess." She kissed Sophie's forehead. "Don't keep Mr. Langdon out too late."

Langdon and Sophie watched her grandmother walk back toward the fieldstone house. When Sophie turned to him, her eyes were awash in deep emotion. "Not exactly the ending I expected."

*That makes two of us,* he thought. Langdon could see she was overwhelmed. The news she had received tonight had changed everything in her life. "Are you okay? It's a lot to take in."

She smiled quietly. "I have a family. That's where I'm going to start. Who we are and where we came from will take some time."

Langdon remained silent.

"Beyond tonight, will you stay with us?" Sophie asked. "At least for a few days?"

Langdon sighed, wanting nothing more. "You need some time here with your family, Sophie. I'm going back to Paris in the morning."

She looked disappointed but seemed to know it was the right thing to do. Neither of them spoke for a long time. Finally Sophie reached over and, taking his hand, led him out of the chapel. They walked to a small rise on the bluff. From here, the Scottish countryside spread out before them, suffused in a pale moonlight that sifted through the departing clouds. They stood in silence, holding hands, both of them fighting the descending shroud of exhaustion.

The stars were just now appearing, but to the east, a single point of light glowed brighter than any other. Langdon smiled when he saw it. It was Venus. The ancient Goddess shining down with her steady and patient light.

The night was growing cooler, a crisp breeze rolling up from the lowlands. After a while, Langdon looked over at Sophie. Her eyes were closed, her lips relaxed in a contented smile. Langdon could feel his own eyes growing heavy. Reluctantly, he squeezed her hand. "Sophie?"

Slowly, she opened her eyes and turned to him. Her face was beautiful in the moonlight. She gave him a sleepy smile. "Hi."

Langdon felt an unexpected sadness to realize he would be returning to Paris without her. "I may be gone before you wake up." He paused, a knot growing in his throat. "I'm sorry, I'm not very good at—"

Sophie reached out and placed her soft hand on the side of his face. Then, leaning forward, she kissed him tenderly on the cheek. "When can I see you again?"

Langdon reeled momentarily, lost in her eyes. "When?" He paused, curious if she had any idea how much he had been wondering the same thing. "Well, actually, next month I'm lecturing at a conference in Florence. I'll be there a week without much to do."

"Is that an invitation?"

"We'd be living in luxury. They're giving me a room at the Brunelleschi."

Sophie smiled playfully. "You presume a lot, Mr. Langdon."

He cringed at how it had sounded. "What I meant—"

"I would love nothing more than to meet you in Florence, Robert. But on *one* condition." Her tone turned serious. "No museums, no churches, no tombs, no art, no relics."

"In Florence? For a week? There's nothing else to do."

Sophie leaned forward and kissed him again, now on the lips. Their bodies came together, softly at first, and then completely. When she pulled away, her eyes were full of promise.

"Right," Langdon managed. "It's a date."

# Epilogue

Robert Langdon awoke with a start. He had been dreaming. The bathrobe beside his bed bore the monogram *HOTEL RITZ PARIS*. He saw a dim light filtering through the blinds. *Is it dusk or dawn?* he wondered.

Langdon's body felt warm and deeply contented. He had slept the better part of the last two days. Sitting up slowly in bed, he now realized what had awoken him . . . the strangest thought. For days he had been trying to sort through a barrage of information, but now Langdon found himself fixed on something he'd not considered before.

*Could it be?*

He remained motionless a long moment.

Getting out of bed, he walked to the marble shower. Stepping inside, he let the powerful jets message his shoulders. Still, the thought enthralled him.

*Impossible.*

Twenty minutes later, Langdon stepped out of the Hotel Ritz into Place Vendôme. Night was falling. The days of sleep had left him disoriented . . . and yet his mind felt oddly lucid.

He had promised himself he would stop in the hotel lobby for a café au lait to clear his thoughts, but instead his legs carried him directly out the front door into the gathering Paris night.

Walking east on Rue des Petits Champs, Langdon felt a growing excitement. He turned south onto Rue Richelieu, where the air grew sweet with the scent of blossoming jasmine from the stately gardens of the Palais Royal.

He continued south until he saw what he was looking for—the famous royal arcade—a glistening expanse of polished black marble. Moving onto it, Langdon scanned the surface beneath his feet. Within seconds, he found what he knew was there—several bronze medallions embedded in the ground in a perfectly straight line. Each disk was five inches in diameter and embossed with the letters N and S.

*Nord. Sud.*

He turned due south, letting his eye trace the extended line formed by the medallions. He began moving again, following the trail, watching the pavement as he walked. As he cut across the corner of the Comédie-Française, another bronze medallion passed beneath his feet. *Yes!*

The streets of Paris, Langdon had learned years ago, were adorned with 135 of these bronze markers, embedded in sidewalks, courtyards, and streets, on a north-south axis across the city. He had once followed the line from Sacré-Coeur, north across the Seine, and finally to the ancient Paris Observatory. There he discovered the significance of the sacred path it traced.

*The earth's original prime meridian.*
*The first zero longitude of the world.*
*Paris's ancient Rose Line.*

Now, as Langdon hurried across Rue de Rivoli, he could feel his destination within reach. Less than a block away.

The Holy Grail 'neath ancient Roslin waits.

The revelations were coming now in waves. Saunière's ancient spelling of Roslin . . . the blade and chalice . . . the tomb adorned with masters' art.

*Is that why Saunière needed to talk with me? Had I unknowingly guessed the truth?*

He broke into a jog, feeling the Rose Line beneath his feet, guiding him, pulling him toward his destination. As he entered the long tunnel of Passage Richelieu, the hairs on his neck began to bristle with anticipation. He knew that at the end of this tunnel stood the most mysterious of Parisian monuments—conceived and commissioned in the 1980s by the Sphinx himself, François Mitterrand, a man rumored to move in secret circles, a man whose final legacy to Paris was a place Langdon had visited only days before.

*Another lifetime.*

With a final surge of energy, Langdon burst from the passageway into the familiar courtyard and came to a stop. Breathless, he raised his eyes, slowly, disbelieving, to the glistening structure in front of him.

*The Louvre Pyramid.*

Gleaming in the darkness.

He admired it only a moment. He was more interested in what lay to his right. Turning, he felt his feet again tracing the invisible path of the ancient Rose Line, carrying him across the courtyard to the Carrousel du Louvre—the enormous circle of grass surrounded by a perimeter of neatly trimmed hedges—once the site of Paris's primeval nature-worshipping festivals . . . joyous rites to celebrate fertility and the Goddess.

Langdon felt as if he were crossing into another world as he stepped over the bushes to the grassy area within. This hallowed ground was now marked by one of the city's most unusual monuments. There in the center, plunging into the earth like a crystal chasm, gaped the giant inverted pyramid of glass that he had seen a few nights ago when he entered the Louvre's subterranean entresol.

*La Pyramide Inversée.*

Tremulous, Langdon walked to the edge and peered down into the Louvre's sprawling underground complex, aglow with amber light. His eye was trained not just on the massive inverted pyramid, but on what lay directly beneath it. There, on the floor of the chamber below, stood the tiniest of structures . . . a structure Langdon had mentioned in his manuscript.

Langdon felt himself awaken fully now to the thrill of unthinkable possibility. Raising his eyes again to the Louvre, he sensed the huge wings of the museum enveloping him . . . hallways that burgeoned with the world's finest art.

Da Vinci . . . Botticelli . . .

Adorned in masters' loving art, She lies.

Alive with wonder, he stared once again down-ward through the glass at the tiny structure below. *I must go down there!*

Stepping out of the circle, he hurried across the courtyard back toward the towering pyramid en-trance of the Louvre. The day's last visitors were trickling out of the museum.

Pushing through the revolving door, Langdon descended the curved staircase into the pyramid. He could feel the air grow cooler. When he reached the bottom, he entered the long tunnel that stretched beneath the Louvre's courtyard, back toward *La Pyramide Inversée*.

At the end of the tunnel, he emerged into a large chamber. Directly before him, hanging down from above, gleamed the inverted pyramid—a breathtaking V-shaped contour of glass.

*The Chalice.*

Langdon's eyes traced its narrowing form downward to its tip, suspended only six feet above the floor. There, directly beneath it, stood the tiny structure.

A miniature pyramid. Only three feet tall. The only structure in this colossal complex that had been built on a small scale.

Langdon's manuscript, while discussing the Louvre's elaborate collection of goddess art, had made passing note of this modest pyramid. *"The miniature structure itself protrudes up through the floor as though it were the tip of an iceberg—the apex of an enormous, pyramidical vault, submerged below like a hidden chamber."*

Illuminated in the soft lights of the deserted entresol, the two pyramids pointed at one another, their bodies perfectly aligned, their tips almost touching.

The Chalice above. The Blade below.

*The blade and chalice guarding o'er Her gates.*

Langdon heard Marie Chauvel's words. *One day it will dawn on you.*

He was standing beneath the ancient Rose Line, surrounded by the work of masters. *What better place for Saunière to keep watch?* Now at last, he sensed he understood the true meaning of the

Grand Master's verse. Raising his eyes to heaven, he gazed upward through the glass to a glorious, star-filled night.

She rests at last beneath the starry skies.

Like the murmurs of spirits in the darkness, forgotten words echoed. *The quest for the Holy Grail is the quest to kneel before the bones of Mary Magdalene. A journey to pray at the feet of the outcast one.*

With a sudden upwelling of reverence, Robert Langdon fell to his knees.

For a moment, he thought he heard a woman's voice . . . the wisdom of the ages . . . whispering up from the chasms of the earth.

# THE STRANGE POWER

*For Max,*
*who brought sunshine*

# CHAPTER 1

You don't invite the local witch to parties. No matter how beautiful she is. That was the basic problem.

*I don't care,* Kaitlyn thought. *I don't need anyone.*

She was sitting in history class, listening to Marcy Huang and Pam Sasseen plan a party for that weekend. She couldn't help but hear them: Mr. Flynn's gentle, apologetic voice was no competition for their excited whispers. Kait was listening, pretending not to listen, and fiercely wishing she could get away. She couldn't, so she doodled on the blue-lined page of her history notebook.

She was full of contradictory feelings. She hated Pam and Marcy, and wanted them to die, or at least to have some gory accident that left them utterly broken and defeated and miserable. At the same time there was a terrible longing inside her. If they would only let her *in*—it wasn't as if she insisted on being the most popular, the most admired, girl at school. She'd settle for a place in the group that was securely her own. They could shake their heads and say, "Oh, that Kaitlyn—she's odd, but what would we do without her?" And that would be fine, as long as she was a *part*.

But it wouldn't happen, ever. Marcy would never think of inviting Kaitlyn to her party because she wouldn't think of doing something that had never been done before. No one ever invited the witch; no one thought that Kaitlyn, the lovely, spooky girl with the strange eyes, would *want* to go.

And I don't care, Kaitlyn thought, her reflections coming around full circle. This is my last year. One semester to go. After that, I'm out of high school and I hope I never see anyone from this place again.

But that was the other problem, of course. In a little town like Thoroughfare she was bound to see them, and their parents, every day for the next year. And the year after that, and the year after that. . . .

There was no escape. If she could have gone away to college, it might have been different. But she'd screwed up her art scholarship . . . and anyway, there was her father. He needed her—and there wasn't any money. Dad needed her. It was junior college or nothing.

The years stretched out in front of Kaitlyn, bleak as the Ohio winter outside the window, filled with endless cold classrooms. Endless sitting and listening to girls planning parties that she wasn't invited to. Endless exclusion. Endless aching and wishing that she *were* a witch so she could put the most hideous, painful, debilitating curse on all of them.

All the while she was thinking, she was doodling. Or rather her hand was doodling—her brain didn't seem to be involved at all. Now she looked down and for the first time saw what she'd drawn.

A spiderweb.

But what was strange was what was *underneath* the web, so close it was almost touching. A pair of eyes.

Wide, round, heavy-lashed eyes. Bambi eyes. The eyes of a child.

As Kaitlyn stared at it, she suddenly felt dizzy, as if she were falling. As if the picture were opening to let her in. It was a horrible sensation—and a familiar one. It happened every time she drew one of *those* pictures, the kind they called her a witch for.

The kind that came true.

She pulled herself back with a jerk. There was a sick, sinking feeling inside her.

Oh, *please,* no, she thought. Not today—and not here, not at school. It's just a doodle; it doesn't mean anything.

*Please let it be just a doodle.*

But she could feel her body bracing, ignoring her mind, going ice-cold in order to meet what was coming.

A child. She'd drawn a child's eyes, so some child was in danger.

But *what* child? Staring at the space under the eyes, Kait felt a tugging, almost a twitch, in her hand. Her fingers telling her the shape that *needed* to go there. Little half circle, with smaller curves at the edges. A snub nose. Large circle, filled in solid. A mouth, open in fear or surprise or pain. Big curve to indicate a round chin.

A series of long wriggles for hair—and then the itch, the urge, the *need* in Kait's hand ebbed away.

She let out her breath.

That was all. The child in the picture must be a girl, with all that hair. Wavy hair. A pretty little girl with wavy hair and a spiderweb on top of her face.

Something was going to happen, involving a child and a spider. But where—and to what child? And *when?*

Today? Next week? Next year?

It wasn't enough.

It never was. That was the most terrible part of Kaitlyn's terrible gift. Her drawings were always accurate—they always, always came true. She always ended up seeing in real life what she'd drawn on paper.

*But not in time.*

Right now, what could she do? Run through town with a megaphone telling all kids to beware of spiders? Go down to the elementary school looking for girls with wavy hair?

Even if she tried to tell them, they'd run away from her. As if Kaitlyn brought on the things she drew. As if she *made* them happen instead of just predicting them.

The lines of the picture were getting crooked. Kaitlyn blinked to straighten them. The one thing she wouldn't do was cry—because Kaitlyn never cried.

Never. Not once, not since her mother had died when Kait was eight. Since then, Kait had learned how to make the tears go inside.

There was a disturbance at the front of the room. Mr. Flynn's voice, usually so soft and melodious that students could comfortably go to sleep to it, had stopped.

Chris Barnable, a boy who worked sixth period as a student aide, had brought a piece of pink paper. A call slip.

Kaitlyn watched Mr. Flynn take it, read it, then look mildly at the class, wrinkling his nose to push his glasses back up.

"Kaitlyn, the office wants you."

Kaitlyn was already reaching for her books. She kept her back very straight, her head very high, as she walked up the aisle to take the slip. KAITLYN FAIRCHILD TO THE PRINCIPAL'S OFFICE— AT ONCE! it read. Somehow when the "at once" box was checked, the whole slip assumed an air of urgency and malice.

"In trouble again?" a voice from the first row asked snidely. Kaitlyn couldn't tell who it was, and she wouldn't turn around to look. She went out the door with Chris.

In trouble again, yes, she thought as she walked down the stairs to the main office. What did they have on her this time? Those excuses "signed by her father" last fall?

Kaitlyn missed a lot of school, because there were times when she just couldn't stand it. Whenever it got too bad, she went down Piqua Road to where the farms were, and drew. Nobody bothered her there.

"I'm sorry you're in trouble," Chris Barnable said as they reached the office. "I mean . . . I'm sorry *if* you're in trouble."

Kaitlyn glanced at him sharply. He was an okay-looking guy: shiny hair, soft eyes—a lot like Hello Sailor, the cocker spaniel she'd had years ago. Still, she wasn't fooled for a minute.

Boys—boys were no good. Kait knew exactly why they were nice to her. She'd inherited her mother's creamy Irish skin and autumn-fire hair. She'd inherited her mother's supple, willow-slim figure.

But her eyes were her own, and just now she used them without mercy. She turned an icy gaze on Chris, looking at him in a way she was usually careful to avoid. She looked him straight in the face.

He went white.

It was typical of the way people around here reacted when they had to meet Kaitlyn's eyes. No one else had eyes like Kaitlyn. They were smoky blue, and at the outside of each iris, as well as in the middle, were darker rings.

Her father said they were beautiful and that Kaitlyn had been marked by the fairies. But other people said other things. Ever since she could remember, Kaitlyn had heard the whispers—that she had strange eyes, evil eyes. Eyes that saw what wasn't meant to be seen.

Sometimes, like now, Kaitlyn used them as a weapon. She stared at Chris Barnable until the poor jerk actually stepped backward. Then she lowered her lashes demurely and walked into the office.

It gave her only a sick, momentary feeling of triumph. Scaring cocker spaniels was hardly an achievement. But Kaitlyn was too frightened and miserable herself to care. A secretary waved her toward the principal's office, and Kaitlyn steeled herself. She opened the door.

Ms. McCasslan, the principal, was there—but she wasn't alone. Sitting beside the desk was a tanned, trim young woman with short blond hair.

"Congratulations," the blond woman said, coming out of the chair with one quick, graceful movement.

Kaitlyn stood motionless, head high. She didn't know what to think. But all at once she had a rush of feeling, like a premonition.

*This is it. What you've been waiting for.*

She hadn't known she was waiting for anything.

*Of course you have. And this is it.*

*The next few minutes are going to change your life.*

"I'm Joyce," the blond woman said. "Joyce Piper. Don't you remember me?"

# CHAPTER 2

The woman did seem familiar. Her sleek blond hair clung to her head like a wet seal's fur, and her eyes were a startling aquamarine. She was wearing a smart rose-colored suit, but she moved like an aerobics teacher.

Memory burst on Kaitlyn. "The vision screening!"

Joyce nodded. "Exactly!" she said energetically. "Now, how much do you remember about that?"

Bewildered, Kaitlyn looked at Ms. McCasslan. The principal, a small woman, quite plump and very pretty, was sitting with her hands folded on the desk. She seemed serene, but her eyes were sparkling.

All right, so I'm not in trouble, Kait thought. But what's going *on?* She stood uncertainly in the center of the room.

"Don't be frightened, Kaitlyn," the principal said. She waved a small hand with a number of rings on it. "Sit down."

Kait sat.

"I don't bite," Joyce added, sitting down herself, although she kept her aquamarine eyes on Kait's face the entire time. "Now, what do you remember?"

"It was just a test, like you get at the optometrist's," Kaitlyn said slowly. "I thought it was some new program."

Everyone brought their new programs to Ohio. Ohio was so representative of the nation that its people were perfect guinea pigs.

Joyce was smiling a little. "It *was* a new program. But we weren't screening for vision, exactly. Do you remember the test where you had to write down the letters you saw?"

"Oh—yes." It wasn't easy to remember, because everything that had happened during the testing was vague. It had been last fall, early October, Kait thought. Joyce had come into study hall and talked to the class. That was clear enough—Kait remembered her asking them to cooperate. Then Joyce had guided them through some "relaxation exercises"—after which Kaitlyn had been so relaxed that everything was foggy.

"You gave everybody a pencil and a piece of paper," she said hesitantly to Joyce. "And then you projected letters on the movie screen. And they kept getting smaller and smaller. I could hardly write," she added. "I was *limp*."

"Just a little hypnosis to get past your inhibitions," Joyce said, leaning forward. "What else?"

"I kept writing letters."

"Yes, you did," Joyce said. A slight grin flashed in her tanned face. "You did indeed."

After a moment, Kaitlyn said, "So I've got good eyesight?"

"I wouldn't know." Still grinning, Joyce straightened up. "You want to know how that test really worked, Kaitlyn? We kept projecting the letters smaller and smaller—until finally they weren't there at all."

"Weren't there?"

"Not for the last twenty frames. There were just dots, absolutely featureless. You could have vision like a hawk and still not make anything out of them."

A cold finger seemed to run up Kaitlyn's backbone. "I saw letters," she insisted.

"I know you did. But not with your eyes."

There was perfect silence in the room.

Kaitlyn's heart was beating hard.

"We had someone in the room next door," Joyce said. "A graduate student with very good concentration, and *he* was looking at charts with letters on them. That was why you saw letters, Kait. You saw through his eyes. You expected to see letters on the chart, so your mind was open—and you received what he saw."

Kaitlyn said faintly, "It doesn't work that way." Oh, *please*, God . . . all she needed was another power, another curse.

"It does; it's all the same," Joyce said. "It's called remote viewing. The awareness of an event beyond the range of your ordinary senses. Your drawings are remote viewings of events—sometimes events that haven't happened yet."

"What do you know about my drawings?" A rush of emotion brought Kait to her feet. It wasn't fair: this *stranger* coming in and playing with her, testing her, tricking her—and now talking about her private drawings. Her very private drawings that people in Thoroughfare had the decency to only refer to obliquely.

"I'll tell you what I know," Joyce said. Her voice was soft, rhythmic, and she was gazing at Kaitlyn intently with those aquamarine eyes. "I know that you first discovered your gift when you were nine years old. A little boy from your neighborhood had disappeared—"

"Danny Lindenmayer," the principal put in briskly.

"Danny Lindenmayer had disappeared," Joyce said, without looking away from Kait. "And the police were going door to door, looking for him. You were drawing with crayons while they talked to your father. You heard everything about the missing boy. And when you were done drawing, it was a picture you didn't understand, a picture of trees and a bridge . . . and something square."

Kaitlyn nodded, feeling oddly defeated. The memory sucked at her, making her dizzy. That first picture, so dark and strange, and her own fear . . . She'd *known* it was a very bad thing that her fingers had drawn. But she hadn't known why.

"And the next day, on TV, you saw the place where they'd

found the little boy's body," Joyce said. "Underneath a bridge by some trees . . . in a packing crate."

"Something square," Kaitlyn said.

"It matched the picture you'd drawn exactly, even though there was no way you could have known about that place. The bridge was thirty miles away, in a town you'd never been to. When your father saw the news on TV, he recognized your picture, too—and he got excited. Started showing the drawing around, telling the story. But people reacted badly. They already thought you were a little different because of your eyes. But this—this was a whole lot different. They didn't like it. And when it happened again, and again, when your drawings kept coming true, they got very frightened."

"And Kaitlyn developed something of an attitude problem," the principal interjected delicately. "She's naturally rebellious and a bit high-strung—like a colt. But she got prickly, too, and cool. Self-defense." She made *tsk*ing noises.

Kaitlyn glared, but it was a feeble glare. Joyce's quiet, sympathetic voice had disarmed her. She sat down again.

"So you know all about me," she said to Joyce. "So I've got an attitude problem. So wh—"

"You do *not* have an attitude problem," Joyce interrupted. She looked almost shocked. She leaned forward, speaking very earnestly. "You have a gift, a very great gift. Kaitlyn, don't you understand? Don't you realize how unusual you are, how wonderful?"

In Kaitlyn's experience, unusual did not equate to wonderful.

"In the entire world, there are only a handful of people who can do what you can do," Joyce said. "In the entire United States, we only found five."

"Five what?"

"Five high school seniors. Five kids like you. All with different talents, of course; none of you can do the same thing. But that's great; that's just what we were looking for. We'll be able to do a variety of experiments."

"You want to *experiment* on me?" Kaitlyn looked at the principal in alarm.

"I'm getting ahead of myself. Let me explain. I'm from San Carlos, California—"

Well, that explained the tan.

"—and I work for the Zetes Institute. It's a very small laboratory, not at all like SRI or Duke University. It was established last year by a research grant from the Zetes Foundation. Mr. Zetes is—oh, how can I explain *him?* He's an incredible man— he's the chairman of a big corporation in Silicon Valley. But his real interest is in psychic phenomena. Psychic research."

Joyce paused and pushed sleek blond hair off her forehead. Kaitlyn could feel her working up to something big. "He's put up the funds for a very special project, a very *intense* project. It was his idea to do screening at high schools all over the country, looking for seniors with high psychic potential. To find the five or six that were absolutely the top, the cream of the crop, and to bring them to California for a year of testing."

"A *year?*"

"That's the beauty of it, don't you see? Instead of doing a few sporadic tests, we'd do testing daily, on a regular schedule. We'd be able to chart changes in your powers with your biorhythms, with your diet—" Joyce broke off abruptly. Looking at Kait directly, she reached out and took Kait's hands.

"Kaitlyn, let down the walls and just *listen* to me for a minute. Can you do that?"

Kait could feel her hands trembling in the cool grasp of the blond woman's fingers. She swallowed, unable to look away from those aquamarine eyes.

"Kaitlyn, I am not here to hurt you. I admire you tremendously. You have a wonderful gift. I want to study it— I've spent my life preparing to study it. I went to college at Duke—you know, where Rhine did his telepathy experiments. I got my master's degree in parapsychology—I've worked at the Dream Laboratory at Maimonides, and the Mind Science Foundation in San Antonio, and the Engineering Anomalies Research Laboratory at Princeton. And all I've ever wanted is a subject like *you*. Together we can prove that what you do is real. We can get hard, replicable, scientific proof. We can show the world that ESP exists."

She stopped, and Kaitlyn heard the whir of a copier in the outer office.

"There are some benefits for Kaitlyn, too," Ms. McCasslan said. "I think you should explain the terms."

"Oh, yes." Joyce let go of Kaitlyn's hands and picked up a manila folder from the desk. "You'll go to a very good school in San Carlos to finish up your senior year. Meanwhile you'll be living at the Institute with the four other students we've chosen. We'll do testing every afternoon, but it won't take long—just an hour or two a day. And at the end of a year, you'll receive a scholarship to the college of your choice." Joyce opened the folder and handed it to Kaitlyn. "A very generous scholarship."

"A *very* generous scholarship," Ms. McCasslan said.

Kaitlyn found herself looking at a number on a piece of paper. "That's . . . for all of us, to split?"

"That is for you," Joyce said. "Alone."

Kaitlyn felt dizzy.

"You'll be helping the cause of science," Joyce said. "And you could make a new life for yourself. A new start. No one at your new school needs to know why you're there; you can just be an ordinary high school kid. Next fall you can go to Stanford or San Francisco State University—San Carlos is just half an hour south of San Francisco. And after that, you're free. You can go anywhere."

Kaitlyn felt *really* dizzy.

"You'll love the Bay Area. Sunshine, nice beaches—do you realize it was seventy degrees there yesterday when I left? Seventy degrees in winter. Redwoods—palm trees—"

"I can't," Kaitlyn said weakly.

Joyce and the principal both looked at her, startled.

"I can't," Kait said again, more loudly, pulling her walls close around her. She needed the walls, or she might succumb to the shimmering picture Joyce was painting in her mind.

"Don't you want to get away?" Joyce said gently.

Didn't she? Only so much that she sometimes felt like a bird beating its wings against glass. Except that she'd never been quite sure what she'd *do* once she got away. She'd just thought, There must be some place I belong. A place where I'd just fit in, without trying.

She'd never thought of *California* as being the place, California was almost too rich, too heady and exciting. It was like a dream. And the money . . .

But her father.

"You don't understand. It's my dad. I've never been away from him, not since my mom died, and he needs me. He's not . . . He really needs me."

Ms. McCasslan was looking sympathetic. Ms. McCasslan knew her dad, of course. He'd been brilliant, a philosophy professor; he'd written books. But after Kaitlyn's mother had died, he'd gotten . . . vague. Now he sang a lot to himself and did odd jobs around town. He didn't make much doing them. When bills came in, he shuffled his feet and ruffled his hair, looking anxious and ashamed. He was almost like a kid—but he adored Kait and she adored him. She would never let anything hurt him.

And to leave him so soon, before she was even old enough to go to college—and to go all the way to California—and for a *year*—

"It's impossible," she said.

Ms. McCasslan was looking down at her plump hands. "But, Kaitlyn, don't you think he'd want you to go? To do what's best for you?"

Kaitlyn shook her head. She didn't want to listen to arguments. Her mind was made up.

"Wouldn't you like to learn to control your talents?" Joyce said.

Kaitlyn looked at her.

The possibility of control had never occurred to her. The pictures came when she wasn't expecting them; took over her hand without her realizing it. She never knew what had happened until it was over.

"I think you can learn," Joyce said. "I think you and I could learn, together."

Kaitlyn opened her mouth, but before she could answer, there was a terrible sound from outside the office.

It was a crashing and a grinding and a shattering all together. And it was a *huge* noise, so huge that Kaitlyn knew at once it could come from nothing ordinary. It sounded very close.

Joyce and Ms. McCasslan had both jumped up, and it was the plump little principal who made it to the door first. She

21

rushed out through the office to the street, with Kait and Joyce following her.

People were running up on either side of Harding Street, crunching through the snow. Cold air bit Kaitlyn's cheeks. The slanting afternoon sunlight threw up sharp contrasts between light and shadow, making the scene in front of Kaitlyn look frighteningly focused and distinct.

A yellow Neon was facing the wrong way on Harding Street, its back wheels on the sidewalk, its left side a wreck. It looked as if it had been broadsided and spun. Kaitlyn recognized it; it belonged to Jerry Crutchfield, one of the few students who had a car.

In the middle of the street, a dark blue station wagon was facing Kaitlyn directly. Its entire front end was accordioned. The metal was twisted and deformed, the headlights shattered.

Polly Vertanen, a junior, was tugging at Ms. McCasslan's sleeve. "I saw everything, Ms. McCasslan. Jerry just pulled out of the parking lot—but the station wagon was going too fast. They just hit him. . . . I saw everything. They were going too fast."

"That's Marian Günter's station wagon," Ms. McCasslan said sharply. "That's her little girl in there. Don't move her yet! Don't move her!" The principal's voice went on, but Kait didn't hear any more.

She was staring at the windshield of the station wagon. She hadn't seen before—but she could see now.

People around her were yelling, running. Kaitlyn hardly noticed them. Her entire world was filled with the car windshield.

The little girl had been thrown up against it—or maybe it had crunched back up against her. She was actually lying with her forehead touching the glass, as if she were looking out with open eyes.

With wide eyes. Wide, round, heavy-lashed eyes. Bambi eyes.

She had a small snub nose and a round chin. Wavy blond hair stuck to the glass.

The glass itself was shattered like a spiderweb, a spiderweb superimposed on the child's face.

"Oh, no—please, no . . ." Kaitlyn whispered.

She found herself clutching, without knowing what she was clutching at. Somebody steadied her.

Sirens were wailing closer. A crowd was gathering around the station wagon, blocking Kaitlyn's view of the child.

She knew Curt Günter. The little girl must be Lindy, his baby sister. Why hadn't Kait realized? Why hadn't her picture shown her? Why couldn't it have shown her cars crashing, with a *date* and a *place,* instead of that pathetic kid's face? How could it all be so *useless,* so completely freaking *useless . . . ?*

"Do you need to sit down?" the person holding her asked, and it was Joyce Piper, and she was shivering.

Kait was shivering, too. Her breath was coming very fast. She clutched harder at Joyce.

"Did you mean that, about me learning to control . . . what I do?" Kait couldn't call it a talent.

Joyce looked from her to the accident scene with something like dawning realization. "I think so. I hope so."

"You have to *promise.*"

Joyce met her gaze full on, the way people in Thoroughfare never did. "I promise to try, Kait."

"Then I'll go. My dad will understand."

Joyce's aquamarine eyes were brilliant. "I'm so glad." She shivered violently. "Seventy degrees there, Kait," she added softly, almost absently. "Pack light."

That night, Kaitlyn had a strangely realistic dream. She was on a rocky peninsula, a spit of land surrounded by cold gray ocean. The clouds overhead were almost black and the wind blew spray into her face. She could actually feel the wet of it, the chill.

From just behind her, someone called her name. But when she turned, the dream ended.

# CHAPTER 3

K ait got off the plane feeling giddy and triumphant.
She'd never been on a plane before, but it had been
easy as anything. She'd chewed gum on takeoff and
landing, done twists in the tiny bathroom every hour to keep
limber, and brushed her hair and straightened her red dress as
the plane cruised up to the gate. Perfection.

She was very happy. Somehow, once the decision to go was
made, Kait's spirits had lifted and lifted. It no longer seemed a
grim necessity to come to the Institute; it was the dream Joyce
had described, the beginning of a new life. Her dad had been
unbelievably sweet and understanding—he'd seen her off just
as if she were going to college. Joyce was supposed to meet her
here at San Francisco Airport.

But the airport was crowded and there was no sign of
Joyce. People streamed by. Kaitlyn stuck close to the gate, head

high, trying to look nonchalant. The last thing she wanted was anyone to ask if she needed help.

"Excuse me."

Kaitlyn flicked a sideways glance at the unfamiliar voice. It wasn't help; it was something even more disturbing. One of those cult people who hang around airports and ask for money. He was wearing reddish robes—Tuscan red, Kait thought. If she were going to draw them.

"I'd like a moment of your time, please." The voice was civil, but persistent—authoritative. It sounded foreign.

Kait edged away—or started to. A hand caught her. She looked down at it in amazement, seeing lean fingers the color of caramel locked around her wrist.

*Okay, jerk, you asked for it.* Outraged, Kait turned the full power of her smoky blue, strangely ringed eyes on him.

He just looked back—and when Kait looked deeply into *his* eyes, she reeled.

His skin was that caramel color—but his eyes were slanting and very dark, with an epicanthic fold. The phrase "lynx-eyed" came to Kaitlyn's mind. His softly curling hair was a sort of pale shimmery brown, like silver birch. None of it went together.

But that wasn't what made her reel. It was a feeling of *age* from him. When she looked into his eyes, she had the sense of centuries passing. Millennia. His face was unlined, but there were ice ages in his eyes.

Kait couldn't remember ever really screaming in her life, but she decided to scream now.

She didn't get a chance. The grip on her wrist tightened and before she could draw a breath, she was jerked off balance, moving. The man in the robes was pulling her backward into the jetway—the long corridor that led to a plane.

Except that there was no plane now and the corridor was empty. The double doors closed, cutting Kaitlyn off from the rest of the airport. She was still too shocked to scream.

"Don't move and you won't get hurt," the man in the robes said grimly. His lynx eyes were hard.

Kaitlyn didn't believe him. He was from some cult and he was obviously insane and he'd dragged her into this deserted place. She should have fought him before; she should have screamed when she had the chance. Now she was trapped.

Without letting go of her arm, the man fumbled inside his robes.

For a gun or a knife, Kaitlyn thought. Her heart was pounding violently. If he would just relax his grip on her arm for an instant—if she could get to the other side of those doors where there were people . . .

"Here," the man said. "All I want is for you to look at this."

He was holding not a weapon but a piece of paper. Glossy paper that had been folded. To Kaitlyn's dazed eyes it looked like a brochure.

I don't believe it, she thought. He *is* insane.

"Just *look*," the man said.

Kaitlyn couldn't help looking; he was holding the paper in her face. It seemed to be a full-color picture of a rose garden. A walled rose garden, with a fountain in the center, and something thrusting out of the fountain. Maybe an ice sculpture, Kaitlyn thought dizzily. It was tall, white, and semitransparent—like a faceted column. In one of its many facets was the tiny, perfect reflection of a rose.

Kaitlyn's heart was still pounding violently. This was all *too* weird. As frightening as if he were trying to hurt her.

"This crystal—" the man began, and then Kaitlyn saw her chance.

The iron grip on her arm loosened just the slightest bit as he spoke, and his eyes were on the picture. Kaitlyn kicked backward, glad that she was wearing pumps with her red dress, slamming a two-inch heel into his shin. The man yelped and let go.

Kaitlyn hit the double doors with both hands, bursting out into the airport, and then she just ran. She ran without looking behind her to see if the man was following. She dodged around chairs and phone booths, heading blindly into the crowd.

She didn't stop until someone called her name.

"Kaitlyn!"

It was Joyce, heading the other way, toward the gate. Kait had never been so relieved to see anyone.

"I'm so sorry—the traffic was terrible—and parking in this place is always—" She broke off. "Kaitlyn, what's wrong?"

Kaitlyn collapsed in Joyce's arms. Now that she was safe, she somehow wanted to laugh. Hysteria, probably, she told herself. Her legs were shaking.

"It was too strange," she gasped. "There was this guy from some cult or something—and he grabbed me. He probably just wanted money, but I thought—"

"He *grabbed* you? Where is he now?"

Kaitlyn waved a hand vaguely. "Back there. I kicked him and ran."

Joyce's aquamarine eyes flashed with grim approval, but all she said was, "Come on. We'd better tell airport security about this."

"Oh—I'm okay now. He was just some nut. . . ."

"Nuts like that, we put away. Even in California," Joyce said flatly.

Airport security sent people looking for the man, but he was gone.

"Besides," the guard told Joyce and Kaitlyn, "he *couldn't* have opened the doors to the jet bridge. They're kept locked."

Kaitlyn didn't want to argue. She wanted to forget all about it and go to the Institute. This was *not* how she'd planned her grand entrance to California.

"Let's go," she said to Joyce, and Joyce sighed and nodded.

They picked up Kaitlyn's luggage and carried it to a sharp

little green convertible—Joyce's car. Kait felt like bouncing on the seat as Joyce drove. Back home it was freezing, with twenty inches of snow on the ground. Here they drove with the top down, and Joyce's blond hair ruffled like down in the wind.

"How's the little girl from the crash?" Joyce asked.

Kaitlyn's spirits pitched.

"She's still in the hospital. They don't know if she'll be okay." Kaitlyn clamped her lips together to show that she didn't intend to answer any more questions about Lindy.

But Joyce didn't ask any more questions. Instead, she said, "Two of your housemates are already at the Institute; Lewis and Anna. I think you'll like them."

Lewis—a boy. "How many of the five of us are boys?" Kaitlyn asked suspiciously.

"Three, I'm afraid," Joyce said gravely, and then gave Kait a sideways look of amusement.

Kaitlyn declined to be amused. Three boys and only one other girl. Three sloppy, meaty-handed, too-big-to-control, hormone-crazed Power Rangers.

Kaitlyn had tried boys once, two years ago when she was a sophomore. She'd let one of them take her out, driving up to Lake Erie every Friday and Saturday night, and she'd put up with what he wanted—*some* of what he wanted—while he talked about Metallica and the Browns and the Bengals and his candy-apple-red Trans Am. All of which Kait knew nothing about. After the first date, she decided that guys must be an alien species, and just tried to deal with him without listening to him. She was still hoping that he'd take her to the next party with his crowd.

She had it all planned out. He'd escort her into one of those big houses on the hill that she'd never been invited to. She'd wear something a little dowdy so as to not show up the hostess. With her boyfriend's arm around her shoulder, she'd be modest and self-effacing, complimenting everything in sight. The whole crowd would see she wasn't a monster. They'd let her in—maybe not all at once, but over time, as they got used to her being around.

Wrong.

When she brought up the party, her lake-loving boyfriend blustered around, but eventually the truth came clear. He wasn't going to take her anywhere in public. She was good enough alone in the dark with him, but not good enough to be seen with him in the daylight.

It was one of the times when it was hardest not to cry. Stiff-lipped, she'd ordered him to take her home. He got angrier and angrier as they drove. When she jerked the car door open, he said, "I was going to dump you anyway. You're not like a normal girl. You're *cold*."

Kait stared after the car when it had gone. So she wasn't normal. Fine, she knew that already. So she was *cold*—and the way he'd said it made it obvious that he didn't just mean her personality. He meant more.

Well, that was fine, too. She'd rather be cold all her life than feel anything with a guy like that. The memory of his humid palms on her arms made her want to wipe her own hands on the skirt of her red dress.

So I'm cold, Kait thought now, shifting in the front seat of Joyce's convertible. So what? There are other things in life to be interested in.

And really, she didn't care how many boys were at the Institute. She'd ignore them—she'd stick with Anna. She just hoped Anna wasn't boy-crazy.

*And that she likes you,* a small, nerve-racking voice in her head added. Kaitlyn squashed the thought, tossing her head to feel the wind snapping her hair back, enjoying the motion and the sunshine.

"Is it much farther?" she asked. "I can't wait."

Joyce laughed. "No, it's not far."

They were driving through residential streets now. Kaitlyn looked around eagerly, but with a tingling in her stomach. What if the Institute was too big, too sterile, too intimidating? She'd pictured a large, squat redbrick building, something like her old high school back in Thoroughfare.

Joyce turned the convertible in to a driveway, and Kait stared.

"Is *this* it?"

"Yup."

"But it's *purple.*"

It was extremely purple. The shingled sides were a cool but vivid purple, the wood trim around the windows was darker purple; the door and wraparound balcony were glaring high-gloss purple. The only things that weren't purple were the slate gray roof and the bricks in the chimney.

Kait felt as if someone had dropped her into a swimming pool full of grape juice. She didn't know if she loved the color scheme or hated it.

"We haven't had time to paint it yet," Joyce explained, parking. "We've been busy converting most of the first floor to labs—but you can have the full tour tomorrow. Why don't you go up and meet your housemates?"

Thrills of nervousness wound through Kait's stomach. The Institute was so much smaller, so much more intimate, than she'd imagined. She'd really be *living* with these people.

"Sure, that's fine," she said, and held her head very high as she got out of the car.

"Don't worry about the luggage yet—just go on in. Go straight past the living room and you'll see a staircase on your right. Take that upstairs—the whole second floor is for you kids. I told Lewis and Anna that you can work out the bedroom situation for yourselves."

Kaitlyn went, trying not to either dawdle or hurry. She wouldn't let anyone see how nervous she was. The very purple front door was unlocked. The inside of the house wasn't purple—it looked quite ordinary, with a large living room on the right and a large enough dining room on the left.

Don't look at it now. Go on up.

Kaitlyn's feet carried her down the tiled foyer that separated them, until she reached the staircase.

Take it slow. Just keep breathing.

But her heart was going quickly, and her feet wanted to leap up the steps. The stairs made a U-turn at a landing and then she was at the top.

The hallway was crowded with odds and ends of furniture, piled haphazardly. In front of Kait and to the left was an open door. She could hear voices inside.

Okay, who *cares* if they're nice? They're probably creeps— and I don't care. I don't need anyone. Maybe I can learn to put curses on people.

The last-minute panic made her reckless, and she plunged through the door almost belligerently.

And stopped. A girl was kneeling on a bed without sheets or blankets. A lovely girl—graceful and dark, with high cheekbones and an expression of serenity. Kaitlyn's belligerence seeped away and all the walls she normally kept around her seemed to dissolve. Peacefulness seemed to come from the other girl like a cool wind.

The girl smiled. "You're Kaitlyn."

"And you're . . . Anna?"

"Anna Eva Whiteraven."

"What a wonderful name," Kaitlyn said.

It wasn't the sort of thing people said back at Warren G. Harding High School—but Kaitlyn wasn't at Warren G. Harding High School anymore, and Anna's serene expression broke into another smile.

"*You've* got wonderful eyes," she said.

"Does she?" another voice said eagerly. "Hey, turn around."

Kait was already turning. On the far side of the room was an alcove with a bay window—and a boy coming out of it. He didn't look threatening. He had a cap of black hair and dark, almond-shaped eyes. From the camera in his hands Kaitlyn guessed he'd been taking pictures out the open window.

"Smile!" A flashbulb blinded Kaitlyn.

"*Ouch!*"

"Sorry; I just wanted to preserve the moment." The boy let go of the camera, which bounced as the strap around his neck caught it, and stuck out a hand. "You do have kind of neat eyes. Kind of weird. I'm Lewis Chao."

He had a sweet face, Kaitlyn decided. He wasn't big and gross, but rather small and neat. His hand wasn't sweaty when she took it, and his eyes weren't hungry.

"Lewis has been taking pictures since we got here this morning," Anna said. "We've got the entire block on record."

Kaitlyn blinked away blue afterimages and looked at Lewis curiously. "Really? Where do you come from?" It must be even farther away than Ohio, she thought.

He smiled beatifically. "San Francisco."

Kaitlyn laughed, and suddenly they were all laughing together. Not malicious laughter, not laughing *at* anyone, but wonderful torrents of giggles *together*. And then Kait knew.

I'm going to be happy here, she realized. It was almost too big a concept to take in at once. She was going to be happy, and for a year. A panorama opened before her. Sitting by the fireplace she'd seen downstairs, studying, the others all doing their own projects, everyone joined by a warm sort of togetherness even while they did their own things. Each of them different, but not minding the differences.

No need for walls between them.

They began to talk, eagerly, friendship flying back and forth. It seemed quite natural to join Anna sitting on the bed.

"I'm from Ohio—" Kait started.

"Aha, a Buckeye," Lewis put in.

"I'm from Washington State," Anna said. "Near Puget Sound."

"You're Native American, aren't you?"

"Yes; Suquamish."

"She talks to animals," Lewis said.

Anna said gently, "I don't really talk to them. I can influence them to do things—sometimes. It's a kind of thought projection, Joyce says."

*Thought projection with animals?* A few weeks ago Kait would have said it sounded insane—but then, wasn't her own "talent" insane? If one was possible, so was the other.

"I've got PK," Lewis said. "That's psychokinesis. Mind over matter."

"Like . . . spoon bending?" Kait asked uncertainly.

"Nah, spoon bending's a trick. Real PK is only for little things, like making a compass needle deflect. What do you do?"

Despite herself, Kaitlyn's heart bumped. She'd never in her life said aloud the thing she was going to say.

"I . . . kind of see the future. At least, I don't, but my drawings do, and when I look back at them, I see that they did. But usually only after the thing has already happened," she finished incoherently.

Lewis and Anna looked thoughtful. "That's cool," Lewis said at last, and Anna said, "So you're an artist?"

The relief that flooded Kaitlyn was painful, and its aftermath left her jubilant. "I guess. I like to draw."

I'd like to draw right now, she thought, dying to get hold of some pastels. She'd draw Anna with burnt umber and matte black and sienna. She'd do Lewis with blue-black—his hair was that shiny—and some sort of flesh-ocher mixture for his skin.

Later, she told herself. Aloud she said, "So what about the bedrooms up here? Who goes where?"

"That's just what we've been trying to figure out," Anna said. "The problem is that there are supposed to be five of us students, and they've only got four bedrooms. There's this one and another one even bigger next door, and then two smaller ones on the back side of the house."

"And only the big ones have cable hookup. I've explained and explained," said Lewis, looking tragic, "that I *need* my MTV, but she doesn't understand. And I need enough outlets for my computer and stereo and stuff. Only the big rooms have those."

"It's not fair for us to take the good rooms before the others even get here," Anna said, gently but firmly.

"But I *need* my MTV. I'll *die*."

"Well, I don't care about cable," Kaitlyn said. "But I'd like a room with northern light—I like to draw in the mornings."

"You haven't heard the worst part—all the rooms have different things," Lewis said. "The one next door is *huge,* and it's got a king-size bed and a balcony and a Jacuzzi bath. This one has the alcove over there and a private bathroom—but almost no closet. And the two rooms in back have okay closets, but they share a bathroom."

"Well, obviously the biggest room should go to whoever's rooming together—because two of us are going to *have* to room together," Kaitlyn said.

"Great. I'll room with either of you," Lewis said promptly.

"No, no, no—look, let me go check out the light in the smaller rooms," Kaitlyn said, jumping up.

"Check out the Jacuzzi instead," Lewis called after her.

In the hallway, Kait turned to laugh at him over her shoulder—and ran directly into someone cresting the top of the stairs.

It wasn't a hard knock, but Kaitlyn automatically recoiled, and ran her leg into something hard. Pain flared just behind her knee, rendering her momentarily speechless. She clenched her teeth and glared down at the thing that had hurt her. A nightstand with one sharp-edged drawer pulled out. What was all this furniture *doing* in the hall, anyway?

"I'm really sorry," a soft southern voice drawled. "Are you all right?"

Kaitlyn looked at the tanned, blond boy who'd run into her. It *would* be a boy, of course. And a big one, not small and safe like Lewis. The kind of boy who disturbed the space around him, filling the whole hallway with his presence. A very *masculine* presence—if Anna was a cool wind, this boy was a golden solar flare.

Since ignoring was out of the question, Kaitlyn turned her best glare on him. He returned the look mildly and she realized with a start that his eyes were amber-colored—golden. Just a few shades darker than his hair.

"You *are* hurt," he said, apparently mistaking the glare for suffering. "Where?" Then he did something that dumbfounded Kaitlyn. He dropped to his knees.

He's going to apologize, she thought wildly. Oh, God, everyone in California *is* nuts.

But the boy didn't apologize—he didn't even look up at her. He was reaching for her leg.

"This one here, right?" he said in that southern-gentleman voice.

Kaitlyn's mouth opened, but all she could do was stare at him. She was backed against the wall—there was nowhere to escape.

"Back here—this spot?" And then, deftly and unceremoniously, he turned up the skirt of her red dress. Kaitlyn's mind went into shock. She simply had no experience that had prepared her to deal with this situation—a perfect stranger reaching under her dress in a public place. And it was the *way* he did it; not like a grabby boy at all, but like . . . like . . . a doctor examining a patient.

"It's not a cut. Just a knot," the boy said. He wasn't looking at her or the leg, but down the hallway. His fingers were running lightly over the painful area, as if assessing it. They felt dry but warm—unnaturally warm.

"You'll have a bad bruise if you leave it, though. Why don't you hold still and let me see if I can help?"

This, at last, catapulted Kait out of silence.

"Hold *still? Hold still for what* . . . ?"

He waved a hand. "Be quiet, now—please."

Kaitlyn was stupefied.

"Yes," the boy said, as if to himself. "I think I can help this some. I'll try."

Kaitlyn held still because she was paralyzed. She could feel his fingers on the back of her knee—a terribly intimate place, extremely tender and vulnerable. Kait couldn't remember *anyone* touching her there, not even her doctor.

Then the touch changed. It became a burning, tingling feeling. Like slow fire. It was almost like pain, but—

Kait gasped. "What are you *doing* to me? Stop that—what are you *doing?*"

He spoke in a soft, measured voice, without glancing up. "Channeling energy. Trying."

"I said *stop*—oh."

"Work with me, now, please. Don't fight me."

Kaitlyn just stared down at the top of his head. His gold-blond hair was unruly, springing in curls and waves.

A strange sensation swept through Kait, flowing up from her knee and through her body, branching out to every blood vessel and capillary. A feeling of refreshment—*of renewal*. It was like getting a drink of clean, cold water when you were desperately thirsty, or being drenched with delicious icy mist when you were hot. Kaitlyn suddenly felt that until this moment, she had only been half-awake.

The boy was making odd motions now, as if he were brushing lint off the back of her knee. Touch, shake off. Touch, shake off. As if gathering something and then shaking drops of water off his fingers.

Kaitlyn suddenly realized that her pain was completely gone.

"That's it," the boy said cheerfully. "Now if I can just close this off . . ." He cupped a warm hand around the back of her knee. "There. It shouldn't bruise now."

The boy stood up briskly and brushed off his hands. He was breathing as if he'd just run a race.

Kaitlyn stared at him. She herself felt *ready* to run a race. She had never felt so refreshed—so alive. At the same time, as she got another glimpse of his face, she thought maybe she ought to sit down.

When he looked back at her, she expected . . . well, she didn't know what. But what she *didn't* expect was a quick, almost absentminded smile from a boy who was already turning around to leave.

"Sorry about that. Guess I'd better go down and help Joyce with the luggage—before I knock anyone else over." He started down the stairs.

"*Wait* a minute—who are you? And—"

"Rob." He smiled over his shoulder. "Rob Kessler." He reached the landing, turned, and was gone.

"—and how did you *do* that?" Kait demanded of empty air.

Rob. Rob Kessler, she thought.

"Hey, Kaitlyn!" It was Lewis's voice from the bedroom. "Are you out there? Hey, Kaitlyn, come quick!"

# CHAPTER 4

Kaitlyn hesitated, still looking down the stairs. Then she gathered her self-possession and slowly walked back into the room. Lewis and Anna were in the alcove, looking out the window.

"He's here," Lewis said excitedly, and brought his camera up. "That's got to be him!"

"*Who's* here?" Kaitlyn asked, hoping no one would look at her too closely. She felt flushed.

"Mr. Zetes," said Lewis. "Joyce said he had a limo."

A black limousine was parked outside the house, one of its rear doors open. A white-haired man stood beside the door, dressed in a greatcoat which Kaitlyn thought must be terribly hot on this Californian afternoon. He had a gold-topped cane—a real gold-topped cane, Kaitlyn thought in fascination.

"Looks like he's brought some friends," Anna said, smiling. Two large black dogs were jumping out of the limo. They started for the bushes but came back at a word from the man and stood on either side of him.

"Cute," Kaitlyn said. "But what's *that?*" A white van was turning in the driveway. Lettering on its side read DEPARTMENT OF YOUTH AUTHORITY.

Lewis brought his camera down, looking awed. "Jeez. That's the California Youth Authority."

"Which is . . . ?"

"It's the last stop. It's where they put the *baaaaad* boys. The hard-core kids who can't make it at any of the regular juvie places."

Anna's quiet voice said, "You mean it's jail?"

"My dad says it's the place for kids who're on their way to state prison. You know, the murderers and stuff."

*"Murderers?"* Kait exclaimed. "Well, what's it doing here, then? You don't think . . ." She looked at Anna, who looked back, serenity a bit clouded. Clearly, Anna did think.

They both looked at Lewis, whose almond-shaped eyes were wide.

"I think we'd better get down there," Kaitlyn said.

They hurried downstairs, bursting out onto the wooden porch and trying to look inconspicuous. No one was looking at them, anyway. Mr. Zetes was talking to a khaki-uniformed officer standing by the van.

Kaitlyn could only catch a few words of what was said—"Judge Baldwin's authority" and "CYA ward" and "rehabilitation."

". . . your responsibility," the officer finished, and stepped away from the van's door.

A boy came out. Kaitlyn could feel her eyebrows go up.

He was startlingly handsome—but there was a cold wariness in his face and movements. His hair and eyes were dark, but his skin was rather pale. One of the few people in California without a tan, Kaitlyn thought.

*"Chiaroscuro,"* she murmured.

"What?" Lewis whispered.

"It's an art word. It means 'light and shade'—like in a drawing where you only use black and white." As Kaitlyn finished, she suddenly felt herself shiver. There was something strange about this boy, as if—as if—

As if he weren't quite canny, her mind supplied. At least, that's the phrase people back home used to use about *you,* isn't it?

The van was driving off. Mr. Zetes and the dark-haired boy were walking up to the door.

"Looks like we've got a new housemate," Lewis said under his breath. "Oh, boy."

Mr. Zetes gave a courtly nod to the group on the porch. "I see you're here. I believe everyone has arrived now—if you'll come inside, we can commence with the introductions." He went in, and the two dogs followed him. They were rottweilers, Kaitlyn noted, and rather fierce-looking.

Anna and Lewis stepped back silently as the new boy

approached, but Kaitlyn held her ground. She knew what it was like to have people step back when you walked near them. The boy passed very close to her, and turned to give her a direct look as he did. Kaitlyn saw that his eyes weren't black, but a very dark gray. She had the distinct feeling that he wanted to unsettle her, to make her look down.

I wonder what he did to get in prison, she thought, feeling chilled again. She followed the others into the house.

"Mr. Zetes!" Joyce said happily from the living room. She caught the old man's arm, smiling and gesturing with enthusiasm as she spoke to him.

Kait's attention was caught by a blond head near the stairs. Rob Kessler had a duffel bag—*her* duffel bag—slung over his shoulder. He saw the group that had just come in, and started toward them . . . and then he stopped.

His entire body had stiffened. Kaitlyn followed his gaze down the foyer—to the new boy.

Who was equally stiff. His dark gray eyes were fixed on Rob with complete attention and icy hatred. His body was held as if ready for an attack as Rob came closer.

One of the two rottweilers by Mr. Zetes began to growl.

"Good dog, Carl," Lewis said nervously.

*"You,"* the new boy said to Rob.

*"You,"* Rob said to the new boy.

"You two know each other?" Kaitlyn said to both of them.

Rob spoke without looking away from the other boy's pale,

wary face. "From a ways back," he said. He let the duffel bag down with a thump.

"Not a long enough ways," the other boy said. In contrast to Rob's soft southern tones, his voice was harsh and clipped.

Both dogs were growling now.

Well, there goes any chance of harmony between housemates, Kaitlyn thought. She noticed that Mr. Zetes and Joyce had broken off talking and were looking at the students.

"We all seem to be together," Mr. Zetes said rather dryly, and Joyce said, "Come over here, everybody! This is the moment I've been waiting for."

Rob and the new boy slowly turned away from each other. Joyce gave the group a brilliant smile as they gathered around. Her aquamarine eyes were sparkling.

"Kids, it's an honor and a privilege to introduce you to the man who brought you all here—the man who's responsible for this project. This is Mr. Zetes."

Kaitlyn felt for a moment as if she ought to applaud. Instead, she murmured "Hello" with the others. Mr. Zetes bent his head in recognition, and Joyce went on.

"Mr. Zetes, these are the troops. Anna Whiteraven, from Washington." The old man shook hands with her, and with each of them as Joyce introduced them. "Lewis Chao from California. Kaitlyn Fairchild from Ohio. Rob Kessler from North Carolina. And Gabriel Wolfe from . . . here and there."

"Yeah, depending on where the charges are pending,"

Rob drawled, not quite aloud. Mr. Zetes gave him a piercing look.

"Gabriel has been released into my custody," he said. "His parole allows him to go to school; for the rest of the time, he's confined to this house. He knows what will happen if he tries to violate those conditions—don't you, Gabriel?"

Gabriel's dark gray eyes moved from Rob to Mr. Zetes. He said one word, expressionlessly. "Yes."

"Good." Mr. Zetes looked at the rest of the group. "While you're here, I expect you all to try to get along. I don't think any of you can realize, at your age, just how great a gift has been given to you. Your one job here is to see that you *use* that gift wisely, and make the most of it."

Now for the pep talk, Kait thought, studying Mr. Zetes. He had an impressive shock of white hair on his handsome old head and a broad and benevolent brow. Kaitlyn thought suddenly, *I* know what he looks like. He looks like Little Lord Fauntleroy's grandfather, the earl.

But the earl wasn't giving any ordinary pep talk. "One thing you need to realize from the start is that you're different from the rest of humanity. You've been . . . chosen. Branded. You'll never be like other people, so there's no reason even to try. You follow different laws."

Kaitlyn felt her eyebrows pull together. Joyce had said similar things, but somehow Mr. Zetes's words had another tone. She wasn't sure she liked it.

"You have something inside you that won't be repressed. A hidden power that burns like a flame," he went on. "You're *superior* to the rest of humanity—don't ever forget that."

Is he trying to flatter us? Kait wondered. Because if he is, it isn't working. It all sounds . . . hollow, somehow.

"You are the pioneers in an exploration that has infinite possibilities. The work you do here may change the way the entire world looks at psychic powers—it may change the way the human race looks at itself. You young people are actually in a position to benefit all humankind."

Suddenly Kait felt the need to draw.

Not the ordinary need, like the desire she'd had to draw Lewis and Anna. This was the need that came with an itch in her hand—and the internal shiver that meant a premonition.

But she couldn't just walk away while Mr. Zetes was talking. She glanced around the room in distraction—and met Gabriel's eyes.

Right now those eyes looked dark and wicked, as if something in Mr. Zetes's speech amused him. Amused him in a cynical way.

With a shock, Kaitlyn realized that he looked as if he also found Mr. Zetes's words hollow. And the way he was gazing at her seemed to show that he knew she did, too.

Kaitlyn felt herself flushing. She looked quickly back at Mr. Zetes, freezing her face into an interested, deferential expression. After all, he was the one paying her scholarship.

He might be a little eccentric, but he obviously had a good heart.

By the time the speech was over, her need to draw was gone.

After Mr. Zetes was finished, Joyce said a few words about how she wanted them to do their best in the next year. "I'll be living at the Institute with you," she added. "My room is back there"—she pointed to a set of French doors beyond the living room that looked as if they led outside—"and you can feel free to come to me at any time, day or night. Oh, and here's someone else you'll be working with."

Kaitlyn turned and saw a girl coming through the dining room. She looked college age, and had tumbled mahogany hair and full lips which looked a bit sullen.

"This is Marisol Diaz, an undergrad from Stanford," Joyce said. "She won't live here, but she'll come daily and help with your testing. She'll also help me cook. You'll find a schedule for meals on the dining room wall, and we'll go over the other house rules tomorrow. Any questions?"

Heads were shaken.

"Good. Now, why don't you go upstairs and fix up your rooms? It's been a long day, and I know some of you must be tired from jet lag. Marisol and I will throw together something for dinner."

Kaitlyn *was* tired. Although her watch said 5:45, it was three hours later by Ohio time. Mr. Zetes said good-bye to each of them, and shook their hands. Then Kait and the others headed upstairs.

"What did you think of him?" she whispered to Lewis and Anna as they reached the second floor.

"Impressive—but a little scary. I kept expecting him to introduce 'Masterpiece Theater,'" Lewis whispered back.

"Those dogs were interesting," Anna said. "Usually I can sort of read animals, tell if they're happy or sad or whatever. But those two were very guarded. I wouldn't want to try to influence them."

Something made Kait glance behind her—and she found that Gabriel was looking at her. She felt disconcerted, so she immediately went on the attack.

"And what did *you* think?" she asked him.

"I think he wants to use us for his own reasons."

"Use us how?" Kaitlyn said sharply.

Gabriel shrugged, looking bored. "How should I know? Maybe to improve his corporation's image—'Silicon Valley Company Benefits Humankind.' Like Chevron financing wildlife programs. Of course, he was right about one thing— we *are* superior to the rest of the human race."

"And some of us are more superior than others, right?" Rob asked, from the stairs. "Some of us don't have to follow the rules—or the laws."

"Exactly," Gabriel said, with a rather chilling smile. He was walking around the hallway, glancing into each bedroom.

"Well, Joyce told us to pick our rooms. I think I'll take . . . this one."

"Hey!" Lewis squawked. "That's the biggest room—the one with the cable hookup and the Jacuzzi and . . . and *everything*."

Gabriel said blandly, "Thanks for telling me."

"It's much bigger than any of the others," Anna said with quiet heat. "We decided it should go to whoever rooms together."

"You can't just grab it for yourself," Lewis finished. "We ought to *vote*."

Gabriel's gray eyes narrowed and his lip lifted in something like a snarl. With one step he was close to Lewis. "You know what a lockup cell looks like?" he said, his voice cold and brutal. "It has a two-foot-wide bed and a metal toilet. One metal stool attached to the wall and one built-in desk. That's all. I've been in a cell like that on and off for two years. So now I figure I'm entitled. Are *you* going to do something about it?"

Lewis scratched his nose, looking as if he were considering it. Anna pulled him back a step.

"MTV isn't worth it," she told him.

Gabriel looked at Rob. "You, country boy?"

"I won't fight you, if that's what you mean," Rob drawled. He looked half-disgusted, half-pitying. "Go ahead, take the room—you sad bastard."

Lewis made a faint sound of protest. Gabriel stepped inside

his newly acquired room and began to shut the door.

"By the way," he said, turning, "everyone else had better keep out of here. After you spend so much time in lockup, you get to like your space. You get kind of territorial. I wouldn't want anybody to get hurt."

As the door closed, Kait said, "Gabriel—like the angel?" She could hear the heavy sarcasm in her own voice.

The door opened again, and Gabriel gave her a long, measuring look. Then he flashed a brilliant, unsettling smile. "*You* can come in any time you like," he said.

This time after the door slammed, it stayed shut.

"*Well,*" Kaitlyn said.

"*Jeez,*" Lewis said.

Anna was shaking her head. "Gabriel Wolfe—he's not like a wolf, really, because they're very social. Except for a lone wolf, an exile. One that's been driven out of the pack. If wolves get driven out far enough they go a little crazy—start attacking anything that comes near them."

"I wonder what his talent is," Kaitlyn mused. She looked at Rob.

He shook his head. "I don't really know. I met him back in North Carolina—at a place in Durham, another psychic research center."

"Another one?" Lewis said, looking surprised.

"Yeah. My parents took me to see if they could make any

sense of the weird stuff I was doing. I guess his parents did the same thing. He wasn't interested in working with the staff, though. He just wanted his own way, and the hell with other people. A girl ended up . . . getting hurt."

Kait looked at him. She wanted to ask, "Hurt *how?*" but from the closed-off expression on his face, she didn't think she'd get an answer.

"Anyway, that was over three years ago," Rob said. "He ran away from the center right after it happened, and I heard he just went from state to state, getting in a heap of trouble everywhere. *Making* a heap of trouble everywhere."

"Oh, terrific," Lewis said. "And we've got to live with this guy for a *year?*"

Anna was looking at Rob closely. "What about you? Did that center help you?"

"Sure did. They helped me figure out just what it was I was doing."

"And just what *is* it you do?" Kaitlyn put in, staring significantly from him to her leg.

"Healing, I guess," the blond boy said simply. "Some places call it therapeutic touch, some places call it channeling energy. I try to use it to help."

Looking into his steady golden eyes, Kaitlyn felt oddly ashamed. "I'm sure you do," she said, which was as close as she could come to saying "thank you." Somehow she didn't want the others to know what had happened between her and Rob earlier. She felt strangely confused by him—and by her reaction to him.

"I'm sure we all do," Rob said, again simply. His smile was slow but infectious—irresistible, in fact.

"Well, we *try*," Anna said. Kait glanced at Lewis, who just widened his eyes without saying anything. She had the feeling that, like her, he hadn't worked too hard at helping people with his powers.

"Look," Lewis said, clearing his throat. "I don't want to change the subject, but . . . can I pick my room next? Because I'd like . . . ummmm, that one."

Rob glanced into the room Lewis had indicated, then stepped down the hall and looked into two other doors. He turned and gave Lewis an oh-come-on look.

Lewis wilted. "But this is the only one left with cable. And I *need* my MTV. And my computer and my stereo and—"

"There's only one fair thing to do," Rob said. "We should make that room a communal place. That way, everybody can watch TV—there isn't one downstairs."

"But then what do *we* do?" Lewis demanded.

"We double up in the small rooms," Rob said briefly.

Kaitlyn and Anna glanced at each other and smiled. Kaitlyn didn't mind rooming with Anna—she was actually glad. It would be almost like having a sister.

Lewis groaned. "But what about my stereo and stuff? They

won't even fit in one of those small rooms, especially if there's two beds in there."

"Good," Rob said relentlessly. "Put 'em in the common room. We can all listen to them. Come on, we'd better start moving furniture."

The first thing Gabriel did was scan the room, prowling around it with silent, wary steps.

He looked in every corner, including the bathroom and closet. It was big, and luxurious, and the balcony offered a quick escape route—if it turned out that escape was necessary.

He liked it.

He flopped on the king-size bed and considered whether he liked anything else about this place.

There was the girl, of course. The one with the witch eyes and the hair like flame. She might be an interesting diversion.

But something inside him twisted uncomfortably. He found himself on his feet and pacing again.

He'd have to make sure it was *just* a diversion. That kind of girl might be too interesting, might tempt you to get involved. . . .

And that could never happen again.

Never. Because . . .

Gabriel wrenched his thoughts away. Aside from the girl, there wasn't much to like here—and several things to hate. Kessler. The restrictions on his freedom—being under house arrest. Kessler. The stupidity of the whole study these people had planned. Kessler.

He could do something about Kessler if he wanted. Take care of him permanently. But then he'd have to run, and if he got caught, he'd end up in lockup until he was twenty-five. It wasn't worth it—not yet.

He'd see how annoying Kessler turned out to be. This place was tolerable, and if he could last out the year, he'd be rich. With that much money, he could *buy* freedom—could buy anything he wanted. He'd wait and see.

And as for them testing his powers—he'd see about that, too. Whatever happened, it was their problem. Their fault.

He settled down on the bed. It was early, but he was tired. In a few minutes he was asleep.

Kait and the others didn't get much moved before Joyce called them down for dinner. Kait rather liked the feeling of eating at the big dining room table with five other people—five, because Gabriel hadn't come out of his room, ignoring all knocks at his door. It was like being part of a large family, and everyone seemed to have a good time—except maybe Marisol, who didn't talk much.

After dinner they went back to furniture arranging. There was plenty of furniture to pick from; the jumble in the hall and rooms seemed to include every style ever invented. Kait and Anna's room ended up with two mismatched single beds, a cheap pressed-wood bookcase, a beautiful French Provincial chair, a Victorian rolltop desk, and the nightstand that had attacked Kait in the hall. Kaitlyn liked all of it.

The bathroom in between the two small rooms was designated the girls' bathroom—by Rob's decree. "Girls need to be nearer to their stuff," he said obscurely to Lewis, who by then only shrugged. The boys would use the bathroom off the common room.

Going to bed, Kaitlyn was happy. Indirect moonlight came in the window behind her bed—*north* light, she noted with pleasure. It shone on the beautiful cedar-and-cherry-bark basket Anna had placed in their bookcase, and on the Raven mask Anna had hung on the wall. Anna herself was breathing peacefully in the other bed.

Kaitlyn's old life in Ohio seemed worlds away—and she was glad.

Tomorrow's Sunday, she thought. Joyce promised to show us the lab, and after that, maybe I'll do some drawing. And then maybe we can look around town. And on Monday we'll go to school and I'll have a built-in set of friends.

What a *wonderful* idea. She knew that Anna and Lewis, at least, would want to eat lunch together. She hoped Rob would, too. As for Gabriel—well, the farther off *he* was, the better. She didn't feel sorry for him at all. . . .

Her thoughts drifted off. The vague discomfort she'd felt

about Mr. Zetes had entirely disappeared. She slipped easily into sleep.

And then, suddenly, she was wide-awake. A figure was standing over her bed.

Kaitlyn couldn't breathe. Her heart seemed to fill her mouth and throat, pounding. The moonlight was gone and she couldn't make out any details of the figure—it was just a black silhouette.

For a wild instant—without knowing why—she thought, *Rob? Gabriel?*

Then a dim light came through the window again. She saw the halo of mahogany hair and the full lips of Marisol.

"What's wrong?" she whispered, sitting up. "What are you *doing* here?"

Marisol's eyes were like black pits. "Watch out—or get out," she hissed.

"*What?*"

"Watch out . . . or get out. You kids think you're so smart—so *psychic*—don't you? So superior to everyone else."

Kaitlyn couldn't speak.

"But you don't know anything. This place is different than you think. I've seen things . . ." She shook her head and laughed roughly. "Never mind. You'd just better watch out—" She broke off suddenly and looked behind her. Kaitlyn could see only the black rectangle of the doorway—but she thought she heard a faint rattling sound down the hall.

"Marisol, what—"

"Shut up. I've got to go."

"But—"

Marisol was already leaving. An instant later, the door to Kaitlyn's room silently closed.

# CHAPTER 5

The next morning, Kait had forgotten about the strange visit.

She woke up to a distant clanging, feeling as if it were very late. A glance at her bedside clock showed that it was seven-thirty, which, of course, meant it was ten-thirty in Ohio.

The clanging was still going on. Anna sat up in bed.

"Good morning," she said, smiling.

"Good morning," Kaitlyn said, feeling how wonderful it was to have a roommate to wake up with. "What's that noise?"

Anna cocked her head. "I have no idea."

"I'm going to find out." Kaitlyn got up and opened the bathroom door. She could hear the clanging more clearly now, and along with it, a weird shouting voice—and a sound like *mooing*.

Impulsively she knocked on the door that led from the bathroom into Rob and Lewis's room. When she heard Rob's voice calling, "Yeah, come in," she opened the door and peered around it.

Rob was sitting up in bed, his rebellious blond hair tousled into a lion's mane. His chest was bare, Kaitlyn noticed with an unreasonable feeling of shock. In the other bed there was a lump of blankets which presumably contained Lewis.

Kaitlyn suddenly realized she was wearing a T-shirt nightgown that only came down to her knees. It had seemed quite natural to walk around in it—until she was confronted by the indisputable reality of *boys*.

She looked desperately around for the source of the clanging and mooing as a distraction. Then she saw it.

It was a cow. A cow made of white porcelain, with a clock in its stomach. The measured, hoarse voice coming from it was shouting in a marked Japanese accent, "Wake . . . *up!* Don't sleep your life away! Wake . . . *up!*"

Kaitlyn looked at the talking alarm clock, and then she looked at Rob. Rob smiled his slow, infectious smile—and suddenly everything was all right.

"It *has* to be Lewis's," Kait gasped, and began to giggle.

"It's great, isn't it?" said a muffled voice from under the blankets. "I got it at Sharper Image."

"So *this* is what I can expect from my housemates," Kait said. "Mooing in the morning." She and Rob were both laughing together now, and she decided it was time to shut the door.

After she closed it, she looked at herself in the bathroom

mirror. She didn't usually spend much time at mirrors, but just now . . .

Her hair was rather disheveled, falling in fine tangles to her waist. Wispy red curls had formed on her forehead. Her strangely ringed eyes looked back at her sarcastically.

So you don't care about boys, huh? they seemed to ask. So how come you're thinking that next time you ought to brush your hair before barging in on them?

Kaitlyn turned abruptly toward the shower—and that was when she remembered Marisol's visit.

*"Watch out or get out. . . . This place is different than you think. . . ."*

God, had that really *happened?* It seemed more like a dream than anything else. Kaitlyn stood frozen in the middle of the bathroom, her happiness in the morning draining away. Was Marisol crazy? She must be—she must have some kind of mental trouble, creeping around in the middle of the night and standing over people in bed.

I've got to talk to someone about it, Kait realized. But she didn't know who. If she told Joyce, Marisol might get in trouble. It would be like snitching—and then again, what if it *had* all been a dream?

In the sunlit, bustling morning, with sounds of laughing and washing all around, it was impossible to even consider the idea that Marisol's warning had been genuine. That there really was something wrong at the Institute.

Marisol herself was in the kitchen when Kait went down for breakfast, but she returned Kaitlyn's questioning look with one of sullen blankness. And when Kait said politely, "Marisol, could I talk to you?" she just frowned without looking up from the orange juice she was pouring.

"I'm busy."

"But it's—it's about last night."

She was more than half expecting Marisol to say, "What are you talking about?"—which would mean that it *had* all been a dream. But instead Marisol shook back her mahogany hair and said, "Oh, *that*. Didn't you get it? That was a joke."

*"A joke?"*

"Of course, stupid," Marisol said roughly. "Didn't you know that? You superpsychics are all so stuck-up—couldn't you tell?"

Kaitlyn's temper hit flashover.

"Well, at least we don't sneak around at night acting like lunatics!" she snapped. "The next time you do that, *you'd* better watch out."

Marisol smirked. "Or what?"

"Or . . . you'll see!" Just then the others began arriving for breakfast, so Kaitlyn was spared having to think up a more specific threat. She muttered, "Nut," and snagged a muffin.

Breakfast was lively, just as dinner had been the night before—and just like the night before, Gabriel didn't show up. Kaitlyn forgot all about Marisol as Joyce told them the house rules and described some of the experiments the kids would be doing.

"We'll do one session of testing this morning, just to get some baselines," Joyce said. "But first, anybody who wants to call their parents can do it now. Kaitlyn, I don't think you called your dad yesterday."

"No, but this would be a great time. Thanks," Kait said. She was actually rather glad to get away from the table—looking at Rob's hair in the morning sunlight made her feel strange. She called her father from a phone at the foot of the stairs.

"Are you having a good time, hon?"

"Oh, yes," Kaitlyn said. "It's *warm* here, Dad; I can go out without a sweater. And everybody's nice—almost everybody. Most people. Anyway, I think it's going to be great here."

"And you've got enough money?"

"Oh, *yes*." Kaitlyn knew her father had scraped together everything he could for her before she left. "I'm going to be fine, Dad. Honest."

"That's terrific, honey. I miss you."

Kaitlyn blinked. "I miss you, too. I'd better go now—I love you." She could hear voices in the room just in front of her. She went around behind the staircase and saw an open door in the little hallway below the landing. Joyce and the others were in a room beyond.

"Come on in," Joyce said. "This is the front lab, the one that used to be a family room. I'm just giving the grand tour."

The lab wasn't at all what Kait had expected. She'd envisioned white walls, gleaming machines, tile floor, a hushed atmosphere. There *were* machines, but there was also an attractive folding screen, lots of comfortable chairs and couches, two bookcases, and a stereo playing New Age music.

"They proved a long time ago at Princeton that a homey atmosphere is best," Joyce said. "It's like the observer effect, you know—psi abilities tend to fade any time the subject is uncomfortable."

The back lab, which had been a garage, was much the same, except that it also had a steel room rather like a bank vault.

"That's for complete isolation in testing," Joyce said. "It's soundproof, and the only communication with the inside is by intercom. It's also like a Faraday cage—it blocks out any radio waves or other electronic transmissions. If you put someone in there, you can be *sure* they're not using any of their normal senses to get information."

"I bet," Kaitlyn murmured. She could feel a creeping sensation along her spine—somehow she didn't *like* that steel room. "I . . . You're not going to put me in there, are you?"

Joyce glanced at her and laughed, her eyes sparkling like green-blue jewels in her tanned face. "No, we won't put you in there until you're ready," she said. "In fact, Marisol," she added to the college girl behind Kaitlyn, "why don't you go bring Gabriel down here—I think we'll test him in the isolation room for starters."

Marisol left.

"Right, everybody, show time," Joyce said. "This is our first day of experiments, so we'll keep them a bit informal, but I do want everyone to concentrate. I won't ask you to work all the time, but when you *do* work, I ask that you give it your all."

She directed them into the front lab, where she installed Anna and Lewis at what looked like study carrels on either side of the room—study carrels with mysterious-looking equipment. Kaitlyn didn't hear all the instructions she gave them, but in a few minutes both Anna and Lewis seemed to be working, oblivious to anything else in the room.

"Gabriel says he's coming," Marisol announced from the door. "And the volunteers are here. I could only get two so early on Sunday morning."

The volunteers turned out to be Fawn, an extremely pretty blond girl in a motorized wheelchair, and Sid, a guy with a blue Mohawk and a ring in his nose. Very California, Kait thought approvingly. Marisol took him into the back lab.

Joyce gestured at Kait to sit down on a couch over by the window. "You'll be working with Fawn, but you'll have to share her with Rob," she said. "And I think we'll let him go first. So just relax."

Kaitlyn didn't mind—she was both excited and nervous about her own testing. What if she couldn't perform? She'd never been able to use her power on cue—except at Joyce's "vision screening," and then she hadn't *known* she was using her power.

"Now, Rob," Joyce said. She had attached a blood pressure gauge to one of Fawn's fingers. "We'll have six trials of five minutes each. What I'm going to ask you to do is to pull a slip of paper out of this box. If the slip says 'Raise,' I want you to try to raise Fawn's blood pressure. If it says 'Lower,' I want you to try to lower it. If it says 'No change,' I want you to do nothing. Understand?"

Rob looked from Fawn to Joyce, his brow wrinkled. "Yes, ma'am, but—"

"Call me Joyce, Rob. I'll be charting the results. In each case, don't tell anyone what the slip says, just do it." Joyce checked her watch, then nodded at the box. "Go ahead, pick."

Rob started to reach in the box, but then he dropped his hand. He knelt in front of the blond girl's wheelchair.

"Your legs give you much trouble?"

Fawn looked at Joyce quickly, then back at Rob. "I have MS—multiple sclerosis. I got it early. Sometimes I can walk, but it's pretty bad right now."

"Rob . . ." Joyce said.

Rob didn't seem to hear her. "Can you lift this foot here?"

"Not very high." The leg lifted slightly, fell.

"*Rob,*" Joyce said. "Nobody expects you to . . . We can't *measure* this kind of thing."

"Excuse me, ma'am," Rob said softly, without looking

around. To Fawn: "How about this one? Can you lift it some?"

"Not as high as the other." The foot lifted and fell.

"That's just fine. Okay, now, you just hold still. You may feel some heat or some cold, but don't you worry about that." Rob reached forward to clasp the girl's bare ankle.

Joyce tilted her sleek blond head to look at the ceiling, then sighed and went to sit beside Kaitlyn.

"I suppose I should have known," she said, letting her hands with the watch and notebook fall on either side of her.

Kaitlyn was watching Rob.

His head was turned toward her, but he clearly wasn't seeing her. He seemed to be *listening* for something as his fingers moved nimbly over Fawn's ankle. As if looking at the ankle would only distract him.

Kaitlyn was fascinated by his face. Whatever she thought of boys in general, her artist's eye couldn't prevaricate. Words from a book she'd once read ran through her mind: "A beautiful, honest face with the eyes of a dreamer." And the stubborn jaw of a fighter, she added to herself, with an amused sideways glance at Joyce.

"How does that feel?" Rob asked Fawn.

"I . . . sort of tingly," she said, with a breathless, nervous laugh. "Oh!"

"Try to lift this foot again."

Fawn's sneaker came up—almost ten inches off the footrest.

"I did that!" she gasped. "No—*you* did that." She was staring at him with huge eyes full of wonder.

"You did it," Rob said, and smiled. He was breathing quickly. "Now we'll work on the other one."

Kaitlyn felt a stab of jealousy.

She'd never felt anything quite like it before—it was similar to the ache she'd gotten back in Ohio when she'd heard Marcy Huang planning parties. Just now, the way Rob was concentrating on Fawn—and the way Fawn was looking at Rob . . .

Joyce chuckled. "Same thing I saw at his school," she said to Kait in a low voice. "Every girl swooning when he goes by— and him not even knowing what's going on. That boy has no idea he's so sexy."

*That's it,* Kait realized. He has no clue. "But *why* doesn't he?" she blurted.

"Probably because of the same thing that gave him his talent," Joyce said. "The accident."

"What accident?"

"He didn't mention it? I'm sure he'll tell you all about it if you ask. He was hang gliding and he crashed. Broke most of his bones and ended up in a coma."

"Oh, my God," Kaitlyn said softly.

"They didn't expect him to live, but he did. When he woke up, he had his powers—but he also had some deficits. Like not knowing what girls are for."

Kaitlyn stared at her. "You're kidding."

"Nope." Joyce grinned. "He's pretty innocent about the world—in a lot of ways. He just doesn't see things quite the way other people do."

Kaitlyn shut her eyes. Of course, that explained why Rob casually reached up girls' skirts. It explained everything—except why just looking at him made her heart pound. And why just the thought of him lying in a coma hurt her. And why she had a very uncharitable desire to run over and physically drag him away from pretty Fawn right now.

There's a word for your condition, her mind told her snidely. It's called—

*Shut up,* Kaitlyn thought. But it was no use. She knew.

"That's enough for now," Rob was saying to Fawn. He sat back on his heels and wiped his forehead. "If we kept working on it every week, I think I could maybe help more. Do you want to do that?"

All Fawn said was, "Yes." But it was the *way* she said it, and the melty, awed way she looked into Rob's eyes, Kait thought. Fortunately, at that moment Joyce stood up.

"Rob, you might talk to *me* about arranging that," she said.

He turned and looked at her mildly. "I knew you'd want me to," he said.

Joyce muttered something under her breath. Then she said, "Right, we'll work something out. Why don't you take a break now, Rob? And, Fawn, if you're too tired for another experiment . . ."

"No, I feel *great*," Fawn said, not sappily but buoyantly. "I feel so strong—ready for anything."

"Energy transfer," Joyce murmured, taking off the blood pressure cuff. "We'll have to explore that." Then she looked up as the door connecting the front and back labs opened. "What is it, Marisol?"

"He is *not* cooperating," Marisol said. Gabriel was right behind her. He looked particularly gorgeous and somehow elegant—but his expression was one of cold contempt.

"Why not?" Joyce asked.

"You know why," Gabriel said. He seemed to sense Kait's eyes on him, and he gave her a long, deadly look.

Joyce put a hand to her forehead. "Right, let's go talk about it."

Rob reached out and caught her arm. "Ma'am—Joyce—I don't know if that's such a good idea. You want to be careful—"

"I'll handle this, Rob, please," Joyce said, in a voice that indicated she'd had enough. She went into the back lab, taking Marisol and Gabriel with her. The door shut.

Anna and Lewis were looking up from their study carrels. Even Fawn was staring.

Kaitlyn braced herself to look at Rob this close. "What'd you mean by that?" she said, her voice as casual as she could make it.

His gaze seemed to be turned inward. "I don't know—but I remember what happened at that center in Durham. *They* tried to make him do experiments, too." He shook his head. "I'll see y'all later," he said softly, and left. Kaitlyn was pleased that he didn't turn to look back at Fawn, and displeased that he didn't turn to look back at *her.*

A few minutes later Joyce returned, looking slightly frazzled. "Now, where were we? Kaitlyn, it's your turn."

Oh, not now, Kaitlyn thought. She felt raw and throbbing from her new discoveries about Rob—as if she'd had a layer of skin stripped off. She wanted to go off by herself somewhere and think.

Joyce was thumbing through a folder distractedly. "Informal; we'll keep this informal," she murmured. "Kaitlyn, I want you to sit down here." She guided Kaitlyn behind the folding screen, where there was a plush reclining chair. "In a minute I'm going to have you put on these headphones and this blindfold." It was a weird-looking blindfold, like goggles made of the two halves of a tennis ball.

"What's *that?*"

"Poor man's version of a Ganzfeld cocoon. I'm trying to get the money to set up a proper Ganzfeld room, with red lights and stereo sound and all. . . ."

"Red lights?"

"They help induce relaxation—but never mind. The point of Ganzfeld testing is to cut off your ordinary senses, so you can concentrate on the psychic ones. You can't see anything with the blindfold; you can't hear anything because the headphones fill your ears with white noise. It's supposed to help you be receptive to any images that come into your head."

"But images *don't* come into my head," Kait said. "They come into my hand."

"That's fine," Joyce said, and smiled. "Let them come—here's a pencil and paper on a clipboard. You don't need to see to draw; just let the pencil move as it wants to."

It sounded crazy to Kaitlyn, but Joyce was the expert. She sat down and put on the blindfold. Everything went dark.

"We'll try just one target image," Joyce said. "Fawn will be concentrating on a photograph of a certain object. You try and receive her thought."

"Sure," Kaitlyn muttered, and put on the headphones. A sound like a waterfall filled her ears. Must be white noise, she thought, leaning back in the chair.

She felt Joyce put the pencil in her hand and the clipboard in her lap.

Okay, relax.

It was actually rather easy. She knew no one could see her behind the screen—which was a good thing, because she must look pretty silly. She could just stretch out and let her thoughts drift. The darkness and the waterfall noise were like a slippery chute—there was nothing to hold on to. She felt herself sliding down . . . somewhere.

And she began to be afraid. The fear swept up and engulfed her before she knew what was happening. Her fingers clenched on the pencil.

Easy—calm down. Nothing to be scared of . . .

But she *was* scared. There was a terrible sinking in her stomach and she felt as if she were smothering.

Just let images come—but what if there were horrible images out there? Frightening things in the dark, just waiting to get into her mind . . . ?

Her hand began to cramp and itch.

Joyce had said to let the pencil move as it wanted to. But Kaitlyn didn't know if *she* wanted it to move.

Didn't matter. She had to draw. The pencil was moving.

Oh, God, and I have no idea what's coming out, she thought.

No idea—except that whatever it was, was scary. Formless darkness writhed in Kaitlyn's mind as she tried to picture whatever it was that the pencil was drawing.

*I have to see it.*

The tension in her muscles had become unbearable. With her left hand, Kaitlyn pulled the goggles and headphones off.

Her right hand was still moving, like a disembodied hand from a science fiction movie, without her mind having any idea of where it was going to go next. It didn't seem part of her. It was horrible.

And the drawing—the drawing was even more horrible. It was . . . grotesque.

The lines were a little wobbly, but the picture perfectly recognizable. It was her own face. Her face—with an extra eye in the forehead.

The eye had dark lashes all around, so it looked almost insectlike. It was wide and staring and unbelievably repulsive. Kaitlyn's left hand flew to her own forehead as if to make sure there was nothing there.

Only skin puckered with worry. She rubbed hard.

So much for remote vision. She'd bet anything Fawn wasn't out there concentrating on a picture like *this*.

Kaitlyn was about to sit up and tell Joyce that she'd ruined the experiment when the screaming began.

# CHAPTER 6

It was very loud even though it seemed to be coming from far away. The rhythm sounded almost like a baby's crying—the frantic, desperate howls of an abandoned infant—but the voice was much deeper.

Kait dropped the clipboard and vaulted out of the chair. She darted around the folding screen.

Joyce was opening the door to the back lab. Everyone else was staring, apparently frozen. Kait dashed up behind Joyce—just as the screaming stopped.

"Calm down! Just calm down!" Marisol was saying. She was standing in front of the blue-Mohawk guy, who was cringing against the wall. His eyes were wild, his mouth loose and wet with saliva. He seemed to be crying now.

"How long?" Joyce said to Marisol, approaching the Mohawk guy with hands outstretched in an I-mean-no-harm gesture.

Marisol turned. "About forty-five seconds."

"Oh, my God," Joyce said.

"What happened?" Kaitlyn burst out. She couldn't stand to watch this college-age guy cry anymore. "What is going *on* here? What's wrong with him?"

"Kaitlyn, please," Joyce said in a harassed voice.

Kaitlyn looked around the room—and saw that the door to the steel room was opening. Gabriel stepped out with a sneer on his arrogant, handsome face.

"I warned you," he said coldly to Joyce's back.

"This volunteer is a psychic," Joyce said in a thin voice.

"Not psychic enough, obviously," Gabriel said.

"You don't care at all, do you?" a voice said from behind Kaitlyn. She felt herself start—she hadn't heard Rob walk up.

"Rob—" Joyce said, but just then the Mohawk guy made a movement as if to dash away, and she broke off, fully occupied in restraining him.

"I said, you really don't care," Rob was saying, stalking up to face Gabriel. To Kait he looked like a golden avenging angel—but she was worried about him. In contrast to Rob's light, Gabriel looked like dangerous darkness. For one thing, Gabriel had been in jail; if it came to a fight, Kaitlyn would bet he'd fight dirty. And for another, he'd obviously done *something* to that volunteer. He might do it to Rob.

"I didn't arrange this experiment," Gabriel was saying in a frightening voice.

"No, but you didn't stop it, either," Rob snapped.

"I warned them."

"You could have just said no."

"Why should I? I told them what might happen. After that, it's their problem."

"Well, now it's my problem, too."

They were snarling right in one another's faces. The air was thick and electric-feeling with tension. And Kaitlyn couldn't stand it any longer.

"Both of you—*just stop it,*" she exploded, reaching them with three long steps. "Yelling at each other doesn't help anything."

They went on glaring at each other.

"*Rob,*" Kaitlyn said. Her heart was pounding. He looked so handsome, blazing with anger like this—and she could sense he was in danger.

Strangely, it wasn't Rob who responded to her. Gabriel turned his dark, cold gaze away from Rob's face to look at Kaitlyn. He gave her one of his disturbing smiles.

"Don't worry," he said. "I'm not going to kill him—yet. It would violate my parole."

Kaitlyn felt a chill as his gray eyes looked her up and down. She turned to Rob again.

"Please?"

"Okay," Rob said slowly. He took a long breath and she could feel the tension go out of his body. He stepped back.

Everyone seemed to feel the change in atmosphere and relax. Kaitlyn had almost forgotten about the volunteer in the last few minutes, but now she saw that Joyce and Marisol had coaxed him into a chair. He sat with his head bent nearly to his knees.

"Oh, man, what did you do to me?" he was muttering.

"What *did* you do to him?" Rob said to Gabriel. Kaitlyn wanted to know, too—she was *wild* to know—but she was afraid of another flare-up.

Instead, Gabriel just looked grim—almost bitter. "Maybe you'll find out someday," he said significantly, making it a threat.

It was then that Kaitlyn heard Lewis's hesitant voice calling from the front lab.

"Uh . . . Joyce, Mr. Zetes is here."

"Oh, God," Joyce said, straightening up.

Kaitlyn didn't blame her. All the experiments disrupted, everybody standing around, one volunteer practically writhing on the ground . . . It was a lot like getting a visit from the school principal when the class is in a total uproar.

Mr. Zetes was wearing a black coat again, and the two dogs were behind him.

"Problems?" he said to Joyce, who was quickly smoothing down her short blond hair.

"Just a slight one. Gabriel had some difficulties—"

"It looks as if that young man had some, too," Mr. Zetes

said dryly. He walked over to the Mohawk guy, looked down at him, then up at Joyce.

"I was going to call an ambulance," she said. "Marisol, would you—"

"There's no need," Mr. Zetes interrupted. "I'll take him in the car." He turned to look at Gabriel, Rob, and Kait, who were all standing by the steel room. "The rest of you young people can take a break," he said.

"Yes, go on. Testing is finished for today," Joyce said, still flustered. "Marisol, why don't you escort Fawn back home? And . . . make sure she's not upset about anything."

Marisol headed for the front lab without changing her sullen expression. Gabriel went, too, with the smooth, long steps of a wolf. Rob hesitated, looking at the Mohawk guy.

"Can I maybe help—"

"No, *thank you,* Rob. If you want some lunch, there are cold cuts in the fridge," Joyce said, in such a voice that Rob had to leave.

Kaitlyn followed, but she paused in the doorway as if trying to shut the door very quietly. It was sheer curiosity; she wanted to know if Mr. Zetes was going to yell at Joyce.

Instead, he said, "How long?"

"About forty-five seconds."

"Ah." It sounded almost appreciative. Kaitlyn got one glimpse of Mr. Zetes, tapping his cane thoughtfully on the ground, and then she had to shut the door.

Gabriel was already gone. Marisol and Fawn were leaving, Marisol looking sullen and Fawn looking back at Rob. Rob was chewing his lip, staring at the floor. Lewis was looking from one person to another. Anna was petting a white mouse she held in her hand.

"Where'd you get that?" Kaitlyn asked. She felt someone ought to say something.

"He was in my experiment. See? This box has different-numbered holes, and I'm supposed to make him go into one of them. Whichever number the monitor shows."

"There must be a sensor inside the hole to register whether you get it right," Lewis said, coming over.

Anna nodded, but she was looking past him. "Don't worry, Rob," she said. "Joyce and Mr. Zetes will take care of that guy. It'll be all right."

"Yeah, but can Mr. Z take care of *Gabriel?*" Lewis said. "That's the question."

Kaitlyn smiled in spite of herself. "Mr. Z?"

"Sure. 'Mr. Zetes' is too long."

"I just don't think he should be here," Rob said broodingly. "Gabriel. I think he's trouble."

"And *I* think I'm going to go crazy wondering what it is he *does,*" Kaitlyn said. "But I don't think Joyce is going to tell us."

"Gabriel has a right to privacy, if he wants it," Anna said gently, putting the mouse in a wire cage. "*I* think we ought to do something to get our minds off it, since we have the afternoon off. We could go into town—or we could finish setting up the common room upstairs."

As always, just being around Anna calmed Kaitlyn down. Serenity drifted from the Native American girl and filled the room.

"Let's do the room," Kaitlyn said. "We can take lunch up there. I'll make sandwiches."

"I'll help," Rob said, and Kaitlyn's heart gave a startled leap.

What do I say, what do I *say?* she thought in the kitchen. Lewis and Anna had gone upstairs; she and Rob were alone.

At least her hands knew what to do. She was used to fixing meals for her dad, and now she spun the lids off mustard jars and stacked cold cuts efficiently. They were very Californian cold cuts: turkey baloney and chicken slices, low-fat salami, Alpine Lace cheese.

Rob worked just as efficiently—but he seemed abstracted, as if his mind were on other things.

Kaitlyn couldn't stand the silence. Almost at random, she said, "Sometimes I wonder if it's really a good idea to try and develop our powers. I mean, look at Gabriel."

She'd said it because she had a vague notion Rob would agree. But he shook his head vigorously and came out of his brown study.

"No, it *is* good—it's important for the world. What Gabriel needs is to develop some *control*—he's bad off for that. Or maybe he just doesn't want to control himself." Rob shook his head and slapped a piece of sprouted whole wheat bread on a sandwich. "But I think everybody ought to develop their talents. D'you realize most people have ESP?" He looked at Kait earnestly.

She shook her head. "I thought we were special."

"We've got more of it. But just about everybody has some. If everybody could work on it—don't you see? Things might start getting better. And they look pretty bad right now."

"You mean . . . for the world?"

He nodded. "People don't care much about each other. But, you know, when I channel energy I feel people's pain. If everybody could feel that, things would be different. There wouldn't be any murder or torture or stuff—because nobody would want to cause pain to anybody else."

Kaitlyn's heart had picked up. He'd "channeled energy" for her—did that mean he felt close to her?

But all she said, very gently, was, "Not everybody can be a healer."

"Everybody has some talent. Everybody could help in some way. When I get out of college I'd like to do the kind of work Joyce is doing—only try to get *everybody* involved in it. Everybody everywhere."

Kaitlyn was staggered by the vision. "You want to save the world?"

"Sure. I'd do my bit," he said, as if saying, *Sure, I'd do my bit for recycling.*

Dear God, Kait thought. I believe him.

There was something about this boy with the golden dreamer's eyes and the quiet voice that commanded her respect. A person like this, Kait thought, comes along only once in a very long time. A person like this can make a difference.

That was what she *thought*. What she felt was . . . was . . . well . . .

Anyway, there was no fighting against it anymore, she thought as they took the sandwiches upstairs.

All through the afternoon, which was spent moving furniture, arguing, and arranging things, Kait hugged her new knowledge to herself. It was both pleasure and pain, just as it was both a pleasure and painful to be able to watch Rob, to be in his company.

She would never have believed she could fall in love on one day's acquaintance.

But there it was. And every minute she was around Rob, the feeling grew stronger. She had trouble focusing on anything else when Rob was in the room, her heart began to beat hard when he looked at her, his voice made her shiver, and when he said her name . . .

By dinnertime, she was a basket case.

The strange thing was, now that she'd admitted it to herself, she wanted to talk about it. To explain to somebody else how she felt. To share it.

Anna, she thought.

When Anna went into their room to clean up before dinner, Kait followed her. She shut the door, then ducked into the bathroom and turned on the faucet.

Anna was sitting on her bed, brushing her long black hair. "What's that for?" she said, amused.

"Privacy," Kait said grimly. She sat down on her own bed, although she could hardly keep herself sitting still. "Anna— can I talk to you?"

"Of course you can."

Of course she could. Kaitlyn knew that suddenly. "It's so strange—back home I never had any friend I could really talk to. But I *know* I can talk to you. I just don't know how to start," she added explosively, discovering this.

Anna smiled, and Kaitlyn felt more peaceful, less agitated. "It wouldn't have anything to do with Rob, would it?"

"Oh, my God," Kaitlyn said, stiffening. "Is it that obvious? Do you think *he* knows?"

"No . . . but I'm a girl, remember? I notice things boys don't notice."

"Yes, well, that's the problem, isn't it?" Kaitlyn murmured, sitting back. She felt crushed suddenly. "I've got this feeling *he* isn't ever going to notice."

"I heard what Joyce said about him."

Kaitlyn was very glad—she wouldn't have to repeat the story, like gossip. "Then you know it's practically hopeless," she said.

"It's not hopeless. You just have to *get* him to notice you, that's all. He likes you; he just doesn't realize you're a girl."

"You think he likes me?"

"Of course he does. And you're beautiful—any normal guy wouldn't have any trouble seeing you're female. With Rob, you're just going to have to do something extra."

"Like take off my shirt?"

"I was thinking of something less extreme."

"I've *thought* of things," Kaitlyn said. "All afternoon I've been thinking of ways . . . well, like trying to get him into romantic situations. But I don't know if it's right. Isn't that like tricking him?"

Anna smiled—a very wise smile, Kait thought. "See that mask?" she said, nodding to the one on the wall. "That's Skauk, the Raven. He was my greatgrandfather's guardian spirit—and when the missionaries came along and gave my family the name 'White,' he was the one who stuck 'Raven' on, so we would always know who we were. Friends of Raven the Trickster."

Kaitlyn stared at the mask, with its long, blunt beak, in fascination.

"Raven was always doing things for his own good—but they turned out to be for everybody's good in the end. Like the time when he stole the sun."

Kaitlyn grinned, sensing a story. "When he what?"

"He stole the sun," Anna said gravely, only her eyes smiling. "Gray Eagle had the sun, but he hated people so much that he kept it hidden in his house, and everybody else lived in darkness. Raven wanted the sun for his own, but he knew Gray Eagle would never let him inside. So he turned himself into a snow white bird and tricked Gray Eagle's daughter into letting him in."

"*Tch,*" Kaitlyn said. Anna's eyes smiled.

"As soon as she did, Raven grabbed the sun and flew away—but Gray Eagle flew after him. Raven got so scared that he dropped the sun . . . and it landed in the sky, where it lit up the world for everybody."

"That's nice," Kaitlyn said, pleased.

"There're lots of stories about Raven. But the point is, sometimes a little trickery isn't so bad." Anna flashed Kait a dark-eyed glance. "And especially where boys are concerned, I think."

Kaitlyn stood up, feeling excitement churn inside her. "Then I'll do it! If I can think of something good."

"You can start with cleaning up a little," Anna said, laughing. "Right now he'll only notice you for the dirt on your nose."

Kaitlyn not only washed but changed her clothes and pulled her hair back with a gold barrette—but she didn't see that it made any difference in Rob's attitude at dinner. Dinner was novel mostly because Gabriel put in an appearance.

"He eats," Kaitlyn whispered to Anna under cover of passing the brown rice. "I was beginning to wonder."

After dinner, Gabriel vanished again. Lewis and Rob went into the common room, which they now called the study, although Kaitlyn didn't think there was much chance of anyone studying in it. Not with U2 on the CD player competing with a horror movie on the TV. It didn't seem to bother Anna, who curled up in the alcove with a book, but Kaitlyn wanted to get away.

She needed to be by herself because of Rob—and because school was tomorrow, her new school, her new chance. Her feelings were all mixed up, flying around in confusion and bumping into each other and ricocheting off even faster.

But most important, she needed to draw.

Not the ESP kind of drawing. Just regular drawing, which always helped smooth out her thoughts. She hadn't really drawn for two days.

That reminded her of something. The drawing she'd done in the lab—she'd just left it there, behind the folding screen. She should go pick it up sometime; she certainly didn't want anyone else to see it.

"I'll be back in a little while," she said to the others in the study, and then she stopped to be grateful a moment because everybody said good-bye as she left. That had always been one of her dreams, to say to a roomful of people, "I'm going" and have them all say good-bye.

The drawing wasn't in the lab. As she let herself out the back door, she hoped someone had thrown it away.

She took only her sketchbook and a couple of sticks of charcoal—it was too dark outside to really see colors. But there was enough moonlight to see trees, and the air was deliciously fresh and cold.

This is more like winter, she thought. Everything was silver and shadows. In back of the house a narrow dirt road sloped down to a stand of redwood trees. Kaitlyn followed it.

At the foot of the hill was a little, almost dry streambed, with a low concrete bridge crossing it. The road looked as if it were never used. Kaitlyn stood in the middle of the redwoods, breathing in the night and the tree smell.

What a wonderful place. The trees cut off the lights of the house, and not even U2 could penetrate this far. She felt quite alone.

She sat on a concrete curb with her sketch pad on her knees.

Although the moonlight was beautiful, the coolest kind of light imaginable, there wasn't really enough of it to draw properly. Oh, well, Kaitlyn thought, Joyce wants me to learn how to draw blind. With loose, fluid motions, she sketched in the shapes of some redwoods across the streambed. It was interesting to get only the shape and no detail.

What a peaceful place. She added a bush.

She was feeling much better already. She added a dark, sinuous line for the stream.

A night like this made you believe in magic. She started to add a few rocks—and then she heard a sound.

A thump. Like, Kaitlyn thought, freezing, someone falling out of a tree.

Or jumping.

Strange, how she knew right away it was human. Not an animal sound, and certainly nothing natural.

Someone was out here with her.

She looked around, moving only her head, keeping her body still. She had good eyes, artist's eyes, and when she'd walked down here she'd noticed the shape of the trees and bushes. She ought to be able to spot anything different.

But she couldn't. She couldn't see anything new, and she couldn't hear anything, either. Whoever was out there wasn't speaking.

That made it not funny. Not a joke. When somebody hides at night and doesn't let you know who they are—when you can *feel* eyes on you, but you don't know whose—that wasn't funny. Kaitlyn's hands felt cold and her throat felt very tight.

Just get up. Leave. *Now,* she thought.

She managed two steps up the hill and saw movement among the trees. It was a person, moving out from the cover of the redwoods.

Kaitlyn's body prepared to fight or flee—but not until she

saw who it was. She had to see the face before she could be released from paralysis.

The person came closer, feet crunching on dead leaves. Moonlight shone on his face, on slanting eyes and softly curling brown hair. It was the man who'd grabbed her in the airport.

He was wearing regular clothes now, not the red robe he'd worn before. And he was coming straight at her, very quickly.

# CHAPTER 7

Fight, Kait decided. Or rather, her body decided it for her, seeming to feel instinctively that she'd never make it up that hill.

Her sketchbook was spiral-bound with heavy wire, and one end was slightly uncoiled—it had been poking her for weeks. Now she dropped the charcoal sticks and brought the book up, poised for attack.

Aim for the eyes, she thought.

She knew she should be screaming, but her throat was too constricted.

All this passed through her mind in the few seconds it took the stranger to reach her. Kaitlyn hadn't been in a fight since elementary school, but now her body seemed to know what to do. The stranger grabbed for her arm—Kaitlyn jerked it away.

*Now,* she thought, and lashed out with the sketchbook.

And it worked—the heavy wire caught him in the cheek, tearing a long bloody scratch.

Fierce triumph surged up in Kait. But the next instant the stranger had her wrist and was twisting it, trying to make her let go of the sketch pad. It hurt, and the pain freed her voice.

"Let go of me," she gasped. *"Let go!"*

He twisted harder. Blood was running down his cheek, black in the moonlight. Kaitlyn tried to kick, but he turned his body and her kicks glanced off harmlessly. He had both her arms now. He was pushing her down onto the sloping ground of the hill. He was winning.

*Scream,* her mind told her.

Kaitlyn sucked in a deep breath and screamed. But it was cut off almost before it started, by the stranger's hand.

"Shut up!" he said, in a furious whisper.

Kaitlyn stared up at him over his smothering hand, knowing her eyes were wide with fear. He was so strong, and so much heavier than she was—she couldn't move at all.

"You're so reckless—you never *think,*" the stranger hissed. The moon was behind him, so his face was in shadow—but she could feel his anger.

He's going to kill me. And I'll never even know why, a small, clear part of her mind said. The rest of her was engulfed in sheer black terror as his hand stayed over her mouth. It was getting very hard to breathe. . . .

Something reared up behind the stranger.

Kaitlyn's dazed mind couldn't tell at first what it was. Just a shape silhouetted against the moonlit sky. Then she saw it was a human shape, with something shining in its hand.

There was a movement quicker than Kait's eyes could follow, and the stranger on top of her was jerked backward slightly. The moonlight reflected off a knife blade.

"Let go of her," a clipped, harsh voice said, "or I'll cut your throat."

*Gabriel?* Kaitlyn thought in disbelief. But it was true, and now her panicked senses could interpret the scene in front of her. Gabriel was holding the stranger at knifepoint.

The stranger's hands lifted away from Kaitlyn. She drew in a gasping, wheezing breath.

"Now get up," Gabriel said. "Nice and easy. I'm in a bad mood tonight."

The stranger rose in one slow, coordinated motion, like a dancer. The knife stayed at his throat the whole time.

As soon as his weight was removed, Kaitlyn got her feet under her and took two scrambling steps up the hill. Adrenaline was still flooding over her in painful, useless waves. Her hands were shaking.

I should help Gabriel, she thought. No matter how tough he is, he's a kid, and that stranger's a man. A strong man.

"Want me to go back to the house and tell them?" she gasped, trying to make herself sound hard and competent.

"Why?" Gabriel said briefly. He made some movement and

the stranger went spinning, landing on his back on the ground.

"Now get out," he said, looking down at the supine figure. "And don't come back unless you're tired of living. If I see you around again, I'll forget I just did two years for murder."

A shock went through Kait. But she didn't have time to think—Gabriel was speaking again.

"I said, get out. Run. Show me a four-minute mile."

The stranger got up, not nearly as smoothly and gracefully as before. From what Kait could see of his expression, he was both furious and frightened.

"You're *both* so stupid—" he began.

"*Run,*" Gabriel suggested, holding the knife as if ready to throw it.

The stranger turned and went, half running, half angrily stalking.

When the crunch of his footsteps had died, Kaitlyn looked at Gabriel, who was folding up the knife and putting it in his back pocket all in one practiced gesture.

Murder, she thought. He was in jail for murder.

What she said, rather unsteadily, was, "Thank you."

He glanced up at her briefly, and she could swear he was amused, as if he knew the difference between her thoughts and her words. "Who was he? An old boyfriend?" he asked.

"Don't be ridiculous," Kait snapped, and then wished she hadn't. One ought to be more polite to a murderer, especially when one was alone with him in the dark. "I don't know *who* he is," she added. "But he was at the airport when I came yes-terday. He must have followed Joyce and me home."

Gabriel looked at her skeptically, then shrugged. "I don't think he'll come back." He started toward the house without turning to see if Kait was following.

Kaitlyn picked up her sketchbook and went after him.


*"What happened?"* Rob said, vaulting to his feet. He and Lewis and Anna were in the study—as was Joyce. Kaitlyn had looked for her on the first floor, then come up here.

Rob was staring from Kaitlyn, who was just realizing that she had bits of dead leaves and grass in her hair, to Gabriel, who was behind her. "What happened?" he repeated, in a more controlled but more frightening voice.

"What does it look like?" Gabriel taunted, at his very nastiest.

Rob started toward him, golden eyes blazing.

*"No,"* Kaitlyn said. "Rob, don't. He didn't hurt me; he saved me."

She felt a surge of dizzy excitement—Rob was angry *for* her, protective. But she couldn't let him fight Gabriel.

"*He* saved you?" Rob said, with open scorn. He was on one side of the doorway, staring at Gabriel as if trying to bore holes in him. Gabriel was on the other side, almost lounging against the wall and looking devastatingly handsome. Kait was caught in between them.

She appealed to Joyce, who was rising from the study couch.

"It was that guy, the guy from the airport," she said. "He was out back." She explained what had happened, watching the alarm grow on Joyce's face.

"Jeez, we'd better call the police," Lewis said when she was done. He sounded more impressed than scared.

"He's right," Anna said, her dark eyes sober.

"Oh, sure, call them," Gabriel sneered. "I only just got paroled. They love to see people like me with switchblades."

Joyce grimaced. She squeezed her eyes shut and did some stretching exercises with her shoulders.

Kaitlyn's heart sank. Gabriel would be in trouble—he might even get sent back to jail. His part of the experiment would be ruined, and he might never learn to control his powers. All because he'd helped her.

Rob was suddenly looking quite cheerful. "Well, we've *got* to report it."

"Fine. Just give me ten minutes' start," Gabriel said through his teeth.

"Stop it, both of you," Kaitlyn said. Then she sighed. Being in love wasn't easy. She didn't want to make Rob unhappy, but she had no choice.

"I have an idea," she said hesitantly. "We could call the police, but not tell them Gabriel was involved. I'll just say I got away from the guy out there. Then nobody would get in trouble, but the police could do whatever they need to."

Rob's smile faded. Gabriel was still glaring. But Joyce opened her aquamarine eyes and beamed.

"Trust you, Kait," she said. "Now, where's a phone?"

Gabriel didn't stay to hear the call.

He went into his room and shut the door behind him. And then, tired but too restless to even sit down, he began to pace.

Images kept floating through his mind. Kaitlyn lying in the moonlight—with some maniac on top of her. What if he hadn't come along just then?

The maniac had been right about one thing—she *was* reckless. She shouldn't be *allowed* out alone at night. She didn't have the right instincts for danger, she wasn't tough enough to protect herself. . . .

So . . . what? his mind asked. So you're going to protect her?

Gabriel flashed one of his best disturbing smiles at nothing. Hardly.

He was going to keep away from her, was what he was going to do. She was a nuisance—and she was stuck on Kessler. Gabriel could see that, even if Kessler was too stupid.

Keep away from her. Yes. And he'd bet—he smiled again—that after what she'd seen tonight, she'd keep away from him.

Two hours later Kait was lying in bed, trying to calm down enough to go to sleep.

There had been a lot of fuss with the police, who'd gone

down into the backyard but had found nothing. They'd promised to have a cruiser patrol the area, and Joyce had told the kids to check the door locks and keep a close lookout for strangers from now on.

"And I don't want you going anywhere alone," she told Kait firmly. "Especially at night." Kait was happy to agree.

But now she couldn't sleep. It had all been too weird, too disturbing. Why would some cult guy from the airport follow her home? *Was* he some cult guy? If not, why had he been wearing the robes? A disguise? A stupid one.

What did he *want?*

And beneath all her other thoughts ran a continuous whispering thread. . . .

Gabriel was a murderer.

The others didn't know. Except Rob—Kaitlyn felt sure Rob knew. But even not knowing, they'd treated him pretty badly tonight. No one had said anything complimentary about him saving Kait. Lewis and Anna had kept their distance, as if they expected him to pull a switchblade on *them* at any minute, and Rob had watched him with steady, smoldering fury.

Rob—she *wouldn't* think about Rob now. She couldn't take the agitation.

Anna was breathing peacefully on the other side of the bedroom. Kaitlyn glanced at her, a motionless shape in the darkness, then very carefully and quietly got out of bed.

She shouldered into her robe and slipped noiselessly out the door.

The study was dim. Kait sat on the window seat in the alcove, her chin on her knees. Outside, a few lights shone through waving tree branches. Then she noticed that light was also shining through the curtains in Gabriel's room.

What she did then was born of sheer impulse. If she'd thought about it, she never would have gone through with it. But she didn't give herself time to think.

She jumped off the window seat and went to knock on his door.

A very quiet knocking, in case he was asleep with the light on. But after only an instant the door opened.

He was wearing a rather sleepy scowl.

"What?" he said ungallantly.

"Come into the study," Kaitlyn whispered.

The scowl disappeared, changing into a dazzling bared-teeth smile. "No, *you* come in *here.*"

He was daring her, Kaitlyn realized. All right; great. She'd prove she trusted him.

Head very high, back straight, she swept by him. She sat down on the desk chair. She glanced around unobtrusively—the room was as nice as Lewis had said. Huge bed, matching furniture, *acres* of space. It seemed bare of personal possessions, though. Maybe Gabriel didn't have any.

Slowly, watching her, Gabriel sat down on the bed. He'd

left the door a little ajar. Kaitlyn, motivated by she didn't know what, got up and closed it.

"You're crazy, you know," Gabriel said unemotionally, as she resumed her seat.

"I wanted to say thank you," Kaitlyn said. *And that I'm not afraid of you,* she added silently. She still couldn't figure out what she felt about Gabriel—even whether she liked him or hated him.

But he had saved her from a very bad situation.

Gabriel didn't look gratified by the thanks. "And that's all?" he said mockingly.

"Of course."

"You're not just a little curious?" When Kaitlyn blinked at him, he leaned forward. His teeth were bared again. "You don't even want to know?"

Kaitlyn felt distaste pinching her features. "You mean . . . about . . ."

"The murder," Gabriel said, his dazzling grin getting nastier by the minute.

Fear uncoiled in Kaitlyn's stomach. He was right—she *was* crazy. What was she doing sitting here in his bedroom? Two days ago she wouldn't have sat in *any* guy's bedroom, and now she was chatting with a killer.

But Joyce wouldn't have brought him to the Institute if he was really dangerous, she thought. Joyce wouldn't take that risk.

Kaitlyn said slowly, "Was it really murder?" Then she looked straight up at Gabriel.

His expression changed as he met her eyes—as if she'd startled him. Then he seemed to regain his balance.

"*I* called it self-defense, but the judge didn't agree," he said. His eyes were now cold as ice.

Something inside Kaitlyn relaxed. "Self-defense," she said.

Gabriel looked at her for a long moment, then away. "Of course, the other one wasn't self-defense. The first one."

He's trying to shock you, Kaitlyn told herself.

He's succeeding, her mind whispered back.

"I'd better go," she said.

He was *very* fast. She was closer to the door, but before she could reach it, he was in front of her, blocking it.

"Oh, no," he said. "Don't you want to hear all about it?"

Those dark gray eyes were strange—almost fixed, as if he were looking through her. His expression was strange, too. As if he were covering unbearable tension with mockery and derision. Kaitlyn could see the glint of clenched teeth between his parted lips.

"Stop it, Gabriel," she said. "I'm going."

"Don't be shy."

"I'm not *shy,* you jerk," she snapped. "I'm just sick of you." She tried to push past him and he wouldn't let her. They tussled.

Kaitlyn found out very quickly how much stronger he was.

Stupid, *stupid*, she thought, trying to get a hand free to hit him. How had she gotten herself *into* this mess? Her heart was going like a trip-hammer, and her chest felt as if it would burst. She was going to have to scream—unless he stopped her. Choked her, maybe. Was that what he'd done to the others?

Maybe he'd used a knife. Maybe he cut them. Or maybe it had been something even worse. . . .

She and Gabriel had been struggling silently, their faces inches apart. Kaitlyn's mind was dark with imaginings of how he might have killed before.

And then . . .

And then it all stopped. Kaitlyn's fantasies were cut off as if somebody had slammed down a window in her mind. And all because of the look in Gabriel's eyes.

Grief. Guilt, too, plenty of that, but mainly grief. A kind Kaitlyn recognized, the kind that makes you nearly bite through your lip so you won't make a noise. The kind Kaitlyn could remember from when she was eight years old, when her mother died.

Gabriel, with his handsome, arrogant face, and his savage bared teeth, was trying to make the tears go away.

Kaitlyn stopped struggling with him, realizing in the moment she did that he hadn't hurt her. He'd been blocking her, restraining her, but he hadn't bruised her.

"Okay," she said, her voice loud in the silence. "So tell me, then."

It caught him off guard. Actually rocked him backward. For a moment he looked shocked—and vulnerable.

Then his face hardened. He was taking it as a challenge.

"I will," he snarled back. He let go of her and stepped away—a hunted, constrained movement. His chest was rising and falling quickly.

"You've all been wondering what I *do*," he said. "Haven't you?"

"Yes," Kait said. She moved cautiously away from the door. "Is that so surprising?"

"No." He laughed—a very bitter laugh. "It's what everyone wants to know. But when they find out, they don't like it." He turned and looked at her with mock bewilderment. "For some reason, they seem to be scared of me."

Kaitlyn didn't smile. "I know what it's like," she said flatly to the carpet. "When they're scared of you. When they can't look you in the eye and they kind of edge away when you get close . . ." She looked up at him.

Something flickered in his eyes; then he shook his head, turning away. "You don't know what it's like when they're so scared that they *hate* you. When they want to *kill* you because they're so scared that you'll . . ."

"That you'll what?"

"Read their minds. Steal their souls. Take your pick."

There was a silence. Ice crept along Kaitlyn's spine. She was bewildered—and afraid.

"Is that what you do?" she said, fighting to keep her voice above a whisper.

"No." The cold knot in Kaitlyn's stomach loosened slightly—until he turned around and looked at her with the calm gray eyes of a madman. "It's not as simple as that. Do you want to know how it works?"

Kaitlyn didn't move, didn't speak. She just looked at him.

He spoke precisely, as if giving a lecture. "Any time two minds make contact, there's a transfer of energy. That's what contact *is,* the transfer of a certain kind of energy. Back and forth, energy carrying information. You understand?"

Rob had talked about energy—channeling energy. But maybe that had been a different kind.

"Go on," Kaitlyn said.

"The problem is that some minds are stronger than others. More powerful. And if a strong mind contacts a weaker one— things can get out of control." He stopped, looking at the dark, curtained window.

"How?" Kaitlyn whispered. He didn't seem to hear her. "How can it get out of control, Gabriel?"

Still looking at the window, he said, "You know how water flows from a high place to a low place? Or how electricity keeps trying to find a ground for its force? Well, when two minds touch, energy flows. Back and forth. But the stronger mind always has more pull."

"Like a magnet?" Kaitlyn asked quietly. She'd never been

great at science, but she did know that—the bigger the magnet, the stronger it was.

"A magnet? Maybe at first. But if something happens—if things get off balance—it's more like a black hole. All the energy flows out of the weaker mind. The strong one drains it. Sucks it dry."

He was standing very still, every muscle rigid. His hands were shoved in his pockets, fingers clenched. And his gray eyes were so bleak and lonely that Kaitlyn was glad he wasn't looking at her.

She said, evenly, "You're a telepath."

"They called it something different. They called me a psychic vampire."

And I felt sorry for myself, Kaitlyn thought. Just because I couldn't help people, because my drawings were useless. But his gift makes him kill.

"Does it *have* to be that way?"

He flicked a glance at her, eyes narrowing. He'd heard the pity in her voice.

"Not if I keep the contact short. Or if the other mind is fairly strong."

Kaitlyn was remembering. *How long? About forty-five seconds. Oh, my God.*

And the Mohawk guy had come out screaming.

*This volunteer is a psychic. Not psychic enough, obviously.*

How strong did a mind need to be to hold up to Gabriel?

"Unfortunately," Gabriel said, still watching her with narrowed eyes, "even a little thing can upset the balance. It can happen before you know it."

Kaitlyn was afraid.

A bad thing to be around Gabriel. He saw it, sensed it. And it obviously triggered some instinct in him—to go for the throat.

He gave one of his wild, disturbing smiles. There was bright sickness in his eyes. "That's why I have to be so careful," he said. "I have to stay in control. Because if I lose control, things can happen."

Kaitlyn struggled to breathe evenly. He was moving closer to her, like a wolf scenting something it wanted. She forced herself not to cower, to look at him without flinching. She put steel into her neck.

"That was how it happened the first time," Gabriel told her. "There was a girl at that center in Durham. We liked each other. And we wanted to be together. But when we got close— something happened."

He was directly in front of her now. Kaitlyn felt her back flatten against the wall.

"I didn't mean it to happen. But I got emotional, you see. And that was dangerous. I wanted to be closer, and the next thing I knew, we were linking minds." He stopped, breathing quickly and lightly, then went on. "She was weak—and afraid. Are you afraid, Kaitlyn?"

# CHAPTER 8

L ie, Kaitlyn thought. But she felt sure he could detect a
lie. She also felt sure the truth might kill her.
  Nothing to do but take the offensive.

"Do you want me to be? Is that what you want—for it all
to happen again?"

A veil-like spiderweb seemed to fall over his gray eyes, taking out their dark brightness. He even pulled back a fraction.

Kaitlyn stayed on the attack, "I don't think you meant to
hurt that girl. I think you loved her."

He stepped back even farther.

"What was her name?" Kaitlyn said.

To her surprise, he answered. "Iris. She was just a kid. We
were both kids. We had no idea what we were doing."

"And she was there because she was psychic?"

His lip curled. "'Not psychic enough,'" he quoted, as if

giving Kait the answer she was expecting. Stark bitterness was in his eyes. "She didn't have enough . . . whatever. Life force. Bioenergy. Whatever it is that makes people psychic—and keeps them alive. That night at the center . . . by the time I was able to let go of her, she was just limp. Her face was white, blue-white. She was dead."

His chest heaved, and then he said deliberately, "No life. No energy left. I'd drained her dry."

Kaitlyn wasn't on the offensive any longer, and she couldn't hold his gaze. Her own chest felt as if there were a tight band around it. After a moment she said quietly, "You didn't do it on purpose."

"Didn't I?" he said. He seemed to have conquered whatever emotion had possessed him; he was breathing easily again. When Kait looked up, she saw his gray eyes were no longer bitter, or even shielded. They were . . . empty.

"The people at the center had a different idea," he went on. "When I realized she wasn't breathing, I called for help. And when they came and saw her—all blue like that—they thought the worst. They said I'd attacked her. They said I'd tried to force her, and when I couldn't, I killed her."

Kait felt a wash of pure, dizzying horror. She was glad there was a wall behind her; she let her weight rest on it, and only then realized she'd shut her eyes.

"I'm sorry," she whispered, opening them. Then, trying to find some comfort, she said, "Rob was right. What Joyce is doing *is* important for the world. We all need to learn how to control our powers."

Gabriel's face twisted. "You believe that country-boy stuff?" he said with utter contempt.

Kaitlyn was taken aback. "Why do you hate Rob so much?"

"Didn't you know? The golden boy was there, in Durham. They practically worshiped him—everything he did was right. And *he* was the one who figured out what had happened to Iris. He didn't know how I'd done it, but he knew her energy had been tapped, like blood if you cut an artery. They hunted me, you know. Like an animal. The center and the police and everyone." His voice was dispassionate.

But that wasn't Rob's fault, Kait thought. It *wasn't*. Aloud she said, "So you went on the run."

"Yeah. I was fourteen and stupid. Lucky for me, they were stupider. It took them a year to find me, and by then I was in California. In jail."

"For another murder," Kaitlyn said steadily.

"When the world is so stupid, you take your revenge, you know? People deserve it. Anybody that weak deserves it. The guy I killed tried to mess with me. He wanted to shoot me over the five dollars in my pocket. I got him first."

Revenge, Kaitlyn thought. She could picture the parts of the story Gabriel hadn't told. Him running away, not caring what happened to him, not caring what he did. Hating everything:

the universe, for giving him his power; the stupid weak people in the universe, for being so easy to kill; the center, for not teaching him how to control his gift—and himself. Especially himself.

And Rob, the symbol of someone who'd succeeded, whose powers brought only good. Who was in control. Who still *believed* in something.

"He's an idiot," Gabriel said, as if reading her thought. He did that too much; it bothered Kaitlyn. "Him and those other two, they're all idiots. But you have some common sense—or at least I thought you did."

"Thanks," Kait said dryly. "Why?"

"You see things. You know something's wrong here."

Kaitlyn was startled. "Something wrong? You mean, at the Institute?"

He gave her a look of knowing contempt. "I see. That's how you're going to play it."

"I'm not *playing* anything—"

He flashed a disturbing smile and turned, walking to the center of the room. "After all, if you leave, you don't stand much chance of getting him. Can't reel him in from Ohio."

Kaitlyn felt herself flush with anger.

It was over—the confidences, Gabriel's almost-decency, his letting down of walls. He was going to be as nasty and objectionable as possible now, just so she wouldn't get the wrong idea about him. Like that he was an okay person.

Well, I won't rise to it, Kaitlyn thought. I won't even dignify that with an answer. And however it sounds, he can't really *know* what Anna and I talked about behind closed doors.

She pushed herself off the wall and moved one step toward Gabriel. She said, very formally, "I'm sorry for what happened to you. It was all terrible. But I think that you should start thinking about what you can do to change things from now on."

Gabriel smiled silkily from behind his walls. "But what if I don't want to change things?"

Two minutes ago, Kaitlyn had been dizzy with sympathy for him. Now she wanted to kick him in the shins.

*Boys,* she thought.

"Good night, Gabriel," she said.

You jerk.

He widened his eyes. "Don't you want to stay? It's a big bed."

Kaitlyn didn't bother to answer that at all. She went out with her head very high, muttering words that would have shocked her father.

One thing was fortunate. For a while there, she'd felt quite close to Gabriel—and that could have meant trouble. Imagine her, Kaitlyn the cold, falling for not just one but *two* boys. But he'd taken care of that. He'd pushed her away, and she felt certain he wouldn't let her ever get close again.

No, thank God, she wasn't in any danger. She found Gabriel interesting—even, in a weird way, heartbreaking—and he was certainly gorgeous. But . . . well, anyone with the bad luck to fall in love with *him* would have to disembowel herself with a bamboo letter opener.

She wouldn't tell anyone what he'd told her about his power. That would be betraying a confidence. But she thought she might talk with Rob about him someday. It might change Rob's views, to know that Gabriel could feel regret.

Strangely, when Kait got back to bed, she fell asleep at once.

The next day Joyce took them to San Carlos High School. They were already registered for classes, and Kait was delighted to find that she shared sociology and British literature with Anna and Rob. In fact, she was delighted with everything. She'd never dreamed school could be like this.

It was different from Ohio. The campus itself was bigger, more sprawling, more open in design. Instead of one big building, there were lots of little ones, connected by covered paths. Ridiculous if it snowed—but it *never* snowed here. Never.

The buildings were more modern, too. Less wood, more plastic. Smaller rooms with more crowding. No brick, no peeling paint, no wheezing furnace.

The students seemed friendly—Rob's blond good looks had something to do with that, Kaitlyn thought. He was clearly a high-status, desirable boy, and he ate lunch with her and Anna and Lewis. Kait could see the glances other girls shot at their table.

Anna was clearly high-status, too—because she was beautiful, not at all nervous, and she didn't seem to care if anyone approached her. By the end of lunch, several girls had come by offering to show the newcomers around. They stayed to chat. One mentioned a party on Saturday.

Kait was very happy.

The thing she'd worried most about was explaining why she and the others were living together. She didn't want to tell these California girls anything about psychic powers and the Institute. She didn't want to be different at this school. She wanted to *fit in*.

But fortunately Lewis took care of that. Between snapping pictures of the girls, he grinned and said that a nice old man had given them a lot of money to go to school here. No one believed him, but it created an irresistible aura of mystery that enhanced their status even more.

At the end of the day, Kaitlyn walked out of art studio class feeling blissful. The art teacher had called her portfolio "impressive" and her style "fluid and arresting." All she wanted to make the world perfect was Rob.

Gabriel, of course, didn't associate with anyone, and ate lunch alone. Kaitlyn saw him several times that day, always away from people, always with his lip curled. He could have had tremendous status himself, she thought, because he looked so handsome and moody and dangerous, but he didn't seem to want it.

Marisol collected them after school in a silver-blue Ford van—all except Gabriel, who didn't show up at the pickup point. Kaitlyn thought about his parole and hoped he was on his way back to the Institute.

"Now for some testing," Joyce said when they got home.

That was fine with Kaitlyn. She was jubilant from her first day at school, and an afternoon of testing meant an afternoon with Rob. She still hadn't figured out a plan for helping him discover she was female, but it was always at the back of her mind. Maybe an opportunity would come up spontaneously.

But the first thing Joyce did was send Rob upstairs, saying she'd call him after she got the others settled.

"The REG is ready, Lewis," she added. She sat Lewis down at the same study carrel as before. This time Kait was bold enough to come up behind them.

"What is that thing?" she asked, looking at the machine in front of Lewis. It looked like a computer, but the monitor had a grid-marked screen with a wiggly green line running across the middle. Like a hospital monitor charting a patient's heartbeat.

"This is a random event generator," Joyce said. "It's a computer that only does one thing—it spits out random numbers. It's producing numbers right now, some positive, some negative, all completely random. That's what the green line is charting. Lewis's job is to make the line go up higher—to influence the machine to spit out more positive numbers than negative ones."

"You can do that?" Kait asked, looking at Lewis in surprise. "With your mind?"

"Yeah, that's what PK is. Mind over matter. This is actually a lot easier than making dice come up a certain number—but I can do that, too, sometimes."

"Stay away from Vegas, kid," Joyce said, rapping him on the head with her knuckles. "They'd shoot out your kneecaps."

She turned to Anna. "Right, you. Same as yesterday. I want you to tell that mouse which hole to go in."

Anna already had the white mouse out of its cage. "Come on, Mickey. Let's go make history."

"Right. Now, Kaitlyn," Joyce said. She nodded Kait toward the folding screen, where Marisol was wheeling up a machine on a cart. Kaitlyn eyed the dials and wires apprehensively.

"Don't be nervous. It's just an EEG machine," Joyce said. "An electroencephalograph. It records your brain waves."

"Oh, great."

"That isn't the part you're not going to like. You're going to really hate *this*." She held up what looked like a tube of toothpaste. "It's electrode cream, and it's murder to get out of your hair."

Kaitlyn sat in the reclining chair, resigned.

Marisol's thickly lashed brown eyes met Kait's only for the briefest of moments. Her full lips were curved in a bored, unchanging pout.

"This is just prep stuff to clean your skin," she said, squeezing a plastic bottle over a ball of cotton. She swabbed several places on Kaitlyn's head, forehead, and temples.

"Don't move your head." She dabbed some of the toothpaste on Kaitlyn's temple, then dabbed more on an electrode. Kaitlyn watched out of the corner of her eye as the wicked-looking little thing was stuck to her.

It didn't hurt. It tickled slightly. Kait shut her eyes and relaxed until Marisol finished wiring her up.

"Now, Medusa," Joyce said. "As I said, we're going to monitor your brain waves while you're doing your stuff. Brain wave levels change depending on what you're doing: Beta waves show you're attending to something, theta waves show you're drowsy. We're looking for alpha waves—the ones usually associated with psychic activity."

She saw Kaitlyn's expression and added, "Just try to ignore all this equipment, right? You'll be doing exactly the same thing as yesterday."

Kaitlyn looked sideways without moving her head, and saw Marisol bringing two strangers into the lab. New volunteers. Kaitlyn felt a sudden sharp twinge.

"Joyce, is one of those volunteers . . . for Gabriel?"

"I don't know where Gabriel is—although I'd like to," Joyce said grimly, handing Kait a pencil and clipboard. "Now relax, kiddo. No blindfold or earphones this time."

Kaitlyn shut her eyes again. She could hear some activity

on the other side of the folding screen—Joyce giving a photo to the volunteer.

"Right," Joyce said. "The subject is concentrating, Kait. You try and receive her thought."

It was only then that Kait discovered how anxious she was. Yesterday she hadn't known what to expect. Today she did know, and she was uneasy. Worried that she wouldn't be able to perform—and worried that she would.

She didn't feel like sliding down that mental chute into nothingness again. And if she did succeed . . . what if she drew something as grotesque as yesterday's picture?

Don't think about it. Take it easy. This is what you're *here* for, remember?

Don't you want to learn to control your power?

Kaitlyn gritted her teeth, then made a supreme effort to relax, to tune the world out. She could hear muted voices.

"Still beta waves on the EEC." That was Marisol.

"Give her time." That was Joyce.

Be calm, Kaitlyn thought. Ignore them. The chair's comfortable. You didn't get much sleep last night.

Slowly, gradually, she felt herself sink into drowsiness.

"Theta waves."

Blackness, falling . . .

"Alpha waves."

"Good!"

Kaitlyn's hand began to cramp and itch. But as she lifted

the pencil, eyes shut, she suddenly remembered yesterday's picture. Anxiety twisted in her stomach.

"Back to beta waves," Marisol said, as if announcing a death in the family.

Joyce peered around the screen. "Kaitlyn, what's wrong?"

"I don't know." Now Kait felt guilty as well as anxious. "I just can't focus."

"Hmm." Joyce seemed to hesitate, then she said, "Right, wait a sec," and disappeared.

She was back again quickly. "Shut your eyes, Kait."

Kaitlyn obeyed automatically. She felt a quick dab and then the touch of something cold on her forehead. Very cold.

"Now try again," Joyce said, and Kait heard her go.

Again Kait tried to relax. This time she felt the darkness swirl around her immediately. Then she had an odd sensation, a feeling of pressure in her head. Like an explosion building. And then—

—pictures. Images rushing in, almost with more force than Kaitlyn could stand.

"Alpha waves like crazy," a faraway voice said. Kaitlyn scarcely heard it.

Nothing like this had ever happened to her before—but she was too startled to be afraid. The pictures were kaleidoscopic, each passing in a flash almost before she could recognize it.

Gabriel. Something purple. Joyce—or someone like her.

Something purple and irregular. A doorway with someone standing in it. A bunch of purple round things. Something tall and white—a tower? A bunch of purple . . . grapes.

She could feel her hand moving, drawing small circles over and over on the paper. She couldn't help opening her eyes— and the instant she did, the images in her head vanished.

She'd drawn a bunch of grapes. Made sense. That was the picture she'd gotten most frequently.

Recklessly, ignoring the wires, she stood up and looked around the screen.

"What happened?" she demanded of Joyce. "I saw pictures in my head—what did you *do?*"

Joyce stood up quickly. "Just put on another electrode."

Kaitlyn put a hand to her forehead. It felt as if there was something between the electrode and the skin.

"Over your third eye," Marisol added stonily.

Joyce glanced back at her. Marisol's olive-skinned face was expressionless.

Kaitlyn had frozen. Her drawing yesterday . . . "What's— what's a third eye?"

"According to legend, it's the seat of all psychic power," Joyce said lightly. "It's in the center of your forehead, where the pineal gland is."

"But—but why would an electrode—"

"God, she's still in alpha waves," Marisol interrupted.

"Time to get you unwired," Joyce said briskly. She began pulling electrodes off. Kaitlyn felt the forehead one go, but Joyce's hands moved so quickly, she didn't see what became of it.

"By the way, what did you get?" Joyce asked, taking the clipboard from her. "Oh, *terrific*," she cried. "Oh, look at this, everybody!"

The warmth in her voice made Kaitlyn forget what she'd been upset about.

"I don't believe it—you got the target picture exactly, Kait! *Exactly*, down to the number of grapes on the bunch."

Anna and Lewis were crowding around. The volunteer, a tall girl with night-dark skin, showed Kait the photo she was holding. It was a bunch of grapes—and Kait's own drawing might have been traced directly from it.

"That's impressive," a warm, drawling voice said from behind Kaitlyn. She felt her heart pick up speed.

"I think it was an accident," she told Rob, turning.

"No accident," Joyce said. "Good concentration. And a good volunteer; we'll have to have you back."

Rob was looking at Kaitlyn's face, his golden eyes darkening. "Are you okay? You look kind of tired."

"Actually—this is so strange—I just got a headache." Kait put her fingers to the center of her forehead, where pain like an ice pick had suddenly begun jabbing. "Oh—I guess I didn't get enough sleep last night. . . ."

"I think she needs a break," Rob said.

"Of course," Joyce said at once. "Why don't you go upstairs and lie down, Kait? We're done here."

Kait was wobbly on her feet.

"I'll help," Rob said. "Hold on to me."

It was the perfect opportunity; better than any plan or trick Kaitlyn could have thought up. And it was *useless,* because all at once her head hurt so badly that she only wanted to lie down and go to sleep.

The pain came in throbbing waves. Rob had to lead her into her bedroom because she couldn't see straight.

"Lie down," he said, and turned off the bedside lamp.

Kaitlyn eased down, then felt the mattress give under Rob's weight beside her. She didn't open her eyes. She couldn't; even the diffuse afternoon light from the window hurt.

"It sounds like a migraine," Rob said. "Is the pain all on one side?"

"It's here. In the middle," Kaitlyn whispered, indicating the spot. Now she was feeling waves of nausea. Oh, *wonderful.* How romantic.

"Here?" Rob said, sounding surprised. His fingers on her forehead were blessedly cool. Strange; they'd been warm last time.

"Yes," Kaitlyn whispered wretchedly. "I'll be all right. Just go away." And now, to top everything off, she'd told the boy she loved to get lost.

Rob ignored the suggestion. "Kait, I was wrong. It's not

a migraine; it's not even an ordinary headache. I think you're sick from burning energy too fast—psychic energy. You've run yourself dry."

Kaitlyn managed a feeble "So?"

"So—I can help you. If you'll let me."

For some reason, that frightened Kaitlyn. But a stab of agony made up her mind. "All right . . ."

"Good. Now, relax, Kaitlyn." Rob's voice was soft but commanding. "It may feel strange at first, but don't fight it. I have to find an open transfer point. . . ."

Cool, deft fingers touched either side of Kaitlyn's neck, paused for a moment as if searching for something. Then lifted, not finding it. They moved to probe delicately at the tender area behind the jaw. "No . . ." Rob murmured.

Kaitlyn felt her hand gently taken. Rob's thumb centered on her palm, his index finger directly opposite it on the back of her hand. Again he seemed to be searching for something, moving his fingers minutely. Almost like a nurse feeling for a vein before taking blood.

"No."

Rob shifted. "Let's try this—move that way a little." Kaitlyn followed his urging and scooted toward the side of the bed. She opened her eyes automatically—and then quickly shut them in alarm. Rob was bending over her, his face very close. Suddenly a pounding heart added to her pain.

"What . . . ?" she gasped.

"This is just one of the most direct ways to transfer energy," he said simply. "You need a lot."

His lack of embarrassment or self-consciousness saved her. Kaitlyn kept her eyes shut and held still as he put his forehead to hers. Their lips were almost touching.

"Got it," he murmured. His mouth actually brushed hers, but he didn't seem to notice. "Now . . . think about where it hurts. Concentrate on the place."

A minute ago she hadn't been able to think about anything else. But now . . . Kaitlyn's awareness was flooded with *him*. She didn't want to move or breathe. She could sense his entire body, even though only his forehead was touching her. Third eye to third eye, she thought dizzily.

Then, all at once, a new sensation rushed in and drove out all thought of anything physical. It was so new that she didn't have any way to classify it.

It wasn't like sight, or touch, or taste, but Kaitlyn's fogged brain tried to interpret it that way. If it had been sight, it would have been millions of sparkling lights that glowed and glittered like jewels. A dynamic, changing pattern of multicolored sparks, twinkles, and flares.

If it had been touch, it might have been pressure—not an uncomfortable pressure, but one that swept away all the pain of her headache. Like a river rushing through her mind, clearing out everything stagnant and clotted and decayed.

If it had been taste, it would have been like fresh, pure

water—water she drank greedily, like an exhausted runner whose mouth has been full of choking dust.

It was electrifying—overwhelming. It didn't simply take away the pain. It filled her with life.

Kaitlyn never knew how long she lay drinking in the life-giving energy. But some time later, she realized that Rob was slowly sitting up. She opened her eyes.

They looked at each other.

"I . . . thank you," Kaitlyn said, barely above a whisper.

She expected him to smile and nod. Instead he blinked. It was the first time she'd seen him at a loss for words.

And then, as they looked at each other, a simple thing happened. Neither of them looked away. With ordinary friends you always look away after a moment—or you speak.

But Rob didn't speak and he didn't look away.

The air between them seemed to shimmer.

# CHAPTER 9

It was as if Rob were seeing her for the first time. More than that—it was as if he were seeing a *girl* for the first time. He looked astonished and wondering, like a person who had never heard music before suddenly catching a few notes of a beautiful melody on the wind. Catching it and wanting desperately to follow it.

His expression was that of someone on the brink of the greatest discovery of his life.

"Kaitlyn?" he whispered, and his voice was awed and questioning and almost frightened.

Kaitlyn couldn't speak. They were both on the threshold of something so big—so *transforming*—that it terrified her. It would change everything, forever. But she *wanted* it. She wanted it to happen.

The whole universe seemed to be hushed and waiting, breath held.

But Rob didn't move. He was on the brink of discovery—but not there yet.

He needs help, Kaitlyn thought. He still doesn't understand what's going on.

It was up to her to show him, to help him take that first step—if she wanted to. And she did. Kaitlyn suddenly felt calm and clear. She saw in her mind what was going to happen, like a picture already finished.

She would cradle his face with her hands and kiss him—very softly. And Rob would look at her with such surprise. So completely innocent—but not stupid. Rob wasn't slow to catch on. After she kissed him the second time, the astonishment would turn to dawning wonder. His golden eyes would start smoldering the way they did when he was angry . . . but for a very different reason.

Then he'd put his arms around her, and kiss her—so lightly—and the energy, the healing energy, would flow between them. And everything would be wonderful.

Breath held, Kaitlyn reached up to touch Rob's face, seeing her own graceful artist's fingers on his jaw. Even that little contact sent sparks dancing up her palm. It all seemed so simple and natural—as if she knew what to do without thinking. As if she'd always known, in some wise place inside.

Imagine it—Kaitlyn the cold, knowing what to do, feeling so sure. It was all about to happen.

Then voices broke into her reverie. Laughing, ordinary

voices that didn't belong at all to the beautiful new world Kaitlyn was inhabiting. She looked up in confusion.

Lewis and Anna were just outside the door. Gabriel was behind them.

"Hey, Kait," Lewis began cheerfully. And then, seeing her face, "Uh, oops."

Anna's dark eyes were stricken and apologetic. "We didn't mean to interrupt," she said, grabbing Lewis's shoulder as if to propel him away.

"A little therapeutic touch in the dark?" Gabriel asked blandly.

Sick dismay swept through Kaitlyn. The discovery, the wonder, in Rob's face was shattered. It had been so fragile, something that was about to be born rather than something that already existed—and now it was gone. Snatched away, leaving only Rob's usual kindness and concern. His affection for Anna and Lewis.

And his hatred for Gabriel.

"Kait had a headache," he said, standing up to face Gabriel directly. "If it's any of your business."

"She seems to be better now," Gabriel observed, looking around him at Kaitlyn. Kaitlyn glared at him with deadly heat.

"It would help if people would leave me alone," she said.

"We were just going," Anna said, her eyes telegraphing her contrition to Kaitlyn. "Come on, Lewis."

"That's right," Rob said, and then, to Kait's utter frustration and disbelief, he walked out the door himself. "Want me to close this?" he asked.

If it had been a ploy to make sure Gabriel and the others stayed away, Kaitlyn would have understood. But it wasn't. Rob had reverted completely. The only emotion she could see in his golden eyes now was brotherly affection.

And there was no way to get through to him, no way to change things back. At least for today, it was over.

She didn't know who to be angry with—Gabriel and the others or Rob himself. She might just kill Rob—but she loved him more than ever.

"Yes, please close the door," she said.

When they were all gone, Kaitlyn lay on her bed, watching as cool violet twilight replaced the warm light of afternoon. The room became shadowy, mysterious. She shut her eyes.

A sound alerted her—a sound like paper rustling. Sitting up quickly, she stared around the room. There it was, something white glimmering out of the shadows, creeping in under the door. No, not creeping—being *pushed.*

Kaitlyn quietly got off the bed and padded to the door. Yellow light from the hallway was shining through the crack beneath the door—and the paper was still moving. She ignored it, grabbed the doorknob, and yanked the door open.

Marisol was kneeling on the hallway floor.

The older girl's chin jerked up, and for a moment her brown eyes met Kaitlyn's. They looked shocked and surly. Then she was on her feet and heading for the stairs.

"Oh, no, you don't!" Fired by all the emotions of the past afternoon, Kait pounced. Frustration, excitement, and fury gave her the strength to seize Marisol and spin her around.

"What were you doing pushing stuff under my door? What *is* that?" Kaitlyn demanded, pointing to the piece of folded paper lying on the threshold. Marisol just tossed her hair out of her eyes and looked defiant.

Kaitlyn let go of her long enough to pick up the paper, then blocked her as she headed for the stairway again.

"This is my picture!" It was the one Kait had done yesterday, the one of her own face with the extra eye, the one she'd left on the lab floor.

Except that now it had writing on it.

Scrawled across the bottom in heavy black pen were the words: WATCH OUT. THIS COULD HAPPEN TO YOU.

"Another joke?" Kaitlyn said grimly, drawing herself up.

Marisol, who was several inches taller, just looked down at her with smoldering brown eyes. Kaitlyn, reckless of the consequences, grabbed Marisol's arm and *shook* her.

"Why are you trying to scare me? Is it because you hate psychics?"

Marisol laughed shortly.

"Do you want me to go *away?* Is it . . . oh, I don't know, some jealousy thing or something?" Kaitlyn was desperately groping for a reason that made sense.

Marisol pressed her full lips together.

"Okay, fine," Kaitlyn said, her voice slightly shaky. "I guess I'll just have to go and ask Joyce."

She got halfway to the stairs before Marisol spoke.

"Joyce can't help you. She doesn't know what's really going on. She wasn't around for the pilot study—but I was."

"What's a pilot study?" Kaitlyn asked, without turning.

"Never mind. The point is, you won't get help from Joyce. All she cares about is getting her experiments done, getting her name in the journals. She's blind to what's really happening. That's why Zetes hired her."

"But what does this thing *mean?*" Kaitlyn asked, shaking the paper.

Silence. Kaitlyn turned around. More silence.

"God, you're dumb," Marisol said at last. "Don't you remember the experiment today? Didn't you wonder at all how you got that picture of the grapes?"

Kaitlyn remembered that kaleidoscopic flood of images. "I assume because I'm psychic," she said, but she could hear the stiff defensiveness in her own voice.

"If you were *really* psychic, you'd figure out why you're here. And then you'd be on the next plane home."

Kaitlyn had had it with innuendo. "What are you *talking*

about? Why can't you say something straight instead of all this secret stuff?" she almost shouted. "Unless you don't really have anything to say—"

Marisol had flinched at the volume of Kaitlyn's voice— and now she suddenly shoved past her, elbowing Kait hard in the arm. As she reached the stairway, she glanced back and snapped, "I came up to tell you you're late for dinner."

Kaitlyn sagged against the wall.

This had been the most confusing roller coaster of a day . . . and Marisol seemed to be *crazy,* that was all. Except that didn't explain what had happened during Kait's experiment. When Joyce had put that "electrode" on Kaitlyn's forehead . . .

Over my third eye, Kait thought. She looked at the now crumpled paper. The extra eye in the picture stared up at her grotesquely, as if trying to tell her something.

I've got to talk to somebody. I can't deal with this alone. I need *help.*

The decision made her feel better. Kaitlyn wadded the paper up and stuck it in her pocket. Then she hurried down the stairs to dinner.

"What's it got to do with me?" Gabriel said, flicking the paper back toward Kaitlyn. He was lying on his bed reading a magazine about cars—expensive cars. "It's not my problem."

Kaitlyn caught the paper in midair. It had taken a great deal of control to come here. She probably wouldn't have done it except that she couldn't face Rob alone just now, and Anna had been on the phone with her family since dinner.

Grimly Kaitlyn held on to her precarious calm.

"If there's anything to what Marisol is saying, then it's *everybody's* problem," she told Gabriel tightly. "And *you* were the one who said that there was something wrong here."

Gabriel shrugged. "What if I did?"

Kaitlyn felt like screaming. "You really think something's wrong—but you don't care about finding *out?* You wouldn't want to *do* anything about it?"

A faint smile touched Gabriel's lips. "Of course I'm going to do something. I'm going to do what I do best."

Kaitlyn saw it coming, but couldn't avoid feeding him the straight line. Feeling like Sergeant Joe Friday at the end of a scene, she rapped out, "And what's that?"

"Taking care of myself," Gabriel said smugly. His dark eyes were full of wicked delight at having the last word.

Kaitlyn didn't bother to hide her disgust as she left.

Outside his door, she leaned against the wall again. Lewis was in the study playing Primal Scream's newest CD at tooth-vibrating levels. Anna was still in the bedroom on the phone. And as for Rob . . .

"Did the headache come back?"

Kaitlyn whirled, somehow feeling cornered against the wall. Why didn't she ever hear Rob coming?

"No," she said. "I'm fine. At least . . . No, I *am* fine." She couldn't deal with Rob right now, she really couldn't. She was afraid for him—afraid of what she might do to him if she got the chance. It seemed equally likely that she'd kiss him or kill him.

"What's that?" he said, and the next thing Kait knew, he was taking the paper out of her hand. She tried to snatch it back, but he was too fast.

"That's nothing—I mean—"

Rob smoothed the paper, glanced at it, then looked up at her sharply. "Did *you* draw this?"

"Yes . . . but I didn't do the writing. I don't—Oh, it's all so confusing." Kaitlyn had come to the end of her resources. She was tired of fighting, of pushing, of badgering people. She was *tired.*

"Come on," Rob said gently. The hand that cupped her elbow was gentle, too, but irresistible. He guided her without hesitation to the one room on the second floor that wasn't occupied—the bedroom he and Lewis shared.

"Now, tell me all about it." He sat beside her on the bed, as naturally as if he were her brother, as close as that. And with as little ulterior motive. It was agonizing—and wonderful at the same time.

And his eyes—he was looking at her with those grave golden eyes, extraordinary eyes. *Wise* eyes.

I can trust him, Kait thought. No matter what else happens between us, I can trust him.

"It's Marisol," she said, and then she was telling him everything. About waking up that first night to find Marisol in her room, about the strange things Marisol had said. *Watch out or get out. This place is different than you think.* About Marisol claiming it was all a joke the next morning. About the experiment today, and how the pictures had come into her mind—after Joyce put the cold thing on her forehead. About Marisol pushing the drawing under her door.

"And then I tried to get her to explain—but all she talked about was some pilot study, and how if I knew why I was *really* here, I would be on the next plane home. And how Joyce didn't know what was really going on, either."

She stopped. She half expected Rob to laugh, but he didn't. He was frowning, looking puzzled and intent.

"If Joyce doesn't know what's going on, then who does?"

"I guess Mr. Zetes. But, Rob, it's all so crazy."

Rob's mouth tightened. "Maybe," he said under his breath. "But I wondered about him. . . ."

"That first day? The speech about us psychics being so superior and following different laws?"

Rob nodded. Kaitlyn was meeting his eyes without self-consciousness now, as grim as he was. He believed her, and that made this whole thing much more serious than before. This was *business.*

"And why he brought Gabriel here," Rob said.

"Yes," Kaitlyn said slowly. Someday she really would have to talk to Rob about Gabriel—but not now. "But what does it all add up to?"

"I don't know." Rob looked at the drawing again. "But I know we have to find out. We have to talk to Joyce."

Kaitlyn swallowed. It had been a lot easier to threaten to tell Joyce in the heat of anger than it was to consider going to her now. But of course, Rob was right.

"Let's do it," she said.

Joyce's room was off the little wood-paneled hallway under the stairs that led to the front lab. It had originally been a solarium, a glass-enclosed porch. Not only that, but the French-door entrance was so large that anyone in the living room or foyer could see straight in. Only Joyce, Kait thought, could live in a room like this without any privacy. It probably had something to do with the fact that Joyce *always* looked good, whether she was doing business in a tailored suit or lounging in layered pink sweats—like tonight.

"Hi, guys," she said, looking up from a laptop computer. Light from her bedside lamp reflected off the glass walls.

Kaitlyn sat gingerly on the bed, and Rob pulled up the desk chair. He was still holding the drawing.

Joyce looked from one of them to the other. "Why so serious?"

Kaitlyn took a deep breath at the same time as Rob said, "We need to talk to you."

"Yes?"

Kait and Rob exchanged glances. Then Kaitlyn burst out, "It's about Marisol."

Joyce's eyebrows lifted toward her sleek blond hair. "Yes?"

"She's been saying things to Kaitlyn," Rob said. "Weird things, about the Institute being dangerous. And she wrote . . . this . . . on a drawing Kaitlyn did."

Still looking puzzled, Joyce took the paper, scanned it. Kait felt her stomach knot. She had stopped breathing completely.

When Joyce threw back her head, Kait thought for a moment she was going to scream. Instead, she burst into laughter.

Peals of laughter, musical and uncontrollable. After a minute she calmed down into snorts, but when she looked at Kaitlyn and Rob, she went off again.

Kaitlyn felt her own mouth stretch into a smile, but it was the polite, unhappy smile of someone waiting to be let in on a joke. At last Joyce collapsed against the mounded pillows, wiping tears from her eyes.

"I'm sorry . . . it's not really funny. It's just . . . it's her medication. She must not be taking it."

"Marisol takes medication?" Rob asked.

"Yes. And she's fine when she *does* take it; it's just that sometimes she forgets or decides she doesn't need it, and then . . . well. You see." Joyce waved the paper. "I suppose she means it symbolically. She's always been a little worried about psychics misusing their powers." Joyce turned to Kaitlyn, obviously struggling not to grin. "You didn't take her *literally,* I hope?"

Kaitlyn wanted to drop through the floor.

How could she have been so stupid? Of course, it had all been a terrible mistake—she should have realized that. And now she'd blundered in on Marisol's emotional problems, or mental problems, or whatever.

"I'm sorry," she gasped.

Joyce waved a hand, biting her lip to keep from laughing. "Oh, look."

"No, I'm really sorry. It was just—it was kind of spooky, and I didn't understand. . . . I *thought* there must be some simple explanation, but . . ." Kaitlyn took a breath. "Oh, God, I hope we haven't gotten her into trouble."

"No—but maybe I should let Mr. Zetes in on this," Joyce said, sobering. "He was the one who recruited her; she was actually hired before I was. I think she's a friend of his daughter's."

Mr. Zetes had a daughter? She must be pretty old, Kaitlyn thought. It was surprising she would have a friend as young as Marisol.

"Anyway, don't worry about it," Joyce said. "I'll talk to Marisol about her meds tomorrow and get everything straightened out. By the way, Kait, when did you draw this?"

"Oh—yesterday, during the remote viewing experiment. I dropped it when I heard that guy with the Mohawk screaming."

"How is that guy?" Rob asked softly. He was looking at Joyce with steady golden eyes.

"He's fine," Joyce said, and Kaitlyn thought she sounded slightly defensive. "The hospital gave him a tranquilizer and released him."

"Because," Rob went on, "I still think you should be careful with Ga—"

"Yes, right. I'm going to change the protocol with Gabriel's experiment." Joyce's tone closed the subject and she glanced at her clock.

"I'm so embarrassed," Kaitlyn said as she and Rob walked back up the stairs.

"Why? After what Marisol did, you had every right to ask what was going on."

It was true, but Kait still felt that somehow she should have realized. She should have more faith in Mr. Zetes, who, after all, had paid a lot of money to give the five of them a new life. She should have *known* that Marisol was having paranoid delusions.

The new life felt a bit lonely as Kait and Rob parted in the hallway. It was maddening to have him say good night so cheerfully, as if he *enjoyed* being her big brother. As if being anything else had never crossed his mind—which, in his view, it probably hadn't. He seemed to have wiped the entire incident this afternoon out of his consciousness.

Anna sat up as Kaitlyn came in the bedroom. "Where've you been?"

"Downstairs." Kaitlyn wanted to talk to Anna, but she was

very, very tired. She fumbled in a drawer for her nightgown. "I think I'll go to sleep early—do you mind?"

"Of course not. You're probably still sick," Anna said, instantly solicitous.

Just before falling asleep, Kaitlyn murmured, "Anna? Do you know what a pilot study is?"

"I think it's a kind of practice experiment—you do it first, before the real experiment. Like a pilot episode for a TV show comes first."

"Oh. Thanks." Kaitlyn was too sleepy to say more. But it occurred to her that maybe Marisol had told the truth about one thing. Marisol had claimed to have been "around for the pilot study," and Joyce had said that Marisol had been recruited before *her*.

The rest was nonsense, though. Like the idea that Joyce had put something weird on her forehead—God, she was glad Rob hadn't mentioned that to Joyce. Joyce would have thought Kaitlyn needed medication, too.

And Rob . . . But she wouldn't think about Rob now. She'd deal with him tomorrow.

All that night she had strange dreams. In one she was on a windswept peninsula, looking out over a cold gray ocean. In another she was with Marisol and a group of strangers. All of them had eyes in their foreheads. Marisol smirked and said, "Think you're so smart? You're growing one, too. The seed's been planted." Then Gabriel appeared and said,

"We've got to look out for ourselves. You see what can happen otherwise?"

Kaitlyn did see. Rob had fallen into a deep crevasse and he was shouting for help. Kaitlyn reached out to him, but Gabriel pulled her back, and Rob's voice kept echoing. . . .

All at once she was awake. The room was full of pale morning light, and the shouting was real.

# CHAPTER 10

The shouts were distant and muffled, but unmistakably hysterical. The clock said 6:15 A.M.

Gabriel, Kait thought wildly, jumping out of bed. What has he done now?

Anna was up, too, her long black hair loose. Her eyes were alert, but not panicked. "What is it?"

"I don't know!"

She and Kait spilled out into the hallway without bothering to put on robes. Rob was just emerging from his room, wearing a tattered pair of pajama bottoms. Kait felt a surge of relief that he wasn't the one doing the shouting.

"It's coming from downstairs," he said.

He took the stairs two at a time, with Kait and Anna right behind him. Kait could hear words in the shouting now.

"Help! God! Somebody help! Quick!"

"It's Lewis!" she said.

The three of them swung around through the dining room and into the kitchen. The shouting stopped.

"Oh, *no,*" Anna said.

Lewis was standing by the kitchen sink, panting. There was a sort of heap at his feet, a heap with mahogany-colored hair at one end.

Marisol.

*"What happened?"* Kait gasped. Lewis just shook his head. Rob had dropped to his knees at once, and was gently turning Marisol over. A trembling started in Kait's legs as she saw the face. Under her olive complexion, Marisol looked chalky. Even her lips were pale. Her eyes were open a little, showing slits of white eyeball.

"Did you call nine-one-one?" Anna asked quietly.

"It's no use," Lewis said in a strangled voice. He was braced against the sink for support, looking down. His face, normally sweet and impish, was drawn with horror. "She's dead. I know she's dead."

Waves of chills swept over Kaitlyn. What Rob was moving was now Marisol's *body,* not Marisol. That one word, "dead," made all the difference. Suddenly Kait didn't want to touch . . . *it.* The body.

She knelt by it anyway, and put a hand on its—Marisol's— chest. Then she jumped a little.

"I think she's breathing."

"She's not dead," Rob said positively. His eyes were shut,

his fingers at Marisol's temples. "Her life force is really low, but she's alive. I'm going to try to help." He stopped talking and sat still, his face lined with concentration.

In the background, Kait could hear Anna calling 911.

"What *happened*, Lewis?" she demanded again.

"She had a sort of . . . It looked like a seizure. I came down early because I was hungry, and she was in here cutting up grape-fruits, and I said hi, and she was kind of crabby, and then all of a sudden she fell down." Lewis swallowed and blinked rapidly. "I tried to pick her up, but she just kept jerking and shaking. And then she stopped moving. I thought she was dead."

Medication, Kait thought. If Marisol had been on medica-tion for seizures—and she stopped taking it . . . Or for diabe-tes. Could diabetes give you seizures?

"Where's Joyce?" she said, getting up suddenly. It was the first question she should have asked. Joyce was always down here before the kids, drinking mugs of black coffee and helping Marisol make breakfast.

"Here's a note on the fridge," Anna said. Underneath a magnet shaped like a strawberry was a note in spiky, casual handwriting.

*Marisol—*

*Coffee filters you bought ystdy wrong kind. I'm going to exchange. Start*

*bkfst—cut 3 grapefruit, make muffins.
Muff mix in blue bowl in fridge. Where
did you put receipt?*

*—J*

"She's at the store," Kait said, and at that moment heard the front door open.

"Joyce!" She and Lewis shouted it together. Kaitlyn rushed to the dining room entrance. "Joyce, something's happened to Marisol!"

Joyce came running. When she saw Marisol on the floor, she dumped her ecological cloth grocery bag on the counter, where several apples and a box of coffee filters spilled out.

"Oh, my God—what happened?" she said sharply. "Is she breathing all right?" Her hands flew from Marisol's wrist to her neck, searching for a pulse.

Rob didn't answer. He was sitting lotus style by Marisol's head, eyes shut, fingers on her temples. Early sun slanted in the east window and shone on his tanned shoulders.

"I think she's breathing okay now," Lewis whispered. "He said he would try to help her."

Joyce looked hard at Rob, then the strain in her face eased. "Good," she said.

"Is she epileptic?" Kaitlyn asked softly but urgently. "Because Lewis said she had a seizure."

"What? No." Joyce spoke absently. "Oh—you mean the medication? No, it's for something else entirely; he said a psychiatrist prescribed it. God knows, maybe she took an overdose. I never even got to talk to her about it."

"I know. We saw your note," Kait began. "But—"

"Listen—sirens," Anna said.

After that, things happened very quickly. Kait and Anna ran to the front door to wave down the paramedics. Just as the rescue van arrived, a black limousine pulled up behind it. Mr. Zetes got out.

And then there was a lot of confusion. Mr. Z was walking very quickly, despite his cane—and the paramedics were rushing inside with equipment—and the rottweilers were barking—and Kait was behind everyone, trying to see into the kitchen. The noise was deafening.

"Get those dogs out!" one of the paramedics shouted.

Mr. Zetes snapped an order and the dogs backed into the dining room.

"Clear this room!" another paramedic said. She was pulling at Rob, trying to get him away from Marisol. Rob was resisting.

Then Mr. Zetes spoke, in a voice that quieted everyone. "All you young people—go upstairs. You, too, Rob. We'll let the professionals take care of this."

"Sir, she's barely hanging on—" Rob began, his voice thick with worry.

"Move!" the pulling paramedic shouted. Rob moved.

On her way up the stairs, Kait came face-to-face with Gabriel, who was coming down.

"They don't want us," she said. "Go back up. How come it took you so long, anyway?"

"I never get up until seven," Gabriel murmured, backing up. He was fully dressed.

"Didn't you hear the yelling?"

"It was hard to ignore, but I managed."

Rob glared at him as he passed. Gabriel returned it with a derisive look that started with Rob's bare feet and ended with Rob's tousled head.

"We can see from the study window," Lewis said, and they all followed him into the alcove—except Gabriel, who went to one of the other windows.

In a few moments the paramedics came out with a stretcher. Lewis's hand made a slight movement toward his camera, which was lying on the window seat. Then it dropped to his side again.

They all watched as the stretcher was loaded into the back of the paramedics' van. Kait felt both frightened and strangely remorseful. Marisol's face had looked so small among all the big rescue workers and the equipment.

"I hope she's all right. She's got to be all right," she said, and then she sat down on the window seat. Her legs were very shaky.

Anna sat down and put an arm around her. "At least Joyce is going, too," she said in her quiet, gentle voice. A little of her calm penetrated Kaitlyn, like a cool wind blowing. Below, Joyce climbed into the van and it pulled out. The black limo stayed.

Rob was leaning against the window glass, one knee on the seat beside Kait. He was completely unselfconscious about his lack of dress.

"Mr. Z sure does have bad luck," he said softly. "Every time he comes here, he finds trouble."

The cool wind blowing through Kaitlyn turned cold. She looked quickly at Rob. "What are you saying?"

"Nothing," he said, still gazing out the window. "It's just too bad for him, that's all."

Lewis and Anna looked puzzled. Kait stared down at the black limousine, feeling an uneasy stirring in her stomach.

After a while, Mr. Zetes called them down to go to school. Nobody wanted breakfast. Kait didn't want to go to school, either, but Mr. Zetes didn't ask her opinion. He escorted them out to the limousine and ordered the driver to take them.

"Oh, God, I left my sociology book," Kait said when they reached the corner. The limousine, instead of turning around, backed up.

Kait ran up the porch steps and yanked the door open, conscious of the five people waiting on her in the car. She burst inside—and then stopped in middash. Mr. Z's two rottweilers were running toward her, toenails clacking and skidding on the hardwood floor. A terrible baying struck her with the force of a physical blow.

Kaitlyn had never been afraid of a dog in her life—but these weren't dogs, they were salivating monsters whose barking made the ceiling ring. She could see their pink and black gums.

She looked around desperately for a weapon—and saw Mr. Zetes.

He was standing in the little hallway just in front of Joyce's room. The strange thing was that Kaitlyn hadn't seen him arrive—and she was sure he hadn't been there when she burst in. She'd been looking in that direction, because that was where the dogs had come from.

Even stranger, she would have sworn that no door had opened or closed over there. The door to the front lab, just behind him, was shut. So were the French doors to his left— the ones that opened on Joyce's room.

But there *wasn't* any other door—to Mr. Z's right was only a solid wall that supported the staircase. So he *had* to have come from the lab or Joyce's room.

Kait saw his mouth move, and the dogs shut up. He gave her a courtly nod, his piercing dark eyes on her face.

"I forgot my sociology book," Kaitlyn said unsteadily. Her pulse was hammering, and for some reason she felt as if she were being caught in a lie.

"I see. Run up and get it," was all he said, but he waited until she came downstairs with it, and saw her out the door.

The drawing came, appropriately, during art studio class.

Kaitlyn had been thinking about Mr. Zetes all day, and had made the interesting discovery that it's quite possible to be miserable during lunch even though important people are being nice to you. Several cheerleaders and three or four attractive guys had sat down to talk to her group—but it didn't matter. However Kaitlyn tried to listen to them, her mind kept drifting to Mr. Zetes standing in that cul-de-sac of a hallway. Like a magician appearing in a sealed cabinet.

In art class, Kaitlyn was supposed to be doing a project for her portfolio—that important collection of pictures that might get her college credit next year—but she couldn't focus. The busy, creative classroom around her was only a blur and a hum.

Almost mesmerized, she flipped to a blank page in her sketchbook and reached for her oil pastels.

She loved pastels because they made it so easy to get what she saw from her eyes to the paper. They were quick, fluid, vigorous—free. For a normal picture, she would start by rapidly sketching the major shapes, then layering on detail. But for the *other* kind of picture, the kind she didn't control . . .

She watched her hand dot tiny strokes of carmine and crimson lake in a rectangular shape. A tall rectangle. Around the rectangle, strokes of Van Dyke brown and burnt umber. The close dots of the browns gradually formed a shimmering pattern, with whorls and lines like wood grain.

Her hand hesitated over the box of pastels—what color next? After a moment she picked up black.

Black strokes clustered heavily inside the rectangle, forming a shape. A human silhouette, with broad shoulders and body lines that swept straight down. Like a coat. A man in a coat.

Kaitlyn sat back and looked at the drawing.

She recognized it. It was one of the images she'd seen in that visionary mosaic yesterday—the doorway. Only now she could see the full picture.

A man in a coat in front of the rectangle of an open door. The red of the doorway gave an impression of energy around him. Framing the door was wood—wood paneling.

The solid wall across from Joyce's door was wood-paneled.

"Nice broken color technique," a voice above her said. "Do you need a squirt of fixative?"

Kaitlyn shook her head and the teacher moved on.

The limousine picked them up after school. Joyce was still at the hospital, Mr. Zetes told them when they got home. Marisol was still unconscious. There wouldn't be any testing today.

Kait waited until everyone had drifted upstairs, and then quietly, one by one, she began to gather them. "We've got to talk. In the study," she said. Anna, Lewis, and Rob all came at once. Gabriel came when she stuck her head in his room and hissed at him.

When they were together in the study, she shut the door and turned the TV on. Then she showed them the picture and told them what she'd seen that morning.

"So you think, like . . . what? There's really a door there?" Lewis asked. "But what does that *mean?* I mean, so what?"

Kaitlyn looked at Rob, whose eyes were dark, dark gold.

"There's more," she said, and she told Anna and Lewis what she'd told Rob and Gabriel the night before. All of it, about Marisol's warnings and the strange things that had been happening.

When she was through, there was no sound except the blaring of a music video on TV.

Anna sat with her head slightly tilted, her long braid falling into her lap, her eyes faraway and sad. Lewis rubbed his nose, forehead puckered. Rob's face was set, his fists resting on his knees. Kaitlyn herself gripped the sides of her sketchbook tensely.

Gabriel was sitting back with one knee hooked over the arm of the couch. He was playing with a quarter, flipping it over and catching it. He seemed completely unconcerned.

Finally Anna said, "*Something's* going on. Any one of those things—like what Marisol said, or the cold thing on your forehead—any one of them could be explained. But when you put them all together, something's . . ."

"Amiss," Rob supplied.

"Amiss," Anna said.

Lewis's face cleared. "But look. If you think there's a door down there, why don't we just go down and *see?*"

"We can't," Anna said. "Mr. Z's in the living room, and so are the dogs."

"He's got to leave sometime," Rob said.

Lewis squirmed. "Look—you're really saying that the Institute is, like, evil? You really think so?" He turned to Rob. "I thought you loved this place, the whole idea of it."

Gabriel snorted. Rob ignored him. "I do love the idea of it," he said. "But the reality . . . I've just got a bad feeling about it. And Kait does, too."

Everyone looked at Kait, who hesitated. "I don't know about feelings," she said finally, looking down at the picture of a door. "I don't even know whether to trust my drawings. But there's only one way to find out about this one."

It took them half an hour to plan the burglary. Actually, it only took five minutes to do the planning. The other twenty-five were spent trying to force Gabriel to help.

"No, thanks. Include me out," he said.

"You wouldn't have to go inside," Kaitlyn said through her teeth. "All you need to do is sit in the alcove and watch for cars coming in the driveway."

Gabriel shook his head.

Anna tried gentle reasoning with him; Lewis tried bribery. None of it worked.

At last Rob stood up with an exclamation of disgust and turned toward the door. "Stop catering to him. He's afraid. It doesn't matter; we can do it without him."

Gabriel's eyes went hard. "Afraid?"

Rob barely glanced back at him. "Yeah."

Gabriel stood up. "Care to say that again?"

This time Rob turned. He stood face-to-face with Gabriel and their eyes locked, silently fighting it out.

Kaitlyn watched them both without breathing. Thinking again that they were so different, such opposites. Rob all gold, radiant energy, his waving hair tousled, his eyes blazing. And Gabriel darkness, his skin paler than usual, his hair looking black in contrast. His eyes bottomless and cold.

Like the sun and a black hole, side by side, Kait thought. In that moment the image was etched into her mind, a picture she would never draw. It was too frightening.

Once again, she was afraid for Rob. She knew what Gabriel could do—with or without a knife. If they started fighting . . .

"I'm going downstairs," she said abruptly. "To ask Mr. Z if we can order a pizza."

Everyone looked at her, startled. Then Kait saw understanding flash in Anna's eyes.

"That's a good idea. I'm sure nobody wants to cook dinner," Anna said, standing and gently taking Rob's elbow. She nudged Lewis with her foot.

"Uh, fine with me," Lewis said, putting his baseball cap on backward. He was still looking at Gabriel.

Slowly, to Kaitlyn's great relief, the two combatants broke their locked stare and stepped away from each other. Rob submitted to Anna's gentle tugging. Kaitlyn made sure he got out the door.

Then she looked back at Gabriel.

His eyes were still dark as black holes, but his mouth was mocking and sardonic. "You can put it off, but it's going to happen someday," he said. Before Kaitlyn could defiantly ask *what* was going to happen, he added, "I'll watch for cars up here. But that's all. I won't risk my neck to help you. If something goes wrong, you're on your own."

Kaitlyn shrugged. "I've always been on my own," she said, and went downstairs to order pizza.

Mr. Zetes didn't leave until eleven o'clock. Kaitlyn was afraid to have the group stay downstairs with him after dinner, afraid that one of them might give something away. They sat in the study, pretending to do homework, and all the time listening for a sign that Mr. Z was going.

When he finally did go, he called them to the staircase and said that Joyce would undoubtedly be coming soon.

"But you won't be alone until then. I'll leave Prince and Baron," he said.

Kaitlyn studied his face, wondering how much he suspected they suspected. Were those dark eyes fierce or just acute? Was there the shadow of a grim smile on his lips?

He can't *know* anything, she thought.

Acting for all she was worth, she said, "Oh, thank you, Mr. Zetes."

When the front door shut behind him, Kaitlyn looked at Anna, who looked back helplessly.

"Prince and Baron?" Kait said.

Anna sighed, fingering the end of her black braid. In anyone else it would have been a nervous gesture. "I don't know. I *will* try, but they look very hard to influence."

"You'd better go if you're going," Gabriel said curtly.

"You just go hide—I mean *stand guard*—in the dark," Rob said. Kaitlyn grabbed his wrist and dragged him a step or two down the stairs. Dearly as she loved Rob, there were times when she wanted to bash his head in.

Gabriel retreated into the darkened study, his handsome face inscrutable.

"You first, Anna," Kaitlyn said. Anna walked down the stairs, so slowly and gracefully that she might have been drifting. Rob and Kait followed, with Lewis behind.

"Careful. Easy," Anna said as she reached the bottom. A low growl sounded from somewhere behind the staircase.

One dog was in the paneled hallway, Kaitlyn saw as they rounded the corner. The other was in the darkened living room, almost blending into the shadows. Both were watching Anna intently.

"Easy," Anna breathed, and that was the last word she said.

She stood perfectly still, looking at the dog in the living room, her left hand raised toward the dog in the hallway, the way you'd gesture to a person to wait.

The growl died away. Anna's upraised hand slowly closed, as if she'd caught something in her fist. She turned, smoothly and without haste, to look at the dog in the hallway.

"Look out!" Rob yelled, jumping forward.

In absolute silence, with its lips peeled back and the hair on its back bristling, the dog in the living room was stalking toward Anna.

# CHAPTER 11

Everything happened too quickly for Kaitlyn to take in. She only knew that she grabbed desperately for Rob's arm to hold him back, thinking that only Anna could deal with the dog, and anyone else was likely to distract her. And then Anna was holding up her hand in a commanding gesture—*stop*—but the dog was still coming. Moving eerily, as if on oiled machinery, every tooth showing.

"*No!*" Anna said sharply, and added some words in a language Kaitlyn didn't know. "Hwhee, Sokwa! Brother Wolf—go to sleep! It's not hunting time now. Rest and sleep."

Then, without showing the slightest sign of fear, she reached for the snarling muzzle. She locked one hand over it, grabbing the hair at the dog's neck with the other. Her eyes gazed straight into the animal's, unflinching and unwavering.

"I'm the pack leader here," she said clearly. "This is not your territory. I am dominant." Kaitlyn had the feeling that the words were only part of the communication. Something unspoken was passing between the graceful girl and the animal.

And the dog was responding. His lips slid down to cover his teeth again. The hair on his back flattened. More—his entire back flattened, drooped, until his belly almost touched the floor. His tail tucked between his legs. His eyes shifted. His entire attitude was one of submission.

Anna held out a hand to the other dog, which moved toward her slowly, tail down, almost crawling on its elbows. She clamped a hand over its muzzle, clearly establishing dominance.

Rob's eyebrows were up. "How long can you sustain that?"

"I don't know," Anna said without turning. "I'll try to keep them right here—but you guys had better work fast." She tilted her head and, still looking at the dogs, began chanting something softly. Kaitlyn didn't understand the words, but the rhythm was soothing. The dogs seemed mesmerized, cringing a little, pushing at her gently with their noses.

"Let's go," Rob said.

The paneling in the hallway was dark—walnut or mahogany, Kaitlyn thought vaguely. She and Rob both scanned it intently, while Lewis squinted doubtfully.

"There," she said, pointing to the middle panel. "That looks like a crack, doesn't it? It could be the top of a door."

"That means there must be a release somewhere around here," Rob said, running his fingers over the smooth wood and into the grooves between panels. "But we'll probably never find it by accident. You may have to push more than one place, and do it in a certain sequence or something."

"Okay, Lewis," Kait said. "Do your stuff."

Lewis edged between them, muttering, "But I don't know what *to* do. I don't know anything about secret doors."

"You don't know exactly what you're doing when you use PK on the random number machine, either, do you?" Kaitlyn demanded. "So how do you manage that?"

"I just kind of . . . nudge at the thing with my mind. It's not conscious. I just nudge and see what happens, and if something works, I keep doing it."

"Like biofeedback," Rob said. "People don't know *how* they slow down their heart rate, but they do."

"Well, nudge this panel and see what happens," Kait told Lewis. "We've got to find that door—if there is a door."

Lewis began, stroking the panel lightly with outspread fingers. Every so often he would stop and push on the wood, his entire body tense. Kaitlyn knew he was pushing with his mind, too.

"Come on, where are you?" he muttered. "Open, open."

Something clicked.

"Got it!" Lewis said, sounding more astonished than triumphant.

Kaitlyn stared, her knees going weak.

There *was* a door. Or a passage, anyway. The middle panel had recessed and slid smoothly behind the panel on the left. There was a gaping hole in the formerly solid wall.

It looked just like Kaitlyn's drawing, except that there was no figure in the doorway. There were only stairs leading downward, faintly illuminated by half-covered reddish lights at foot level. They seemed to have been activated by the door opening.

Lewis breathed one word. "Jeeeeeez."

"Why is it so dark?" Kait murmured. "Why not put some real lights in?"

Rob nodded toward the French doors to Joyce's room just opposite. "Maybe because *she's* there. This way, you could walk into this place without being seen, even at night."

Kaitlyn frowned, then shrugged. There was no time to wonder about it. "Lewis, you stay up here. If Gabriel yells that he sees lights coming up the driveway, tell us. We'll come up fast, and you can close the door."

"*If* I can close the door," Lewis said. "It's like trying to learn how to wiggle your ears—you don't know how until you do it." But he stationed himself by the panel like a resolute soldier.

"I'll go first," Rob said, and began cautiously making his way down the stairs. Kaitlyn followed, wishing that she'd brought a flashlight. She didn't at all like this journey into red-hazed dimness—although the lights illuminated the steps themselves, they showed nothing around them. The stairway seemed suspended in an abyss.

"Here's the bottom," Rob said. "It feels like another hallway—wait, here's a switch."

Light blossomed, cool, greenish fluorescent light. They were in a short hallway. The only door was at the end.

"We may need Lewis again," Kaitlyn said, but the door opened when Rob turned the handle.

Kaitlyn didn't know what she expected to see, but it certainly wasn't what she saw. An ordinary office, with a corner desk and a computer and filing cabinets. After the sliding panel and the dark staircase, it was something of a letdown.

She looked at Rob. "You don't think . . . I mean, what if we're completely wrong here? What if he just has a hidden room because he's eccentric? It's possible."

"Anything's possible," Rob said, so shortly that she knew he wondered, too. He went to the filing cabinet and pulled out a drawer with a sliding rattle.

The sound made Kaitlyn's skin jump. If they *were* wrong, they had no business poking into things.

Defiantly she went over to the desk and thumbed through some papers from the letter tray. They were business letters, mostly from important-sounding people, addressed to Mr. Zetes. They all seemed to be photocopies, duplicates. Big deal.

"You know what?" she asked grimly, still pawing. "I just realized. If Mr. Z *was* trying to hide something, he'd never hide it *here*. Why should he? He's got to have better places. He's got a *house*, doesn't he? He's got a *corporation*, somewhere—"

"Kaitlyn."

"Well?"

"I think you should look at this." Rob was holding a file from the cabinet. There was a photograph of Kait clipped on the jacket, and in bold letters: KAITLYN BRADY FAIRCHILD, PROJECT BLACK LIGHTNING.

"What's Project Black Lightning?"

"I don't know. There's a file like that for each of us. Inside there's just a bunch of papers—all kinds of information. Did you know they have your birth certificate?"

"The lawyers told Dad they needed stuff. . . . What's that?"

"A graph about your testing, I think." Rob's tanned finger traced the bottom axis. "Look, this is dated yesterday. It says *First Testing with*—and then there's a word I can't read."

"First testing with something," Kaitlyn repeated slowly. She touched her forehead. "But what does it mean?"

Rob shook his head. "There's another set of files here, with other names." He held up a file jacket with a photo of a smiling girl with dark brown hair. It was labeled SABRINA JESSICA GALLO, BLACK LIGHTNING PILOT STUDY.

Running diagonally across the label, in thick red ink, the word TERMINATED was scrawled.

Kaitlyn and Rob looked at each other.

"Which was terminated?" Kait breathed. "The study or the girl?"

Silently, with one impulse, they turned back to their search.

"Okay, I've got a letter," Kait said after a moment. "It's from the Honorable Susan Baldwin—a judge. It says, 'Enclosed is a list of potential clients who might be interested in the project.' *The project.*" Kaitlyn's eyes scanned down the list. "'Max Lawrence—up for sentencing May first. TRI-Tech, Inc.—settlement conference with Clifford Electronics Limited, June twenty-fourth.' It's all like that, names and trial dates and stuff."

"Here's another file," Rob said. "It's hard to figure out, but I think it's an old grant from NASA. Yeah, a grant from NASA for half a million, back in eighty-six. For"—he paused and read carefully—"investigation into the feasibility of the development of psychoactive weaponry."

"What of the what?" Kaitlyn said hopelessly. "Psycho-*what?*"

Rob's eyes were dark gold and bleak.

"I don't know what it all adds up to. But it's not good. There's a *lot* Mr. Z didn't tell us."

"'This place is different than you think,'" Kaitlyn quoted. "And there *was* a pilot study before us—so Marisol told the truth. But what happened to those kids? What happened to Sabrina?"

"And what's going to happen to—" Rob broke off. "Did you hear that? A noise up there?"

Kaitlyn listened, but she didn't hear anything.

Upstairs, Gabriel was seething.

The whole plan was stupid, of course. Why did they want to go meddling in what was obviously not their business? The time to worry about Zetes was when he was trying to *do* something to you, not before. Then fight—kill him, if necessary. He was only an old man. But why ruin what had so far proved to be a very comfortable deal?

It was all *his* idea, Gabriel felt sure. Kessler's. Rob the Virtuous probably felt there was something unspiritual about coming into so much money. He had to wreck it somehow.

And Kaitlyn was just as bad these days. Completely under Kessler's spell. Why should Gabriel care about her, a girl who was in love with a guy he hated? A girl who only disturbed him . . .

A girl with hair like fire and witch eyes, his mind whispered.

A girl who hounded him, badgered him . . .

Who challenges you, his mind whispered. Who could be your equal.

A girl who interfered with him, trying to get inside his guard . . .

Whose spirit is like yours.

Oh, shut up, Gabriel told his brain, and stared broodingly into the darkness beyond the study window.

The street in front of the Institute was silent and deserted. Naturally, it was midnight—and here in the suburbs that meant everyone was tucked nice and snug in their beds.

Nevertheless, Gabriel felt uneasy. Little sounds seemed to be nagging at his subconscious. Cars on the streets behind the Institute, probably.

Cars . . . Suddenly Gabriel stiffened. Eyes narrowed, he listened for a moment, then he left the alcove.

Nothing out the west window of the study. With the silent

steps of a housebreaker he headed for the back of the house, to Rob and Lewis's bedroom. He looked out the back window, the one facing north.

And there it was. The limo. It had obviously come up the narrow dirt road in back. Now the only question was whether Zetes was just about to get out, or—

Directly beneath him, in the kitchen, Gabriel heard a door open.

The back door, he thought. And those idiots downstairs are all waiting for him to come from the front.

There wasn't any time to go down and warn them—and Zetes would hear a shout.

Gabriel's lip curled. Tough. Kaitlyn knew the truth. He'd told her he wouldn't risk his neck for her. Not that there was anything he could do anyway, except . . .

He shook his head slightly. Not that. In the darkened window his reflected eyes were cold and hard.

Below, the kitchen door slammed.

No, he told himself. He wouldn't. He wouldn't . . .

On the bottom of the letter tray was a scribbled page like something you might doodle while on the telephone. Kaitlyn could make out the scrawled words "Operation Lightning Strike" and "psychic strike team."

"This is weird—" she began. She never finished the sentence because *it* hit her.

Just what *it* was, she couldn't tell at first. Like Rob's healing transfusion of energy, it wasn't something you could see or hear or taste. But while Rob's energy flow had been wonderful, invigorating, an intense pleasure, this was like being hit by a runaway train. Kaitlyn had the feeling of being violated.

And while it didn't trigger any of her normal senses, it mimicked them. Kaitlyn smelled roses. She felt a burning in her head—a painful searing that built until a light like one of Lewis's flashbulbs went off in her brain. Then, through the explosion, she heard a voice.

Gabriel's voice.

*Get out of there! He just came in the back door!*

For a moment Kait stood paralyzed. Knowing that Gabriel could communicate directly with her mind was very different from *feeling* it. Her first reaction was that she was hallucinating; it was impossible.

Rob was gasping. "God. He's a telepath."

*Shut up, Kessler. Move. Do something. You're about to get caught.*

Kaitlyn felt another wave of astonishment. The communication was two-way—Gabriel could hear Rob. Then some primitive instinct within her awoke and shoved all speculation aside. This wasn't the time to think—it was time to *act*.

She threw the letters back in the tray and slid the drawers of the file cabinet shut. Then she had an idea and she tried to do something she'd never done before. She tried to send a thought. She didn't know *how* to send one, but she tried, concentrating on the burning-roses sensation in her head. *Gabriel—can you hear me? You need to tell Anna he's here. Tell her to hang on to the dogs until—*

*I can hear you, Kaitlyn. It's Anna.* The answer was lighter, calmer, than Gabriel's communication. It was a lot like Anna's speaking voice.

Kaitlyn realized something. Not only could she hear Anna, but she had a sense of where Anna was, and what Anna was doing. It was as if she could feel Anna's presence. And Lewis's . . .

*Lewis, shut the panel,* she thought. *And then get upstairs. Anna, let the dogs go as soon as he does.*

*And what are you going to do?* Lewis asked. Kait could sense that he was working on the panel.

*Hide,* Rob said briefly, turning off the fluorescent lights in the hallway and the office.

Although it seemed like hours since the explosion in Kaitlyn's mind, she knew it was only a few seconds. This strange telepathy might be very, very disconcerting, but it was an extraordinarily efficient way to communicate.

*I've got the panel shut. I'm going upstairs,* Lewis said.

*I'm letting the dogs go—quick, Lewis! Come on!* Anna's voice sharpened, and Kait felt a surge of urgency from her.

*What's happening?* Kait demanded.

*Wait—I think it's all right. Yes.* Now what Kait felt from

Anna was relief. *He was coming around through the dining room just as we went up the stairs, but I don't think he saw us. He was looking down at the dogs.*

*You two had better get into bed. He might come upstairs,* Rob said. Kaitlyn turned toward him in the dark. It was fascinating—his silent mental voice sounded just like his ordinary voice, but more so. It was more honest, it seemed to carry more of *him* in it. Right now it was full of quiet concern for Anna and Lewis.

"Or he might come down here," Rob's real voice whispered to Kait. "Come on."

He took her hand. How he could navigate in the dark was beyond her, but he guided them both to the corner desk.

"Get under it," he whispered. "The file cabinets block off the view from the door."

Kaitlyn found herself squeezing into a very tight place.

And then they waited. There was nothing else to do. Kaitlyn's heart was beating violently, seeming loud in the quietness. Her hand in Rob's was slick. Sitting still was much harder than moving and talking had been.

Another fear had gripped her. This was Gabriel's power, right? The one that had killed Iris, the girl in Durham; that had driven the Mohawk volunteer crazy after forty-five seconds. How long had Gabriel kept their minds linked up tonight? And how much longer before he started to suck *their* brains out?

*It has to get unstable,* she reminded herself. *That's what he said. He can control it if he keeps the contact short.*

She was still afraid. Even though Gabriel hadn't said anything since the beginning, she could *feel* him out there. A strong presence, surrounded by smooth, hard walls. He was keeping them all in contact. And every second that ticked by made the contact more dangerous.

Beside her, Rob stiffened. *Listen,* he said.

Kaitlyn heard. A sliding, rattling sound. The panel.

*I don't think that's Lewis,* Rob said.

*It's not. I'm in bed,* Lewis said.

Anna's mental voice was clear and purposeful. *Do you want us to do anything, Kait?*

Kait took a deep breath, then sent the thought, *No, just sit tight. We'll be fine.* At the same time she felt Rob squeeze her hand. There were some things that could be said without even telepathy. She and Rob both knew that they wouldn't be fine—but she couldn't think of any way for Anna to help.

Light suddenly showed in a diffuse fan pattern on the office floor. Mr. Zetes had turned on the fluorescents in the hallway.

Please don't let him come in. Please don't let him come in, Kaitlyn thought. Then she tried to stop thinking, in case the others could hear her panic.

The office door was opening, light spilling in.

Beneath the desk, Kaitlyn buried her face in Rob's shoulder, trying to keep absolutely still. If he didn't actually *come* in—if he only looked in . . .

More light. Mr. Z had turned on the office switch. Now he

had only to step beyond the file cabinets to see them.

I wonder if we'll be terminated, Kait thought. Like Sabrina. Like Marisol. She wanted to jump out and get it over with, to confront Mr. Zetes. They were lost anyway. The only thing that kept her from moving was Rob's arm around her.

Upstairs, she heard a wild clamor. An explosion of barking and baying.

*What is it?* she thought.

Gabriel's voice, cool sarcasm underlaid with heated anger, came back. *I've riled the dogs a little. I figure that should bring him up.*

Kaitlyn held her breath. There was a pause, then the lights in the office went off and the door shut. A minute later the light in the hallway went off, too—and then she heard a rattle.

She sagged against Rob. He squeezed her with both arms and she clung back, even though it was really too warm for clinging.

Above, the barking went on and on. Then, gradually, it faded as if getting more distant.

Gabriel's voice came again. *He's taking them out to the limo. I don't think he's coming back, but Joyce might be—any minute now.*

*Lewis,* Rob said, *get us out of here.*

Ten minutes later, they were all upstairs in the study.

It was perfectly dark except for the moonlight coming in the window. They could barely see each other, but that didn't matter. They could *feel* each other.

Kaitlyn had never been so aware of other people in her life. She knew where each of them was; she had a vague sense of what each was doing. It was as if they were not quite separate creatures—isolated and yet attached somehow.

Like insects caught in a huge web, she thought. Tied together by almost invisible threads. Every pull on the strands lets you know someone else is moving. Her artist's mind gave her an image: the five of them hanging trapped, spread-eagled, and the silken strands between them humming with power.

"Nice picture. But I don't want to be trapped in a web with you," Lewis said mildly.

"And I don't want to have you reading my thoughts," Kaitlyn told him. "That was private."

*How am I . . .* "I mean, how am I supposed to tell?" Lewis asked, changing from mental voice to ordinary voice in midsentence.

"Nobody likes it," Rob said. "Switch it off, Gabriel."

There was a silence which Kaitlyn sensed with both mind and ears.

Everyone turned to look at Gabriel. He looked back with cold defiance.

"Fine," he said. "Just tell me how."

# CHAPTER 12

Kaitlyn stared into the darkness where Gabriel was sitting.

*What do you mean?* Rob asked, deadly quiet. He didn't even seem to notice he wasn't speaking out loud.

"What have you done before?" Anna put in quickly. "I mean, how does it stop, usually?"

Gabriel turned to her. "Usually? When people drop dead or start screaming."

There was another blank silence, then a sudden gabble of voices, both mental and otherwise.

*Are you saying it's going to kill us?*—that was Lewis.

"Just a minute; let's all stay calm."—Anna.

*I think you'd better start explaining, buddy!*—Rob.

Gabriel sat for a moment, and Kait had the feeling of raised hackles and bared teeth from him—like one of the rottweilers. Then, slowly and coldly, he began to explain.

It was the story he'd told Kaitlyn about his powers: about how Iris, the girl in Durham, had died, about his escape afterward, about the man who'd tried to kill him, the man he'd killed instead. He told it without emotion—but Kaitlyn could feel the emotion that was suppressed behind the wall. They all could—and Kaitlyn could tell that, too.

*I hate this as much as you do,* Gabriel finished. *The last thing I want is to see what's in your helpless little minds. But if I knew how to control it, I wouldn't be here.*

*He feels more trapped than anyone else. Like a spider caught in its own web,* Anna commented, and Kaitlyn wondered if it was meant to be a shared insight, or if Anna was just thinking it.

"But then why did you do it to *us* tonight?" Rob demanded. Kait could feel the bewilderment emanating from him. Direct contact with Gabriel's mind had shaken his view of Gabriel as a selfish, ruthless killer—Kaitlyn could tell that. Which was funny, she thought, because the image of a selfish, ruthless killer was exactly what Gabriel was trying so hard to project right now. "If you knew you couldn't control it, why did you use telepathy on us?" Rob said angrily.

*Because I couldn't think of any other way to save your useless necks!* Gabriel's reply had the force of a knockout blow.

Rob sat back.

"There probably *wasn't* another way," Kaitlyn said judiciously. "Mr. Zetes was just about to walk in on us when the dogs started barking. What did you do to them, by the way?"

*Threw a shoe at them.*

At those *dogs? Jeeeez,* Lewis said.

Gabriel seemed to give a mental shrug. *I figured he'd have to come up and see what was going on. Then he couldn't get them to shut up, so he finally had to take them outside.*

"Look," Anna broke in, "maybe we shouldn't be using this thing so much. Maybe it'll go away sooner if we all just ignore it."

"It'll go away when we go to sleep," Gabriel said flatly—but aloud, Kaitlyn noticed.

"Are you sure?" Lewis asked.

"Yes."

Kaitlyn decided not to mention that Gabriel didn't *feel* as sure as he sounded.

"We really should go to sleep, anyway," she said. It was only now, when all the panic and excitement were over, that she could begin to realize how tired she was. She was stiff from tension and from sitting under that desk. And her mind was exhausted from trying to take in everything that had gone on today. From Marisol's seizure, to Mr. Zetes appearing by the hidden door, to her drawing in art class, to the burglary—so much had happened that her brain was simply giving up.

"But you didn't tell us what was down there behind the panel," Lewis said. "Did you find *anything?*"

"We found plenty, all bad," Rob said. "But Kaitlyn's right. We can talk about it tomorrow."

Kaitlyn could feel Anna biting her lip on questions, judging that it was wiser to wait. She could feel Lewis sighing. But it was all muffled by an enormous sense of weariness—even of dizziness, of illness. She wasn't just feeling her own fatigue, she realized. Gabriel was on the verge of collapse. He was—

*Rob,* she said urgently.

Rob was already moving. In trying to stand up, Gabriel had staggered and fallen to his knees. Kaitlyn helped Rob put him back on the couch.

"He's bad off—like you when you burned up so much energy yesterday, Kait," Rob told her. He was holding Gabriel's arm—and Gabriel was resisting feebly.

"I don't burn energy doing this. I take energy," he said.

"Well, you burned something this time," Rob said. "Maybe because you were connecting so many people. Anyway . . ." Kaitlyn could hear him take a deep breath—and sense him getting a better grip on Gabriel's arm. "Anyway, maybe I can help you. Let me—"

*"No!"* Gabriel shouted. "Let go of me."

"But you need energy. I can—"

*I said, let go!* Once again, the thought itself was an attack. Kaitlyn winced and everyone backed up a little—everyone except Rob. He stood his ground.

Lewis said weakly, "I think he's got enough energy right now."

Gabriel's attention was still on Rob. "I don't need anything from anyone," he snarled, trying to pull out of Rob's grip. "Especially not from you."

"Gabriel, listen—" Kait began. But Gabriel wasn't in a mood to listen. She could feel waves of defensive, destructive fury beating at her like the icy battering of a storm.

*I don't need any of you. This doesn't change anything, so don't think it does. By tomorrow it'll be gone—and until then, just leave me alone!*

Rob hesitated, then released Gabriel's arm. "Whatever you want," he said almost gently. He stepped back.

Now, Kaitlyn thought, comes the interesting part. Whether Gabriel can make it to his room on his own or not.

He did. Not very steadily, but belligerently. Not needing words to send the message that they'd all better keep away.

The door to the large bedroom shut hard behind him. Kaitlyn could still feel his presence on the other side, but it was a feeling of walls, of spiky barriers. She herself used to have walls like that.

"Poor guy," Lewis muttered.

"I think we'd all better go to bed," Anna suggested.

They did. Kaitlyn's clock said 2:52 A.M. She wondered vaguely how they were going to make it to school tomorrow, and then exhaustion overcame her.

The last thing she remembered, as her defenses lowered

in sleep, was thinking, *By the way, Gabriel, thanks. For risking your own neck.*

She got only nasty images of icy walls and locked doors as an answer.

She was dreaming, and it was the old dream about the peninsula— the rocky peninsula and the ocean and the cold wind. Kaitlyn shivered in the spray. The sky was so dark with clouds that she couldn't tell if it was day or evening. A single, lonely gull circled over the water.

What a desolate place, she thought.

"Kaitlyn!"

Oh, yes, Kaitlyn remembered. The voice calling my name; that was in my first dream, too. And now I turn around and there's no one there.

Feeling resigned, she turned. And started.

Rob was climbing down the rocks. His gold-blond hair was flecked with spray and there was damp sand on his pajama bottoms.

"I don't think you're supposed to be here," Kaitlyn told him with the confused directness of dreams.

"I don't *want* to be here. It's freezing," Rob said, hopping and slapping his bare arms with his hands.

"Well, you should have worn more sensible clothes."

"I'm freezing, too," a third voice said. Kaitlyn looked.

Lewis and Anna were behind her, both looking chilled and windswept. "Whose dream is this, anyway?" Lewis added.

"This is a very strange place," Anna said, gazing around with dark, thoughtful eyes. Then she said, "Gabriel—are you all right?"

Gabriel was standing a little way down the peninsula, his arms folded. Kaitlyn felt that this dream was getting crowded—and ridiculous. "It's funny—" she began.

*I don't think it's funny, and I'm not going to play.* Gabriel's voice said in her head.

. . . if it was a dream.

Suddenly Kaitlyn was very much in doubt.

"Are you *really* here?" she asked Gabriel. He just looked at her coldly, with eyes the color of the ocean around them.

Kaitlyn turned to the others. "Look, you guys, I've had this dream before—but not with all of *you* in it. But is it really you, or am I just dreaming you?"

"You're not dreaming *me*," Lewis said. "I think I'm dreaming you."

Rob ignored him and shook his head at Kait. "There's no way for me to prove I'm real—not until tomorrow."

Strangely, that convinced Kait. Or maybe it was just the nearness of Rob, the way her pulse quickened when she looked at him, the certainty that her mind couldn't be making up anything this vivid.

"So now we're sharing *dreams?*" she asked edgily.

"It must be the telepathic link. That web of yours," said Anna.

"If Kaitlyn's had the dream before, it's *her* fault," said Lewis. "Isn't it? And where are we, anyway?"

Kaitlyn looked up and down the narrow spit of land. "I don't have a clue. I've only had this dream a couple of times before, and it never lasted this long."

"Can't you dream us somewhere warmer?" Lewis asked, teeth chattering.

Kaitlyn didn't know how. This dream didn't *feel* like a dream exactly—or, rather, she felt much more like the waking Kaitlyn than the fuzzy Kaitlyn who moved semiconsciously through dreams.

Anna, who seemed least affected by the cold, was kneeling near the edge of the water. "This is strange," she said. "You see these piles of stones everywhere?"

It was something Kaitlyn hadn't noticed before. The peninsula was bordered with rocks, most of which looked as if they had just washed up. But some of the rocks were gathered into stacks, piled one on top of another to form whimsical towers. Some rocks had their long axis up and down, some were placed horizontally. Some of the towers looked a bit like buildings or figures.

"Who did it?" Lewis asked, aiming a kick at a pile.

"Hey, don't," Rob said, blocking the kick.

Anna stood up. "He's right," she told Lewis. "Don't spoil things. They're not ours."

*They're not anyone's. This is just a dream,* Gabriel said, throwing a look more chilling than the wind at them.

"If it's *just* a dream, how come you're still in it?" Rob asked.

Gabriel turned away silently.

Kaitlyn knew one thing: This particular dream had gone on *much* longer than any of the others. And they might not really be here, but Rob's skin was covered with gooseflesh. They needed to find shelter.

"There must be somewhere to go," she said. Where the peninsula joined the land, there was a very wet and rocky beach. Above that, a stony bank, and then trees. Tall fir trees that formed a dark and uninviting thicket.

On the other side, water . . . and across the water, a lonely cliff, bare in some places, black with forest in others. There was no sign of human habitation, except—

"What's that?" she said. "That white thing."

She could scarcely make it out in the dimness, but it looked like a white house on the distant cliff. She had no idea how one might get to it.

"It's useless," she murmured, and at the same moment a surge of warmth swept over her. How strange—everything was getting cloudy. She was suddenly aware that while she was standing on the rocky peninsula, she was also lying down . . . lying down in bed. . . .

For a moment it seemed as if she could choose where she wanted to be.

Bed, she thought firmly. That other place is too cold.

And then she was turning over, and she *was* in bed, pulling up the covers. Her brain was too foggy to think of calling to the others, of finding out if it really had been a shared dream. She just wanted to sleep.

The next morning she woke up to: *Oh, no.*

*Lewis?* she thought hazily.

*Hi, Kaitlyn. Hi. Rob.*

*G'way, Lewis. I'm sleeping,* Rob said indistinctly. Only, of course, he didn't say it, not with his voice. He was in his own bedroom, and so was Lewis. Kait could *feel* them there.

She looked up over hummocks of sheets and blankets, to see Anna looking at her from the other bed. Anna looked flushed with sleep, sweet, and resigned.

*Hi. Anna.* Kaitlyn said, feeling somewhat resigned herself.

*Hi, Kait.*

*Hi, Anna,* Lewis said chirpily.

*And good night, John-boy!* Gabriel shouted from across the house. *Shut the hell up, all of you!*

Anna and Kaitlyn shared a look. *He's crabby when he wakes up,* Kaitlyn observed.

*All boys are,* Anna told her serenely. *At least he seems to have got his strength back.*

*I thought,* Rob said, his mental voice seeming more awake, *that you said it would be gone by this morning.*

Thunderous silence from Gabriel.

*We might as well get dressed,* Kaitlyn said at last when the silence went on. *It's almost seven.*

She found that if she concentrated on herself, the others receded into the background—which was just as well, she thought as she showered and dressed. There were some things you *needed* to be alone for.

But no matter what she did, they were there. Lurking around the edges of her mind like friends just within earshot and shouting range. Paying attention to any one of them brought that one closer.

Except Gabriel, who seemed to have locked himself off in a corner. Paying attention to him was like bouncing off the smoothness of his steely walls.

It wasn't until she was dressed that Kaitlyn remembered her dream.

"Anna—last night—did you dream anything in particular?"

Anna looked up from beneath the glistening raven's wing of her dark hair. "You mean about that place by the ocean?" she said, brushing vigorously. She seemed quite undisturbed.

Kaitlyn sat down. "Then it was real. I mean, you were really there." *You guys were all in my dream,* she added silently, so the others could hear it.

*Well, it's not really that surprising, is it?* Rob asked from his room. *If our minds are linked telepathically, and one of us has a dream, maybe the others get dragged in.*

Kaitlyn shook her head. *There's more to it than that,* she told Rob—but what more, she didn't know. Just then Lewis interrupted anyway, from the stairway.

*Hey, I think Joyce is home! I hear somebody in the kitchen. Come on down!*

All thoughts of the dream vanished. Kaitlyn and Anna ran out and met Rob on their way to the staircase.

"Joyce!" Lewis was saying when they got to the kitchen. He was also saying *Joyce!* but Joyce didn't seem to notice.

"Are you all right?" Kaitlyn asked. Joyce looked very pale, and there were huge dark circles under her eyes. She looked . . . young, somehow, like a kid with a short haircut that's turned out wrong.

Kaitlyn swallowed, but couldn't manage the next words. Anna said them for her. "Is Marisol . . . ?"

Joyce put down a box of Shredded Wheat as if it were heavy. "Marisol is . . . stable." Then her adult control seemed to desert her and she blurted, lips trembling, "She's in a coma."

"Oh, God," Kaitlyn whispered.

"The doctors are watching her. I stayed with her family at the hospital last night, but I didn't get to see her." Joyce fished in her purse, found a tissue, and blew her nose. She picked up the Shredded Wheat box and looked at it blankly.

"Now, you just let go of that and sit down," Rob said gently. "We'll take care of everything."

"That's right," Kaitlyn said, glad for the guidance. She herself felt sick and terrified. But *doing* something made her feel better, and in a few minutes they had Joyce sitting at the kitchen table, with Anna stroking her hand, Kaitlyn making coffee, and Rob and Lewis setting out bowls and spoons.

"It's all so confusing," Joyce said, wiping her eyes and crumpling the tissue in her fist. "Marisol's family didn't know she was on medication. They didn't even know she'd been seeing a psychiatrist. I had to tell them."

Kaitlyn looked at Rob, who, shielded by the pantry door, returned the look with grim significance. Then, carefully measuring scoops of ground coffee, she asked Joyce, "Who told *you* she was seeing a shrink?"

"Who? Mr. Zetes." Joyce passed a hand over her forehead. "By the way, he said you kids behaved really well last night. Went to bed early and all."

Anna smiled. "We're not children." She was the only one who could talk; the others were all engaged in a torrent of silent communication.

*I knew it,* Kaitlyn was telling Rob. *Joyce doesn't know anything about Marisol except what comes from Mr. Z. Don't you remember—when I asked about Marisol's medication, she told me, "He said a psychiatrist prescribed it." It was Mr. Zetes who told her that. For all we know, Marisol wasn't on any medication at all.*

Rob's face was tight. *And now she's in a coma because—*

*Because she knew too much about what was going on here. What was really going on,* Kait finished.

*Which you guys still haven't told us,* Lewis reminded her. *But look, why don't we tell* Joyce *what's going on? I mean, what's going on with us. She might know how this telepathy thing works—*

*NO!*

The thought came like a clap of thunder from upstairs. Kaitlyn involuntarily glanced upward.

Gabriel's mental voice was icily furious. *We can't tell anyone— and especially not Joyce.*

"Why not?" Lewis said. It took Kaitlyn a moment to realize he'd said it aloud. Anna was casting alarmed glances from the table.

"Uh, anybody want sugar or Equal or anything on their cereal?" Rob interjected. *Lewis, be careful!* he added silently.

"Sugar," Lewis said, subdued. *But why can't we tell Joyce? Don't you trust her?* he added in what came across as a mental stage whisper.

"Equal," Kaitlyn said, to Rob. *I do trust her—I think. I don't believe she knows anything—*

*You idiot! You can't trust anyone,* Gabriel snarled from upstairs. The volume of his thoughts was giving Kaitlyn a headache.

Looking pained, Rob and Lewis sat down at the table. Kaitlyn poured Joyce a cup of coffee and joined them. The spoken and unspoken conversations formed an eerie counter-point to each other.

*I hate to say this, but I think he's right,* Rob said silently, when the echoes of Gabriel's forceful message had died. *I want to trust Joyce, too—but she tells Mr. Zetes everything. She told him about Marisol and look what happened.*

"Everything's going to be all right," Anna told Joyce. *She's very upset over Marisol. That's genuine,* she told the others.

*She's an adult,* Gabriel said flatly. *You can't trust any adult, ever.*

*And if she's innocent, she could get hurt,* Rob added.

"If there's anything we can do to help Marisol, let us know," Kaitlyn said to Joyce. *All right. We won't tell her,* she conceded. *But we need to get information about telepathy from somewhere. And we need to talk about what Rob and I found in that hidden room.*

Rob nodded, and covered it with a violent spasm of coughing. *We'd better meet at school—alone. Otherwise talking like this is going to drive me crazy.*

Kaitlyn felt agreement from everywhere, except upstairs.

*That means you, too, Gabriel,* Rob said grimly. *You're the one who started this. You're going to be there, boy.*

Aloud he said, "Could somebody pass that orange juice, please?"

# CHAPTER 13

They met at lunch, and Kaitlyn and Rob told about everything they'd found in Mr. Zetes's hidden office below the stairs. Anna and Lewis were as puzzled as Kait had been over the various files and papers.

"Psychoactive weaponry," Gabriel said, seeming to relish the words. By unanimous agreement they were all talking out loud, and Kaitlyn couldn't tell what Gabriel was thinking behind his barriers.

"Do you know what it means?" Rob asked. His attitude toward Gabriel had changed overnight. There was a new tolerance in him—and a new combativeness. Kaitlyn had the slightly alarmed feeling that he meant to push and challenge Gabriel whenever he thought it was good for Gabriel.

"Well, psychoactive should be obvious even to a moron," Gabriel said. "It means something activated by psychics."

*As opposed to something activated by psychos?*

"Lewis!" Kaitlyn, Anna, and Rob all said. Gabriel contented himself with a withering look.

"I couldn't help it. I'm sorry. I'm not saying anything, see?" Lewis took a desperate chug of milk.

"Something . . . activated . . . by psychic power," Gabriel repeated coldly, one eye on Lewis. When there was no interruption, he turned to Rob. "Do I have to explain weaponry, or can you manage that alone?"

Rob leaned forward. "Why . . . would NASA . . . want him . . . to develop weaponry?"

Kaitlyn slammed a fork on the table between them to get their attention. "Maybe NASA didn't want him to actually develop it—but to find out if somebody *else* could be developing it. Eighty-six was the year the *Challenger* shuttlecraft exploded, right? Well, what if NASA thought the explosion was, like, sabotage? *Psychic* sabotage?"

"Sabotage by who?" Rob asked quietly.

"I don't know—the old Soviet Union? Somebody else who didn't want the space program to go ahead? If you got psychics to develop PK that could work over really long distances, you could have them throw switches in the shuttlecraft while they were sitting here on earth. I know it's not a nice idea, but it's possible."

"We're not dealing with nice people," Anna said.

"Look, what about all the other things in that room?"

Lewis asked. "The pilot study stuff, and the letter from the judge—"

"Forget it. All of it," Gabriel said sharply, and when several people turned to protest, he added, *Forget it! We've got something else to worry about first. Understand?*

Kaitlyn nodded slowly. "You're right. If this . . . web . . . that connects us gets unstable . . ."

"Even if it doesn't, we've got to get rid of it," Gabriel said brutally. "And the only place to get information about telepathy—*hard* information, in detail—is the Institute."

"That's right, Joyce has a bunch of books and journals and things in the lab," Lewis said. "But she's going to think it's weird that we're suddenly interested."

"Not if we go now," Gabriel said. "She's probably asleep."

"She *might* be asleep," Kaitlyn said cautiously. "And she might not be—and Mr. Zetes might be there. . . ."

"And pigs might fly. We'll never find out unless we go see." Gabriel stood, as if everything were decided.

*Jeez, he's sure active all of a sudden. Now that he's got a stake in things.*

"Lewis," Kaitlyn said mildly. But Lewis was right.

Joyce was asleep, with the French doors to her room wide open. Kaitlyn glanced at Rob, and what otherwise would have been just a meaningful look took on words.

*Too bad,* she told him. *I was hoping we might get a chance to go back into that hidden room—but it's too risky. She'd hear us.*

He nodded. *It would have been too risky anyway. Those doors are mostly glass—and if she woke up, she'd be looking straight out at that panel.*

Lewis was screwing his face into an unaccustomed frown. *I thought we were supposed to be talking out loud.*

*Not when we're standing outside Joyce's door,* Kaitlyn said. *This thing is useful when we need to be quiet.* She moved stealthily away.

They found Gabriel already in the front lab, kneeling by a bookcase, scanning the journals inside. Kaitlyn went to help him.

"There are more bookcases in the back," Anna said, and she and Lewis went through the door. Rob joined Kaitlyn. He didn't need to say anything—she could feel his watchful protectiveness. He meant to keep an eye on her when Gabriel was around.

*There's no need,* Kaitlyn thought, and then wondered if anyone had heard her. Oh, she didn't *like* this—this *exposure.* Not being sure if your own thoughts were private. She reached crossly for a book.

*We've got to get rid of this thing.*

On either side of her, Rob and Gabriel were radiating agreement.

They looked for what seemed like hours. Kaitlyn scanned journals with names like *Journal of the American Society for Psychical Research* and *Research in Parapsychology.* Some were translations of foreign journals with tongue-twisting names like *Sdelovaci Technika.*

There were articles about telepathy, thought projection, suggestibility. But nothing that looked remotely helpful to their situation.

At last, when Kaitlyn was beginning to worry that Joyce *had* to wake up soon, Anna called excitedly from the other room.

*People, I've found something!*

They all hurried to the back lab and gathered around her.

"'On stability in telepathic linkage as a function of equilibrium in self-sustaining geometric constructs,'" she said, holding a journal with a red cover. "It's about groups in telepathic links—groups like *us*."

"What on earth is a self-sustaining geometric construct?" Kaitlyn asked, very calmly.

Anna flashed a smile. "It's a web. You said it yourself, Kaitlyn—we're like five points that are joined to form a geometrical shape. And the point is that it's *stable*—that's what this article is saying. Two minds connected aren't stable. Three or four minds connected aren't stable. But five minds connected are. They form a—a sort of stable shape, and the whole thing stays in balance after that. That's why we're still linked."

Rob glanced at Gabriel. "So it's your fault. You shouldn't have connected all five of us."

Gabriel ignored him, reaching for the journal. "What I want to know is how to get *un*connected."

"I'm getting there," Anna said, holding it away from him. "I haven't read that part yet, but it's got a section here about how to disrupt the stability and break the connection." Her eyes scanned down the page as she continued to hold the journal away from Gabriel.

The others waited impatiently.

"This says that it's all theoretical, that nobody's ever really gotten five minds linked together. . . . Wait . . . then it says that some *larger* groups may be stable, too. . . . Okay, here. Got it." Anna began to read aloud. "'Breaking the link would be harder than initiating it, would require a far greater amount of power. . . .' But wait, it says there *is* one certain way of breaking it—" Anna stopped abruptly, eyes fixed on the page. Kaitlyn could feel her shock and dismay.

"What?" Gabriel demanded. "What does it say?"

Anna looked up at him. "It says the only certain way of breaking the connection is for one of the group to die."

Everyone stared at her, stunned. There was no sound, either mental or vocal.

"You mean," Lewis said shakily, at last, "that the web won't kill us—but that the only way to get rid of it is for one of us to *be* killed?"

Anna shook her head—not a negative, merely a helpless gesture. "That's what the article says. But—it's only a theory. Nobody can really know—"

Gabriel snatched the journal from her. He read rapidly, then stood for a moment very still. Then, with a furious gesture, he threw the journal at a wall.

"It's permanent," he said flatly, turning to stare at the wall himself.

Kaitlyn shivered. His anger frightened her, and it mixed with her own feelings of shock and fear.

In a lot of ways she'd enjoyed the connection. It was interesting, exciting. Different. But to *never* be able to break it . . . to know you'd be stuck in a web until one of them died . . .

My whole life has changed, she thought. Forever. Something . . . irrevocable . . . has happened, and there's no way to undo it.

I will never be alone, unconnected, again.

"At least we know it's not going to kill any of us," Anna said in a quiet voice.

Kaitlyn said slowly, "Like you said, that article might be wrong. There might be some other way to break it—we can read other books, other journals, and see."

"There is a way. There *has* to be," Gabriel said, in a cracked, almost unrecognizable voice.

He's the most desperate of all of us, Kait realized with something like dispassion. He can't stand being this close—having us all this close to him.

*Until we find it, you all stay away from me,* Gabriel's mental voice said, as if in answer to Kaitlyn's thought. Had he heard her?

"Meanwhile," Rob said in a quiet, level voice, "we might work on learning how to control it—"

*Just stay away!* Gabriel shouted, and he strode out of the room.

Lewis, Anna, Rob, and Kaitlyn were left staring after him.

"Why's he so mad at *us?*" Lewis asked. "If it's anyone's fault, it's his."

Rob smiled faintly. "That's why he's mad," he said in a dry voice. "He doesn't like being wrong."

"It's more than that," Kaitlyn said. "He helped us—and look where it got him. So it just confirms what he thought in the first place, that you should never help."

There was another silence, while everyone just stood. We still haven't taken it all in, Kaitlyn thought. We're in shock.

Then she gave herself a mental shake. "Those bookcases look pretty bad. We'd better clean things up quick. We can look for other articles about breaking the web later, when we know Joyce won't be around."

They straightened the books and the rows of plastic journal holders in both labs. It was as she was putting on the final touches that Kaitlyn found another article that intrigued her.

Someone had marked the page with a red plastic Post-it flag. The title was simply "Chi and Crystals."

*You guys? What's chi?* she asked, scarcely aware that she wasn't asking it out loud.

"It's a Chinese word for your life energy," Lewis said, coming to her. "It flows all through your body in different channels, sort of like blood—or electricity. Everybody has it, and psychics have more of it."

"So chi is what Rob channels?" Kaitlyn said.

"That's one name for it," Rob said. "At the other center they told me lots of others—like in India they call it *prana,* and the ancient Egyptians used to call it *sekhem.* It's all the same thing. All living things have it."

"Well, according to this article, crystals store it," Kaitlyn said.

Rob frowned. "Crystals aren't alive. . . ."

"I know, but this says that theoretically a crystalline structure could store it up, kind of like a charged battery," Kaitlyn said. She was still looking at the article thoughtfully. Something was tugging at her, whispering significance, demanding that she pay attention to it. But she didn't know *what.*

The article looked as if it had been read a lot. . . .

"She's up," Rob said. Kaitlyn could hear it, too—water running in the single downstairs bathroom. Joyce was awake and washing.

Anna checked her watch. *It's three-thirty. We can just tell her that we walked home from school.*

Kaitlyn nodded and she felt agreement from the others. She straightened her back, kept her head high, and went to face Joyce.

The week that followed was hectic. There was school to go to during the days, and testing with Joyce in the afternoons. Any leisure time was filled with two things: trying to find a way to break the web, and trying to find out more about Mr. Zetes's plans. The problem was that they didn't make much progress with either.

They didn't get into the hidden room again. Although Kait and Rob waited for a chance, Joyce never left the Institute again and she slept with her doors open.

Kaitlyn lived in a perpetual state of astonishment and nervousness. It was hard to be constantly on her guard with Joyce, to keep from talking about the only two things that were now important in her life. But somehow she managed it—they all managed it.

Marisol remained in a coma. No one outside her family was allowed to visit her, but Joyce called every day. Every day the news was the same: no change.

Mr. Zetes visited the Institute several times, always unexpectedly. They kept their secrets from him, too—or at least, Kaitlyn was pretty sure they did. Occasionally, when she saw Mr. Z's penetrating dark eyes lingering on Gabriel, she wondered.

Gabriel himself was . . . disturbing. Disturbed. Not taking things well.

For Kaitlyn, even though this new intimacy was strange and terrifying, it was exciting, too. She'd never been so close to other people in her life. The sparkling enthusiasm of Lewis's thoughts—the cool serenity of Anna's—that was *good*. And the closeness to Rob was almost painful delight.

But for Gabriel, it was all torture. He spent every minute of his free time reading journals and books, trying to find a way to break the web. He convinced Joyce he was simply interested in researching his talent, and she was delighted. She let him go to the library and get more books, more journals.

He didn't find anything helpful. And every day he didn't, he withdrew further from the others. He learned how to wall himself off telepathically so that Kaitlyn could barely sense his presence.

*We're trying to leave you alone,* she told him. And it was true, they were, because they were all worried. Gabriel seemed to be getting wound tighter and tighter, like something waiting to explode.

On Tuesday, one week after the web was established, Joyce tested Kaitlyn with the EEG machine again.

Kaitlyn had been waiting for this. *I think she's going to do it,* she told Rob. They had gotten pretty good at sending messages to specific people.

*I can come in any time you want,* he said. *But what do you want me to do—just try to watch her?*

Kaitlyn debated as she followed Joyce's instructions to sit down and close her eyes. *No—if there's anything she doesn't want you to see, she won't let you watch. Could you make a distraction when I tell you to? It only needs to last a minute.*

*Yes,* Rob said simply.

Now that Marisol wasn't there to help, Joyce had stopped

testing Gabriel at all, and usually sent Rob and a volunteer to the back lab while the other three did their testing in the front. Rob was there now with Fawn, the girl who had MS. Kaitlyn could feel him waiting, alert and vigilant.

"Right; you know how to do this," Joyce said, sticking a final electrode in place—in the center of Kaitlyn's forehead. Over her third eye. "I'll concentrate on the picture. You relax."

Kait murmured something, concentrating on the feel of that single electrode. Cold. It was definitely colder than all the others, and her forehead had a prickling feeling.

When she relaxed, letting her mind fall into darkness, she knew what to expect.

It came. First the feeling of incredible pressure behind her forehead. It turned into a feeling of inflation, like a balloon being blown up. Then came the pictures.

They flashed through her mind with bewildering speed, and she could only recognize a few. She saw roses and a horse. She saw Mr. Zetes in front of the hidden doorway again. She saw a white house with a caramel-colored face in the window.

And—unexpectedly—she heard voices.

Anna's voice: *Kait—I can't think—what's happening?*

Lewis's: *Jeeeeeeeez.*

Rob's: *Just hang on, everybody.*

At the same time, to Kait's astonishment, she could clearly hear Gabriel. *What the hell is this? What are you trying to do?*

She forced herself to ignore the distracting pictures. *Gabriel, where are you?*

*Just coming up on Exmoor Street.*

Kaitlyn was amazed. Exmoor Street was blocks away from the Institute. They'd found that their telepathy fell off sharply with distance, and anything more than a block was too far for clear communication.

But Gabriel was clear now—painfully clear.

*I'll explain later,* Kait told him. *Just try to deal with it for a few minutes.* Then she told Rob, *Now.*

Immediately she heard a thud, and then Fawn's voice shouting. "Joyce! Oh, please—Rob's hurt!"

Kaitlyn remained perfectly still, eyes shut. She heard a rustle on the other side of the screen, then Anna's voice saying, *She's going. She's in the back lab now.*

Kaitlyn opened her eyes, reaching up to her forehead. The little electrode came away easily, but something remained behind. She could feel it with her fingertips, something stuck to her skin by the electrode cream.

Carefully, her heart beating violently, she peeled it off.

When she looked at it, pinched between thumb and forefinger, she got a shock of disappointment. It wasn't anything after all—just a lump of white electrode cream. Then her fingernails scraped at it and she saw that beneath the coating of paste was something hard. It was white, too, or translucent, which made it difficult to see. It was about the size and shape of her little fingernail, and quite smooth and flat.

It looked like crystal.

All this time she could hear faint voices in the other room. Now Rob said, *Watch out, Joyce is standing up.*

Quickly Kaitlyn stuck the small crystal back onto her forehead. She jammed the electrode on over it, praying they both would stay.

*She's coming back,* Lewis reported.

*Here she is,* Anna said.

Kait rubbed the telltale paste from her fingers onto her jeans. She picked up the pencil and clipboard and began to draw. It didn't matter what. She sketched a rose.

The folding screen was moved. "Kaitlyn, I'm going to unhook you," Joyce said in a rapid, harassed voice. "Rob's completely collapsed—I think he's overdone things with that girl. Anna, Lewis, can you help get him to the couch here? I want him to lie down for a while."

Kaitlyn held still, fingers curled because she was guiltily aware that there was still electrode cream under her fingernails. She was relieved that Joyce didn't seem to notice anything peculiar about the forehead electrode. What *Kaitlyn* noticed, though, was that after taking that one off, Joyce's hand went quickly to her shirt pocket. As if palming something and putting it away.

*Rob, you okay?* Kaitlyn asked, as Lewis and Anna helped him in, and Joyce turned to settle him on the couch.

She got the mental impression of a wink. *Just fine. Did you see anything?*

*A crystal,* Kait told him. *We need to talk about this, try to figure it all out.*

Rob said, *Sure thing. Just as soon as she lets me get up.*

"Before you go, what did you draw?" Joyce asked, looking up as Kait headed for the door.

Kaitlyn got the clipboard and showed her the rose picture.

"Oh, well—better luck next time. It was supposed to be a horse. I'm sorry we had to interrupt your testing."

"It doesn't matter." Kaitlyn said. "I'm going upstairs to get this electrode stuff out of my hair." Silently she added, *We'd better meet before dinner.*

She went upstairs. She wanted to think, but somehow her head seemed cloudy, her thoughts slow.

Rob's voice came to her. *Kaitlyn—are you feeling okay?*

Kaitlyn started to answer, and then *realized* just how she was feeling. *Oh, Rob, I'm stupid. I forgot what happened to me last time she did this.*

She could sense revelation and sympathy from Lewis and Anna, but Rob put it into words. *A headache.*

*A bad one,* Kaitlyn admitted. *It's coming on fast and getting worse.*

Rob's frustration was almost palpable. *And I'm stuck down here with Joyce fussing over me.*

*It doesn't matter,* Kait told him quickly. *You're supposed to be in a collapse, so stay collapsed. Don't do anything to make her suspicious.*

To distract herself, she looked out the window, squinting against the mild light. And then she saw something that made her heart jump into her throat.

Instantly there was an answering wave of alarm from downstairs. *What, what?* Lewis said. *What's wrong?*

*It's nothing,* Kaitlyn said. *Don't worry. I've just got to check something out.* It was the first time she'd tried to deceive the others, but she wanted a moment to think alone. She pulled away from them mentally, knowing they'd respect that. It was like turning your back in a crowded room: the only kind of privacy any of them had now.

She hesitated by the window, looking out at the black limousine parked on the narrow dirt road—and the two figures beside it. One was tall, white-haired, wearing a greatcoat. The other lithe, dark-haired, wearing a red pullover.

Mr. Zetes and Gabriel. Talking in a place where no one could hear them.

# CHAPTER 14

K aitlyn hurried downstairs and slipped out the back
door.

Quietly, she told herself as she made her way
down the hill behind the Institute. Quietly and carefully. She
kept to the blurred shadows of the redwood trees, creeping
up on her prey.

She got close enough that she could hear Gabriel and Mr.
Zetes talking. She knelt behind a bush, looking at them cautiously through the prickly winter-green foliage.

It gave her a grim satisfaction to realize that Gabriel's wall-building could have some drawbacks. He'd barricaded himself from the rest of them so efficiently that he didn't sense her a few yards away. Fortunately, Mr. Zetes's dogs didn't seem to be around to spot her, either.

Shamelessly eavesdropping, Kaitlyn strained her ears.

One dread pounded inside her, sharper than her headache.

She had a terrible fear that they were talking about the web.

In a way, she wouldn't be surprised. The strain on Gabriel had been growing every day. He was desperate, and desperate people look for desperate cures.

But if he'd betrayed them, if he'd gone to Mr. Zetes behind their backs . . .

As she listened, though, her heartbeat calmed a little. It didn't seem to be that kind of conversation. Mr. Zetes seemed to be stroking Gabriel's ego, complimenting Gabriel in a vague and extravagant way. Like somebody buttering up a fraternity pledge, Kaitlyn thought. It reminded her of the speech Mr. Zetes had given the first day at the Institute.

"I know how you must feel," he was saying. "Repressed, hemmed in by society—forced into this *ordinariness*. This *mediocrity*." Mr. Zetes gestured around him, and Kaitlyn instinctively scrunched lower behind her bush. "While all the time your spirit feels caged."

That's nasty, Kaitlyn thought. Talking about cages to someone just out of a boys' prison . . . that's *low*.

"Alienated. Alone," Mr. Zetes continued, and Kait allowed herself a grin. She knew for a fact that one thing Gabriel was *not* feeling these days was alone.

Mr. Zetes seemed to sense that he was off the mark, too, because he went back to harping on the repressed and caged bit. He was manipulating Gabriel; that was clear enough. But why? Kaitlyn thought. She could barely feel Rob, Lewis, and

Anna from here, and she didn't dare try to get in touch with them. It would certainly alert Gabriel, and she wanted to find out what was going on.

"Society itself will someday realize the injustice that's been done to you. It will realize that extraordinary people must be allowed a certain liberty, a certain freedom. They must follow their own paths, without being caged by laws made for ordinary individuals."

Kaitlyn didn't like the expression on Gabriel's face, or the dim feelings she could sense from him behind his walls. He looked . . . *smug,* self-important. As if he were taking all this crap seriously.

It's the strain, Kaitlyn thought. He's so sick of us that he's gone right round the bend.

"I think we should continue this discussion at my house," Mr. Zetes was saying now. "Why don't you come up with me this evening? There's so much we have to talk about."

Horrified, Kaitlyn saw that Gabriel was shrugging. Accepting. "I've been wanting to get away," he said. "In fact, I'd do just about anything to get out of here."

"We might as well go from here," Mr. Zetes said. "I was going to pay a visit to the Institute, but I'm sure Joyce can carry on without me."

Alarm flashed down Kaitlyn's nerves and her heart thumped. Gabriel was getting in the car. They were going to leave right *now*—and there was no time to do anything.

Only one thing. She stood up, trying to look bold and casual at once, and to think clearly despite the pain in her head.

"Take me, too," she said.

Two heads snapped around to look at her. Gabriel had paused with one foot inside the limousine. Both he and Mr. Zetes looked very startled, but in an instant Mr. Zetes's expression had changed to fierce, pitiless scrutiny.

"I've been listening," Kaitlyn said, since this was obvious. "I just came down to—to think, and I saw you, and I listened."

Gabriel's eyes were dark with fury—he was taking it as another invasion of his privacy. "You little—"

"Different rules for extraordinary people," Kaitlyn told him imperiously, standing her ground. "Society shouldn't cage me in." It was the best she could do trying to remember the gibberish Mr. Z had been spouting.

And it seemed to soften Mr. Z's fierce expression. His grim old lips curved a little. "So you agree with that," he said.

"I agree with freedom," Kaitlyn said. "There're times when I feel just like a bird hitting a pane of glass—and then flying back a little and hitting it again—because I just want to get *out*."

It was the truth, in a way. She *had* felt like that—back in Ohio. And the ring of truth seemed to convince Mr. Zetes.

"I often thought you might be the second one to come around," he murmured, as if to himself. Then he looked back at her.

"I should very much like to talk to you, my dear," he said,

and there was a tone of formality, of *finality*, in his voice. As if the simple words were part of some ceremony. "And I'm sure Gabriel will be delighted to have you along."

He made a courteous gesture toward the limo.

Gabriel was gazing at Kaitlyn darkly, looking unconvinced and not at all delighted to have her. But as she slowly got into the car, he shrugged coldly. "Oh, sure."

"Shouldn't we go to the Institute first?" Kaitlyn asked, as Mr. Zetes got in and the limousine began to move, backing up smoothly toward the bridge. "I could change my clothes. . . ."

"Oh, you'll find things quite informal at my home," Mr. Zetes said, and smiled.

They were getting farther away from the purple house every second. *Rob,* Kaitlyn thought, and then with more force. *Rob! Rob!*

She got only a distant sense of mental activity as an answer. Like hearing a muffled voice, but being totally unable to make out the words.

*Gabriel, help me,* she thought, deliberately turning her face away, looking out the limousine window. It frightened her to be using telepathy with Mr. Zetes in the car, but she didn't have a choice. She sent the thought directly at Gabriel, jarring through his walls. *We need to tell Rob and the others where we're going.*

Gabriel's response was maddeningly indifferent. *Why?*

*Because we're going off with a nut who could have anything in mind for us, that's why! Don't you remember Marisol? Now, just help me! I can't get through to them!*

Again Gabriel seemed completely unaffected by her urgency. *If he were going to put us in a coma like Marisol, he would hardly need to take us to San Francisco,* he said contemptuously. *And besides, it's too late now. We're too far away.*

He was right. Kaitlyn glared out the window, trying not to let her tension show in her body.

*Nobody asked you to come and invite yourself along,* Gabriel told her, and she could feel the genuine coldness behind his words. The resentment and anger. *If you don't like it, that's your own fault.*

He hates me, Kaitlyn thought bleakly, putting up walls of her own. She wasn't as good at it as he was, but she tried. Right now, she didn't want to share anything with him.

It was getting dark, the swift chilly darkness of a winter evening. And every mile the limousine went north was taking her farther and farther away from Rob and the Institute, and closer to she didn't know what.

By the time they reached San Francisco, it was fully dark, and the city lights twinkled and gleamed in skyscraper shapes. The city seemed vaguely menacing to Kaitlyn—maybe because it was so beautiful, so charming and cheerful-looking. As if it were decked out for a holiday. She felt there had to be something beneath that lovely, smiling facade.

They didn't stay in the city. The limo headed toward dark hills decorated with strings of white jewels. Kaitlyn was surprised at how quickly the tall buildings were left behind, at how soon they were passing streets of quiet houses. And then the houses began to be farther and farther apart. They were driving through trees, with only an occasional light to show a human habitation. The limousine turned up a private driveway. "Nice little shack," Gabriel said as they pulled up in front of a mansion. Kaitlyn didn't like his voice at all. It was mocking, but dry and conspiratorial, as if Mr. Zetes would appreciate the joke. As if Gabriel and Mr. Zetes shared something.

Something *I* don't share, Kaitlyn thought. But she tried to put the same tone in her own voice. "Really nice."

Under heavy eyelids, Gabriel gave her a glance of derisive scorn.

"That's all for tonight," Mr. Zetes told the chauffeur as they got out. "You can go home."

It gave Kaitlyn a tearing sensation to watch the limousine cruise away. Not that she'd ever said more than "hello" to the driver, but he was her last connection with . . . well, normal human beings. She was alone now, with Mr. Zetes and a Gabriel who seemed to resent her very existence.

"I live very simply, you see," Mr. Zetes was saying, walking up the columned path to the front door. "No servants, not even the chauffeur. But I manage."

Prince and Baron, the two rottweilers, came bounding

up as he opened the door. They calmed at a glance from Mr. Zetes, but followed closely behind him as he and his visitors walked through the house. Just another thing to make Kaitlyn nervous and unhappy.

Mr. Zetes took off his coat and hung it on a stand. Underneath he was wearing an immaculate, rather old-fashioned suit. With real gold cuff links, Kait thought.

The inside of the house was as impressive as the outside. Marble and glass. Thick, velvety carpets and polished, gleaming wood. Cathedral ceilings. All sorts of foreign and obviously expensive carvings and vases. Kaitlyn supposed they were art, but she found some of them repulsive.

Gabriel was looking around him with a certain expression— one it took her a moment to categorize. It was . . . it was the way he'd been looking at the magazine with the expensive cars. Not greedy; greed was too loose and unformed. This expression had *purpose;* it was sharp and focused.

Acquisitive, Kaitlyn thought. That was it. As if he's planning to *acquire* all this. As if he's determined to.

Mr. Zetes was smiling.

I should look like that, too, Kaitlyn thought, and she tried to stamp an expression of narrow-eyed longing on her own face. All she wanted was to fool Mr. Zetes until he let them go home. At the beginning she'd had some idea about finding things out about Mr. Zetes—but not anymore. Now she was just hoping to live through whatever was coming and get back to the Institute.

"This is my study," Mr. Zetes said, ushering them into a room deep in the large house. "I spend a great deal of time here. Why don't you sit down?"

The study was walnut-paneled and darkly furnished, with leather chairs that creaked when you sat on them. On the walls were gold-framed pictures of horses and what looked like fox hunts. The curtains were a deep, lightless red, and the lamps all had rust-colored shades. There was a bust of some old-fashioned-looking man on the mantelpiece and a black statue of a foreign-looking woman on the floor.

Kaitlyn didn't like any of it.

But Gabriel did, she could tell. He leaned back in his chair, looking around appreciatively. It must be a guy thing, Kaitlyn thought. This whole place is so masculine, and so . . . Again, she had trouble finding a word. The closest she could come was *old money.*

She supposed she could see why Gabriel, used to living on the road or in a cell with one bunk and a metal toilet, might like that.

The dogs lay down on the floor. Mr. Zetes went over to the bar—there was a full bar, with bottles and silver trays and crystal decanters—and began pouring something. "May I offer you a brandy?"

My God, Kaitlyn thought.

Gabriel smiled. "Sure."

*Gabriel!* Kaitlyn said. Gabriel ignored her completely, as if she were a fly buzzing around the perimeter of the room.

"Nothing for me, thanks," she said, trying not to sound as frightened as she felt. Mr. Zetes was coming back with only two glasses, anyway—she didn't think he'd even meant to include her in the offer.

He sat down behind the desk and sipped golden liquid out of a ballooning glass. Gabriel sat back in his chair and did the same. Kaitlyn began to feel like a butterfly in a spider's web.

Mr. Zetes himself seemed more aristocratic and imposing than ever, more like an earl. Someone important, someone who ought to be listened to. This whole study was designed to convey that impression, Kaitlyn realized. It was a sort of shrine that drew your attention to the figure behind the large, carved desk. The figure with the immaculate suit and the real gold cuff links and the benevolent white head.

The atmosphere was beginning to get to her, she realized.

"I'm so glad we're able to have this talk," Mr. Zetes said, and his voice went with the atmosphere. It was both soothing and authoritative. The voice of a man who Knew Best. "I could see right away at the Institute that you were the two with the most potential. I knew that you'd outstrip the others very quickly. You both have so much more capacity for understanding, so much more sophistication."

Sophisticated? Me? Kaitlyn thought. But a part of her, a tiny part, was flattered. She'd been more sophisticated than other kids in Thoroughfare, she knew that. Because while all they'd been thinking about was cheerleading or football games, she'd been thinking about the world. About how to get out into the world.

"You can conceive of . . . shall we say, broader horizons," Mr. Zetes was saying, as if he'd followed her train of thought. It was enough to bring Kait up short, to make her look at him in alarm. But his piercing old eyes were smiling, bland, and he was going on. "You are people of vision, like myself," he said. He smiled.

"Like myself."

Something in the repetition made Kaitlyn very nervous.

It's coming, she realized. Whatever it is. He's been building up to something, and here it is.

There was a long silence in the room. Mr. Zetes was gazing at his desk, smiling faintly, as if lost in thought. Gabriel was sipping his drink, eyes narrowed but on the floor. He seemed lost in thought, too. Kaitlyn was too uneasy to speak or move. Her heart had begun a slow, relentless hammering.

The silence had begun to be terrible, when Gabriel raised his head. He looked Mr. Zetes in the eyes, smiled faintly, and said, "And just what is your vision?"

Mr. Zetes glanced toward Kaitlyn—a mere formality. He seemed to assume that Gabriel spoke for both of them.

When he started talking again, it was in a dreadful tone of

complicity. As if they *all* shared a secret. As if some agreement had already been reached.

"The scholarship is only the beginning, of course. But naturally you realize that already. The two of you have such . . . enormous potential . . . that with the right training, you could set your own price."

Again Gabriel gave that faint smile. "And the right training is . . . ?"

"I think it's time to show you that." He put his empty glass down. "Come with me."

He stood and turned to the walnut-paneled wall of the study. As he reached out to touch it, Kaitlyn threw Gabriel a startled glance—but he wasn't looking at her. His entire attention seemed fixed on Mr. Zetes.

The panel slid back. Kaitlyn saw a black rectangle for one instant, and then a reddish glow flicked on as if activated automatically. Mr. Zetes's form was silhouetted against it.

My picture! Kaitlyn thought.

It wasn't, exactly. Mr. Zetes wasn't wearing a coat, for one thing, and the red light wasn't as bright. Her picture had been more a symbol than an actual rendition—but she recognized it anyway.

"Right this way," Mr. Zetes said, turning to them almost with a flourish. He expected them to be surprised, undoubtedly, but Kaitlyn couldn't work herself up to pretending. And when Gabriel entered the gaping rectangle and started down the stairway, she realized she couldn't protest, either. It was too late for that. Mr. Zetes was looking at her, and the dogs were on their feet and right behind her.

She had no choice. She followed Gabriel.

This stairway was longer than the one at the Institute, and it led to a hallway with many doors and several branching corridors. A whole underground complex, Kaitlyn realized. Mr. Zetes was taking them to the very end.

"This is . . . a very special room," he told them, pausing before a set of double doors. "Few people have seen it. I want you to see it now."

He opened one of the doors, then turned toward them and stopped where he was, gesturing them in, watching their faces. In the greenish fluorescent light of the hallway his skin took on an unhealthy chalky tone and his eyes seemed to glitter.

Kaitlyn's flesh began to creep. She knew, suddenly and without question, that whatever was in there was terrible.

Gabriel was going in. Mr. Zetes was watching her with those glittering eyes in a corpselike face.

She didn't have a choice.

The room was startling in its whiteness. All Kaitlyn could think at first was that it was exactly what she'd imagined the laboratories at the Institute would be like. White walls, white tile, everything gleaming and immaculate and sterile. Lots of unfamiliar machinery around the edges, including one huge metal-mesh cage.

But that was all incidental. Once Kaitlyn was able to focus on anything, she focused on the thing in the center of the room—and then she forgot everything else.

It was . . . what? A stone plant? A sculpture? A model spaceship? She didn't know, but she couldn't look away from it. It drew the eye inevitably and then held it fast, the way some very beautiful paintings do—except that it wasn't beautiful. It was hideous.

And it reminded Kaitlyn of something.

It was towering, milky, semitranslucent—and that should have given her a clue. But she couldn't get over her first impression that it was some horrible parody of a plant, even when she realized that it couldn't be.

It was covered with—things. Parasites, Kait thought wildly. Then all at once she realized that they were growths, smaller crystals sprouting from a giant parent. They stuck out in all directions like the rays of a star, or some giant Christmas decoration. But the effect wasn't festive—it was somehow obscene.

"Oh, God—what *is* it?" Kaitlyn whispered.

Mr. Zetes smiled.

"You feel its power," he said approvingly. "Good. You're quite correct; it can be terrible. But it also can be very useful."

He walked over to the . . . thing . . . and stood beside it, the dogs padding at his heels. When he looked at it, Kaitlyn saw that his eyes were admiring—and acquisitive.

"It's a very ancient crystal," he said, "and if I told you where

218

it came from, you wouldn't believe me. But it will amaze you, I promise. It can provide energy beyond anything you've ever imagined."

"This is the training you were talking about?" Gabriel asked.

"This is the means of training," Mr. Zetes said softly, almost absently. He was still looking at the crystal. "The means of sharpening your powers, increasing them. It has to be done gradually to avoid damage, but we have time."

"*That* thing can increase our powers?" Gabriel said with scorn and disbelief.

"Crystals can store psychic energy," Kaitlyn said in a small voice. It sounded small and distant even to her. She had the feeling of someone who'd walked into a nightmare.

Mr. Zetes was looking at her. "You know that?" he said.

"I . . . heard it somewhere."

He nodded, but his eyes lingered on her as he said, "You two have the potential—this crystal has the power to develop that potential. And I have . . ." He stopped, as if thinking how to phrase something.

"What do you have?" Gabriel said.

Mr. Zetes smiled. "The contacts," he replied. "The . . . clients, if you will. I can find people who are willing to pay considerable amounts for your services. Amounts that will climb as your powers are honed, of course."

Clients, Kaitlyn thought. That letter—the letter from Judge Baldwin. A list of potential clients.

"You want to hire us out?" she blurted before she could stop herself. "Like—like—" She was too overwrought to think of an analogy.

Gabriel could think of one. "Like assassins," he suggested. His voice chilled Kaitlyn—because it wasn't at all outraged or indignant. He sounded quite calm—thoughtful, even.

"Not at all," Mr. Zetes said. "I think there would be very few assassinations involved. But there are a number of business situations in which your talents would be invaluable. Corporate espionage—industrial sabotage—influence of witnesses at certain trials. No, I would prefer to call you a psychic strike team, available for handling all sorts of situations."

A strike team. Project Black Lightning, Kaitlyn thought. The words scribbled on that piece of paper. He wanted to turn them into a paranormal dirty tricks team.

"I hadn't meant to explain all this to you so quickly," Mr. Zetes was going on. "But the truth is that something has come up. You remember Marisol Diaz, of course. Well, there has been a bit of a problem with Marisol's family. Several of them have become . . . unexpectedly difficult. Suspicious. I'm afraid that money has little influence on them. I need to quiet them some other way."

There was a pause. Kaitlyn couldn't say anything because she felt as if she were choking, and Gabriel simply looked sardonic.

"I thought we weren't assassins," he said.

Mr. Zetes looked pained. "I don't need them killed. Just quieted. If you can do it some other way, I'm very happy."

Kaitlyn managed to get words through the blockage in her throat. "You did it to Marisol," she said. "You put her in the coma."

"I had to," Mr. Zetes said. "She had become quite unstable. Thank you for bringing that to my attention, incidentally— if you hadn't mentioned it to Joyce, I wouldn't have realized so soon. Marisol had been with me for several years, and I thought she understood what we were doing."

"The pilot study," Kaitlyn said.

"Yes, she told you about that, didn't she? It was a very great pity. I didn't know then that only the strongest minds, the most gifted psychics, could stand contact with one of the great crystals. I gathered six of the best I could find locally—but it was a terrible disaster. Afterward I realized that I would have to expand my search—cover the whole nation—if I wanted to find students who could tolerate the training."

"But what happened to *them?*" Kaitlyn burst out. "To the ones in the pilot study—"

"Oh, it was a dreadful waste," Mr. Zetes said, as if repeating something she should have gotten the first time. "Very good minds, some of them. Genuine talent. To see that reduced to idiocy and madness is very sad."

Kaitlyn couldn't answer. The hair on her arms and the back of her neck was standing up. Tears had sprung to her eyes.

"Marisol, now—I did think she understood, but in the end she proved otherwise. She was a good worker in the beginning. The problem was that she knew too much to be simply bribed, and she was too temperamental to be controlled by fear. I really had no other choice." He sighed. "My real mistake was to use drugs instead of the crystal. I thought a seizure might be very effective—but instead of dying, she wound up in the hospital, and now her family is posing a problem. It's really very difficult."

He might look like an earl—but he was insane, Kaitlyn thought. Truly insane, insane enough that he didn't realize how insane all this would sound to sane people. She looked at Gabriel—and felt a shock that sent chills up from her feet.

# CHAPTER 15

Because Gabriel didn't look as if he found it insane. Slightly distasteful, maybe, but not crazy. In fact, there was something like agreement in his face, as if Mr. Z were talking about doing something unpleasant but necessary.

"But we can take care of that problem," Mr. Zetes said, looking up and speaking more briskly. "And once it's over, we can get to our real work. Always assuming you're interested, of course?"

His voice had a note of gentle inquiry, and he looked from Gabriel to Kaitlyn, waiting for an answer. Again Kaitlyn felt a shock of disbelief. Those dark, piercing eyes of his looked so acute—how could he not realize what she was feeling? How could he look at her as if he expected agreement?

She had exploded into speech before she knew what was happening. All the fear, all the fury, all the disgust and horror, that had been building inside her burst out.

"You're *insane,*" she said. "You're completely insane, don't you know that? Everything that you've said is completely *insane.* How can you talk about people being reduced to idiots as if—as if—" She was degenerating into sobs and incoherence. "And *Marisol,*" she gasped. "How could you do that to *her?* And what you want to turn us all into—you're just completely, totally *crazy.* You're *evil.*"

She was having hysterics, she supposed. Raving. Shouting as if shouting were going to do any good. But she couldn't stop herself.

Mr. Zetes seemed less surprised than she did. Displeased, certainly, but not astonished. "Evil?" he said, frowning. "I'm afraid that's a very emotional and inexact word. Many things seem evil that are, in a higher sense, good."

"You don't *have* any higher sense," Kaitlyn shouted. "You don't care about anything except what you can get out of us."

Mr. Zetes was shaking his head. "I'm afraid I can't waste time in arguing now—but I honestly hope you'll see reason eventually. I think you will, in time, if I keep you here long enough." He turned to Gabriel. "Now—"

Then Kaitlyn did something she realized was stupid even as she was doing it. But her anger at Mr. Zetes's insufferable smugness, his indifference to her words, drove her beyond any caution.

"You won't get any of the others to join you," she said. "Not any of them back home. Rob wouldn't even *listen* to it.

And if I don't come back, they'll know something's wrong. They already know about the hidden room there at the Institute. And they're linked, we're all linked telepathically. All five of us. And—"

*"What?"* Mr. Zetes said. For the first time, a real emotion was showing on his face. Astonishment—and anger. He looked at Gabriel sharply. "What?"

"We are, aren't we?" Kaitlyn demanded. "Tell him, Gabriel." *And tell him he's crazy, because you know he is. You* know *he is!*

"It's something that happened," Gabriel told Mr. Zetes. "It was an accident. I didn't know it would become permanent. If I had"—he glanced at Kaitlyn—"it never *would* have happened."

"But this is—You're telling me that the five of you are involved in a stable telepathic link? But don't you realize . . . ?" Mr. Zetes broke off. There was plenty of emotion in his face now, Kaitlyn noted. It was dark with blood and fury. "Don't you realize that you're useless within a linked group like that?"

Gabriel said nothing. Through their connection, Kaitlyn could feel that he was as angry as Mr. Zetes.

"I was counting on you," Mr. Zetes said. "I *need* you to help me take care of the Diaz problem. If that isn't controlled . . ." He stopped. Kaitlyn could see he was making a great effort to get hold of himself. And, after a moment or two, he apparently succeeded. He sighed, and the fury drained out of his face.

"There's no help for it now," he said. "It's a very great pity. You don't know how much work is wasted." He looked at Kaitlyn. "I had great hopes for you."

Then he said, "Prince, back."

Kaitlyn had almost forgotten about the dogs—but now one came straight for her, hair bristling, teeth showing to the gums. It was completely silent, which only made it scarier.

Involuntarily Kaitlyn took a step backward—and the dog kept coming. As it reached her, she stepped back again and again—and then she realized what was happening. She was standing inside the metal cage.

Mr. Zetes had gone over to a kind of console across the room. He pressed a button and the door to the cage slid shut.

"I told you," Kaitlyn said tensely. "If you keep me here, they'll know—"

Mr. Zetes interrupted as if he didn't notice her speaking. Turning to Gabriel, he said, "Kill her."

Shock washed over Kaitlyn like an icy bath—and again and again. She'd realized, all at once, just *how* stupid she'd been. The cold reality of her situation left her unable to breathe. Unable to think.

"Don't worry; it's just a Faraday cage," Mr. Zetes was telling Gabriel. "It's built to keep out normal electromagnetic waves, but it's quite transparent to your power. It's like the steel room at the Institute, and you projected easily through that."

Gabriel was silent. His stony expression told Kaitlyn

nothing, and she couldn't feel anything from him through the web. Maybe she was just numb.

"Go on," Mr. Zetes said. He was beginning to look impatient. "Believe me, there's no other alternative. If there were, I would save myself the work of getting another subject like her—but there's no choice. The link has to be broken. The only way to break it is to kill one of the five of you."

Gabriel's chest rose and fell with a sudden deep breath. "The link has to be broken," he repeated, grimly. Kaitlyn did feel something then. She felt that he meant it.

"Then go on," Mr. Zetes said. "It's unfortunate, but it has to be done. It's not as if it's the first time you've killed." He glanced at Kaitlyn. "Have you heard about that? Drains his victims' life energy dry. An extraordinary power." There was a kind of macabre satisfaction in his face.

Then it turned to impatience again. "Gabriel, you know what the rewards will be with me. You can literally have anything you want, in time. Money, power—your rightful position in the world. But you must cooperate. You must prove yourself."

Gabriel stood like a statue. Except for that one sentence, he hadn't said a word. Something artistic in Kaitlyn's brain watched him with mad clarity, thinking about how really beautiful his face was in repose. He looked a bit like his namesake, like an angel carved in white marble. Except for his eyes, which were definitely not an angel's eyes. They were dark and fathomless— and right now rather pitiless. Cold as a black hole.

One could very easily imagine an assassin having eyes like that.

Then something like sadness entered them. Because he's sorry to have to kill me? Kaitlyn wondered.

She felt nothing at all through the telepathic web. It was like being connected to a glacier.

"Go on," Mr. Zetes said.

Gabriel glanced at Kaitlyn, then at the white-haired man.

"I'd rather kill you," he said conversationally, to Mr. Zetes.

Kaitlyn didn't get it at first. She thought he might just be stating a preference, rather than refusing.

Mr. Zetes, though, looked unamused. Forbidding. He put one hand behind him.

"If you're not for me, you're against me, Gabriel," he said. "If you won't cooperate, I'll have to treat you as an enemy yourself."

"I don't think you'll have time," Gabriel said, and took a step toward him.

Kaitlyn grabbed at the metal mesh of her cage. Her numbed brain was finally getting things together. She wanted to laugh hysterically—but it didn't seem right.

*Don't kill him,* she thought wildly to Gabriel. *Don't really kill him—he's crazy, don't you see? And we've got to do things— police, an institution—but we can't actually* kill *people.*

Gabriel tossed her the briefest of glances. "*You're* the one who's crazy," he said. "If anybody ever deserved it, it's him. Not that your idea didn't have its points," he added to Mr. Zetes. "Especially in the rewards department."

Mr. Zetes's eyes shifted from Kaitlyn to Gabriel during this exchange. They narrowed, and he nodded slightly.

Kaitlyn was waiting for some sign of fear. It didn't come. Mr. Zetes seemed calm, even resigned.

"You won't change your mind?" he asked Gabriel.

Gabriel took another step toward him. "Good night," he said.

Mr. Zetes brought his hand from behind his back, and Kaitlyn saw that he was holding a dark and very modern, very nasty-looking gun.

"Baron, Prince—guard," he said. And then he added, "If you make a move now, these dogs will jump up and tear out your throat. And then there's the gun—I've always been a very good shot. Do you think you can dispose of all three of us with a knife before we can kill you?"

Gabriel laughed—a very disquieting sound. Although his back was to Kaitlyn now, she knew that he was giving Mr. Zetes his most dazzling, disturbing smile. "I don't need a knife," he said.

Mr. Zetes shook his head, gently and disparagingly. "There's something I'm afraid you haven't realized. Joyce hasn't tested you since you formed this . . . unfortunate linkage, has she?"

"So what?"

"If she had, you would have discovered by now that it's quite difficult for a telepath who is already in a stable link to reach outside that link. Nearly impossible, I believe. In other words, young man, except for communications within your group of five, you've lost your power."

Kait could feel the disbelief surging in Gabriel. His walls were lowered now, his attention was focused elsewhere. Then she felt something like the drawing back of the ocean just before a tsunami—a sort of gathering in Gabriel's mind. She braced herself—and felt him unleash it.

Or try to. The wave, instead of crashing down on Mr. Zetes, seemed to crash around her and Gabriel instead.

It was true. He couldn't link with anyone else. Not to communicate with them—and not to harm them.

"And now, if you'll sit down in that chair," Mr. Zetes said.

Kaitlyn's eyes shifted to the chair. She'd barely noticed it before. It stood on the opposite side of the room from the door, and it looked frighteningly high-tech. It was made of metal.

With the gun in front of him and a dog on either side, Gabriel backed up to the chair. He sat.

Mr. Zetes went over and made some quick movements, stooping once. When he stood, Kaitlyn realized that Gabriel was now restrained in the chair by metal cuffs at his wrists and ankles.

Then Mr. Zetes stepped behind the chair. Two winglike

devices swung forward. In another instant, Gabriel's head was held motionless by a device that looked as if it were meant for brain surgery.

"The crystal can do more than just amplify power," Mr. Zetes said. "It can cause excruciating pain—even madness. Of course, that was what happened with the pilot study." He stepped back. "Are you quite comfortable?" he asked.

Kaitlyn was remembering the pain that had resulted from being in contact with a tiny shard of the crystal, a piece the size of her fingernail.

Mr. Zetes went over to the towering thing with the jagged growths in the center of the room. For the first time, Kaitlyn realized that the metal stand that supported it was mobile. The entire structure, though obviously heavy, could be moved.

Very carefully and delicately, Mr. Zetes was bringing the crystal to Gabriel. Tipping it slightly. Adjusting it. Until one of the jagged terminals, one of the growths, was resting against Gabriel's forehead.

In direct contact with the third eye.

"It will take a while for it to build. Now I'm going to leave the room," Mr. Zetes said. "In an hour or so I'll come back— and by then I think you might have changed your mind."

He walked out. The dogs went with him.

Kaitlyn was alone with Gabriel—but there was absolutely nothing she could do.

She looked wildly at the door of the metal cage, pulled at

it with the strength of desperation. She only succeeded in cutting her fingers. It took her about two minutes to discover that there was no way she could affect it, with fists or feet or the weight of her body.

"Don't bother," Gabriel said. The strain in his voice frightened her into going over to look at him.

He was completely immobile, his face white as paper. And now that Kaitlyn was still, she could feel his pain through the web.

He was trying to hold it back, to close himself—and the pain—off from her. But even what little got through to her was terrible.

The pressure behind the forehead—like what she had experienced with the crystal Joyce had used, but indescribably worse. As if something alive were swelling there, trying to get out. And the heat—like a blowtorch directed against that spot. And the sheer black agony—

Kaitlyn's knees gave out. She found herself half lying on the floor of the cage.

Then she pulled herself up to a sitting position.

*Oh, Gabriel . . .*

*Leave me alone.*

"I'm sorry," she whispered, saying it and sending it at once. *I'm so sorry. . . .*

*Just leave me alone! I don't need you. . . .*

Kaitlyn couldn't leave him alone. She was locked into it with him, sharing the waves of agony that kept building. She could feel them break over her, spread out infinitely around her. Spreading, swelling . . . to include all of them. All five who shared the web.

*Kaitlyn!* a distant voice shouted.

The connection was shaky, tenuous. But Kaitlyn recognized Rob.

It wasn't just pain. It was power. The crystal was feeding Gabriel power.

*Rob—can you hear me? Lewis, Anna—can you hear me?*

*Kaitlyn, what's happening? Where* are *you?*

*It's them, Gabriel! We've got them! It's them!* For a minute, despite the screaming of her nerves, Kaitlyn was simply delirious with joy.

*We might lose them any second,* Gabriel said. But Kaitlyn could feel what he felt—there were no walls between them now. The crystal had annihilated those. And his relief and joy were as strong as hers.

*Rob, we're in Mr. Zetes's house. You've got to find out somehow where that is—and fast.* Kaitlyn told them about the study, and the panel. *It might be closed again, but Lewis can open it. But you have to hurry, Rob—come quick.*

*If you want to find us alive,* Gabriel added. Kaitlyn was amazed that he was even speaking coherently. She knew that he was taking the worst of the pain himself. She felt a surge of admiration for him.

*Keep it to yourself, witch,* he told her.

It was an endearment, she realized. *Witch.* She supposed she'd better learn to like it.

*You could have told Mr. Zetes you'd think about killing me. You could have bought yourself time,* she said.

*I don't bargain with people like him.*

Kaitlyn, through the waves of pain that were starting to be tinged with crimson and carmine, felt an intense pride and triumph. *You see?* she thought to Rob. *Mr. Zetes was wrong about all of us. You see how wrong?*

But Rob wasn't there anymore. The connection had been too fragile—or now the pain was wiping everything out.

She leaned against the metal cage, dimly feeling its coolness. *Hang on,* she thought. *Hang on. Hang on. He's coming.*

She didn't know if she was saying it to Gabriel or to herself, but he answered. *You believe that?*

It roused her a little. *Of course,* she said. *I know he is. And so do you.*

*It's dangerous. He's risking his own neck by coming here,* Gabriel said.

*You know he's coming,* Kaitlyn said, able to say it with perfect assurance because she could *feel* it, directly.

"Rob the Virtuous," Gabriel said, aloud. He made a contemptuous sound like a snort—which was marred because he almost immediately gasped in pain.

Kaitlyn could never really remember the time that passed after that. It wasn't time to her, so much as a series of terrible, endless waves that eventually turned brilliant, bursting red and white like molten rock. She had no means of keeping track of them, and no consciousness of anything but them. She was alone with the waves of colored agony, thrown about by them like a swimmer caught in a riptide.

Alone—except for Gabriel. He was there, always connected. They were both being thrown around by the pain, dimly aware of each other. Kaitlyn didn't think it did Gabriel much good to know she was there, but she was glad of his presence.

It seemed a very long time, centuries maybe, but at last she sensed another presence in the maelstrom that was her world.

*Kaitlyn—Gabriel. Can you hear us now? Kaitlyn! Gabriel!*

*Rob.* Her own response was so weak and faltering, so small in the huge waves, that she didn't think he would hear it.

*Thank God! Kait, we're here. We're in the house. Everything is going to be all right—Joyce is with us. She's on our side. She didn't know anything about what he was doing. We're coming to help you, Kait.*

There was a near frenzy to Rob's words. Emotion—an emotion Kait had never sensed from him before. But she couldn't think now. Too much pain.

She lost awareness until she felt a presence very close.

Rob. She dragged herself up. The room was both too bright and strangely gray and dim. Alternating, like lightning. Rob was there, golden as an avenging angel, somehow coming between her and the pain. And Lewis was there, and Anna, both crying. And Joyce, her sleek blond hair all ruffled like a dandelion. They were running toward the crystal, although Kaitlyn saw their movements as discontinuous, as if under a strobe lamp.

And then—like a light switch being turned off—the pain was gone.

It left echoes, of course, and normally Kaitlyn would have found even the echoes unbearable. But it was so different from the actual pain that she felt wonderful. Able to think again, able to breathe. Able to see.

She saw that Joyce had pulled the terminal of the crystal away from Gabriel. His forehead was bleeding freely, the skin torn. He must have moved his head somehow, in spite of the metal restraints. The blood ran down his face in streams, as if he were crying.

He'd hate that, Kaitlyn thought. But Gabriel wasn't awake to be hating it. She realized now that it was some time since she'd felt any sort of communication from him, even a scream. He was unconscious.

The door of the Faraday cage was opening. Rob was beside her. Rob was holding her.

*Are you all right? Oh, God, Kait, I thought I might lose you.*

There it was again. The new emotion. The one that felt almost like pain, but was different.

Kaitlyn looked up into Rob's eyes.

*I didn't know,* he said. *I didn't realize how much I had to lose.*

It was like being transported back to the afternoon when he'd looked at her with awe and wonder, on the brink of a discovery that would change both their lives. Except that now he wasn't just on the brink. The full discovery was in those golden eyes, shining with terrible clarity. A pure light that was almost impossible to look at.

*It would have been like losing me, like losing my own soul,* Rob said, but it wasn't really like him saying it to her, it was as if he were simply realizing these things himself. *And now it's like finding my soul again. The other half of me.*

Kaitlyn felt it again, the universe around her hushed and waiting, enclosing the two of them. This time, though, there was a trembling joy to the hush, a *certainty.* They weren't on the threshold anymore. They were passing through. Everything being said between them, without spoken words or even words of the mind. It was simply as if their souls were mingling, joining in an embrace that wasn't quite the web and wasn't quite Rob's healing power, although it had elements of both.

It was beyond all that. It was a union, a *togetherness,* that Kaitlyn had never dreamed of.

*I'm with you. I belong to you.*

*I'm a part of you. I will be forever.*

Kaitlyn didn't even know which of them was speaking. The feelings were in both of them.

*We were born for this.*

He was holding her hands, she was holding his. She could

feel the power flowing between them, the energy like millions of sparkling lights, like fresh, cleansing water, like music, like stars. But she felt she was healing him as much as he was healing her. Giving him back what the accident had taken from him, the part of him that had been missing.

And then it was all so simple and natural. As if they both knew what to do without thinking—as if they'd always known what to do.

She tilted her face up, he bent down.

His lips touched hers.

In a minute they were exchanging the softest, most innocent kisses imaginable.

Kait had *never* thought that kissing a boy would be like this.

Not even Rob. She'd thought that kissing Rob would be wonderful. But this wasn't like something physical at all. It was simply like falling into the color of Rob's eyes. It was like falling endlessly into sunlight and gold.

*Born for each other. For this.*

A long sunlit wave, a wave of gold, came and carried them away.


Dimly, gradually, Kaitlyn was aware of a loud sound. A loud *vocal* sound.

"I said, I'm sorry to interrupt you, but really. Rob, there's something to do here!"

It was Joyce, sounding sadly unmusical after the lovely

voices Kaitlyn had been hearing. Joyce was looking at them, impatient and worried, and the tears on Anna's face were still wet. It had only been a minute or so since they'd all come in.

Impossible, of course. Kaitlyn in her heart knew it had been hours, but that was *real* time, soul time, and not the time that was ticking away on this dreary planet. She and Rob had been floating around for hours, but it had only taken a minute *here*.

Rob disengaged himself, letting go of Kaitlyn's hands. A small parting, but a hard one. Kaitlyn's fingers curled, empty.

"I'm sorry. I think I can help Gabriel," Rob said. He got up, took a step, then turned back to Kait. He knelt down by her again. *I forgot to say, I love you.*

Kaitlyn gave a half-gasping laugh. As if *that* needed to be said. "You go help Gabriel," she whispered.

"No, I need both of you," Joyce was saying. "And *quickly.* You can't solve this with energy channeling, Rob—he needs to be brought back from wherever he is. I need all four of you to get in contact with the crystal."

That broke through the lingering gold haze in Kaitlyn's vision. *"What?"* she said, standing up. She noticed dimly that she felt good, physically. Strong. Healing power *had* flowed between her and Rob.

"I need you all to get in contact with the crystal," Joyce said patiently. "And Gabriel, too—"

"No!"

"It's the only way, Kaitlyn."

"You saw what it did!"

"This time it will only be for a moment. But I need *all* of you to touch the crystal, everyone who's in the link. Now, for God's sake, hurry. Don't you realize that Mr. Zetes may be back at any minute?"

Kaitlyn staggered as she made her way out of the cage. To let the crystal touch Gabriel again—impossible. It couldn't be done, it was too cruel. And the crystal was *evil;* Kaitlyn knew that. . . .

But Joyce said it was the only way.

Kaitlyn looked at Joyce, who looked back with clear aquamarine eyes. Eyes that looked anguished but earnest.

"Don't you want to save him, Kait?"

Kaitlyn's hand began to itch and cramp.

She needed to draw—but there wasn't any time. No time. And nothing to draw with. Not a pen or paper in this entire sterile lab.

"*Please* trust me, everyone. Come on, Lewis. Just get your hand ready to touch it. When I say *now,* grab a terminal."

Lewis took a deep breath and then nodded. He held his hand ready.

"Anna? Good. Thank you. Rob?"

Rob looked at Kaitlyn.

If she could draw . . . But she couldn't. Looking back at Rob, Kaitlyn made a helpless motion that ended with a nod.

"We'd better do it," she whispered.

Joyce shut her eyes and sighed in relief. "Good. Now, I'll get behind Gabriel. When I say *now,* I'll move him in contact. Each of you grab a terminal and hold on, right?"

Kaitlyn could vaguely sense the others agreeing. She herself was moving to stand in front of the crystal, one hand outstretched. But her mind was whirring with frantic speed.

I can't draw . . . not with my hands. But the power's not in my hands. It's in my head, in my mind. If I could draw in my mind . . .

# CHAPTER 16

E ven as Kaitlyn thought it, she was doing it. Desperately visualizing oil pastels, her favorite, sweeps of color. First I'd take lemon yellow, fluffy sweeps, with dashes of palest ocher. Then curves of flesh tint—and two small pools of light blue and Veronese green, dotted together.

All right! What is it? Step back! Step back and look.

In her mind, she stepped back, and the sweeps and dots made a picture. Joyce. Unmistakably Joyce.

Then gray. Curves and lines of gray. A shape—a glass. With flesh tones holding it—Joyce holding a glass.

"Everyone ready?" Joyce said.

Kaitlyn didn't move, didn't open her eyes. She was concentrating on the next part of the picture. Rich olive-hued flesh, with a mass of burnt umber and deep madder for hair. The brown and red went together to make mahogany.

Marisol. A picture of Joyce and Marisol. And Joyce was holding out to Marisol a glass—

"I've got his head," Joyce said. "And—*now*—"

Kaitlyn's scream, both mental and verbal, cut through the words. *"Don't do it! Don't do it! She's with him—Mr. Zetes!"*

In the split second that followed, she wondered if she might be wrong. Joyce might have given Marisol something unknowingly—but the picture hadn't said that. It might not even be a picture of a real event, but for once, the *meaning* was clear to Kaitlyn. And the meaning was one of menace and danger. It felt to her the way the picture of the old witch giving Snow White a poisoned apple had felt to Kaitlyn the child.

And, even as Kaitlyn opened her eyes, she saw that she *hadn't* been wrong. Joyce had thrust Gabriel's head against the crystal and was holding it, and her face had an expression that Kaitlyn had never seen before. A look of twisted, bestial fury.

*She knew all the time. She was in on everything,* Kaitlyn thought, sickened. She could feel the shock and pain of the others—especially Rob. But her shout had reached them in time. Not one of them had touched the crystal.

Except Gabriel—Gabriel, who was now being roused from unconsciousness by the white-hot lightning bolts of pain.

Kaitlyn started to move—to tear Joyce away from Gabriel. Rob started at the same moment she did. But before they could get there, the doors burst open and chaos exploded on them.

It was Mr. Zetes—and the dogs. Something knocked into Kaitlyn with the force of a speeding truck and she fell. A dog was ripping at her. Mr. Zetes had the gun.

Still holding Gabriel against the crystal, Joyce was shouting. "I'll break the link! I'll break it!"

Rob was fighting the other dog. Anna was trying to pull the animal off him, her own calls to it lost in the clamor.

"There's an easier way to break it! Only one of them needs to die!" Mr. Zetes shouted. He was aiming the gun at Lewis.

And this is how it ends, a part of Kaitlyn's mind thought, curiously detached. None of them could help Lewis. None of them could do anything before Mr. Zetes could shoot.

She seemed to sense the old man's finger tightening on the trigger. At the same time she saw the room as one large picture, every detail etching itself into her mind as if with the burst of a flashbulb. Rob and Anna tangled with the rottweiler, Lewis standing in almost comical horror, Joyce's twisted face over the face of Gabriel, whose cheeks were masked in blood and who was just opening his eyes . . .

She felt Gabriel's awakening at the same instant, felt his pain—and his fury. Someone was hurting him. Someone was threatening a member of his web.

Gabriel lashed out.

Mr. Zetes had said that a telepath in a stable link couldn't reach outside that link—but Gabriel was now connected to a source of unthinkable power. His mind blazed out like the flare of a supernova—in four directions. With absolute precision and deadly force, he sent a torrent of fire through Mr. Zetes and Joyce and the two dogs.

Kaitlyn felt the dim shadows of it through the web, the reverberations of what Gabriel had unleashed on them. It knocked her flat.

Mr. Zetes fell without firing a shot. Behind Gabriel, Joyce hit the wall. The dog tearing Kaitlyn's arm spasmed as if it had been electrocuted and was still.

Then Gabriel stopped it. He had sagged back from the crystal, collapsing. The entire room was silent and motionless.

*Let's get out of here,* Rob gasped.

Kaitlyn was never sure how they got out of the house. Rob was the main force in moving them. He practically carried Gabriel. She and Anna and Lewis helped each other. There was a long time of stumbling and dragging and finally they were on grass.

Grass cool with dew. It felt wonderful. Kaitlyn rested against it gratefully, as if she'd just staggered out of a fire.

At last Lewis whispered thickly, "Are they dead?"

*The dogs are, I think,* Anna said. Kaitlyn agreed, but didn't mention that she'd seen blood coming out the eyes and nose and ears of the one on top of her.

*But Mr. Zetes and Joyce—I don't know,* Anna finished. *I think they might be alive.*

"And so Joyce didn't want to save Gabriel," Lewis said.

"She wanted to break the web somehow," Kaitlyn said, not surprised to find her voice hoarse. "Even if it killed us. Gabriel wasn't any good to them linked to us. . . . Don't ask why. I'll explain everything later."

"But Joyce was bad," Lewis said sadly. The simple innocence of the statement caught Kait—and did something to her.

Joyce was bad. She'd been against them, ready to use them, the whole time. Marisol had been wrong; Joyce had clearly known everything. She'd known about the big crystal and had had no hesitation about using it. She must have known all about the hidden room, too.

"God," Kaitlyn whispered. "How could I have been so dumb? It was probably *her* room—everything was copies, remember, Rob? Duplicates. Mr. Zetes had his stuff here, and she had hers in the Institute."

"Kaitlyn," Rob whispered, and there was both pain and tenderness in his voice, although he couldn't reach her since he was cradling Gabriel. "Don't. It's not worth it."

Kaitlyn looked at him in surprise—and realized she was crying. Thick streams of tears. She put a hand to her cheek and touched the wetness. As soon as she did, she felt something swell up in her chest.

And then she was sobbing, huge sobs, the kind she hadn't cried since she was eight years old.

Anna held her. *Leave her alone,* she told Rob. *She deserves to cry. We all do.*

The shaking sobs passed quickly, and Kaitlyn began to feel better.

Gabriel was stirring.

"This time," Rob told him, "you don't have any choice. You're half-dead—and we can't stay here. You *have* to take help." He added, silently, where it would mean more, *You saved my life a little while ago. There's only one way I can repay that.*

Gabriel blinked. He looked terrible—the blood and the pain had distorted his handsome face. But he managed a trace of the old arrogance as he whispered, "Only because I can't stop you."

Kaitlyn stopped sniffling and smiled. *It's not much good to talk like that when all your walls are down,* she told him. Then she added, *I like you this way. Walls can be very bad things.*

Gabriel ignored her, which was all he could do at the moment.

Now Rob was touching Gabriel with gentle, irresistible fingers, and Kaitlyn could feel strength flowing into Gabriel. Through Rob's healing points, through the telepathic web. She put her hand on Rob's and added her own strength, letting Rob take her energy and channel it into Gabriel. Lewis and Anna crowded close and touched Rob's hand, too, adding their contribution. All four of them, linked tightly, willing life and energy into Gabriel.

Kaitlyn could sense his need and his fear—which rapidly turned into astonishment. He'd never felt energy freely given before, she realized. Now she knew what he was feeling and she could feel it with him—the sparkling lights, the pure water, the refreshment. The awakening from half-sleep into real, vivid life.

She could feel astonishment and joy from Anna and Lewis, too.

*And I never believed them about kundalini rising,* Lewis said. *Jeeeez, was I wrong.*

*About what?* Anna asked, laughing in her mind.

*Kundalini—old Chinese health concept. Relating to chi, you know. Remind me to tell you about it sometime.*

Anna, still laughing, said, *I will.*

When they were all feeling ready to ride tigers and fight elephants bare-handed, Rob lifted his hands.

"That's enough," he said, and then added gently, "We really shouldn't stay here. I think Anna was right, and that Joyce and Mr. Zetes are alive. We need to keep moving."

"But where?" Kaitlyn said. She could stand, she found; she could even move easily.

Gabriel was on his feet, too. "Well, out of San Francisco for a start," he said, wiping his face with his dew-wet shirt. Even in the simple act of standing up he had pulled away from them all a little, mentally.

It's only to be expected, Kaitlyn told herself. Don't be disappointed. He needs his space.

"Well, of course, out of San Francisco. But then—where? Home?"

Even as she said it, she knew she couldn't go. If Mr. Zetes and Joyce survived, they would come after her. Kaitlyn knew about them now—Kaitlyn was a danger in the way that Marisol had been a danger. They'd want to have Kaitlyn . . . quieted.

And as much as Kaitlyn adored her father, she knew him very well. He was loving, impractical—vague. Happiest in his own small world, singing and doing odd jobs. What protection could he offer her? He wouldn't even be able to understand her story, much less help her deal with it.

In fact, she'd probably be putting *him* in danger by going home. Nothing would be easier than for Joyce and Mr. Zetes to find her there. And once they found her, she'd be dead—along with anyone else who had heard her story.

Kaitlyn didn't have the least doubt that Mr. Zetes had ways to get people killed. He had contacts. He had clients. He would find a way.

Looking around at the others, she could see them reaching the same conclusion about their own families. She could feel their dawning bewilderment.

"But then . . . where do we go?" Lewis said, in a croaking whisper.

"We have to do something to stop them. Not just Mr. Zetes and Joyce, but whoever else is involved. There must be others—like that judge. We have to find a way to stop them all."

Kaitlyn felt her breath snatched away. She looked at Rob.

Yes, she loved him, but really . . . really, she'd just been thinking about how to keep herself and her friends safe. That was going to be hard enough.

"If we don't stop them," Rob said, turning and looking directly at her, "then they'll do it again. They'll try again, with some other group of kids."

Rob was counting on her. Trusting her. And of course, he was right.

"It's true," Kaitlyn said quietly. "We can't let that happen."

"I agree," Anna chimed in softly.

There was a pause, and then Lewis said, "Oh, jeez . . . Count me in."

They all looked at Gabriel.

"I don't even have a home," he said mockingly. "All I know is that I'm not going back into a lockup cell."

"Then come with us," Rob said.

"You don't even know where you're going."

Kaitlyn said, "I might."

Everyone looked quickly at her.

"It's just an idea," she said. "I don't even know exactly why it's come into my head . . . but do you remember that dream, the one we were all in together?"

There were nods.

"Well, what if . . . what if the place in the dream was a real place? When I think about it, I get this sort of feeling that it might be. Does anybody else?"

Everyone looked doubtful, except Anna, who looked thoughtful.

"You know," she said, "I had the same feeling while I was there—in the dream, I mean. That beach felt real. It was a lot like the beaches where I live, up North. It felt almost . . . familiar. And that white house—"

"Wait," Kaitlyn said. "The house. The white house." Her brain was whirring again. She'd seen a white house somewhere else. In her mind this afternoon—could it only be this afternoon?—when Joyce had tested her with the shard of crystal.

She'd never drawn that picture—it had disappeared in a flash. But now she suddenly felt she might be able to reach it again.

Don't think—draw. Draw with your mind. Let your mind go.

Whether it was the recent contact with the great crystal, or simply desperation, she'd never know. But her mind began to draw, sketching with easy, fluid strokes. Vigorous clean strokes. She didn't even have to think about what colors to use. They simply appeared before her, shimmering, in a picture that was completed in a few heartbeats.

A white house, yes. With red roses growing at the door. A lonely house, but an eerily beautiful one. And a face in the window—a caramel-colored face, with slanting eyes and softly curling brown hair.

The man who'd attacked her—but *had* he attacked her? He'd grabbed her and tried to talk with her when she was waiting to meet Joyce. He'd grabbed her in the backyard of the Institute—and she'd hit him. And then he'd called her reckless and told her she never *thought*.

She was thinking now. Whoever he was, he had been in the house in her dream. And he had showed her a picture of a rose garden, with a crystal in the fountain.

She hadn't recognized it as a crystal then. But when she'd seen the big crystal, that monstrosity that Mr. Zetes had owned, she'd almost remembered.

The crystal in the rose garden hadn't looked . . . perverted. It had been clean and clear, with no obscene growths sprouting out. It had looked . . . pure.

So what did it all add up to? Kaitlyn didn't know, but she took a deep breath and tried to explain it to the others.

When she was done, there was a silence.

"So we're following our dreams," Gabriel said with mock sentimentality, his lip still slightly curled.

The words pleased Kait somehow. "Yes," she said, and smiled at him. "And we'll see where they take us."

"Wherever it is, we're going together," Rob said.

Kaitlyn looked at him. She was cold and battered and she knew that the danger was just beginning. And they had no clear idea of which way to travel and even less idea of *how* to travel.

But somehow it didn't matter. They were all alive, and all together. And when she looked into Rob's golden eyes, she knew that it was going to be all right.

# THE POSSESSED

*For Rosemary Schmitt,*
*with thanks for all her good wishes*
*and support*

# CHAPTER 1

"Hurry!" Kaitlyn gasped as she reached the top of the staircase. And she added with her mind, in case it might make more of an impression that way: *Hurry.*

From four different directions she felt acknowledgment, and an urgency just as strong as her own. Felt it with a sense that wasn't one of the ordinary five, but that was like seeing music or tasting color.

Telepathy was strange.

But sometimes comforting. Right now Kait was grateful for Rob's presence in her mind. It burned with a strong golden glow that warmed and steadied her. She could sense him in the next room, working fast but without panic, flipping through drawers and stuffing jeans and socks into a canvas bag.

They were leaving the Institute.

Not exactly the way they'd intended to, when they'd come to be part of a year-long psychic research project. Kaitlyn had expected to leave the Zetes Institute next spring with a band playing, a college scholarship under her arm, and her father looking on proudly. Instead, she was scrambling in the middle of the night to get her belongings together and get out before Mr. Zetes caught up with them.

Mr. Zetes, the head of the Institute, the one who wanted to turn them into psychic weapons and sell them to the highest bidder.

Only maybe now he just wanted them dead. Because they'd found out what he was up to and fought back and beaten him. Impossible as that might sound, with all Mr. Z's power, they'd *won.* They'd left him knocked out cold in the secret rooms of his San Francisco mansion.

When he woke up he was going to be mad enough to kill.

"What are you taking?" Anna asked, and her usually calm voice had a hurried sound.

"I don't know. Clothes—warm clothes, I guess. We don't know where we'll be sleeping at night." Kait repeated the last thought mentally, so Rob and Lewis and Gabriel could hear. *Warm clothes, everybody!*

A mental voice answered her, sharp as a knife and cool as midnight. *And money,* it said. *Take all the money you can get your hands on.*

"Always practical, Gabriel," Kaitlyn murmured and stuffed her purse into a duffel bag, recklessly piling jeans and sweaters and underwear on top of it. She took her lucky hundred dollar bill out of a jewelry box on the dresser and jammed it in her pocket.

"What else?" she said aloud. She found herself grabbing crazy things: a velvet cap with gold embroidery, a necklace that had been her mother's, the paperback mystery she'd been reading. Finally she jammed in her smallest sketchbook and the plastic box that held her oil pastels and colored pencils. She *couldn't* leave without her art kit—she'd rather go naked.

And her drawings weren't just recreation; they were far more important than that. They were how she told the future.

Hurry, quick, she thought.

Anna was hesitating, looking at a carved wooden mask on the wall. It was Raven, the totem of Anna's family, and it was much too big to take with them.

"Anna . . ."

"I know." Anna touched the blunt beak of the mask once with graceful fingers, then turned from it. She smiled at Kaitlyn, her dark eyes serene over high cheekbones. "Let's go."

"Wait—soap." Kait dashed into the bathroom and snagged a bar of Ivory, catching a glimpse of herself in the mirror. Nothing like as serene as Anna—her long red hair was in elf-locks, her cheeks were flushed, and the strange blue rings in her eyes were burning smokily. She looked like a feverish witch.

"Okay," Rob said as they all met in the hall. "Everybody ready?"

Kaitlyn looked at them, at the four people who'd become

closer to her than she would have imagined any people could be.

Rob Kessler, all warmth and color, gold-blond hair and golden eyes. Gabriel Wolfe, arrogant and handsome, like a drawing done in black and white. Anna Eva Whiteraven, her expression gentle even under pressure. Lewis Chao with his almond-shaped eyes glittering with anxiety, slapping a baseball cap onto smooth black hair.

Thanks to Gabriel's power going out of control, they were linked by a telepathic web. None of them would ever be alone again—unless they could find a way to break the link.

"I want to get something from downstairs," Gabriel was saying.

"Me, too," Rob said, "and I need Lewis to help. All right, let's get moving. You all right, Kait?"

"Just breathless," Kaitlyn said. Her heart was pounding, and there was a shakiness in every limb that made her not want to stand still.

Rob reached to take her duffel bag with the ruthless courtesy of his North Carolina lineage. For just an instant their hands touched; his strong fingers wrapped around hers.

*It'll be all right,* he told her in a swift private communication meant for no one else.

The feeling that flooded Kaitlyn was almost painful. For God's sake, not *now,* she thought and ignored the sparks that swarmed where he'd touched her skin.

"Be careful, you—healer," she said and started down the stairs.

Lewis kept glancing over his shoulder. "My computer," he mourned softly. "My stereo, my TV set . . ."

"Why don't you go back and get them?" Gabriel asked nastily. "What could be more inconspicuous?"

"Keep *moving*," Rob ordered. At the bottom of the stairs he said, "Lewis, come with me."

Kait followed them. "What are you doing?"

"Getting the files," Rob said grimly. "Okay, Lewis, open that panel."

Of course, Kaitlyn thought. Mr. Zetes's files, the ones he kept in the hidden room here under the stairway. They were full of all kinds of information, most of it cryptic, some of it undoubtedly incriminating.

"But what can we *do* with them? Who can we show them to?"

"I don't know," Rob said. "But I want them anyway. They *prove* what he's been up to."

Lewis was running sensitive fingertips over the dark paneling on the wall. Kaitlyn could feel what he was doing, trying to locate the spring release with his mind. "It's not easy to perform on demand like this," he muttered, but then there was a click and the panel slid back.

"Mind over matter," Rob said, grinning.

*Hurry,* Kaitlyn told him sharply.

She didn't wait to see him start down into the dimly lit hallway behind the door. She took her duffel bag into the front laboratory where Anna was opening a wire cage.

"Go on," she was saying. "Go on, Georgie Mouse, go on, Sally Mouse . . ." She knelt to hold the cage by the open side door.

"You're letting them out?"

"I'm *sending* them away, telling them to find a field. I don't know what Mr. Z will do to them," Anna said. "I don't even trust Joyce anymore." Joyce Piper was the parapsychologist who actually ran the Institute for Mr. Zetes, the one who'd recruited Kaitlyn. Even now, Kaitlyn couldn't think about her without feeling a twinge of betrayal.

"Okay, but *hurry.* We don't have time to waste," she said and moved restlessly back into the hallway. Lewis was tugging at his baseball cap nervously.

Gabriel, in the small bedroom beyond, was going through Joyce's purse.

*Gabriel!* Kait said. She could feel her shock reverberating in the telepathic web, and she tried to muffle it.

He merely slanted her an ironic glance. "We need money."

"But you can't—"

"Why not?" he said. His gray eyes were so dark they looked almost black.

"Because it isn't . . . it's not . . ." Kaitlyn could feel herself sagging. "It's wrong," she said finally.

Gabriel didn't admit to concepts like "wrong."

"Joyce is our enemy," he said shortly. "If it wasn't for her, we wouldn't be running away in the middle of the night in the first place. It's necessary—and you know it, don't you, Kait?"

It was dangerous to look into Gabriel's eyes for more than an instant. Kaitlyn turned away without answering, then turned back to hiss, "All right, but don't take any credit cards. They can trace those. And don't let Rob know, or he'll go ballistic. And *hurry*."

That one word had begun to pound relentlessly in her brain: hurry, hurry, hurry. Faster than a heartbeat. She had a feeling—no, a certainty—that every second they stayed here was too long.

A premonition? But she didn't have that kind of premonition. It was only by drawing that she could get an image of the future.

Hurry. Hurry. Hurry.

Trust yourself, she thought suddenly. Go with your feelings.

"Gabriel," she said abruptly, "we've got to leave now." She added in an urgent mental shout, *Lewis, Rob, Anna—we have to leave! Right now, this second! Something's going to happen—I don't know what, but we've got to get out of here—*

"Take it easy." She felt Gabriel's hand on her arm and only then realized how agitated she was. As soon as she'd spoken her feelings out loud, she'd realized how strong they were, how urgent.

"I'm all right, but Gabriel, we've got to go. . . ."

He looked into her eyes briefly and nodded. "If you feel like that—come on."

In the hallway Rob was hurrying out of the open panel with an armful of file folders. Anna was emerging from the lab.

"What's wrong? Is someone coming?" Rob asked.

"I don't know, I just know we have to hurry—"

"We'll take Joyce's car," Gabriel said.

Rob hesitated, then nodded. "Come on, out the back door." He hustled Lewis and Anna ahead of him. Kaitlyn followed right on his heels, feeling she couldn't move fast enough.

"We'll just use the car to get out of the area," Rob was saying, when a wave of adrenaline broke over Kaitlyn. It left a metallic taste of fear in her mouth.

Behind her the front door burst open.

# CHAPTER 2

Kaitlyn looked back.

Mr. Zetes.

Light from the porch shone behind him so he appeared as a dark silhouette, but somehow Kait could still see his face. When she'd first come to the Institute a week ago, she'd thought that Mr. Z was a handsome, aristocratic old gentleman—like Little Lord Fauntleroy's grandfather. Now she knew the truth, and the leonine head with its shock of white hair appeared completely evil to her. Those piercing dark eyes seemed to burn like—

Like a demon's, Kaitlyn thought. Except he's not a demon, just an insane genius, and we've got to get *out* of here. . . .

They were all paralyzed. Even Gabriel, who was in front of Kaitlyn now that she had turned around, closer to Mr. Zetes. Something about the man stopped them all dead, drained the will out of them.

They were held by pure fear.

*Don't look at him,* Rob's voice said in Kaitlyn's mind, but it was faint and distant. The terror reverberating in the web was much stronger.

"Come here," Mr. Zetes said. His voice was strong and rich and utterly commanding. He stepped forward and Kaitlyn could see him more clearly in the living room lights. There was blood in his thick white hair and on his starched shirt collar. Gabriel's mental attack had done that, knocked him out, made him bleed. But Gabriel was exhausted now. . . .

As if he were part of the web and could hear her thoughts, Mr. Zetes said, "You're all tired. I don't think you can use your powers any further tonight. Why don't we sit down and talk together?"

Kait had been too frightened to speak, but this struck fire in her. "We don't have anything to talk about," she said caustically.

"Your futures," Mr. Zetes said. "Your lives. I realize that I was too harsh earlier tonight. It was a shock to find you'd gotten yourselves into a permanent telepathic link. But I still think we can work together. We'll find another way to break the link—"

"You mean besides killing one of us?" Kaitlyn snarled.

*Don't stick around and argue with him,* Gabriel said, his cold mental voice cutting through the thrumming fear in the web. *You four go—start heading for the back door. I'll keep him here.*

"No," Kaitlyn said aloud, before she could help it. Even in

the middle of this danger, she felt a wash of emotion. Gabriel, who'd always claimed he didn't care about anybody, was risking himself to protect them. . . .

And he was moving now, putting himself directly between her and Mr. Zetes. Once she could no longer see Mr. Zetes's face, she felt her paralysis break.

*But we can't leave you,* she told Gabriel. *You nearly died once tonight already—*

Gabriel didn't glance back. His posture was wolflike, his attention fixed on Mr. Zetes. *Kessler, get them out. I'll handle the old man.*

But Rob's mental voice was sharp. *No! None of us can stay. Don't you see, he wants to keep us here—and we haven't seen Joyce yet.*

The instant he said it, Kaitlyn knew he was right. It was a trap.

"Come on!" she shouted, both mentally and aloud—but even as she was shouting it, a shape appeared in the kitchen doorway beside her. Hands grabbed for her.

"Let me go!"

Kait found herself kicking and screaming. Other shouts hurt her ears. All she could see was the venemous, twisted face in front of her.

Joyce Piper's sleek blond hair was plastered flat to her head with sweat and blood. Dried rivulets ran down her cheeks. Her aquamarine eyes were full of heated poison, and her lips were drawn back.

Oh, God, she wants to kill me; she really wants to kill me. I trusted her and she's crazy, she's as crazy as Mr. Zetes is—

Hands were pulling her away from Joyce, shoving her toward the back of the house. Rob's voice rose over the background shouting.

"Run, Kaitlyn! Go! Everybody run!"

Looking back, Kaitlyn had a brief glimpse of Rob and Gabriel grappling with Joyce, of Mr. Zetes coming toward them, his face suffused with fury. Then she was running, with Lewis and Anna jostling around her. She didn't realize she still had her duffel bag until she got to the back door and had to put it down to undo the locks.

She yanked the door open—and there was Mr. Zetes's chauffeur. Looking immovable as a mountain, blocking the way.

*Get him!*

Kaitlyn wasn't sure who shouted it, but she and Anna and Lewis were all moving at once. It was as if they suddenly had only one mind, divided into three bodies. Lewis put his head down and ran at the man's stomach; Kait swung her duffel bag at his face; Anna slammed a foot into his shin. He toppled over and they ran on, stampeding toward the green convertible in the driveway.

It was Joyce's car, the car they'd taken from Mr. Zetes's mansion to get back to the Institute. The keys were still inside.

"Get in the back," Kaitlyn told Lewis and Anna, throwing

her duffel bag into the backseat. *Rob! Gabriel! Get out here! Come on; we're ready for you!*

She twisted the key in the ignition, yanked at the gearshift, and turned the wheel hard. She wasn't a very good driver—she hadn't had much practice back in Ohio—but now she sent gravel flying as she swung the convertible in a tight arc on the driveway.

"Headlights—" Lewis gasped. Kait reached down blindly and wrenched a dial. The blaze of light illuminated the chauffeur, who was on his feet again in front of them.

Kaitlyn headed right toward him.

She could hear yelling, but everything seemed to be happening in slow motion. The chauffeur's mouth was open. For endless seconds the car kept getting closer and closer to him, and then suddenly he was diving sideways. He got out of the way just as Rob and Gabriel burst through the back door.

*Get in!* Kait hit the brake, jolting the car. Rob and Gabriel scrambled in, climbing over Lewis and Anna. Kaitlyn didn't wait for them to untangle themselves; she put her foot on the accelerator and pressed—hard.

*Go,* she was thinking—or maybe it was somebody else thinking it, she couldn't tell. *Go, go, go, go.*

Tires squealed as she reached the street, turned, and sped away from the purple house that was the Zetes Institute for Psychic Research.

It was a great relief to be moving this fast. She overshot

stop signs, shrieked around corners. She didn't know where she was going, just that she had to get as far away as possible.

"Kait." It was Rob's voice. Rob was in the front seat beside her, an armful of folders clutched to his chest. He put a hand on her arm. *Kait.*

Kaitlyn was breathing hard and shivering—a fine all-over tremor. She'd reached El Camino Real, the main street in San Carlos. She ran a red light.

*Kait, ease up. We got away. It's all right.* His fingers tightened on her arm, and he repeated, "It's all right."

Kaitlyn felt her breath come out more slowly. She was able to ease her grip on the steering wheel. "Are you guys okay?"

"Yeah," Rob said. "Gabriel knocked them out again. They're both lying unconscious in the lab." He turned to look into the backseat. "Nice going."

"Oh, glad you thought so," Gabriel said in a voice as cold as Rob's had been warm. But through the web, Kaitlyn could feel Gabriel's desperate tiredness.

She sensed a rush of concern from Rob and knew he felt it, too. "Look," he said, "you're wiped out. Do you want me to—"

*No,* Gabriel said flatly.

Kaitlyn's heart sank. Just an hour or so ago Gabriel had been willing to accept Rob's help—all their help. Back at the mansion he'd let Rob use his healing power, let him channel energy from the rest of them to save Gabriel's life. Gabriel had come to trust all of them, when he'd never trusted anyone before. They'd actually gotten through to him, broken down the walls. And now . . .

Gabriel was reverting again. Shutting them out, pretending he wasn't part of them. And there was nothing they could do about it.

Kaitlyn gave it a try anyway. Sometimes Gabriel seemed to . . . respect her more than the others, or at least he listened to her opinions more. "You've got to keep your strength up," she began lightly, trying to catch his eye in the rearview mirror.

He cut her off with a terse, *Leave me alone.*

Kait got an image of walls, high walls with nasty spikes sticking out of them. Gabriel trying to cover his vulnerability. She knew what he wouldn't verbalize, that he didn't want to be indebted to Rob ever again.

Anna's quiet voice broke into her thoughts. "Where are we going?"

"I don't know." It was a good question and Kait's heart started pounding again. "You guys, where *can* we go?"

She could sense consternation all around her. None of them except Lewis was familiar with the San Francisco area.

"Well—jeeez," Lewis said. "Okay, we don't want to go into the city, right? My parents live up in Pacific Heights, but—"

"But that's the first place Mr. Z will look," Rob said. "No, we agreed before, we can't go to our parents. We'll only get them in trouble, too."

"The truth is," Gabriel began, "we don't know *where* we're going—"

"It doesn't matter," Kaitlyn interrupted him. "It doesn't matter where we're going eventually. What we need to figure out is what to do *now*. It's two A.M. and it's dark and it's cold and Mr. Zetes is going to be after us . . ."

"You're right about that," Gabriel said. "And he'll have the police after us, too, when he wakes up from being knocked out. We're in a stolen car."

"Then we'd better get away from San Carlos fast," Lewis said, alarm sharpening his voice. "There's Highway 101, Kait. Get on it going north."

Kaitlyn clenched her teeth and got on the freeway, which was a big one, five lanes in each direction. She knew the others must be aware of how nervous she was, but no one mentioned it.

"Now, let's see . . . we don't want to go to San Francisco. . . . Okay, take the San Mateo bridge there, and when you get across, go on 880 north. That's the East Bay; you know, Hayward and Oakland."

The bridge started out wide but narrowed to a ribbon of concrete that seemed to barely clear dark water. In a few minutes they were cruising up another freeway.

"Good job," Rob said softly, and Kaitlyn felt a flash of warmth. "Now, don't speed too much; we don't want to draw attention to ourselves."

Kaitlyn nodded and kept the red hand of the speedometer quivering just below sixty miles per hour. They hadn't been driving two minutes before Lewis said, "Uh-oh."

"What 'uh-oh?'" Kaitlyn asked tightly.

"There's a car behind us with antlers," Anna said.

*"Antlers?"*

"Police light bar," Lewis said. His voice was thin.

Rob stayed calm. "Don't panic. They won't pull you over for going three miles over the speed limit, and Mr. Z probably isn't even awake yet. . . ."

Lights sprang to life on the roof of the car behind Kaitlyn. Blue and yellow flashing lights.

Kaitlyn's stomach plunged as if she'd stepped into an elevator. Her heart had begun a sick pounding.

"Can we panic now?" Lewis gasped. "I thought you said Mr. Z wouldn't be awake yet."

"We forgot," Anna said. "He had plenty of time to call the police and report the car stolen back at the mansion. When he *first* woke up."

Kait had a wild impulse to run. She'd run from the police a time or two back in Ohio, mainly when they wanted her to make some prediction about a case they were working on. But that had been on foot, out in the farmland that surrounded Thoroughfare—and she hadn't been a criminal then.

Now she was in a stolen car, and she'd just helped assault three grown-ups.

*And you've got* me *in the car, and I'm violating my parole,*
Gabriel's voice said in her mind. *Remember? I'm not supposed to
leave the Institute except to go to school.*

"Oh, God," Kaitlyn said aloud. She gripped the wheel
with palms that were slick with sweat. The need to run, to jam
on the accelerator and get *out* of here, was swelling in her like
a balloon.

"No," Rob said urgently. "We won't be able to get away
from them, and the last thing we want is a high-speed chase."

"Then what do we do, Rob?" Anna asked.

"Pull over." Rob looked at Kait. "Pull over and we'll talk
to them. I'll show them *this.*" He hefted the files. "And if
they take us to the police station, I'll show it to everyone
there."

Kaitlyn felt a surge of incredulity from Gabriel. "Are you
joking? How naive are you, Kessler? Do you think anybody is
going to believe five kids—especially any cop—" He broke off.
When he spoke again, it was in a different voice, taut and yet
somehow expressionless. "Fine. Pull over, Kait."

Walls. Kait could feel Gabriel's walls go up, but she had
more critical things to think about. She took the next exit
off the freeway and the flashing blue and yellow lights followed her.

She went quite a way down the street before she could
make herself slow and stop. The police car glided up behind
her like a shark and stopped, too.

Kaitlyn was breathing hard. "Okay, you guys . . ."

"I'll do the talking," Rob said, and Kait was grateful. She watched in the rearview mirror as a figure got out of the cruiser. There was only one officer, a policeman.

With numb fingers, Kaitlyn rolled down the window. The policeman bent down a bit. He had a neat dark mustache and a very solid-looking chin.

"Driver's license," he said, and Rob, leaning over Kait, said, "Excuse me." And then Kait felt it.

A pulling-back, like the ocean gathering for a tsunami. It came from the backseat. Before she could move or say anything, Gabriel struck.

Dark power shot out of him toward the policeman, a wave of crashing, destructive mental energy. The policeman made a sound like a hurt animal and dropped his notebook, clapping his hands to his head.

"No!" Rob shouted. "Gabriel, stop!"

Kaitlyn could only feel the echoes of the attack through the web, but it was blinding her, making her sick. Dimly she saw the policeman fall to his knees. Anna was gasping. Lewis was whimpering.

*Gabriel, stop!* Rob roared in a voice to cut through all the confusion. *You'll kill him. Stop!*

I have to help him, Kaitlyn thought. We can't become murderers . . . I have to help. . . .

It took a tremendous effort of will to turn around, to focus on Gabriel's mind. She wanted to shield herself from the terrible power still pouring out of Gabriel. Instead, she opened herself to it, trying to break through to him.

*Gabriel, you're not a killer, not anymore,* she told him. *Please stop. Please stop.*

She had a sense of wavering, and then the black torrent eased. It seemed to flow back into Gabriel, where it disappeared without a trace.

Trembling, Kaitlyn leaned her head against the seat back. There was absolute silence in the car.

Then Rob erupted. "*Why?* Why did you *do* that?"

"Because he would never have listened to us. Nobody's going to listen, Kessler. Nobody's on our side. We've got to *fight* if we want to live. But you don't know anything about that, do you?"

"I'll show *you* something about it—"

"Stop it!" Kaitlyn shouted, grabbing Rob, who was lunging at Gabriel. "Shut up, both of you. We don't have time to fight—we've got to get out of here, now." She fumbled with the door handle and flung the door open, dragging her duffel bag behind her.

The policeman was lying still now, but to Kaitlyn's relief he was breathing.

*Who knows if his mind's okay, though,* she thought. Gabriel's power could drive people into screaming insanity.

The others were scrambling out of the car. Lewis was

ghastly pale in the police car's headlights, and Anna's dark eyes were huge—owl eyes. When Rob knelt by the policeman, Kaitlyn could feel the tension in his body.

Rob passed a hand over the policeman's chest. "I think he'll be all right—"

"Then let's *go*," Kaitlyn said, casting a desperate look around and pulling at him. "Before somebody sees us, before they send more police . . ."

"Take his badge first," Gabriel suggested nastily, and that got Rob on his feet. And then something seemed to break in all of them simultaneously, and they were running away from the deserted police car.

At first Kaitlyn didn't care where she was running. Gabriel was in the lead, and she blindly followed his twists and turns onto side streets. Eventually, though, when a stabbing pain in her side slowed her down to a walk, she began to notice her surroundings.

Oh, God, where *are* we?

"It's not Mister Rogers' neighborhood," Lewis muttered and jammed his baseball cap on backward.

It was the most eerie and menacing street Kait had ever seen. The gas station they were passing was derelict: no glass in the windows, no gas pumps. So was the station across the road. The Dairy Belle snack shop was enclosed by a very solid-looking chain-link fence—a fence that had barbed wire on the top.

Beyond the Dairy Belle was a liquor store with a flickering yellow sign and iron bars in front of the glass windows. It was open and several men stood in the doorway. Kaitlyn saw one of them look across the street—directly at her.

She couldn't see his face, but she saw teeth flash in a grin. The man elbowed one of his companions, then took a step toward the street.

# CHAPTER 3

Kaitlyn froze, her legs suddenly refusing to move. Rob moved up beside her, put an arm around her, urging her on. "Anna, come here," he said quietly, and Anna obeyed without a word. Lewis crowded up close.

The man across the street had stopped, but he was still watching them.

"Just go on walking," Rob said. "Don't look back." There was calm conviction in his voice, and the arm around Kait's shoulders was hard with muscle.

Gabriel turned around to sneer. "What's the matter, Kessler? Scared?"

*I'm scared*, Kaitlyn told him, before Rob could respond. She could feel Rob's anger—he and Gabriel were spoiling for a fight. *I'm scared of this place, and I don't want to stay here all night.*

"Well, why didn't you say so?" Gabriel nodded down the

street. "Let's go there, where the factories are. We'll find some place to hole up where the cops won't find us."

They crossed railroad tracks, passed huge warehouses and yards full of trucks. Kaitlyn kept glancing behind her nervously, but the only sign of life here was the white smoke billowing out of the Granny Goose factory's smokestacks.

"Here," Gabriel said abruptly. It was a vacant lot, fenced and barb-wired like everything else around here. A sign inside read:

SALE LEASE 4+ ACRES

APPROX. 180,000 SQ. FEET

PACIFIC AMERICAN GROUP

Gabriel was standing by a gate in the fence, and Kaitlyn saw that the barbed wire on top of the gate was squashed flat. "Give me a sweater or something," he said. Kaitlyn took off her ski jacket, and Gabriel spread it over the flattened barbed wire.

"Now climb."

In another minute they were inside the lot, and Kait had her jacket back—now dotted with perforations. She didn't care; all she wanted to do was huddle down like a duckling in some place where nothing could get her.

The lot was a good place. A huge rampart of dirt clods

screened the middle of it off from the street. Kaitlyn stumbled over to a corner where two walls of dirt met and collapsed against it. The adrenaline that had fueled her for the last eight or nine hours had run out, leaving every muscle like jelly.

"I'm so tired," she whispered.

"We all are," Rob said, sitting beside her. "Come on, Gabriel, get down before somebody sees you. You're half dead."

Right, Kaitlyn thought. Gabriel had been exhausted before knocking out the policeman, and now he was almost shaking with fatigue.

He stayed on his feet for a moment, just to prove that he wasn't listening to Rob, then sat down. He sat across from the rest of them, keeping his distance.

Lewis and Anna, though, scooted in close to Kaitlyn. She shut her eyes and leaned back, glad of their closeness, and of Rob. Rob's warm, solid body seemed to radiate protectiveness. He won't let anyone hurt me, she thought foggily.

*No. I won't,* Rob's voice in her mind said, and she felt immersed in gold. An amber glow that warmed her and even fed her, somehow, pouring radiance into her. Like cuddling up with a sun, she thought.

I'm so tired. . . .

She opened her eyes. "Are we going to sleep here?"

"I think we'd better," Rob said, his voice dragging. "But maybe one of us should stay up—you know, to keep watch in case somebody comes."

"I'll watch," Gabriel said briefly.

*"No."* Kaitlyn was appalled. "You need sleep more than any of us. . . ."

*Not sleep.* The thought was so fleeting, so faint, that Kaitlyn wasn't sure if she'd really heard it or not. Gabriel was the best at screening his thoughts from the rest of them. Right now Kaitlyn could sense nothing from him in the web, except that he was drained. And that he was adamant.

"Go ahead, Gabriel, suit yourself," Rob was saying grimly.

Kaitlyn was too tired to argue with either of them. She'd never imagined that she could sleep outdoors like this, sitting on the bare ground with nothing over her head. But it had been the longest night of her life—and the *worst*—and the dirt wall behind her felt amazingly comfortable. Anna was pressed up against her on one side and Rob on the other. The March night was mild and her ski jacket kept her warm. She felt—almost safe.

Kaitlyn's eyes closed.

Now I know what it's like to be homeless, she thought. Uprooted, out in the world, adrift. Heck, I *am* homeless.

"What city are we in?" she mumbled, feeling somehow that this was important.

"Oakland, I guess," Lewis muttered back. "Hear the planes? We must be near the airport."

Kaitlyn could hear a plane, and crickets, and distant

traffic—but they all seemed to be fading into a feature-less hum. In a few moments she stopped thinking and was dreaming instead.

Gabriel waited until all four of them were asleep—fast asleep— and then he stood up.

He supposed he was putting them in danger by leaving. Well, he couldn't help it—and if Kessler couldn't protect his girl, that was his own lookout.

It had become painfully obvious that Kaitlyn was Kessler's girl now. Fine. Gabriel didn't want her anyway. He should be grateful to Rob the Golden Boy for saving him—because a girl like that could trap you, could get under your skin and change you. And this particular girl, with hair like autumn fire and skin like cream and the eyes of a witch, had already shown that she wanted to change *him.*

Almost succeeded, too, Gabriel thought as he picked his way through the scraggly brush poking its way between dirt clods. She'd gotten him in a state to accept help from Kessler, of all people.

Never again.

Gabriel reached the fence and boosted himself over it, clearing the barbed wire. When he came down, his knees almost buckled.

He was weak. Weak in a way he'd never been before. And

there was a feeling inside him—a *hunger.* A burned-out feeling, as if a fire had passed over him, leaving him blackened and parched. Like cracked earth thirsty for summer rain.

He'd never felt like this before. And part of him, a small part that sat back from the rest of his mind and sometimes whispered judgment, said that there was something dangerous about feeling this way. Something *wrong.*

Ignore it, Gabriel thought. He made his legs move down the uneven sidewalk, tightening muscles so they wouldn't shake. He wasn't afraid of this kind of neighborhood—it was his native environment—but he knew better than to show weakness here. The weak got picked off in a place like this.

He was looking for someone else weak.

The whispering part of his mind twinged at that.

Ignore it, Gabriel thought again.

The liquor store was up ahead. Beside it was a long brick wall decorated with the remains of tattered posters and notices. Men stood against the wall, or sat on crates in front of it.

Men—and one woman. Not a beauty. She was skin and bones, with hollow eyes and unhealthy hair. A tattoo of a unicorn covered the calf of one leg.

Now there was irony. A unicorn, the symbol of innocence, virginity.

Better this scrawny ratbag than the innocent witch back in the lot, he thought, and flashed his most brilliant, disturbing smile at nothing.

That thought demolished the last of his hesitation. It had to be someone. He'd rather it be this bit of human garbage than Kaitlyn.

The burned, parched feeling was overwhelming him. He was a scorching void, an empty black hole. A starving wolf.

The woman turned toward him. She looked startled for a moment, then smiled in appreciation, her eyes on his face.

Think I'm handsome? Good, that makes it easy, Gabriel thought, smiling back.

He put his hand on her shoulder.

The ocean hissed and spat among the rocks. The sky was an uneasy color, more metallic violet or grayed lavender than real gray, Kaitlyn thought. She was standing on a narrow rocky peninsula. On either side of her was the ocean. Ahead the peninsula stretched out like a bony finger into the water.

A strange place. A strange and lonely place . . .

"Oh, no. Here *again?*" Lewis said from just behind her. Kait turned to see him—and Rob and Anna, as well. She smiled. The first time she'd found them in her dream she'd been confused and almost angry. Now she didn't mind; she was glad of the company.

"At least it's not so cold this time," Anna said. She looked as if she fit into this wild place where nature seemed to rule without human interference. The wind blew her long dark hair behind her.

"No, and we should be *glad* to be here," Rob said, his voice full of suppressed excitement. He was scanning the horizon alertly. "This is where we're *going*, remember—if we can find it."

"No," Kait said. "*That's* where we're going." She pointed across the water to a distant shore where a cliff rose, black with thick-growing trees. Among the trees, shining in the eerie light, was a single white house.

It was the white house Kaitlyn had seen in a vision at the Institute. The one in the photograph shown to her by a lynx-eyed man with caramel-colored skin. She knew nothing about the man except that he was an enemy of Mr. Zetes, and nothing about the house except that it was connected to the man.

"But it's our only chance," she said aloud. The others were looking at her, and she went on, "We don't know who they are, but they're the only people who even have a chance to help us against Mr. Z. We don't have any choice but to try and find them."

"And maybe they can help us with"—Lewis changed to telepathic speech in midsentence—*this thing. Maybe they'll know how to break the link.*

Anna spoke quietly. "You know what the research says. One of us has to die."

"Maybe they can find some way around that."

Kaitlyn said nothing, but she knew they all felt the same way. The web that tied them together had brought them very close, and there were some wonderful things about it. But all the same, in the back of her mind there was always the pounding insistence that it *had* to be broken. They couldn't live the rest of their lives like this, welded together this way. They *couldn't*. . . .

"We'll find the answers when we get there," Rob said. "Meanwhile, we'd better look around. Examine everything about this place. There must be some clue as to where it *is*."

"Let's walk up there," Kait suggested, nodding toward the end of the peninsula. "I'd like to get as close to that house as possible."

They kept a close watch as they walked. "Same old ocean," Lewis said. "And back there"—he gestured behind them—"same old beach with trees. If I had my camera we could get a photo to compare to other things. Like, you know, pictures in books or travel brochures."

"There's just not enough to distinguish it from other beaches," Kaitlyn said. "Except—look, does it seem to you that there are more waves on the right side?"

"It does," Rob said. "That's weird. I wonder what would cause it?"

"And then there are these," said Anna. She dropped to one knee beside a pile of rocks, some long and thin, some nearly square. They were stacked like a child's blocks, but much more whimsically, forming an irregular tower that had appendages sticking out at intervals—like airplane wings.

The piles were all over the peninsula, resting on the huge

boulders that lined either side. They ranged from small to gargantuan. Some, to Kaitlyn's eye, looked like crude depictions of people or animals.

"I have the feeling I should *know* this," Anna said, her hands framing the stack, not quite touching it. "It should have some meaning to me." Her face was troubled, her full lips pinched, her eyes clouded.

"Never mind," Rob said. "Keep walking and maybe it'll come to you. Is it a place you've seen before?"

Anna shook her head slowly. "I don't *think* I've seen it. And yet it's *familiar*—and it's north, I'm sure of that. North of California."

"So we look at all the beaches north of California?" Lewis muttered, with unaccustomed bleakness. He kicked at a rock pile.

"Don't!" Anna said quickly—with unaccustomed sharpness. Lewis ducked his head.

At the end of the peninsula Kait tilted her face to the wind. It felt good and it was exhilarating to have the ocean crashing around her on three sides, but they still weren't much closer to the white house.

"Who's giving us these dreams, anyway?" Lewis asked from a little way behind her. "I mean, do you think it's *them,* in that house? Do you think they're in there now?"

"Let's ask," Rob said, and without warning he cupped his hands around his mouth and shouted across the water. "Hey, you! You out there! Who are you?"

Kaitlyn's heart jolted at the first bellow. But the shout had a *good* sound, a sound to combat the ghostly violet sky and the vast stretch of moving water. This was a big place, and big sounds fit here.

She cupped her own hands around her mouth. "Whooo are yooeou?" she shouted, sending her voice across the ocean as if she really expected someone in the white house to hear.

"That's it," Anna said, and she threw her head back and gave a long-drawn-out cry that sent gooseflesh up Kait's spine. "Whooo are yooeou? Where are weeee?"

Lewis joined in. "Thiiiis suuucks! Talk to us! Can't you be a little clearer?"

Kaitlyn choked on laughter, but kept calling. The racket caused a pair of gulls to soar upward, alarmed.

And then, amidst their own clamor, came an answer.

It was louder than their shouting voices, but it was a breathless whisper nevertheless. As if, Kaitlyn thought suddenly, a thousand people were whispering at once, almost in chorus but not quite. A thousand people crowded around you in a small, echoing room.

It shut them all up immediately. Kait stared wide-eyed at Rob, who had grasped her shoulder in an automatic impulse to protect her.

"Griffin's Pit! Griffin's Pit! Griffin's Pit!" the urgent whispers said.

Kaitlyn's lips formed the word "What?" but no sound came out. The cacophony of sound was beating at her from all sides. She could see Lewis grimace. Anna had her hands to her head.

"Griffin's Pit Griffin's Pit Griffin's Pit . . ."

*Rob, it hurts. . . .*

*Then wake up, Kaitlyn! It's your dream; you have to wake up!*

She couldn't. But she could see that the pounding noise was hurting Rob, too. His face was tense, his golden eyes dark.

*"GriffinsPitGriffinsPitGriffinsPit—"*

Kaitlyn gave a jerk and the peninsula disappeared.

She was staring into the night sky. A lopsided moon was dipping toward the horizon. A single airplane roared slowly among the stars, red lights winking.

Rob was stirring beside her, Anna and Lewis sitting up.

"Everybody all right?" Kaitlyn said anxiously.

Rob smiled. "You did it."

"I guess. And we got our answer—I guess." She rubbed at her forehead.

"Maybe that's why they didn't try to communicate in words before," Anna said. "Maybe they knew it would hurt us. And what they were saying wasn't too clear, anyway."

"Griffin's Pit," Kaitlyn said. "It sounds—ominous."

Lewis wrinkled his nose. "Griffin's—*what? Oh,* you mean Whippin' Bit."

"*I* heard something like 'Wyvern's Bit,'" Anna put in. "But that doesn't make much sense."

"Neither does Whiff and Spit," Rob said. "Unless it's some kind of combination perfume and tobacco factory. . . ."

"C'mon down to the Whiff and Spit; snuff it up and cough it out," Lewis chanted, giving it a catchy rhythm. "But, look, if none of us heard the same thing, it means we're back where we started."

"Wrong," Rob said and twisted Lewis's cap down over his eyes. He grinned; Kaitlyn could tell he was in a good mood. "We know there's somebody out there, and they're trying to talk to us. Maybe they'll get better. Maybe we'll get lucky. Anyway, we have a direction to go—north. And we know what to look for—a beach like that. The search is on!"

His enthusiasm was infectious. His smile, the lights dancing in his golden eyes—all infectious, Kaitlyn thought.

Kaitlyn had a feeling—wild, inappropriate, but consuming—of hope. All her life she'd wanted to belong somewhere, wanted it with a deep-down, gut-wrenching ache. And she'd always had the strange conviction that she *did* belong somewhere. That there was a place where she fit in perfectly—if only she could find it.

Since Gabriel had locked them into the web, she'd found *people* to belong to. Whether she wanted it or not, she was bonded for life to her four mind-mates. And now—well, maybe the dream was calling them to a *place* to belong. The place she'd sensed in the back of her mind all along, the place where all her questions would be answered and she would understand who she really was and what she was supposed to do with her life.

She smiled at Rob. "The search is on." She scooted closer to him, knee to knee, and added in a private message, *And I love you.*

*Strange coincidence,* Rob's voice said in her mind.

Amazing how he could make her feel. Safe in a vacant lot, warm in the middle of the night. Just being this close to him, being able to touch his thoughts and feel his presence, was comforting—and dizzying.

*I like being close to you, too,* he said. *The closer I get, the closer I want to get.*

Kaitlyn was floating, drowning in the gold of Rob's eyes. She began, *I wish we could be like this forever—*

She was cut off. Anna, who had been sitting with her chin on her knees, now suddenly raised her head.

"Wait a minute—where's Gabriel?"

Kait had forgotten about him. Now she realized that the rampart of earth across from them was deserted.

"He must have gone to check on something," Lewis said hopefully.

"Or maybe he's gone for good," Rob said—and there was a sort of grim hope in his voice, too.

"Sorry. No deal." A shower of earth fell from the dirt wall, and Gabriel appeared, wearing a rather chilling smile.

And he looked—well. Refreshed. Not tired anymore.

Kaitlyn felt the shadow of alarm. She brushed it away before anyone else could notice it. Of *course* Gabriel was all right. There was nothing wrong with him looking so . . . rejuvenated. He'd had a chance to rest, that was all.

"It's getting light," Gabriel was saying. "I checked around; there's no activity out there: no cops, nothing. If we're going to get out, now's the time."

"Okay," Rob said. "But first, sit down a minute. We have to figure out what the plan is, what we're doing next. And we have to tell you what happened to us tonight."

"Something happened?" Gabriel looked around sharply. "I was—only gone for a few minutes."

"It wasn't anything real; it was a dream," Kaitlyn said, and she tried to quash her alarm again. That hesitation between "I was" and "only gone for a few minutes"—Gabriel was lying. She couldn't feel it in the web, but she knew.

Where had he been?

Rob was telling him about the dream. Gabriel listened to the whole story, looking amused and slightly contemptuous.

"If that's where you really think you're going, I don't care," he said when Rob finished. His handsome lip was curled. "All I care about is getting away from the California Youth Authority."

"Okay," said Rob. "Now, we ought to take stock—what have we got with us here? What're our assets?" He gave a rueful grin.

"'Fraid I don't have anything but my wallet and these files."

For the first time Kait consciously realized that neither Rob nor Gabriel had their duffel bags with them. Lost in the fight with Mr. Zetes, she guessed.

"I've got my bag," she said. "And a hundred dollars in my pocket"—she checked to make sure—"and maybe fifteen in my purse."

"I've got *my* bag," Lewis said. "But I don't think any of my clothes are going to fit either of you guys." He eyed Rob and Gabriel doubtfully—they were both several inches taller than he was. "And about forty dollars."

"I've only got a few dollars in change," Anna said. "And my bag of clothes."

"And I've got—oh, twelve-fifty," Rob said, flipping through his wallet.

"Jeez, only a hundred and fifty-something—remind me never to run away with you guys again," Lewis said.

"It's not even enough to buy bus tickets—and then we have to eat," Rob said. "And it's not as if we have just one destination—we've got to *look* for the place, so we don't really know where we're going. Gabriel, how much—"

Gabriel had been shifting where he sat, noticeably impatient. "I've got about ninety dollars," he said shortly—without, Kait noticed, mentioning that he'd gotten it from Joyce's purse. "But we don't need bus tickets," he added. "I've taken care of it. We've got transportation."

"Huh?"

Gabriel shrugged and stood, brushing crumbs of dirt off his clothes. "I've got us a car. I hotwired it and it's ready. So if you're finished talking . . ."

Kaitlyn leaned her head into her hands. "Oh, God."

She could *feel* the golden-white blaze of anger beside her. And now Rob was standing, moving up to get right in Gabriel's face. He was absolutely furious.

"You did *what?*" he said.

# CHAPTER 4

Gabriel gave one of his wildest smiles. "I stole us a car. What about it?"

"What about it? It's *wrong,* that's what. We are not going around stealing people's cars."

"We stole Joyce's," Gabriel said musically and mockingly.

"Joyce was trying to *kill* us. That makes it—not right, maybe, but justifiable." He got even closer to Gabriel and said with deadly anger, emphasizing each word, "There is *no* justification for stealing things from innocent people."

Gabriel was clearly enjoying himself, relaxed but ready for action any minute. He wanted to fight, Kaitlyn realized—he was dying for it. Almost as if he were feeding off the blazing energy Rob radiated. "What's *your* idea, country boy? How do we get out of here?" he said.

"I don't know, but we don't steal. It's wrong. That's all." And for Rob, it *was* all, Kaitlyn knew. It was that simple for him.

She was chewing her lips, uneasily aware that it wasn't so simple for her. Half of her was impressed that Gabriel had gotten a car, and she had a sneaking feeling she'd be happy to ride away in it if she weren't nervous that they'd get caught. A car would be something to hold on to, an anchor against the uprooted, drifting feeling of being homeless.

But Rob would never go for it. Dear Rob. Dear honorable Rob, who was completely and utterly pigheaded and who could be the most exasperating boy on earth. Who was now glaring at Gabriel challengingly.

Gabriel bared his teeth in response. "And what about the old man? You don't think he's going to give up, do you? He'll have the police after us—and maybe other people. He has a lot of friends, a lot of connections."

It was true. Kaitlyn remembered the papers she had seen in Mr. Z's hidden room. There had been letters from judges, CEOs of big companies, people in the government. Lists of names of important people.

"We need to get out of here—*now*," Gabriel said. "And that means we need transportation." His eyes were locked on Rob's. Neither of them willing to give in.

They're going to fight, Kaitlyn thought, and she looked at Anna in despair. Anna had paused in the middle of brushing the dark and shining raven wing of her hair. She looked back worriedly at Kait.

*We've got to stop them,* she said.

*I know,* Kait thought back. *But how?*

*Come up with another solution.*

Kaitlyn couldn't think of another solution—and then it came to her.

*Marisol,* she thought.

Marisol. The research assistant back at the Institute. She'd been with Mr. Zetes even before Joyce, and she'd known about his plans. She'd tried to warn Kaitlyn—and Mr. Z had put her in a coma for it.

Kait said it aloud, with mounting excitement. "Marisol!"

It broke into Rob and Gabriel's stareout. "What?" Rob said.

Kaitlyn scrambled to her feet. "Don't you see—if anybody would help us, if anybody would believe us—and we're in *Oakland.* I'm sure Joyce said she was from Oakland."

"Kait, calm down. What are you—"

"I'm saying we should go to Marisol's *family.* They live here in Oakland. We could probably walk. And they might help us, Rob. They might understand this whole horrible thing."

The others were staring at Kait—but it was a good staring, full of dawning wonder.

"You know, they might, at that," Rob said.

"Marisol may even have told them something about it— maybe not in detail, but she might have given hints. She liked to give hints," Kait said, remembering. "And they've got to be upset over what happened. Their daughter's fine, a little moody but perfectly healthy—and then one day she falls down in a coma. Don't you think they'd have their suspicions?"

"It depends," Gabriel said. He looked dark and cold—cheated of his confrontation. "If she was taking drugs—"

"*Joyce* said she was taking drugs. And personally, I'm not inclined to trust anything Joyce said—are you?" Kaitlyn tilted her chin at him and to her surprise got a flash of amusement from the gray, chill eyes.

"Anyway, it's the best chance we've got," Lewis said. Always quick to see the bright side of things, he was smiling now, his dark eyes sparkling. "It's someplace to go—and maybe they'll *feed* us."

Anna twisted her hair into a long tail and stood gracefully, and Kaitlyn realized it was settled. Two minutes later they were walking down the sidewalk, looking for a phone book. Kaitlyn felt unkempt and empty—she hadn't eaten since lunch yesterday—but surprisingly fit.

The street was deserted, now, and although the fenced-in buildings were just as decrepit, the whole place looked a little safer. Lewis was cheerful enough to pull out his camera and take a picture.

"For posterity," he said.

"Maybe it's better not to look like a tourist," Anna suggested in her gentle voice.

"If anybody comes near us I'll take care of them," said

Gabriel. His thoughts were still black with jagged red streaks—leftover from his fight with Rob.

Kait looked at him. "You know, I was meaning to ask you. Mr. Z said you couldn't link with another mind once you were in a stable link with us—but you linked with that policeman, and with Mr. Z and Joyce earlier."

Gabriel shrugged. "The old man was wrong," he said briefly.

Again, Kaitlyn felt a whisper of anxiety in her blood. Gabriel was hiding something from all of them. Only Gabriel, she thought, could manage that so easily in the web.

And despite his barriers, she could sense something—strange—in him. Something that had changed in the last night.

The crystal, she thought. Mr. Zetes had forced Gabriel into contact with a giant crystal, a monstrosity of jagged edges that housed unthinkable psychic power.

What if it had done something to Gabriel? Something . . . permanent?

"Gabriel," she said abruptly, "how's your forehead?"

He put his fingers to it quickly, then, deliberately, dropped his hand to his side. "Fine," he said. "Why?"

"I just wanted to look at it." Before he could stop her, she reached up herself, brushing his dark hair aside. And there on his forehead she could see it, shadowy on the pale skin. Not the kind of scab she would have expected from the cut the crystal had given him. It looked more like a scar or a birthmark—a crescent-shaped dimness.

"Right over your third eye," Kaitlyn said involuntarily, just as Gabriel grabbed her wrist in a bruising grip. She and he had both stopped dead. He stared at her, and there was something frightening in his gray gaze. Something menacing and alien that she'd never seen before.

The third eye—the seat of psychic power. And Gabriel's powers had been greater ever since his contact with the crystal. . . .

He'd always been the strongest of all of them, psychically. It scared Kait to think what he might become if he got any stronger.

"What's *wrong* with you guys?" Lewis was demanding. The others were far ahead. Rob was walking back toward them, his brows drawn together.

Then Anna, who was farthest down the street, called, "I see a phone!"

Gabriel released Kait's wrist, almost throwing it, and started toward Anna briskly.

Leave it alone, Kaitlyn told herself. For now. For now, concentrate on surviving.

They found Marisol's name among a flood of Diazes in the phone book. Lewis wasn't familiar with Ironwood Boulevard, the street where she lived, but they studied a map at a gas station.

It was almost nine-thirty before they arrived, and Kaitlyn was hot, dusty, and starving. It was what Lewis called a pueblo house, a fake adobe house covered with pinky-brown stucco. No one answered the doorbell.

"They're not home," Kaitlyn said in despair. "I was stupid. They're at the hospital with Marisol; Joyce said they went every day."

"We'll wait. Or come back," Rob said firmly, his resolution and his temper undisturbed. They were heading toward the shade of the garage when a boy, a little older than they were, came around from the back of the house.

He had no shirt and his thin, sinewy body looked tough. Kait would never have dared approach him on the street. But he also had curly hair that shone in the morning light like mahogany, and a full, rather sullen mouth.

In other words, thought Kaitlyn, he looks like Marisol.

For several heartbeats they all just stared at each other, the boy obviously resenting these intruders on his property, ready to fight them off. Rob and Gabriel were reacting by bristling. Then Kaitlyn stepped forward impulsively.

"Don't think we're crazy," she said. "But we're friends of Marisol's and we've run away from Mr. Zetes and we don't know where else to go. We've been on the road since last night and it took us hours to walk here. And—well, we thought you might help us."

The boy stared harder, through narrowed eyes that had long, dark lashes. Finally he said slowly, "Friends of Marisol's?"

"Yes," Kaitlyn said firmly, tucking away in her mind all the memories of how Marisol had snubbed her and terrorized her. That didn't matter now.

The boy looked each of them over, his expression sour. Just when Kaitlyn was convinced he was going to tell them to go away, he jerked his chin toward the house.

"Come on in. I'm Tony. Marisol's brother."

At the door he asked casually, "You a *bruja?* A witch?" He was looking at her eyes.

"No. I can do—things. I draw pictures and eventually they come true."

He nodded, still casual. Kaitlyn was vastly grateful that he seemed to believe her. He accepted the idea of psychic powers without surprise.

And despite his surly looks, he was—thoughtful. Generous. One minute after they were in the house he rubbed his chin, cast a sideways glance at Lewis, and muttered, "You been on the road, huh? You guys hungry? I was going to eat breakfast."

A lie, Kaitlyn thought. He must have seen how Lewis was sniffing at a lingering aroma of eggs and bacon. She warmed to him immediately.

"There's a lot of stuff people brought over when Marisol got sick," he said, leading them into the kitchen. From the refrigerator he pulled out a giant baking dish full of what looked like corn husks and a smaller one full of noodles. "Tamales," he said hefting the big one. He put down the small one. "And chow mein."

Fifteen minutes later they were all seated around the big kitchen table, and Kait was finishing up the story of their flight from the Institute. She told how Joyce had recruited them, how they'd come to California, how Marisol had warned them that things at the Institute weren't what they seemed, and how Mr. Zetes had finally revealed himself last night.

"He's completely evil," she said finally and looked at Tony uncertainly. But again he seemed unsurprised, merely grunting. Rob had his pile of folders and papers ready as proof, but it didn't seem necessary.

Staring down into a tamale, Kaitlyn asked the others, *Now how do we tell him Mr. Zetes put his sister in a coma?*

From every one of them—except Gabriel—she felt discomfort. Gabriel was toying with his food, apparently not interested in eating. He sat a little away from the rest of them, as usual, and looked as if he were farther away mentally.

Anna spoke up. "How is Marisol?"

"The same. The doctors say she's always going to be the same."

"We're sorry," Lewis said, wiggling his fork inside a corn husk.

"Did you ever think," Rob said quietly, "that there was anything—strange—about what happened to her?"

Tony looked at him directly. "Everything was strange. Marisol didn't take drugs. I heard some stuff last week about how she was supposed to be on medication—but it wasn't true."

"Joyce Piper told *us* she was on medication. She told us Marisol was seeing a psychiatrist. . . ." Rob's voice trailed off, because Tony was shaking his head vigorously. "Not true?"

"She saw a shrink once or twice last year, because of the really weird stuff that was going on. That was when she worked at Zetes's house. He had some sick people there—for a study, Marisol said."

"The pilot study? You know about that?" Kaitlyn leaned forward eagerly. "Marisol mentioned it—a study with other psychics like the one Mr. Zetes was doing with us."

Rob was sorting through the folders, pulling out one Kaitlyn had seen before. It was a file jacket with a photo of a brown-haired girl labeled SABRINA JESSICA GALLO, BLACK LIGHTNING STUDY.

Scrawled across the label in thick red ink was the word TERMINATED.

Tony was nodding. "Bri Gallo. She was one of them. I think they had six all together. They were into some really bizarre crap. Sick. Zetes had this mental domination over them."

He shifted, seemed to consider, then said, "I'll tell you a story. There was a guy who worked with Marisol, another assistant. He didn't like the boss, thought Zetes was crazy. He used to fight, you know? Talk back. Show up late. And finally he decided he was going to talk to a newspaper about what was going on at that house. He told Marisol that one night. She said the next morning when she saw him, he was—different. He didn't talk back anymore, and he sure didn't talk about any newspapers. He just did his work like he was sleepwalking. Like somebody *enbrujado*—under a spell."

"A spell?" Kait wondered. "Or drugs?"

"Stranger than drugs. He kept on working there, and he kept on getting paler and sleepier. Marisol said he had this blank look, like he was there but his soul wasn't." Tony glanced toward the hallway where a large candle burned in a niche beneath a statue of the Virgin Mary. Simply and unemotionally he said, "I think Boss Zetes works black magic."

Kaitlyn glanced at Rob, who was listening intently, his eyes amber-brown and grim. He met her gaze and said silently, *It's as good a word as any for what he does with that crystal. And maybe Mr. Z does have some mental powers we don't know about.*

Aloud, Kaitlyn said, "He used drugs on Marisol. Joyce Piper gave her something—I don't know what, but I saw it in a vision."

At first Tony seemed not to have heard. He said, "I told her to get out. A long time ago. But she was ambitious, you know? She made money, she bought a car, she was going to get her own place. She said she could handle things."

Kaitlyn, who had always been poor, could understand that.

"She did try to get out in the end," Rob said. "Or at least to get us out. And that was why Mr. Z had to stop her."

Tony grabbed a kitchen knife and slammed it into the wooden table.

Kait's heart almost jumped out of her body. Anna froze, her dark owl eyes on Tony's face. Lewis winced, and Rob frowned.

Gabriel, his eyes on the quivering knife handle, smiled.

*"Lo siento,"* Tony muttered. "I'm sorry. But he shouldn't have done that to Marisol."

Almost without thinking, Kaitlyn put her hand on his. Back in Ohio she would have laughed at the idea. She'd hated boys, loud, smelly, interfering boys. But she understood exactly what Tony was feeling.

"Rob wants to stop him—Mr. Zetes," she said. "And we have this idea that if we can get to this certain place, we might get help. There are people there who act like they're against the Institute."

"Can those people help Marisol?"

Kaitlyn had to be honest. "I don't know. But if you want, we'll ask them. I promise."

Tony nodded. He took his hand from under Kaitlyn's and wiped his eye absently.

"We're not even sure who they are," Rob said. "We think they live somewhere up north, and we have an idea of what the location looks like. We figure it may take us a while to find them, and we'll be on the road all that time. The only problem is that we don't know how to get there."

"No," Gabriel broke sarcastically, speaking for the first time since they'd arrived. "That's not the only problem. The other problem is that we're broke. And stranded."

Tony looked at him, then smiled. It was a crooked smile, but genuine, as if he liked Gabriel's directness.

"We thought we might talk to your parents," Kaitlyn said delicately. "If we go to our own parents they'll find us, you see. And our parents wouldn't understand."

Tony shook his head. He stared out the window into a neat backyard as if thinking. At last he said, "Don't wait for my parents. It'll only upset them."

"But—"

"Come on outside."

Kaitlyn and the others exchanged looks. The web was as blank with surprise as their faces. They followed.

The backyard was filled with dormant rosebushes. There was an extension of the driveway behind an iron gate. On the driveway was a silver-blue van.

"Hey, that's the van from the Institute," Lewis said.

Tony had stopped and was regarding it with folded arms. He shook his head. "No, it's Marisol's. It was hers. It is hers." He stood for a moment, shaking his head as if trying to figure this out, then turned abruptly to Kait. "You take it."

*"What?"*

"I'll get some stuff—sleeping bags and things. We've got an old tent in the garage."

Kaitlyn was overwhelmed. "But—"

"You need stuff for a trip, right? Otherwise you're going to die out there. You're never going to make it." He shook off

Kaitlyn's reaching hand and backed up, but he met her eyes. His voice was almost a growl. "And you're going to fight *him*, the bastard that hurt Marisol. Nobody else is. Nobody else *can*, because you need magic to fight magic. You take the van."

His eyes were Marisol's eyes, too, Kaitlyn realized. Rich brown almost the color of his hair. She could feel her own eyes filling, but she held his gaze. "Thank you," she said softly.

*And we'll do whatever we can to get them to help Marisol,* she thought. She knew the others could hear her, but it was really a private promise.

"We better get you out of here before my mom gets back," Tony said. He took Rob and Lewis into the garage. Kait, Anna, and Gabriel examined the van.

"It's perfect," Kaitlyn whispered, looking around the inside. She'd ridden in it before, to and from school, but she'd never really *looked* at it. To her eyes now, there seemed to be square miles of room. There were two bucket seats in front and two long bench seats in back, with lots of space between them.

There still seemed to be miles of room once Tony piled in blankets, sleeping bags, and pillows. Riches untold, Kaitlyn thought, fingering a thick down-filled comforter. He even took Gabriel and Rob back into the house and lent them spare clothes. Finally he put groceries from the refrigerator into a paper bag.

"It won't last long with five of you, but it's something," he said.

"Thank you," Kait said again as they got ready to leave. Rob was in the driver's seat; Gabriel in the other front bucket seat. Anna and Lewis were in the bench seat behind them. Kaitlyn had ended up in the rear bench seat—too far from Rob, but no matter. They'd change places later.

"You just get Zetes, right?" Tony said, then slid the door of the van shut.

*We're going to try,* Kaitlyn thought. She waved as Rob backed out of the driveway.

"Keep going down this street and I'll tell you how to get back on Highway 880," Lewis said. He was studying a map of California that Tony had supplied. When they were on the highway, he changed it for a map of the United States.

"Well, we've got clothes, we've got food, and we've got sleeping gear. And we certainly have transport," Rob said, settling back in his bucket seat and running a caressing hand over the steering wheel. "Now—exactly where are we going?"

# CHAPTER 5

"Let's just get out of California as fast as possible," Gabriel said. Rob wouldn't agree.

"We ought to think about this before we just start driving blindly. We're looking for a beach, right? There are a lot of beaches in California—"

"But we *know* it's not in California," Kait interrupted. "Anna and I know that. We're sure." In front of her, Anna was nodding.

"And we've got to get *out* of this state," Gabriel said. "This is where the cops will be looking for us. Once we're in Oregon we can relax a little."

Kaitlyn was afraid Rob would argue just for the sake of arguing with Gabriel—she wasn't sure how things stood between them just now—but he just shrugged and said, "Okay, then," peaceably.

Lewis rattled the map. "The fastest way is to go up Interstate 5," he said. "I'll tell you how to get there. We still won't make it to Oregon before dark."

"We can change drivers every few hours," Kaitlyn said. "Oh, and everybody, try and look like you're on a field trip or something, at least until one o'clock or so. People might think it's strange for a bunch of teenagers to be riding around in a van during school hours."

The country kept changing as they drove. At first it was beige and flat, with scrubby grass and an occasional gray-purple bush beside the road. As they got farther north it became more hilly, with trees that were either bare or dusty green. Kait watched it all with an artist's eye and eventually picked up her sketchpad.

It felt like a long while since she'd had time to draw. It had only been twenty-four hours, since yesterday's art studio class—but her entire life of yesterday felt years away. The oil pastels spread smoothly onto the fine-toothed paper, and Kaitlyn felt herself relax. She needed this.

She blocked out the shape of the distant hills with side strokes of the pastel stick, catching an impression of them before the scene changed. That's what she liked about pastels—you could work fast on a burst of inspiration. She filled the hills in with loose, vigorous strokes, and the picture was done in minutes.

That was practice. Now turn the page. Reach for cool colors—pale blue and icy mauve. Maybe acid green and blue-purple, too.

A picture was coming alive under her fingers without her conscious intent.

Kaitlyn was used to letting her fingers go at moments like this, while her mind simply drifted. Right now her mind had drifted to thoughts of Gabriel.

She was going to have to talk with him, and soon. As soon as she could find any privacy. Something serious was wrong. She had to find out what it was. . . .

With a shock Kaitlyn recognized what she'd drawn on the sketch pad.

Gabriel. Not the stark black-and-white portrait she'd always imagined, but a form arising out of a dense network of colored lines. It was unmistakably Gabriel . . .

. . . and in the center of his forehead, blazing with cold blue brilliance, was a third eye.

It seemed to glare at her balefully, and Kaitlyn suddenly felt faint. As if she were about to fall into the picture.

She jerked back, and the sensation disappeared, but chills ran down her neck.

Stop it, she told herself. There was nothing strange about a picture of the third eye. Gabriel was psychic, wasn't he? And this just a metaphor showing he was. She'd drawn a picture of herself with a third eye once.

The reassurances didn't reassure. Kaitlyn knew in her bones that the drawing foretold something evil.

*Kait, what's wrong?*

Rob's voice in her head. Kaitlyn looked up from the maze of colors to see that everyone was looking at her. Gabriel had turned around in the front, and Lewis and Anna were looking over the back of their seat. She could see Rob's worried eyes in the rearview mirror.

While she'd been drawing she'd forgotten about the web, hadn't even felt the presence of the others. And she could tell from their confusion that they hadn't heard *her* thoughts, either, just gotten a general sense that she was upset.

Interesting, one part of her mind said. So drawing is a way to screen my thoughts. Or maybe it's just concentrating.

Meanwhile, the rest of her mind was answering Rob.

*It's nothing. Just a drawing.*

She felt Rob's alarm. "A precognition?" he said aloud.

"No—I don't know." It was horribly impossible to lie in the web. "Whatever it is, I don't want to talk about it now."

She didn't, either. Not with Gabriel sitting there hearing every word, not with Lewis and Anna looking on. Gabriel would be furious at the violation of his privacy, and the others might panic. No, Kaitlyn had to talk to him alone about this first.

She could feel frustration from Rob—he could tell she was hiding something, but not *what*. Anna's clear dark eyes were questioning.

Time to change the subject. "Shouldn't we stop and switch drivers?" she said.

Lewis grinned. "Let's wait a couple of exits and stop at the

Olive Pit. There was a sign back there advertising free samples."

"This must be olive country," Kait said, glad of a distraction. "I keep seeing groves of olive trees."

She kept talking until they stopped, and then there was the complexity of selecting olive samples—chili olives and Cajun olives and Texas olives and Deep South olives—and by the time they all got back into the van everyone seemed to have forgotten their questions.

Gabriel drove. Rob sat in the rear with Kaitlyn, who leaned against him.

"You all right?" he said, too softly for the others to hear.

Kaitlyn nodded, avoiding his golden eyes. She didn't *want* to have any secrets from Rob, but she was afraid to upset the precarious balance between him and Gabriel.

"Just tired," she said. She didn't feel like drawing anymore, not even when a huge and beautiful mountain appeared before them in the distance. Its single peak was white with snow, accented by black ridges of rock.

"Mount Shasta," Lewis said.

They passed rolling hills and crossed riverbeds, mostly dry. The motion and the sound of the van was lulling. Kait's head drooped onto Rob's shoulder and her eyes shut.

She woke with a start and a shiver. How strange—it was *cold* suddenly. Icy cold, as if she'd stepped into a restaurant freezer.

She looked around, dazed with sleep. Mount Shasta was

behind them, glowing like a huge watermelon jewel in the sunset. The sky was murky mauve.

In the front bench seat Anna's black head was lifting. "Gabriel, turn down the air conditioning!" she pleaded.

"It's not on."

"But it's *cold*," Kait said and was caught by another shiver.

Shivering himself, Rob wrapped his arms around her. "It sure is," he said. "We haven't gone *that* far north—is it usually like this, Lewis?"

Lewis didn't answer. Kait saw Anna look at him curiously, and at the same time realized she could sense nothing from him in the web.

"Is he asleep?" she asked Anna.

"His eyes are open."

Kaitlyn's heart rate seemed to quicken. *Lewis?* she thought, sending the word to him.

Nothing.

"What's happening?" she said aloud as Rob let go of her to lean around the front seat and look into Lewis's face. She had a bad feeling—a very bad feeling. Something was *strange*. The air wasn't just cold, it was full of electricity. And there was a smell, a smell like a sewer drain.

And a sound. Kaitlyn heard it suddenly over the soft roar of the van's engine. A sharp, sweet sound, one note, as if somebody had run a wet finger around the rim of a crystal goblet. It hung in the air.

"What the *hell* is going on?" Rob demanded. He was shaking Lewis. At the same moment Gabriel snarled from the front, "What are you guys *doing* back there?"

"We're not doing anything," Kait called—just as Lewis jumped up and dived for the empty bucket seat beside Gabriel.

His hands grabbed and beat at the air. His body slammed into Gabriel, who cursed and wrestled with the steering wheel. The van swerved.

"Get out of here! Get him out of here!" Gabriel shouted. "I can't see—"

Rob twisted in behind Lewis, trying to pull him back. The van kept swerving and skidding as Lewis's elbows hit Gabriel. Kaitlyn clung to the seat in front of her, frozen.

"Come *on!*" Rob yelled. *Lewis, come on back! There's nothing there!*

Lewis kept on fighting, and then all at once he went limp, and like a cork popping out of a bottle, he shot backward with Rob. They both crashed into Anna, who yelped. Then they fell in a tangle on the floor.

"Hey—what's the matter? You getting fresh or something?" Lewis said. "Let go of me."

It was an ordinary, complaining voice. Lewis was disentangling himself, looking mildly bewildered but absolutely normal.

Rob sat up and stared at him.

Gabriel had finally gotten the van on course again. He shot

a glare over his shoulder. "You crazy jerk," he said. "What'd you think you were doing?"

"Me? I wasn't doing anything. Rob was grabbing me." Lewis looked around at all of them, his round face honestly puzzled.

"Lewis—you really don't remember?" Kaitlyn asked. She could tell by his expression, by his presence in the web that he didn't. "You jumped up and started beating on something in that seat," she said, nodding. "Only there was nothing there."

"Oh . . ." A sort of light was dawning on Lewis's face. Then his expression turned sheepish. "I guess—I was dreaming, you know? I don't really remember the dream, but I thought I saw somebody sitting there. A kind of whitish shape—a person. And I knew I had to get it. . . ." His voice trailed off. He gave another look around and hunched his shoulders apologetically.

"A dream," Gabriel said in disgust. "Next time keep your dreams to yourself."

A dream? Kaitlyn thought. No. It didn't make sense; it couldn't be the whole explanation. Why should Lewis suddenly start having dreams that made him attack things? And what about the cold—it had disappeared as quickly as it had come; the air felt fine now. And the drain smell, and that sound . . .

*We're all tired,* Anna's gentle voice said in her head, reminding her that she hadn't been trying to shield her thoughts. *Not just tired but exhausted. And we've been under so much stress—it could come out in strange ways.*

"We could all have been dreaming a little," Rob said with a laugh.

"I suppose," Kaitlyn said. She tried to put any further doubts out of her mind—for now, at least. Lewis obviously believed his own story, and Anna and Rob believed him because he believed it. There was no point in harping on it.

We'll wait and see what happens, she told herself. She settled back on the seat, and Rob returned to sit by her again. The light was fading in a way that made her want to check if she was wearing sunglasses. To the west and in front of them were huge flaming hot cherry clouds.

"Should we stop?" Rob asked, peering at his watch in the dimness.

Gabriel turned the van's headlights on. "We're still in California. We can stop when we get to Oregon."

The sky went gray and then black. Ghost trucks with dazzling headlights came and went on the other side of the highway. It was nearly eight o'clock when they reached a sign saying WELCOME TO OREGON.

They drove on until they found a rest stop and then ate dinner sitting on the cool dark grass outside the van. Dinner was peanut butter sandwiches and one apple apiece, drawn from the grocery bag Tony had given them. Dessert was some cherry cough drops Lewis had found in the glove compartment and the last of the Cajun olive samples.

"We can stay here tonight," Rob said, looking around the

almost-deserted rest stop. There were few cars on the highway nearby. "Nobody will bother us."

Kait found she'd brought toothpaste but no toothbrush. In the women's rest room she rubbed her teeth with a corner of a cotton shirt she'd packed. They all wanted to go to bed early.

"But *how?*" Kaitlyn said when she got back, confronted at last with the logistics of five of them sleeping in the van. Suddenly there no longer seemed to be acres of room. "Where do we all *fit?*"

"The rear seat reclines," Rob said. He and Lewis had the back of the van open and were fiddling with the bench seats. "See, it folds back into a flat bed. That's room for two people there. Somebody else can sleep on the other bench seat, and then the two bucket seats in front recline."

"I'll take one of those," Lewis said. "Unless somebody wants to share the back . . . ?" He looked from Anna to Kait hopefully.

"The girls can have the back," Rob said.

Anna's dark eyes were laughing. "Oh, no . . . I think you and Kaitlyn should have the back. I'll sleep on the other bench."

"And *I'll* sleep outside," Gabriel said shortly, leaning in from the front and yanking a sleeping bag out of the pile.

Daggers and broken glass, that was what Kait felt from him through the web. She and Rob hadn't even *agreed* yet, although she knew they would. She liked to sleep close to Rob, it felt safe. And she knew Rob liked to have her close, because then he didn't worry about her as much.

"It's just convenience," she began, but Gabriel cut her off with a look. He seemed pale and tense under the van's interior lights.

"Look, I don't think it's such a good idea, sleeping outside," Rob said in a mild voice. Gabriel gave him the look, too.

"I can take care of myself," he said and showed his teeth.

He left the van. Kaitlyn helped Rob spread out blankets automatically, trying to screen her thoughts from the others. She still hadn't had a chance to speak to Gabriel privately. She was going to have to *make* a chance, and soon.

Sleeping in the back of the van was cramped and a little stuffy—like sleeping in a compartment on a train, Kaitlyn guessed. But she didn't really mind being crowded in with Rob. He was warm and nice to hang on to. Comfortingly solid.

It was the first time they had been alone together—and Kaitlyn was so tired her eyelids felt like lead weights. There were no golden sparks at his touch now, just a steady shining light that seemed to pour reassurance into her.

"I love you," she murmured sleepily, and they kissed. A sweet kiss that made her cling to him afterward.

*I love you,* Rob thought back. His thought carried the essence of *him* with it—pure Rob. Warm as sunlight, with an underlying hint of strength that made Kait think of lions basking in the savanna. Rob had a fine stubborn temper of his own, but he cared too much about other people to let it rule him.

And he didn't care who heard him say he loved her. A vocal whisper would have been much more private than telepathy. Distantly Kaitlyn could feel tolerant amusement laced with envy from Lewis and peaceful approval from Anna—but from outside the van, from Gabriel, a wave of dark repudiation. Bitterness. An anger that frightened her.

*He feels that he's been cheated of something,* she thought, even as she clung harder to Rob. *But that's not right; I never led him on. . . .*

*We've got to find a way to break this link,* Rob said stiffly. *It's all right when you want it, but having people spying on your thoughts when you don't want—*

"Rob, don't annoy him," Kait whispered. Rob was broadcasting loud and clear, and Gabriel was getting angrier by the minute. The two of them together were like flint and iron—sparking off each other at every opportunity.

*I've said from the beginning that we've got to get rid of it,* Gabriel said from outside. *And I know of one certain way, at least.*

He meant for one of them to die. It had come to that, Gabriel threatening them again, acting as if he hated them all.

"Leave it alone," Kaitlyn hissed before Rob could answer. "Oh, *please,* Rob, just leave it; I'm so tired." To her surprise she felt on the verge of tears.

Rob immediately gave up the argument, mentally turning his back on Gabriel. *We'll find a way to break it—another way,* he promised Kaitlyn. *The people in the white house will help us. And if they don't,* I'll *find a way.*

"Yes," Kaitlyn murmured, her eyes shutting. Rob was holding her close, and she believed him, as she'd believed in him from the beginning. She couldn't help it; Rob *made* you believe.

"Go to sleep, Kait," he whispered, and Kaitlyn sank into the darkness fearlessly.

*As long as you're with me I'm not afraid,* she thought.

The last thing she heard before sleep was a distant whisper from Anna. "I wonder if we'll dream again?"

Gabriel twisted inside the sleeping bag. There was nothing but grass underneath him, but he felt as if he were lying on roots—or bones.

Ghoulish thought. The bones of the dead beneath him. Maybe the bones of his personal dead, the ones he'd dispatched himself. That would be poetic justice, at least.

Though he wouldn't have admitted it to anyone, Gabriel believed in justice.

Not that he regretted having killed the guy in Stockton. The one who'd been ready to shoot him over the five crumpled dollar bills in his jeans pocket. He was quite happy to have sent that particular home boy to hell.

But that had been his second murder. The first had been unintentional—the product of what happened when a strong mind came in contact with a weaker one. He'd been strong, and Iris—sweet Iris—had been weak. Fragile as a little white mouse, delicate as a flower. Her life energy had poured into him as if one of her arteries had been cut. And he—

—hadn't been able to stop it.

Not until it was over and she was lying limp and motionless in his arms. Her face blue-white. Her lips parted.

Gabriel found that he was lying rigid, staring straight up into the endless darkness of the night sky. His hands were clenched into fists and he was sweating.

I'd die if it would bring her back, he thought with sudden clarity. I'd change places with her. I belong in hell with home boy, but Iris belongs here.

It was strange, but he couldn't really remember her face anymore. He could remember loving her, but not what she'd looked like alive, except that her gaze had been wide-open and defenseless, like a deer's.

And he couldn't take her place. Things weren't that *simple* in the universe; he wasn't going to get off that easy. No, his part was to lie here on grass that felt like bones and think about the new murders, the ones that he was going to commit, inevitably, in the future.

There wasn't any other way for him.

The girl in Oakland—that scrawny ratbag with the tattoo—

he hadn't killed her, quite. He'd left her in an alley with her life force almost drained, but still flowing. She'd live.

But tonight . . . the need was stronger. Gabriel hadn't expected that. He'd been feeling it for hours, the parched, cracked-earth sensation, and by now it was almost unbearable. It was all he could do not to rip into Kessler, who was a constant beacon of energy, radiating it like a lighthouse or one of those stars that flared regularly. The temptation was almost unendurable, especially when Kessler was being annoying, which was almost always.

No. He couldn't touch any of his own group. Aside from the fact that it would blow his secret, it was—impolite. Impolitic. Uncivil.

And wrong, the distant part of his mind whispered.

Shut up, Gabriel told it.

He was out of his sleeping bag in one lithe twist.

Since Rob the Wonder Boy was off limits, he would have to go hunting elsewhere. Through the web, Gabriel could feel the deep sleep of his mind-mates; through the windows of the van he saw nothing. Nobody was going to miss him.

He looked around under the stars for someone to quench his thirst.

# CHAPTER 6

The people were leaning over her. The first thing Kait noticed was that they looked like pencil drawings—monochrome, all the color sucked out. The second thing was that they were evil.

She didn't know how she knew that, but it was clear. Clearer than the faces of the people. It wasn't that they didn't have features, but the features seemed blurred, as if they were moving back and forth thousands of times a second, or as if something about them had affected Kait's sight.

Aliens, she thought wildly. Little gray people from flying saucers. And then: Lewis's white shape.

Kaitlyn's heart began pounding with deep sick thuds that seemed to choke off her breath.

She wanted to scream, but that was impossible. She didn't even know if she were awake or asleep, but she was paralyzed.

If I could move—if I could just move I could tell. I could make them go away. . . .

What she wanted to do was to kick upward with her legs and lash out with her arms to see if the visions were solid. But she couldn't even lift her knee. The things were leaning over her from all sides. There was a strange property about them—when Kaitlyn looked at any one of them, it seemed to be rushing toward her, but the group stayed in the same place. They were *looking* at her. Staring with a fixed blank gaze that was worse than any malevolence. And they seemed to be bending farther down, coming closer . . .

With a violent jerk Kaitlyn managed to lift her arm. At least, it felt like a violent jerk to her, but what she saw was her arm rising feebly and almost dreamily toward the figures. It brushed through one monochrome leaning face, and she felt a shock of coldness on the skin.

Refrigerated air . . .

The figures were gone.

Kait lay on her back, blinking. Her eyes were open now, and she thought they'd been open the whole while—but how could she tell? She was staring into darkness as black as the blackness behind closed lids. The only thing she could see was the faint shape of her arm waving in the cold air.

Cold—the air was definitely cold. And there had been a sudden drop in temperature just before Lewis saw *his* vision.

I don't believe it was a dream, Kaitlyn thought. Or not an ordinary dream.

But then, what? A premonition? She didn't have premonitions that way, and Lewis didn't have them at all. Lewis had psychokinesis, PK, the power to move objects with his mind.

Whatever it had been, it had left her with a terrible sick feeling. There was a—a *running* in her middle, a hot restless feeling that made it agony to lie still. She felt cramped and her eyes ached and her whole body was vibrating with adrenaline.

Rob was lying peacefully beside her, his breathing even. Deeply asleep. Kaitlyn hated to wake him; he needed the rest. Lewis and Anna were sleeping soundly, too—she could feel that through the web.

And Gabriel outside? Kait sent her mind searching, doing something she couldn't have described to an outsider. It was like wondering how your foot was feeling, concentrating your attention on a particular part of yourself in a particular location. Somehow she could wonder how Gabriel was doing, and then feel . . .

. . . that he wasn't there, she realized with a shock. Not outside the van where he had been before. She could sense him dimly—somewhere else—but she couldn't locate him exactly, and she couldn't tell what he was doing.

Fine. *Good.* With sudden determination Kaitlyn inched her legs up, pulling the blanket off her by degrees. Just as slowly, she sat up and then stood, crouching, edging sideways to the door in the middle of the van.

She passed Anna, curled neatly on her short bench, black hair swathing her face. Lewis's bucket seat was reclined so far she had to reach under it to get the door open. But finally, with a clank, the door slid back.

Kaitlyn could feel everyone stir, then settle again. She dropped lightly out of the van and shut the door as quietly as she could.

Now. She was going to find Gabriel. Her nervous energy would be put to good use—she was going to *talk* to him, confront him about the strangeness she'd felt inside him, about what he'd been doing when he'd left them all last night. It was the perfect opportunity; with the others asleep, they'd have complete privacy. And if Gabriel didn't like it—tough. Kaitlyn was wound up and ready for a fight herself.

She turned from the van and looked around the rest stop. Aside from the lighted bulk of the rest rooms, everything was dark. There were only three cars to be seen—a battered Volkswagen Bug, a lowslung Chevy, and a white Cadillac.

And no Gabriel. Kaitlyn couldn't get a location on him. She peered into the darkness behind and in front of her, then shrugged and started walking.

He was here *somewhere*. Just walled off so she couldn't feel him. As if he lived in a private fortress. Well, she'd explain differently to him; he was *part* of them, and he couldn't keep denying it.

And he shouldn't be wandering around alone like this in the dark. Kait passed the Bug and the Chevy, noting absently that Oregon license plates had pictures of mountains on them. She passed the Cadillac, which was parked under the last streetlight, and hesitated on the brink of the darkness beyond.

That way . . . she had an urge to go that way. An instinct. If there was one thing Kait had learned recently, it was to trust her instincts—but it was lonely-looking out there, lit only by a half-full moon just beginning to rise.

Bracing herself, she began to move cautiously forward, stepping off the sidewalk onto grass. The ground curved down, leading toward a lonely clump of trees—Kait could see their upper branches against the lighter black of the night sky.

It was very quiet, and Kaitlyn's skin was prickling, tiny hairs lifting. Well, that wasn't surprising: Oregon was cooler than California. It was just the night air.

But where *was* Gabriel? Kaitlyn was moving blindly toward the trees, but it wasn't like Gabriel to go sit under a tree. Maybe instinct had been wrong this time.

All right, she'd go just down to that first tree—she could see it fairly well now that her eyes were adjusting to the darkness— and then she'd turn back. She was far enough from the van that she could only feel Rob and Lewis and Anna very dimly, and she knew that communication would be impossible.

I'm truly alone, she thought. The only way any of us can be alone now, by getting out of range of the others. Maybe that's why Gabriel's been wandering off at night; I could understand that. Simply to get some distance.

She almost had herself convinced by the time she got to the tree.

What she found there she discovered with all her senses at once. Her ears picked up some slight sound of movement and the hiss of a ragged breath. Her eyes made out a shape half concealed behind the tree. And her psychic senses felt a disturbance in the web—a *shimmering,* as if she'd stepped near a charged field.

All the same, she could hardly make herself believe what she was witnessing. Heart beating madly, she stepped closer, moving around the tree. The shape—in the moonlight it looked like a romantic painting of Romeo and Juliet, a kneeling boy holding a limp girl in his arms. But the sound, the quick panting breath—that was more like an animal.

What she felt through the web was animalistic, too. It was hunger.

Please, no, Kaitlyn thought. She'd begun to shake, an uncontrollable trembling that started in her legs and went everywhere. Please, God, I don't want to see this. . . .

But then the kneeling boy raised his head, and there was no way to deny it anymore.

Gabriel. It was Gabriel and he was holding a girl who looked unconscious or dead, and when he looked up, it was straight into Kaitlyn's eyes.

She could see the shock on his face—and in the web she felt a shattering. A crashing-down of walls as the barriers he'd been holding around himself collapsed. She'd taken him off guard, and suddenly she could feel—everything.

Everything he was going through. Everything he was experiencing at that moment.

"Gabriel—" she gasped aloud.

*Hunger,* she got back. She could feel it pounding at her. Hunger and desperation. An intolerable, agonizing pain—and the promise of relief in the girl he was holding. A girl who wasn't dead, Kaitlyn realized, but comatose and bursting with life energy. What Lewis called *chi.*

"Gabriel," Kaitlyn said again. Her legs were wobbling; they weren't going to support her much longer. She was overwhelmed by the need she felt—*his* need.

"Get away," Gabriel said hoarsely.

She was surprised he could talk. There wasn't much rationality in his presence in the web. What Kait felt there seemed less like Gabriel than some shark or starving wolf. A desperate, merciless hunter ready to make his kill.

Run, something inside Kaitlyn said. He's about to kill, and it could be you as easily as that girl. Be smart and *run . . .*

"Gabriel, listen to me. I won't hurt you." Kaitlyn got the words out raggedly, on separate breaths, but she managed to hold her hands out toward him almost steadily. "Gabriel, I understand— I can *feel* what you need. But there has to be another way."

"Get *out* of here," Gabriel snarled.

Ignoring the terrified sickness in her stomach, Kaitlyn took a step toward him. Think, she was telling herself frantically. Think, be rational—because *he* certainly isn't.

Gabriel's lips peeled back from his teeth, and he jerked the girl to him. As if protecting his prey from an intruder. "Don't come any closer," he hissed.

"It's energy, isn't it?" Kaitlyn didn't dare take another step, so she dropped to her knees instead. She was at Gabriel's level now, and she could see that his eyes were like two windows opening on darkness. "It's life energy you need. I can feel that. I can feel how much it hurts—"

"You can't feel anything! Get out before you really do get hurt!" It was a tortured cry, but almost instantly afterward Gabriel stilled. A deathly calm spread over his face, and his eyes went like black ice. Kaitlyn could feel his purposefulness in the web.

Without looking at her, ignoring her completely, he turned his attention to the girl in his arms. The girl had soft curly hair—dark blond or light brown, Kaitlyn thought. She looked almost peaceful. Gabriel had undoubtedly stunned her with his mind somehow.

Now he turned her head to one side, pushing the disordered curls off the back of her neck. Kaitlyn watched in horror, frozen by the cool deliberation of his movements.

"Right here," Gabriel whispered, and he touched the nape

of the girl's neck, a point at the upper part of the spine, just between vertebrae. "This is the transfer point. The best place to take energy. You can stay and watch if you want."

His voice was like an Arctic wind, and his presence in the web like ice. He was looking at the girl's neck with cold hunger, eyes narrowed, lips skinned back a little.

And then, as Kaitlyn watched, he bent to put his lips to the girl's skin.

*"No!"*

Kait didn't know what she was going to do until she did it. But suddenly she was moving, she was throwing herself across the little distance to Gabriel. She was putting her hands between the girl and him—one hand on the girl's neck, the other on Gabriel's face. She felt his lips, and then the brush of teeth.

*Keep out of this!* Gabriel's mental shout was so powerful it sent shockwaves through Kaitlyn. But she hung on.

*Give her to me!* he shouted. Kaitlyn's vision was red; she could see nothing, feel nothing, but the all-encompassing fury of Gabriel's hunger. He was a snarling, clawing animal now— and she was fighting him.

And losing. She was weaker, both physically and psychically, and he was utterly ruthless. He was tearing the girl away from her, his mind a black hole ready to consume. . . .

*No, Gabriel,* Kaitlyn thought—and she kissed him.

That was the result, anyway, of her sudden darting movement. She'd meant for a different contact—forehead

to forehead, the way Rob had touched her to channel healing energy once. But at the touch of his lips against hers she
felt a shock of a different sort and it was an instant before
she could pull back to get the position right.

She'd shocked Gabriel, too—shocked him into stillness.
He seemed too astonished to fight her or jerk away. He simply
sat, paralyzed, as Kaitlyn shut her eyes, and, gripping his shoulders, thrust her forehead against his.

*Oh.*

That simple contact, skin to skin, third eye to third eye,
brought the biggest shock of all. A jolt that went through Kait
like lightning—as if two ends of electric wiring had touched,
sending a violent current coursing through.

Oh, she thought. *Oh . . .*

It was frightening—terrifying in its power. And for the first
instant it hurt. She felt a tearing in her body, in her bloodstream—
as if something was being pulled out of her. A vital pain at the
roots of her being. Dimly, with some part of her mind that could
still think, she remembered what Gabriel had said once. That
people were afraid he would steal their souls. That was what this
felt like.

And yet, at the same time, it was compelling. It swept
her along with it, helpless to resist. It demanded that she sur-
render. . . .

You wanted to help him, the part of Kait that could still
think said. So help him. *Give.* Give what he needs.

Kaitlyn felt a wrenching—and then a bursting. It was as if some barrier in her had been broken, ripping under pressure. She trembled violently—and felt herself *give*.

It still hurt, but in a new way. A strange way that was almost pleasure. Like the release of something painful, blocked . . . backed-up.

Kait had received psychic energy before, taking Rob's healing power when she'd been drained and exhausted. But she'd never given it, not on this scale. Now she felt a torrent of energy flowing from her into Gabriel, like a flood of golden sparks. And she could feel him responding, drinking in the energy greedily, gratefully. The darkness inside him, the black hole, being lit up by the gold.

Life, Kaitlyn thought dizzily. It's life I'm giving him really. He needs this or he'll die.

And then: Is this how healers feel? Oh, no wonder Rob likes doing it. There's nothing like it, nothing . . . especially if you *want* to help.

For the most part, though, she couldn't think at all. She simply *experienced*, feeling Gabriel's hunger gradually being sated, the burning need in him slowly cooling as it was met. And feeling his amazement, his wonder.

He was less of an animal now, and more Gabriel. The Gabriel who had tried to protect her from the pain of Mr. Zetes's great crystal, the Gabriel who'd had tears in his eyes when he spoke of his past. Kaitlyn realized suddenly that she'd gotten behind his walls again. She was seeing, touching, the Gabriel that was kept hidden from the world.

*It's different—like this.* The thought was almost a whisper, but it shook Kaitlyn with its strength. Its—intensity. She could feel the astonished gratitude behind it, and something like awe. *Different . . . when I took energy before—when I took it last night—it wasn't like this.*

And because Gabriel's mind was open to her, Kait knew what he meant. She could *see* the girl from last night, the one with the straggly hair and the unicorn tattoo. And she could taste the girl's fear, her anguish and aversion.

*She was unwilling,* Kaitlyn told Gabriel. *You forced her; she didn't want to help you. I do.*

*Why?*

One word, with the force of a blow behind it. Kaitlyn felt Gabriel's hands tighten on her shoulders as he projected the thought. She hadn't been aware of her physical body for some time, but now she realized that she and Gabriel were clinging to each other, still in contact at the transfer point. The curly-haired girl, the new victim, had fallen or been shoved aside.

*Why?* Gabriel repeated, almost brutally, demanding an answer.

*Because I care about you!* Kaitlyn shot back. The violence of the first channeling of energy was gone, but she could still feel it flowing from herself to him. And she could feel, in some distant way, an approaching dizziness, a weakness. She ignored it. *Because I care what happens to you, because I—*

Abruptly, with no warning at all, Gabriel pulled away. Whatever Kaitlyn had been about to say was lost.

The jolt of broken contact was almost as bad as the moment of initiation. Kaitlyn's eyes flew open. She could see the world again, but she felt blind. Blind and horribly alone. Even feeling Gabriel in the web was nothing to the intimacy of direct energy transfer.

*Gabriel . . .*

"It's enough," he said, speaking instead of returning her thought. She could feel him trying to gather his walls again. "I'm all right now. You did what you meant to do."

"Gabriel," Kaitlyn said. There was a terrible wistfulness inside her. Without thinking, she raised a hand to touch his face.

Gabriel flinched back.

Hurt and loss flooded over Kait. She clamped her lips together.

"Don't," Gabriel said. Then he looked away, shaking his head. "I'm not trying to hurt you, damn it!" he said sharply. "It's just—don't you realize how dangerous that was? I could have drained you. I could have killed you." He turned back and looked directly into her eyes again, with a sudden fierceness that frightened Kaitlyn. *"I could have killed you,"* he repeated with vicious emphasis.

"You didn't. I feel fine." The dizziness had gone, or never come. She looked steadily at Gabriel. In the moonlight his eyes were as black as his hair, and his pale face was almost supernaturally beautiful. "I'm psychic, so I have more of the energy than normal people. Obviously I've got enough to spare."

"It was still a risk. And if you touch me, there's the risk I'll take more."

"But you're all right now. You said so, and I can feel it, too. You don't need more; you're all right."

There was a pause and Gabriel's eyes dropped. Then, slowly, almost grudgingly, he said, "Yes." Kaitlyn could feel him trying to think, could sense his confusion. "And—I'm grateful," he said at last. He said it awkwardly, as if he hadn't had much practice, but when he lifted his eyes again she saw that he meant it. She could feel it, too, a childlike, marveling gratitude that was totally at odds with those chiseled features and grim mouth.

Kait's throat tightened. It was all she could do not to reach out to him again. Instead she said, as dispassionately as she could manage, "Gabriel, was it the crystal?"

"What?" He looked away from her again, as if realizing he'd revealed too much.

"You weren't like this before. You didn't *need* energy, not before Mr. Zetes hooked you up with that crystal. But now you've got a mark on your forehead, and you've changed—"

"Into a real psychic vampire." Gabriel laughed shortly. "That's what the people at the research center in Durham said—but they didn't know, did they? Nobody can know what the reality is like."

"That isn't what I was going to say. I was going to say that you'd changed, and I'd noticed it before tonight. I think you've become—more powerful. You can link up with minds outside the web, and before you couldn't."

Gabriel was rubbing his forehead absently but roughly. "I suppose it had to be the crystal," he said. "Who knows, maybe that's what it's for. Maybe it's what Zetes wanted, all of us slaves to this—need."

The idea took Kaitlyn's breath away. She'd been thinking of it as some side effect, something that had happened accidentally because the crystal had burned too much of Gabriel's energy. But the idea that anyone would do this deliberately—would make someone like this on *purpose* . . .

"It's nauseating, isn't it?" Gabriel said conversationally. "What I've become is nauseating. And I'm afraid it's permanent, or at least I don't see any reason why it shouldn't be."

He'd seen her horror and was hurt by it. Kait tried to think of some way to make him feel better, and settled on brisk normalcy.

"Well, at least we have a way of dealing with it," she said. "For now, we'd better get this girl back to where she came from, don't you think? And then we should go and tell Rob. He'll want to help and he may even be able to think—"

She broke off with a gasp. She'd been getting to her feet, but now Gabriel hauled her back down again with one powerful yank.

Kaitlyn found herself looking into eyes that were black and glittering with menacing fury.

# CHAPTER 7

"No," Gabriel snarled. "We will not tell Rob—*anything.*"

Kaitlyn was bewildered. "But—the others have to know—"

"They don't have to know. They're not my *keepers.*"

"Gabriel, they'll *want* to know. They care about you, too. And Rob may be able to help you."

"I don't want his help."

It was said flatly, and with absolute finality. Kaitlyn realized that on this issue Gabriel was inflexible, and there was no use in arguing.

He went on anyway, just in case she needed convincing. "Of course, I can't stop *you* from telling them," he said, releasing her arm and giving a sudden disarming smile. "But if you do I'm afraid I'll have to leave this little expedition . . . and our group . . . permanently."

Kaitlyn rubbed her arm. "All right, Gabriel. I get the

point. And," she added with sudden conviction, "I'll still help you. But you've got to *let* me help. You've got to tell me when you're feeling—like you did tonight. You've got to come to me, instead of wandering around looking for girls to attack."

Gabriel's expression was suddenly bleak. "Maybe I don't want your help, either," he said stonily. Then he burst out, "How long do you think you can keep this up? This *donation?* Even a psychic doesn't have endless energy. What if you get weak?"

That's why I wanted to tell Rob, Kaitlyn thought, but she knew better than to start debating again. She simply said, "We'll deal with that when we come to it." She tried to hide the flicker of unease inside her. What *would* they do—if Gabriel had one of these fits and she was too weak to help him? He'd kill an ordinary person, drain him dry.

Think about it later, she decided. And then pulled out the old hope, the one that had been comforting her since they'd left the Institute.

"Maybe the people in the white house can help," she said. "Maybe they'll know a way to cure you—undo what the crystal did."

"If it was the crystal," Gabriel said. With a faint self-mocking smile he added, "It seems to me that we're expecting a lot from these people in the white house."

That's because we don't have any other hope. Kaitlyn didn't say it, but she knew Gabriel understood. She and Gabriel sometimes understood each other too well.

"Let's get this girl back. What car did she come from?" she asked, turning away from those ironic dark gray eyes.

They put the girl back in the Cadillac. According to Gabriel, she'd been alone, which was fortunate. Nobody would have noticed she was missing, or called the police. And Gabriel said that she'd never seen him—he'd come up behind her and put her to sleep with one touch of his mind.

"I seem to be developing new talents by the hour," he said and smiled.

Kaitlyn wasn't amused, but she had to admit to some relief. The girl would just think she'd fallen asleep and would drive away never knowing what had happened to her. Or at least that was what Kait hoped.

"You'd better get in the van with the rest of us," she said. "You need *sleep.*"

Gabriel didn't object. A few minutes later he was settling down in the other bucket seat, while Kait was creeping into the back of the van again.

I need sleep, too, she thought, snuggling in beside Rob's warm body with a feeling of gratitude. And, please, please, I don't want any more dreams.

When Kaitlyn woke again, it was daylight. Rob was sitting up, and all around her were the noises of people stirring and yawning.

"How is everybody?" Rob asked. His blond hair was tousled

and he looked terribly young, Kaitlyn thought. Young and vulnerable when you compared his sleepy golden eyes to the dark gray ones she'd seen last night. . . .

"Kinked up," Lewis moaned from the front. He was wriggling his shoulders. Kaitlyn had a few kinks herself, and she saw that Gabriel was stretching cautiously.

"You'll be fine," Anna said and got up. She opened the side door and jumped lightly out, with no sign of stiffness.

"I feel like I swallowed a fuzz ball," Rob said, running his tongue over his teeth. "Does anybody—"

*Oh, my God. What is it?*

The exclamation came from outside the van, from Anna. The four inside immediately broke off what they were doing and started for the door.

*What's wrong, Anna?* Kaitlyn thought even before she got out.

*I've never seen anything like it.*

Anna's grave dark eyes were wide, fixed on the van itself. Kaitlyn turned and looked, but at first couldn't quite grasp what she was seeing. It looked almost *beautiful* at first.

The entire van was swathed with glittering ribbons—as if someone had painted stripes of shining stuff all over it, even over the windows. In the crisp morning light the stripes took on rainbow colors. There were hundreds of the bands, crossing and recrossing.

And yet it wasn't beautiful, really. It evoked a feeling of

revulsion in Kait. When she looked closely at one of the stripes, she saw it was tacky . . . slimy, almost. Like . . . like *mucus* . . .

"Slug trails!" Rob said and pulled Kaitlyn away from the van.

Kaitlyn's stomach lurched. She was glad she hadn't eaten more for dinner last night. "Slug trails—but it *can't* be," Gabriel said, sounding angry. "Look around you—there's no sign of a trail anywhere but on the van."

It was true. Kaitlyn swallowed and said, "I've never seen a slug big enough to leave a trail like *that*."

"I have, in *Planet of the Giant Gastropods*," Lewis said.

"I have, too, in my backyard," Anna said. She nodded when the others looked at her. "I'm serious. In Puget Sound there are slugs that big, banana slugs. Some people eat them."

"Thank you for sharing that with us," Kaitlyn whispered, stomach lurching again.

Gabriel still looked angry. "How did they get there?" he demanded, as if Anna had put them there personally. "And why aren't there any on those cars?" He pointed toward a gray Buick parked nearby, and the middle-aged couple in the Buick looked at him curiously.

"Leave her alone. She doesn't know," Rob said before Anna could answer.

"Do *you?*"

Rob slanted a dangerous golden glare at Gabriel and started to shake his head. Then he stopped and looked thoughtful. He turned to the van again, frowning.

"It could be—"

"What?" Kaitlyn asked.

Rob shook his head slowly. In the early sunlight he looked like a ruffled golden angel. "Oh, nothing," he said and shrugged.

Kait had the feeling that he was suppressing something, and the next minute he gave her a half-laughing look, as if to say she wasn't the only one who could hide things in the web.

A nasty *stubborn* angel, Kait thought, and Rob grinned.

"Come on, let's get out of this place," he said, turning to the others, who were looking displeased. "It's just slug stuff. Let's find a car wash."

Until that moment Kaitlyn had forgotten her dream about the colorless people. The episode with Gabriel had swamped it, somehow, driving it back into her subconscious. But now, suddenly, she remembered, and she looked at the van sharply.

"Heads up!" Lewis hissed before she could say anything. "It's the law!"

A police car was cruising into the rest stop. Kaitlyn's heart gave one thump, and then she was following the others in a quick but orderly retreat into the van.

*Just keep your heads down and stay calm,* Rob told them. *Pretend you're talking to each other.*

"A lot of good that's going to do," Gabriel said acidly.

The police car drove past them. Kait couldn't help glancing sideways at it. A uniformed woman in the passenger seat glanced up at the same moment, and for an instant their eyes met.

Kaitlyn's breath stopped. She only hoped her face was as utterly blank as her mind felt. If that policewoman saw her terror . . .

The car cruised on.

Kait could feel her pulse in her throat. *Somebody start driving,* she thought. *Fast but casual.* Rob was already sliding into the driver's seat.

Kaitlyn was still terrified the police car would turn around, or follow them when they left. But it didn't. It seemed to have stopped at the other end of the rest stop.

Where the white Cadillac was, Kait's mind supplied, and she tried to squash the thought and the memories it evoked instantly. She didn't dare look at Gabriel or let herself wonder if the curly haired girl *had* remembered something after all.

"Don't be scared," Lewis said when they were once again on Highway 5. He'd felt her turmoil even if he didn't know the reason. "We're okay now."

Kaitlyn gave him a watery smile.

They found a do-it-yourself car wash in a town called Grants Pass, and Kaitlyn disbursed ninety-nine cents from their funds to buy paper towels. She also paid for breakfast burritos and coffee at a McDonald's, since none of them could face peanut butter this early in the morning.

"And now we should cut over to the coast," Rob said when

they were done eating. They'd washed themselves as well as the car at the car wash, a novel experience that Kait wasn't sure she wanted to repeat.

"Well, you have two choices," said Lewis, who had by default become the Keeper of the Map. "There's a road that goes through the Siskiyou National Forest, and then a little north of that there's a regular highway."

After a short discussion they decided on the highway. As Anna said, the white house might be surrounded by trees, but it wasn't in a landlocked forest. It was someplace where the ocean came between two wooded arms of land.

"Some place called Griffin's Pit," Lewis said, his eyes crinkling as he looked at Kait.

"We might try looking that up in a library somewhere," Rob said, steering the van back to the freeway. "That and all the other variations we can think of."

"Maybe we'll just *find* the place first," Kaitlyn said wistfully.

But at Coos Bay, where the highway finally reached the coast, she slumped and shook her head.

"Not north enough," she said and glanced at Anna for confirmation.

Anna was nodding resignedly. They all stood around the van, staring down at the ocean. It was vast and blue and sparkling—and *wrong*. Not at all like the water they'd seen in the dream.

"It's way too civilized," Anna said. She pointed to a large

freighter loaded with logs that was passing through the bay entrance. "See that? It's putting junk in the water—oil or gasoline or something—and the water we saw wasn't *like* that. It wasn't traveled like this. It felt clean."

"Felt clean," Gabriel repeated, almost sneering.

"Yes," Kaitlyn said. "It did. And look at those sand dunes. Did anybody see sand in the dream?"

"No." Rob sighed. "Okay, back in the van. Yukon ho."

"Can't we eat first?" Lewis pleaded. It had taken them until noon to get to the bay.

"Eat while we drive," Rob said. In the van Kaitlyn made and passed out peanut butter sandwiches.

They chewed on them apathetically, looking out the windows. The view as they drove north up the Oregon coast was not inspiring.

"Sand," Lewis said after half an hour. "I never knew there was so much sand in the world."

The dunes seemed endless. They were huge and rolling, sometimes blocking off the view of the ocean. In places they were hundreds of feet high.

"How horrible," Kaitlyn said suddenly. In the sand she could see distant trees—buried trees. Only the top third of their trunks emerged from the dune, standing but quite dead. It was as if the dunes had swallowed a forest . . . and digested it.

"Jeez, there's even vultures circling," Lewis said, eyeing a large bird.

"That's an osprey," Anna said almost unkindly.

Kait glanced at her, then sat back, relapsing into silence. She felt depressed, and she didn't know if it was the dunes, the prospect of endless traveling to an unknown destination, or the peanut butter sandwiches.

Everyone else was silent, too. There was a heavy feeling to the air. Oppressive. Laced with something Kaitlyn couldn't quite put her finger on. . . .

"Oh, come on," she said, half aloud. "Cheer up, everybody. This is only our second day." She groped in her mind for an interesting topic to distract them. After a moment she found one, not only interesting but slightly dangerous. Oh, well, nothing ventured, nothing gained.

"So, Lewis, about this *chi* stuff," she said. He glanced at her lethargically. "So, I was wondering, how much can somebody afford to lose before they get sick?"

She could see Gabriel stiffen in the front passenger seat.

"Um," Lewis said. "It depends. Some people have a lot—they generate it all the time. If you're healthy you do that, and it just kind of flows freely inside you, without any blocks. Through strange channels."

Kaitlyn laughed. "Through what?"

"Strange channels. Really. That's what my grandfather called some of the arteries the *chi* runs through. He was a master of *chi gong*—that's the art of manipulating *chi,* kind of like what Rob does when he heals."

Gabriel by now was deliberately *not* looking at Kait, all the while willing her fiercely to shut up. Unable to send a reassuring message, Kaitlyn ignored him.

"So it's sort of like blood," she said to Lewis. "And if you lose it, you manufacture more."

"In the Middle Ages people thought blood *was* the life energy," Rob said from the driver's seat. "They thought some people had too much—that's what they had in mind when they bled you with leeches. They thought if they could drain some of the extra blood off, it would relieve the pressure; help you produce better, clearer blood afterward. But of course they were wrong—about blood."

He looked over his shoulder as he said it, and Kait thought his glance encompassed Gabriel as well as her. Alarm shot through her. Rob wasn't stupid. What if he'd guessed . . . ?

Gabriel was radiating cold fury.

"Well, that's interesting," Kait gabbled. She now wanted to find a boring topic to make them all forget this. Even silence would be fine—but Rob was speaking again.

"Some people think that's how the legends of vampires started," he said. "With psychics that drained their victims of life energy, *sekhem, chi,* whatever you want to call it. Later the stories got twisted and people called it blood."

Kaitlyn sat frozen. It wasn't just what Rob was saying, it was the *way* he was saying it. His disgust and loathing filled the web.

"I've heard legends about that, too," Anna said, and her repugnance was equally clear. "About evil shamans who live by stealing power from others."

"That's sick," said Lewis. "If a *chi gong* master did that, he'd be ostracized. It completely violates the Tao."

Their abhorrence was reverberating in the web, shuddering over Kaitlyn in waves. Very distantly she could sense Gabriel's stony presence.

No wonder he didn't want them to know, she thought, knowing that no one else could sense her through the all-pervading horror and aversion. None of them can understand. They just think it's awful.

She wished she could tell Gabriel she was sorry, but Gabriel was looking out the window, his shoulders tense.

To Kaitlyn's vast relief, Lewis changed the subject. "And of course there are the people whose energy fields are too *strong*," he said with a sly look at Rob. "You know, the people you agree with even when you don't know why. The ones that put you under a spell with their charisma—their energy just knocks you out."

Rob's eyes in the rearview mirror were innocent. "If I see somebody like that I'll tell you," he said. "Sounds dangerous."

"It is. You can find yourself fighting evil magicians just because some nut thought it was a good idea."

There was an edge to Lewis's voice that showed the remark wasn't entirely benign. Kaitlyn was glad they weren't talking about vampires anymore, but discouraged when everyone lapsed into silence again.

Something's wrong with us, she thought, and shivered.

The silence lasted for endless miles up the coast. The dunes ran out eventually and were replaced by black basalt headlands that plunged down to the sea. Huge waves crashed around strange rocks rising like monoliths out of the water.

At one point they passed a deep fissure in the cliffs, where the pounding sea had whipped the water into a froth like cream.

"Devil's Churn," Lewis said sepulchrally, raising his head from the map.

"Looks like it," Kaitlyn said. She meant to sound light-hearted, but somehow it came out grim.

Silence again. They passed offshore islands, but these were inhabited only by gulls and other birds. No trees, no white house. Kaitlyn shivered again.

"We're never going to find it," Lewis said.

This was so unlike him that Kait felt only surprise, but Anna turned sharply. "I wish you wouldn't be so pessimistic. Or if you have to be, I wish you'd keep your opinions to yourself!"

Kaitlyn's jaw dropped. The next moment she felt a rush of protective anger. "You don't have to be so nasty to him," she told Anna heatedly. "Just because you're so—so *stoic* all the time. . . ." She stopped and almost bit her tongue. What had made her say that?

Hurt flashed in Anna's dark eyes. Lewis scowled. "I can fight my own battles," he said. "You're always jumping in."

"Yes, she's a real little do-gooder," Gabriel said from the front.

Rage exploded in Kaitlyn. "And you're a cold-blooded *snake!*" she shouted. Gabriel gave her a brilliant, unsettling smile.

"She got that one right, anyway," Rob said. The van was swerving erratically. Rob was looking at Gabriel rather than at the road. "And you shut up, Lewis, if you know what's good for you."

"I think you're all horrible," Anna gasped. She seemed on the verge of tears. "And I've *had* it, all right? You can let me off here because I'm not going with you any farther."

Tires squealed as Rob hit the brakes. A horn blared behind them.

"Fine," Rob said. "Get out."

# CHAPTER 8

·

"Go on," Rob said curtly. "Don't keep us all waiting."

The horn blared again behind them.

Anna rose without any of her usual grace. Her movements were jerky, full of repressed energy. She snatched up her duffel bag and began to fumble with the door handle.

Kait sat stiffly, her shoulders tense, her head high. Her heart was pounding with defensive fury. *Let* Anna go if she wanted. It just showed she'd never cared for the rest of them in the first place.

Ridiculous.

The thought came out of nowhere, like a tiny glint of light in her mind, there and gone in an instant. It was enough to shock Kaitlyn into some kind of sense.

Ridiculous—of course Anna cared for the rest of them. Anna cared about everything, from the earth itself to the animals she loved to just about any person that crossed her path.

But then why was Kait so *angry* with her? Kait could feel all the physical symptoms. The pounding heart, the shortness of breath—the flushed face and tight feeling at her temples. More, there was a wild need to *move* in her muscles, like the desire to hit something.

Physical symptoms. It was another glint, surfacing from Kaitlyn's subconscious. And suddenly she understood.

"Anna, wait. *Wait,*" she said just as Anna wrestled the door open. She tried to make her voice calm, when it kept wanting to come out panicked or seething.

Anna stopped but didn't turn.

"Don't you see—everybody, don't you *see?*" Kaitlyn looked around at the others. "This isn't real. We're all upset, but we're not really upset at each other. We're just *feeling* angry, so our minds think there must be a reason to *be* angry."

"It's just nerves, I suppose," Gabriel sneered. His lip was curled and his gray eyes were savage. "We couldn't possibly really hate each other."

"No! I don't know what it is, but—" Kaitlyn broke off, realizing that in addition to all the other physical symptoms she was shivering. It was *cold* in the van, colder than could be explained by the open door. And there was a strange odor in her nostrils, a sewer stench.

"Do you smell that? It's the same thing I smelled yesterday when Lewis did his sleepwalking bit. And it's cold like yesterday, too." Kaitlyn could see confusion mingling with the anger in the faces around her, and she turned to the one person she trusted absolutely.

*Rob,* she said fervently, *please listen. I know it's hard because you feel like you're angry, but just try. Something's going on.*

Slowly Rob's face cleared. The smoldering fury went out of his amber-colored eyes, leaving them golden and somewhat bewildered. He blinked and put a hand to his forehead.

"You're right," he said. "It's like that psychology experiment— give someone an injection of adrenaline, and then put them in a room with someone acting angry. The first person gets angry, too, but it's not real anger. It's been *induced.*"

"Someone's doing that to us," Kaitlyn said.

"But how?" Lewis demanded. He sounded scoffing, but not as exasperated as before. "Nobody's given us any injections."

"Long distance," Rob said. "It's a psychic attack."

His voice was flat and positive. His eyes had gone dark gold. Outside, the blaring horn had given way to several horns sounding continuously.

"Shut the door, Anna," Rob said quietly. "I'll find a place to pull over. There's something I ought to have told you before."

Anna slid the door shut. A few minutes later they had pulled over by the roadside and Rob was looking at the rest of them soberly.

"I should have mentioned it this morning," he said. "But I wasn't sure, and I didn't see any point in you all worrying.

Those slug tracks . . . well, back at Durham I heard stories about people waking up to find those around their house. Slime trails or sometimes footprints of people or animals. They almost always went along with nightmares—people having terrible dreams the night before."

Nightmares. Now Kaitlyn remembered. "I had a terrible dream last night," she said. "There were all these people leaning over me. Gray people—they looked like pencil sketches. And it was cold—just the way it was a few minutes ago." She looked at Rob. "But what *is* it?"

"They said all those things were signs of a psychic attack."

"A psychic attack," Gabriel repeated, but his tone was less sarcastic than it had been.

"The stories were that dark psychics could do things even over long distances. They could visualize you and use PK, telepathy, even astral projection." His troubled eyes turned back to Kait. "Those gray people you saw—I've heard that astral projections are colorless."

"Astral projections as in letting your mind do the walking? Leaving your body behind?" Lewis asked, cocking an eyebrow. The atmosphere had changed; the web was no longer quivering with animosity. Kait thought that everyone looked like themselves again.

Rob was nodding. "That's it. And I've heard that psychic attacks can make you weak or nervous—even make you think you're going crazy."

"I thought *I* was going crazy just now," Anna said. Her eyes were large and bright with unshed tears. "I'm sorry, everybody."

"I'm sorry, too," Kaitlyn said. She and Anna looked at each other a moment and then simultaneously reached forward to hug each other.

"Sure, everybody's sorry," Gabriel said impatiently. "But we've got more important things to think about. A psychic attack means one thing—we've been found."

"Mr. Zetes," Rob said.

"Who else? But the question is, who's he gotten to do it? What psychics are attacking?"

Kaitlyn tried to visualize the faces in her dream. It was impossible. The features had been too blurred.

"Mr. Z had a lot of contacts," Rob said wearily. "Obviously he's found some new friends."

Anna was shaking her head. "But how can he have found such powerful ones so fast? I mean, *we* couldn't do what they're doing, and we're supposed to be the best."

"The best of our age group," Rob began, but Kaitlyn said, "The crystal."

Understanding flared immediately in Gabriel's eyes. "That's it. The crystal is amplifying their power."

"But it's *dangerous*," Kaitlyn started, and then she shut up at an ominous glance from Gabriel.

Intent on his own thoughts, Rob didn't seem to notice.

"Obviously, they don't care about the danger, and while they're using the crystal they're much stronger than we are. The point is that we've got to be prepared. They're not finished with us—and the attacks will probably get worse. We've got to be ready for anything."

"Yeah, but ready how?" asked Lewis. "What can you do against that kind of attack?"

Rob shrugged. "At the Durham Center I heard people talk about envisioning light—protective light. The problem is that I never really listened. I don't know how you do it."

Kaitlyn let out her breath and sat back. The others were doing the same, and a sense of apprehension ran through the web. Apprehension—and vulnerability.

There was a long silence.

"Well, I suppose we'd better get back on the road," Kait said finally. "It's no good sitting around and thinking about it."

"Just everybody be on the lookout for anything unusual," Rob said.

But nothing unusual happened on the rest of the drive. Anna took the wheel and they resumed their beach-scanning, agree-ing that nothing on the Oregon coast looked like the place in their dreams. The rock was too black—volcanic, apparently—and the water too open.

"And it's still not north enough," Kait said.

They stopped that night at a little town called Cannon Beach, just below the Washington border. It was already dark by the time Anna pulled the van into a quiet street that dead-ended on the beach.

"This may not be legal, but I don't think anybody's going to bother us," she said. "For that matter, I've hardly seen anybody around here."

"It's a resort town," Rob said. "And this is off season."

It certainly seemed like off season to Kaitlyn. The sky was clouding over, and it was cold and windy outside.

"I saw a little store back there on the main street," she said. "We've got to buy something for dinner—we ate the last of the bread and peanut butter for lunch."

"I'll go," Anna said. "I don't mind the cold."

Rob nodded. "I'll go with you."

It was only once they were gone that Kait wished Lewis had gone, too. She was getting worried about Gabriel.

He seemed tense and distant, staring out the window into the dark. In the web Kaitlyn could feel only coldness and a sense of walls—as if he were living in a castle of ice.

He put the highest walls up when he had the most to hide, Kaitlyn knew. Right now she was worried that he was suffering—and that he wouldn't come to her for help.

And she'd noticed something else. He was still sitting in the front passenger seat. The rest of them had changed places every so often, but Gabriel always stuck to the front.

I wonder, Kait thought, if it could have anything to do with the fact that *I* always stick to the back.

She was getting fairly good at screening her thoughts when she concentrated. Neither Lewis nor Gabriel seemed to have heard that.

Rob and Anna returned windblown and laughing, clutching paper bags to their chests.

"We splurged," Rob said. "Microwave hot dogs—they're still pretty hot—and Nachos and potato chips."

"And Oreos," Anna said, puffing back wisps of black hair that had blown in her face.

Lewis grinned as he unwrapped a hot dog. "Pure junk food. Joyce would die."

Kaitlyn glanced at him, and for a moment everyone stilled. We still can't really believe it, Kait thought. We all *know* Joyce betrayed us, but we can't accept it. How could anyone put on an act the way she did?

"She was so—*alive*," Anna said. "Effervescent. Energetic. I liked her from the minute I saw her."

"And she used that," Gabriel snarled. "She was recruiting us; making us like her was just a technique."

So tense, Kaitlyn thought. He's incredibly on edge. She watched Gabriel tearing into a hot dog almost savagely, and worry shifted in her stomach.

"Really hits the spot, doesn't it?" she said. Her eyes were on Gabriel, and she tried to keep her presence in the web completely neutral. She added casually, "But maybe it's not enough."

"We got two for everybody and a couple of extras," Anna

said, following Kait's gaze to Gabriel. "You can have one of the extras, Gabriel."

He waved her off impatiently. His gray eyes, fixed on Kaitlyn, were full of angry warning.

"Just trying to be helpful," Kaitlyn said. She leaned close to Gabriel to fish a potato chip out of the bag and added in a low voice, "I wish you'd let me."

*You can help by leaving me alone.*

The thought was swift and brutal—and meant only for her. Kaitlyn could tell that none of the others had heard it. Trust Gabriel to have perfected the art of private communication.

So he wasn't going to come to her. He needed to, she was sure of that now. His face seemed even paler than usual, almost chalky, and there was a repressed violence to his movements. As if he were under some terrible internal pressure, and in danger of flying apart at any minute.

But he was stubborn, and that meant he wouldn't come. Gabriel didn't know how to ask for help, he only knew how to take.

Never mind, Kaitlyn thought, watching him surreptitiously. I'm stubborn, too. And I'm *damned* if I'm going to let you kill yourself—or anybody else.

Gabriel waited until they were all asleep.

Kaitlyn had been the last to succumb, fighting even the warmth they'd produced by running the van's heaters before they bedded down. He'd felt the red-gold shimmer of her thoughts running on when all the others were still and silent. She was trying to outwait him.

But it didn't work. Gabriel could be patient when he had to be.

When even Kaitlyn's thoughts had faded into a humming blank, Gabriel quietly sat up in the driver's seat and opened the door beside him. He slid out and had the door shut again almost before anyone could stir. Then he waited a moment, his senses focused on the inside of the van.

Still asleep. Good.

The wind out here was bitterly cold. Not the sort of night for any sensible person to be out wandering. That was a problem, and Gabriel thought about it as he trudged through the dry, loose sand above the high tide line.

Then he looked up. There were cottages and duplexes on the beach, as well as motel units. And some of them must be occupied.

He tried to dredge up a killing smile, but he couldn't quite manage. Breaking and entering was one crime he'd never committed before. Somehow it seemed different from picking a victim at random off the streets.

But the other choice was Kaitlyn.

This time the killing smile came easily. It was a smile for himself, and full of self-mockery. Because Kaitlyn was the obvious choice—the girl was warm and willing and definitely pleasant to link up with. Her life energy encased her in a scintillating ruby glow; her mind was a place of blue pools and blazing meteors. He'd been tempted all day by the aura that surrounded her like a charged field.

It had been all he could do not to plunge into that halo and drink it in gulps. Find a transfer point and fix on to it like a leech. He'd needed her desperately.

Only a complete fool would have turned down her help when it was freely offered.

Fighting his way through crumbling sand while the wind lashed around him like a lost spirit, Gabriel smiled.

Then he began to trudge toward one of the cottages that had a light in the window.

Kait woke up and cursed herself.

She'd been absolutely determined not to fall asleep. And now Gabriel was gone, of course. She could feel his absence.

How could she have been so *stupid?*

She'd had practice, now, in disentangling herself from Rob and slipping away soundlessly.

Kait almost yelped as she stepped away from the van and into the wind. She should have brought a jacket—but it was no use thinking about that now. Head bent, arms wrapped around herself, she cast her thoughts wide.

She'd had practice now in searching for Gabriel, too. He was good at concealing himself, but she knew what to look for. In only a moment she had found it—a faraway sense of glittering ice. Like a blue-white spark on the edge of her mind. Kait turned her body toward it and started walking.

It was rough going. The wind blew sheets of sand away from her. When the moon came out, it showed particles whisking through the air like ghosts. It also showed a gigantic rock shaped like a haystack rearing out of the ocean, where no rock had any business being.

A spooky place. Kaitlyn tried not to think about psychic attacks and Mr. Zetes. She was crazy to have come out here alone, of course—but what else could she do?

The wind smelled of saltwater. From her left came the soft-but-loud crashing of waves. Kait swerved to avoid driftwood and then turned sharply, heading for a cluster of cottages. There. Gabriel was very close; she could feel it.

The next moment she saw him; a dark silhouette against a lighted window. Alarm spurted through her. That window—she knew what he was doing loitering around a cottage. What if he'd already . . .

*Gabriel!*

The call was involuntary, wrung out of her by panic. Kaitlyn's heart thumped before she realized that Rob and the others were out of range.

Gabriel wasn't. His head whipped around.

*What are you doing here?*

*What are* you *doing?* she countered. *What have you done, Gabriel?*

She saw him hesitate, then saw him abandon the cottage window abruptly and come striding toward her. She walked to meet him, and he pulled her into the shelter of a carport.

"Can't I take a walk without being followed?" he said venomously.

Kaitlyn gave herself a moment before answering. She was trying to smooth her hair, which the wind had turned into a mane of elf-locks and fine tangles. And she needed to catch her breath.

At last she looked at him. A streetlight outside illuminated half his face, leaving the other half in shadow. Kaitlyn could see enough. His skin looked tight, as if it had been stretched over his bones. There were black circles under his eyes. And there was something about his expression . . . the way he stared at her, eyes narrowed, lips drawn back a little as he breathed quickly.

Gabriel was on the breaking point. And, no, he hadn't gotten into that cottage yet.

"Is that what you were doing?" she said. "Taking a walk?"

"Yes." His lips drew back a little farther. His eyes had turned defiant—he was going to brazen this out. "I need to get away from the rest of you once in a while. There's only so much of Kessler's mind I can stand."

"So you just wanted some privacy." She took a step toward

him. "And you decided now was the time for a little stroll."

With startling suddenness he flashed his most dazzling smile. "Exactly."

Kait took another step. The smile disappeared as suddenly as it had come, leaving his mouth grim. "In the middle of the night. In the freezing cold."

He looked dangerous now. Dark and dangerous as a wolf on the hunt. "That's right, Kait. Now be a good girl and go back to the van."

Kaitlyn moved again, close enough that she could feel his warmth—and he could feel hers. She could feel the instant tension in his body, could see his eyes darken. She could hear his breath become uneven.

"I've never been a good girl. Ask anybody back home—they said I have an attitude problem. So you were just hanging around that cottage by accident."

He took the sudden change in subject without blinking, but when he spoke it was through clenched teeth. "What else would I be doing?"

"I thought"—Kaitlyn tilted her head back to look up at him—"that you might need something."

"I don't need anything from anyone!"

She'd accomplished something astonishing just then—she'd made Gabriel give way before her. He'd retreated, stepping back until the concrete wall behind him stopped him.

Kait didn't give him a chance to regroup. She knew the risk

of what she was doing. Gabriel was on the verge of snapping—and he was capable of violence. But she wouldn't let herself think about the danger; she could only think about the shining torment in Gabriel's eyes.

She moved to him again, this time so close that they were touching. Carefully, deliberately, she put her hands on his chest. She could feel the running-stag clamor of his heart.

Then she looked up at him, her face inches from his.

"I think you're lying," she whispered.

# CHAPTER 9

Something in Gabriel's eyes fractured. It was like watching gray agate shatter into pieces.

He caught Kaitlyn by the shoulder. His other hand clamped in her hair, twisting her head to the side.

Black terror washed over Kait, but she didn't move. Her fingers tightened on the sleeves of Gabriel's borrowed shirt.

Then she felt his lips on the back of her neck.

The first sensation was a piercing, as if a single sharp tooth had penetrated at the upper part of her spine, just below her neck.

Vampires, Kait thought dazedly. She knew Gabriel was just opening a transfer point, but it felt as if he had punctured her skin. She could easily see how the legends about vampires had started.

The next instant the sharp pain had gone, replaced by a *tugging*, as if something inside her was being plucked up by the roots. She felt her own momentary resistance—like the earth clinging to a handful of weeds being pulled. And then a giving, a yielding. As if the weeds had come free in the pulling hand.

Energy fountained out of the open wound in a narrow stream. Kaitlyn felt a flare of heat—and pleasure.

*All right. It's going to be all right,* she thought, scarcely knowing whether she was speaking to herself or Gabriel. The experience itself was frightening—it was like working with high-voltage electricity. But she refused to be afraid on other grounds.

*I trust you, Gabriel,* she thought.

She could feel the energy pouring into him, and once again she felt his gratitude, his appreciation. His relief as his need was met.

*I trust you.*

The energy was still flowing steadily, and Kait had a sense of cleansing. Her entire body felt light and airy, as if her feet weren't touching the ground. She relaxed in Gabriel's arms, letting him support her.

*Thank you.*

The thought wasn't Kaitlyn's, and no one else was in range—so it had to be Gabriel. But it didn't sound like Gabriel. There was no anger, no mockery. It was the free and joyous communication of a happy child.

Then, all at once, the current streaming between them was broken. Gabriel released her and lifted his head.

Dizzy, Kaitlyn clung to him for a moment, hearing her own breath slowing.

"No more," Gabriel said. He was breathless, too, but calm. The starving emptiness inside him filled—at least partly.

Then he said, "Kait . . ."

Kaitlyn made herself let go of him. She stepped back, keeping her eyes down.

"Are—are you sure it's enough? You'll be okay now?" She spoke because sharing thoughts was too intimate.

It had occurred to her—finally—that she was courting another kind of danger here. Being this close to Gabriel, *giving* to him, and feeling his joy and gratification—it had bound them together in a way even the web could not match. It had brought down Gabriel's walls . . . again.

And that was unfair, because on her part it was just caring. It's not like what I feel for Rob, she told herself. It isn't—love. . . .

She could sense Gabriel looking at her. Then she felt an indefinable change in him, a mental straightening of shoulders.

"We need to get back," he said. His voice was short and he ignored her question.

Kait looked up. "Gabriel—"

"Before we're missed." Gabriel turned away and started out into the night.

But he waited for her after a few steps, and he stayed close as they made their way across the beach. Kaitlyn said nothing as they walked. She couldn't think of anything that wouldn't make matters worse.

As soon as they got within sight of the van, she saw that something was wrong.

The van should have been dark inside, but each window was glowing. For one instant Kait thought the others had turned on the dome light, and then she thought of fire. But the glow was too bright for the dome light and too cool for fire. And it had a strange opaque quality about it—almost like a phosphorescent mist.

Fear, icy and visceral, gripped at Kaitlyn.

"What is it?" she whispered.

Gabriel pushed her back. "Stay here."

He ran to the van, and Kait followed, scrambling up behind him when he opened the door. Instantly the trip-hammer beating of her heart seemed to double.

She could see the mist clearly now. And she could see Lewis in the front passenger seat and Anna curled on the first bench seat. They were both asleep—but not peacefully.

Lewis's face was twisted into a grimace, and he was moving his arms and legs jerkily as if trying to escape from something. Anna's long black hair hid her face, but she was writhing, one hand a claw.

"Anna!" Kaitlyn grasped her shoulder and shook her. Anna made a moaning sound, but didn't wake up.

"Rob!" Kaitlyn turned to him. He was lying on his back, thrashing helplessly. His eyes were shut, his expression one of agony. Kaitlyn shook him, too, calling his name mentally. Nothing helped.

She looked over to see how Gabriel was doing with Lewis—and froze.

The gray people were here.

She could see them hanging in the air between her and Gabriel. Lewis's seat cut right through one of them.

"It's an attack!" Gabriel shouted.

Kait was reeling. She felt giddy and confused, almost as if she might faint. It was the web, she realized—she was picking up the sensations of the three dreamers.

Oh, God—she had to do something fast, before she and Gabriel collapsed, too.

"Visualize light!" she shouted to Gabriel. "Remember what Rob said? You defend against psychic attacks by envisioning light!"

Gabriel turned his gray eyes on her. "Fine—just tell me how. And what *kind* of light?"

"I don't know." Panic was rioting inside Kaitlyn. "Just think about light—picture it all around us. Make it—a golden light."

She wasn't quite sure why she'd picked gold. Maybe because the mist was a sort of silvery-green. Or maybe because she always thought of gold as Rob's color.

Pressing her hands to her eyes, Kaitlyn began to envision light. Pure golden light surrounding all of them in the van. As an artist, she found it easy to hold the picture in her mind.

*Like this,* she thought to Gabriel and sent him the image. The next moment he was helping her, his conviction adding to hers. She felt she could actually *see* the light now; if she opened her eyes it would be there.

*It's working,* Gabriel told her.

It was. Kait's giddiness was fading, and for the first time since entering the van she felt warmth. The mist had been as cold as the outdoors.

It slipped away now, like an oppressive blanket sliding off Kait. Still visualizing the golden light, she opened her eyes.

The sleepers had quieted. The last traces of the mist were vanishing, curling in on themselves and disappearing. The gray people were still hanging in air.

The next instant they had vanished, too, but not before Kaitlyn got a strange impression. For just a moment she had looked into one of those gray faces—and recognized it. It seemed *familiar,* although she couldn't put her finger on why.

Then the thought was driven out of her mind as she realized that Rob was stirring. He groaned and blinked, dragging himself to a sitting position.

"What—? Kaitlyn—?"

"Psychic attack," Kaitlyn told him calmly and precisely. "When we got back the whole van was filled with mist and you wouldn't wake up. We got rid of it by visualizing light. Oh, Rob, I was so scared." Abruptly her knees folded and she sat down on the floor.

Anna was sitting up, too, and Lewis was moaning.

"Are you guys okay?" Kaitlyn asked shakily, from the floor.

Rob clenched one hand in his unruly blond hair. "I had the most terrible nightmare. . . ." Then he looked at Kait and said, "'When we got back?'"

Kaitlyn's mind went blank, which was probably a good thing. She was too shaken to summon a lie. But behind her Gabriel said smoothly, "Kait had to go to the bathroom, and she didn't want to go alone. I escorted her."

It was a good story. Rob and Anna had found a public rest room down the beach. But Kaitlyn felt little triumph when Rob nodded, accepting it. "Very gallant of you," he said wryly.

"We also saved you," Gabriel added pointedly. "Who knows what that mist was going to do?"

"Yes." Rob's face sobered. He tugged at his hair a moment and then looked up at Gabriel. "Thank you," he said, and his voice was frank and full of genuine emotion.

Gabriel turned away.

There was an awkward moment, and then Anna spoke up.

"Look, why don't you two explain just exactly how you 'visualized light,'" she said. "That way we'll know what to do if they attack again."

"And then maybe we can go back to *sleep*," Lewis added.

Kait explained without much help from Gabriel. By the time she finished she was yawning hugely and her eyes were watering.

They settled down to sleep prepared for the worst, but nothing else happened that night, and Kaitlyn had no dreams.

She woke in the morning to Rob's mental exclamation. She hurried out of the van to find him and Anna bent over, staring at the ground beside the van.

The asphalt was covered with a thin layer of sand blown from the beach. In that sand, all around the van, were delicate tracks and footprints.

"They're animal tracks," Anna said. "You see these? These are the tracks of a raccoon." She pointed to a footprint three inches long, with five long splayed toes, each ending in a claw. "And these are from a fox." She moved her finger to a series of delicate four-toed marks.

"And those oval ones are from an unshod horse, and the little ones are from a rat," Anna finished. Then she looked up at Kait.

Kaitlyn didn't even bother saying, "But *all* of those animals couldn't have been here last night." She remembered very well what Rob had said yesterday—sometimes victims of a psychic attack found the footprints of people or animals.

"Great," she muttered. "I have the feeling we should get out of here."

Rob stood up, brushing sand from his hands. "I agree."

It wasn't quite so easy, though, since the van picked that morning to be obstreperous. Rob and Lewis fiddled with the engine but could find nothing wrong, and in the end it started.

"I'll drive for a while," Anna said. She'd been sitting in the driver's seat, starting the engine when Rob told her to. "Just tell me where to go."

"Stay on 101 and we'll head into Washington," Lewis instructed. "But maybe we'd better stop at a McDonald's for breakfast first."

Kaitlyn wasn't sorry to say goodbye to the black basaltic Oregon coast. Gabriel had been edgy and silent all morning and she was beginning to wonder if what she'd done on the beach last night had been a mistake. She knew she would have to catch him sometime and talk it out, and the idea sent humming bees and butterflies into her stomach.

Please let us find the white house soon, she thought. And then, with a twinge, realized that Gabriel had been right. She *was* expecting a lot of the people in the white house. And what if they couldn't solve all the problems she was bringing them?

Kait shook her head, then turned to look at the dismal, slate-gray day outside.

They passed stands of what Anna said were alder trees, which from a distance looked like big pink clouds. The alder branches were mostly bare, but there were a few reddish leaves hanging on each twig, which gave the stand an overall reddish cast.

By the side of the road were little kiosks which held huge bunches of daffodils, yellow as spring. Signs on the kiosks said $1.00 A BUNCH, but there was no one to take the money. It's the honor system, Kaitlyn thought. She longed for the pure gold of the daffodils, but she knew they couldn't spare the money.

Doesn't matter, she thought. I'll draw instead. She opened her kit and pulled out aureolin yellow, one of her favorite colors. In a few minutes she was drawing, glancing up only occasionally as they crossed a high bridge over the Columbia River. A sign proclaimed:

WELCOME TO WASHINGTON

THE EVERGREEN STATE

"You're home, Anna," Rob said.

"Not yet. It's a long way to Puget Sound if we're sticking to the coast," Anna replied, but Kaitlyn could tell from her voice that she was smiling.

"And we may not get there," Lewis put in. "We may find the white house first."

"Well, it's not here," Gabriel said shortly. "Look at the water."

The left side of the road, which dipped down to the ocean,

was lined with large brown rocks and boulders. Nothing like the gray rocks in the dream.

Kaitlyn opened her mouth to say something—and her hand began to cramp.

A sort of itching cramp, a *need* that had her picking up a pastel stick before she knew what she was doing. She knew what the sensations meant. Her gift was kicking in. Whatever she drew now would be not just a picture but a premonition.

Cool gray and burnt umber, steel and cloud blue. Kaitlyn watched her hand dotting and stroking the colors on, with no idea of what image was forming. All she knew was that it needed a touch of sepia here—and just two round circles of scarlet lake in the center.

When it was finished, she stared at it, feeling a strange creeping between her shoulderblades.

A goat. She'd drawn a *goat,* of all things. It was standing in what looked like a river of silvery-gray, surrounded by cloudy surrealistic fog. But that wasn't what frightened Kait. It was the eyes.

The goat's eyes were the only dash of color in the drawing. They were the color of burning coals, and they seemed to be looking straight out of the picture at Kaitlyn.

Rob's quiet voice made her jump. "What is it, Kait? And don't say 'nothing' this time—I know there's something wrong."

Mutely Kaitlyn held out the picture to him. He studied it, brows drawing together. His lips were a straight line.

"Do you have any idea what it means?" he asked.

Kaitlyn rubbed pastel dust between her fingers. "No. But then I never do—until it happens. All I know is that somewhere, somehow, I'm going to see that goat."

"Maybe it's symbolic," suggested Lewis, who was leaning over the back of the other bench seat to look.

Kaitlyn shrugged and said, "Maybe." She had a nagging sense of guilt—what good was a gift that gave you this kind of premonition? She had produced the picture; she ought to be able to tell what it meant. Maybe if she concentrated . . .

She thought about it while they passed beaches of packed sand and mudflats—none of them like the white house terrain—and while they got lunch at a Red Apple Market. But all the concentration brought was a headache and a feeling of wanting to *do* something, something physical, to let off tension.

"I'll drive now," she said as they left the market.

Rob glanced at her. "Are you sure? You hate driving."

"Yes, but it's only fair," Kaitlyn said. "You've all taken a turn."

Driving the van wasn't as hard as she'd thought it would be. It was less responsive than Joyce's convertible, but the single-lane road was almost deserted and easy to follow.

After a while, though, it began to rain. It started with cat's-paw splatters that made a pleasant sound, but it got worse and worse. Soon it was raining violently—huge sheets that turned the windshield opaque in between sweeps of the wipers. As if someone were throwing buckets of silvery paint against the glass.

"Maybe someone else should drive now," Gabriel said from the bench seat behind Kaitlyn. He'd relinquished the front passenger seat when Kait had taken the wheel—as Kait had suspected he would.

She glanced at Rob, who'd taken the vacated seat. If it had been Rob's suggestion, she might have acquiesced. But Gabriel had a mocking, goading way of saying things that made you want to do just the opposite.

"I'm fine," she said shortly. "I think the rain is easing up."

"She's fine," Rob agreed, giving her one of his slow infectious smiles. "She can cope."

And then, of course, Kaitlyn was stuck with it. Tongue pressed against her front teeth, she peered into the rain and did her best to prove Rob right. The road straightened out and she drove faster, trying to demonstrate casual competence.

When it happened, it happened very suddenly. Later, Kaitlyn would wonder if it might have changed anything if Rob had been driving. But she didn't really think so. Nobody could have coped with what appeared on that narrow road.

Kait was almost convinced of her own competence when she saw the shape in the road. It was directly in her path but far enough ahead to avoid.

A gray shape. A low horned shape—a goat.

If Kaitlyn hadn't seen it before, she might not have recognized it—there was so little time. But she knew every line of that goat; she'd stared at it for hours this morning. It was exactly like her picture, down to the red eyes. They seemed to blaze at her, the only wink of color in the gray and rainy landscape.

Silver, some part of her mind thought wildly. The silvery-gray river hadn't been a river at all but a road. And the fog had been the rain-vapor rising from the ground.

But most of her mind wasn't thinking at all, it was just reacting. *Brakes,* it told her.

Kait's foot hit the brakes, pressing and releasing the way her driver's ed teacher had advised for bad weather.

Nothing happened.

Her foot slammed down in utter defiance of the driver's ed teacher. And again, nothing happened. The van didn't skid; it didn't slow in the least.

The goat was dead ahead. There was no time to scream, no time even to think. No time to pay attention to the sudden clamor in the web as the others realized that something was wrong.

Kaitlyn wrenched at the steering wheel. The van swerved and careered to the left, into the opposite lane. She got a flash of trees getting close very fast.

*Turn right! Swerve back!*

Kait wasn't sure whose thought it was, but she was already obeying. The van swung right—too far.

I'm going off the road, she thought with a curious calm.

Then everything was confusion.

Kaitlyn could never really remember what happened next, except that it was awful. Trees whipped by. Branches hit the windshield. There was an impact—shocking—but it didn't seem to slow them.

Then the van seemed to leap and go rocketing downward.

Kaitlyn had a sense of being rattled around like a pea in a tin can. She could hear screaming—she thought it might be her own voice. And then there was another impact and every-thing went dark.

# CHAPTER 10

Kaitlyn could hear water—a musical gurgling sound. It was soothing and part of her wanted to listen to it and rest.

But she couldn't. There was something . . . someone she had to worry about. Someone . . . *Rob.*

Not just Rob. The others. Something terrible had happened and she had to make sure they were all right.

Strangely, she wasn't sure just what had happened.

All she knew was that it had been awful. She had to piece together just what the awful thing might have been from what she could see around her.

Opening her eyes, she found that she was in Marisol's van. The van wasn't moving and it wasn't on the road anymore. Through the windshield she could see trees, their branches dripping with green moss. Stretching in front of her she could see water. A creek.

For the first time, she realized that there was water around her feet.

Idiot! There was an accident!

As soon as she thought it, she looked over to Rob. He was blinking, trying to undo his seat belt, seeming as dazed as she felt.

*Rob, are you okay?* Instinctively Kait used the most intimate form of speech.

Rob nodded, still looking stupefied. There was a cut on his forehead. "Yeah—are you?"

"I'm sorry; I'm so sorry. . . ." If pressed, Kaitlyn couldn't have said what she was apologizing about. She only knew that she'd done something dreadful.

*Forget sorry. We have to get out of here,* Gabriel said.

Kaitlyn twisted to look behind her. "Are you guys all right? Is anybody hurt?"

"We're okay—I think," Lewis said. He and Anna were getting up. They didn't seem to be injured, but their faces were drained of color and their eyes stared wildly.

"Help me get this open," Gabriel said sharply, wrenching at the side door.

It took all three of them to get the door open, and then Kait and Rob had to crawl over the center console of the van to go out the same way. Jumping out of the van, Kaitlyn landed in water so cold it took her breath away. With Rob's help, she waded painfully over irregular stones to the bank.

From here she could see what had happened to the van. They'd gone off the road, hit a few trees, and then plunged down a steep embankment into the creek. Kaitlyn supposed it was lucky they'd finished right side up. The silver-blue van was dented and battered—the right front fender a mass of twisted metal.

"I'm sorry," she whispered. She now remembered what she had to be sorry for. She was doubly guilty—she'd lost control of the van and she'd failed to interpret her own drawing, the drawing that might have warned her.

"Don't worry, Kait," Rob said gently, putting his arms around her. But then he winced.

"Oh, Rob, your head—there's a terrible cut." He put a hand to it. "Not that bad." But he squatted down on the fern-covered embankment. Rain dripped from the trees around him.

"We should wash it," Anna said. "We've got water, but we need some cloth—"

"My duffel bag!" Kaitlyn started into the water, but Gabriel held her back, seizing her arm ungently.

"That's dangerous, you idiot," he said. His gray eyes were hard.

"But I *need* it," Kaitlyn said. She felt that she could stop the shaking inside her if she just had something to *do,* some action to perform.

Gabriel's mouth twisted. "For God's sake—oh, all *right.*

You stay here." Letting go of her so roughly it was almost a push, he turned and waded to the van. A moment later he was splashing back, holding not only Kait's bag, but Anna's, which contained the files Rob had taken from the hidden room.

"Thank you," Kaitlyn said, trying to look him in the eye.

"The blankets and sleeping bags are all soaked," Gabriel said briefly. "Not worth saving—we'll never dry them out in this weather."

Anna used a T-shirt of Kaitlyn's to wash Rob's cut and staunch the bleeding. Then she said, "Hold this, Kait," and went hiking up the embankment. She returned with a handful of something green.

"Hemlock needles," she said. "They're good for burns; maybe they'll help a cut, too." She applied them to Rob's head.

Lewis had been staring around at the dripping trees, twirling his baseball hat on one finger. Now he said abruptly, "Look, what happened? Did we skid or—"

"It was my fault," Kaitlyn said.

"No, it wasn't," Rob said stubbornly. The T-shirt bandage Anna had made hung over one eye, giving him the rakish look of a pirate. "There was a goat in the road."

Lewis stopped twirling his hat. "A goat."

"Yes. A gray goat . . ." Rob's voice trailed off and he looked at Kaitlyn. "Gray," he said. "Colorless, really."

Kaitlyn stared at him, then shut her eyes. "Oh."

Anna said, "You think it was an apparition? Like the gray people?"

"Of course it was," Kaitlyn said. She'd been so shaken by the accident that she'd forgotten what had happened just before. "I'm so stupid—it had red eyes. Like some sort of demon. And— oh, Rob!" She opened her eyes. "The brakes didn't work. I kept pressing and pressing, but they didn't work!" The trembling at her core seemed to expand suddenly until her whole body was shivering violently.

Rob put his arm around her, and she clung to him, trying to calm herself. "So it was a psychic attack," he said. "The goat was some kind of illusion—maybe an astral projection. At Durham I heard of psychics who could project a part of themselves in the shape of an animal. And the brakes had been tampered with—it must have been long-distance PK. The whole thing was a setup."

"And we could have been killed," Anna said thinly.

Gabriel's laugh was harsh. "Of course. They're playing for keeps."

Rob straightened his shoulders. "Well, the van's not worth salvaging—and besides, we'd better not let anybody find us here. They'll ask questions, want to call the police."

Kaitlyn could feel her heart skip a beat. She lifted her head to stare at Rob in dismay. "But—but, then, what do we *do?*"

"We go to my house," Anna said quietly. "My parents will help us."

Rob hesitated. "We agreed, no parents," he said. "We could end up putting them in danger—"

"But we don't have a *choice*," Anna said, just as quietly but with steel behind the softness. "We're stuck without a car or food, we don't have anywhere to sleep. . . . Listen to me, Rob. My parents can take care of themselves. Right now *we're* the ones in trouble."

"She's right," Lewis said soberly. "What else can we do? We can't afford a hotel and we can't sleep out here."

Rob nodded reluctantly. Kaitlyn allowed herself to feel some relief. Just the thought of having somewhere specific to go was comforting. But Anna's next words dispelled the comfort.

"It means we'll have to give up following the coast," Anna was saying. "We should just cut straight across to the Sound. We'll have to hitchhike, I guess."

"*Five of* us?" Gabriel said. "Who's going to pick up five teenagers?"

Secretly Kaitlyn agreed. Standing in the rain trying to get a ride—in a strange state—when there were five of you—and you had to be on the alert for the police . . . well, it wasn't her idea of fun. But what other choice did they have?

"We've got to try," Rob was saying. "At least, maybe somebody will take Anna and Kait with 'em—and then maybe the girls can find a phone and call Anna's folks."

Helping each other, they climbed through the wet ferns

and bracken, up the embankment, and to the road. Rob said they had better walk a little distance away from the van to lessen the chance that they'd be connected with it.

"We're lucky," he said. "You can't see the creek from the road, and nobody was around to actually see the accident."

Kaitlyn tried to keep reminding herself she was lucky as she stuck her thumb out, staring down the lonely road.

There weren't many cars. A long truck carrying huge logs passed without stopping. So did a black Chevy pickup full of orange and green fishing net.

Kaitlyn looked around as they waited. The rain had eased to a drizzle, but the world had a sodden look that was rather menacing. All the trees here, including the alders, were covered with thick mint-colored moss. It was a disturbing sight, all those branches that weren't white or brown, but lumpy unnatural green.

She felt a glow in the web just as Lewis asked, "What are you doing, Rob?"

Rob was standing with his eyes shut, an expression of concentration on his face. "Just moving energy around," he said. "I could think better if this cut would start healing." He opened his eyes, pulling the T-shirt bandage off. Kait saw with relief that the cut had stopped bleeding. There was even a little color in Rob's face.

"Okay," he said and smiled. "Now, how about the rest of you? Anybody starting to hurt?"

Lewis shrugged; Anna shook her head. Gabriel kept looking down the road, ignoring the question.

Kaitlyn shifted, then said, "No, I'm fine." She wasn't; she was chilled and miserable and her entire left side had begun to ache. But she felt somehow that she didn't merit healing. She didn't *deserve* it.

"Kait—I can *feel* you're not," Rob was beginning, when Lewis said, "Another car!"

It was approaching slowly, an old Pontiac the color of pumpkin pie.

"It won't stop," Gabriel said sourly. "*Nobody's* going to stop for five teenagers."

The car passed them, and Kait got a glimpse of a young woman behind the rain-splattered window. Then brake lights flashed, and the car slowed to a stop.

"Come on!" Rob said.

As they reached the car, the driver's window opened. Kaitlyn heard the beat of Caribbean music, and then a voice. "You looking for a ride?"

It wasn't a young woman, Kaitlyn realized. It was a girl. A girl who didn't look any older than they were. She was slender and small-boned, with a pale and delicate face that contrasted sharply with her heavy shock of dark hair. Her eyes were gray-green.

"We sure are," Lewis said eagerly. Kaitlyn could feel his admiration in the web. "We're a little wet, though," he added apologetically. "Well, more than a little. A lot."

"Doesn't matter," the girl said carelessly. "The seats are vinyl—it's my granny's car. Get in."

Kaitlyn hesitated. There was something about this girl—she seemed fragile, but there was something almost furtive about her.

*Rob? I'm not sure we should.*

Rob glanced at Kait in surprise. *What's wrong?*

*I don't know. She's just—does she seem okay to you?*

*She seems great to me,* Lewis interrupted. *Jeez, what a babe. And I'm freezing out here.*

Kaitlyn still wasn't sure. *Anna?*

Anna had been walking around the back of the Pontiac, but had stopped at Kaitlyn's first message. Now she said gently, *You're probably still shaken up, Kait. I think she's fine—and besides, we can all fit in this car!*

"Yes, we can, can't we?" Gabriel said aloud, not seeming to mind the girl's inquisitive glance. Kaitlyn wondered how they must appear to the girl—all five of them standing frozen and silent—and then Gabriel suddenly coming out with this strange rhetorical question.

*All right, let's do it,* Kait said hastily. She was embarrassed, and she didn't want to argue anymore. But as Rob opened the door, she asked Gabriel, *What did you mean?*

*Nothing. It's just an interesting coincidence that we fit, that's all.*

Anna and Lewis got in the front with the girl. Kaitlyn slid

in the back seat after Rob, and Gabriel followed her. The white vinyl seats creaked under their weight.

"My name's Lydia," the girl said in that same careless voice. "Where are you going?"

They introduced themselves—or rather Lewis introduced them—and Anna said, "We're trying to get to Suquamish, near Poulsbo—but that's pretty far away. Where were you headed?"

Lydia shrugged. "I wasn't headed anywhere, really. I took the day off school to drive around."

"Oh, do you go to North Mason High? I have a cousin there."

Anna's question was perfectly innocent, but Lydia seemed affronted. "It's a private school," she said briefly. Then she said, "Are you getting enough heat back there? If I turn it too high, the windows steam up."

"It feels great," Rob said. He was holding Kaitlyn's hands in his own, rubbing them. And he was right, being in a warm dry car was wonderful. Kaitlyn's brain felt almost stupefied at the sudden luxury.

She was aware, though, that Lydia was watching them keenly, casting glances at Lewis and Anna beside her, then looking up into the rearview mirror to examine the three in the back. Although Lewis seemed to enjoy the scrutiny it made Kait uncomfortable, particularly when Lydia began frowning and chewing her lip in a speculative way.

"So what were you doing back there?" Lydia asked finally, very casually. "You're awfully wet."

"Oh. We were . . ." Lewis fumbled for words.

"We went for a hike," Gabriel said evenly. "We got caught in the rain."

"Looks more like you got caught in a flood."

"We found a creek," Gabriel said before Lewis could answer.

"So you guys are from around here?"

"From Suquamish," Anna said—and for her, at least, that was the truth.

"You take long hikes," Lydia said, looking in the rearview mirror again. Kait noticed that she had exactly three freckles on her small nose.

Somehow Lydia's skepticism had calmed Kait's own suspicions. It wasn't really furtiveness lurking in those gray-green eyes, she decided. It was more defensiveness, as if Lydia had been beaten up by life a great deal. Kaitlyn felt sympathetic.

They were driving inland, now, through stands of evergreen trees with tall bare trunks. To Kaitlyn, they looked like hundreds of soldiers standing at attention.

Lydia shook back her hair and tilted her chin up. "I hate going to private school," she said suddenly. "My parents make me."

Kaitlyn, relaxing in the warmth of the car, tried to think of something to say to that. But Lewis was already sympathizing. "That's too bad."

"It's so strict—and boring. Nothing exciting ever happens."

"I know. I went to private school once," Lewis said. Lydia changed the subject abruptly.

"Do you always take duffel bags when you go hiking?"

"Yes," Gabriel said. He seemed to be able to handle Lydia best. "We use them like backpacks," he said, seeming amused.

"Isn't that a little awkward?"

Gabriel didn't answer. Lewis just smiled engagingly.

There was another minute or so of fidgeting from Lydia, and then she burst out, "You're running away, aren't you? You don't really live around here at all. You're hitchhiking across the country or something—aren't you?"

*Don't tell her anything,* Gabriel thought to Lewis, just as Lydia said, "You don't have to tell me. I don't care. But I wish *I* could have an adventure sometime. I'm so tired of private riding clubs and country clubs and Key Clubs and the Assistance League." She was silent for a moment and then added, "I'll drive you to Suquamish if you'll tell me the way. I don't care how far it is."

Kaitlyn didn't know what to make of the girl. She was a strange, excitable creature—that was certain. And she felt left out, an outsider looking in on the five of them.

Kaitlyn remembered how that felt—being outside. Back in Ohio she had been outside everything. She'd been too different; her blue-ringed eyes had been too strange, her psychic drawings had been too spooky. No one at her old high school had wanted to consort with the local witch.

But she still wasn't sure about Lydia—and she didn't like the way Lydia pushed so hard to get in.

*Don't tell her anything,* she advised Lewis, echoing Gabriel's opinion. After a moment Lewis lifted his shoulders in acquiescence.

"We'd be grateful if you'd take us to Suquamish," Rob said gently, and then they all shut up and listened to the radio.

"Turn here," Anna said. "It's just down this street—there, that house with the Oldsmobile in front of it."

It was twilight, but Kaitlyn could see that the house was the same red-brown color as Anna's cedar basket. It must be made of cedar, she realized. The spruce and alder trees around it were becoming mere towering shapes as dark fell.

"We're here," Anna said softly.

A house, Kaitlyn thought. A real house with parents in it, adults who would help take care of them. For the moment it was all Kait wanted. She stretched her stiff, clammy legs and watched Gabriel reach for the door handle.

Lydia blurted, "I guess you weren't running away. I didn't know you really had somewhere to go. Sorry."

"It doesn't matter. Thanks for the ride," Rob said.

Lydia hunched her shoulders. "Sure," she said. It was the voice of someone who hasn't been invited to a party. Then she said in subdued tones, "Could I use your bathroom?"

"Oh—sure," Anna said. "Hang on, I'd better go inside first." *Mom isn't going to be expecting us,* she added silently.

Moving quickly and lightly, Anna ran up to the house. The others waited in the car, looking through steam-clouded windows. After a few minutes Anna came back, leading a short, motherly woman who looked bewildered but humorously resigned. Kait thought suddenly that she knew where Anna got her serenity.

"Come inside, all of you," the woman said. "I'm Mrs. Whiteraven, Anna's mother. Oh, my goodness, you're wet and half-frozen. Come in!"

They went in, and Lydia went with them.

Inside, Kaitlyn got a quick impression of a crowded, comfortable living room and two identical boys who looked about nine or ten. Then Anna's mother was hustling them into the back of the house, running hot baths and gathering clean clothes.

"You boys will just have to wear some of my husband's things," she said. "They'll be big, but they'll have to do."

Some time later Kaitlyn found herself warm and faintly damp from a bath, dressed in Anna's clothes and sitting in front of the fireplace.

"Your mother's nice," she whispered to Anna. "Isn't she a little surprised to have us turn up like this? Did she ask you any questions?"

*Not yet. She's more interested in feeding us and getting us warm. But I know one thing—she hasn't heard anything from the Institute. She thought I was still at school.*

They had to stop talking then because Anna's little brothers came in and started asking her about California. Anna managed to tell them about it without mentioning Mr. Zetes or the Institute.

Mrs. Whiteraven bustled back in. "Anna, your other friend was just waiting in the hall. I sent her to wash up. We'll have dinner in a few minutes, as soon as the boys are ready."

"But she isn't—" Anna began. She broke off as Lydia walked into the room, looking small and almost pathetic. It would be too rude to say "she isn't my friend" when Mrs. Whiteraven had just invited her to dinner.

*After all, she did give us a ride,* Anna said to Kaitlyn, who shrugged.

Rob, Gabriel, and Lewis appeared wearing billowing flannel shirts and jeans tightly belted to keep them on. Kaitlyn and Anna nobly refrained from giggling, but Lydia grinned. Lewis grinned back at her, unabashed. They sat down with Anna's mother and father at the table.

Dinner was hamburgers and smoked salmon, corn and broccoli and salad, with berry pie for dessert and Thomas Kemper's Old Fashioned Birch Soda to wash it down. Kaitlyn had never been so happy to see vegetables. All five of them from the Institute dug in with an enthusiasm that made Mrs.

Whiteraven's eyes widen, but she didn't ask any questions until they'd finished eating.

Then she wiped her hands on a dish towel, pushed her chair back, and said, "Now, suppose you kids explain what you're doing in Washington?"

# CHAPTER 11

Kaitlyn looked from Anna's mother to Anna's father, a grave man with steady eyes who'd scarcely spoken during dinner. The kitchen was warm and quiet. Yellow light shone from the overhead lamp onto unfinished pine cupboards.

Then Kaitlyn looked at Rob. They were all looking at one another, all five who shared the web.

*Should we?* Anna asked.

*Yes,* Kaitlyn thought back, feeling agreement from the others. *But only your parents. Not . . .*

Anna waved a hand at her twin brothers. "You guys go play, okay? And . . ." She glanced at Lydia and faltered. Kaitlyn knew the problem; Anna was gentle by nature, and it was difficult to say "get out" to a guest who'd just eaten at the same table.

*You're too soft-hearted,* she thought, but Gabriel was already speaking.

"Maybe Lydia and I could take a walk outside," he said. "It's stopped raining now." Standing, he looked every inch the gallant gentleman—if you didn't count the mocking glint in his eyes. He extended his hand to Lydia courteously.

There wasn't much Lydia could do. She went rather pale, so that her three freckles stood out more prominently. Then she thanked Anna's parents and took Gabriel's hand. Lewis gave her a hurt look.

*Be careful,* Kaitlyn thought to Gabriel as he and Lydia walked out.

*Of what? Psychic attacks—or her?* he sent back, amused.

Anna's brothers went, too. And then there was no further excuse for delay. With one final look at her mind-mates, Anna took a deep breath and began telling her parents the whole story.

*Almost* the whole story. She left out some of the more grue-some bits and didn't mention the mind-link at all. But she told about Marisol, and the crystal that enhanced psychic power, and Mr. Zetes's plans for making his students into a psychic strike team. Rob went and got the files he'd taken from the hidden room.

"And we've been having these dreams," Anna said. "About a little peninsula with gray water all around it, and across from it is a cliff with trees and a white house. And we think that the people in the house might be sending us the dreams, trying to help us." She told about Kaitlyn's two encounters with the caramel-skinned man who came from the white house.

"He didn't seem to like the Institute," Kait put in. "And he showed me a picture of a garden with a huge crystal in it—like Mr. Z's crystal. We figure that maybe they know about these things."

Mrs. Whiteraven frowned. Her black eyes had been snapping and flashing throughout Anna's story, especially when Anna told about Mr. Z's plans. Mr. Whiteraven had merely gotten more and more grave-looking, one of his hands slowly clenching into a fist. Like Tony, they seemed to have no trouble accepting the reality of what Anna was saying.

Now Anna's mother spoke. "But—you're saying you set out for this white house without any idea where it is?"

"We have *some* idea," Anna said. "It's north. And we'll know it when we see it—the peninsula is lined with these strange rock piles. I keep thinking they're familiar somehow. They look like this." She got a pencil and began drawing on the back of one of the file folders. "No—Kait, you're the artist. Draw one."

Kaitlyn did her best, sketching one of the tall, irregular rock stacks. It came out looking a bit like a stone snowman with outspread arms.

"Oh, it's an *inuk shuk*," Mrs. Whiteraven said.

Kaitlyn's head jerked up. "You *recognize* it?"

Anna's mother turned the paper, studying it. "Yes—I'm sure it's an *inuk shuk*. The Inuit used them for signals, you know, to show that a certain place was friendly or that visitors were welcome—"

"The *Inuit?*" Anna interrupted, choking. "You mean we have to go to Alaska?"

Her mother waved a hand, brow puckering. "I'm sure I've seen some of these much closer. . . . I know! It was somewhere on Vancouver Island. We took a trip there when you were about five or six. Yes, and I'm sure we saw them there."

Everyone began talking at once.

"Vancouver Island—that's Canada—" Rob said.

"Yes, but it's not far—there's a ferry," Anna said. "No *wonder* those things were familiar—"

"I've never been to Canada," said Lewis.

"But do you remember exactly *where* they were?" Kaitlyn was asking Mrs. Whiteraven.

"No, dear, I'm afraid not. It was a long time ago." Anna's mother chewed her lip gently, frowning at the picture. Then she sighed and shook her head.

"It doesn't matter," Rob said. His eyes were alight with excitement. "At least we know the general area. And somebody on the island has *got* to know where they are. We'll just keep asking."

Anna's mother put the paper down. "Now, just a minute," she said. She and her husband exchanged a glance.

Kaitlyn, looking from one of them to the other, had a sudden sinking feeling.

"Now," Mrs. Whiteraven said, turning away from her

husband. "You kids have been very brave and resourceful so far. But this idea about finding the white house—it's not practical. This isn't a problem for children."

"No," said Mr. Whiteraven. He'd been looking through the files Rob had brought. "It's a problem for the authorities. There's enough proof here to get your Mr. Zetes put away for a long time."

"But you don't understand how powerful he is," Anna said. "He's got friends everywhere. And Marisol's brother said that only magic could fight magic—"

"I hardly think Marisol's brother is an expert," her mother said tartly. "You should have gone to your parents in the first place. And that reminds me, you have to *call* your parents, now—all of you."

Kait hardened herself. "We can't tell them anything that would make them feel better. And if Mr. Zetes has some way of tapping the call—well, he'd know exactly where we are."

"If he doesn't already," Anna said softly.

"But . . ." Mrs. Whiteraven sighed and exchanged another look with her husband. "All right, *I'll* call them in the morning. I don't need to tell them exactly where you are until we get this thing straightened out."

"Straightened out how, ma'am?" Rob asked. His eyes had darkened.

"We'll talk to the elders, then to the police," Anna's mother said firmly. "That's the right thing to do."

Anna opened her mouth, then shut it again. *It's no good,* she told the others helplessly.

*No. It isn't,* Rob agreed.

Lewis said, *Jeeeez. I guess we should be relieved, but—*

Kaitlyn knew what he meant. Adults were in the picture now, taking charge, handling things. The authorities were going to be told. The five of them didn't have to worry anymore. She should have been happy.

So why did her chest feel so tight?

Two thoughts jostled in her brain. One was: After we got so far . . .

The other was: The adults don't know Mr. Z.

"Now we'll have to find places for you to sleep," Anna's mother was saying briskly. "You two boys can have the twins' room, and I'll put your friend Gabriel on the couch. Then Anna can share her room with you, Kait, and Lydia can go in the guest room—"

"*Lydia's* not sleeping here," Kaitlyn blurted, before thinking about how rude this sounded. "She's not one of us; she just gave us a ride."

Mrs. Whiteraven looked surprised. "Well, you can't expect her to drive all the way home now. It's too late, and she told me before dinner that she was tired. I've already invited her to stay overnight."

Kaitlyn started to groan, then realized that Rob and Anna and especially Lewis were looking at her reproachfully. In the web she could feel their bewilderment—they didn't understand what she had against Lydia.

Oh, well, what difference did it make anyway? Kait shrugged and bent her head.

Gabriel and Lydia came strolling through the door a few minutes later. Lydia didn't look particularly disappointed to have missed the kitchen conference. She kept glancing up at Gabriel through her lashes—a stratagem that seemed to amuse Gabriel and annoy Lewis. Kait and Anna left Rob to fill Gabriel in on what had happened while they helped make up the guest room bed.

*So the quest is over?* Gabriel asked. Kaitlyn could hear him perfectly even though he was in the kitchen and she was giving a final punch to Lydia's pillow.

*We'll talk about it tomorrow,* she told him grimly. She was tired.

And she was worried about Gabriel. Again. Still. She could tell that he was in pain—she could feel the tension shimmering under his surface. But somehow she didn't think he was going to let her help tonight.

He didn't. He wouldn't talk about it, either, not even when she managed to sneak a moment alone with him while the others were getting ready for bed.

"But what are you going to do?" She had dreadful visions of him sneaking into Anna's parents' room, too crazed to know what he was doing.

"Nothing," he said shortly, and then, with icy fury, "I'm a *guest* here."

So he'd caught her vision. And he had his own code of honor. But that didn't mean he could hold out all night. . . .

He was already walking away.

Kaitlyn climbed into Anna's double bed feeling uneasy and discouraged.

It was just dawn when she woke. She found herself staring at the luminous green numbers on Anna's clock radio, a knot twisting in her stomach. She could sense the others sleeping—even Gabriel. He was so restless that she could tell he hadn't been out anywhere.

Strangely, of all the things she had to worry about, the one bothering her was Lydia.

Forget Lydia, she told herself. But her mind kept spinning out the same questions. Who was Lydia, and why was she so eager to be with them? What was wrong with the girl? And why did Kait keep feeling she wasn't to be trusted?

There should be some way to tell, Kait thought. Some test or something. . . .

Kait sat up.

Then, quickly but as stealthily as possible, she slid out of bed and picked up her duffel bag. She took the bag into the bathroom and locked the door.

With the light on she fished through the bag until she found her art kit. The sealed Tupperware had survived the creek, and her pastels and erasers were safe. The sketchpad was damp, though.

Oh, well. Oil pastels didn't mind the damp. Kaitlyn picked up a black pastel stick, held it poised over the blank page, and shut her eyes.

She'd never done this before; trying to *make* a picture come when she didn't already feel the need to draw. Now she made use of some of Joyce's techniques, deliberately relaxing and shutting out the world.

Clear your mind. Now think of Lydia. Think of drawing Lydia. . . . Let the picture come. . . .

Black lines radiating downward. Kaitlyn saw the image and let her hand transfer it to the paper. Now some black grape mixed in. Blue for highlights—it was Lydia's hair. Then pale fleshtones for Lydia's face and celadon green for Lydia's eyes.

But she felt she needed the black again. Heavy strokes of black, lots of them, above and around Lydia's portrait, forming a silhouette that seemed to be cradling Lydia, encompassing her.

Kaitlyn's eyes opened all the way, and she stared at the drawing. That broad-shouldered silhouette with body lines that swept straight down like a man in a coat . . .

In one furious motion she was on her feet.

I'll kill her. Oh, my God, I'm going to *kill* her. . . .

She jerked open the bathroom door and headed for the guest room.

Lydia was a slender shape under the covers. Kait turned her over and grabbed her by the throat.

Lydia made a noise like Georgie Mouse. Her eyes showed white in the darkness.

"You nasty, spying, sneaking little *weasel,*" Kait said and shook her a few times. She spoke softly, so as not to wake Anna's parents, and put most of her energy into the shaking.

Lydia made more noises. Kaitlyn thought she was trying to say, "What are you talking about?"

"I'll tell you what I'm talking about," she said, punctuating each word with a shake. Lydia was gripping her wrists with both hands, but was too weak to break Kait's hold. "You're working for Mr. Zetes, you little worm."

Squeaking feebly, Lydia tried to shake her head.

"Yes, you are! I *know* it. I'm psychic, remember?"

As Kaitlyn finished speaking, she sensed activity behind her. It was her mind-mates, crowding in the doorway. So much emotion, so close, had gotten through to all of them even in their sleep.

"Hey! What are you doing?" Lewis was saying in alarm, and Rob said, "Kait, what's happening? You woke everybody up. . . ."

Kaitlyn barely turned. "She's a spy!"

"What?" Charming in too-big pajamas, Rob came to stand beside the bed. When he saw Kaitlyn's grip on Lydia's throat, he reached instinctively. Lewis was right behind him.

"Don't, you guys. She's a spy—aren't you?" Kaitlyn tried to bang Lydia's head against the headboard, but didn't have enough leverage.

"Hey!"

"Kait, just calm down—"

"Admit it!" Kait told the struggling Lydia. "Admit it and I'll let you go!"

Just as Rob was putting his arms around Kait, trying to pull her away, Lydia nodded.

Kaitlyn let go. "I did a drawing that showed she's working for Mr. Zetes," she said to Rob. To Lydia, she added, "Tell them!"

Lydia was coughing and choking, trying to get enough air. Finally she managed to wheeze, "I'm a spy."

Rob dropped his arms, and Lewis looked almost comically dismayed. "What?"

A wave of ugly emotion came from Gabriel. Images of Lydia being chopped into little pieces and thrown in the ocean. Kaitlyn winced and for the first time realized that her hands were sore.

The others had gathered around the bed now. Anna was somber, and Lewis looked hurt and betrayed. Rob crossed his arms over his chest.

"All right," he said to Lydia. "Start talking."

Lydia sat up, small and ghostly in her white nightgown. She looked at each of the five rather threatening figures surrounding her bed.

"I am a spy," she said. "But I'm not working for Mr. Zetes."

"Oh, come off it," Kaitlyn said, and Gabriel said, "Of course you're not," in his silkiest, most sinister manner.

"I'm *not*. I don't work for him. . . . I'm his daughter."

Kaitlyn felt her jaw sag. Unbelievable—but, wait. Joyce *had* mentioned that Mr. Zetes had a daughter. . . .

*She said the daughter was friends with Marisol,* Rob agreed.

Kaitlyn remembered. She also remembered thinking that any daughter of Mr. Zetes's would have to be old, strangely old to be friends with Marisol.

"How old are you?" she said suspiciously to Lydia.

"Eighteen last month. Look, if you don't believe me, my driver's license is in my purse."

Gabriel picked a black Chanel purse off the floor and dumped its contents on the bed, ignoring Lydia's murmur of protest. He extracted a wallet.

"Lydia Zetes," he said, and showed the driver's license to the others.

"How did you *get* here?" Rob demanded.

Lydia blinked and swallowed. She was either on the verge of tears or an excellent actress, Kaitlyn thought. "I flew. On a plane."

"The astral plane?" Gabriel asked. He was very angry.

"On a *jet*," Lydia said. "My father sent me, and I got the car from a friend of his, a director of Boeing. My father called and told me where you'd be—"

"Which he knew because he set up a trap for us," Rob interrupted, seizing on this. "A trap with a goat. He knew if we didn't get killed in the accident, we'd be stranded—"

"Yes. And I was supposed to come along and help you—if any of you were still alive."

"You—little—" Words failed Kaitlyn. She grabbed for Lydia's throat again, but Gabriel was faster.

"Don't bother with it. *I'll* take care of her," he said. Kaitlyn sensed cold hunger.

Everyone in the web knew what he meant. The interesting thing was that *Lydia* seemed to know what he meant, too. She flinched, scooting back against the headboard.

"You don't understand! I'm not your enemy," she said in a voice laced with raw panic.

"Sure you're not," Lewis said.

"No, you're just his daughter," said Kaitlyn. Then she felt Anna's hand on her arm.

"Wait a minute," Anna said quietly. "At least let her say what she wants to." To Lydia, she said, softly but severely, "Go on."

Lydia gulped and addressed herself to Anna. "I know you won't believe me, but what I told you in the car was true. I *do* hate private school, and riding clubs, and country clubs. And I hate my father. All I ever wanted was to get away—"

"Yeah, yeah," Lewis said. Gabriel just laughed.

"It's *true*," Lydia said fiercely. "I hate what he does to people.

I didn't want to come after you, but it was my only chance."

Something about her voice made Lewis falter in his sneering. Kaitlyn could feel his indecision in the web.

"You weren't going to tell us, though, were you?" Kaitlyn said. "You'd never have told us who you were if I hadn't found out."

"I *was* going to," Lydia said. She squirmed. "I *wanted* to," she amended. "But I knew you wouldn't believe me."

"Oh, stop sniveling," Gabriel said.

Kaitlyn was looking at Rob. *I know I'm going to hate myself for asking this—but do you think it could be true?*

*I . . . don't know.* Rob grinned suddenly. *But maybe we can find out.*

He sat on the bed, taking Lydia by the shoulders, and looked into her face. She shrank back.

"Now listen to me," he said sternly. "You know that we're psychics, right? Well, Kaitlyn has the power to tell if you're lying or not." To Kait he said, *Go get your drawing stuff.*

Kaitlyn hid a smile and brought it from the bathroom. Rob went on, "All she has to do is make a drawing. And if that drawing says you're not telling the truth . . ." He shook his head darkly. "Now," he said, looking hard at Lydia again, "what's your story this time?"

Lydia looked at Kait, then at Rob. She lifted her chin. "It's the same. Everything I told you was true," she said steadily.

Kaitlyn made a few scribbles on the pad. Her gift didn't

work that way, of course, but she knew that the real test here was of Lydia's demeanor.

*Well?* she asked Rob.

*Either she's telling the truth or she's the greatest actress in the world.*

*Like Joyce?* Gabriel put in pointedly. *You know, I could probably tell if she's telling the truth. I could mind-link with her.*

*Yeah, but what are the chances that she'd survive?* Rob asked.

Gabriel shrugged. The hunger flickered again.

"Look, what was it you were supposed to do when you found us?" Kaitlyn asked Lydia.

"Keep you guys from going wherever you were going," she said promptly. "Convince you to go to the police or something instead—"

"He *wants* that? Your father?"

"Oh, yes. He knows he can fix the police. He's got lots of friends, and he can do things with the crystal. He's not afraid of police; he's afraid of *them.*"

"Who?" Kaitlyn demanded.

"Them. The people of the crystal. He doesn't know where they are, but he's afraid you'll find them. They're the only ones who can stop him." She looked around. "*Now* do you believe me? Would I have told you that if I were your enemy?"

Kaitlyn could feel the wavering in the web, and the sudden resolution. Rob and Anna believed her. Lewis not only believed her but liked her again. Gabriel was cynical, but that was typical Gabriel. And Kait herself was convinced enough to have a new worry.

"If Mr. Z *wants* us to go to the police—" she began.

"Right," Rob said grimly.

"But we'll never convince my parents," Anna said.

"Right," Rob said again.

A feeling was stirring in Kaitlyn, part terror, part dismay, and part wild excitement.

Lewis gulped. "But that means—"

"Right," Rob said a third time. He grinned at Kait, his grin reflecting her bewildering mix of emotions. "The search," he announced to the room at large, "is back on."

Gabriel cursed.

Lydia was looking from one of them to another in bewilderment. "I don't understand."

"It means we're going to have to run away again," Rob said. "And if you really want to help us—"

"I do."

"—you can drive us to Vancouver Island. There's a ferry, right?" He glanced at Anna, who nodded.

"I'll do it," Lydia said simply. "When do we go?"

"Right *now*," Kaitlyn said. "We've got to get out of here before Anna's parents wake up."

"Okay, everybody," Rob said. "Grab your things and let's get moving."

# CHAPTER 12

"The ferry leaves from Port Angeles at eight-twenty," Anna said as she and Kaitlyn hurriedly changed their clothes in her bedroom.

"It's started raining again," said Kaitlyn.

They all met a few minutes later in the front hallway. There were ominous stirring noises from the back of the house.

"Shouldn't you leave a note?" Lewis whispered.

Anna sighed. "They'll know," she said briefly.

"I'll leave them the files," Rob said. "Maybe they can do something with them."

Gabriel snorted.

Outside, the sky was cold and gray. The rain seemed to come at them horizontally as they drove to Port Angeles. If they kept the defroster on maximum, it cleared the windshield but scorched their skin; if they turned it down, the windshield immediately steamed over. If they opened the windows, it cleared everything but they froze.

At the ferry the water was navy blue with just a hint of green. They waited in a line of cars and finally drove onto a large boat. It cost twenty-five dollars, and Kaitlyn paid because Lydia only had credit cards.

On the passenger deck Kaitlyn watched the deep blue water slipping away on either side. We're on our way, she thought. To Canada. She had never been to a foreign country.

She was drinking a vending-machine Coke that Rob had brought her when Lewis rushed up, breathless.

"Trouble," he said. "I just talked to some kids in the bathroom. They said if you're under eighteen, you're supposed to have a letter of authorization to get into Canada."

"*What?*"

"A letter. From your parents or something, I guess. Telling who you are and how long you're going to be there."

"Oh, *terrific*." Kaitlyn looked at Rob, who shrugged.

"What can we do? We'll just hope they don't ask for one."

"I'm eighteen, anyway," Lydia said. "I'll drive and maybe the rest of you can fake it."

An hour later they cruised into Victoria Harbor. Kaitlyn's breath caught. The sun had come out, and the harbor was a picture begging to be painted. There were lots of little sailboats and lots of clean-looking pink and white buildings.

But she couldn't keep staring; they had to go downstairs

again and get in the car. They waited in another line at the customs checkpoint while the knot in Kaitlyn's stomach wound tighter and tighter.

"Where do you live?" a sunglassed customs officer asked Lydia.

Lydia's fingers barely tightened on the wheel. "In California," she said, smiling.

The customs officer didn't smile back. He asked to see Lydia's driver's license. He asked where they were going in Canada and how long they'd be staying. Lydia answered everything in a careless, sophisticated murmur. Then the officer bent a little at the waist to examine the inside of the car.

*Look old,* Kaitlyn told the others. They all sat up straight and tried to look mature and bored.

The customs officer didn't change expression. He glanced at each of them, then straightened.

"Any of you under eighteen?" he asked Lydia.

Kaitlyn's stomach gave a final sickening twist. Their driver's licenses would show the rest of them were *all* under eighteen. And then he'd ask for a letter. . . .

Lydia hesitated imperceptibly. Then she said "Oh, no." She said it lightly, with something like a toss of her head. Kaitlyn admired that. Although Lydia was slight, her manner was sophisticated and assured.

The customs officer hesitated. He was looking at Lewis— the one of them who looked youngest. Lydia glanced back at Lewis, too, and although her face was calm, her gaze was almost desperate. Pleading. Lewis's jaw set, and Kaitlyn felt a ripple in the web.

The customs officer had something hanging at his belt, a pager or walkie-talkie or something. Suddenly it began to shriek.

Not beep. *Wail.* It went off with a sound like an air-raid siren, a vibrating sound that put Kaitlyn's teeth on edge. People turned to look.

The customs officer was shaking the walkie-talkie, pressing buttons. The shrieking only went up in volume.

The officer looked from the device to the car as if hesitating. Then he grimaced, trying to muffle the electronic shrilling. With an impatient hand, he waved Lydia on.

"Go, go," Lewis whispered excitedly.

Lydia put the car in gear, and they glided off at a majestic five miles an hour. When they reached a main street, Kaitlyn let out her breath. They'd made it!

"Easier than I thought," Rob said.

In the back seat Lewis was chortling. "How about that? One for the home team!"

Kaitlyn turned on him. That ripple she'd felt in the web just before the shrieking began . . . "Lewis—did *you?*"

Lewis's grin widened, his eyes sparkling. "I figured if those creeps could sabotage us with long distance PK, I could handle a walkie-talkie. I just made a few little adjustments to give it some feedback."

Lydia glanced back at him again, and for the first time there was something like appreciation in her gray-green eyes. "Thanks," she said. "You saved my you-know-what." Lewis beamed.

Even Gabriel seemed grudgingly impressed. But he asked Lydia smoothly, "Who are those creeps, by the way? The ones who've been trying to kill us with psychic attacks."

"I don't know. Truly, I *don't.* I know my father has been doing something with the crystal—and he may have people helping him. But I don't know who."

"I wonder if they've stopped," Anna said suddenly. "I mean, there wasn't an attack last night. Maybe they've lost track of us."

"And maybe they're relying on somebody else to keep track," Gabriel said, with a meaningful look at Lydia. She gave something very much like a flounce without interfering with her driving.

"Where am I supposed to go now?" she asked.

There was a pause. Then Rob said, "We're not sure."

"You came here without knowing where you're *going?*"

"We don't know exactly. We're looking for—"

"Something," Gabriel said, interrupting Rob. Lewis frowned and Kaitlyn gave Gabriel an impatient look.

*We decided to trust her. And she's going to find out anyway, as soon as we find it. . . .*

"Then let her wait until we find it," Gabriel said aloud. "Why trust any further than we have to?"

Lydia's lips tightened, but she didn't say anything, and she didn't flounce again.

"I figure we have two choices," Rob said. "We can drive up and down the coast blindly, or we can *ask* people around here if they know where the—" He changed for an instant to silent speech: *the rock towers are.* "If Anna's mom recognized them, people on the island should know them."

"Can't *you* remember anything, Anna?" Lewis asked. "Your mom said you were on that trip, too."

"I was five," Anna said.

They decided to ask around. A man at a tourist shop sold them a map and directed them to the Royal British Columbia Museum. But although the museum people recognized Kaitlyn's sketch of an *inuk shuk,* they had no idea where any might be found on the island. Neither did anyone at the camera shop, or the bookstore, or the British imports store, or the native crafts shop. Neither did the librarians at the Victoria Library.

"Is it time to start driving around blindly?" Gabriel asked.

Lewis pulled out the map.

"We can drive either northeast or northwest," he said. "This island's sort of like a big oval and we're at the bottom. And before you ask, *nothing* on here looks like our Griffin's Pit. There're thousands of little peninsulas and things all over the coast, and no way to tell any of them apart."

"It's probably too small to be on the map, anyway," Rob said. "Flip a coin: Heads we go east, tails we go west."

Kaitlyn flipped a coin and it came up heads.

They drove northeast, following the coastline, stopping to check the ocean every few miles. They drove until it was dark, but they found nothing resembling the place in their dream.

"But the ocean is right," Anna said, standing on a rock and looking down into the blue-gray water. Gulls were crowded thickly around her—they took off when Kaitlyn or the others came near, but tolerated Anna as if she were a bird.

"It's *almost* right," Kaitlyn temporized. "Maybe we need to go farther north, or to try going west." It was frustrating to feel she was so close to the place, but not to be able to sense where it was.

"Well, we're not going to find anything tonight," Gabriel said. "The light's gone."

Kaitlyn heard the note of tension in his voice. Not just ordinary Gabriel-tension, but a fine edge that told her he was in trouble.

All day he'd been quieter than usual, withdrawn, as if he were wrapping himself around his private pain. His control was getting better, but his need was getting worse. It had been nearly thirty-six hours since Kaitlyn had caught him on the beach in Oregon.

And what on earth is he going to do tonight? Kaitlyn wondered.

"I beg your pardon?" Rob said, looking at her quickly.

She'd forgotten to screen her thoughts. Desperately hoping

he'd only caught the last bit, she said, "I was wondering what on earth we're going to do tonight. To sleep, I mean. We're almost broke—"

"And starving," Lewis put in.

"—and we certainly can't all sleep in this car."

"We'll have to find a cheap motel," Anna said. "We can afford one room, anyway, since it's off season. We'd better head back for Victoria."

In Victoria they found the Sitka Spruce Inn, which let them have a room with two twin beds for thirty-eight dollars and didn't ask any questions. The paint inside the room was peeling and the door to the bathroom didn't shut properly, but, as Anna pointed out, it did have beds.

At Rob's direction the girls got the beds. Lydia chose to share with Anna—clearly she hadn't forgotten the strangling. Kaitlyn curled up on the other, pulling the thin coverlet over her. The boys, sleeping on the carpet, had usurped the blankets.

She slept, but lightly. All that evening Gabriel had avoided her, refused to speak with her. Kait could tell by his cold determination that he was bent on solving his problem alone—and she didn't think that he was going to lie there and quietly endure it again tonight. By now she was closely enough attuned to him that she thought she'd wake up when he did.

It worked—mostly. Kaitlyn woke when the hotel door closed with a click. She could sense that Gabriel wasn't in the room.

Getting out of bed stealthily was almost routine now. The only shock came when Kaitlyn looked at the other bed and realized that there was only one figure in it.

Lydia was gone. Not in the bathroom, either. Just gone.

Kaitlyn crept out of the room feeling very grim.

She tracked Gabriel by his presence in the web, feeling him move away from her, following. She wondered if Lydia was with him.

Eventually she came out by the harbor.

Kaitlyn hadn't been afraid walking down the quaint, old-fashioned streets of Victoria. There were a few people out, and an atmosphere of sleepy safety blanketed the town. But here by the harbor it was very quiet, very lonely. The lights of boats and buildings reflected in the water, but it was still dark and the wharf was deserted.

She found Gabriel pacing in the shadows.

He looked something like a wild animal, a captured predator pacing out the confines of his cage. As Kaitlyn got closer, she could sense the intensity of his hunger.

"Where's Lydia?" she said.

He swung around to stare at her. "Can't you leave me alone?"

"*Are* you alone?"

There was no sound but the soft swish of water for a moment. Then Gabriel said with careful precision, "I have no idea where Lydia is. I came out by myself."

"Was she still in bed then?"

"I didn't look."

Kaitlyn sighed. All right, then, forget about Lydia, she told herself. There's nothing you can do. "Actually, I came out here to talk about *you*," she said to Gabriel.

Gabriel gave her a searing glance. All he said was "No."

"Gabriel—"

"It can't go on, Kaitlyn. Don't you see that? Why can't you just leave me to deal with things my way?"

"Because your way means people get hurt!"

He froze. Then he said distinctly, "So does yours."

Kaitlyn didn't understand—she wasn't sure she *wanted* to understand. Gabriel seemed . . . vulnerable . . . just now. She slapped down the strange, impossible thought that sprang to mind and said, "If you mean me, I can handle myself. If you mean Rob . . ."

The vulnerability disappeared instantly. Gabriel straightened and gave one of his most disturbing smiles.

"Let's say I meant Rob," he said. "What's he going to do when he finds out?"

"He'll understand. I wish you'd let me *tell* him. He might be able to help."

Gabriel's smile just grew more unpleasant. "You think so?"

"*I'm positive.* Rob likes to help people. And, believe it or not, I think he likes *you*. If you weren't so touchy—"

Gabriel waved a hand in sharp dismissal. "I don't want to talk about him."

"Fine. Let's talk about what you're going to do tonight. Going hunting? Going to find some girl walking alone and grab her?" Kaitlyn stepped closer as she spoke. Dim as it was, she could see the immediate wariness on Gabriel's face.

That's it, she thought. All I have to do is get near enough. His control is so close to breaking . . .

Gabriel didn't say anything, so she went on. "Whoever she is, she won't know what you're doing. She'll fight you, and that will hurt her. And she probably won't have enough energy, so you'll probably kill her. . . ."

Kaitlyn was very near now. She could see Gabriel's eyes, see the tortured struggle there. She could feel just the flash of his thought, quickly muffled. *Danger.* Quietly she said, "Is that what you want to happen?"

A muscle in his jaw jerked. "You know it isn't," he raged, equally quiet. "But there isn't any other choice—"

"Oh, Gabriel, don't be *stupid,*" Kaitlyn said and put her arms around him.

He managed to resist for about one and a half seconds.

Then, with shaking hands, he pushed her hair off her neck. His lips were so near the place already. Kaitlyn bent her head to make it easy for him.

A feeling of something blowing open, breaking through . . .

and then something being released. Something like an electric current or a streak of lightning. Kaitlyn relaxed, giving willingly.

And felt her emotions rising to the surface, like blood rising to the surface of heated skin. Her caring for Gabriel, her longing to help him. She could sense his feelings, too.

It was only then that she realized, that she remembered, what the true danger in this was. Only then that she understood what Gabriel had meant by his warnings.

Because she could *feel* what he felt. And along with the gratitude, the sheer satisfaction and relief, were other emotions. Appreciation, joy, wonder, and—oh, dear God, *love.* . . .

Gabriel loved her.

She could see herself in his mind, an image so cloaked in glamour and ethereal grace that she could scarcely recognize it. A girl with red-gold hair like a meteor trail and smoky-blue eyes with strange rings in them. An exotic creature that burned like an eager flame. More witch than human.

How could she have been so *stupid?*

But it had never occurred to her that Gabriel, prickly, untouchable Gabriel, could fall in love with anyone. He'd changed too much since he'd loved Iris—and killed her. He'd become too hard, too bitter.

Only he hadn't.

There was no possibility of misunderstanding. Kaitlyn

could feel his emotions clearly—she was surrounded by them, immersed in them. After two days of deprivation Gabriel's control had splintered and his barriers dissolved completely. He realized what she was seeing, but he couldn't stop her, because he was too desperate in his feeding to fight.

Kait had the sense that they were staring at each other across a narrow chasm, both frozen in place, unable to hide from the other. She was seeing into Gabriel's naked soul. And that wasn't right, that wasn't fair, because she knew what he'd be seeing in her. Friendship and concern, that was all. She couldn't love Gabriel; she was already in love. . . .

But with Gabriel's emotions swirling around her, crashing around both of them like a storm-swelled wave, it was hard to remember that. It was hard to keep any rational thought in mind. Gabriel's love was pulling at her, dragging at her, demanding that she return it. That she give herself completely, open and give him everything. . . .

*What are you doing to her?*

Kaitlyn's heart stopped.

It was Rob's voice, and it shattered her world like a bolt of lightning. In one instant the sea-swept warmth of Gabriel's passion disappeared. The connection between them was cut off, and they sprang apart . . .

Like guilty lovers, Kaitlyn thought.

Rob was standing just below one of the wrought-iron

Victorian streetlights. He was fully dressed, but his hair was still rumpled into a lion's mane from sleep. He looked angry—and bewildered.

And despite his words, he hadn't grabbed Gabriel or tried to pull them apart. Which meant he knew. He must have sensed in the web that Kait wasn't being attacked.

There was a long moment when all three of them just stood. Like statues, Kaitlyn thought wildly. Pillars of salt. She knew that every second she delayed explaining made the thing look worse. But she still couldn't believe it was happening.

Gabriel seemed to be in shock, too. He stood as paralyzed as Kait, his gray eyes dilated.

At last Kait managed to speak through dry lips. "Rob, I was going to tell you—"

It was a terrible choice of words. Rob's face drained of color, and his golden eyes went so dark they were lightless.

"You don't need to," he said. "I saw." He swallowed and then said in an odd, husky voice, "I understand."

Then he turned quickly, almost running. Running away.

*Rob, no! That's not what I meant! Rob, wait—*

But Rob was almost at the concrete stairs leading to the harbor street. Hurrying to get out of range.

Kaitlyn cast one wild look after him. Then she looked at Gabriel, who was still standing motionless in the shadows. His face revealed nothing, but Kaitlyn could feel his pain.

Her heart was pounding madly. They both needed her,

and she could only help one of them. There was no more than a moment to choose.

With an agonized look at Gabriel, she whirled and ran after Rob.

She caught Rob beneath another streetlight, one with hanging baskets of flowers suspended from a crosspiece.

"Rob, please—you have to *listen* to me. You—"

She was almost hysterical, unable to finish her sentence. He turned, his eyes the wide hurt eyes of a child.

"It's all right," he said. With a jolt Kaitlyn realized something else. Those eyes were *blind*—he wasn't really seeing her. And he certainly wasn't listening.

"Rob, it's not what you think." The dreadful cliché rolled off her tongue before she could stop it. Then she said, with ferocious intensity, "It *isn't.* Aren't you even going to give me a chance to explain?"

That got through. Rob winced and recoiled just a bit, as if he'd rather run away again. But he said, "Of course you can explain."

She could see him bracing himself, waiting for an explanation of why she wanted to leave him. Frustration crested in her, overriding her fear. Words came out in a breathless rush.

"Gabriel and I weren't—we weren't doing anything wrong. I was giving him *energy,* Rob—like you do when you're healing. The crystal did something awful to him, and now he needs life energy every day. He's been in hell this last week. And if I don't help him, he'll hunt somebody down on the streets, and maybe kill them."

Rob blinked. He still looked like some tousled kid who'd been dealt a mortal blow, but now doubt was creeping into his expression. He repeated slowly, "The crystal?"

"I think that's what did it. He was never like this before. Now he needs the energy to stay alive. Rob, you *have* to believe me."

"But—why didn't you tell me?" Rob was shaking his head now, as if he had water in his ear. He looked dazed.

"I wanted to tell you, I did, but he wouldn't let me." And now I've betrayed his confidence, Kaitlyn thought. But there had been nothing else to do. She had to make Rob understand. "And no wonder he wouldn't, after the way you guys all talked about psychic vampires. He knew you'd be disgusted, and he couldn't stand that. So he kept it a secret."

Rob was wavering. Kait could see that he wanted to believe her, and that he was having trouble. Struggling for a leap of faith.

A voice behind Kaitlyn said, "It's all true."

# CHAPTER 13

Kaitlyn whirled to see the most unlikely person imaginable. Lydia. Looking fragile and wistful, her blue-black hair a liquidy mass under the streetlight's soft illumination.

"You!" Kaitlyn said. "Where have you been? Why did you leave the room?"

Lydia hesitated, then shrugged. "I saw Gabriel leave. I wondered where he was going in the middle of the night, so I followed him to the wharf. And then I saw you come—"

"You spied on us!" It must have been Lydia she'd heard going out the door, Kaitlyn realized. Gabriel had already left.

"Yes," Lydia said, half miserably, half defiantly. "I spied on you. But it's a good thing I did!" She looked at Rob. "Kaitlyn kept saying she wanted to tell you. And she was only doing it because otherwise Gabriel would hurt people, maybe kill them. I don't understand exactly what it's all about, but I know she wasn't messing around with him."

Rob's whole body had relaxed—uncrumpling, Kaitlyn thought. And her own heartbeat was easing. Some of the nightmare feeling of unreality was fading away.

She looked at Rob and he looked at her. For a moment even communication in the web was unnecessary. Kait could see his love, and his longing.

Then, without quite knowing how she'd gotten there, she was in his arms.

"I'm sorry," Rob whispered. And then: *I'm so sorry, Kait. I thought . . . But I could understand why you might want to be with him. You're the only one he cares about. . . .*

*It's my fault,* Kaitlyn thought back, clinging to him as if she could make them into one body, fuse them together permanently. *I should have told you before, and I'm sorry. But—*

*But we won't talk about it any more,* Rob said, holding her more tightly. *We'll forget it ever happened.*

*Yes.* In that moment it seemed to Kaitlyn that she *could* forget. "But we have to make sure Gabriel's all right," she said aloud. "I left him by the wharf. . . ."

Slowly and reluctantly Rob let go of her. "We'll go now," he said. His face still bore the marks of recent emotion; there were shadows under his eyes and his mouth was not quite steady. But Kaitlyn could feel the quiet purpose in him. He wanted to help. "I'll explain to him that I didn't understand. All that talk about psychic vampires—I didn't know."

"I'll go, too," Lydia said. She had been watching them with open curiosity. For once, Kaitlyn didn't mind, and she gave Lydia a look of gratitude as they started walking. The girl might be nosy, she might be sneaky, and she might have a father who belonged in a horror movie—but she'd done Kaitlyn a good turn tonight. Kaitlyn wouldn't forget that.

Gabriel wasn't at the wharf.

"Hunting?" Rob said, looking at Kait with concern.

"I don't think so. He took enough from me—" Kaitlyn broke off as Rob's arm around her tightened. Rob was shaking his head.

"He can't do that anymore," he muttered. "It could hurt you. We'll have to figure something out. . . ." He shook his head again, preoccupied.

Kaitlyn said nothing. Her happiness was dimming a bit. She was all right with Rob again—but Gabriel was in bad trouble, worse even than Rob knew. She couldn't tell Rob what she'd seen in Gabriel's mind.

But she was dead certain Gabriel wasn't going to accept help from Rob—or from her, ever again.

The next morning Gabriel was back. Kaitlyn was surprised. She and Rob had returned to the hotel the night before to find

Anna and Lewis still sitting up. Rob had awakened them both when he found Kait, Gabriel, and Lydia missing.

At Rob's insistence Kait had explained as best she could about Gabriel's condition. Anna and Lewis had been shocked and sorry—and had promised to do anything they could to help.

But Gabriel didn't want help. The next morning he wouldn't talk to anyone and would barely glance at Kait. There was a strange, glittering look in his eyes, and all Kait could sense from him was determination.

*He's hoping that the people in the white house can help him,* she guessed. *And other than that, he doesn't care about anything.*

"We're in deep trouble financially," Anna was saying. "There's enough for gas and breakfast, maybe lunch, and then . . ."

"We'll just have to find the place today," Rob said, with typical Rob-ish optimism. But Kaitlyn knew what he left unspoken. They found the place today or they had to quit, resort to robbery, or use Lydia's credit cards and risk being traced.

"Let's go over what we're looking for," she said. What she really meant was that it was time to tell Lydia. *I think we can trust her,* she added, and Rob nodded. Lewis, of course, agreed wholeheartedly. Kaitlyn was getting a little worried about him—it was clear that he was more than infatuated with Lydia, but Lydia seemed to be the type to play the field.

Gabriel was the only one who might have objected, and he was sitting by the window, ignoring them all.

"A little peninsula thing with rocks on it," Lewis said promptly with a grin at Lydia.

"With *inuk shuk*," Anna said. "Lining both sides. And the shore behind it is rocky, and behind that is a bank with trees. Spruce and fir, I think. And maybe some scotch broom."

"And the ocean is cold and clean and the waves only come from the right," Kaitlyn put in.

"And it's called something like Griffin's Pit," Rob finished and smiled at her. There was still something of apology, of regret, about his slow smile this morning. Kait felt a twinge in her chest.

"Or Whiff and Spit or Wyvern's Bit," she said lightly, smiling back. Then she said, turning back toward Lydia, "And across from it is a cliff—although heaven knows how that can be, unless it's another little island. And on the cliff is a white house, and that's where we're going."

Lydia nodded. She wasn't stupid; she'd taken all of this in. Her eyes said "thank you" to Kait. "So where do we search today?"

"Flip a coin again," Lewis began, but Rob said, "Let Kaitlyn decide." When Kait looked at him, he added seriously, "Sometimes you have intuitions. And I trust . . . your instinct."

Kaitlyn's eyes stung. She understood; he trusted *her*.

"Let's go the other way today, west. The water didn't feel

quite right yesterday. Not . . . enclosed . . . enough." She herself wasn't sure what she meant by that, but everyone else nodded, accepting it.

They skipped breakfast and started driving northwest.

The weather was lovely for a change, and Kaitlyn found herself pathetically grateful for sunshine. Huge puffy white clouds drifted overhead. The coastal road quickly narrowed to one lane and trees crowded around them.

"It's the rain forest," Anna said. To Kaitlyn it was an almost frightening display of plant life. The road seemed to cut through a *solid* swath of vegetation. It was like a puzzle shaped like a wall on either side of the road—the pieces were different colors for different plants, but they interlocked solidly to fill all the space between the ground and the sky.

"We can't even *see* the ocean," Lewis said. "How're we supposed to tell if we're near the place?"

He was right. Kaitlyn groaned inwardly; maybe west had been a bad idea after all. Rob just said, "We'll have to go down side roads every so often and check. And we'll ask people again."

The problem was that there were few side roads and fewer people to ask. The road simply went on and on, winding through the forest, allowing them only occasional glimpses of the coast.

Kaitlyn tried not to feel discouraged, but as they drove farther and farther, her head began to buzz and the emptiness in her middle to expand. She felt as if they'd been driving for-ever, through three states and a foreign country. And they were never going to find the white house—in fact, the white house probably didn't exist. . . .

"Hey," Lewis said. "Food."

It was another of the kiosks, like the ones that had sold daffodils in Oregon. But this sign said BREAD DAYS: FRIDAY, SATURDAY, SUNDAY.

"It's Sunday," Lewis said. "And I'm starving." They took two loaves of multigrain bread—and paid for them, because Rob insisted. Kaitlyn hadn't realized how hungry she was until she took the first bite. The bread was dense and moist, cool from the cold air outside. It had a nutty, nourishing flavor, and Kait felt strength and optimism flowing back through her.

"Let's stop *there*," she said as they passed a small build-ing. A sign proclaimed it to be the SOOKE MUSEUM. She didn't have much hope, first of all because the big museum in Victo-ria hadn't helped them, and second because this place looked closed, but she was in the mood to try anything.

It *was* closed, but a woman finally answered Rob's persis-tent knocking. There were piles of books on the floor inside, and a man with a pencil behind his ear, taking inventory.

"I'm sorry," the woman began, but Rob was already talking.

"We don't want to bother you, ma'am," he said, turning the southern charm on full force. "We just have one question—

we're looking for a place that might be around here, and we thought you could maybe help us find it."

"What place?" the woman said with a harassed glance behind her, obviously impatient to get back to her work.

"Well, we don't exactly know the name. But it's like a little peninsula, and it's got these rock towers all up and down it."

Kaitlyn held up her drawing of the *inuk shuk*. Please, she was thinking. Oh, please . . .

The woman shook her head. Her look said she thought Kaitlyn and Rob were crazy. "No, I don't know where you'd find anything like that."

Kaitlyn's shoulders sagged. She and Rob glanced at each other in defeat. "Thank you," Rob said dully.

They both turned away and were actually leaving when the man inside the museum spoke up.

"Aren't there some of those things out at Whiffen Spit?"

Every cell in Kaitlyn's body turned into ice.

Whiffen Spit. Whiffen Spit, Whiffenspit, *Whiffenspit* . . . It was as if the whispering chorus of voices was once again in her mind.

Rob, fortunately, seemed able to move. He spun and got a foot in the door the woman was closing.

*"What did you say?"*

"Out at Whiffen Spit. I've got a map here somewhere. I don't know what the rocks are for, but they've been there as long as I can remember. . . ."

He went on talking, but Kait couldn't hear him over the roaring in her own ears. She wanted to scream, to run around crazily, to turn cartwheels. Anna and Lewis were clutching each other, laughing and gasping, trying to maintain their composure in front of the museum people. The whole web was vibrating with pure joy.

*We found it! We found it!* Kaitlyn told them. She had to tell someone.

Yeah, and it's Whiffenspit, Lewis said, running it together into one word as Kaitlyn had. *Not Griffin's Pit or Whippin' Bit—*

*Rob was closest,* Anna said. Whiff and Spit was actually pretty good.

Kaitlyn looked toward the car, where Lydia and Gabriel were standing as if declaring themselves both outsiders. Lydia was wide-eyed, watching with interest. Gabriel—

*Gabriel, aren't you happy?* Kaitlyn asked.

*I'll be happy when I see it.*

"Well, you're *going* to see it, ol' buddy," Rob said, turning and calling with a reckless disregard for the museum people. "I've got a map here!" He waved it triumphantly, his grin nearly splitting his face.

"Well, don't just stand around talking!" Kait said. "Let's go!"

They left the museum people staring after them.

"I can't believe it's real," Kaitlyn kept whispering as they drove.

"Look at this," Lewis was saying excitedly over her. "This map shows why there are only waves coming from the right. It's in the mouth of a little bay, and on the right side is the ocean. The other side is Sooke Basin, and there wouldn't be any waves there."

Rob turned on a narrow side road, nearly invisible between the trees. When he parked at the end, Kaitlyn was almost afraid to get out.

"Come on," Rob said, extending his hand. "We'll see it together."

Slowly, as if under a spell, Kaitlyn walked with him to the edge of the trees and looked down.

Then her throat swelled and she just stared.

It was the place. It looked exactly as it had in her dreams, a little spit of land pointing like a crooked finger into the water. It was lined with the same boulders, many with *inuk shuk* piled on top of them.

They walked down the rocky beach and onto Whiffen Spit.

Gravel crunched under Kaitlyn's feet. Gulls wheeled in the air, crying. It was all *so familiar.* . . .

"Don't," Rob whispered. "Oh, Kait." It was then that she realized she was crying.

"I'm just happy," she said. "Look." She pointed across the water. Far away, on a distant cliff covered with trees so green they were black, was a single white house.

"It's real," Rob said, and Kait knew he was feeling what she was. "It's really there."

Anna was kneeling by the edge of the spit, moving rocks. "Lewis, get that big one."

Lewis was showing Lydia around. "What are you doing?"

"Building an *inuk shuk*. I don't know why, but I think we should."

"Let's make it a good one," Rob said. He took hold of a large, flat rock, tried to lift it. "Kait—"

He didn't finish. Gabriel had taken hold of the other side.

The two of them looked at each other for a moment. Then Gabriel smiled, a thin smile touched with bitterness, but not with hatred.

Rob returned it with his own smile. Not as bright as usual, with something like apology behind it, and hope for the future.

Together, they lifted the stone and hauled it to Anna.

Everyone helped build the *inuk shuk*. It was a good big one, and sturdy. When they were done, Kait wiped wet dirt off her hands.

"Now it's time to find the white house," she said.

From the map they could see why there was land across the water. It was the other side of the mouth of Sooke Basin. They would have to drive back the way they'd come, and then all the way around the basin—or as far as the side roads would take them.

They drove for well over an hour, and then the road ran out.

"We'll have to walk from here," Rob said, looking into the dense mass of rain forest ahead.

"Let's just hope we don't get lost," Kait muttered.

It was cool and icy fresh in the forest. It smelled like Christmas trees and cedar and wetness. With every step Kaitlyn could hear her own feet squishing in the undergrowth and feel herself sinking—as if she were walking on cushions.

"It's sort of primeval, isn't it?" Lydia gasped, picking her way around a fallen log. "Makes you think of dinosaurs."

Kaitlyn knew what she meant. It was a place where people didn't belong, where the plant kingdom ruled. All around her things were growing on other things: ferns on trees, little seedlings on stumps, moss on everything.

"Did anybody ever see the movie *Babes in Toyland*?" Lewis asked in a muted voice. "Remember the Forest of No Return?"

They walked for several hours before they were certain they were lost.

"The problem is that we can't see the sun!" Rob said in exasperation. The sky had gone gray again, and between the clouds and the canopy of green above them, they had no way to get their bearings.

"The problem is that we shouldn't have just barged in here in the first place," Gabriel snapped back.

"How else are we supposed to get to the white house?"

"I don't know, but this is stupid."

Another argument, shaping up to be a classic. Kaitlyn turned away, to find Anna staring fixedly at something on a branch. A bird, Kaitlyn saw, blue with a high pointed crest.

"What is it?"

Anna answered without looking at her. "A Steller's jay."

"Oh. Is it rare?"

"No, but it's smart," Anna murmured. "Smart enough to recognize a clearing with a house. And it can get above the trees."

Understanding crashed in on Kaitlyn, and she had to suppress a whoop. She said in a choked voice, "You mean—"

"Yes. Hush." Anna went on staring at the bird. In the web, power thrummed around her, rose from her like waves of heat. The jay made a harsh noise like *shaaaack* and fluttered its wings.

Rob and Gabriel stopped arguing and turned to goggle.

"What's she *doing?*" Lydia hissed. Kait shushed her, but Anna answered.

"Seeing through its eyes," she murmured. "Giving it my vision—a white house." She continued to stare at the bird, her face rapt, her body swaying just slightly. Her fathomless owl's eyes were mystical, her long dark hair moved with her swaying.

She looks like a shaman, Kaitlyn thought. Some ancient priestess communing with nature, becoming part of it. Anna was the only one of them who really seemed to belong in the forest.

"It knows what to look for," Anna said at last. "Now—"

With a rapid-fire burst of noise like *shook, shook, shook,* the jay took off. It went straight up, into the canopy of branches—and disappeared.

"I know where it is," Anna said, her face still intent and trancelike. "Come on!"

They followed her, scrambling over mossy logs, splashing through shallow streams. It was rough going over steep ground, and Anna always seemed to be just on the verge of vanishing into the trees. They kept following until the light began to dim and Kaitlyn was ready to drop.

"We've got to take a rest," she gasped, stopping by a stream where huge fleshy yellow flowers grew.

"We can't stop now," Anna called back. "We're there."

Kaitlyn jumped up, feeling as if she could run a marathon. "Are you sure? Can you see it?"

"Come here," Anna said, standing with one hand on a moss-bedecked cedar. Kaitlyn looked over her shoulder.

"Oh . . ." she whispered.

The white house stood on a little knoll in a clearing. This close Kaitlyn could see it was not alone. There were several outbuildings around it, weathered and splintery. The house itself was bigger than Kaitlyn had thought.

"We made it," Rob whispered, behind her. Kaitlyn leaned against him, too full of emotion to speak, even in the web.

When they'd found Whiffen Spit, she'd felt like singing

and shouting. They had all been rowdy in celebration. But, here, shouting would have been wrong. This was a deeper happiness, mixed with something like reverence. For a long while they all just stood and looked at the house from their visions.

Then a harsh, drawn-out *shaaaak* broke into their reverie. The jay was fluttering on a branch, scolding them.

Anna laughed and looked at it, and it swooped away. "I told it thank you," she said. "And that it could leave. So now we'd better go forward, because we'll never find our way back."

Kaitlyn felt awkward and self-conscious as she walked out of the shelter of the trees, down toward the house. What if they don't want us here? she thought helplessly. What if it's all a mistake . . . ?

"Do you see any people?" Lewis whispered as they came abreast of the first outbuilding.

"No," Kaitlyn began, and then she did.

The building was a barn, and there was a woman inside. She was forking hay and dung, handling the big pitchfork very capably for someone as small and light as she was. When she saw Kaitlyn she stopped and looked without saying a word.

Kaitlyn stared at her, drymouthed. Then Rob spoke up.

"We're here," he said simply.

The woman was still looking at each of them. She was tiny and elegant, and Kait couldn't tell if she were Egyptian or Asian. Her eyes were tilted but blue, her skin was the color of coffee with cream. Her black hair was done in some complicated fashion, with silver ornaments.

Suddenly she smiled.

"Of course!" she said. "We've been expecting you. But I thought there were only five."

"We, uh, sort of picked up Lydia on the way," Rob said. "She's our friend, and we can vouch for her. But you do know us, ma'am?"

"Of course, of course!" She had an almost indefinable accent—not like the Canadians Kaitlyn had heard. "You're the children we've been calling to. And I'm Mereniang. Meren if that's too long. And you must come inside and meet the others."

Relief sifted through Kaitlyn. Everything was going to be all right. Their search was over.

"Yes, you must all come inside," Mereniang was saying, dusting off her hands. Then she looked at Gabriel. "Except him."

# CHAPTER 14

"What?" Kaitlyn said, and Rob said, "What do you mean, except him?"

Mereniang turned. Her face was still pleasant, but Kait suddenly realized it was also remote. And her eyes . . .

Kaitlyn had seen eyes like that only once before, when the man with the caramel-colored skin had stopped her in the airport. When she'd looked into his eyes, she'd had the sense of centuries passing. Millennia. So many years that the very attempt to comprehend them sent her reeling.

There were ice ages in this woman's eyes, too.

Kaitlyn heard her own gasp. "Who *are* you?" she blurted before she could stop herself.

The enigmatic blue eyes dropped, veiled by heavy lashes. "I told you. Mereniang." Then the eyes lifted again, held steady. "One of the Fellowship," the woman said. "And we don't have many rules here, but this one can't be broken. No one may come into the house who has taken a human life."

She looked at Gabriel and added, "I'm sorry."

A wave of pure fury swept over Kait. She could feel herself flushing. But Rob spoke before she could, and he was as angry as she'd ever seen him.

"You can't do that!" he said. "Gabriel hasn't—what if it was self-defense?" he demanded incoherently.

"I'm sorry," Mereniang said again. "I can't change the rules. Aspect forbids it." She seemed regretful but composed, perfectly willing to stand here all evening and debate the issue. Relaxed but unbending, Kait thought dazedly. Absolutely unbending.

"Who's Aspect?" Lewis demanded.

"Not who. What. Aspect is our philosophy, and it doesn't make exceptions for accidental killing."

"But you can't just shut him out," Rob stormed. "You *can't.*"

"He'll be taken care of. There's a cabin beyond the gardens where he can stay. It's just that he can't enter the house."

The web was singing with outrage. Rob said flatly, "Then we can't enter it, either. We're not going without him!"

There was absolute conviction in his voice. And it rallied Kaitlyn out of her speechless daze. "He's right," she said. "We're not."

"He's one of us," Anna said.

"And it's a stupid rule!" Lewis added.

They were all standing shoulder to shoulder, united in their determination. All but Lydia, who stood aside looking uncertain—and Gabriel.

Gabriel had moved back, away from them. He was wearing the thin, faint smile he'd given Rob earlier.

"Go on," he said directly to Rob. "You have to."

"No, we don't." Rob was right in front of him now. Golden in the blue twilight, contrasting with Gabriel's pale face and dark hair. Sun and black hole, Kaitlyn thought. Eternal opposites. Only this time they were fighting *for* each other.

"Yes, you do," Gabriel said. "Go in there and find out what's going on. I'll wait. I don't care."

A lie Kait could feel clearly in the web. But no one mentioned it. Mereniang was still waiting with the patience of someone to whom minutes were nothing.

Slowly Rob let out his breath. "All right," he said at last. His voice was grim and the look he turned on Mereniang not friendly.

"Wait here," Mereniang told Gabriel. "Someone will come for you." She began walking toward the house.

Kaitlyn followed, but her legs felt heavy and she looked back twice. Gabriel looked almost small standing there by himself in the gathering darkness.

The white house was made of stone, and spacious inside, with a cathedral hush about it. The floor was stone, too. It might have been a temple.

But the furniture, what Kaitlyn could see of it, was simple. There were carved wooden benches and chairs that looked Colonial. She glimpsed a loom in one of the many recessed chambers.

"How old is this place?" she asked Mereniang.

"Old. And it's built on the remnants of an older house. But we'll talk about that later. Right now you're all tired and hungry—come in here and I'll bring you something to eat."

She ushered them into a room with an enormous fireplace and a long cedar table. Kaitlyn sat on a bench, feeling flustered, resentful, and *wrong*.

She went on feeling it as Mereniang returned, balancing a heavy wooden tray. A young girl was behind her, also carrying a tray.

"Tamsin," Mereniang introduced her. The girl was very pretty, with clusters of curly yellow hair and the profile of a Grecian maiden. Like Mereniang and the man at the airport, she seemed to have the characteristics of several different races, harmoniously blended.

*But they're not what I expected,* Kaitlyn told Rob wretchedly.

It wasn't that they weren't magical enough. They were almost *too* magical, despite their simple furniture and ordinary ways. There was something alien at the core of them, something disturbing about the way they stood and watched. Even the young girl, Tamsin, seemed older than the giant trees outside.

The food was good, though. Bread like the loaves they'd bought at the kiosk, fresh and nutty. Some soft, pale yellow cheese. A salad that seemed to be made of more wild plants than lettuce—flowers and what looked like weeds. But delicious. Some flat purply-brown things that looked like fruit roll-ups.

"They *are* fruit roll-ups," Anna said when Lewis asked. "They're made of salal berries and salmonberries."

There was no meat, not even fish.

"If you're finished, you can come meet the others," Mereniang said.

Kaitlyn bridled slightly. "What about Gabriel?"

"I've had someone take food to him."

"No, I mean, doesn't *he* get to meet the others? Or do you have a rule against that, too?"

Mereniang sighed. She clasped her small, square-fingered hands together. Then she put them on her hips.

"I'll do what I can," she said. "Tamsin, take them out to the rose garden. It's the only place warm enough. I'll be along."

*The rose garden's warm?* Lewis asked as they followed Tamsin outside.

Strangely enough, it was. There were roses blooming, too, all colors, crimson and golden-orange and blush pink. The light and warmth seemed to come from the fountain in the center of the walled garden.

No, not the fountain, Kaitlyn thought. The crystal in

the fountain. When she'd first seen it in a picture, she hadn't known what it was; she'd wondered if it was an ice sculpture or a column.

It wasn't like Mr. Z's crystal. That monstrosity had been covered with obscene growths, smaller crystals that sprouted like parasites from the main body. This crystal was clean and pure, all straight lines and perfect facets.

And it was glowing gently. Pulsing with a soft, milky light that warmed the air around it.

"Energy," Rob said, holding a hand up to feel it. "It's got a bioenergetic field."

Kaitlyn felt a ripple in the web and was turning even as Gabriel said, "Beats a campfire."

"You're here!" Rob said. They all gathered around him happily. Even Lydia was smiling.

At the same moment Mereniang came through the other entrance in the wall with a group of people.

"This is Timon," she said. The man who stepped forward actually looked old. He was tall but frail and white-haired. His lined face was gentle, the skin almost transparent.

*Is he the leader?* Kaitlyn asked silently.

"I am a poet and historian," Timon said. "But as the oldest member of the colony, I am sometimes forced to make decisions." He gave a gently ironic smile.

Kaitlyn stared at him, her heartbeat quickening. Had he *heard* that?

"And this is LeShan."

"We've already met," Gabriel said and showed his teeth.

It was the caramel-skinned man from the airport. His hair was a pale shimmery brown, like silver birch. His eyes were slanting and very dark, and they flashed at Gabriel dangerously.

"I remember," he said. "The last time I saw you, you had a knife at my throat."

"And you were on top of Kaitlyn," Gabriel said, causing some consternation among the rest of the Fellowship.

"I was trying to warn you!" LeShan snapped, moving forward.

Mereniang was frowning. "LeShan," she said. LeShan went on glaring. "LeShan, Aspect!"

LeShan subsided, stepping back.

If Aspect was a nonviolent philosophy, Kait had the feeling that LeShan had a little trouble with it. She remembered that he'd had a temper.

"Now," Timon said. "Sit down if you'd like. We'll try to answer your questions."

Kaitlyn sat on one of the cool stone benches that lined the wall. She had so many questions she didn't know which to ask first. In the silence she could hear the singing of frogs and the gentle trickle of water in the fountain. The air was heady with the scent of roses. The pale, milky light of the crystal gave a gentle radiance to Timon's thin hair and Mereniang's lovely face.

No one else was speaking. Lewis nudged her. *Go on.*

"Who are you people?" Kait asked finally.

Timon smiled. "The last survivors of an ancient race. The people of the crystal."

"That's what I heard," Lydia said. "I've heard people use that name, but I don't know what it *means*."

"Our civilization used crystals for generating and focusing energy. Not just any crystals—they had to be perfectly pure and faceted in a certain way. We called them great crystals or firestones. They were used as power stations; we extracted energy from them the way you extract the energy of heat from coal."

"Is that possible?" Rob said.

"For us it was. But we were a nation of psychics; our society was based on psychic power." Timon nodded toward the crystal in the fountain. "*That* is the last perfect crystal, and we use it to generate the energy to sustain this place. Without it, we would be helpless. You see, the crystals do more than just supply technical power. They sustain *us*. In the old country they could rejuvenate us; here they merely stop the ravages of time."

Is that why so many of them have young faces and old eyes? Kaitlyn wondered. But Lewis was speaking up.

"There's nothing like that in history books," he said. "Nothing about a country that used crystals for power."

"I'm afraid it was before what you consider history," Timon

456

said. "I promise you, the civilization did exist. Plato spoke of it, although he was only repeating stories *he'd* heard. A land where the fairest and noblest race of people lived. Their country was formed of alternating rings of land and water, and their city was surrounded by three walls. They dug up a metal called *orichalcum,* which was as precious as gold and shone with a red light, and they used it to decorate the inner wall."

Kaitlyn was gasping. For as Timon spoke, she *saw* what he described. Images were flooding into her mind, as they had when Joyce had pressed a tiny shard of crystal to her third eye. She saw a city with three circular walls, one of brass, one of tin, and one which glowed red-gold. The city itself was barbaric in its splendor—buildings were coated with silver, their pinnacles with gold.

"They had everything," Timon said in his gentle voice. "Plants of every type; herb, root, and leaf. Hot springs and mineral baths. Excellent soil for growing things. Aqueducts, gardens, temples, docks, libraries, places of learning."

Kaitlyn saw it all. Groves of beautiful trees intermingled with the beautiful buildings. And people living among them without racial strife, in harmony.

"But what *happened?*" she said. "Where did it all go?"

LeShan answered. "They lost respect for the earth. They took and took, without giving anything back."

"They destroyed the environment?" Anna asked.

"It wasn't quite as simple as that," Timon said softly. "In

the final days there was a rift between the people who used their powers for good and those who had chosen the service of evil. You see, the crystals could just as easily work evil as good, they could be turned to torture and destruction. A number of people joined the Dark Lodge and began to use them this way."

"And meanwhile the 'good' psychic masters were demanding too much of their own crystals," LeShan put in. "They were greedy. When the energy broadcast from the crystals was tuned too high, it caused an artificial imbalance. It caused earthquakes first, then floods."

"And so the land was destroyed," Timon said sadly. "Most of the people died with it. But a few clairvoyants escaped—they'd been able to predict what was going to happen. Some of them went to Egypt, some to Peru. And some"—he lifted his head and looked at Kait's group—"to Northern America."

Kaitlyn narrowed her eyes. There had been no pictures in her head to accompany Timon's last words. "This—destruction," she said. "It wouldn't have involved a continent sinking or anything, would it? Like a lost continent?"

Timon just smiled. "Ours is certainly a lost race," he said, then went on without answering the question. "This little enclave is all that remains of our people. We came here a long time ago, with the hope of living simply, in peace. We don't bother the outside world, and most of the time it doesn't bother us."

Kaitlyn wanted to pursue her question, but Rob was asking another one. "But, you know, Mr. Zetes—the man we ran away from—he has a crystal, too."

Members of the Fellowship were nodding grimly. "We're the only pure survivors," Mereniang said. "But others escaped and intermarried with the natives of their new lands. Your Mr. Zetes is a descendent of one of those people. He must have inherited that crystal—or possibly unearthed it after it had been hidden for centuries."

"It *looks* different from yours," Rob said. "It's all covered with things like spikes."

"It's evil," Mereniang said simply, her ageless blue eyes clear and sad.

"Well, it did something to Gabriel," Rob said. In the web Kaitlyn could feel Gabriel tense in anticipation. Although he was keeping himself under tight control, she could tell he was both hopeful and resentful. And that he was beginning to suffer as he did every night—he needed energy, soon.

"Mr. Z hooked Gabriel up to it," Rob was going on. "Like you said, for torture. But afterward—well, it had permanent effects."

Mereniang looked at Gabriel, then moved to look at him more closely. She put a hand on his forehead, over his third eye. Gabriel flinched but didn't step back.

"Now, just let me . . ." Mereniang's sentence trailed off. Her eyes were focused on something invisible, her whole attitude one of listening. Kaitlyn had seen Rob look like that when he was healing.

"I see." Mereniang's face had become very serious. She took her hand away. "The crystal stepped up your metabolism. You burn your own energy now so quickly that you need an outside supply."

The words were dispassionate, but Kait was certain she could detect something less impartial in those ageless blue eyes. A certain fastidious distaste.

Oh, God, no, Kait thought. If Gabriel senses that . . .

"There's one thing that might help," Mereniang said. "Put your hands on the crystal."

Gabriel looked at her sharply. Then, slowly, he turned to the crystal in the center of the garden. His face seemed particularly pale in the cool white light as he approached it. After a brief hesitation, he touched one hand to a milky, pulsating facet.

"Both hands," Mereniang said.

Gabriel put his other hand on the crystal. As soon as it touched, his body jerked as if an electrical current had been sent through it. In the web Kaitlyn felt a flare of power.

She was on her feet in alarm. So was Rob, so were the others. But what she felt in the web now was energy flowing, flowing *into* Gabriel. It was cold, and it elicited none of the wild gratitude and joy she'd felt in Gabriel when he took energy from her—but it was feeding him nevertheless. Sustaining him.

She sat down again. Gabriel took his hands away. He stood with his head down for a moment, and Kaitlyn could see that he was breathing quickly. Then he turned.

"Am I cured?" he asked, looking straight at Mereniang.

"Oh—no." For the first time the dark woman looked uncomfortable. She couldn't seem to hold Gabriel's eyes. "I'm afraid there *is* no cure, except possibly the destruction of the crystal that made you this way. But any crystal which produces energy can help you—"

Rob interrupted, too overwrought to be polite. "Just a minute. You mean destroying Mr. Zetes's crystal will cure him?"

"Possibly."

"Well, then, what are we waiting for? Let's destroy it!"

Mereniang looked helplessly at Timon. All the members of the Fellowship were looking at one another in the same way.

"It isn't that easy," Timon told Rob gently. "To destroy that crystal, we would first have to destroy *this* crystal. The only way to shatter it would be to unite it with a shard from a crystal that is still pure. Still perfect."

"And this is the last perfect crystal," Mereniang reminded them.

"So—you can't help us," Rob said after a moment.

"Not in that, I'm afraid," Mereniang said quietly. Timon sighed.

Kait was looking at Gabriel. His shoulders had sagged abruptly, as if taking on a heavy weight. His head was slightly bent. In the web all she could feel were the walls he was doggedly building brick by brick. She could only guess what he must be feeling.

She knew what her other mind-mates were feeling, though—alarm. The Fellowship couldn't cure Gabriel's psychic vampirism. Well, then, what about their other problem?

"There's something else we wanted to ask you about," Lewis said nervously. "See, when we were trying to figure out what Mr. Z was up to—well, it's a long story, but we ended up with this telepathic link. All of us, you know. And we can't get rid of it."

"Telepathy is one of the gifts of the old race," Timon said. His old eyes rested on Kait briefly, and he smiled. "The ability to communicate mind to mind is a wonderful thing."

"But we can't *stop*," Lewis said. "Gabriel got us linked, and now we can't get unlinked."

Timon looked at Gabriel. So did Mereniang and several of the others, as if to say, "You again?" Kaitlyn had the distinct impression that they thought he was a troublemaker. She sensed a flash of anger from Gabriel, quickly stifled.

"Yes, well, I'm afraid there's not much we can do about that, either," Mereniang said. "We can study it, of course, but a five-way link is a stable pattern. Usually it can only be broken by—"

"The death of one of the members," Kaitlyn and Anna said in chorus. They looked at each other in despair.

"Or distance," Timon said. "If you were to put physical distance between the members—that wouldn't break the link, of course, but you wouldn't feel it as much."

Rob was rumpling his already tousled hair. "But, look, the really important thing is Mr. Zetes. We understand if you can't fix Gabriel or break the link—but you *are* going to help us against Mr. Z, aren't you?"

There was one of those dreadful pauses which spoke louder than words.

"We are a peaceful race," Timon said at last, almost apologetically.

"But he's *afraid* of you. He thinks you're the only threat to him." Rob glanced for confirmation at Lydia, who nodded.

"We don't have the power of destruction," Mereniang said. LeShan was grinding one fist into his palm—Kaitlyn sensed that he, at least, wished they did.

Rob was still protesting. "You mean there's nothing you can do to stop him? Do you realize what he's *up* to?"

"We are not warriors," Timon said. "Only the youngest of us can even leave this place and travel in the outside world. The rest are too feeble—too old." He sighed again and rubbed his lined forehead.

"But can't you do something psychically?" Kaitlyn asked. "Mr. Z's been attacking us long distance."

"It would give away our location," LeShan said grimly, and Timon nodded.

"Your Mr. Zetes *does* have the power of destruction. If he discovers this place, he will attack us. We are only safe as long as it remains a secret."

Gabriel lifted his head and spoke for the first time in a long while. "You're awfully trusting of *us,* then."

Timon smiled faintly. "When you first came here, Mereniang looked into your hearts. None of you has come to betray us."

Kaitlyn had been listening with growing frustration. Suddenly she couldn't keep quiet any longer. She found herself standing, words bursting out of her throat.

"You can't help Gabriel and you can't help break the link and you won't help us fight Mr. Zetes—so what did you *bring* us here for?"

There was age-old sadness in Mereniang's eyes. Endless regret, tempered with the serenity of resignation.

"To give you a refuge," the dark woman said. "We want you to stay here. Forever."

# CHAPTER 15

"But what about Gabriel?" Kaitlyn said. It was the first thing she could think of.

"He can stay, too."

"Without going in the *house?*"

Before Mereniang could answer, Rob spoke. "Look, *nobody's* deciding to stay right now. This is something we've got to think over—"

"It's the only place you'll be safe," Mereniang said. "We've had a lot of visitors over the years, but we've asked very few to stay with us. We do it when they have no choice—no other safety."

"Are there any here now?" Kait asked, looking at the Fellowship behind Mereniang.

"The last died a long time ago. But he lived longer than he would have in the outside world—and so will you. You are part of our race, and the crystal will help sustain you."

Lewis was twisting his baseball cap. "What do you mean, 'part of your race'?"

Timon spread his hands. "All psychics are descendants of the old race. Somewhere among your ancestors was one of the people of the crystal. The old blood has awakened in you." He looked at each of them earnestly. "My children, you *belong* here."

Kait didn't know what to say. She'd never felt so confused and disoriented in her life. The Fellowship was nothing that she had expected, and the discovery left her numb, in shock. Meanwhile, the web was a jumble of conflicting emotions that made it impossible for her to tell what any particular one of the others was thinking.

It was Rob who saved them, speaking steadily. "We're proud that you think we're good enough to join you, sir," he said to Timon. He'd regained his natural courtesy. "And we'd like to thank you. But this is something we're going to have to talk over a bit. You understand that." It was a statement, but Rob scanned the faces of the Fellowship questioningly.

Mereniang looked vaguely annoyed, but Timon said, "Of course. Of course. You're all tired, and you'll find it easier to think tomorrow. There's no hurry."

Kaitlyn still felt like arguing with somebody—but Timon was right. She was swaying on her feet. Tomorrow they'd all be fresh, and less emotional.

"We'll talk to them again about Mr. Zetes then," Rob

whispered to her under cover of the meeting breaking up.

Kaitlyn nodded and glanced around for Gabriel. He was talking to Lydia, but he stopped when he saw her looking.

"Are you going to be all right?" she asked him.

His eyes were opaque—as if they'd filmed over with gray spiderweb. "Sure," he said. "They've got a little cot for me in the toolshed."

"Oh, Gabriel . . . Maybe we should all stay there with you. Do you want me to ask Meren—"

*"No,"* Gabriel said vehemently. Then he added more smoothly, "Don't worry about me. I'll be fine. Get your sleep."

Walls, walls, walls. Kaitlyn sighed.

Then, oddly, he said: "Good night, Kait."

Kaitlyn blinked. Had he ever said good night to her before? "I—good night, Gabriel."

Then Mereniang gathered them up and took them into the house, leaving Gabriel with a couple of the men.

It was as they were entering the house that Kaitlyn remembered a question she'd forgotten to ask. "Meren, do you know about the *inuk shuk* on Whiffen Spit?"

"Timon knows the most about them."

"Well, I was just wondering why they were there. And if they meant anything."

Timon was smiling reminiscently. "Ancient peoples started the tradition. They came down as traders from the north and left some of their stone language here. They called this a place of good magic, and they built their friendship signs on the spit that points to it."

Timon was still smiling, lost in thought. "That was a very long time ago," he said. "We've watched the world change all around us—but we have remained unchanged."

There was a note of pride in his voice, and a tinge of arrogance in Mereniang's face.

Kait looked at Timon. "Don't you think change is sometimes good?"

Timon came out of his reverie, looking startled. But no one answered her.

Kaitlyn's bedroom was very plain, with a bed built into the wall, a chair, and a washbasin under a mirror. It was the first time she'd slept alone—without the others—in a week. She didn't like it, but she was so tired she fell asleep quickly anyway.

Alone in the tool shed, Gabriel was awake.

So Mereniang had "looked into their hearts," had she? He smiled wryly. What the Fellowship didn't seem to realize was that hearts could change. *He* had changed since he'd come here.

It was a change that had started last night. Last night on the wharf when he'd discovered his feelings for Kaitlyn—and Kaitlyn had made her choice.

It wasn't her fault. Strangely enough, it wasn't Kessler's, either. They belonged together, both honest, both good.

But that didn't mean Gabriel had to stick around and watch it.

And now, tonight, his last hope had disappeared. The people of the crystal couldn't free him. They didn't even *want* to. And he'd seen the disgust and condemnation in their eyes.

Live here? In their outbuildings? Face that condemnation every day? And watch Kessler and Kait romancing each other?

Gabriel's lips drew back from his teeth in a fierce smile. He didn't think so.

I should be grateful to the Fellowship, he thought. They've shown me what I really am, simply in contrast to what *they* are. Back in the old days I'd have joined the Dark Lodge and hunted these gutless wimps out of existence.

It was a fairly simple equation. He didn't belong with the good guys, the white hats. Therefore, he must belong with the other side.

Not a new revelation, but a rediscovery. Kait had almost made him forget what he really was. She'd almost convinced him that he could live on the light side, that he wasn't a killer by nature. Well, tomorrow she'd see how wrong she'd been.

Gabriel stepped back a little to look at the body on the toolshed floor.

The man's name had been Theo. The Fellowship had sent him to spend the night out here—whether as companion or guard Gabriel didn't know. Now he was in a coma. Not quite dead, but getting there.

Gabriel had mind-linked with him to take knowledge from his brain. Including the knowledge of a secret trail through the otherwise impassable forest.

The extra energy had been nice, too.

Now the only thing Gabriel was waiting for was Lydia. He'd whispered a few words to her in the rose garden, asking her to come tonight and meet him. He was fairly certain she'd show up.

And then Gabriel would ask her if she really wanted to spend the next seventy years with a commune of doddering old hippies. Or if life might not be better back in sunny California, where Gabriel had the feeling that Mr. Zetes was setting up a little Dark Lodge of his own.

Lydia was weak. He thought he could persuade her. And if he couldn't—well, she could join Theo on the floor. Lewis would be unhappy, but what did Lewis matter?

For just an instant an image flashed through his mind of what would happen if he *could* persuade her. What would happen here, to the Fellowship, once he gave Mr. Zetes the information needed to home in on the white house. It wouldn't be a pretty picture. And Kait would be in the middle of it. . . .

Gabriel shook the thought off and bared his teeth again.

He had to at least have the courage of his convictions. If he was going to be evil, he'd *be* evil, all the way. From now on there were no half measures.

And besides, Kessler would be here. He'd just have to take care of Kaitlyn himself.

A footstep sounded outside the shed. Gabriel turned to meet Lydia, smiling.

Someone was shouting.

Kaitlyn could hear it even in her sleep, as she slowly drifted toward consciousness. By the time she was fully awake, it was more than one person, and the web was singing with alarm.

She ran out, pulling on her clothes. Broadcasting *What's happening?* to anyone that could hear.

*I don't know,* Rob sent back. *Everyone's upset. Something's happened. . . .*

People were running in the hallways of the white house. Kaitlyn spotted Tamsin and swooped on her. "What's going *on?*"

"Your friends," Tamsin said. She had olive-dark eyes, contrasting strangely with her golden hair. "The boy outside and the small girl . . ."

"Gabriel and Lydia? *What?*"

"They're gone," Mereniang said, appearing from a recessed room. "And the man we had guarding Gabriel is nearly dead."

Kaitlyn's heart plummeted. Endlessly, it seemed. She couldn't move or breathe.

It couldn't be true. It *couldn't.* Gabriel wouldn't have done a thing like that. . . .

But then she remembered how he'd looked last night. His gray eyes so opaque, his walls so high. As if he'd lost all hope.

And she certainly couldn't sense him anywhere in the web. She could feel only Rob and Lewis and Anna, who were coming to join her now in the hallway.

Rob put an arm around her to support her. Kaitlyn needed it; she thought her knees might give out.

Lewis was looking wretched and unbelieving. "Lydia went, too?" he asked pathetically. Mereniang just nodded.

"But they can't have gone far," Kait whispered, finding her voice. "They can't get through the forest."

"The guard knew a path. Gabriel entered his mind. He knows what the guard knew." Mereniang spoke with very little emotion.

"It must have been Lydia," Rob exploded. "Gabriel wouldn't have done it on his own. Lydia must have talked him into it, somehow." Kaitlyn could feel his pain and Lewis's fighting each other, building exponentially, magnifying her own distress.

Mereniang shook her head once, decisively. "If anything, it was the other way around. I realized last night that Gabriel was dangerous; that was why I sent Theo to watch him. But I underestimated *how* dangerous he was."

Kaitlyn felt a wave of sickness. "I still can't believe it. It couldn't have been his fault—"

"And I still don't think it was Lydia's fault," Lewis began.

"It doesn't matter whose fault it is," Mereniang said sharply, interrupting both of them. "And there's no time to argue. We have to prepare for an attack."

Lewis looked confused and horrified. "You're going to attack—?"

"No! We're going to *be* attacked. As soon as those two communicate with your Mr. Zetes. They must have run away to join him."

This time the wave of sickness almost drowned Kaitlyn. She heard Anna whisper, "Oh, no . . ."

And she tried to convince herself that Gabriel wouldn't tell Mr. Zetes, that he'd just run away. But the violent beating of her own heart contradicted her.

"Mereniang! We need you in the garden!" The voice came from a doorway.

Mereniang turned. "I'm coming!" She looked back at Kaitlyn's group. "Stay inside. The worst of it will be out there." And then she was running.

Kaitlyn held on to Rob, her only anchor in a spinning world. *Do you think he'll do it?*

Rob's arms tightened around her. *I don't know.*

*Rob, is it our fault?*

The hardest question, the one she knew would haunt her dreams if she lived through today. She could feel Lewis's hurt despair. Before Rob could answer, the attack began.

A cold wind blew down the corridor. Not just cold air; a gale. It whipped Kaitlyn's hair against her cheeks and tore loose strands from Anna's braid. It cut through their clothing like a newly sharpened knife.

And with it came a rattling. The wooden bench against the wall began to tremble, at first with a fine vibration, then more and more violently. Kaitlyn could hear the banging of doors swinging on their hinges, and the crash of things falling off shelves and walls.

It was so sudden that for a moment all she could do was stand and cling to Rob. Her temperature seemed to have dropped by degrees. A violent shivering racked her body.

"Stay together," Rob shouted, reaching out for Anna and Lewis. They grabbed hold, all four of them clutching each other. It was like trying to stand in a blizzard.

There was a wild ringing in Kaitlyn's ears—like the sound she'd heard once in the van. The sound of a crystal glass being stroked, only this went on and on, and it was pitched at a frequency that hurt. That pierced like needles, making it almost impossible to think.

And the *smell.* The odor of rotting flesh, of raw sewage. The wind forced it into her nostrils.

"What are they trying to do? Stink us all out?" Lewis shouted.

"Meren said it would be worse outside!" Anna shouted back. It was no good using telepathy, the entire web was vibrating with that piercing note.

"And they said she was needed in the *garden!*" Rob shouted. "The garden—where the crystal is. Come on!"

"Come on *where?*" Lewis yelled.

"To the rose garden! Maybe we can do something to help!"

They stumbled and staggered getting out of the house. Outside, the wind was worse, and the sky was black with clouds. It didn't seem to be morning at all, but an eerie and unnatural twilight.

"Come on!" Rob kept shouting, and somehow they made it to the garden.

The smell was coming from here, and so was the ringing sound. The roses were tattered, their petals torn off by the wind. A few petals still whirled in the air.

"Oh, God—the crystal!" Anna shouted.

Most of the Fellowship seemed to be gathered around it, and many of them, including Timon and Mereniang, had their hands on it. The crystal itself was pulsating wildly, but not with the gentle milky light Kait had seen before. Every color of the rainbow seemed to be fighting and flashing in its depths. It was dazzling, almost impossible to look at.

But that wasn't what Anna had meant. It was something much worse. Superimposed on the rose garden crystal was another, a phantom crystal without any color. A monstrosity with growths sprouting from every facet.

The crystal from Mr. Z's basement, Kait thought dazedly. Or, rather, its astral image. And around that corrupted crystal were the astral images of the attackers, visible like ghosts among the bodies of the Fellowship.

The gray people, the ones she'd seen in the van. She just hadn't seen the crystal then. They were leaning around it, touching it with their hands and foreheads. Using its power—

—to do what? Kaitlyn thought suddenly. "What are they trying to do?" she shouted to Rob.

"They're trying to destroy our crystal," one of the Fellowship answered. A sturdy woman who was in the outer circle around the fountain. "They've set up a vibration to shatter it. They won't be able to do it, though, not while all our power is protecting it."

"Can we help?" Rob yelled.

The woman just shook her head, looking back at the crystal. But Rob and Kaitlyn both moved past her, struck by a common impulse to get as close as possible to what was happening. They squeezed through the crowd and ended up behind Timon and Mereniang.

Timon's frail body was shaking so hard that Kaitlyn felt a stab of fear. She was shaking herself—not with cold, now, but with the vibrations of the crystal. The ground, the fountain, everything was trembling, as if resonating to a single, terrible note.

"So much—evil. So much—"

It was a gasp, and Kaitlyn could barely hear it. But she saw Timon's lips moving and she caught the words. His lined face was white, his eyes wide and clouded.

"I didn't know," he gasped. "I didn't realize—and to do such things to *children* . . ."

Kaitlyn didn't understand. She looked at Mereniang and saw that the dark woman's face was also twisted with horror. Those blue eyes narrowed and streamed with tears.

Then Kait looked at the gray people.

They were more defined than she'd ever seen them before. It was almost as if they were actually materializing here, as if they might appear physically at any moment. She could see their bodies, their hands—and their faces.

One of them was familiar. Kaitlyn had seen that face before—or at least a picture of it. On a folder labeled SABRINA JESSICA GALLO.

But Mr. Zetes had told her they'd all gone insane. Every one of his first students, everyone in the pilot study.

Maybe he didn't mind them being insane. Maybe it was easier to control them that way. . . .

Kaitlyn could feel tears on her own cheeks. Timon was right. Mr. Zetes was absolutely evil.

And he seemed to be winning. The crystal in the fountain was vibrating ever more frenetically. The kaleidoscope of colors disappearing into the misty gray of the other crystal. She could actually see the corrupted crystal more clearly now.

"Timon, let go!" Mereniang was calling. "You're too old for this! The crystal should be sustaining you, not the other way around."

But Timon didn't seem to hear her. "So evil," he said again and again. "I didn't realize how evil. . . ."

"Rob, we've got to do something!" Kaitlyn shouted.

But it was Timon who answered, in a telepathic voice that cut through the ringing in the web. A voice so strong that Kaitlyn whirled to stare at him.

*Yes! We must do something. We must let go of the crystal!*

Mereniang was staring, too, her eyes and mouth open. "Timon, if we release it—"

*Do it!* the telepathic voice roared back. *Everyone, do it now!*

And with that, Timon stepped away, taking his hands off the crystal.

Kaitlyn's head was spinning. She watched as the other members of the Fellowship looked at each other wildly, in obvious distress. Then, suddenly, she saw another figure step back.

It was LeShan, his lynx eyes flashing, holding his empty hands in the air.

Another one of the Fellowship stepped away, and another. Finally only Mereniang was holding on.

*Let go!* Timon shouted.

The crystal was trembling visibly. The piercing note rang higher and higher in Kaitlyn's ears.

"Let go," Timon whispered, as if his strength had suddenly given out. "Someone—make her . . . She'll be destroyed. . . ."

Rob surged forward. He grabbed Mereniang around the waist and pulled. Her palms came away from the crystal, and they both fell to the ground.

The terrible ringing became a terrible crashing. The sound

of a million goblets falling to the floor. A sound that deafened Kaitlyn, echoing in every nerve.

The great crystal was shattering.

It was almost like an explosion, although the only thing flying outward was light. A burst of radiance that left Kaitlyn blind as well as deaf. Imprinted on her eyelids she had a picture of thousands of shards hanging in air.

She fell to her knees, arms wrapped around her head protectively.

When she opened her eyes, the world had changed. The wind was gone. So was the smell.

So were the crystals—both of them. The gray crystal had simply vanished, along with the gray people. The other one, the last perfect crystal in the world, was lying in splinters in the water of the fountain.

Dizzy and unbelieving, Kaitlyn looked around.

Timon was lying on the grass, one hand curled on his chest. His eyes were shut, his face waxen.

Rob was picking himself up from under Mereniang, who was crying.

"Why?" the dark woman demanded. It was what Kait wanted to know herself. "Why, why?"

Timon's eyelids fluttered.

"Take a shard and give it to the children," he whispered.

# CHAPTER 16

Mereniang looked both bewildered and horrified. She didn't move. But LeShan took two quick steps and thrust a hand into the fountain.

"Here," he said, holding out one of the shards toward Rob.

Rob didn't glance up. He was kneeling by Timon, one hand on the old man's upper chest.

"Hang on," he said. Then he glanced up at Mereniang. "He's so weak! It's as if his life-force has disappeared. . . ."

"The crystal was sustaining him," Mereniang said. Her blue eyes, though still fixed on Timon, were dull. She had withdrawn into herself, arms wrapped around her body. "When it shattered, his life ended."

"He's not dead yet!" Rob said fiercely. He shut his eyes,

placing his free hand on Timon's forehead. Kaitlyn could sense the healing energy flowing from him.

"No," Timon whispered. "It's no use, and I need you to listen to me."

"Don't talk," Rob ordered, but Kait went to kneel by the old man. She needed to understand what was happening.

"Why did you do it?" she asked.

Timon's eyes opened. There was a strange serenity in their depths. He even managed something like a smile.

"You were right," he said faintly. "Change is good—or at least necessary. Take the shard."

LeShan was still holding out the crystal. Kaitlyn looked from him to Timon. Then she reached out her hand.

The shard was almost as thick as her wrist and a foot long. It was cold and heavy and the facets were very sharp. One sliced into her thumb when she tested the edge.

"Take it back with you, and do what needs to be done," Timon whispered. His voice was almost inaudible now. Rob was sweating, his hands trembling, but Timon seemed to be fading away.

"Some things are so evil they must be fought. . . ."

A shiver went through Timon's frame, and a strange sound came from his lungs. Death rattle, Kaitlyn thought, too numb to move. It was almost like hearing a soul leave a body.

Timon's eyes were wide, staring at the sky. But now they were unseeing.

Kaitlyn's throat felt tight and swollen. Her eyes filled, tears spilling over. All around her the members of the Fellowship were milling about, like a flock of birds thrown into confusion. They didn't seem to know what to do now that Timon was dead and the crystal shattered.

And Rob's chest was heaving. His hair was dark with sweat, his eyes dark with grief. A healer who had lost the battle.

Kaitlyn scooted over to him, glad to have some problem she could understand. She put her arms around him. She felt a ripple in the newly free web and saw Lewis and Anna come to kneel beside her.

They put their arms around both Kait and Rob. All of them holding on as they had in the blizzard. Clinging to one another because they were all they had.

"All right, you lot!" LeShan was shouting. "Timon's gone, but we're still alive. We're going to have to think for ourselves. And we don't have time to stand around!"

"We're going to have to leave, of course," LeShan said. He seemed to have taken charge while Mereniang was grieving. Kaitlyn was glad; LeShan might be aggressive and quick-tempered, but she found him much easier to understand than the rest of the Fellowship.

They were all standing in the central hallway of the white house. Around them the Fellowship was busying itself, packing and carrying, moving and loading. "You think Mr. Zetes will attack again," Rob said. It wasn't a question.

"Yes, that was just the beginning. He's removed our defenses—and that was probably all he *could* do at one go. Next time it'll be for the kill." A tall woman looked in from another hallway. "LeShan, are the children coming with us? I'm trying to arrange transportation."

LeShan looked at Kait and the others.

"Well?" he said.

No one spoke at first. Then Rob said, "Let me get this clear. Timon's idea was that we should go back down to Mr. Zetes, and use the shard of your crystal to destroy *his* crystal."

"It's the only way to do it," LeShan said. "But that doesn't mean you have to."

"Timon *died* so we could have a shard," Anna said. Her normally gentle face was severe.

"And I *still* don't understand," Kait burst out. "Why did everyone listen to him? You were dead-set against fighting before—what made you all change your minds?"

LeShan's lip curled. "I don't think they all *did* change their minds. They're just used to obeying Timon. He might not have considered himself the leader, but everyone let him do the thinking."

"And he changed his mind because of the attack?" Lewis said uncertainly.

"Because of Sabrina," Kaitlyn said. Everyone looked at her. "Didn't you *see?*" she asked.

Lewis blinked. "Who's Sabrina?"

"Sabrina Jessica Gallo. She was one of the gray people. I didn't realize it before because I couldn't see her face."

"Are you sure?" Rob asked.

"Positive. I saw her clearly this time. And I guess that means the other gray people are the other old students. They all looked young to me."

"That was what Timon sensed," LeShan said. His lips were still curled slightly, as if he had an unpleasant taste in his mouth. "We all sensed it, everyone who was touching the crystal. The attackers were *children*—none of them over twenty. And their minds were twisted . . . I can't explain it."

"They were insane," Kaitlyn told him rather calmly. "That's what Mr. Zetes said, that the crystal had driven them crazy. And that's why I never thought of him using them to attack us. I had the idea they were in institutions somewhere."

"Maybe Mr. Z got them out," Lewis said hollowly.

LeShan grimaced. "In any case, we could feel their agony— and their evil. None of us realized evil like that still existed in the world. I think *we* had the idea that it died when our country died."

"And you're not going to tell us what that country was, are you?" Kaitlyn asked. She'd been meaning to get the question in since yesterday.

LeShan seemed not to hear her. "If you four go back down to fight this man, it will be dangerous," he said. "I won't pretend otherwise. And you can't rely on any help from us. I've got to make sure all these people get settled somewhere—and by the time I'm free, it may be all over with you."

"Thanks," Rob said dryly.

"If I can help after that, I will. But it's your decision."

"We'd be safe if we went with you?" Kaitlyn asked. She felt almost wistful.

"Reasonably safe. Nobody can promise perfect safety."

Kaitlyn sighed. She looked at Rob, and at Lewis and Anna. They were all looking at one another, too.

*Do we really have a choice?* Rob asked.

*The longer we wait, the stronger Mr. Z will get,* Anna said. Her thought smoldered with conviction.

*We might as well finish what we started,* Lewis put in, sounding resigned. He'd bounced back remarkably quickly from his upset. With his natural resilience and optimism, he was even now hoping for the best in Lydia—Kait could tell.

Kaitlyn had a different reason for wanting to go back. Yes, she wanted to stop Mr. Zetes, but there was something more important.

*Gabriel,* she told the others.

There was an immediate swell of emotion. Some of it was anger, bewilderment, feelings of betrayal. But there was sympathy, too, and determination—and love.

*You're right,* Rob thought. *If he really is going to join Mr. Zetes—*

*I'm afraid he is,* Kaitlyn broke in. *I should have thought of it last night. Meren said that any crystal that produces energy could feed him. And Mr. Z's crystal certainly produces energy.*

*You think that's why he left?* Anna asked.

*I don't know. I doubt that's all of it. But I think he'd rather get energy from a crystal than from people. And the more contact he has with that crystal—*

"The worse he'll get," Rob said aloud. "The more like Sabrina and those other poor jerks."

"We've got to stop *that,*" Lewis said, startled.

Rob looked at him, and then smiled. It was just the ghost of his normal grin, but it warmed Kaitlyn immeasurably.

"You're right," he said. "We've got to stop it."

"My parents may be able to help," Anna said. "I'm sure they've been trying."

LeShan said, "I'll arrange your transportation."

That was all he said, but his lynx eyes flashed at Kaitlyn. She had the impression that he was desperately proud of them.

"Wait, there's one more thing," she said anxiously. "I wanted to ask you before, but I never got the chance. There's this girl back in California. Mr. Zetes put her into a coma somehow—with drugs, we think. I told her brother that we'd ask you for help, but . . ."

Her voice trailed off. She could feel Rob's concern regarding Marisol, and his chagrin over forgetting—but LeShan's face was impassive.

*Of course they won't be able to help,* she thought. *They're not doctors. I was stupid for even asking . . .*

She didn't want to imagine Marisol's brother's face when she told him.

LeShan was nonchalant. "The perfect crystals had the virtue of curing most diseases," he said. "Even a shard ought to do something to help your friend."

Kaitlyn's breath came out in a rush. She hadn't even realized she was holding it, but suddenly her heart was lighter.

LeShan was walking away, but he glanced back over his shoulder and grinned.

"So it's just us again," Lewis said. They were waiting for LeShan to bring them a guide through the forest. Kaitlyn was carrying her duffel bag, which held her clothes—all dirty by now—and her art kit. She had the crystal shard in her other hand.

"We're the only ones we have to rely on," Kaitlyn agreed.

Anna said, "That's all anybody ever has, really."

"Yeah, but all that driving, all that searching," Lewis said. "All for nothing."

Rob looked at him quickly. "It *wasn't* for nothing. We're stronger now. We know more. And we finally have a weapon."

"Right," Anna said. "We set out to find this place and we did. We wanted to find a way to stop Mr. Z and we have."

"Sure. It's all over but the screaming," Lewis said, but he smiled.

Kaitlyn looked back at the white house, now looted and empty. She was wondering if she *could* have stayed if things had been different. If Gabriel hadn't betrayed them, if the Fellowship were staying, could she have made her home here? Would it have been a place where she could have belonged?

"If we can destroy the crystal, we can cure Gabriel, too," Rob was saying.

Kaitlyn looked at him fondly. No, she thought. I don't belong with the Fellowship. I belong with Rob—and Lewis, and Anna, and Gabriel, too. Wherever they are, I'm home.

"Right," she said to Rob. "So let's go do it. The search is on again."

She looked down at the shard. As a ray of sun broke through the clouds, it flashed like diamond.

# THE PASSION

*For Pat McDonald, editor extraordinaire,*
*whose keen insight helped shape my visions, and whose*
*boundless patience allowed me to perfect them*

# CHAPTER 1

A dog barked, shattering the midnight silence. Gabriel glanced up briefly, his psychic senses alert. Then he went back to breaking into the house.

In a moment, the lock on the door gave way to his lock-pick. The door swung open.

Gabriel smiled.

There were four people awake in the house. One of them Kaitlyn. Beautiful Kaitlyn with the red-gold hair. A pity he might have to destroy her—but he was her enemy from now on. He couldn't afford weakness.

He was working for Mr. Zetes now. And Mr. Zetes needed something—a shard from the last perfect crystal in the world. Kaitlyn had it . . . Gabriel was going to take it.

As simple as that.

If anyone tried to stop him, he was going to have to hurt them. Even Kaitlyn.

For just an instant there was a tightening in his chest. Then his face hardened and he moved stealthily into the dark house.

"Give up, Kaitlyn."

Kaitlyn looked into Gabriel's dark gray eyes.

"How did you get *in* here?" she said.

Gabriel smiled silkily. "Breaking and entering is one of my new talents."

"This is Marisol's house," Rob said from behind him. "You can't just—"

"But I *have* just. Don't expect help; I've put everybody outside to sleep. I'm here, and I think you know why."

They all stared at him: Kaitlyn and Rob and Lewis and Anna. They were refugees, runaways from the Zetes Institute for Psychic Research, and Marisol's family had taken them in. Marisol herself was absent; once a research assistant at the Institute, she'd found out too much and ended up in a coma. But her family had been kind—and now Kaitlyn had brought more trouble on them.

It was past midnight. The four of them had been sitting up in the room Marisol's brother had assigned the girls, talking and trying to figure out what to do next. And then the door had opened to reveal Gabriel.

Kaitlyn, who was standing directly in front of the handsome mahogany desk by Marisol's bed, made her face utterly blank. She tried to make her mind blank, too.

Anna and Lewis, who were sitting on the bed, were looking just as blank, and Rob's mind was just one wash of golden
light. Nothing for Gabriel to grab onto.

It didn't matter. He looked past Kaitlyn, at the desk, and
his smile was dazzling and dangerous.

"Give up," he said again. "I want it, and I'm going to get it."

"We don't know what you're talking about," Rob said flatly,
taking a step toward him.

Gabriel answered without turning to look at Rob. He was
still smiling but his eyes were dark. "A shard of the last perfect crystal," he said. "Do you want to play hot and cold—or
should I just take it?" He looked at the desk again.

"*If* we did have it, we wouldn't be giving it to you," Rob
said. "We'd use it to destroy your boss—he is your boss now,
isn't he?"

Gabriel's smile froze. His eyes narrowed slightly, and Kaitlyn could see darkness filling them. But his voice was calm
and easygoing. "Sure, he's my boss. And you'd better stay away
from him or you're going to get hurt."

Kaitlyn could feel a stinging behind her eyes. She didn't
believe this was happening, she *didn't*. Gabriel was standing
here like a stranger, warning them away from Mr. Zetes. From
*Mr. Zetes,* the man who'd tried to make them into psychic
weapons to sell to the highest bidder, who'd tried to kill them
when they rebelled. Who'd hounded them all the way up to
Canada when they ran away from him, and who was clearly

still after them now that they'd returned to fight him. They'd hoped Marisol's house would be a safe place to hide from him—but they'd been wrong.

"How *can* you, Gabriel?" Anna said in her low, clear voice, and Kaitlyn knew she was feeling the same thing. Anna Eva Whiteraven's face—usually serene between its dark braids of hair—was now clouded. "How can you join him? After everything he's done—"

"—and everything he's going to do," Lewis put in. Lewis Chao was normally as cheerful as Anna was serene, but now his almond-shaped eyes were bleak.

"He's bad, Gabriel; he's bad, and you know it," Rob said, closing in from behind. Rob Kessler wasn't built for menace either, but just now with his tousled blond hair and blazing golden eyes he looked like an avenging angel.

"And he'll turn on *you* in the end," Kaitlyn said, adding her voice to the chorus against Gabriel. In her mind she added herself to the group: Kaitlyn Fairchild, not as gentle as Anna and Lewis or as good as Rob, a girl with fiery hair and a temper. And eyes that people called witchy, smoky blue with darker blue rings in them. Right now, Kait fixed these eyes mercilessly on Gabriel, staring him down.

Gabriel Wolfe threw back his head and laughed.

As always, it almost took Kaitlyn's breath away. Gabriel was so handsome it was frightening. His pale skin made his dark hair look even darker, like the silky pelt of some animal—

like his namesake. A wolf, a predator in his bones, who enjoyed stalking and toying with his prey.

*Of course he's bad,* Gabriel said. Kaitlyn heard the words in her head, rather than with her ears, and the tone was amused and mocking. *I'm bad, too—or hadn't you noticed?*

Tiny needles of pain jabbed into Kaitlyn's temples.

She managed not to gasp, but she could sense Anna's alarm, and Lewis's and Rob's.

Gabriel had gotten stronger.

Kaitlyn could feel it through the psychic web that connected the five of them, the web that Gabriel had created. The web that would link them until one of the five died. They were all psychics: Rob was a healer and Kaitlyn saw the future, Lewis was psychokinetic and Anna controlled animals—but Gabriel was a telepath. He fused minds. He'd fused *their* minds, the five of them, by accident, and now they were like the arms of a starfish: separate but part of one being.

Gabriel's power had always been strongest, but now it rocked Kaitlyn with its force. His mental voice had been amused, yes—but it had also been like a white-hot poker burning the words directly into her brain.

By contrast, Lewis's thought sounded weak and distant. *I'm scared.*

Kaitlyn glanced at him quickly and saw that he hadn't meant it to be heard. That was the problem with telepathy, with the web that connected them, held them close. It held them *too* close, sometimes, throwing their private thoughts into the public forum. Leaving them totally exposed, naked to one another. Unable to hide anything.

Realization flashed through her, and she looked back at Gabriel.

"That's it, isn't it?" she said. "Why you left. It was too much for you, being so close. It was too intimate—"

"No."

"Gabriel, we all feel the same way," Anna said, picking up on Kaitlyn's theme. "We'd all like some privacy. But we're your friends—"

Gabriel's smile was savage. "I don't need friends."

"Well, you've got them, boy," Rob said softly. He moved in another step and his hand closed on Gabriel's shoulder. With a gesture that made it look easy, he turned Gabriel around.

Kaitlyn could feel Gabriel's startled outrage in the web. Rob ignored it, speaking quietly and seriously, looking Gabriel straight in the face. His anger was gone, and so was the usual defensiveness that flared between him and Gabriel, the male rivalry, the jostling for position. Rob was struggling with his pride, his internal honesty conquering it. Forcing himself to be vulnerable with Gabriel.

"We're more than friends," he said. "We're part of each other, all of us. You made us that way. You linked us together to save our lives—and now you're telling us you've defected to the bad guys? That you're our enemy?" He shook his head. "I don't believe it."

"That's because you're an idealistic idiot," Gabriel hissed, his voice as soft as Rob's, but feral and menacing. He didn't try to move out of Rob's grip. "Believe it, country boy—because if you mess with me, you're going to be sorry."

Rob shook his head. He had a look in his eyes that Kaitlyn knew well, and his jaw was at his most stubborn. "You can't fool me, Gabriel. You act like a dumb tough guy but you're not, you're smart. One of the smartest people I've ever met. You could make something of yourself—"

"I *am*—" Gabriel began, but Rob went on, gentle and relentless.

"You act like you don't care about people, but that's not true either. You saved us all from the crystal when Joyce and Mr. Z were trying to kill us with it. You saved us again when they trapped us at the Institute. You helped Kaitlyn save us from that psychic attack in the van."

And then Rob did something that astonished Kaitlyn. He actually *shook* Gabriel. Once again, startled outrage washed through the web, but before Gabriel could say anything Rob was speaking again, fierce and insistent.

"I don't know what you're trying to prove, but it's no good. *It's no good.* You care about us; you can't change that. Why don't you just give in and admit it, Gabriel? Why don't you stop this nonsense right now?"

Kaitlyn's breath was caught in her throat. She didn't *dare* breathe, didn't dare move. Rob was walking on a tightrope above razors and knives. He was insane—but it was working.

Gabriel's body had relaxed slightly, some of the predator-tension draining out of it. And though Kaitlyn couldn't see his eyes, she guessed that they were lightening, a warm gray instead of cold. His presence in the web was warming, too; Kaitlyn no longer got images of stalactites and glaciers. Under the burning heat of Rob's golden eyes, Gabriel's icebergs were cracking up.

"We all care about you," Rob said, never letting up the intensity. "And your place is right here. Come back to us and help us get rid of Mr. Z, okay? Okay, Gabriel?"

And then he made his mistake.

He'd been speaking vehemently, throwing his words into Gabriel's face, and Gabriel had been listening as if he couldn't help it. Almost as if he were hypnotized. But now Rob switched to nonverbal communication to punch his message directly into Gabriel's mind. Kaitlyn knew why he did it—telepathy was forceful and intimate. Too intimate. Her cry of warning was lost as Gabriel snapped.

*Come back,* Rob was saying. *Come back, Gabriel—okay?*

Kaitlyn felt fury building in Gabriel like a tsunami. *Rob,* she thought. *Rob, don't—*

*Leave me ALONE!*

The mental shout was like a physical blow. Literally. It

threw Rob backward, body spasming in total reflex as the signals from his own brain scrambled. He fell with every muscle contracted, his face twisted, his fingers clawed. Kaitlyn felt a spasm of sheer terror on his behalf. She wanted to run to him, but she couldn't. Gabriel was between them and her legs wouldn't move. Anna and Lewis stood frozen as well.

*I don't need any of you,* Gabriel said, still with enough force to numb Kaitlyn's mind. *You're wrong about me. I'm no part of you. You can't even imagine what I am, what I've become.*

"I can," Kaitlyn gasped. She was thinking of what Mr. Zetes's crystal had done to him, what it had made him. A psychic vampire, who needed to drain life energy from others to live himself. She could feel the ghost of teeth in her spine, just at the base of the neck. As if a single sharp tooth were piercing the skin there.

The memory brought a certain fear, but no revulsion. And anxious as she was to get to Rob and help him, she wanted to help Gabriel, too.

"It's not your fault, Gabriel," she whispered. "You think you're evil because of what you can do with your mind, because of what the crystal made you do. But it's not your fault. You didn't ask for it. And you're not evil."

"That's where you're wrong." Gabriel had turned to face her, and she saw that he was calmer. But the ice was back in his eyes, the cold, lucid madness that was more terrifying than any rage. When he smiled, goose-flesh broke out on Kait's arms.

"I've known what I am for a long time," he said conversationally. "The crystal didn't change me, it just enhanced my abilities. And it made me accept myself." His smile widened, and Kaitlyn had a primal instinct to run. "If you've got the darkness in your nature, you might as well enjoy it. Might as well go where you belong."

"To Mr. Zetes," Anna whispered, her lovely, high-cheekboned face drawn with disgust.

Gabriel shrugged. "He has a vision. He thinks psychics like me have a place in the world—on top. I'm superior to the rest of the lousy race, I'm smarter, stronger, *better*. I deserve to *rule*. And I'm not going to let any of you stop me."

Kaitlyn shook her head, struggling with words. "Gabriel—I don't believe that. You're *not*—"

"I *am*. And if you try to keep me from getting that shard, I'm going to prove it to you."

He was looking at the desk again. Kaitlyn drew herself up a little. Rob was still lying helpless on the floor, Lewis and Anna seemed frozen. There was nobody but her to stop him.

"You can't have it," she said.

"Get out of the way."

"I said, you can't have it." To her amazement, her voice was fairly steady.

He moved closer to her, his gray eyes filling her field of vision, filling the world. *Don't make me do it, Kaitlyn. I'm not your friend anymore. I'm your hunter. Go home and stay away from Mr. Z and you won't get hurt.*

Kaitlyn looked into his handsome pale face. *If you want the shard, you'll have to take it by force.*

"Whatever you say," Gabriel murmured. His eyes were the color of a spiderweb. Kaitlyn felt the touch of his mind like a searing caress and then the world exploded in pain.

# CHAPTER 2

"Kaitlyn!"

Dimly Kait heard Rob's shout, felt him struggling to get to his feet. Then, when he couldn't, beginning to crawl. She could barely sense him for the overwhelming pain in her head.

Anna and Lewis were closer and she could hear them shouting, too.

"Let go of her!"

"What are you doing to her?"

Gabriel brushed them away and kept on doing it. The pain increased—like fire. Kaitlyn had only one memory that would compare to it: being connected to the crystal. The big crystal, the impure one, the one Mr. Zetes used for enhancing psychic powers—and for torture.

Waves of red-streaked agony that peaked very quickly and died away just as another wave was coming. Kaitlyn's own muscle tension held her rigid, standing motionless under it. Kept her from getting away, kept her from screaming. It wasn't heroism. She didn't have the air.

*Stop it, damn you! Stop it!*

Rob had gotten to her, somehow. His hands were on her, and golden healing energy flooded up to combat the red-streaked anguish. His powers were protecting her.

"Leave her alone," Rob said hoarsely, and pulled Kaitlyn away from Gabriel, toward the bed.

Gabriel regarded the cleared path in front of him thought-fully. "That was all I wanted," he murmured.

He opened the middle drawer of the mahogany desk and took out the crystal shard.

Kaitlyn was gasping for breath. Rob put her down on the bed, one arm still around her protectively. Kait could sense his trembling anger, and the shocked fury of Lewis and Anna—and she was surprised to find that she herself felt very little resentment toward Gabriel. There had been a look in his eyes just before he blasted her—as if he'd had to turn himself off to do it. To squelch his own emotions.

Now he turned to face them, and the shard flashed in the bright light of Marisol's halogen lamp. It was the size and shape of a small unicorn's horn, a foot long, multifaceted. It glittered not like crystal, but like diamond.

"It's not yours," Anna said in a low voice. She and Lewis had flanked Rob and Kaitlyn, the four of them presenting a united front to Gabriel. "The Fellowship gave it to Kait."

"The Fellowship," Gabriel sneered. "Those gutless do-gooders. If I'd lived in the old days, I'd have joined a Dark Lodge and hunted them out of existence."

Not gutless, Kaitlyn thought. Gabriel's words brought the faces of the Fellowship to her mind: Timon, frail but wise; Mereniang, cool and discerning; LeShan, lynx-eyed and impatient. They were the last survivors of an ancient race, the race that had used the crystals. They didn't interfere with the affairs of humanity—but they'd made an exception for Kaitlyn's group. They'd given up their own power to give Kaitlyn a weapon against Mr. Zetes.

"And now Mr. Z is forming a Dark Lodge of his own," she said, looking at Gabriel steadily.

"You could call it that. A psychic strike team. And *I'm* going to lead it," Gabriel said negligently, stroking the crystal. That was dangerous, as Kait could have told him. One of the facets cut his finger and he frowned at the drop of blood absently. He seemed to feel no danger from the others; he didn't even bother to look at them.

"This would have been useless to you anyway," he said. "You were planning to take it to the crystal, right? Put them together and set up a resonance that would shatter both."

Kaitlyn didn't know *what* the scientific theory was. LeShan had told them that this shard would destroy Mr. Z's crystal, that was all. She watched a drop of Gabriel's blood fall onto the hardwood floor.

"But to do that, you'd have to get to the crystal," Gabriel continued. "And you can't. The old man has it under a combination lock—and PK won't help with that, will it, Lewis? Eight random numbers to guess?"

He sounded almost jolly—and he was right, Kaitlyn knew. Lewis could move objects with his mind using psychokinesis, but that wouldn't help him figure out a combination.

Lewis had flushed slightly, but he didn't answer Gabriel's question. Instead he said, "Is Lydia still in this with you?"

"Your little sweetheart?" Gabriel grinned nastily. "Better give up on her, too. She's back under her father's thumb. She never liked you, anyway."

Pity, Kaitlyn thought. Lydia Zetes was a spy and a traitor, sent by her father to snoop on them as they traveled to Canada to find the Fellowship—but Kaitlyn felt vaguely sorry for her. Being under Mr. Z's thumb was a fate she wouldn't wish on anybody.

"It's like I told Kaitlyn," Gabriel said calmly. "You might as well all go home. You can't get at the crystal. The police wouldn't believe you—the old man has them taken care of. He's taking care of the ones Anna's parents contacted, too, by the way. And the Fellowship can't even help themselves. So there's really no point in you staying. Why don't you go home before I have to hurt you again?"

Rob had been silent so far—too angry with Gabriel to find words. Now he found them, standing up to face Gabriel directly once again. Kaitlyn didn't need the web to sense his rage—it was written in every line of his body, in the burning of his golden eyes.

"You're a traitor," he told Gabriel simply. "And if you won't join us, we'll fight you. With everything we've got."

His voice was quiet, but it shook. Not just rage, Kaitlyn thought suddenly. Rob was *hurt*—he felt personally betrayed. He hadn't believed Gabriel would hurt Kait—and Gabriel had proved him wrong. It had become a battle between them, Rob and Gabriel, the two in the group who had always fought most fiercely together, felt the most antagonism for each other, taken the positions farthest apart.

And who knew how to push each other's buttons. Rob was going on, his voice not quiet now but rushed and reckless.

"You know what I think? I think Kait was wrong—it's not the web you can't stand. It's not the intimacy. It's the *freedom*. Having to make your own choices, be responsible for yourself. That's what you can't take. You'd rather be a slave to the crystal than deal with freedom."

Gabriel lowered the shard, his eyes darkening. Kaitlyn grabbed for Rob's arm, but he seemed oblivious to her.

"I'm right, aren't I?" Rob said, with a short, strange laugh, as if delighted to have hurt Gabriel. It was so vicious and contemptuous it didn't sound like Rob. "Mr. Z tells you what to do—and you *like* that. It's what you're used to, after all those years locked up in CHAD. Hell, you probably *miss* being in jail—"

Gabriel went white and hit him.

Not mentally—Kaitlyn had the impression that he was too angry for that. He hit with his fist, catching Rob square in the mouth. Rob's head jerked back and he went down.

With the fluid, easy movements of a predator, Gabriel reached for him again. Kaitlyn found herself on her feet and between them.

*"No!"* She fumbled for Gabriel, meaning to restrain him or at least hinder him—and somehow found herself grabbing the crystal. It was cold and hard. She held onto it and Gabriel, still trying to get to Rob, let go.

Lewis and Anna were around Gabriel now, seizing any part of him they could reach and clinging. Kaitlyn managed to detach herself from the group and back away, clutching the crystal to her chest. Gabriel didn't seem to care; his eyes were fixed on Rob.

Who was scrambling up, wiping blood from his mouth with the back of his hand. He looked savagely triumphant at having gotten Gabriel to lose control. Kaitlyn realized he wasn't thinking anymore, just feeling. He was lost in his hurt and betrayal and anger, lashing out in a way she'd never seen before.

God, we've changed, she thought, sick with dismay. We've all changed from being in such close contact with one another. Rob used to be so pure and now he's furious . . . just like a regular human being, her mind added, unasked.

And he's *wrong*—and I've got to stop this. Before the two of them actually kill each other.

"Come on," Rob was saying. "D'you have the guts to go one on one with me? No hocus-pocus, just our fists. You man enough for that, boy?"

Gabriel pulled off his jacket, despite the efforts of Anna and Lewis to keep him still. Strapped to his forearm was a knife in some kind of spring-loaded mechanism.

Oh, *great*, Kaitlyn thought. She held on to the crystal shard more tightly. She knew she should get it to safety—but where *was* safety? Gabriel could follow anywhere she went; could take the knowledge of where it was hidden out of her mind. And besides, she couldn't leave and let Gabriel and Rob fight.

She decided to gamble.

"Here's the crystal, Gabriel," she said. "I've got it—and the only way you're going to get it is the way you did before." *But I'm hoping you won't,* she added mentally. *You said yourself that it's not going to do us any good. We can't get to Mr. Z's crystal—so what difference does it make? Why not just go back and tell him you couldn't find it?*

She was trying to give him a way out. If he didn't *really* want to hurt them . . .

Gabriel hesitated. His mouth was tight; his eyes hard. But she could see uncertainty in his face. He stood very still a moment, then, abruptly, he started toward her.

Kaitlyn's mind blanked out in fear and surprise. Behind her, the door opened.

"Hey, are you guys still up—?" The sleepy voice broke off.

It was Tony, Marisol's brother, wearing cutoff shorts as pajama bottoms. He was rubbing his eyes and frowning. Clearly whatever Gabriel had done to keep the Diaz family asleep had worn off.

"Who's that?" Tony demanded, staring at Gabriel. Then he blinked and the frown disappeared.

"Hey, it's you. I remember you from last time. Come back to get the *brujo*, huh?"

He seemed happier to see Gabriel than he had been to see the rest of them, Kait thought. Maybe because Gabriel was somebody he could relate to—another tough guy. Or maybe because he thought that of all of them, Gabriel was most likely to be able to get Mr. Zetes. Tony hated Mr. Z with a passion; called him "El Diablo" or "El Gato"—both names for the devil, and longed for him to be sent *abajo*—down below to hell—where he belonged.

The five who shared the web were all frozen by the presence of a stranger, like figures in a tableau. Tony went on talking cheerfully; he didn't seem to feel the tension in the room or see the blood on Rob's chin.

"I see you got the *cuchillo*—the magic knife for Marisol. I couldn't believe it when they told me. A real old-fashioned charm, right? After all those doctors said she'd never wake up— we'll show 'em!" He grinned, his usually sullen features almost glowing. He did everything but slap Gabriel on the back.

Kaitlyn looked at Gabriel sharply, saw what she'd suspected—

that he hadn't known the shard could cure Marisol. Maybe she should have told him, but she hadn't liked the idea of giving Mr. Z any further information. He'd find a way of using it against them somehow.

For now, though, it had given Gabriel pause. He seemed thrown off balance by Tony's gratitude and good humor. Embarrassed.

"Well, Gabriel certainly helped us to get the shard," Kait said—and that was true enough. If Gabriel hadn't defected, the Fellowship's crystal wouldn't have been reduced to shards in the first place. "And he would want Marisol to get well."

Rob was quietly wiping his bloody mouth again. He'd backed off when Tony came in, and Kaitlyn could feel through the web that he was calming down. Gabriel looked at him, then at Kaitlyn, and finally at Tony.

"We'll have a big party when all this is over," Tony said. "A real blowout. I've got some friends in a garage band. As soon as Marisol is better." He ran a hand through his curly mahogany hair.

Kaitlyn pressed the crystal to her chest and looked at Gabriel.

He held her gaze a minute with eyes as dark and unfathomable as storm clouds. For the first time that night she consciously noticed the scar on his forehead—a crescent-shaped mark left by his encounter with Mr. Z's crystal. Right now it seemed to stand out against the pale skin.

Then, looking suddenly tired, Gabriel shrugged. His eyelids drooped, hooding those depthless eyes.

"I've got to go," he said.

"You can stay," Tony offered immediately. "There's plenty of room."

"No, I can't. But I'll be back." He said the last to Kaitlyn and Rob, with heavy emphasis. Kait couldn't mistake his meaning. "I'll be back—soon."

He picked up his jacket and walked out the door. Kaitlyn felt her breath come out in a rush. She found she was holding the crystal so hard it hurt.

Tony yawned. "So, are you guys coming to bed? I put sleeping bags on the floor."

"Just give us a minute," Rob said. "We have to talk something over."

Tony left. Rob shut the door after him, then turned to face the others.

He isn't as calm as I thought, Kaitlyn realized. Rob's jaw was set, his skin pale under its tan.

"Now," Rob said. "What to do."

Kaitlyn shifted. "He did go away," she pointed out. "Without the crystal."

Rob angled a sharp glance at her. "Are you defending him?"

"No. But—"

"Good. Because it doesn't matter if he went away. He'll be back. You heard him."

Anna opened her mouth, then shut it and sighed. She put a hand to her forehead. Her usual serenity was in tatters, but she seemed to be regaining it, gathering it around her like a cloak. "Rob's right, Kaitlyn," she said slowly. "Gabriel did say that—and he *meant* it."

Kaitlyn lowered her arms and looked at the crystal. It was heavy and cold, and on one facet was a pinkish smear. Gabriel's blood. "But what can we *do?*" she said.

"That's what I want to know." Lewis's round, open face was tense. "What can we do against him? He knows where we are—"

"We'll have to get out," Rob said. "That's obvious. And another thing that's obvious—Gabriel's our enemy now. I meant it when I said we'd fight him. We've got to do whatever's necessary from now on."

Kaitlyn felt very cold.

Lewis was sober. "Geez," he breathed. Then he said, "I guess if we have to stop him, we will."

"Not just that. If we have to hunt him, we will, too. We may have to destroy Mr. Zetes—and that may include Gabriel. If it does, it does. We'll do whatever it takes," Rob said. "We don't have any choice."

Lewis looked even less happy, but he nodded slowly, scratching his nose. Frightened, Kaitlyn turned to Anna.

Anna's lovely face was set. "I agree," she said quietly. "Although I hope he'll come to his senses and it won't be necessary—for now he's our enemy. We have to treat him that way." Her dark eyes were sad but stern. Kaitlyn understood—Anna's nature was peaceful, but she had the pragmatism of Nature itself. Sometimes hard choices had to be made, sometimes even sacrifices.

They were all in agreement, all united against Gabriel. And they were looking at Kaitlyn.

That was when Kaitlyn realized what she had to do.

It came to her in a dazzling burst of inspiration, almost like one of her pictures. A crazy plan, completely insane—but she had to do *something*. She couldn't let Rob destroy Gabriel—not only for Gabriel's sake, but for Rob's. If he succeeded, he would be changed forever.

The first item in her plan was not to let anyone know she was planning it.

So she composed her face and did her best to veil her thoughts. It wasn't easy to hide things from mind-mates, but she'd gotten a lot of practice in the past week or so. Looking as resigned and grim as possible, she said, "I agree, too."

She was worried that they might be suspicious—but she was with three of the most unsuspicious people in the world. Rob nodded, looking genuinely grim and resigned himself, Anna shook her head sadly, and Lewis sighed.

"We'll hope for the best," Rob said. "Meanwhile, I guess we should get some sleep. We'll have to get up early and get moving."

Which means I don't have much time, Kaitlyn thought, and then she tried to smoke-veil that, too. "It's a good idea," she said, going over to the desk and putting the crystal shard back in.

Lewis said good night and left, chewing one thumbnail and looking wistful. About Gabriel? Kaitlyn wondered. Or Lydia? Anna departed for the bathroom and Kait and Rob were left alone.

"I'm sorry about all this," Rob said. "And especially sorry he hurt you. That was—unspeakable." His eyes were dark, dark gold.

"It doesn't matter." Kaitlyn was still cold—and drawn to Rob's warmth like a moth to a flame. Especially now, when there might be no tomorrow . . . but he couldn't know that. She reached for him and he took her in his arms.

Their first kiss was a little desperate, on both sides. Then Rob calmed down, and his tranquility spread to Kait. Oh, nice. Warm tingles, warm golden haze.

It was harder now to cloak her thoughts from him. But she had to, he couldn't suspect that they were going to be separated for the first time since they'd met. Kaitlyn clung to him and concentrated on thinking about how much she loved him. How she wanted to engrave him on her memory . . .

"Kait, are you all right?" he whispered. He held her face between his hands, searching her eyes.

"Yes. I just—want to be close." She couldn't get close enough.

You've changed me, she thought. Not just showing me that boys aren't all pond scum. You've made me different, made me look at the broader picture. Given me vision.

Oh, Rob, I love you.

"I love you, Kait," he whispered back.

And *that* meant it was time to stop. She was losing her control; he was reading her thoughts. Reluctantly Kaitlyn pulled back.

"You said it yourself. We're going to need our sleep," she told him.

He hesitated, grimacing. Then nodded, yielding. "See you tomorrow."

"Sleep well, Rob."

You're so good, Rob, she thought as the door closed behind him. And so protective of me. You wouldn't let me do it. . . .

There was a map of Oakland on the desk; they'd bought it to find their way back to Marisol's house. She put it in her duffel bag with the rest of her worldly possessions—a change of clothes bought with the Fellowship's money and her art kit—and pulled a pair of underwear over it. Maybe there was a way to leave the bag in the bathroom . . . yes, and she could wear a nightgown over her clothing. . . .

"Need something?" Anna's voice said from behind her. Guilt stricken, Kaitlyn froze in place.

# CHAPTER 3

**B**lank your mind! Kaitlyn told herself.

She'd been caught red-handed, thinking about things that would *make* Anna suspicious—if Anna had been listening. And everything tonight depended on Anna not suspecting.

"Just trying to figure out what to wear tomorrow," Kait said lightly, giving the bag a final rummage-through. "Not that I have much choice; I'm beginning to feel like Thoreau."

"With his one old suit?" Anna laughed, and Kaitlyn felt the knot in her stomach ease. "Well, I'm sure Marisol would lend you something if she knew what an emergency it was. Why don't you look in the closet?" Anna was going to the closet herself as she spoke. "Whew! This girl liked clothes. I bet we can both find something to fit."

I love you, Kaitlyn thought, as Anna pulled out a long slim

cotton-knit dress and said, "This looks like you, Kait." I love you and Lewis almost as much as I do Rob. You're all so *decent*—and that's why he's going to beat you if you're not careful.

She forced her mind away from that and looked around the room. Marisol's room was like Marisol herself—an unpredictable mixture. Neat with messy, old with new. Like the big mahogany desk, with its silky-ruddy finish scratched and stained, as if it had been given by a loving grandmother to a careless teenager who used it for mixing perfume and storing a CD player. Or the leather miniskirt peeping out of a hamper just below the picture of the Virgin Mary.

A pair of expensive sunglasses were lying half under the bed's dust ruffle. Kait picked them up and absently twisted one gold earpiece back into shape.

"How about this?" Anna was saying, and Kait whistled. It was a very sexy, very feminine dress: spandex bodice fitting to just below the hips then flaring to a sheer chiffon skirt. Tiny gold clasps held the cap sleeves. A *radical* dress, black, that would make the wearer look slim as a statue.

"For you?" Kait said.

"No, you, dummy. It would make the boys swallow their tongues." Anna started to put the dress back. "Come to think of it, you don't need any more boy trouble. You've got two panting after you already."

"This kind of dress might get a girl *out* of trouble," Kait said hastily, taking the hanger. Spandex and chiffon wouldn't wrinkle, and she would need all the weapons she could gather if her plan went through. An outfit like this might make Gabriel sit up and take notice, and seducing Gabriel was item number one on her date book.

She folded the dress small and put it in her duffel bag. Anna chuckled, shaking her head.

Is this really me doing this? Kait wondered. Kaitlyn Brady Fairchild, who used to think Levi's jeans were high fashion? But if she was going to be Mata Hari, she might as well do it thoroughly.

What she said was, "Anna? Do you think about boys?"

"Hmm?" Anna was peering into the closet.

"I mean, you seem so *wise* about them. You always seem to know what they'll do. But you don't seem to go after them."

Anna laughed. "Well, we've been pretty busy lately with other things."

Kaitlyn looked at her curiously. "Have you ever had one you really liked?"

There was the barest instant of hesitation before Anna answered. She was looking at another dress, fingering some sequins that were coming off. Then smiled and shrugged. "Yeah, I guess I found somebody worth caring for once."

"What happened?"

"Well—not much."

Kaitlyn, still watching curiously, realized with surprise that Anna's thoughts were veiled. It was like seeing lights behind a paper wall—she could sense color but not shape. Is that what my veiling looks like? she wondered, and barely had the wits to ask, "Why not?"

"Oh—it would never have worked out. He was together with somebody already. My best friend."

"Really?" Thoughts of veiling had led to thoughts of *what* she was veiling, and Kaitlyn was by now utterly distracted. She hardly knew what she was saying, much less what Anna was. "You should have gone for it. I'll bet you could have *taken* him. With your looks . . ."

Anna grinned ruefully and shook her head. "I would never do that. It would be wrong." She put the sequinned dress back in the closet. "Now, bed," she said firmly.

"Um." Kaitlyn was still distracted. Thinking: I'm casual, I'm calm, I'm confident. She hurried to the bathroom and came back with her clothes still on under the billowing flannel nightgown she'd gotten at Anna's house.

She'd acquired it on the trip *up* to Canada, because they hadn't stopped by Anna's home in Puget Sound on the way back down. They'd accepted money and a 1956 Chevy Bel Air from the Fellowship and taken Route 101 all the way down the coast, driving all day for three days, avoiding Anna's parents. Avoiding *any* parents—they hadn't contacted Lewis's in San Francisco or Rob's in North Carolina or Kaitlyn's father in Ohio. They'd agreed on this early as a necessity; parents would only get worried and angry and would never, never agree to their kids doing what had to be done.

But from what Gabriel had said, Anna's parents had gone to the police anyway. They'd had proof of what Mr. Z was up to—files Rob had stolen from the Institute, detailing Mr. Z's experiments with his first group of students . . . but obviously even proof wasn't enough. Mr. Z had the police sewn up.

No one from the outside could take him down.

Kaitlyn sighed and pulled the covers more tightly over herself. She was focused on Anna, lying beside her in Marisol's bed; listening to Anna's breathing, monitoring Anna's presence in the web.

When she was certain Anna was asleep, she quietly slipped out from under the covers.

*I'm going out to see Rob,* she projected, not loud enough to wake the other girl, but loud enough, she hoped, to wiggle into Anna's subconscious. That way, if Anna noticed her missing in the next few hours, she might assume Kaitlyn was in the living room and not worry.

Kait tiptoed to the bathroom, where she'd managed to leave her duffel bag. She stripped off the flannel nightgown and crammed it on top of the black dress and Marisol's designer sunglasses. Then she crept down the hallway and noiselessly let herself out the back door.

There was no moon, but the stars were frosty-pale in the night sky. Oakland was too big a city for them to make much of a show, and for a moment Kaitlyn felt a pang of homesickness.

Out by Piqua Road in Thoroughfare, the sky would be pitch-black, huge, and serene.

No time to think about that. Keep moving and find a phone booth, girl.

Back in Thoroughfare, she would have been terrified of walking around a strange city at night—not to mention daunted by the task of trying to get to *another* strange city, at least thirty or forty miles away. But she was a different Kaitlyn than she'd been back in Thoroughfare. She'd dealt with things then *that* Kaitlyn had never dreamed of, she'd traveled all the way to Canada without any adult to help, and she'd learned to rely on her own resources. Now she had no choice. She couldn't wait until morning—she'd never get away from the others in the daytime. She didn't have money for a cab. Still, there must be a way to get across the bay to San Carlos; she just had to find it.

With an almost frightening coolheadedness, she set out to find the way.

This wasn't a bad area of town, and she found a phone booth with an undamaged phone book. She looked up Public Transportation in the local area pages—thank heaven, it said that most of the buses ran twenty-four hours a day. She could even see the basic route she'd have to take: up to San Francisco to get across the water, then south down to San Carlos.

But now, how to *find* a bus that was running at this hour? Well, first thing was to find the bus line. Wincing a little, she tore the AC Transit map out of the phone book—a rotten thing to do, but this was an emergency. Using that and the map of Oakland she navigated her way to MacArthur Street, where the map showed the "N" bus running all night.

Once there, she heaved a sigh of relief. A twenty-four-hour gas station at the corner of MacArthur and Seventy-third. The attendant told her that the bus ran hourly, and the next one would come at 3:07. He seemed nice, a college age boy with shiny black skin and a flattop, and Kaitlyn hung around his booth until she saw the bus approaching.

The bus driver was nice, too, and let her sit behind him. He was a fat man with an endless supply of ham sandwiches wrapped in greasy paper, which he took from a bag under his seat. He offered Kait one; she accepted politely but didn't eat it, just looked out the window at the dark buildings and yellowish streetlights.

This was *really* an adventure. Going to Canada, she'd been with the others. But now she was alone and out of mind-shot—she could scream mentally and none of them would hear. As they approached the Bay Bridge, its swooping girders lit up like Christmas, Kaitlyn felt a thrill of joy in life. She clutched her duffel bag with both hands, sitting up very straight on her seat.

When they got to the terminal where she'd have to change buses, the driver scratched under his chins. "What you want now is the San Mateo line, okay? You go across the street and wait for the Seven B—it'll be along in about an hour. They keep the terminal closed because of homeless people, so you got to wait outside." He closed the bus door, shouting, "Good luck, sweetie."

Kaitlyn gulped and crossed the street.

I'm not afraid of homeless people, she told herself. I *was* a homeless person; I slept in a vacant lot, and in a van on the beach, and . . .

But when a man with a plaid jacket over his head came toward her pushing a shopping cart, she felt her heart begin to pound.

He was coming closer and closer. She couldn't see what was in the cart; it was covered with newspapers. She couldn't see his *face* either, she only thought it was a man because of the husky build.

He kept coming, slowly. Why slowly? So he could check her out? Kaitlyn's heart was going faster and faster, and her joy in life had disappeared. She'd been stupid, stupid to go wandering around at night by herself. If she'd only stayed in her nice safe bed . . .

The figure under the plaid jacket was almost on her now. And there was no place to run. She was on a deserted street in a dangerous city and she couldn't even see a phone booth. The only thing she could think of to do was sit up straight and pretend she didn't even see him. Act as if she weren't afraid.

He was right in front of her now. For an instant a streetlight shone into the hood of his jacket, and Kaitlyn saw his face.

An old man, with grizzled hair and gentle features. He looked a little baffled and his lips moved as he walked—as he *shuffled*. That was why he was going so slowly, because he was old.

Or, Kaitlyn thought suddenly, maybe because he's weak or hungry. It would make *me* hungry to push a shopping cart around at four o'clock in the morning.

It was one of those moments when impulse overrode thought. Kaitlyn pulled the ham sandwich out of her duffel bag.

"Want a sandwich?" she said, which was exactly what the bus driver had said to her. "It's Virginia ham."

The old man took the sandwich. His eyes wandered over Kaitlyn for a moment and he gave a smile of astonishing sweetness. Then he shuffled on.

Kaitlyn felt very happy.

She was cold and tired, though, by the time the bus came. It wasn't a nice bus like the "N." It had a lot of graffiti on the outside and split vinyl seats on the inside. There was chewing gum on the floor and it smelled like a bathroom.

But Kaitlyn was too sleepy to care, too sleepy to ask to sit behind the driver. She didn't pay much attention to the tall man in the torn overcoat until he got off the bus with her.

Then she realized he was following her. It was nine or ten

blocks walk to the Institute, and by the third block she was sure. What hadn't happened in the depths of Oakland or the wilds of San Francisco was happening here.

Or . . . he might be okay. Like the man with the shopping cart. But the man of the cart hadn't been following her.

What to do? Knock on somebody's door? This was a residential neighborhood, but all the houses were dark. Run? Kaitlyn was a good runner; she could probably outdistance the man if he wasn't in good shape.

But she couldn't seem to make herself do *anything*. Her legs just kept walking mechanically down Exmoor Street, while shivers ran up her spine at the thought of him behind her. It was as if she were caught in some dream, where the monsters couldn't get her as long as she didn't show she was afraid.

When she turned a corner she glanced back at him. Foxy red hair—she could see that under a streetlight. His clothes were ragged but he looked strong, athletic. Like somebody who could easily overtake a seventeen-year-old girl running.

That was what she saw with her eyes. With her other sense—the one that sometimes showed her the future—she got no picture but a distinct impression. *Bad.* This man was *bad,* dangerous, full of evil thoughts. He wanted to do something bad to *her.*

Everything seemed to go clear and cold. Time stretched and all Kait's instincts were turned to survival. Her brain was whirring furiously, but no matter which way she turned the situation looked the same. Very bad. No inspiration came about to save herself.

And underneath her thoughts ran a sickening litany: I should have known I couldn't get away with this. Wandering around at night on my own . . . I should have *known*.

Think of something, girl. *Think*. If you can't run, you'd better find shelter, fast.

All the houses around her looked asleep, locked-up. She had a horrible certainty that no one would let her in . . . but she had to do *something*. Kait felt a sort of wrenching in her guts—and then she had turned and was heading for the nearest house, taking the single porch step in a jump and landing on the welcome mat. Something inside her cringed from banging on the door, even in this extremity, but she clamped down on the cringe and *did* it. Hollow bangs echoed—not loud enough, to Kait's ears. She saw a doorbell, pushed on it frantically. She kept pounding, using the side of her fist because it hurt less than using her knuckles.

Inside, she could hear only silence. No reaction to her noisy intrusion. No footsteps running to the door.

Oh, God, *answer!* Come here and answer your door, you idiots!

Kaitlyn looked behind her and her heart nearly jumped out of her body.

Because the foxy man was *there;* he was standing on the walkway of the house. Looking at her.

And he was veryveryvery bad. His mind was full of things that Kaitlyn couldn't sense directly, but that when put together sounded like one long scream. He'd done things to other girls—he wanted to do them to her.

No sound from the house. No help. And she was cornered prey here on the porch. Kait made her decision in an instant. She was off the porch and running, running for the Institute, before the man could move a step.

She heard her own pounding footsteps in the street—and pounding feet behind her. Her breath began to sob.

And it was dark and she was *confused*. She didn't know which way the Institute was anymore. Somewhere around here she turned left—but *where?* It was a street that sounded like a flower or plant—but she couldn't read street signs anyway.

That street looked familiar. Kait swerved toward it, trying to get a glimpse of the sign. Ivy Street—was that right? There was no time to debate. She veered down the street, trying to push her legs into going faster . . . and realized almost instantly that it was a mistake.

A cul-de-sac. When she reached the end, she'd be caught.

She glanced behind her. He was there, running, overcoat flapping like the wings of a bird of prey. He was ungainly but very fast.

She wasn't even going to make it to the end of the cul-de-sac. If she ran to a house, he'd grab her as she stood on the porch. If she slowed, he'd tackle her from behind. If she tried to double back, he'd cut her off.

The only thing she could think of to do was stand and fight.

Once again, the feeling of clear coldness swept over her. Right, then. She pulled up short, staggering a little, and whirled. She was standing in the widest part of the cul-de-sac, surrounded by parked cars.

He saw her and stumbled, slowing down, hesitating. Then, at a shambling half-run, he started toward her again. Kaitlyn stood her ground.

She was glad she hadn't dropped her duffel bag. Maybe she could use it as a weapon. Or maybe there was something *in* it to use. . . .

No, everything was too soft. Except the pencils, but they were in her art kit. She'd never get them out in time.

Then I'll use my fingers to stab his eyes out, she thought savagely. And my knees and my feet and fists. Adrenaline was singing in her veins; she was almost *glad* of the chance to fight. The things she sensed inside him made her want to rip him to pieces. He'd killed, he was a killer.

"Come on, you creep," she said, and realized she was saying it out loud.

He came. He was grinning, a crazy-happy grin. His eyes were crazy, too. Kaitlyn tensed her muscles and then he was on her.

# CHAPTER 4

Gabriel was blocking the world out, but the scream came through.

He was pacing in front of the Institute, loitering. He'd been out all night, and didn't particularly want to go in. Not that anyone inside now would bother him—but he still had an impulse to avoid the place. He'd screwed up; he hadn't gotten the crystal shard. And tonight he'd have to explain to *him*.

Zetes. Gabriel felt a muscle in his jaw twitch. He understood now why Marisol had been so afraid of the old man. He had a sort of malevolent power about him, a power that was best observed in day-to-day living. He seemed to drain the will out of everyone around him. Not suddenly, the way Gabriel drained life energy, but slowly. People around him began to feel nervous and exhausted—and dazed. Like birds looking into the eyes of a snake.

A quiet form of terrorization.

Gabriel didn't intend to be terrorized. But now that he'd chosen his path, he needed Zetes. The old man had the structure, the organization, the contacts. Gabriel planned to use all those things on his journey to the top.

He was debating going in when the scream sliced through his consciousness. It wasn't a vocal sound, purely mental. It was composed of hate and anger as well as fear. And it was Kaitlyn.

*Close.* North and west of him, he thought. He was moving before he thought anything else.

And he probably couldn't have explained why if anyone had asked him.

He moved with the smooth long steps of a hunting wolf. The scream came again—the sound of someone fighting for her life. Gabriel moved faster, homing in on it.

Ivy Street. It was coming from down there—and now he could see it, in the streetlights at the end of the cul-de-sac. He couldn't hear anything except mentally; Kaitlyn never did scream out loud when she was in trouble.

Gabriel reached the grappling figures at a dead run. A red-haired man was on top of Kaitlyn, and she was biting, kicking, and clawing. The man was considerably damaged but sure to win in the end. He was heavier and stronger, he could outlast her.

Déjà vu, Gabriel thought. Once in back of the Institute he'd found another man attacking Kaitlyn—a man who'd turned out to be from the Fellowship. This one, Gabriel thought, eyeing the unwashed hair and unsavory appearance of Kaitlyn's attacker, was unlikely to be anything but a bum.

He could just leave things as they were. The old man would be happy to hear Kaitlyn was dead, and it would mean one less person keeping the shard from them. But . . .

All these thoughts flashed through Gabriel's mind in seconds. Before he'd even consciously come to a conclusion, he was reaching for the man.

He tangled a hand in the back of the dirty overcoat and pulled, yanking the man up. Kaitlyn rolled out from under, and he could hear the surprise in her mind. *Gabriel!*

So she hadn't seen him. Well, she'd been busy trying to stay alive. The man in the overcoat was reacting now, pulling away. He saw Gabriel and threw a punch.

Gabriel ducked around it. He jerked his arm and the knife in his sleeve *snicked* out. His hand closed around it, feeling the welcome weight, the smoothness of the handle.

The man's eyes got big.

Just like Wolverine, Gabriel thought, cutting the knife in front of him in a practice move. The red-haired man's eyes followed it. He was scared; Gabriel could already taste the flavor of his fear.

But don't worry about the knife, he thought, knowing the man couldn't hear him. That's just a distraction, to keep you watching . . . while I do *this*. . . .

Gabriel's other hand rose almost gracefully, gracefully and stealthily, and touched the man on the back of the spine. Just above the soiled collar of the overcoat, just at the nape of the neck.

His fingers made contact with skin, found the transfer point. He could find it easier with his mouth, but he wasn't going any nearer this filthy derelict than he had to. There was a feeling of breakage, as if something was tearing loose. The red-haired man stiffened violently, his muscles jerking. Then Gabriel felt it—the rush of energy, like blue-white light streaking up from the transfer point, fountaining into the air. Into Gabriel's fingers, filling channels and rushing through them, warming his entire body.

Ahhhhh.

It was something like a cold drink on a hot day—a cold drink in a tall glass, with ice cubes clinking against the inside and drops of water condensing on the outside. And it was something like getting your second wind when running—a sudden feeling of strength and peace and vigor. And it was something like standing on the bow of a catamaran with the wind in your face. It wasn't *much* like any of those things, but they were as close as Gabriel could get to the feelings of refreshment and vitality and excitement.

Drinking pure life, that was what it was. And even from a filthy derelict, it tasted pretty good. This guy had been more alive, in his creepy, slimy way, than most. Gabriel let go of him, then pushed the knife back into its casing.

The red-haired man gave a shudder and collapsed, falling as if he'd been deboned. On the ground, he twitched once and was still. He smelled bad.

Kaitlyn, breathing hard, was getting to her feet.

"Is he dead?" she asked.

"No, he's got a gasp or two left. But he's not at all well."

"You enjoyed that." Her eyebrows were arched in scorn and her smoky blue eyes flashed. Wispy red curls clung to her forehead; the rest of her hair was loose in a glorious flame-colored waterfall. She looked flushed and windblown and very beautiful.

Gabriel looked away angrily. He *wouldn't* think about her, he wouldn't see how beautiful she was, how fair her skin was or the way her breathing moved her chest. She belonged to someone else, and she meant *nothing* to him.

He said, looking at the huddled figure on the ground, "You were doing a pretty good job on him yourself."

Kaitlyn shivered, then controlled it. Her voice was softer when she answered. "I could see he was full of nasty things. His mind was . . ." She shivered again.

"You could see into his mind?" Gabriel asked sharply.

"Not exactly. I could *sense* it somehow—sort of like a feeling or a smell. I couldn't tell exactly what he was thinking." She looked up at Gabriel, hesitated, then took a deep breath. "I'm sorry. I didn't say thank you. But I *am* glad you showed up. If you hadn't . . ." Her voice trailed off again.

He ignored this last. "Maybe being in the web has made you slightly telepathic for other people—or maybe that guy was slightly telepathic." He touched the overcoat with the toe of his running shoe. Then he looked at Kait. "Where are the others?"

Kaitlyn drew herself up, looked back calmly. "What others?"

"You know what others." Gabriel stretched out his senses, listening for the slightest hint of their presence. Nothing. He narrowed his eyes at Kaitlyn. "They've got to be around somewhere. You wouldn't come out here alone."

"Wouldn't I? I *am* alone. I came on the bus; it was easy. Aren't you going to ask why?"

Behind her, the sky was green and palest pink, shading to ultramarine in the west. The last stars were going out, the first light was touching her hair with red-gold. She stood slim and proud as some medieval witch princess against the dawn. Gabriel had to work to keep his face expressionless, to keep his presence in the web icy. "All right," he said. "What are you doing here?"

"What do you mean, she's *gone?*" Rob demanded.

"She's gone," Anna repeated miserably. "I woke up and looked and there she wasn't. She isn't *here.*"

Lewis rolled over in his sleeping bag, squinting and scratching. "Did you check in the, uh . . ."

"Of course I've checked in the bathroom. I've looked *everywhere,* and she's just not anywhere. Her bag is gone, too, Rob."

*"What?"* It came out a yell. Anna clapped a hand over his mouth, and Rob stared at her over it.

*If her bag's gone, she's gone,* he said telepathically after a moment.

*That's what I've been telling you,* Anna replied. Her beautiful dark eyes were wide but calm. Anna always could keep her head in a crisis—and Rob was close to losing his. Ever since last night his emotions had been in a turmoil.

With an effort he collected himself. *No, I mean that she's gone for a while—and probably of her own free will. Somebody kidnapping her wouldn't have taken the bag.*

"But—why would she leave?" Lewis asked, sitting up. "I mean, she *wouldn't* leave, but if she did leave—well, why?"

Rob looked past the dark, heavy shapes of the living room furniture to the window. It was just dawn.

"I think . . . she's maybe gone to the Institute."

The other two stared at him.

"No," Anna said.

Rob lifted his shoulders, lip caught between his lower teeth. He was still looking out the window. "I think yes."

"But *why?*" Lewis said. Rob barely heard him. He was looking at the sky, translucently blue, like glass. Kait was out there somewhere. . . .

*"Rob!"* Lewis was shaking him. *"Why* would she have gone to the Institute?" he demanded.

"I don't know," Rob said, coming back to earth. "But she might have an idea she can influence Gabriel—or maybe she wants to try something on Mr. Zetes."

Anna and Lewis audibly let air out of their lungs. "I thought—I mean I thought you were saying . . ."

Rob blinked at him, bewildered.

"He thought you were saying that Kait defected like Gabriel," Anna said crisply. *"I* knew she didn't, but I thought maybe *you* thought she did."

"Of course she wouldn't do that," Rob said, shocked. It was hard for him to understand other people sometimes—they seemed so quick to think the worst about each other, even their friends. He knew better, Kaitlyn wasn't capable of anything evil.

"But she must have gone in the middle of the night," Lewis was saying. "You think she took the car?"

"The car's out front. I looked before I woke you up," Anna said. "I don't know *how* she could make it."

"She'd find a way," Rob said briefly. Kaitlyn was silk and fire—over a steel-hard core of determination. "No, she'll get there, if that's where she's going. The question is, what do we do about it?"

"What *can* we do?" Lewis said.

There were sounds of stirring in the back of the house.

Marisol's parents. Rob glanced that way, then back out the window.

"We'll have to get to her somehow. Find her and get her out of there."

"Get her out," Anna said quietly. It wasn't a question, it was a confirmation.

"We *have* to," Rob said. "I don't know what she has in mind, but it's not going to work. Not in that house of lunatics. They're dangerous. They'll kill her."

"I came to see you," Kaitlyn said, and moved closer to him.

She could tell he wasn't buying it.

"It's *true*. Look at me, feel my thoughts. I came here to see you, Gabriel."

She was taking a chance. But she *had* come to see him, that much was true, and after he'd just saved her life she was genuinely glad to see him. He could sense that much safely. And she was betting he wouldn't search below the surface, because that would mean getting close, letting *her* sense *him*. She had the strong feeling he didn't want that.

He was looking at her hard, his gray eyes narrowed against the light. Beautiful north light, slanting around them, making the modest houses look enchanted, making even Gabriel look golden and warm. She could only guess how it made her look.

Gabriel dropped his eyes. His psychic senses had brushed

her mind as lightly as a moth's wing. "So you came to see me," he said.

"I've missed you," Kaitlyn said, and that was also true. She'd missed his razor wit and the mocking humor that glinted behind his eyes and his strength in the web. "I want to join you."

It was such a whopping huge lie that she expected to *feel* the alarms going off in his head. But he'd withdrawn his mental probing and veiled himself. He wouldn't even look at her properly.

"Don't be stupid," Gabriel said, in a voice suddenly gone weak.

Kaitlyn saw her advantage and pounced. "I *did*. I decided last night. I don't like Mr. Z, but I think some of the things he says are true. We have infinite possibilities—we just need room. Freedom. And we *are* superior to other people."

Gabriel seemed to have gathered himself. "You don't go in for that stuff."

"Why shouldn't I? I'm tired of running. I want to be with you, and I want power. What's wrong with that?"

His mouth had gone hard. "Nothing's wrong—only you don't believe it."

"Test me." Kaitlyn's heart was pounding with the risk. "Gabriel, I didn't know what we had together until you left. I care about you." This was it, the time to see whether she was true Hollywood material. She stepped even closer to Gabriel, almost touching him. "Believe me."

If he wanted, he could reach into her mind and rip the truth out. Her thin shields wouldn't hold against him.

But he didn't try to probe her brain. He kissed her instead.

Kaitlyn surrendered to the kiss deliberately—she knew she had to, and she felt a flash of triumph. Small-town girl makes good. A star is born!

Then the triumph was swept away by something much stronger and deeper. Something fierce and joyous—and *pure.* They were clinging together, he was holding her as hard as she was holding him.

Electricity seemed to arc between them. Everywhere they touched Kaitlyn could feel the sparks. His hand tangled in her hair, and she was frighteningly moved by the tiny tugs, the little pain it caused as his fingers worked. His lips brushed against hers again and again.

An ache was starting inside Kaitlyn. They were together, *together,* so close, and she wanted to be closer. A trembling thrill raced through her—and then a flash of light. His fingers were on the nape of her neck.

A flash of light—it was beginning. The sparks becoming a blue-white torrent. In a moment the transfer point would open, and her energy would flood into him.

The ultimate sharing—but she *couldn't.* Their minds would be open to each other. She would have no shields—he would see everything.

Kaitlyn tried to pull away . . . but it didn't work. He was

holding her and she couldn't seem to let go of him. She didn't have the will—and in a moment he would *see*—

A garage door roared to life.

Kaitlyn jumped and was saved. Gabriel lifted his head, looking at a house near them. Kaitlyn took the moment to step away.

The world was coming to life around them. It wasn't dawn but daylight. The door to another house was opening; a cat was running up a walkway. No one had noticed the tall boy standing in the street kissing a girl, or the crumpled figure at their feet.

"But they'll see us in a minute," Kaitlyn whispered. "Let's go."

They walked quickly. At the intersection, Kaitlyn looked at him. "Which way to the Institute?"

"You really want to go there?" He looked doubtful, but not contemptuous as before. She'd convinced him.

"I want to be with you."

Gabriel was confused. Confused and vulnerable—there was something fragile in his eyes. "But—I hurt you."

"You didn't want to." Kaitlyn was sure of that suddenly. She'd thought so before, but now she was *sure*.

"I don't know," he said shortly. "I don't know anything anymore."

"*I* know. Forget about it." She could tell he was still bewildered, but she figured that was probably good. The more off balance, the less he'd be likely to analyze her. She was still dizzy and bewildered herself from that kiss.

Oh, God, what am I getting myself into?

She decided to think about it later.

"Is Joyce still running things?" Joyce Piper was the woman who'd recruited them both last winter—who'd made the Institute seem like a legitimate place. Even now Kaitlyn had a hard time believing she was as bad as Mr. Z.

"If you can call it running things. She's supposed to be in charge, but—well, you'll see."

Kaitlyn felt a surge of victory, suppressed it. He wasn't arguing anymore. He was assuming she'd come, and that they'd let her in.

I'm going to do it, she thought. She suddenly realized that it was wonderful good luck that she was arriving with Gabriel. He was going to help her immeasurably.

As they neared the Institute she thought, stand tall, walk tall. She held her head up. The first time she'd come here she'd been overwhelmed by anxiety. Worry about her new roommates—would they like her, would they accept her? Now she had much more serious things to worry about, but she had a purpose. She knew she looked cool and confident, almost regal.

She reached into her duffel bag and pulled out Marisol's sunglasses. Put them on, flicked back her hair.

Now I'm ready.

Gabriel glanced at her. "Those new?"

"Well, I don't figure Marisol needs them anymore." She saw him raise his eyebrows at her new hardheartedness.

The Institute was *purple.* Well, of course she remembered that, but it was still a shock to see how truly purple it was. A wild thrill of homesickness ran through her.

"Come on," Gabriel said, and led her to the door. It was locked. He rattled in exasperation.

"I forgot the key—"

"What about your new talent for breaking and entering?"

But the door opened. Joyce was standing there, her short blond hair slick and wet. She was wearing a pink sweater and leggings.

As always, an aura of energy surrounded her, as if she might suddenly spring into action at any moment. Her aquamarine eyes were sparkling with life.

"Gabriel, where have—" She broke off, her eyes widening. She'd seen Kaitlyn.

For a moment they just stood and looked at each other. Under her cool exterior, Kaitlyn's heart was pounding. She *had* to convince Joyce, she had to. But she could feel the waves of suspicion radiating from the blond woman.

Once, Joyce had fooled her, had fooled all of them. Now it was Kaitlyn's turn. Kait felt just like one of those Federal agents infiltrating the Mafia.

And you know what they do to *them,* she thought.

"Joyce—" she began, making her voice gentle and persuasive.

Joyce didn't even glance at her. "Gabriel," she said in a grating whisper, "get her the hell out of here."

# CHAPTER 5

Kaitlyn stared at Joyce in dismay. There was a buzzing in her ears, and she couldn't speak.

Gabriel saved her. "Wait until you hear what she has to say."

Joyce glanced from one of them to the other. Finally she said, "Did you get the crystal shard?"

"I couldn't find it," Gabriel answered without any discernible pause. "They have it hidden someplace else. But what difference does it make?"

"What *dif*—" Joyce clamped her lips together and threw a glance behind her, as if worried she'd be overheard. "The difference is that *he's* going to be here tonight, wanting it."

"Look, are you going to let us in or not?"

Joyce let out a stifled breath, turned her gem-hard eyes on Kaitlyn again. She gazed for a long moment, then she abruptly reached out and snatched the sunglasses from Kaitlyn's face.

Kait was startled but wouldn't show it; she returned the aquamarine gaze steadily.

"All right," Joyce said at last. "Come in. But this had better be good."

"It's good if you want another clairvoyant," Gabriel said once they were in the living room. "You know Frost isn't very good."

Joyce sat down, one trim pink leg crossed over the other. "You've got to be kidding," she said shortly.

"I want to join you," Kaitlyn said. The buzzing was gone from her ears; she could speak in cool, nonchalant tones.

"I'm sure!" Joyce said. *Her* tone was sarcastic.

"Would I bring her here if it wasn't true?" Gabriel asked. He flashed one of his brilliant, unsettling smiles. Before Joyce could reply he added, "I've looked into her mind. She's sincere. So why don't we just cut the bull? I'm hungry."

"*Why* would she want to join us?" Joyce demanded. She looked shaken by Gabriel's conviction.

Kaitlyn went through her speech about believing Mr. Z's theories about psychics and supreme power. She was getting good at it by now. And, she was finding, it was fairly easy to sell it to people who wanted power themselves. It was a motivation they could understand.

At the end of the oration Joyce bit her lip. "I don't know. What about the others? Your friends."

"What about them?" Kaitlyn said coldly.

"You were involved with Rob Kessler. Don't deny it."

Kaitlyn could feel Gabriel waiting for the answer, too. "We broke up," she said. She wished, suddenly, that she had thought more about this part of the story. "I was interested in Gabriel and that made him furious. Besides," she added with happy inspiration, "he likes Anna."

She had no idea what made her say it, but it had an unexpected effect on both Joyce and Gabriel. Joyce's eyebrows went up, but some of the tightness went out of her mouth. Gabriel hissed in a sharp breath—like someone about to say, I knew it all the time.

Kaitlyn was startled. She hadn't *meant* that. Rob had never given any sign—and neither had Anna—or at least she didn't *think* so. . . .

And she couldn't think about it now. She had to stay firmly in the moment. She fixed her eyes on Joyce, who was looking torn.

"Look," Kait said. "This is straight up. I wouldn't come here if I wasn't serious—I wouldn't put my *dad* in that much danger." She held Joyce's gaze. "Because you guys can do things to him, right? I wouldn't risk that." In fact, it wasn't something she had realized until a little while ago. Mr. Z's psychics could attack over any distance, and if they found out the truth about Kait, he'd be an obvious target. Now it was too late to turn back—the only way to protect her dad was to make her act good.

"Hmm. But you went all the way to Canada to *fight* us."

"Sure. I went to the Fellowship and found it was a crock. They can't even help themselves, much less anyone else. And— it's not that I don't care about Rob and the others anymore, but I can't stick with them when they're going to lose. I want to be on the winning side."

"You and Lydia," Joyce said, grimly amused. It was another hit; Kait could tell. "Well, if nothing else I suppose we can use you as a hostage," Joyce murmured.

"In that case, can we get some breakfast?" Gabriel asked, not waiting to see what Kaitlyn's reaction would be.

"Right," Joyce said briefly, handing Kaitlyn the sunglasses. "Nobody else is up yet. Get it yourselves."

*A little different from the cheerful-homemaker attitude you had before,* Kaitlyn thought, not bothering to shield it from Gabriel. He grinned.

The kitchen was different. Dirty, for one thing; there were dishes in the sink and Coke cans spilling out of the wastebasket. A cardboard box full of sloppily shut take-out containers was on the counter.

Chinese food, Kaitlyn saw. Joyce never let *us* have takeout Chinese. And those boxes of Frosted Flakes and Captain Crunch in the pantry—what had happened to Joyce's health food kick? An act?

"I told you she wasn't exactly running things anymore," Gabriel said under his breath, slanting a quirky glance at her.

Oh. Kaitlyn shrugged and poured herself a bowl of Captain Crunch.

When they were finished eating, Joyce said, "Right, go upstairs and get yourself cleaned up. You can go in Lydia's room for now—then we'll see about further arrangements when *he* comes tonight."

Kaitlyn was surprised. "Lydia's living here?"

"I told you," Gabriel said. "Under her father's thumb."

As she and Gabriel reached the landing, Kait said, "Which room do you have now?"

"The same as before." He indicated the best room in the house, the big one that had cable hookup and a balcony. Then he gave her an evil glance. "Want to share it with me? You can use the Jacuzzi. And the king-size bed."

"I think Joyce would put her foot down about *that*," Kaitlyn said.

She didn't know which room was Lydia's, but she knocked lightly on the door of the room she used to share with Anna. Then she looked in.

Lydia, small in an oversize T-shirt, was just getting out of bed. She saw Kaitlyn and squeaked. Her eyes darted around the room, looking for an exit, then she took a sideways step toward the bathroom door.

Kaitlyn chuckled. In a way, it was a relief to see someone more scared than she was. "What's the hurry?" she said, feeling lazy and dangerous. Like Gabriel.

Lydia seemed to be paralyzed. She wriggled a little, like a worm on a hook, then she blurted, "He made me do it. I didn't want to leave you in Canada."

"Oh, Lydia, you're such a liar. You did it for the same reason I did. You wanted to be on the winning side."

Lydia's cat-tilted green eyes opened even wider. She was a pretty little thing, with a pale and delicate face and a heavy shock of black hair. Or she would have been pretty if she hadn't always looked so guilty and slinking, Kait thought.

"The same reason you did?" Lydia breathed. "You mean— Father brought you here—?"

"I came on my own, to join you guys," Kaitlyn said firmly. "Joyce said I could share this room." She swung her duffel bag over the twin bed that wasn't rumpled, and dropped it with a thump.

She'd expected Lydia to look awed or understanding. Instead, Lydia looked as if she thought Kait was crazy.

"You *came on your own* . . ." Then she stopped and shook her head. "Well, you're right about one thing," she said. "My father is going to win. He always wins." She looked away, lip curling.

Kaitlyn eyed her thoughtfully. "Lydia, how come you're at the Institute? You're not psychic—are you?"

Lydia shrugged vaguely. "My father wanted me here. So Joyce could watch me, I think."

And you didn't really answer the question, Kaitlyn thought.

Gabriel had said that if Kait had picked up the red-haired man's thoughts, either she or the red-haired man must be slightly telepathic. But Kaitlyn had been able to tell how Joyce felt about her, and now she was getting strong feelings from Lydia. It wasn't that she could tell exactly what they were thinking; more that she could get a sense of their general mood.

So I'm a telepath? It was a weird and unsettling thought. Telepathy in the web didn't count; Gabriel had hooked them together. But to sense other people's feelings was something new.

Like just now she could tell that Lydia had a lot on her mind—which meant she might be induced to talk.

"So what's it like around here?" Kaitlyn asked casually.

Lydia's lip curled farther, but she just shrugged again and said, "Have you met the others?"

"No. Well, I mean, I've seen their astral forms before, on the way to Canada."

"You'll probably like those better than their real forms."

"Well, why don't you introduce me?" Kait suggested. She wasn't really as interested in the dark psychics as in the routine around here—something that might give her an idea where Mr. Z kept the crystal. But any information would be helpful, and she figured it was better to be aggressive in meeting Mr. Z's new students. She didn't want them to think she was afraid of them.

"You *want* to see them?" Lydia was afraid of them.

"Yeah, come on, show me the psychic psychos." Kaitlyn kept her tone light and was rewarded with a faint, admiring grin. "Let's tour the zoo."

In the hallway, they nearly ran into Joyce. She glanced at them and then knocked briskly at the door of what had once been the common room for Kait's group. Without waiting for an answer, she threw the door open.

"Everybody up! Renny, you have to get to school; Mac, we start testing in ten minutes. If you want any breakfast, you'd better move it."

She moved on, to yell at another door. "Bri! School! Frost! Testing!"

Kaitlyn, with a clear view of the first room, had to keep herself from gasping.

Oh, my God, I don't believe it.

The room was now a bedroom—sort of. Like a bedroom from a flophouse, Kaitlyn thought. No, *worse*. Like a bedroom from one of those abandoned buildings you see on the news. Across one wall the words "NO FEAR" were spray-painted. *Spray-painted.* Most of the curtains were down and one of the windows in the alcove was broken. There was a large hole in the plaster of one wall and another in the door.

And the room was filthy: It wasn't just the motorcycle helmet and the traffic cones on the floor, or the stray bits of clothing draped over every piece of furniture, or the cups over-flowing with cigarette butts. There were cookie crumbs and ashes and potato chips mashed into the carpet, and mud on almost everything. Kaitlyn marveled at how they'd managed to get it so dirty in such a short time.

A boy wearing only boxer shorts was standing up. He was big and lanky, with hair so short it was almost nonexistent, and dark, evil, knowing eyes. A skinhead? Kaitlyn wondered. He looked like the kind of guy you would hire as an assassin, and his mind felt like the red-haired man's.

"Jackal Mac," Lydia whispered. "His real name's John MacCorkendale."

Jackal eyes, Kaitlyn thought. That's it.

The other boy was younger, Kaitlyn's age. He had skin the color of creamed coffee and a little, lean, quick body. His face was narrow, his features clean and sharp. The glasses perched on his nose did nothing to make him look less tough. A smart kid gone bad, Kait thought. The brains of the operation? She couldn't get a clear feeling about his mood.

"That's Paul Renfrew, Renny," Lydia whispered—and ducked. Jackal Mac had thrown a size twelve combat boot at her.

Kaitlyn ducked, too. Then she stood frozen as the huge guy rushed toward them, all arms and legs.

"What are you doing here? What do you want?" he snarled, right in Kaitlyn's face.

Oh, Lord, she thought. His *tongue* is pierced. It was, with what looked like a metal bolt.

Renny had come, too, light as a sparrow, his eyes merry and malicious. He circled Kaitlyn, picked up a strand of her hair by the ends.

"Ouch! That burns!" he said. "But the curves are okay." He smoothed a hand over Kait's behind. "I like her better in the flesh."

Kaitlyn reacted without thinking. She whirled around and her hand made sharp contact with Renny's cheek. It knocked his glasses askew.

"You don't ever do that," she said through her teeth. It brought back every moment of loathing she'd ever felt for a boy. Boys, with their big meaty hands and their big sloppy grins . . . she pulled her arm back in preparation for another slap.

Jackal Mac caught her wrist from behind. "Hey, she fights! I like that."

Kaitlyn jerked her hand out of his grasp. "You haven't seen anything yet," she told them, and gave her best wolfish grin. It wasn't acting. This was genuine, from the heart.

They both laughed, although Renny was rubbing his cheek.

Kaitlyn turned on her heel. "Come on, Lydia. Let's meet the others."

Lydia had been crouching by the stairway. Now she straightened up slightly and hurried toward the second door Joyce had shouted at. It was the room Rob and Lewis had shared in the old days.

The door was ajar; Lydia pushed it open. Kaitlyn braced herself for more destruction.

She wasn't disappointed. Once again the curtains were down, although here they'd been replaced by black sheets. There was a black candle burning on the dresser, dripping wax, and an upside-down pentagram scrawled on the mirror in lipstick. *Glamour* magazines lay open on the floor, and there was the inevitable scattering of clothing and garbage.

There was a girl on each of the twin beds.

"Laurie Frost," Lydia said. She didn't seem quite so afraid of the girls. "Frost, this is Kaitlyn—"

"I know her," the girl said sharply, sitting up. She had blond hair even lighter than Joyce's, and much messier. Her face was beautiful, although the permanently flared nostrils gave it a look of perpetual disdain. She was wearing a red lace teddy and as she raised a hand to flick hair out of her eyes Kaitlyn saw that she had long silvery nails. They were pierced with tiny rings like earrings.

"She's one of *them*. The ones who ran away," Frost said in a menacing hiss.

"Hey, yeah," the other girl said.

There was no need for Lydia to introduce her. Kaitlyn recognized her from a picture on a file folder in Mr. Z's office. Except that the picture had been of a pretty, wholesome girl with dark hair and a vivid face. Now she was still pretty—in a bizarre way. There were streaks of cerulean blue in her hair, and black smudges of makeup surrounding her eyes. Her face was hard, her jaw belligerent.

Sabrina Jessica Gallo, Kaitlyn thought. We meet at last.

"I know you, too," Kaitlyn said. She kept her voice cool and returned Bri's stare boldly. "And I'm not running away now. I came back."

Bri and Frost looked at each other, then back at Kait. They burst into nasty laughter, Bri barking, Frost tittering.

"Right back into the mousetrap," Frost said, flicking her long, silvery nails. "It's Kaitlyn, right? What do they call you, Kaitlyn? Kaitykins? Kitty? Kit Cat?"

Bri took it up. "Kit Kat? Pretty Kitty? Pretty Pretty?"

They dissolved into laughter again.

"We'll have to make the Kitty Kat welcome," Frost said. Her wide, pale blue eyes were spiteful but slightly unfocused. Kaitlyn wondered if she were hung over from something—or maybe that was just the way these people *were*. The Fellowship had sensed insanity in them, and what Kaitlyn sensed now was that each of them was a little bit *off*. Aggressive, malicious—but not very focused. As if there were an inner fogginess in each of them. They weren't even properly suspicious; they weren't asking the right questions.

And Kait wasn't sure what to do with them while they were pointing and giggling at her like kindergartners.

"Sabrina and Frost, I said *now!*" Joyce's voice came from the corridor, cracking like a whip. The girls kept giggling. Joyce pushed past Kaitlyn like a blond meteor and began yelling at them, picking clothes up off the floor.

Kaitlyn shook her head, putting on an expression of genteel astonishment for Joyce's benefit. Then she turned to Lydia.

"I think I've seen enough," she said, and made an exit.

A few minutes later Joyce came into Lydia's room. Her sleek hair was ruffled and she was flushed, but her aquamarine eyes were still hard.

"You can stay in this room today," she said to Kaitlyn. "I don't want you going downstairs while I'm doing testing."

"That's fine with me. I didn't get any sleep last night."

"Good luck napping," Joyce said grimly.

But in a surprisingly short time, the upper floor was still. Lydia, Renny, and Bri had departed for school; Jackal Mac and Frost were presumably being tested. Gabriel's door was locked.

Kaitlyn lay down on her old familiar bed—and realized how tired she really was. She felt wrung out, drained not only of energy, but of emotion. She'd meant to lie awake and make a plan, but she fell asleep almost instantly.

She woke a long time later. Warm, diffuse afternoon light filled the room. Silence filled her ears.

She got up and grabbed for the headboard as a wave of giddiness swept her. Breathing slowly, she held her head down until she felt steadier.

Then she crept in stocking feet to the door.

Still silence. She went to the stairway and turned her head, ear pointed downstairs. No sound. She descended quietly.

If Joyce saw her, she'd say she was hungry, and when was dinnertime anyway?

But Joyce didn't appear. The lower floor seemed deserted. Kaitlyn was alone in the house.

Okay, don't panic. This is terrific, the perfect opportunity. What do you want to look at first?

If I were a big ugly crystal, where would I be?

One obvious place was the secret room in the basement. But Kaitlyn couldn't get in that; Lewis had always used PK to find the hidden spring in the panel. Another place was in Mr. Z's house in San Francisco, where he'd kept it before. But Kaitlyn couldn't do anything about that today. Sometime she'd have to find a way to get to San Francisco.

For now . . . well, Joyce hadn't wanted her to see the testing. So Kait would start with the labs.

The front lab was as she remembered it, weird machines, a folding screen with seashells appliquéd on it, chairs and couches, bookcases, a stereo. There was no graffiti. Kaitlyn looked briefly into each of the study carrels that lined the walls, but she knew already that the crystal could never fit into something so small. She found only more equipment.

I wonder what their powers are? she thought, envisioning each of the students she'd met. I forgot to ask Lydia. Gabriel said something about Frost being clairvoyant, but the others— I'll bet they do something *bizarre*.

She turned to the back lab . . . and found it locked.

*Aha!*

It had never been locked before. Kaitlyn found it extremely suspicious that it should be locked now.

But her jubilation changed to despair a minute later as she realized a basic truth. If it was locked, she *couldn't get in.*

But wait, wait. Joyce had always kept a house key on top of the bulletin board in the kitchen, for anybody to grab when they were leaving the house. Sometimes people had the same locks on the inside doors of a house as the outside. If that key were still there . . . and if it fit . . .

In a moment she was in the quiet, darkening kitchen, fingers searching anxiously on the top of the bulletin board's frame. She found some dust, a dead fly . . . and a key.

Eureka! Praying all the way, Kaitlyn hurried back to the lab. She held key to lock, almost dropping it in her nervousness.

It's *got* to work, it's *got* to work. . . .

The key slipped in. It fit! She waggled it. It turned!

The doorknob turned, too. Kait pushed and the door was open. She stepped in and shut the door behind her.

The back lab was dim—it had been a garage and had only a small window. Kaitlyn blinked, trying to make out shapes. She didn't dare turn on a light.

There were bookcases here, too, and more equipment. And a steel room like a bank vault.

A Faraday cage.

Kaitlyn remembered Joyce telling her about it. It was for complete isolation in testing. Soundproof, electronically shielded. They had put Gabriel in there.

Kait remembered herself begging Joyce to promise *she'd* never have to go in.

Her mouth was dry. She tried to swallow, but her throat seemed to stick together. She walked toward the gray bulk of the steel vault, one hand lifted as if she were blind.

Cool metal met her fingers.

If I were a crystal, I'd be somewhere like this. Shielded, enclosed. With enough room for everybody to get in and crowd around me.

Kaitlyn's fingers slid over the metal. Her former tranquility in the face of danger was gone, and her heart wasn't just pounding, it was *thundering*. If the crystal was really in there, she had to see it. But she didn't really want to see it—and to be alone with that obscene thing . . . in the dark. . . .

Kaitlyn's skin was crawling and her knees felt unsteady. But her fingers kept searching. She found something like a handle.

You can do it. You can do it.

She pulled.

At first, she thought the sound she heard was the vault door clicking. Then she realized it was somebody opening the lab door behind her.

# CHAPTER 6

What does a spy do when she's caught?

Kait's stomach plummeted. She recognized the voice, even before she whirled around to see the figure silhouetted in the door.

Light shone behind him. Broad shoulders, then body lines that swept straight down. A man wearing a greatcoat.

"Are you finding anything to interest you?" Mr. Zetes asked, his gold-headed cane swinging in his hand.

Oh, God. The buzzing was back in Kaitlyn's ears and she couldn't answer. Couldn't move, either, although her heart was shaking her body.

"Would you like to see what's inside there?"

Say something, idiot. Say anything, *anything*.

Her dry lips moved. "I—no. I—I was just—"

Mr. Zetes stepped forward, snapped on the overhead light. "Go on, take a closer look," he said.

But Kaitlyn couldn't look away from his face. The first time she'd seen this man, she'd thought him courtly and aristocratic. His white hair, aquiline nose, and piercing dark eyes made him look like some English earl. And if an occasional grim smile flashed across his face, she was sure that he had a heart of gold underneath.

She'd found out differently.

Now, his eyes held her with an almost hypnotic power. Boring into her mind, gnawing. He looked more telepathic than Gabriel. His measured, imperious voice seemed to resound in her blood.

"Of course you want to see it," he said, and Kaitlyn's throat closed on her protests. He advanced on her slowly and steadily. "Look at it, Kaitlyn. It's a very sturdy Faraday cage. Look."

Against her will, Kaitlyn's head turned.

"It's natural that you would be interested in it—and in what's inside. Have you seen that yet?"

Kaitlyn shook her head. Now that she wasn't looking into those eyes, she found she could speak—a little. "Mr. Zetes—I wasn't—"

"Joyce told me that you had come back to join us." Mr. Z's voice was rhythmic . . . almost soothing. "I was very pleased. You have great talents, you know, Kaitlyn. And a keen, inquiring mind."

As he spoke he unlocked the vault with a key, grasped the handle. Kaitlyn was speechless again with fear. Please, she was thinking. Please, I don't want to see, just let me go.

"And now your curiosity can be satisfied. Go in, Kaitlyn."

He pulled the steel door open. There was a single lamp inside, the battery-driven kind that clamps on walls. It gave enough light for Kaitlyn to see the object below.

Not the crystal. A sort of tank, made of dark metal.

Bewildered, forgetting herself, Kaitlyn took a step forward. The tank was almost like a Dumpster trash can, except that instead of being rectangular it had one side which slanted steeply. A door was set in that steeply slanting side. It looked like the door to a hurricane cellar, leading down.

There were all sorts of pipes, cables, and hoses attached to the tank. One machine beside it looked like the electroencephalograph Joyce had used to measure Kaitlyn's brain waves. There were other machines Kaitlyn didn't recognize.

The tank itself felt like a giant economy-size coffin.

"What . . . is it?" Kaitlyn whispered. Dread was clogging her chest like ice. The thing gave off an aura of pure evil.

"Just a piece of testing equipment, my dear," Mr. Zetes said. "It's called an isolation tank. The ultimate Ganzfeld cocoon. Put a subject inside, and she is surrounded by perfect darkness and perfect silence. No light or sound can penetrate. It's filled with water, so she can't feel the effects of gravity or her own body. There is no sensory stimulation of any kind. Under those conditions, a person—"

Would go insane, Kaitlyn thought. She recoiled from the tank violently, turning away. Just the idea of it, to be abandoned in utter darkness and silence, was making her physically sick.

Mr. Z's hand caught her, holding her lightly but firmly. "Would be undistracted by outside influences, free to extend her psychic powers to the fullest. Just as you did when Joyce blindfolded you, my dear. Do you remember that?"

He had turned to look at her, holding her terrified gaze with his. She hadn't missed his use of personal pronouns. Put a subject inside and *she* can't feel *her* own body.

"As I said earlier, you have very great talents, Kaitlyn. Which I would like to see developed to their fullest."

He was pulling her toward the tank.

And she couldn't resist. That measured voice, that precise grip . . . she had no will of her own.

"Have you heard of the Greek concept of *arete,* my dear?" He had put aside his cane and was opening the hurricane-cellar door. "Self-actualization, becoming all you can be." He was pushing her toward the open door. "What do you think you can be, Kaitlyn?"

A black hole gaped in front of her. Kaitlyn was going into it.

"Mr. Zetes!"

The voice was thin and distant in Kaitlyn's ears. All she could see was the hole.

"Mr. Zetes, I didn't realize you were here. What are you doing?"

The pressure on Kait's neck eased and she could move of

her own volition again. She turned and saw Joyce in the door-way. Gabriel and Lydia were behind her.

Then Kaitlyn simply stood, blinking and trying to breathe. Mr. Z was going over to Joyce, talking to her in an undertone. Kaitlyn saw Joyce look up at her in surprise, then shake her head.

"I'm sorry, but there's no help for it," Mr. Z said, with mild regret, as if saying "I'm sorry, but we'll have to cut expenses."

He's talking about my imminent demise, Kaitlyn realized, and suddenly she was talking, gabbling.

"Joyce, I'm sorry. I know I shouldn't have gone inside here, but I wanted to see what changes you'd made, and there was nobody around to ask, and—I'm *sorry.* I didn't mean anything by it."

Joyce looked at her, hesitated, then nodded. She beckoned Mr. Z into the front lab and began talking to him. Kaitlyn followed slowly, warily.

She couldn't hear everything, but what she heard stopped her breath. Joyce was defending her, championing her to Mr. Z.

"The Institute can use her," Joyce said, her tanned face earnest—and strained with what looked like repressed desperation. "She's well-balanced, conscientious, reliable. Unlike the rest of—" She broke off. "She'll be an asset."

And Gabriel was agreeing.

"I can vouch for her," he said. Kaitlyn felt a surge of gratitude—and admiration for his level, dispassionate gray eyes. "I've probed her mind and she's sincere."

Even Lydia was chiming in—after everyone else, of course.

"She *wants* to be here—and I want her for my roommate. Please let her stay."

Listening to it, Kaitlyn was almost convinced herself. They all sounded so *sure*.

And somehow it worked—or seemed to work. Mr. Z stopped shaking his head regretfully and looked thoughtful. At last he shifted his jaw, drew a deep breath, and nodded.

"All right, I'm willing to give her a chance," he said. "I'd like to see a little more penitence in her—some signs of remorse—but I trust your judgment, Joyce. And we could certainly use another remote-viewer." He turned to give Kaitlyn a benevolent smile. "You and Lydia go along to dinner. I want a word with Gabriel."

It's over, Kaitlyn realized. They're not going to kill me; they're going to feed me. Her heart was only beginning to return to its normal rate. She tried to hide the trembling in her legs as she followed Lydia.

But it slowed her down, and before she could get out of the front lab she heard Mr. Z speak to Joyce again.

"Give her a chance, but watch her. And have Laurie Frost watch her, too. She's intuitive; she'll pick up on anything subversive. And if she finds something . . . you know what to do."

A sigh from Joyce. "Emmanuel . . . you know what I think about your 'final solution'—"

"We'll send her out on a job soon. That ought to prove something."

"Kait, are you coming?" Lydia called from the kitchen.

Kait went through the door, but dawdled on the other side. Mr. Z was speaking again.

"Gabriel, I'm afraid you've been careless."

Gabriel's voice was restrained but defiant. "About the shard? You haven't heard—"

"Not about that," Mr. Zetes said in his unhurried way. "Joyce explained that to me. But there was a man found half-dead on Ivy Street. He had all the signs of someone drained of life energy. The police have been making inquiries."

"Oh."

"*Very* careless of you to do that in our own neighborhood— and the man might talk." Mr. Z's voice dropped to an icy whisper. "Next time, *finish the job.*"

Kaitlyn was shivering when Gabriel came through the door. She was barely able to give him a smile of gratitude.

*Thanks.*

He shrugged. *No problem.*

Dinner started off quietly. Joyce served bacon cheeseburgers, fare that never would have been allowed in the old days. The psychics eyed Kaitlyn from around the long table, but didn't say much. Kait had the feeling they were biding their time.

"So where was everybody this afternoon?" she asked Lydia, trying for normalcy.

"I was in Marin. Riding lessons," Lydia said in subdued tones—she never seemed to talk loudly around the other students.

"I was asleep," Gabriel said lazily.

No one else answered, including Joyce, who returned to the kitchen. Kaitlyn dropped the subject and ate fries. It was interesting, though—the ones who'd been out were also the ones who would have been involved in testing. Could they have been in San Francisco? In Mr. Z's house—with the crystal?

She made a mental note to follow up on the question.

What Joyce said next might have been coincidence.

"So you've seen the isolation tank."

Kaitlyn almost inhaled a fry. "Yes. Have—has anybody really been in that thing?"

"Sure, it's cool," Bri said. She shut her eyes and leaned her head back. "Cosmic, man! Groooovy." Her expression of ecstasy was marred by the fact that her open mouth was full of half-chewed hamburger.

"Shut your face, you slut!" Frost snapped, flicking a pickle chip at her.

"Who's a slut, you bimbo?" Bri returned cordially, chewing. "Jimbo bimbo. Mumbo jumbo."

They both laughed: Frost shrilly, Bri gruffly.

Jackal Mac glared. "Quit with the freakin' noise," he said brutally. "You make me sick with that freakin' noise." He had been eating with fervent single-mindedness, the way Kaitlyn imagined a coyote might eat.

"I like to see girls have a good time," Renny said. He was eating with finicky precision, gesturing with a french fry. "Don't you, Mac?"

"You making fun of me? You making fun of *me*, man?"

Kaitlyn blinked. It was a non sequitur; she didn't follow Mac's logic. But it didn't take logic to read the sudden fury in his slitted eyes.

He stood up, towering over the table, leaning across to stare at Renny. "I said, you makin' fun of *me?*" he bellowed.

Renny let him have it with a hamburger in the face.

Kaitlyn gaped. The hamburger had been dripping with ketchup and Thousand Island dressing. Renny had thoughtfully removed the bun, so Jackal Mac got the full benefit of the condiments.

Bri shrieked with laughter. "What a pitch, what a pitch! Pitch, snitch!"

"Think that's *funny?*" Jackal Mac seized her by the hair and slammed her face into her plate. He began to grind it around and around. The giggles turned to screams.

Kaitlyn was now gasping. Frost plunged her long nails into a bowl of coleslaw and came out with a juicy handful. She threw it at Mac, but it scattered over the table, hitting Renny, too.

Renny seized a bottle of Clearly Canadian water—the fizzy kind.

"Time to go." Gabriel caught Kaitlyn by the arm above the elbow and neatly lifted her from the chair out of the way of a burst of carbonated water. Lydia was already scuttling out of the room.

"But he's going to kill her!" Kaitlyn gasped. Mac was still grinding Bri's face into the plate.

"So?" Gabriel piloted her toward the kitchen.

"No, I mean, *really*. I think that plate cracked; he's going to *kill* her."

"I said, 'so?'"

There was the sound of shattering glass and Kaitlyn looked back. Jackal Mac had stopped grinding Bri's face; Renny was now slashing at him with a broken Clearly Canadian bottle.

"Oh, my *God*—"

"Come on."

In the kitchen, Joyce was washing dishes.

"Joyce, they're—"

"It happens every night," Joyce said shortly. "Leave it alone."

"Every night?"

Gabriel stretched, looking bored. Then he smiled. "Let's go up to my balcony," he said to Kaitlyn. "I need some air."

"No, I—I want to help Joyce with the dishes." There was no point in trying to deceive him about such a minor thing, so she added, *I want to talk to her a minute. I didn't have time earlier.*

"Suit yourself." Gabriel's voice was unexpectedly cold; his expression was stony. "I'll be busy later." He left.

Kaitlyn didn't understand why he was angry, but there was nothing to do about it. She was a spy, she had information to gather. Picking up a dish, she said abruptly, "Joyce, why do you put up with it?"

"With Gabriel? I don't know, why do you?"

"With *them*." Kaitlyn jerked her chin toward the dining room, where yells and crashes could still be heard.

Joyce gritted her teeth and scrubbed viciously at a greasy pan with a soap pad. "Because I have to."

"No really. Everything's so crazy now—and it seems like it's against everything you believe in." Kaitlyn was getting incoherent—maybe the scare before dinner was still affecting her. She had the feeling that she should shut up, but instead she blundered on. "I mean, you seem like the kind of person who really *believes* in things, and I just don't understand—"

"You want to know why? I'll show you!" With a soapy hand, Joyce seized something that had been on the counter, underneath the Chinese take-out containers.

It was a magazine, the *Journal of Parapsychology.*

"My name is going to be in this! The lead article. And not just this." Joyce's face was contorted, it reminded Kaitlyn of the way she'd looked when she'd held Gabriel's bleeding forehead against the crystal, trying to kill him. Overcome by maniacal passion.

"Not just this, but in *Nature, Science, The American Journal of Psychology, The New England Journal of Medicine,*" Joyce raved. "Multidisciplinary journals, the most prestigious journals in the world. My name and my work."

Dear God, she's a mad scientist, Kaitlyn thought. She was almost spellbound by the ranting woman.

"And that's just the beginning. Awards. Grants. A full professorship at the school of *my* choice. And, incidentally, a little trinket called the Nobel Prize."

Kait thought at first that she was joking. But there was no humor in those glazed aquamarine eyes. Joyce looked as insane as any of the psycho psychics.

Could he have hit her with the crystal, too? Kaitlyn wondered dazedly. Or could it be some sort of cumulative effect from being around it, like secondhand smoke?

But she knew that no matter what the crystal had done to warp and magnify the desire, it was Joyce's desire in the first place. Kaitlyn had finally discovered what made Joyce run; she had just seen into the woman's soul.

"That's why I put up with it, and why I'm going to put up with anything. So that the cause of science can be advanced. And so I can get *what I'm due.*"

As suddenly as she had grabbed it, Joyce dropped the magazine she'd been shaking in front of Kaitlyn's eyes. She turned back to the sink.

"Now, why don't you take a walk," she said in a voice suddenly gone dull. "I can wash the dishes by myself."

Numb, Kaitlyn walked out of the kitchen. She avoided the dining room, went through the front lab and up the stairs.

Gabriel's door was locked. Well, she should have expected

that, really. She'd managed to offend two of the three people who'd championed her tonight. Might as well try for a perfect score, she thought philosophically, and headed for the room she was to share with Lydia.

But Lydia proved to be impossible to offend or talk to at all. She was in bed with the covers pulled over her head. Whether she was sulking or simply scared, Kaitlyn didn't know. She wouldn't come out.

So *moody*, Kaitlyn thought.

It was a very long, very dull evening. Kait listened to the other psychics stagger up to their various rooms, then a TV blared from one room, a stereo from the other. It spoiled Kaitlyn's concentration for the one thing that might have relaxed her: drawing.

And this room depressed her. All her possessions had disappeared from it—thrown away when the new students came in. Anna's raven mask was lying in a corner. Like a piece of garbage. Kait didn't dare hang it up where it belonged.

Finally, she decided to take a bath and follow Lydia's example. She had a long soak, curled up in bed—and then there was nothing to do but think.

Scenes from the day kept floating through her mind. The face of the red-haired man . . . Gabriel's face in the dawn light. Mr. Z's silhouette.

I've got to make plans, she thought. Mysteries to investigate. Ways to find the crystal. But her mind couldn't focus on one thing, it kept skipping.

Joyce defended me . . . I fooled the fooler. And what convinced her was that Rob and I had broken up . . . because Rob liked Anna.

What an idea. How odd. And Gabriel fell for it, too.

She must be sleepy. Her mind skipped again, her thoughts becoming less and less cohesive. I hope Gabriel isn't really angry with me. I need him. Oh, God, all the things I said to him . . .

Was that wrong? To let him think I'm in love with him? But it wasn't completely a lie. I do care about him. . . .

As much as I do about Rob?

It was a heretical thought, and one which jerked her fully awake. She realized she had been half-dreaming.

But the thought wouldn't go away.

In Canada she had discovered that Gabriel loved her. Loved her in a vulnerable, childlike way she could never have believed if she hadn't *seen* it, felt it in his mind. He had been completely open to her, so warm, so joyous . . .

. . . the way he was this morning, her mind whispered.

But in Canada she hadn't loved him. Or at least she hadn't been in love.

You couldn't be in love with two people at the same time. You *couldn't* . . .

Could you?

Suddenly Kaitlyn felt icy cold. Her hands were cold, her face was cold. As if someone had opened a window somewhere inside her and let a glacial wind blow in.

If I loved Gabriel . . . if I loved both of them . . .

How could I choose?

*How could I choose?*

The words were ringing so loudly in her head that she didn't notice the very real noise in her room. Not until a shadow loomed on the wall beside her.

Terror swept her. For an instant she thought it was Mr. Z—and then she saw Gabriel beside her bed.

Oh, Lord, did he hear my thought? She groped for shields, found she didn't have any. She was burned out.

But Gabriel was smiling, looking at her from under heavy eyelids. He would never have smiled like that if he had heard. "Ready to try out the balcony now?" he asked.

Kaitlyn looked at him, slowly regaining her composure. He was looking particularly gorgeous, and dangerous as darkness. She felt a magnetic pull drawing her to him.

But she was exhausted. Unshielded. And she had just discovered a crisis within herself that threatened to bring the world crashing down.

I can't go with him. It would be insane.

The magnetic pull only got stronger. She wanted to be held. She wanted him to hold her.

"Come on," Gabriel whispered, and took her hand. He caressed the palm with his thumb. "Kiss me, Kait."

# CHAPTER 7

Kaitlyn was shaking her head at him. What on earth could the girl mean?

Gabriel could tell she wanted to come. He'd read the line in some old book somewhere, probably during one of his stints in solitary. "She trembled at his touch." Reading it, he'd sneered—but now he was seeing the real thing. When he reached down to take her hand, Kaitlyn trembled.

So what was the problem?

*I'm tired,* she projected in a whisper.

*Oh, come on. Sitting on a balcony is relaxing.*

He could tell she was going through some struggle. Mad because of the way he'd acted after dinner? Or . . .

Did it have something to do with what he'd seen this afternoon?

His mood darkened. *Is there something wrong?* he asked silkily.

"No, of course not," she said very quickly. On the other bed a lump under the comforter stirred. Gabriel eyed it with distaste.

Kaitlyn was getting up. Gabriel's lip twitched at the sight of her nightgown—it was flannel and tentlike, covering her from throat to ankle. Quite a bit different from Frost, who had pirouetted in front of him dressed in what looked like a transparent red handkerchief the first night he'd met her. She'd made it clear, too, that she didn't mind if he took the handkerchief off.

Kaitlyn, by contrast, was holding the neck of her nightgown closed as she briskly walked to his room.

She paused there to look at the walls. "You do the graffiti?"

He snorted. *Mac. He was living here.*

"And what did he think when you asked him to get out?"

Gabriel said nothing, waited until she turned around. Then he gave her one of his most disturbing smiles. *I didn't ask.*

"Oh." She didn't pursue it. She stepped through the open sliding glass door onto the balcony. "It's a nice night," she murmured.

It was—a soft moonless night, with stars showing between branches of the olive trees. The air was warm, but Kaitlyn had her arms wrapped around herself.

Gabriel went still.

Maybe it was the simplest explanation after all. Maybe he'd been wrong about her trembling—or wrong about the reason. Not desire . . . but fear.

"Kaitlyn." Instinctively, he used words instead of thoughts, giving her the distance she seemed to need. "Kait, you don't have to . . . I mean, you *know* that, don't you?"

She turned quickly, as if startled. But then she didn't seem to know what to say. He could search her thoughts—he could sense them even now, like silver fish darting and gliding in clear water—but he *wouldn't*. He would wait for her to tell him.

She was staring at him, breathing lightly. "Oh, Gabriel. I do know. And I can't explain—I'm just . . . oh, it's been a hard day."

Then she put her hands over her face. She started to cry, with her hair falling around her, and little quick intakes of breath.

Gabriel stood transfixed.

Kaitlyn the indomitable—crying. She did it so seldom that he was too amazed at first to react. When he could move, he could think of only one thing to do.

He took her in his arms, and Kaitlyn clung to him. Clung tightly—and after a moment lifted a tear-stained face to him.

The kisses were soft and slow and very passionate. It was strange to do this without touching her mind, but he wasn't going to be the first to initiate contact. He'd wait for her. Meanwhile, it was a sort of pleasurable agony to restrain himself.

And it was good just to hold her and touch the softness of her skin. He wanted to hold her hard, not to hurt her but to keep her safe, to show her that he was strong enough to protect her. Her beauty was like fire and strange music, and he loved her.

And he *could* love her, because she didn't belong to anyone else, and she loved him back. She'd given it all up for him.

For an instant he felt a flicker of guilt at that, but it was swept aside by a fierce desire to hold her closer. To *be* closer. He couldn't keep himself in check any longer. He reached for her mind, a tendril of thought extending to caress her senses.

Kaitlyn recoiled. Not just pulling away from his mind, but pulling out of his arms. He could feel her trying to fling up shields against him.

Leaving him stricken, utterly bewildered, and bereft. Cold because she'd taken all the warmth in the universe away with her.

Suspicion knifed through him, unavoidable this time.

*What is it you don't want me to see?*

"Nothing!" She was frightened—no, panicked. His suspicion swelled until it was larger than both of them, until it blocked out everything else. He threw words at her like stones.

"You're lying! Don't you think I can tell?" He stared at her, controlling his breath, forcing his voice into velvety-iron tones. "It wouldn't have something to do with Kessler coming around here this afternoon, would it?"

"Rob—here?"

"Yeah. I felt his mind and tracked him down to the redwood trees out back. You're telling me you didn't know?"

Her eyes were still wide with surprise—but he saw, and felt, the flash of guilt. And his suspicions were confirmed.

"What are you really doing here, Kaitlyn?"

"I told you. I—"

"Stop lying to me!" Again he had to stop to control himself. When he spoke again his voice was like ice because he was made of ice. "You didn't break it off with him, did you? And you're not here to join us. You're a spy."

"That's not true. You won't even give me a chance—"

"I told them all that I'd seen into your mind—but I never really did. You made sure of that. You did a wonderful job of tricking me."

Her eyes were large and fierce with pain. "I didn't trick you," she said in a ragged voice. "And if you think I'm a spy, then why don't you go tell Joyce? Why don't you tell them all?"

He was calm, now, because a block of ice can't feel. "No, I won't do that. I'll let you do it to yourself. And you will, sooner or later—probably sooner, because the old man isn't stupid and Frost will pick things up. You'll betray yourself."

There was a blue flame of defiance in her eyes now. "I'm telling you, I am not a spy," she said.

"Oh, right. You're perfectly sincere. I believe you completely." Quick as a striking snake, he bent over her, thrusting his face close to hers. "That's fine, as long as you remember one thing. Keep out of my way. If you mess with *my* plans, angel—no mercy."

Then he left, stalking out of the room to be alone with his dark bitterness.

Kaitlyn cried herself to sleep.

"Bri—school! Frost—testing!"

The shouting voice in the hall woke Kaitlyn. She felt languid and stupid, with a stuffed-up nose and a bad headache.

The door banged open. "Lydia—school! Kaitlyn, you're going to school, too. I arranged it yesterday, and I'm coming in with you today."

Thanks for telling me, Kaitlyn thought, but she got up—painfully, because every muscle seemed to be aching. She stumbled to the bathroom and began to go through the routine of dressing like a programmed robot. Shower, first.

The warm water felt good on her upturned face, but her mind kept leaping back to what had happened with Gabriel last night. At first everything had been so wonderful—and then . . . it had hurt her to see his eyes like holes in his face and his mouth tight to keep it from working.

You ought to be glad it all turned awful, a voice inside her whispered. Because if it had stayed good—well, what would you do? What would you do about Rob?

She didn't *know* what she would have done. Her entire middle was a tight ball of anguish and she was so confused.

It didn't matter. Gabriel hated her now, anyway. And that

was *good,* because she was going to be true to Rob. It was good—except for the minor fact that Gabriel might denounce her to Mr. Z and get her killed.

Tears mingled with the shower spray on her face. Kaitlyn turned her head aside to take a deep, shuddering breath, and that was why she didn't see the shower curtain being pulled open.

The first thing she knew was a rough hand closing around her wet arm.

"What do you think you're doing? Get out of there!" Bri shouted, adding a string of expletives. Kaitlyn had to step over the side of the tub or fall over it—she was being dragged out. Naked and stunned, she shook her hair back and stared at the other girl.

"You think you can use all the hot water again? Like you did last night?" That was the gist of what Bri was yelling, although actually every other word was a curse. Kaitlyn stood dripping on the tile floor, dumbfounded.

"You think you're better than us, don't you?" Bri shouted. "You're Little Miss Responsible, teacher's pet. You can use all the water you want to. You've never had it hard."

The sentences were disjointed, and again Kaitlyn had that sense of something being *off,* as if Bri couldn't actually get a fix on what was making her angry. But her anger and resentment were clear enough.

"Everybody's darling," she mocked, cocking her head back and forth, with a finger to her chin—a bizarre Shirley Temple impersonation. "Looks so *sweet*—"

Something snapped. Kaitlyn's temper had always been combustible, and now it ignited like rocket accelerant touched with a match. Naked as she was, she seized Bri and slammed her against a wall. Then she pulled her away and slammed her back again. Bri's mouth fell open and her eyes showed white. She fought, but fury gave Kaitlyn inhuman strength.

"You think I've always had things easy?" she yelled into Bri's face. "You don't know how it was back in Ohio. I was from the wrong side of the tracks anyway, but to top it off, *I was a witch.* You think I don't know what it's like to have people cross themselves when you look at them? When I was five the bus driver wouldn't take me to school—she said my mom ought to get me blessed. And then my mom died—"

Tears were sliding down Kaitlyn's cheeks, and she was losing her anger. She slammed Bri again and got it back.

"Kids at school would run up and touch me for a dare. And adults would get so nervous when I talked to them—Mr. Rukelhaus used to get a *twitch* in his eye. I grew up feeling like something that ought to be put in the zoo. Don't tell me I don't know what it's like. *Don't tell me!*"

She was winding down, her breath slowly calming. So was Bri's.

"You dye your hair blue and do stuff to look weird—but you're doing it yourself, and you can change it. I can't change my eyes. And I can't change what I am."

Suddenly embarrassed, Kaitlyn let go of Bri's arms and looked around for a towel.

"You're okay," Bri said in a voice Kaitlyn hadn't heard her use before. Not a sneering tough-girl voice. Kait looked around, startled.

"Yeah, you're okay. I thought you were a goody-goody wimp, but you're not. And I think your eyes are cool."

She looked more sane than she had since Kait had met her.

"I—well, thanks. Thank you." Kait didn't know whether to apologize or not; she settled for saying, "You can use the shower now."

Bri gave a friendly nod.

It's strange, Kait thought as Joyce drove her to school. Bri, Lydia, and Renny had gone in Lydia's car. It's strange, but for a while there she sounded just like Marisol. What was it Marisol said that first night? *You kids think you're so smart—so superior to everyone else.*

But we *didn't* think that; it was just Marisol's paranoia—a very particular kind of paranoia. Kaitlyn shot a look at Joyce under her eyelashes. And Joyce has that kind, too—thinking she isn't getting what she's due.

They *all* think the world is out to get them—that they're special and superior but everybody is persecuting them. Can the crystal do that?

If it can, it's no wonder they're out to get the world first.

Joyce checked her in to school, and Kaitlyn found herself going to the same classes she had when she'd come to the Institute. The teachers put her absence down as a vacation, which was mildly amusing. It was surrealistic, like being in a dream, to sit in British literature again, with all these kids whose lives were quiet and boring and completely safe. Who hadn't had *anything* happen to them in the last few weeks; who hadn't changed at all. Kaitlyn felt out of step with the whole world.

Watch it, kid. Don't *you* get paranoid.

At lunch several people asked her to sit with them. Not just one group, but two, called to her in the cafeteria. It was the sort of thing Kaitlyn had always dreamed about, but now it seemed trivial. She was looking for Lydia—she wanted to talk to that girl.

Lydia wasn't in evidence. Bri and Renny were off in a corner, bullying people and probably extorting lunch money. Kaitlyn wondered how their teachers dealt with them.

I'll look around by the tennis courts, she thought. Maybe Lydia's eating her lunch out there.

She was crossing in front of the PE building when she saw three people crowded in the doorway of the boy's locker room. They were looking out from behind the little wall that kept people from seeing in the open doors, and they seemed ready to duck back at any moment. The weird thing was that one of them was a girl. A girl with long dark braids . . .

And the tallest boy had hair that shone in the sun like old gold. Kaitlyn's heart leaped into her mouth and choked her. She ran.

"Rob—you shouldn't be here," she gasped as she got behind the wall. And then she was hugging him hard, overcome by how dear and familiar and honest, and loyal and safe he was. His emotions wide open—not icy and shielded. She could *feel* how much he cared for her, how glad he was that she was alive and unhurt.

"I'm fine," she said, pulling back. "Really. And I'm sorry for running away without telling you—and I don't know why you're not mad."

Lewis and Anna were crowding around her, smiling, patting her as if to make sure she was real. They were *all* so dear and good and forgiving. . . .

"We were *worried* about you," Anna said.

"We camped out yesterday near the Institute hoping you'd come out," Lewis said. "But you never did."

"No—and *you* can't do that ever again," Kait said shakily. "Gabriel saw you. I don't think anybody else did, thank God, but he's bad enough."

"We won't have to do it again," Rob said, smiling. "Because we've got you now. We'll take you with us—even though we don't exactly have a place to go yet. Tony's working on that."

Kait thought he had never looked so handsome. His eyes were amber-gold, clear and full of light like the summer sky.

His face was full of trust and happiness. She could feel the radiant energy of his love.

"Rob . . . I can't." The change in his expression made her feel as if she'd hit an innocent child in the face.

"You can." Then, as she kept shaking her head: *"Why not?"*

"For one thing, if I disappear, they'll think I've betrayed them and they'll do something to my father. I *know* they will; I feel it in Joyce. And for another thing—Rob, it's *working*. I've got them snowed. They believe I've come back to join them and I've already had a chance to look around the house." She didn't dare tell him what had come of that; she had the feeling that if Rob knew, she'd be slung over his shoulders caveman style, being carried out of San Carlos.

"But what are you looking for? Kait, *why* did you come back here?" Anna said.

"Couldn't you figure that out? I'm looking for the crystal."

Rob nodded. "I thought it was something like that. But you don't need to live there, Kait. We'll break in sometime; we'll find a way."

"No, you won't. Rob, there are *five* psychics there, besides Lydia and Joyce, and they're all crazy-paranoid. Literally. We need somebody on the inside, who can move around the house freely, and who can figure out what's going on. Because I don't just want to find the crystal, I want to find the way to destroy it. I need to know everybody's schedule, figure out a time when we can get to it with the shard. We can't just go running in some afternoon waving it over our heads. They'll slaughter us."

"We'll fight back," Rob said grimly, his jaw at its most stubborn.

"They'll still slaughter us. They're *loonies*. You haven't seen what they've done to the house—" Kaitlyn caught herself. Too much description of the danger—she was about to get slung over Rob's shoulder. She changed tracks fast. "But they trust me. This morning one of the girls said I was okay. And Joyce wants me around because the rest of them are so far into the twilight zone. So I think everything will work out—if you'll just please let me get on with it."

Rob took a long, deep breath. "Kaitlyn, I can't. It's just too dangerous. I'd rather walk in and fight it out with Gabriel myself—"

"I *know* you would." And that's just what you're *not* going to do, Kait thought. "But it's not just Gabriel—you haven't seen the others. There's a guy called Jackal Mac who's about eight feet tall and has a shaved head and muscles like a gorilla. And I don't even *know* what his psychic power is, but I know that they're all hopped up on the crystal. It makes them stronger, and it makes them crazier."

"Then I don't want you with them."

"I *have* to be. Someone has to be. Don't you see that?" Kaitlyn felt her eyes filling—they seemed to do that a lot these days—and then she decided to do something dishonorable. To use those tears. She let them come, and she asked Rob, "Don't you trust me?"

She could see how it hurt him. His own eyes had a suspicious shine, but he answered steadily, "You know I do."

"Then why won't you let me do this? Don't you think I'm capable enough?"

It was completely unfair, as well as being unkind. And it worked. Rob had to admit that he thought she was very capable. The only one of them who could pull such a thing off. He even had to admit, finally, that it was a thing that probably needed to be done.

"Then why won't you *let* me?"

Rob gave in.

"But we'll come back and check on you next Monday."

"It's too dangerous, even at school—"

"Don't push it, Kait," Rob said. "Either you let us check on you regularly or you don't stay at all. We'll be here on Monday at lunch. If you don't show up, we're coming in after you."

Kaitlyn sighed, knowing Rob wasn't going to budge. "Okay. And I'll call when I find the crystal and I know a time we can get to it. Oh, Lewis—I should have thought of this before. How do you make the secret panel slide back?"

Lewis's almond-shaped eyes widened in dismay. "Huh? Kait—I don't know!"

"Yes, you do. Something inside you knows, because you do it."

"But I can't say it in words—and besides, you don't have PK."

"Neither does Joyce or Mr. Z, and the panel was made for them. And if you can't say it in words, just think it to me. Just think *about* it and let me listen."

Lewis was reluctant and doubtful, but he screwed up his face and began to think. "I just sort of feel around with my fingers—I mean with my mind—behind the wood. Like this. And I feel something metallic here. And then when I get to about here . . ."

"It opens! So the springs or whatever have to be in those places. You're a good visual thinker, I can see just what parts of the panel you mean." Kait made a note of the images, freezing them in her memory as she hugged him. "Thanks, Lewis."

*And I'll mention you to Lydia,* she added soundlessly, because a picture of Lydia was running underneath all Lewis's other thoughts.

She felt his shy embarrassment, like a mental blush. *Thanks, Kait.*

Then she hugged Rob again. *I'm glad you came.*

*Be careful,* he sent back to her, and she wished she could just go on hugging him, standing here and feeling safe. He was so good and she cared about him so much.

When she hugged Anna she projected a private message. *Take care of him for me—please?*

Anna nodded, biting her lip to keep the tears back.

Kait left without looking behind her.

The rest of the school day was uneventful, but Kait felt exhausted. She was fumbling in her locker after the last bell rang, when Bri came running interference through the crowd.

"Hurry up," she said in her boyish voice. "Come on; Joyce is waiting for you. She sent me to get you."

"What's the rush?" Kait asked nervously. Bri's dark eyes were snapping; her cheeks were flushed with excitement.

"Black Lightning strikes! Mr. Zetes has a job for us."

# CHAPTER 8

Kait hurried toward Joyce's car with a knot in her stomach. She didn't know what kind of jobs Mr. Z had the kids do, but she knew she wasn't going to like it.

As it turned out, though, Joyce wasn't rushing them to the job. She was taking four of them shopping.

Gabriel, Renny, Frost, and Kaitlyn. They dropped Bri at the Institute where she stood on the sidewalk screaming with rage.

"It's not her fault, but she just doesn't look the part," Joyce said rather calmly as she headed for the freeway. "I told her not to put that blue in her hair."

Kaitlyn, squashed between Frost and Renny in the tiny backseat, felt as if she had lost her only friend. Not that she would rely on Bri, actually, or trust her as far as she could throw her. But the other three were openly hostile; Gabriel wasn't speaking to her, Renny kept whispering obscene suggestions in her ear, and Frost gave her a spiteful pinch whenever she thought Joyce wouldn't notice.

"What part doesn't she look?" Kait asked faintly.

"You'll see." Joyce drove them to a mall and pulled up in front of Macy's. There she ensconced Gabriel and Renny in the men's department and hustled Kait and Frost to the women's. She pushed Kait past Liz Claiborne and into Anne Klein.

"Now we're going to find you each a suit. Tweed, I think. Brown, anyway. Very conservative, only a little slit in the skirt."

Kaitlyn didn't know whether to laugh or groan. She'd never had a suit before, so this should have been exciting—but tweed?

It wasn't so bad when she got it on. Joyce pulled her hair back and Kait eyed herself in the mirror thoughtfully. She looked very trim and serious, like the librarian in a movie who starts out with her hair in a bun and horn-rim glasses and then blossoms by the end of the picture.

Frost's transformation was even more amazing. Her normal attire was a style Kait had privately dubbed "slunge"— a cross between sleaze and grunge. But in a double-breasted brown wool suit, she looked like another librarian—from the neck down.

"When we get home, you'll lose the lipstick—all of it— and half the mascara," Joyce told her. "And you'll put that rat's nest into a French twist. Also lose the gum."

The boys were equally transmogrified by three-piece Mani suits and leather shoes. Joyce paid for everything and hustled them out of the store.

"When do you tell us what we're doing?" Gabriel asked in the car.

"You'll hear the details at home. But basically it's a burglary."

Kaitlyn's stomach knotted again.


"So what now?" Anna asked. They were sitting in a Taco Bell in Daly City. Tony had promised to find them a place to stay with one of his friends—an apartment in San Francisco. But he hadn't found the place yet, and Rob was worried about staying any longer at Tony's house. So they spent as much time as possible outdoors, where they might be hard to find.

For the first time since Kaitlyn had disappeared Rob had an appetite.

But he would never in a hundred years have imagined he'd have left her at the Institute. The little witch—he still wasn't quite sure how she'd persuaded him. Of *course,* she was capable, but even a capable person could easily get killed there.

She'd asked him to trust her, that was it. All right, then, by God, he'd trust her. It was hard to let her go—he didn't think anyone realized how hard. He would very much have preferred to go himself. But . . .

I believe in you, Kaitlyn Fairchild, he thought. Just please God keep yourself safe.

He was so deep in his own thoughts that Anna had to poke him and ask silently, *I said, what now, Rob?*

"Huh? Oh, sorry." He stopped sucking on his Coke, considered. "Well, we've been too busy watching Kait to take care of Marisol. I guess we'd better do that now. Tony said his parents wouldn't be at the hospital till tonight, so it's a good time."

"Should we get Tony to go with us?" Lewis asked.

Rob thought. "No, I guess not. If it doesn't work, it'll be pretty hard on him to watch. We'll find some way to make them let us in." Tony had warned them that Marisol wasn't allowed visitors, except family.

They drove to St. Luke's Hospital in San Francisco, and Rob took the crystal shard out of the glove compartment. It was a crazy place to keep it, but they had to take it with them wherever they went. He slipped it into the sleeve of his sweater—it was just about as long as his forearm—and they strolled into the hospital.

On the third floor Rob beckoned a nurse—"Ma'am? Could I ask you a question?"—and sweet-talked her while Lewis and Anna snuck in Marisol's room. Then when all the nurse's phones began to ring at once, he snuck in himself. The ringing was provided by Lewis's PK, a neat trick, in Rob's opinion.

Inside the room, he felt Anna's shock. She was trying bravely to conceal it, but it showed through. He squeezed her shoulder and she smiled at him gratefully, then she stopped smiling and moved away so abruptly that he was startled.

Upset, probably. Marisol looked bad. Rob remembered her as a vivid, handsome girl, all tumbled red-brown hair and full pouting lips. But now . . .

She was painfully thin. There were all sorts of tubes and wires and monitors attached to her. Her right arm was on top of the blanket, with the wrist cocked at an impossible angle, turned in against the forearm. And she *moved*—her head twisted constantly, writhing on her neck, her brown eyes partway open but unseeing. Her breathing was frightening to hear: She seemed to be sucking air in through clenched teeth as she grimaced.

*I thought people in comas were quiet,* Lewis thought shakily.

Rob knew better. He'd been in a coma himself, after meeting a mountain at fifty miles an hour. He'd been hang gliding at Raven's Roost off the Blue Ridge Parkway, and he'd hit wind shear and stalled out. He'd broken both arms, both legs, his jaw, enough ribs to puncture a lung . . . and his neck. A hangman's fracture—so called because it's the same place your neck breaks when they hang you. Nobody expected him to live, but a long while later he'd woken to find himself in a Stryker frame and his granddaddy crying.

He'd spent months in bed and during those months he'd discovered his powers. Maybe they'd been there all along, and he'd just never sat still long enough to notice them, or maybe they were a gift because God was sorry about smashing a li'l ol' farm boy into that mountain. Either way, it had changed his life, made him see what a dumb sucker he'd always been, how selfish and shortsighted. Before, he'd aspired to being a guard for the Blue Devils at Duke. After, he aspired to help some.

Now, he felt shame flood up to drown him. How could he have left Marisol like this a day longer than she needed to be? He shouldn't have waited, not even to watch out for Kait. There was no excuse for it—he was still a dumb sucker and a selfish jerk. Fat lot of help he'd given Marisol.

This time Anna squeezed *his* shoulder. *None of us realized,* she said. *And we don't even know if we can help her, now. But let's try.*

He nodded, strengthened by her gentle practicality. Then, with one glance up at a picture of the Madonna and Child above the bed, he pulled the crystal out of his sleeve. It was cold and heavy in his hand. He wasn't sure where to apply it— LeShan hadn't said anything about that. After some thought he gently touched it to her forehead, the site of the third eye. A powerful energy center.

And nothing happened.

Rob waited, and waited some more. The tip of the shard rested between lank strands of red-brown hair. Marisol's head kept twisting. There was no change in her energy level.

"It's not working," Lewis whispered.

Fear pricked at Rob like tiny hornet stings. Was it his fault? Had he left it too long?

Then he thought, maybe the crystal needs a little help.

He took a deep breath, shut his eyes, and concentrated.

He never could explain exactly how he did his healing—how he knew what to do. But somehow he could feel what was wrong with a person. He could see different kinds of energy running through them like bright-colored rivers—and sometimes not flowing, but dark and stagnant, stuck. Marisol was almost all stuck. There was some sort of blockage between brain and body, and nothing was flowing either way.

How to fix that? Well, maybe start with the third eye, send energy through the crystal until it pushed hard enough against the plugs to blow them free.

Gold energy, flooding down the crystal. The crystal swirled it in a spiral and amplified it, heightening it with every turn. So that was how this thing worked!

More energy. More. Keep it flowing. He could see it flowing into Marisol, now, or at least trying to. Her third eye was stopped up as if somebody had wedged a cork in there. The energy built up behind it, roiling and gold and getting hotter by the minute. Rob felt sweat break out on his forehead. It dripped into his eyes and burned.

Ignore it. Send more energy. More, more.

Rob was breathing hard, a little frightened by what was happening. The energy was a crackling, spinning mass now, so hot and dense that he could barely hold onto the crystal. It was like trying to control a high-pressure fire hose. And trying to send more energy in was like trying to pump air into a critically overinflated bicycle tire. Something had to give.

Something did. Like a cork blowing out of a bottle, the blockage flew out of Marisol's third eye. The force of the energy behind it chased it down her body and out the soles of her feet almost faster than Rob's eye could follow.

Gold everywhere. Marisol's entire body was encased in gold as the energy raced around, rushing through veins and capillaries, circulating at a wildly accelerated speed. An internal whirlpool bath. God, it was going to kill the girl. Nobody was meant to have that much energy.

Rob jerked the crystal away from her forehead.

Marisol's body had been straining, her back arching as the energy shot through her. Now she fell back and lay completely still for the first time since they'd walked in. Her eyes were shut. Rob realized suddenly that one of her monitors was blaring like an alarm going off.

Then, as he watched, her right hand began to move. The fingers unclenched, the wrist relaxed. It looked like a normal hand again.

"Oh, God," Lewis whispered. "Oh, look at that."

Rob couldn't speak. The alarm went on blaring. And Marisol's eyes opened.

Not halfway. All the way. Rob could see the intelligence in them. He reached out to touch her cheek, and she blinked and looked scared.

"It's okay," he told her, loud over the alarm. "You're going to be all right, you understand?"

She nodded uncertainly.

Running footsteps sounded outside the door. A sturdy nurse burst in, got almost to the bed before she skidded and saw Rob.

"What do you think you're doing in here? Did you touch anything?" she demanded, hands on hips—and then she took a good look at Marisol.

"Ma'am, I think she's feeling a little better," Rob said, and smiled because he couldn't help it.

The nurse was looking from Marisol to the monitors. She broke into a huge grin, switched the monitor off, and took Marisol's pulse.

"How're you feeling, darlin'?" she asked with tears shining in her eyes. "You just hang on one minute so I can get Doctor Hirata. Your mama's going to be so happy." Then she rushed out of the room without yelling at Rob.

"I think we'd better go before Doctor Hirata gets here," Lewis whispered. "He might ask some awkward questions."

"You're right." Rob grinned at Marisol, touched her cheek again. "I'll tell your brother you're awake, okay? And he'll be over here as fast as he can drive. And your parents, too . . ."

"*Rob,*" Lewis whispered urgently.

They made it to the back stairs without being caught. On the second landing they stopped and whacked each other in glee.

"We did it!" Rob whispered, his voice echoing in the empty stairwell. "We did it!"

"*You* did it," Anna said. Her dark eyes were glowing and wise. It wasn't true, it had been the crystal, but her praise made Rob feel warm to the tips of his fingers.

He hugged Lewis and felt happy. Then he hugged Anna and felt a surge of something different from what he felt for Lewis. Stronger . . . warmer.

It confused him. He'd only felt something like it once before—when he'd found Kaitlyn alive down in Mr. Z's basement. It was almost like pain in its intensity, but it wasn't pain.

Then he pulled back, shocked and mortified. How could he let himself feel like that about anyone but Kaitlyn? How could he let himself feel even a little like that?

And he knew Anna could tell, and that she was upset, because she wouldn't meet his eyes and she was holding herself shielded. She was disgusted with him, and no wonder.

Well, one thing was for certain. It would never happen again, never.

They walked down the rest of the stairs with only Lewis talking.

"All right, this is the place," Gabriel said. It was an imposing stone building on a one-way street in the financial district of San Francisco. Through the metal-framed glass doors Kait could see a guard at a little booth.

"Joyce said the guard won't give us any trouble. We sign in with the names she told us. The law firm is Digby, Hamilton, and Miles, the floor is sixteen."

He didn't look at Kaitlyn as he spoke and he didn't glance at her as they went inside. She didn't seem to exist for him anymore. But Joyce had told them to go in pairs, and Kait was supposed to walk by Gabriel. She tried to do it without showing any more expression than he did.

The guard was wearing a red coat and talking on a cell phone. He barely looked at them as Gabriel flipped through papers on a clipboard. Gabriel signed, and then it was Kait's turn. She wrote *Eileen Cullen, Digby, Hamilton, and Miles, 16,* and *11:17,* on the appropriate lines. The 11:17 was the "Time In."

Frost and Renny signed in and they crossed the tile mosaic floor to a bank of brass elevators. A man in jeans was polishing the brass, and Kaitlyn stared at her neat brown Amalfi shoes while they waited—it seemed a long time—for the elevator.

Once inside, Gabriel pushed a large black button for floor sixteen. The button stuck. The elevator started, slowly, and with a wheeze.

Renny was snickering and Frost let out a torrent of gasping giggles.

"Do you know what I signed for my name?" Renny asked, banging the elevator door. "I signed Jimi Hendrix. And I put for the company, Dewey, Cheatum, and Howe. Get it? Dewey, Cheatum, and Howe for a law firm!"

"And I put Ima Pseudonym," Frost said, tittering.

Kaitlyn's heart gave a violent thud and began racing. She stared at them, appalled. They *looked* normal now: Frost's hair was pulled back elegantly and she was wearing only one earring in each ear and Renny could have been a junior accountant. But underneath they were still the same raving loonies.

"Are you guys *nuts?*" she hissed. "If that guard takes a look at that sheet—oh, God, or if the next person who signs in just *glances* up—we are *dead. Dead.* How could you do such a thing?"

Renny just waved a hand at her, weak with laughter. Frost sneered.

Kait turned to Gabriel to share her horror. It was a reflex— she should have known better. However horrified he might have been a minute ago, he now shrugged and flashed a quick, mocking smile.

"Good one," he said to Renny.

"I knew *you* had a sense of humor," Frost purred, running a silvery fingernail up Gabriel's gray wool sleeve. She ran it all the way to his crisp white collar, then toyed with the dark hair behind his ear.

Kaitlyn gave her a blistering glare through narrowed eyes. Then she stared at the elevator buttons, fuming silently. She didn't like this job. She *still* hadn't been told what they were doing—what can you burglarize in a law firm? She didn't even know what psychic powers Frost and Renny had. And now she had to worry about what other insane things they might decide to do.

The elevator doors opened.

"What a dump," Renny said, and snickered. Gabriel cast an appreciative look around. The walls were paneled in some beautiful reddish gold wood and the floor was dark green marble. Through glass doors Kait could see what looked like a conference room.

Gabriel glanced at the map Joyce had given him. "Now we go right."

They passed rest room doors—even those looked opulent—and entered a hallway with dark green carpeting. They stopped when they came to a set of doors blocking their way. The doors were very big and heavy; they looked like metal, but when Kaitlyn touched one it was wood. And locked.

"This is it," Gabriel said. "Okay, Renny."

But Renny was gone. Frost, standing a little way back, said, "He had to go to the little boys' room." She was struggling to keep a straight face.

Kaitlyn clenched her fists. She'd seen the graffiti at the Institute; she could just bet what he was doing in there. "Now what?" she snarled at Gabriel. "Look, are you going in there to get him, or am I?"

Gabriel ignored her, but she could see the tightness of his jaw. He started toward the bathroom, but at that moment Renny came out, his face the picture of innocence.

"I would have thought," Gabriel said without looking at Kait, "that you'd be happy if we screwed this up. After all, you're not really one of us . . . are you?"

Kaitlyn felt chilled. "I am, even if you don't believe it," she said, working to put sincerity in her voice. "And maybe I don't like stealing things, but I don't want to get caught and sent to jail, either." As Renny approached, walking cockily, she added in an undertone, "I don't even know why we *brought* him."

"Then watch and see," Gabriel said tersely. "Renny, this is it. From here on you need a security pass."

The device on the wall looked vaguely familiar. It was like the machines at the gas station that you slide a credit card through to charge gas automatically.

"Yeah, magnetic," Renny muttered. He pushed his glasses back with an index finger on the nosepiece and ran a hand over the security pass reader. "Anybody looking?" he said.

"No, but do it fast," Gabriel replied.

Renny stroked the device again and again. His face was wrinkled up, monkeylike. Kaitlyn chewed her lip and watched the central area from which they'd just come. Anybody stepping out of an elevator would see them.

"There you are, baby," Renny whispered suddenly. And the right hand door swung open.

So now Kaitlyn knew. Renny had PK, psychokinesis; he could move objects by power of mind alone. Including the little mechanisms inside security pass readers, apparently.

Just like Lewis, Kaitlyn thought. I wonder if there's something about short guys.

The door closed behind them when they went through.

Gabriel led them quickly down the hallway. On the left other hallways branched away; on the right were secretaries' carrels with computers on the desks. Behind the carrels were office doors, with names on brass nameplates beside them. Kaitlyn saw one nameplate that said WAR ROOM.

Maybe law is more exciting than I thought.

They came to another set of the big doors and Renny dealt with them in the same way. They walked down another hallway.

The farther they got into private territory, the more frightened Kait was. If anyone caught them here, they would have some explaining to do. Joyce hadn't given them any advice about that—Kaitlyn had the sick feeling that Gabriel might be expected to use his power.

"What are we *looking* for, anyway?" Kait whispered to Gabriel between her teeth. "I mean, have they got the Mona Lisa here or something?"

"Keep your stupid mouth shut. Anyone walking up one of those hallways could hear us."

Kaitlyn was stunned into silence. Gabriel had never spoken to her like that before. And he hadn't said a word about Renny and Frost doing really dangerous things.

She blinked and set her teeth, determined not to speak again, no matter what.

"This is it," Gabriel said at last. The nameplate on the door said E. Marshall Winston. "Locked," Gabriel said. "Renny, open it. Everybody else keep your eyes out. If anybody sees us here, we've had it."

# CHAPTER 9

Kaitlyn stared down the hall until she saw red after-images. She was sweating onto her white silk blouse. Then she heard a snap and the door opened.

"Frost, keep watching out. Renny, come with me."

Kaitlyn felt sure Gabriel wanted her to keep watching, too, but couldn't bring himself to name her. She followed Renny into the dark office. Gabriel was pulling the shades, cutting out the night.

"She said Mr. Z thought it would probably be in the file cabinet—I guess that's this." He went over to a wooden credenza with file drawers built in. "Locked."

Renny took care of that, while Gabriel shone a penlight on the drawers. Kaitlyn's heart was thumping, quick and hard. She was watching a crime being committed—a serious, major crime. And if they got caught, she was as guilty as any of the others.

Renny stepped back and Gabriel pulled the top file drawer out. Then he cursed softly, closed it, and pulled out the lower one.

It was crammed with hanging files in green folders, each one neatly labeled. Kaitlyn watched the penlight illuminate labels: Taggart and Altshuld—Reorganization. Star Systematics— Merger. Slater Inc.—Liquidation. TCW—Refinancing.

"Yes!" Gabriel whispered. He pulled out the thick hanging file that said TCW.

Inside were a lot of manila folders. Gabriel began going through them deftly. It all seemed to be paper, mostly white paper covered with courier type, a few booklets with paper as thin as Bible pages.

In a strange way, Kaitlyn felt relieved. It didn't seem so wrong to steal paper, even if it was important paper. It wasn't like taking money or jewels.

Gabriel's breath hissed out.

He was peering into a manila envelope. He pulled out the papers inside it, scattering them on the credenza's flat top, and shone the light on them.

Kaitlyn squinted, trying to make out what they were. They looked like certificates or something, heavy blue-gray paper, with a fancy border around the edges.

Then her eyes focused on tiny words Gabriel was tracing with his finger. Pay to Bearer . . .

Oh, my *God.*

Kaitlyn stood paralyzed, the print swimming before her eyes. She kept staring at the number on the bond, sure it couldn't be right, but it kept saying the same thing.

U.S. $1,000,000.

One million dollars.

And there were lots of the things. A pile of them.

Gabriel was flipping through, counting under his breath. "Twenty," he said at last. "That's right." He gathered the bonds up in his hands and caressed them. He was wearing the same expression Kaitlyn had seen when they toured Mr. Z's mansion. Like Scrooge counting his gold pieces.

Kaitlyn forgot her vow not to speak. "We're stealing twenty million dollars?" she whispered.

"A drop in the bucket," Gabriel said, and caressed the bonds again. Then he straightened up and began to briskly put the other folders back into the drawer. "We don't want a custodian or somebody to see anything's wrong tonight. Not until we get out of the building."

When the drawer was shut, he put the manila envelope inside his jacket. "Let's go."

Nobody was in the hall and they passed the first set of doors safely. From this side, the doors just pushed open. Kaitlyn didn't know whether to be nauseated or relieved. They were committing a felony. Gabriel was walking around with twenty *million* stolen dollars against his chest. And the horrible thing was that they were getting away with it.

Of course, on the brighter side, they were getting away with it. Kaitlyn wasn't going to jail.

That was when the two men stepped out of an office in front of them.

Kaitlyn's heart jumped into her mouth and then *burst*. Her feet were rooted to the floor and her hands and arms were numb. Her chest was squeezed so tightly that there was no room for her lungs to breathe.

Still, at first she thought the men wouldn't look her way. They did. Then she thought they wouldn't keep looking, wouldn't stare—because surely she was frightened *enough*, she'd been punished enough already. She wanted nothing to do with a life of crime.

But the men kept looking, and then the men were walking toward Kaitlyn's group. And then their mouths were moving. That was all Kaitlyn could take in at first, that the mouths were moving. She couldn't hear what they were saying, everybody seemed to be underwater or in a dream.

But a minute later her mind ran it all back for her, sharp and clear. "What are you doing here? You're not interns."

And there was suspicion in the voices, or at least a sense of wrongness. And Kaitlyn knew that if somebody didn't come up with something quick, that suspicion was going to harden and gel and they'd be trapped like flies in amber.

Think, girl. Think, *think*.

But for once, absolutely nothing came to her. Her quick

brain was useless. All she could think of was the lump under Gabriel's black-flecked gray jacket, which was starting to look as big as an elephant inside a boa constrictor.

That was when Frost stepped in.

She moved forward in a slithery, silky way totally at odds with her brown suit. Kaitlyn saw her smile at the two men and take their hands.

God, not *now*, Kaitlyn thought. Flirting won't stop them. But this passed in a flash, because Frost was talking, and not in a sexy way, but bright and cheerful.

"You must be—Jim and Chris," she said, hanging on to their hands like somebody at a tea party. "My uncle told me about you. You're in the corporate group, right?"

The two men looked at her, then at each other.

"We're just looking around. I'm thinking of coming here in a few years, and these are my friends. My uncle said it would be all right, and he gave me his security pass."

"Your uncle?" one of the men said, not as sharp as before, but bewildered.

"Mr. Morshower. He's a senior partner—but you know him, because he knows you. Why don't you call him at home and check it out? He'll tell you everything's okay."

"Oh, Sam," one of the young men said weakly. Funny that Kaitlyn had suddenly realized they were young. "I mean, Mr. Morshower." He threw a look at the other young man and said, "We won't bother him."

"No, no. I insist," Frost said. "Please call him." She actually picked up a phone from one of the secretaries' desks.

"That's all right," said the second young man. He looked unhappy. For the first time Kaitlyn was able to look at them as people. One had brown hair and one had black hair, but they were both wearing white shirts and striped ties knotted all the way up, even at this hour, and they both looked pale and somewhat harassed.

"Are you sure?" Frost asked, sounding disappointed. She put the phone back. The young men gave wry, watery smiles.

"Can you find your way out?" they asked, and Frost said of course, they could. Kaitlyn hardly dared to say anything, but she managed to smile at them as she walked past, and back down the hall, and toward the elevators.

Her chest was squeezed again, but this time the pressure was from inside. She was so bursting with laughter that she could hardly contain it until they were in the elevator.

Then they were all laughing, howling, shrieking, almost falling down. Renny did fall down, drumming his heels on the elevator floor. They were insane. Kaitlyn very nearly kissed Frost.

"But how did you know?" she said. "Did Joyce tell you?"

"No, no." Frost tossed her ash blond head impatiently. "I got it from them. I could've done it just from a piece of their clothing or one of those stupid fat silver pens they had in their pockets."

"Those were Montblanc pens. And they weren't silver, they

were platinum," Gabriel said quietly, and then they all had to be quiet because they'd reached the lobby. Frost swerved toward the red-coated guard to sign out, but Gabriel pushed her past him and into the street. The guard looked after them, came to the door.

"Step on it," Kait said to Gabriel as they scrambled into Joyce's car.

"It's called psychometry," Frost said to Kait after another period of hilarity. Gabriel was driving wildly through the streets of San Francisco.

Kaitlyn had heard of psychometry. You could tell a person's whole history by handling a personal object. "But why did you pick Mr. Morshower?"

"Because I could tell they were afraid of him. They were supposed to have something—a merger agreement?—sent to his client by the FedEx deadline today and they haven't done it."

Frost reeled the words off glibly, but Kaitlyn could tell she wasn't really interested anymore. And the resourcefulness and sanity that seemed to have taken her over during the crisis was fading. The inner fogginess was coming back. It was as if intelligence were a tool this girl used, and then threw away when it wasn't needed anymore.

That put a damper on Kaitlyn's excitement. The feeling of having brilliantly outwitted a cruel world was dying away. For a while it had made her breathless, but now . . .

We really are crooks, she thought with a mental sigh.

And she was afraid of Frost's powers. Anybody who could find out that much about you with a touch was dangerous. Frost had already touched Kait when they were in the backseat of Joyce's car. Had she found anything out?

Must not have, Kaitlyn concluded, or Joyce wouldn't have sent me. Maybe it helps that I've developed shields in the web. But I'll have to be careful—one false step and . . .

"Just try not to get a ticket," she said to Gabriel, who was rounding a corner wildly.

He didn't answer. Great. He wasn't speaking to her again.

"Did I pass?" Kait asked Joyce.

Joyce looked at her, going through all the signs of being startled.

"What do you mean?"

"It was a test, wasn't it? So, did I pass or fail? I didn't do much."

They were sitting up in Joyce's room, drinking herbal tea in the wee hours of the morning. Renny and Frost had gone upstairs to drink something stronger, and Gabriel had gone with them, never glancing at Kait.

"Yes, it was a test," Joyce said at last. "The money will come in handy, but mostly I had to make sure that you were really one of us. Now you're a full member of the team—and if you ever think of crossing us, remember that you've participated in a felony. The police take a dim view of that."

She took a sip of tea and mused briefly. "You and Gabriel passed," she added. "As for Frost and Renny . . ."

"They did most of the work."

"But from what you've said, they also did a lot of stupid things." For a moment Kait thought Joyce was going to go on, to confide in her. But then Joyce stood up and said shortly, "We'll stick to other kinds of jobs from now on. Long distance, maybe. Mac is good at that."

"Is he?" Kait asked innocently. "What's his power? I don't know what he or Bri do."

She held her breath, sure Joyce wouldn't tell her. But Joyce shrugged and said, "His specialty is astral projection, actually."

Let your mind do the walking, Kait thought. It was Lewis's phrase. So Mac was responsible for the astral projections and psychic attacks against them on the way to Canada. "But we saw at least four figures," she blurted before she thought. "And one of them was Bri—I *recognized* her."

Joyce was setting the clock radio by the bedside and answered impatiently and almost absently. "Mac used to guide them, help them get away and then help them get back into their bodies. But anybody can do astral projection if they have the power of the crys—" She broke off so quickly her little white teeth actually snapped shut. Then she said, "Bed, Kaitlyn. It's way past time."

I knew they used the crystal to project themselves, Kait

thought. I saw it beside their astral forms. But she didn't tell Joyce. She said, "Okay, but are you going to tell me what Bri does?"

"No. I'm going to go to bed."

And that was all Kaitlyn could get out of her.

Upstairs, Kaitlyn could hear the voices in Gabriel's room. Gabriel and Frost and Renny? Gabriel and Frost? There was no way to find out.

"Too bad I can't do astral projection," she muttered.

Lydia was asleep, of course, so there was no chance to talk to her. And no way to try out the secret panel downstairs—it was directly across from Joyce's room.

Nothing to do, then, but go to sleep . . . but it took her a long time to relax, and when she did, she had nightmares.

The next morning she saw Frost coming out of Gabriel's room.

Gabriel came out a moment later, while Kaitlyn was still standing motionless by the stairs. He was shrugging into his T-shirt. He looked particularly handsome in a just-roused, early morning way. His hair was very wavy, as if someone had run fingers through it to release the curl, his eyes were hooded and lazy and there was a faint smile of satisfaction on his lips.

Kaitlyn discovered that she wanted to kill him. The image that came to her mind was of hitting him with a rolling pin, but not in an amusing, comic-book sort of way. In a way that would make splinters of bone fly and splatter the walls with blood.

His expression changed very slightly when he saw her standing there. His eyes narrowed and his mouth soured. But he held her gaze stonily and walked by her without speaking.

"Today you'll do some testing," Joyce said to Kaitlyn after breakfast.

But before starting with Kait, Joyce settled the other psychics in. Testing had changed since the old days, Kaitlyn thought. Then, Joyce's experiments had been scientific, the kind of thing you could report in a journal article. Now, everything seemed oriented toward crime.

Jackal Mac, wearing swim trunks full of holes, was led toward the back lab with the isolation tank, and Kait heard Joyce saying, "Just take a look inside that safe in the city, see if the papers are there. Then try the long-distance job, check out that furnace."

Astral projection for felons, Kait thought. Is that how they knew the twenty million was in that filing cabinet? But how did they know to look in a filing cabinet in the first place?

Renny was practicing his PK, but not on a random event generator as Lewis had done. He had a collection of locks in front of him, as well as diagrams that looked like the insides of locks. Without touching anything, he was making the locks open and close.

Aha, Kait thought. Well, that makes sense. He needs to

know what part of the lock to push with his mind to open it. PK doesn't give you magical knowledge about locks, just the power to poke around inside them.

It explained Gabriel's comment about Lewis not being able to open the combination lock on the crystal—wherever the crystal *was*. Kaitlyn would bet her last dime that Mr. Z had some sort of fiendishly complicated locking device, something that Lewis couldn't get a diagram for. Which meant the only way to open the lock would be to somehow figure out the eight numbers in the combination.

Whoa, girl. Take it easy. You've got to *find* that crystal first.

As soon as she'd thought it, Kaitlyn shifted nervously. Gabriel and Frost were sitting across the room by the stereo. But *he* was studying a pile of CDs and *she* couldn't tell anything unless she touched a person. Besides, she seemed to be studying Gabriel. She was looking more sleazy than grungy today, in an orange top cut so low that you could ski down the bare skin in front. Her hair had returned to its usual uncombed state and her lips were vivid tangerine.

"What are you doing?" Kait asked Bri, as a diversion.

Bri glanced up. "Can't you tell?"

She was holding a plumb bob on its line above a map. The plumb bob and line looked just like what Kaitlyn's father had used to determine if a surface was vertical, just a small weight hanging freely from a cord. The map was upside down to Kaitlyn and she could only make out "—Charlotte Islands."

"I'm dowsing," Bri said. She gave a boyish grin at Kait's surprise.

"I thought you used a forked stick for dowsing."

"No, stupid. That's for dowsing for water or gold or something. This kind is to find things that are far away, and you can do it for *anything*."

"Oh." As Kaitlyn watched, the plumb bob began to swing in circles over a section of the map.

"See? All you got to do is think of what you're looking for. Sasha used to do the other kind of dowsing, only he didn't use a stick. He used coat hangers shaped like *l*s."

"Sasha?"

"Oh, yeah. You never met him." Bri snorted laughter. "He was blond and pretty cute, critty pute. Cute."

"Was he one of Mr. Z's first students?" Kaitlyn asked quickly. "Part of the pilot study, like you?" Bri seemed to be on the verge of one of those bizarre attacks which always ended in her repeating nonsense words until it drove everyone crazy.

"Yeah, him and Parté King. Not his real name. Parté King was a bike messenger in the city, a real skinny guy. Both terrific psychics."

"But what happened to them? Are they dead?"

"Huh? They—" Suddenly Bri's face turned cold, as if someone had turned off a light switch inside her. She looked up at Kait and her face was hard. "Yeah, they're dead," she said. "Sasha and Parté King. You wanna make something of it?"

Joyce was coming out of the back lab. Kaitlyn moved away from Bri's carrel feeling depressed.

The dark psychics were nicer to her now, sure, but it was like a geyser pool bubbling between eruptions. Ready to go off in her face at any minute.

The doorbell rang.

"That's the volunteers—would you get them, Gabriel?" Joyce said bustling around with her clipboard. "Frost, I'm going to have you do some psychometry with them; Kait, I'm going to start you with some remote viewing."

She sat Kaitlyn in a carrel with a photograph in front of her. It was an eight-by-ten glossy of a wall safe.

"I want you to concentrate on the picture and draw anything that comes into your mind," she said. "Try to imagine what might be *in* the safe, okay?"

"Okay," Kaitlyn said, concealing a surge of rebellion. This was *not* legitimate research, and she was losing her taste for larceny.

"I'm going to put this on your forehead," Joyce added, producing a piece of masking tape.

This time the surge was one of alarm, and Kait couldn't hide it. "An electrode over my third eye?" she asked as lightly as she could.

"You know what it is. Since you haven't been exposed to the big crystal, we'll use this to enhance your powers."

"Well, why don't you expose me to the big crystal, then?" Kait asked recklessly. "Those little chips give me a headache, and—"

"Sorry, that's up to Mr. Zetes, and he doesn't want you anywhere near it. Now, hold still." Joyce's tone said she'd had enough. Her eyes had gone as hard as gems and she barely pushed aside Kaitlyn's bangs before slapping the tape on Kait's forehead.

Kait felt the piece of crystal cold against her skin. It was bigger than the piece Joyce had used in the old days, maybe because now Joyce wasn't trying to conceal it. This one felt the size of a quarter.

Knowing where it came from, she could scarcely keep herself from tearing the tape off. But then she saw Gabriel in the doorway, looking sardonic and amused.

*You don't have anything against the crystal, do you? After all, you're one of us. . . .*

Kaitlyn shot back, *I'm not one of* them. *But I guess you are.*

*Right, angel. I'm one of them—and don't you forget it.*

Kaitlyn left the tape alone.

But she didn't want to help Joyce with the safe. She stared at the photograph, then shut her eyes and just scribbled, taking the time to think.

She understood now how the dark psychics had attacked them on the road to Canada. First Bri probably dowsed to figure out where they were. Then Jackal Mac guided their astral forms to the right location. After that, they could assault their victims with weird apparitions or with Renny's long-distance PK. Simple. You could terrorize people without ever going near them.

And now Joyce was expecting her to join in the long-distance crime wave, to help them visualize some safe to break into.

Wait a minute.

If she could see into a safe, why not a room? Why not try to visualize the secret room below the stairway?

Without opening her eyes, Kait groped for a new piece of paper. She'd never tried to visualize a specific place before, but the remote viewing process was old hat by now. Stretch out and let your thoughts drift. Block out any external noises. Let the darkness take you down. . . .

And now, think of the secret room. Think of walking up to the door, visualize that hallway lit by fluorescent greenish light. Walk up to the door . . . and let the darkness take you. . . .

Her hand began to cramp and itch.

Then it was dancing and skidding over the paper, moving of its own accord while Kaitlyn floated in darkness. Sketching fluidly, easily. Kaitlyn held her breath and tried not to be anxious, tried not to think or feel anything.

Okay, slowing down—is it done yet? Can I look?

She couldn't resist the temptation. One eye opened, then both were open and wide. Chills swept over her, as she stared, not at the piece of paper her hand was still working on, but at the first one, the one that was supposed to be only scribbles.

Oh, God, what *is* it? What have I done?

# CHAPTER 10

I t wasn't her usual style. It was cartoonish, but *gruesome* cartoonish, like the new breed of comic books. At first Kait thought it might be a picture of her beating Gabriel to death with a rolling pin.

But those long tear-shaped things flying out at the edges were flames. Flames, fire. It was a fireball or an explosion, circular, with smoke billowing every which way, and the shock waves moving outward like ripples on a pond.

And in the center was a stick figure of a person. Like Itchy the cat after Scratchy hits him with a flamethrower. Arms waving, legs splayed in a grotesque dance.

Ha, ha.

Except that since Kait's drawings always came true, somebody was going to get burned. Somebody involved with that safe, maybe? Kait tried to recapture what she'd been thinking about while scribbling. Too much. Psychic attacks, Canada,

Bri dowsing, Jackal Mac on the astral plane, Renny's PK. And the safe, of course, even though she'd tried not to think about it.

This picture could involve any of those things. Kait had a very bad feeling about it, made worse by a nagging, growing headache.

What about the other picture? The one that was supposed to be visualizing the secret room? Kait looked at it and wanted to slam her fist on the table.

Garbage! Trash! Not literally, but the drawing was useless. It wasn't the inside of a room at all, and it certainly didn't show a crystal. It was a line drawing of a sailing ship on a pretty, wavy ocean. Sitting on the deck, right below the sails, was a Christmas tree. A nice little Christmas tree with garland and a star on top.

Kaitlyn's eyes were stinging with pain and fury. The first picture left her helpless. The second was useless.

And that makes *me* completely hopeless.

Suddenly she couldn't hold her feelings in. She crumpled them up with a savage motion and threw them as hard as she could at Frost. One hit Frost on the cheek, the other hit Frost's volunteer.

"Kaitlyn!" Joyce shouted. Frost leaped up, one hand to her cheek. Then she made a rush for Kait, her nails clawed.

*"Frost!"* Joyce shouted.

Kaitlyn put a foot out to block Frost. In elementary school

she'd been a pretty good fighter, and right now it felt good to fend Frost off. And if Frost whacked her, she was going to whack right back. She felt calm and queenly standing there ready to kick Frost in the chest.

"Come on, snowflake," she said. "Come get me!"

"I will, you!" Frost shrieked, charging again.

"Gabriel, help me! Renny, you stay in that seat!" Joyce shouted.

Joyce and Gabriel dragged Frost back and sat her down hard in a chair. Kait was tempted to go after her, but didn't.

"Now," Joyce said in a voice to cut through steel, "what is going on?"

"I got mad," Kaitlyn said, not at all sorry. "Everything I draw is *trash*."

"Smash," Bri said quietly. Kait had an urge to snicker.

Joyce was staring at Kait, lips compressed, brow furrowed. Abruptly, she pulled the tape off Kait's forehead.

"How do you feel?" she said.

"Bad. I have a headache."

"Right," Joyce muttered. "All right, you go upstairs and lie down. But first you pick up those papers and put them in the trash can where they belong."

Stiff-backed, Kait stalked over to the crumpled wads, picked them up. Then, as Joyce turned back to her clipboard, she faked throwing them at Frost again. Frost went red, and Kait hurried out of the room.

Upstairs, she shut the door of her bedroom and wondered what had come over her.

Was she crazy? No, of course—it was the crystal. Joyce had used a big piece of the crystal and it had made Kaitlyn act like the psycho psychics.

And I must be pretty crazy to start with, because it didn't take much, Kaitlyn thought. Maybe Bri and the others were a lot saner than me to begin with. I wish I could have seen them before . . .

She let out her breath, trying to make sense of her feelings. She'd really been furious there, furious and completely indifferent to any consequences her actions might have. She would happily have scratched Frost's eyes out.

Well, maybe that wasn't so crazy. After all . . .

Kaitlyn sat on the bed heavily. She kept trying to tell herself she didn't care about Gabriel—but if she didn't care, why did she hate Frost so much today?

And Gabriel certainly didn't jump up to defend me, she thought. He probably enjoyed watching us fight.

Kait rubbed her throbbing forehead, wishing she could go outside and lie under a tree. She needed air. Idly, she toyed with the balls of paper in her other hand.

Then she looked up as the door opened.

"Can I come in? My riding lesson was canceled this morning," Lydia said. She sounded depressed.

"It's your room," Kaitlyn said.

She kept rolling the paper balls around, squashing them against each other. She'd taken them so Frost wouldn't pick them out of the trash can and laugh at them—but was that the only reason? Now she wondered if it hadn't also been some survival instinct kicking in.

None of her drawings was really worthless. Maybe she'd better keep them.

"What's the matter?" Lydia asked.

Kait frowned. Lydia was picking *now* to talk? "I've got a headache," she said shortly, and dropped the paper balls in a drawer.

Then she remembered her promise to Lewis. She glanced at Lydia out of the side of her eye.

The smaller girl looked very neat in a brown riding habit. Her heavy dark hair was pulled away from her small pale face, and her green eyes showed up more than ever. Neat and rich—and miserable.

"Have you got a boyfriend?" Kait asked abruptly.

"Huh? No." She hesitated, then added, "I'm not after Gabriel, if that's what you mean."

"It isn't." Kait didn't want to talk about Gabriel. "I was thinking about Lewis—did you ever notice him?"

Lydia looked startled—almost frightened. "Lewis! You mean Lewis Chao?"

"No, I mean Lewis and Clark. Of course Lewis Chao. What do you think of him?"

"Well . . . he was nice to me. Even when the rest of you weren't."

"Well, he thinks you're nice, too. And I told him—" Kaitlyn caught herself. Oh, Lord, this headache was making her stupid. She'd almost said that she'd told Lewis *yesterday* she'd bring him up. Frantically, she tried to think of another way to end the sentence.

"I told him that you'd think you were too good for him. That you'd just laugh at him. That was a long time ago," Kaitlyn finished at random.

Lydia's eyes seemed to turn a darker green. "I wouldn't laugh. I like nice guys," she said. "I don't think *you're* very nice. You're turning out just like them," she added, and left the room, slamming the door.

Kaitlyn leaned back against the headboard, convinced she just wasn't cut out to be a spy.

And she still didn't feel quite herself. One thing was certain, she couldn't let Joyce put her in contact with the crystal again. It made her lose control, and when she lost control anything could happen.

And another thing was certain, too. She couldn't use her power to visualize the hidden room downstairs, and Joyce wasn't going to let her anywhere near it. So the only solution was for her to go down there herself.

But *when?*

Still rubbing her forehead, Kaitlyn toed her sneakers off and lay down.

At first she shut her eyes just to ease the headache. But soon her thoughts began to unwind and her muscles relaxed. This time there were no nightmares.

When she woke she had that feeling of desertion again. The house seemed too quiet, the warm air too still.

At least her headache was gone. Moving slowly, she got off the bed and tiptoed to the door.

Silence.

Oh, they *wouldn't* leave me alone again. Not unless it's a trap. If it's a trap, I'm not going anywhere.

But she had a *right* to go downstairs. She lived here; she was a full member of the team. She could be going down to get a diet soda or an apple.

Down the stairs, then.

And she had a right to look around downstairs. She could be looking for the others; she could be lonely. She kept the right words on her lips.

"Joyce, I just wanted to ask you—"

But Joyce wasn't in her room.

"Are you guys still testing—?"

But the front lab was empty. So was the back lab.

And the kitchen, and the dining room, and the living room. Kaitlyn pushed aside the living room curtains to look outside the house. Nobody playing hacki sack or Frisbee tag. Only juniper hedges and acacia trees. She couldn't even see Joyce's car.

Okay, so maybe it's a trap. But it's too good an opportunity to miss.

Heart beating in her throat, Kaitlyn crept toward the paneled hallway under the staircase.

The middle panel, she thought, with one guilty glance behind her at the French doors leading to Joyce's room. She ran her fingers over the smooth dark wood, reaching up to find the crack that was the top of the door.

Okay, she was in front of it. Now to find the place Lewis had showed her. She shut her eyes and concentrated on the images she'd gotten from Lewis. They weren't exactly visual, more like just a feeling of how she should move her hands. He'd found something around this level—and then he'd pushed with his mind. She would push with her fingers.

And then he'd moved over *this* way, and down, and pushed again. Kaitlyn pushed again, pressing hard.

Something clicked.

Kaitlyn's eyes flew open. I did it! I actually did it!

Excitement bubbled up from her toes, fizzling out to fill every part of her body. She was *impressed* with herself.

The middle panel had disappeared, sliding to the left. Stairs led downward, illuminated only by faint reddish lights at foot-level.

The bubbles seemed to be making a fizzing in her ears now, but Kaitlyn tried to listen over it. Still, silence.

Okay. Going down.

With each step into the red dimness, she felt a little of the effervescence leaving her. This wasn't a nice place. If she'd been a few years younger, it would have made her think of trolls.

At the bottom she groped for the light switch she knew should be there—and then snatched her fingers back. Too much light wasn't good. If there was somebody in the room at the end of the hall, they might notice.

But if she didn't turn on the light, she'd have to walk the whole way in darkness. Just the thought made her knees unsteady.

There was no help for it. Tensing her muscles, she put a hand on the wall to guide her and began walking forward. In a moment she had to put the other hand out to feel for obstacles. She was blind.

Each step was hard, and she had to clench her teeth tighter and tighter to make herself keep going. The red staircase behind her began to feel more and more tempting.

Oh, God, what if somebody came and saw the panel open and closed it *and locked her in here?*

The thought was so terrible that she almost turned around and ran. Instead, she used the energy to force herself forward. And *one* more step, and *one* more step—

Her outstretched fingers encountered a door.

Her need for light was so great that she reached automatically for the knob, without listening to see what might be on the other side. But instead of a knob, her fingers found something like a calculator built into the door.

What was it? She could feel little square bumps in a regular pattern. It really did feel like a calculator.

Oh, you idiot. You *idiot.* You must still be stupid from the testing this morning. It's a combination lock. Not one of those padlock kinds; one of the fancy ones, where you punch numbers on a keypad.

And if this was the combination lock, then behind that door . . .

It was *in* there. That grotesque thing with the obscene crystalline growths all over it. It was squatting in there just a few feet away.

Kaitlyn was swamped by a feeling of evil.

And then—she heard noises.

From behind the door.

*They were in there with it.*

Oh, God, I'm so stupid, I'm so stupid. Of course, they're in there. This is where they go in the afternoons, they go to the crystal, and they're all sitting in there around it *right now.*

Don't panic, don't panic, she told herself, but it was too late. She *was* panicking. She hadn't even asked Lewis how to shut the secret panel. She was incompetent and stupid and they were right inside there and she didn't have time to get away.

Another noise sounded—very close to the door.

Suddenly Kaitlyn was moving, without thinking, without

caring where she was going. With great stocking-footed leaps she was sailing down the hallway toward the red stairs. She reached the first step and began to scramble up, banging her knee, ignoring it, scrambling on. Using her hands. She got to the top of the stairs and the white light of the hallway blazed into her eyes. That light was the only thing that stopped her, kept her from running through the living room and out of the house—or up to her bedroom to hide under the bed. She was almost like an animal in her blind instinct to get under cover.

"Kaitlyn, what on *earth*—?"

The voice was high and light, surprised. Kaitlyn turned terrified eyes on Lydia.

"What happened? Did they do something to you?" Lydia was looking past her down the stairs.

A tiny bit of Kaitlyn's mind returned. There was a chance, just a chance for help—for salvation. Lydia knew about the panel; Lydia seemed worried about Kaitlyn.

"Oh, Lydia," she said, and her voice came out a croak. "I—I . . ."

She'd meant to lie, to say that she'd been down with the others and she'd gotten scared. But somehow what came out was, "Oh, Lydia, I know I shouldn't have gone down there. But Joyce never lets me do anything. I just wanted to see—and now Joyce is going to be *furious*. I don't know how to get the panel shut."

Lydia was looking at her with level green eyes.

s, she couldn't leave when she'd come so far.

tick it out until Monday—and if she could

r the shard—

ould figure out the combination.

get into that room alone.

as she went, Kaitlyn headed for her art kit.

hadn't been concentrating on the right

trying to see inside the room—and heaven

he'd gotten the garbage she had. Maybe

tmas tree in with the crystal. Maybe there

tle in there. Anyway, now she knew what

eeded numbers for that combination lock.

art materials, with her beloved pastels and

ook, she was going to get those numbers.

, ceiling light off. Kaitlyn threw a T-shirt

e nightstand to dim it. Okay, that was the

air swathed in a towel, feet tucked under

paper.

orked so hard at blanking her mind. She

he chute into the waiting darkness. The

over her fingers and she felt them moving,

h new pastel sticks, swirling colors across

er she looked at what she'd done.

can't *believe* it!

"I just want ... blurted, "I'm sor ...

There was a ... was dizzy. Lydia ... caught between ... teeth.

Finally she ... looked up ... do. You're one o ... the left wall qu ...

The panel ...

Kaitlyn st ... floor.

"Be caref ... Kaitlyn ... away before K ...

Kaitlyn stood ... Her legs we ... cent bruise ...

Lydia k ...

There ... no ... house who ... Kaitlyn's li ...

So wh ... the ...

Oh, i ... Kaitlyn fl ...

But t ... safe was t ...

frightened she wa ... If she could just ... get Rob to give h ... —and if she d ... She had to, to ... Drying hersel ... Last time she ... thing. She'd been ... only knew why s ... Joyce kept a Chris ... was a ship in a bo ... to think about.

*Numbers.* She r ... And with her own ... her faithful sketchb ... Door shut tigh ... over the lamp on th ... proper ambiance. H ... her, she put pastel to ... She had never w ... *threw* herself down ... itch and cramp took ... reaching out to snat ... the page.

A few minutes la ... I can't believe it. I ...

It was another ship with a Christmas tree.

This time in color. The ship's sails were dove white, the planks were tinted sienna brown, the pretty curly waves were three shades of blue. And standing proudly on the deck was a celadon green Christmas tree with poppy red garland and a yellow ocher star.

Kaitlyn wadded the paper up in a fury and threw it at the mirror.

She wanted to break things. She wanted to throw something heavier—

The door burst open.

Instantly, Kaitlyn's fury disappeared and terror rushed in to fill the vacuum. Lydia had told them. They had all run up here to get her. She could hear thudding footsteps in the hall behind the figure in her doorway.

"Hey, Kait, how come it's so dark in here?" Bri shouted. Without waiting for an answer, she added, "Come on! Get dressed!"

For what, execution? Kait wondered. She heard her own voice saying almost quietly, "Why?"

"Because we're celebrating! We're all going out to the club! Come on, get dressed, put your best duds on. Plenty of *guys,*" Bri added slyly. "You got something to wear? I could lend you something."

"Uh—that's okay, I've got something," Kaitlyn said hastily. She could just imagine what sort of "duds" Bri might have to lend. But Bri's urgency was contagious, and Kaitlyn felt herself being propelled toward the closet. "I've got a black dress—but why are we celebrating?"

"We did a job this afternoon," Bri said, shaking her clasped hands over her head like a boxer. "An astral job, a real big job. We killed LeShan."

"I met her on the stairs. She said she had to see you," Tony's friend said. Rob, Lewis, and Anna were sitting in the tiny one-room apartment. Rob peered behind Tony's friend at the person who had to see them.

"I've been tracking you from house to house," the girl said. She had clusters of curly yellow hair and the profile of a Grecian maiden. Despite the yellow hair, her complexion was olive and her eyes almond-shaped like Lewis's. She was very pretty.

And familiar. "I know you," Rob said. "You were—you were with the Fellowship."

"Tamsin," Anna said, before the girl could.

The girl—Tamsin—nodded at her. She looked as if she were trying to smile, but it didn't work. The smile turned into a trembling of her lips, then her head went down and she started to cry.

From the doorway, Tony's friend said, "I'll catch you guys later," and left hurriedly.

"What is it?" Rob was trying to lead the girl to a chair. His initial excitement at seeing her had deflated like a pricked balloon. He'd thought the Fellowship had sent someone to help.

"I came to help," the girl choked out, as if she could hear his thought—and probably she could. The Fellowship were all psychics. "LeShan sent me."

"Then what's the matter?" Anna asked quietly, putting a gentle hand on Tamsin's quivering shoulder.

"Nothing was the matter—until a little while ago. Then I felt it. I felt him die. LeShan is dead."

Rob's skin tingled with shock. He had to swallow hard. "Are you sure?"

"I *felt* it. We thought we'd be safe from them on our new island. But they must have found him. I felt him die."

*She's really upset,* Lewis said silently.

She was, Rob thought. Not just upset but helpless—the way the people of the Fellowship tended to be when they didn't have a leader. He didn't send the thought to Lewis because he had the feeling Tamsin could hear.

"And now I don't know what to do," Tamsin said, almost wailing it. "LeShan was going to tell me when I got here. I came all this way and I can't help you at all."

Rob looked at Anna, as if he might find something comforting to say in her face. Anna was so wise. But Anna's gaze, dark and liquid with tears, held his only a moment, then quickly dropped.

Angry with himself, Rob put an arm around Tamsin. He said, "Maybe Meren—"

"Mereniang is dead, too," Tamsin whispered. "She died on the way to the island. There's no help anywhere, no hope!"

# CHAPTER 11

Kaitlyn sat on Lydia's bed with the black dress on her lap. She had been reaching for it, glad that she'd brought it and that it had hung out with no wrinkles, when Bri had told her.

Now she just sat. She didn't need to ask Bri any questions. She knew the whole truth.

*Queen* Charlotte Islands. That's what the map had said. In Canada. That must have been where the Fellowship had gone when they'd left Vancouver Island. Bri had dowsed for them with that map.

And Jackal Mac had checked the furnace out. Some furnace where the Fellowship were living. Kaitlyn knew because she had a picture of it—a picture of a fireball, of a furnace exploding. And a man in the middle of it.

All of them had gathered around the crystal this evening and sent out their astral forms. They'd left their bodies and gone to the Queen Charlotte Islands and then Renny had used his PK.

Oh, LeShan. Kaitlyn twisted the chiffon of the black dress between brutal fingers. I liked you. I really liked you. You were arrogant and angry and impatient and I really, really liked you. You were *alive*.

Caramel-colored skin. Slanting lynx eyes. Softly curling hair that seemed to have an inner luminescence, pale and shimmering brown. And a spirit that burned like midnight fire.

Dead.

And now Kaitlyn had to go and celebrate. No way to get out of it. They would know if she tried to make some excuse. If she was going to be one of them, she had to hate the Fellowship as they did.

Feeling very brittle, very light, and unstable, Kait went over to the mirror. She pulled off the towel and her clothes and put on the black dress. She began to mechanically run her fingers through her wet hair, when she suddenly realized something.

I look like a witch.

In the dim light, with her long hair falling about her shoulders, drying just enough to be a halo of red, with the black dress and her bare feet and the pallor of her face . . .

I do. I look extremely witchy. Like somebody who might go walking down the street like this, barefoot, hair wild in the breeze, singing strange songs, and all the people peeping out at me from behind their curtains.

The fitted spandex bodice *did* make her look slim as a statue, and the sheer chiffon skirt swirled from hip to midcalf. But it wasn't vanity that held her there looking. It was a new sense of her own competence, of determination.

Anybody who looks this witchy *must* be able to call down a curse. And that's what I'm going to do. Somehow, I'll make them all pay, LeShan. I'll avenge your death. I promise.

*I promise.*

People were calling outside. Lydia was opening the door apologetically.

"I just heard," she said. She looked as hangdog and slinking as Kaitlyn had ever seen her, but also bitterly satisfied, as if she'd been proved right. "I told you my father would win. He always does. You were smart to come in on this side, Kait."

"Could I borrow a pair of nylons?" Kaitlyn asked.

Mr. Z was in the living room when they all came downstairs. Kaitlyn supposed he'd been in the hidden room with them, directing the work. He gave Kaitlyn a courtly nod as she walked toward him in a pair of shoes borrowed from Frost.

He looked amiable, but Kaitlyn could *feel* his savage joy. He knew she was hurting and he liked that.

"Have a good time, Kaitlyn," he said.

Kaitlyn lifted her head, refusing to give him the satisfaction.

Gabriel was there, too, handsome in dark clothes. Kaitlyn turned appraising eyes on him. He didn't look disturbed over LeShan's death—but then he had no reason to like the Fellowship.

Their philosophy said they couldn't open their doors to anyone who'd taken a human life . . . no matter what the circumstances. Because Gabriel had killed by accident and in self-defense, they refused to let him in. So now Gabriel wasn't upset.

Everyone else was delirious with happiness.

Mr. Z saw them off, and they took two cars. Kait rode in Lydia's car with Bri and Renny. Joyce took Gabriel, Frost, and Jackal Mac. Kait spent the drive plotting how to make them all pay—Gabriel, too.

The club was called Dark Carnival. Kaitlyn stopped musing on revenge to stare. It was like nothing she'd ever seen before.

There was a line of people waiting to get in the door. People wearing *everything*. Unimaginable outfits. They looked bizarre and more than a little scary.

Traffic stopped the car for a while near the door and Kaitlyn was able to watch what was going on. A doorkeeper with a lip-ring and a Liverpool accent was saying who could get in immediately, who should wait, and who should just go home. Those who got in: a guy with purple glittery lipstick and silver aluminum curlicues for hair. A girl in an evening gown of black spiderweb. A chic Italian-looking girl in a white unitard and black velvet shorts—very short.

"He keeps out people who aren't cool enough," Bri said in Kaitlyn's ear, leaning heavily on her back. "You have to be either famous or completely beautiful or—"

Or dressed like a cross between a Busby Berkeley show and something from a science fiction movie, Kaitlyn thought.

"So how are we going to get in?" she asked quietly.

She was watching the losers—the people who couldn't get in. The normal people who weren't exciting or weird enough, waiting outside behind cords, sometimes crying.

"We've got invitations," Lydia said in a dead voice. "My father has connections."

She was right. The doorkeeper let them right in.

Inside there were strobe lights, super black lights, and colored lights, all flashing in an atmosphere so full of smoke Kaitlyn could hardly see anything but the flashing rainbow.

The music was loud, a throbbing beat that people had to shout over. On the dance floor a girl with long shiny hair was kicking high over her head.

"Isn't it great?" Bri yelled.

Kaitlyn didn't know what it was. Loud. Weird. Exciting, if you were in the mood to celebrate, but surreal if you weren't.

I'm going to avenge you, LeShan. I promise.

She glimpsed Joyce walking toward the dance floor. Jackal Mac, the lights reflecting on his head, was giving an order to a scantily clad cocktail waitress.

Where was Gabriel?

Bri had disappeared. Kait was surrounded by people with wings, people dressed in cellophane, people with spikes for fingernails. Everywhere she looked were falls of Day-Glo hair.

Enormous false eyelashes. Slanted eyebrows, silver-glittering eyebrows. No eyebrows. Pierced bodies.

If she hadn't been so cold with anger over LeShan, Kaitlyn might have been scared. But just now nothing could touch her. A man in a leopard-skin unitard and a mask beckoned her to dance and she followed him to the floor. She didn't really know much about dancing, except what she'd done at home, watching the TV and dreaming.

It was too loud to talk, and she didn't really care what the leopard-man thought of her—so it was the perfect opportunity to muse on revenge again.

And that was how she solved the mystery of the combination lock.

It wasn't like in books, where the faithful sidekick makes some offhand remark and then the famous detective sees all. There was no particular reason why it came to her. But every minute or so her mind would go back to her problem.

I need to get to that crystal. Which means I need to get the combination.

And once when her mind went back to it, she thought, "But maybe I already have the combination. One drawing was a real prophecy. What about the other?"

And then the other thought was simply *there,* fullblown, a question asking itself in her mind: How can a Christmas tree and a ship be eight numbers?

Well, *Christmas* had a number, of course. A date. December

the twenty-fifth, 12/25. Or 25/12 if you were thinking the twenty-fifth of December.

The dark room rocked under Kaitlyn's feet. The leopard-skin man was walking away, but she didn't care. She backed up to a railing, her eyes on the flashing lights.

She was trembling with excitement, her mind racing to follow this new idea to the end, like a spark running down a line of powder.

The ship. The ship is another number. And what number? It could be the number of masts or the number of crew or the number of voyages it made. Or a date, a date when the ship sailed—but what kind of ship is it?

A window opened in her stomach and she felt hollow with dismay. She didn't know anything about ships. How long would it take to research, to speculate?

No, stop. Don't panic. The picture was drawn by your unconscious, so it can't be much smarter than you are. It couldn't take a date and make it into a ship if you didn't *know* the date and ship already.

But I'm so stupid, Kaitlyn argued back. Rotten in history. I only know the simplest dates—like "In fourteen hundred ninety-two . . ."

*Columbus sailed the ocean blue.*

That sparkly, curly blue ocean. Three colors of blue. Drawn with an excess of care.

She'd found the answer.

Kaitlyn knew it, she felt certain. But a nagging murmur of dissent was starting in her brain. Mr. Z wouldn't make the combination that simple. He wouldn't begin it—or end it—with 1492. Anyone *glancing* at it would remember. Someone breaking in might try it at random.

That was when Kaitlyn had her second brainstorm. Supposing the combination didn't begin or end with 1492—not all together. The Christmas tree had been in the middle of the ship, so supposing the combination was 14/12/25/92. Or 14/25/12/92.

Good heavens, or even 1/12/25/492. Or . . .

Kaitlyn cut her busy brain off. I'll think of all the possibilities later. But I'll try the easy ones first. And I'll—

A guy with a bald head was darting a black-stained tongue at her. Kaitlyn recoiled, then realized it was Jackal Mac.

"What's the matter? Scared of me?"

Kaitlyn stared into the jackal eyes. "No," she said flatly.

"Then come dance."

No, Kaitlyn thought. But she was a spy and her most important job was to not get caught until she got the shard to the crystal. Nothing else was important.

"Okay," she said, and they danced.

She didn't like the way he moved in on her. Not like slow dancing, he wasn't trying to hold her, but he kept moving toward her, forcing her to back up. Otherwise his swinging arms and gyrating hips would have made contact.

She saw Frost and Gabriel together on the floor. Frost fit right in here; she was wearing a silver baby doll dress and silver ankle boots. She kept brushing against Gabriel's body as she danced.

Well, at least she wasn't as exposed as that woman wearing a negligee. Or that man painted orange who seemed to be wearing almost *nothing*.

"Hey, baby! Pay attention!"

Jackal Mac was closing in again. Kaitlyn stepped back and collided with a woman in space-age neon sunglasses.

"Sorry," she muttered, inaudibly over the music. She edged away, heading for a deserted space below the bandstand. "Look, Mac, I'm kind of tired—"

"Sit down and rest."

He was backing her farther into the space, below and slightly behind the stage. Kaitlyn tripped over a cord or cable. She couldn't keep walking backward like this.

"I think I just want something to drink. Would you like something?"

It was strange that her voice was so calm. Because suddenly she was very scared.

They were in an isolated little nook here, where the music was loudest. No one from the dance floor could really see them. Certainly no one could hear them. It was smoky and dark and humid and it felt like a trap.

"Yeah, I'm kinda thirsty," Jackal Mac said, but he was

blocking the way out. His eyes gleamed in the dimness. He had one hand up, resting on the stage, and suddenly Kaitlyn got a whiff of his sweat.

Danger.

It was like red warning lights flashing in her head, like the sound of sirens. She could *feel* his mind, cluttered and trashed and nasty as his bedroom. Nasty as the red-haired man had been.

"I'm thirsty, you know, but not for a drink. Gabriel told me how you used to take care of him."

Not like the red-haired man after all. Jackal Mac had a different aberration. He didn't want to hurt her body, he wanted to suck her brain out.

*You bastard,* Kaitlyn thought with white-hot fury, but she didn't mean Jackal Mac. Her hatred was for Gabriel.

He'd told this—animal—about what Kait had done for him. The most private moments she'd ever had with anyone. Kaitlyn felt as if she'd been violated already, ripped open for everyone to see.

"What else did Gabriel tell you?" she said in a voice that was hard and distant and unafraid.

Jackal Mac was surprised. His head bobbed, apelike, then his black-stained tongue came out to lick his lips.

"He said you were always chasing him. I guess you like it, huh?" Sliding his arm down to shoulder level, he moved closer. "So you gonna make this easy, or what?"

Kaitlyn held her ground. "You're not a telepath. I don't know what you think—"

"Who says you need to be a telepath?" Mac laughed. "This is about energy, pretty girl. We all need energy. Everybody who's a friend of the crystal."

The crystal. Of course. Mr. Z's way of keeping them all in line. It had made them all psychic vampires like Gabriel. And it satisfied them all, provided them with energy . . . unless you were like Jackal Mac and wanted something extra.

He wants me to be afraid, Kait thought. He enjoys that, and he'll like draining my energy best if I'm fighting and screaming. That little extra kick.

I hate you, Gabriel. I *hate* you.

But it didn't prevent her from saying what needed to be said.

"And you think Gabriel's going to like it if you mess around with me?" she asked. "He didn't like you messing with his room."

Mac's eyes took on an almost injured expression.

"I wouldn't touch Gabriel's woman," he said. "But that's Frost now. He was the one who said I should check you out."

His teeth shone white in the darkness.

For an instant, Kaitlyn felt only numb. Gabriel had thrown her to Jackal Mac like a bone. How could she *live* with that?

And then survival instinct took over and she realized that she wouldn't have to live with it if she didn't do something fast.

Jackal Mac was reaching for her with his blunt, restless hands. She knew the routine. There were several transfer points, but third eye to third eye or lips to spine were best. She would bet that Mac wanted her spine.

So *relax*. Relax and let him get behind you. No, pretend you're going to cooperate.

A part of her mind was yammering at her, insisting that there was a way to yell for help. A vocal scream would be lost in the throbbing music, but she could scream mentally. Gabriel had come the last time; he might come if he thought Mac was killing her.

But I *won't* scream, she thought, cold washing over her like an icy waterfall. I won't scream even if he does kill me. I wouldn't take Gabriel's help if I knew it would save my life.

Gabriel had set this human beast on her. Let Gabriel live with the consequences. Besides, he might hear her screams and just smile.

"Come on," Kaitlyn said to Mac, aware she hardly sounded seductive. "I don't mind. Just let me get my hair out of the way."

His hands with their ugly, chewed-up nails hovered in the air. She stepped toward him, but to one side, grasping her hair with one hand, pulling it off her neck, watching his eyes follow her movements greedily.

"Okay and just let me do—*this*." While his eyes were on her bare shoulders, she slammed a heel into his shin. He made a thick, startled sound of surprise and pain, more like a pig than a jackal. He lunged toward her—

—but she had kicked the loose cord between his feet. He stumbled, tangled in it. Kaitlyn didn't wait to see if he recovered his balance or not. She was running.

She reached the dance floor, plunged into the crowd. Fell into someone's arms. A poetic-looking young man wearing a shirt with a large collar and flowing white sleeves.

"Hey—"

Kaitlyn reeled away. Where was Joyce? Nobody else could keep Mac from following her out here, from dragging her back. . . .

*There.* Joyce and Lydia. Kaitlyn wove unsteadily toward them through the crowd.

"Joyce—"

She didn't get any farther. A roar was beginning behind her. Jackal Mac was parting the crowd like Moses parting the Red Sea. But unlike Moses, he was doing it with fists and elbows, and the Red Sea was getting mad.

"You don't need to explain," Joyce said tightly to Kaitlyn.

As Kaitlyn watched, Mac ran into a short woman with lacquered hair. He shoved her aside. A large man wearing chains lunged forward to grab him.

"Here comes Renny," Lydia said.

Renny appeared with a bottle. Kait couldn't tell if he was attacking Mac or defending him, but suddenly glasses were flying, people were throwing punches. Jackal Mac picked up a chair and lifted it over his head.

Screams split through the music. Hefty men in suits were running in from all directions.

"You girls get out of here," Joyce said. Kaitlyn could feel that she was angry and exasperated almost to tears. Here she was, out to celebrate in her pink St. John dress with the rhinestones, and Mac was ruining everything. If Kaitlyn hadn't known why Joyce was celebrating, she might have felt sorry for her.

As it was, she took Lydia's arm and propelled her toward the Exit sign. Lydia waited until they were in the car to speak.

"What happened?"

Kait shook her head, then leaned her temple against the cool window. Everything inside her was sick and sore. Not from Mac's attack. From knowing Gabriel had egged him on. And from the hole in the universe where LeShan had been.

It's a filthy world, she thought slowly. But I'm going to do my part to clean it up. And then I'll never have to look at Gabriel again. I'll go as far away from here as I can go.

It was very late when she heard Joyce bring the others home that night. There was a lot of thudding on the stairs, a lot of banging and laughing and cursing.

"They scare me," Lydia said softly from the other bed. "The way they are. What they can do."

They scared Kaitlyn, too. She wanted to say something

comforting about how things were going to change, but she didn't dare. Lydia wasn't evil, but she was weak—and besides, no one was to be trusted. *No one.*

"Think about something else," Kaitlyn said. "Did you ever find a cow alarm clock around here?"

"No. A what?"

"An alarm clock shaped like a cow. It was Lewis's. It used to go off every morning, this sound like a cowbell and then a voice shouting 'Wake up! Don't sleep your life away!' And then it would moo."

Lydia giggled faintly. "I wish I'd seen that. It sounds—like Lewis."

"Actually, it sounded like a cow." Kaitlyn could hear Lydia snorting softly in the darkness for a while, then silence. She pulled the covers over her head and went to sleep.

The next day she was confronted with a problem. Everyone else was exhausted and lethargic, so Joyce had canceled all testing. She had the day to herself—but she couldn't figure out how to get in touch with Rob.

Call the Diaz house? Not from inside the Institute. Much too risky. And she had no excuse for walking off alone to find a pay phone. She didn't want to do anything that might look suspicious.

But she *needed* to talk to Rob, to tell him to bring the shard on Monday. She didn't want to waste any more time.

She was sitting at the desk in her room, tapping a pencil

and wondering if she dared ask to borrow Lydia's car, when a noise at the window made her turn around.

A kitten. A big kitten, almost a cat. It was pawing at the screen.

Kaitlyn almost smiled despite her mood. You funny baby, how did you get all the way up here? she wondered, and went to open the screen. The kitten butted its head against her and rasped her knuckle with a tongue like a furled pink leaf until Kait rubbed the black velveteen fur between its ears.

What a funny collar. Way too thick. That must hurt you. . . .

It was a piece of paper, wrapped around and around the blue nylon stretch collar and secured with masking tape.

A note.

Suddenly Kaitlyn's heart was beating hard. She looked down into the backyard below the window. Nobody in sight. Then she glanced over her shoulder, toward the closed door of the bedroom.

Eyes on the door, she pulled at the tape with her fingernails, tearing the note free.

# CHAPTER 12

THE MAN AT THE AIRPORT AND THE LADY WITH THE
PITCHFORK ARE DEAD. THE WATER S TOO HOT. MEET
ME AT THE OLD RENDEZVOUS SOON AND THE DISH WILL
RUN AWAY WITH THE SPOON. PICK YOUR TIME, JUST LET
ME KNOW. SEND A MESSAGE IN A BOTTLE.

The note was neither addressed nor signed—Rob had
thought it less risky that way, Kaitlyn supposed. But she understood what it said.

Mereniang was dead, too. LeShan was the man who'd
accosted her at the airport, and the first time they'd seen Meren
she'd been pitching cow dung. Rob thought Kaitlyn was in too
much danger now, and he wanted her to come to the gym,
where he'd whisk her away from the Institute permanently. She
was supposed to pick a time when she could get away and send
a note back.

Kaitlyn sat for a moment, rolling the pencil between her fingers. Then she straightened her shoulders, tore a sheet out of her sketchbook and began to write in a heavy, determined hand.

> The hotter the water, the better witches like it. No date today. Same time, same place tomorrow. Bring the magic knife. I've done my homework and know my numbers.

She hoped Rob would remember Tony saying "I see you got the magic knife for Marisol." And she hoped he would understand that she *couldn't* leave now; she knew where the crystal was kept and she knew the combination to get to it.

The kitten was nudging her, rolling, asking for pets. Kaitlyn stroked it, then wrapped the note around its collar and taped it securely. She opened the screen and held her breath.

Out went the kitten, without a backward glance. Anna must have implanted the suggestions very well.

Now, Kaitlyn thought, leaning back. Nothing to do but wait for tomorrow at noon. And hope Rob keeps his date.

"I can't let you do it alone," Rob said.

"But don't you *see?* It's the only possible way."

"No," Rob said flatly.

It was noon on Monday. They were hiding in the gym itself, which seemed safer than the entrance.

Kaitlyn looked at Lewis and Anna for help, but they were both looking pretty helpless. As if they couldn't figure things out. Rob was the one who'd made up his mind.

"I can't let you take it back to the Institute by yourself. I'm going with you—I'll sneak in whenever you do."

He just wasn't thinking it through. "But what if we get caught sneaking into the house?"

"What if *you* get caught with the crystal? That would be just as bad as being seen with me."

"No, it *wouldn't*," Kaitlyn said, straining to keep her voice patient. "I can hide the crystal—or at least there's a chance that I could hide it quick if I heard somebody coming. But I can't hide *you*. What am I going to do, stick you under a sofa pillow?"

Rob was trying to be patient, too—she could see and feel it. And he was losing the battle. "It's . . . just . . . too . . . dangerous," he said with slow emphasis. "Do you really think I'm going to sit around, safe in somebody's apartment, while you take all the risk? What does that make me?"

"Smart. Rob, I'm hoping I can get to the crystal today, but that may not be possible. Joyce could have the lab door open; somebody could be sitting in the living room where they can see the secret panel. I may have to wait around for days and watch for my chance. *You* can't sit that long in the house with me—or even outside," she added, cutting him off. "Gabriel would feel you there, just like he did before. And then it would be all over, he's really our enemy now."

She had thought this through, and she didn't intend to budge. And she could see Rob knew it. His expression suddenly changed; his jaw set, his mouth straightened into a grim line. A golden blaze sparked in his eyes. He looked, Kaitlyn thought, like a good guy pushed too far.

Without a word, he reached for her, grabbed her around the waist. Kaitlyn felt herself lifted, her feet leaving the wooden gym floor.

"I'm sorry, but I've had enough," he said. "You're coming back to the car."

A few days ago, Kaitlyn might have thought this funny. But now . . .

*Put me down!*

The volume of it shocked Rob into loosening his grip. The sheer fury in her eyes kept his mouth shut as Kaitlyn pulled away from him.

Anna and Lewis were shocked, too—and frightened. Kaitlyn knew they could feel the anger pouring off her like invisible waves. She stood like a queen, feeling tall and terrible and when she spoke each word came out like a white-hot chip of steel.

"I am *not* an object, something to be picked up or carried away or passed around. *Gabriel* thought that's what I was. He was wrong. You're both wrong," she said to Rob.

His hair was tousled, making her suddenly think of a

little boy. His eyes were dark amber and wide. There was utter silence in the gym.

"*I* am the only one who can decide what will happen to me," Kaitlyn went on very quietly. "No one else. *Me.* And I've already made my decision. I'm going back to that place and I'm going to try to stop them any way I can. Whether you give me the shard or not is *your* decision, but I'm going back anyway."

She had never spoken to him like this before, and she could see that he was confounded. Stricken. Kaitlyn tried to make her voice gentler, but she could hear the steel underneath it.

"Rob, don't you see, this thing is bigger than just us. You're the one who taught me that things can be bigger than people. You made me *want* to make a difference. And now I have a chance to do it. Timon died and LeShan died and Mereniang died, and if somebody doesn't stop the Institute more people are going to die. I *have* to try and stop that."

Rob was nodding slowly. He swallowed and said, "I understand. But if something happened to you—"

"If something terrible happens to me, then at least I know that *I* chose it. I went because I decided to go. But *you* don't have anything to do with it. . . . Do you understand?"

Anna was crying. Lewis was almost crying.

And Rob—seemed shocked into submission. He looked at Anna as if that were somehow his final appeal.

Anna blinked away tears. Her face was compassionate, sad—and still. Too deep a stillness to be simply resignation.

"Kait's right," she said. "She'll go if she says she'll go. You can't say for her. Nobody can ever say for somebody else."

Then Rob looked back at Kait, slowly, and she knew that he was seeing her as an equal for the first time. An equal not just in brains or psychic power or resourcefulness, but in every way, with exactly as much right to risk her life as he had to risk his.

Equal and *separate*. It was as if at that moment they split apart, became two independent creatures. If Rob had ever had a fault in their relationship, it was thinking he had to protect her. And Kaitlyn had encouraged it in a way, by thinking that she needed to be protected. Now, all at once, they were both realizing it wasn't true.

And once Kait knew that, she realized that in the last few minutes she had grown in his eyes. Rob respected her more, even loved her more than ever before . . . in a different way.

But he was still having a hard time grasping that he was *really* going to have to stand here and watch her walk away and take the risk herself. So he gave it one last try, not with force, but with entreaty.

"You know, I've been wondering if we should maybe wait just a little to use the shard, anyway. It did cure Marisol, you know. You didn't see that, Kait, but it was wonderful. And there are a lot of other people in that hospital. I was kind of hoping . . ." He shrugged, his face wistful.

Kaitlyn was moved. But before she could speak, Anna did.

Anna's face was even more compassionate than before, more sad—and more certain.

"No, Rob," she said quietly. "That's the one thing we *can't* do. It doesn't belong to us; it's just on loan. Timon gave it to us for destroying the crystal. We *can't* just go around using that much power that isn't really ours. Something bad would come of it."

Then she put a gentle hand on Rob's shoulder. "You've got power of your own that you can use to help people—and that should be enough. You'll have your chance, Rob."

Rob stared at her for a long moment, then nodded. He looked from her to Kaitlyn, and through the web, Kaitlyn got just a glimpse of his thought. He was awed and a little confused at being caught between these two farsighted women. She could feel him wondering how they'd gotten so wise while he'd stayed dumb.

And thinking there was nothing for him to do but agree.

"So it's settled," Kaitlyn said quietly. "I'll take the shard and go back to the Institute, and you'll go back to Tony's friend's apartment."

"We left Tamsin there," Anna said. "We'll tell her what you're doing. She'll be rooting for you, Kait, and so will Marisol."

Kaitlyn was glad to talk about something ordinary, because she had the feeling that any minute she might start crying. "Marisol's really that much better?"

"She's still in the hospital because her muscles are weak and she has to learn to use them again. But Tony says it'll only be a few days before she's walking. Oh, Kait, I wish you could have seen his face when he came to see us! And his mom and dad—they called and just thanked us over and over. We couldn't get them off the phone."

"And Tony said he was going to light a candle for you," Lewis put in. "You know, in church. Because Rob told him you were in danger."

Kaitlyn's throat was swollen and her eyes kept filling with warmth. She gulped. "I'd better take it and get going."

Rob knelt and opened the duffel bag he'd brought. He took out the crystal shard, opened Kaitlyn's backpack, and put it in. Kaitlyn knew that he was doing it himself as a sort of symbolic offering, an admission that she was right. She also knew that he had to fight to make every move.

He stood up, very pale, and held the backpack out to her.

"Call us when it's over," he said. "Or if you think you can't do it before tomorrow. And, Kait?"

"Yes?"

"If you don't call us by tomorrow, I'm coming in. That's not negotiable, Kaitlyn; that's *my* choice. If I don't hear from you, I'm assuming that something's gone wrong, and all bets are off."

What could Kaitlyn say?

*Good luck,* Lewis said silently as she hugged him. *I'll be thinking about you.*

*Be careful,* Anna said. *Be as clever as Raven and get yourself out safe.* She added a few words in Suquamish, and Kaitlyn didn't need a translation. It was a blessing.

Last of all, she hugged Rob. His eyes were still sore from the hard lesson he'd just learned. He held on to her very tightly. *Please come back to me. I'll be waiting.*

How many times had women said that to their men who were going off to war?

The swelling in Kaitlyn's throat was getting bigger by the minute. *I love you all,* she told them. Then she turned around and walked toward the back door of the gym, feeling their eyes on her. She knew they stood in perfect silence as she went out onto the blacktop, and then onto the baseball field, watching and watching until she was out of sight.

Kaitlyn was heading straight back for the Institute. It was only about a mile. She'd told Rob that she might have to wait for days to get to the crystal, but she knew that her best chance was right now. Bri, Renny, and Lydia were at school—and Gabriel was supposed to be. That left Frost and Jackal Mac in the house with Joyce.

I should be able to get in without them noticing, she thought. And then maybe they'll all go into the back lab or something, and I can get to the panel.

The walk was actually pleasant. Kaitlyn found herself noticing the sky, which was a beautiful blue with just the right amount of wispy clouds. The sun was warm on her shoulders, and the hedges by the sidewalk were dotted with starlike yellow flowers. It's spring, she thought.

Strange how you enjoyed the world more when you thought there was a chance you might be leaving it soon.

Even the Institute looked exotic and beautiful, like a giant grape monument.

Now came the hard part. She had to sneak in so as not to get caught, but do it without *looking* sneaky. So that if she *were* caught, she could say she'd come home from school sick.

After some thought, she let herself in the kitchen door. The kitchen was right by the front lab, but no one in the lab could see her until she passed the lab doorway.

Music was coming from the lab. Good, that should cover any sounds. Squaring her shoulders, Kait walked boldly by the lab doorway, forcing herself to glance inside casually, forcing herself not to tiptoe.

That one glance showed her Frost sorting through a tray full of watches and keys, while Joyce sat beside her with a notebook. Frost was facing the back lab—great. Joyce was facing Frost, but bent over her notebook. Pretty good.

Jackal Mac was nowhere in sight. Kait prayed he was in the back lab, in the tank.

Still forcing herself *not* to be stealthy, not to creep, she walked through the dining room and out and around the staircase. She looked around the corner and saw the little hallway that led to the other door of the lab.

Okay, how to make this look casual? I've got to wait here . . . maybe I'm tying my shoe.

Without taking her eyes off the figures in the lab, she knelt and undid her shoelace. Then she stayed that way, with the laces in her hands, watching Joyce.

I can't go into the hall until she turns around or goes into the back lab. It takes a few seconds to get the panel to slide back, she could just glance up and see me from where she is now.

Time dragged by. The backpack began to feel heavy, dragging at Kaitlyn's shoulders.

Come on, Joyce. Move. Go get a book from the case or something. Go change the CD. Do anything, just *move*.

Joyce stayed put. After what seemed like an hour, Kaitlyn decided that she was going to have to risk stepping out anyway— and then she saw Joyce was getting up.

Kait's vision seemed to go double. Joyce's face was a tan blur. Then Joyce's back was a pink blur. Joyce was going into the back lab.

Oh, thank you! Thank you!

The instant the last bit of pink disappeared, Kaitlyn stepped into the hall. No time to be stealthy, no point in looking casual. All that mattered was to be *quick*.

Her fingers stabbed out at the wood paneling, once and then again. The click seemed agonizingly loud. She threw a glance at Frost—Frost still had her back turned.

The panel had recessed. Kaitlyn stepped into the gaping hole.

Down the stairs. Quick. Quick.

She'd never learned the secret of closing the panel from inside. Well, it didn't matter much. As long as she got to the crystal. She didn't care if they discovered her after that.

As she reached the bottom stair she shrugged off her backpack and pulled out a flashlight. She'd taken it from the kitchen drawer that morning.

Quick. Move quick. The little circle of light showed her the way.

Aha. There it is.

The combination lock shone softly on the wall by the door, looking like something from a science fiction set. A door to the starship *Enterprise*.

Although her heart was beating in all sorts of funny places—her throat, her ears, her fingertips—Kaitlyn felt calm. She'd rehearsed this all in her mind last night.

Put the backpack down. Flashlight in your teeth. Take out the paper with the possible combinations on it. Make every move count.

Paper in one hand, she began to punch in numbers with the other.

Each little rubber pad gave under her fingertips, and the number she'd punched appeared on an LED display at the top.

1 ... 4 ... 1 ... 2 ... 2 ... 5 ... 9 ... 2. Enter.

Nothing. The LED display blanked out.

Okay. *Next!*

1 . . . 4 . . . 2 . . . 5 . . . 1 . . . 2 . . . 9 . . . 2.

Again, nothing. Tiny threads of panic began to unwind in Kaitlyn's gut. Okay, so she still had six combinations to go, but she'd used the best two. What if Mr. Z had changed the numbers? She should have drawn again last night to make sure. Oh, God, she hadn't even *thought* of that. . . .

Wait a minute. I didn't press Enter.

She pressed it. Immediately she heard a sort of pleasant hum, an accepting sound that reminded her of an ATM machine getting to work.

With a soft click, the door opened away from her.

I did it! It worked! Oh, thank you, Columbus—I'll love you forever!

Her heart was beating all over now, her entire skin tingling with the pulses. Excitement and fear swam inside her, and she had to take a deep breath to keep her head.

Okay, quick, now, *quick*. A light might be seen upstairs, so get the shard out first.

She fumbled getting it out of the backpack. The flashlight kept sliding out from under her chin. The paper with the combinations had fallen on the floor. She ignored it.

Okay. *Got it.*

With both hands, she held the crystal shard.

It had never felt so good to her. Cold and heavy and sharp, it was like a weapon in her hand, strengthening her. It seemed to be telling her, *Don't worry about anything from here on in.*

*All you have to do is get me to the crystal. I'll take care of things from there.*

Yes, Kaitlyn thought. Now.

In the end, it had almost been too easy. Why had Rob been so worried about her?

Standing tall, holding the crystal like a spear, she pushed the door open and stepped into the office. It was dark and she'd lost the flashlight. She reached for the wall, fingers groping across it. She found a light switch and got ready to throw it, planning to charge toward the great crystal as soon as she could see. A battle yell, some legacy of distant Irish ancestors, gathered in her throat.

*Now . . .*

She threw the switch—and froze.

The charge never happened. The crystal was there, all right, huge and deformed and grotesque as she remembered. But it wasn't alone. There were two—other things—in front of it.

Kaitlyn's eyes opened wide as she saw them. She felt her lips stretching open, not for a battle yell, but for a scream. A scream of perfect terror.

# CHAPTER 13

At first all Kaitlyn was able to take in was her feeling of disgust and horror. It was something like the disgust she'd felt at home when her dad would turn over a shovelful of earth in the garden—and reveal something soft and squirmy or hard and chitinous hiding underneath.

A little like that, but magnified hundreds and thousands of times.

She guessed these two things were human. Or had started out that way. But they looked so deformed and felt so *wrong*, they gave her the sick feeling she'd gotten when she first saw a potato bug, that huge, unnatural, semicrustacean-looking insect. Or when she'd seen her first picture by Hieronymus Bosch, the artist who did scenes from hell, with people who had lobsters' claws or windows in their bodies.

The other thing she knew immediately was that they

were guard dogs. Mr. Z's new guard dogs, put here to protect the crystal.

Sasha and Parté King.

She knew them from Bri's descriptions—although it took a lot of imagination. Sasha had skin that was chalky white, unnaturally white, like something that had never seen the sun. Almost translucent, with lines of blue veins showing through. His eyes were like the red eyes of albino mice, or the blind eyes of cave fish.

He did have blond hair, as Bri had said. Hair that was not just unkempt but *full of things.* Bits of garbage and paper like the rubbish that covered the floor.

He looked like a slug: white, flaccid, immobile.

Then there was Parté King—whatever that weird name might mean. Bri had said he was skinny. Now he was skeletally thin, wasted away like someone about to die. Skin stretched across his bones—almost as if he had an exoskeleton, like a bug. His brown hair was falling out in clumps, exposing naked skull.

He looked like some kind of cricket, as if he would rattle if you shook him.

And they were both alive, even though they looked like nothing that could survive long. Kaitlyn realized with a qualm of pure horror that they *lived* down here, alone and insane, chained to the floor. Biting at people's ankles, grinning face-splitting grins.

She thought she was going to vomit.

"Muh-muh-muh," Sasha said, beaming. His teeth were wet; wetness spilled onto his chin. He made a wormlike movement toward her.

I should run, Kaitlyn thought dispassionately. Her thought seemed to die somewhere before it got to her legs. She stood still and watched the swollen white grub thing inching across the floor toward her. It was like a human being in the process of mutating into something. A pupa.

They weren't going to let her get to the crystal. She could feel the power of their minds like a curtain across the room. So strong it almost knocked her over, invading all her senses. The touch of their minds made her think of rotting things, bugs, pus.

Parté King was making a clicking noise in his throat. Pushing himself into a sitting position. They both wore canvas jackets which held their arms behind their backs with many straps.

Straitjackets.

Below that they wore garbage bags. Kaitlyn couldn't make sense of that until she realized: diapers.

Run, you stupid girl. Please run now.

Parté King fell over backward, his stick legs waving slowly in the air.

"Ch-ch-ch-ch-ch." He was still grinning.

So this is what happens to Mr. Z's old students. It could happen to you, too. A little too much time near the crystal and . . .

Hey, but they're still terrific psychics!

Please, *run.*

At last she seemed to tune in to her brain's terrified whimpering pleas. She turned around to run. She saw the open door of the office, took a wavering step toward it.

And ran into a sort of invisible wall, a thickening of the air. Cold air. Or maybe there was nothing wrong with the air, and it was just her muscles.

She couldn't move a step closer to the door. They had her, they were draining her volition, her will to run. She couldn't get away, and maybe she'd known that all the time.

Sasha laughed bubbles, like a baby.

"You poor things," Kaitlyn whispered. Pitying them didn't change an ounce of her loathing for them. She knew somehow that they were beyond any kind of healing. Hurt worse than Marisol in her coma.

Even if they would let her approach them with the crystal shard, even if she were a healer like Rob, it wouldn't help. Kaitlyn *knew.*

Her knees were giving out. She let it happen, sitting on the floor and watching the creatures who shared it with her crawl closer. There was nothing to do.

Nothing except wait for Mr. Zetes to come.

"I thought you'd bring that to me," Mr. Zetes said. "Thank you, my dear."

He held his hand out for the shard. Kaitlyn looked at the

long fingers with their square, perfectly manicured nails. She tried to stab him.

It was stupid. There were the human pupae behind her, dragging her every gesture into slow motion, and there were the psycho psychics behind Mr. Z. They'd all come to see the fun. Besides, Mr. Z himself was strong.

He took the shard from her, hurting her wrist. Deliberately, she thought.

"In a way, it's too bad you decided to come out of the closet now," Mr. Z said. "I wish you'd kept the pretense up for just a few more days. My next job for you was silencing the Diaz family."

His handsome old face was absolutely diabolical.

"I like your old students," Kaitlyn choked out. "The ones with very good minds. What a waste."

"Muh-muh-*muhhhh*," Sasha drooled behind her. "Muhhh."

Mr. Z glanced at him almost fondly. "They're still useful," he said. "The crystal has made them more powerful than ever, in a way, it's allowed them to achieve their true potential. I'm afraid you can't join them, though." He turned slightly, speaking over his shoulder.

"John, please put this in Joyce's room. Laurie and Sabrina, take Kaitlyn upstairs and get her ready. Paul, watch them."

Who are all those people? Kaitlyn thought whimsically. Jackal Mac took the shard and disappeared, presumably heading for Mr. Z's car. Frost and Bri stepped forward and each took her by an arm, leading her out of the office. Renny followed.

Joyce and Lydia were standing in the hallway by the hidden panel. Frost and Bri marched Kaitlyn by them.

As they reached the second floor, Kait spoke. "What's going to happen to me?"

"Never mind." Frost gave her a push and Kaitlyn stumbled into the room Frost and Bri shared. Frost's face was sparkling with malicious triumph. She looked almost beautiful, like a Christmas tree angel with hair made of spun glass. She had on bubble-gum pink lipstick, so glossy it reflected light.

"Bri? You going to tell me?"

Bri looked angry instead of triumphant. "You sneak. You dirty spy." Her deep boyish voice was rough with anger and revulsion. "You get what you deserve."

Renny stood just outside Bri's door, arms folded, his clean-cut narrow features severe. He looked like an executioner.

Frost was groping through a pile of clothes on the floor. "Here. Put this on."

It was a bathing suit, one piece, black-and-white striped.

Kaitlyn thought of saying "Why?"—but there wasn't any point. She said, "I'm not going to undress in front of *him*."

"Mr. Z told me to watch," Renny said. Not lecherously. Flatly.

"You got better things to worry about," Bri said, her voice harsh.

Kaitlyn decided not to argue. Bri was right; what difference did it make at this point? She turned her back to the door and stripped, ignoring Renny like a piece of furniture. She tried to hold her head high, make every movement regal and indifferent. Even so, by the time she had pulled the bathing suit on her face was burning, her eyes full of tears.

Frost tittered and snapped the elastic on Kaitlyn's back. But Bri said nothing and kept her head down. Even Renny seemed to avoid Kaitlyn's gaze as she turned around again.

"I'm ready."

They marched her downstairs.

Not back to the crystal room. Into the front lab. The door to the back lab was open.

And then Kaitlyn knew.

I will not scream, she told herself. I won't whimper and I won't scream. They'll just enjoy it more. They'd love me to start screaming.

But she was afraid she *would* scream. Or that she might even beg.

"Is everything ready?" Mr. Z asked Joyce. Joyce was standing in the doorway to the back lab. She nodded.

Jackal Mac was staring at Kaitlyn as if he wanted to drink her face through his eyes. His evil jackal eyes. His mouth was partly open, making her think of a panting dog.

Loving this. Loving it.

"You're going to end up like the ones downstairs," Kaitlyn told him. Jackal Mac grinned like a fox.

Mr. Zetes made a gesture, a formal gesture that reminded Kaitlyn of the first time she'd heard him speak. When he'd welcomed her and Rob and the others to the Institute, telling them how special they all were. It seemed like years ago.

"Now," Mr. Z said, addressing the whole group, "I think you all know the situation. We've discovered a spy. I'm afraid I suspected this from the beginning, but I decided to give her a chance." He looked at Joyce, who looked back with a blank face. "However, there's no longer any doubt about why she came to us. So I think the best solution is my original one."

He looked at each of the others in the room and spoke with genteel emphasis. "I want you all to witness this, because I want you to understand what happens when you break faith with me. Does anyone have any questions?"

The lab was silent. Dust motes hung in the slanting afternoon light. No one had a question.

"All right. John and Paul, take her in. Joyce will handle the equipment."

*Fight,* Kaitlyn thought. That was different than screaming. As Mac and Renny reached for her, she ducked sideways and tried to run, throwing a mule kick as she went.

But they were ready for her. Mac wasn't going to be faked out again. He simply tackled her as if she'd been a two-hundred-pound quarterback, knocking her to the floor. Kaitlyn saw stars and had a horrible sense of not enough air. She'd had the breath knocked out of her.

There was a confused time, and then she realized she was sitting up, being whacked on the back. She whooped in air. Then, before she could really get her bearings, she was being hauled to her feet.

Fighting was no good. She was helpless.

Then she heard a voice, thin, high, and frightened. To her astonishment, she realized it was Lydia.

"Please don't do it. Please don't—Father."

Lydia was standing in front of Mr. Z. Her pale hands were clenched together at waist level, not as if she were praying, but as if she were trying to hold her guts in.

"She can't fight you anymore, and you know it. You could just send her away. She'd never tell anyone about us; she'd just go away and be quiet and live. Wouldn't you, Kaitlyn?" Lydia turned huge green eyes on Kait. Her lips were white, but there was a fierceness in those eyes that Kaitlyn admired.

Good for you, Lydia, she thought. You finally stood up to him. You spoke out, even when nobody else would.

But someone else was speaking.

"Lydia has a point, Emmanuel," Joyce said in a low, carefully controlled voice. "I really don't know if we have to go this far. I'm not entirely comfortable with this."

Kaitlyn stared at her. Joyce's hair was sleek as seal fur, her tanned face was smooth. Yet Kaitlyn caught a sense of inner agitation almost as great as Lydia's.

Thank you, Joyce. I knew it couldn't all be an act. There's something good in you, deep down.

Kaitlyn glanced at the others.

Bri was shifting from foot to foot, scratching her blue-streaked head. Her face was flushed; she looked as if there were something she wanted to say. Renny was scowling, seeming angry but uncertain.

Only Jackal Mac and Frost still looked eager and enthusiastic. Frost's eyes were shining with an almost romantic fervor, and Jackal Mac was licking his lips with his pierced tongue.

"Anyone else?" Mr. Z asked in a voice of terrible quiet. Then he turned on Joyce. "It's lucky for you that I know you aren't serious. You've managed to overcome your discomfort in much more squeamish situations than this. And you will now, of course—because you wouldn't want to join her in that tank. Or visit the room downstairs overnight."

A sort of shudder passed over Joyce's face. Her aquamarine eyes seemed to unfocus.

"And the same goes for the rest of you," Mr. Zetes said. "Including *you*." He was looking at Lydia. He hadn't raised a fist; he hadn't even raised his voice. But Lydia flinched, and everyone else went still. His very presence cowed them all.

"Every one of you would go to jail for years if the police found out what you've been doing these last weeks," Mr. Zetes said, his face composed and Satanic. "But the police will never have to deal with you. Because *I* will, if you cross me. Your old classmates downstairs will help. There is nowhere you can go to get away from us, nowhere you can hide that we can't find you. The power of the crystal can reach out across the globe and swat you like a fly."

Silence and stillness. The psychics watched the floor. Not even Frost was smirking now.

"Now," Mr. Z said in a grating whisper, "does anyone still have any objections?"

Some people shook their heads. Lydia, her shoulders hunched miserably, was one of them. Others just stayed still and quiet, as if hoping Mr. Z wouldn't look at them.

"Gabriel?" Mr. Zetes said.

Kaitlyn looked up in surprise. She hadn't realized Gabriel had arrived; she'd barely noticed his absence before.

He was frowning, looking like somebody who's arrived at a party to find it had started an hour earlier without him. "What's going on?" he said. He repeated it to Kaitlyn silently, his narrowed eyes on the black-and-white bathing suit. *What's going on? What did you do?*

"A disciplinary matter," Mr. Zetes said. "I hope there won't be any more like it in the future."

Kaitlyn didn't wait for him to finish, but spoke to Gabriel over his words. *None of your business. I despise you.* She threw the full weight of her contempt at him like someone throwing beer cans and rocks and bricks. And then, because Rob had taught her how to hurt him, she added, *Jailbird. You'd better do everything he says or he'll send for the police.*

She hadn't realized how much she hated him before this moment. All the loathing that she somehow hadn't felt toward Renny or even Jackal Mac and Frost, she felt for him. All the anger and betrayal. If she'd been closer, she would have tried to spit on him.

Gabriel's face hardened. She felt him pull away, felt the ice of his shields. He didn't say another word.

"All right," Mr. Z said. "You boys take her in; then we'll all go into the city for dinner. I think this calls for another celebration."

There was no point in fighting any longer. Mac and Renny dragged Kaitlyn into the back lab. She stood motionless in their grip while Joyce forced a mouthpiece into her mouth. It was connected to an air hose like a scuba diver's.

Now Joyce was pulling gloves over her hands and forcing her into a canvas jacket like the ones the creatures downstairs were wearing. Kaitlyn's arms were crossed, useless. Weights were being attached to a belt around her waist, and to her ankles.

She heard a voice behind her: Mr. Zetes. "Goodbye, my dear. Pleasant dreams."

And then Joyce was sticking something in her ears. Some kind of earplugs. Suddenly Kaitlyn was deaf.

They were pushing her forward.

The isolation tank still looked like a Dumpster. A lopsided

Dumpster with a hurricane door. The door was open and they were forcing her inside.

She couldn't help it; she was going into this *thing*. This thing that they were going to close on her, that they were going to bury her in alive.

As the dark metal walls rose around her and the water came up to meet her, Kaitlyn's nerve broke. She did scream. Or at least, she tried. But the thing in her mouth muffled it like a gag and the earplugs dulled the rest of the sound. There was only silence as water enveloped her. And darkness.

She twisted, trying to get on her back, to see the door. To see the light for one last instant . . .

But all she saw was a rapidly diminishing rectangle of white. Then the metal door clanged shut. It was the last sound she was to hear.

Right from the beginning, it was very bad.

Remembering Bri's words ("Sure, it's cool. Cosmic, man!"), she had hoped that the tank might be pleasant at first. Or at least bearable. But it wasn't. It was a death trap, and from the first instant Kaitlyn felt a screaming inside her that wouldn't stop.

Maybe the difference was that she knew she was in here for good. They weren't going to let her out in an hour or a few hours or a day. They were going to keep her in here for as long as it took, until she was a *thing*, a drooling, vacant-eyed lump of flesh with no mind.

Her first thought was to try and beat the system. She would make her own noise; she would make herself feel. But even the loudest humming was dim and soon her throat grew sore. After a while she wasn't sure whether she was humming or not.

It was very difficult to kick with the weights on her legs, and when she did manage, she found the tank was lined with something like rubber inside. Between the drag of weights and water and the give of the rubber padding, she couldn't feel much of anything.

She couldn't pinch with her fingers, either, the gloves prevented that and dulled all sensation. Her arms were immobilized. She couldn't even chew her lips—the mouthpiece prevented it.

More, all these exertions tired her out. After trying everything she could think of, she was exhausted, unable to do anything but float inertly. The weights were gauged to keep her floating right in the middle of the water, away from the top and bottom of the tank, and the water temperature was gauged so that she had no sensation of hot or cold.

It was then that she began to realize the true horror of her situation.

It was dark. She couldn't *see*. She couldn't see *anything*.

And she couldn't hear. The silence was so deep, so profound, that she began to wonder if she really remembered what sound was.

In the endless dark silence, her body began to dissolve.

Once, when she'd just turned thirteen, she'd had a nightmare of a disembodied arm in her bed. She had half-woken one night to find that she'd been lying with her arms pressed together under her body, and that one of them had gone to sleep. She could feel it with her other hand: a cool, unnaturally limp arm. In her not-awake state, it seemed as if someone had put a severed dead arm in her bed. Her own arm was foreign to her.

After that, all her nightmares were of the cool blue arm snuggling up to her chin and then dragging her under the bed.

Now Kaitlyn felt as if *all* her limbs had gone to sleep. At first it seemed that her body had gone dead, and then she realized she didn't *have* a body anymore. At least, there was no way to prove she did.

If there were arms and legs in the tank, they weren't hers. They were dead, unholy, other peoples' limbs, floating around her, ready to kill her.

After a while, even the sense that there were other peoples' limbs around her faded. There was *nothing* around her.

She had no sense of being trapped inside the little Dumpster tank. She had no sense of being anywhere. She was alone in pure space, and around her was nowhere, nothingness, absence, emptiness.

The world had disappeared because she couldn't sense it. She'd never realized it before, but the world *was* her senses. She had never known anything but her internal map of it, made up from what she saw and heard. And now there was no sight, no sound, no map, no world. She couldn't keep hold of the conviction that there *was* a world outside—or that there was an outside.

Did the word *outside* have meaning? Could something be outside the universe?

*Maybe there had never really been anything except her.*

Could she really remember what the color "yellow" was? Or the feeling of "silk"?

No. It had all been a joke or a dream. Neither of those things existed. These ideas of "touch" or "taste" or "hearing"— she'd made them up to get away from the emptiness.

She had always been alone in the emptiness. Just her, just K—

Who was she? For an instant there, she'd almost had a name, but now it was gone. She was nameless.

*She didn't exist either.*

There was no person thinking this. No "I" to make words about it.

There was no . . . no . . . no . . .

A silent scream ripped outward. Then:

*Kaitlyn!*

# CHAPTER 14

Gabriel was frightened.

Frost sat beside him during dinner—Mr. Z's orders, he was certain. She touched him every other minute, stroking his wrist, patting his shoulder. Again, he felt certain, on Mr. Z's orders.

They wanted to know if he would try and reach Kaitlyn with his mind.

But the restaurant in San Francisco was too far from the Institute. Kaitlyn was long out of range, as Joyce must have told Mr. Z. Gabriel didn't even try to stretch out his mind; instead he worked on convincing everyone that he didn't want to. That he hated Kaitlyn as much as Jackal Mac did.

He must have done a good job, because Lydia was looking at him with burning green hatred in her eyes—when her father's head was turned, of course.

She wasn't the only one who looked unhappy. Bri had

eaten almost none of her dinner. Renny kept swallowing as if he felt sick. And Joyce was holding herself rigid and expressionless, her aquamarine eyes fixed on the candle in the center of the table.

The club they went to next was also far away from San Carlos—but not quite as far. Frost left his side to dance with Mac. As soon as she was gone, Gabriel slipped the piece of crystal he had palmed out of his pocket.

It should increase his range—but enough? He wasn't sure. The only time he'd managed a telepathic link over such a long distance was when he'd been in agonizing pain.

He had to try.

With Mr. Z smoking a cigar and smiling benevolently at the dancers on the floor, Gabriel clutched the tiny chip of crystal and sent out his mind.

But the frightening thing was that even when he felt he'd stretched out far enough, he couldn't feel Kaitlyn. Her place in the web was filled with nothingness. Not even a wall, only blankness. Nobody nowhere.

Desperate, he kept calling her name.

There was a vision in her mind.

Whose mind? It didn't matter. Maybe there wasn't a mind at all, but only the vision.

A rose, full and blooming, with lush petals. The petals were a warm color that she had forgotten. At first it was a nice image, all those petals on one stem, separate but connected. It reminded her of something. But then the vision went bad. The petals turned black, the color of the emptiness. The rose began to drip blood. It was hurt, mortally wounded. The petals began to fall . . . and on each there was a face, and the face was *screaming. . . .*

*Kaitlyn! Kaitlyn, can you hear me?*

Petals falling, dripping. Like tears.

*Kaitlyn! Oh God, please answer me. Please, Kaitlyn. Kaitlyn!*

There was desperation in the voice. Whose voice? And who was it talking to?

*I couldn't contact you before. He had Frost sitting by me, touching me. She would have known. But now I have them convinced I don't want to talk to you—oh, please, Kaitlyn; answer. It's Gabriel.*

Suddenly there was another vision. A hand dripping blood. Onto a floor. Gabriel's hand, cut by the crystal shard, dripping onto Marisol's floor.

And she had seen it, she, Kaitlyn. She was Kaitlyn.

She had a self again.

*Gabriel?*

His voice came back, at a volume that hurt her. *Yes. Kaitlyn, talk to me.*

*Gabriel, is it really you? I thought . . . you'd be mad. After I said . . .*

She wasn't sure what she'd said. Or even what "saying" was.

*Kaitlyn, don't be—don't even think about that. Are you all right?*

It was a stupid question. Kaitlyn had no way to answer it in words, so she sent along the thin, quivering strand of the web that connected them a vision of what the emptiness was like. Nothingness, void, absence . . .

*Stop. Please stop now. Oh God, Kait, what can I do?*

Kaitlyn could feel the black well trying to suck her back into it; all she had to hold on to was the slender connection with Gabriel, like a tiny shaft of light in a dungeon. It was keeping her sane at the moment, but it wasn't enough. She needed more, she needed . . .

*You need to see and hear,* Gabriel said.

*I don't even remember what those things are like,* Kaitlyn told him. She could feel hysteria bubbling in her, stealing her rationality.

Gabriel said simply, *I'll show you.*

And then he began to give her things, with his mind. Things *he* had seen and heard, things from his memory. He gave her everything.

"Remember what the sun's like? It's hot and yellow and so bright you can't look at it. Like this. See?" In her sense-starved condition his voice seemed like a real voice not like telepathy. He was giving her the sound of talking. And sending her a picture. As soon as Kaitlyn saw it she remembered. The sun.

*That's good,* she said. *It feels good.*

"That's what it looks like in summer. I grew up in New York, and sometimes in the summer my mom would take me to this place by the ocean—remember the ocean?"

Blue-green coolness. Hot sand between the toes, gritty sand in the bathing trunks. Water foaming and hissing, children shrieking. The smell and taste of salt.

Kaitlyn drank it all in greedily, hungry for every nuance of sight or sound. *More, please. More.*

"We'd go up to the boardwalk, just her and me. She'd always buy me a hot dog and an ice cream. She didn't have much money, because the old man drank it all, but sometimes she'd make him give her a dollar to fix something he really liked for dinner. Then she'd get me the ice cream—remember ice cream?"

Creamy, blobby coldness. Stickiness on her chin. Rich, dark taste of chocolate.

*I remember. Thank you, Gabriel.*

He gave her more. All his best memories, everything he could think of that was good. Every golden afternoon, every skateboard ride, every moment with his mother when he was seven years old and sick with the fever that gave him his power.

Everything he was, he gave to her.

Kaitlyn devoured the sensations, filling herself with the reality of the world outside. She was drenched in sunshine and cool wind and the smell of burning leaves and the taste of

Halloween candy. And music; she hadn't realized how Gabriel loved music. At fourteen, he'd wanted to play in a garage band. He was jamming with the drummer one night, trying to get more in sync—and then the drummer was lying on the floor, clutching his head. Pierced by Gabriel's mind. When Gabriel tried to help him up, he ran screaming.

A week later, Gabriel was on his way to the psychic research center in Durham, where his principal and his mother and the social worker hoped someone could teach him control. His father's last word to him had been: "Freak."

"Never mind about that," Gabriel said. He was giving her only good things, nothing depressing. She could feel that he didn't want her to see his father's stubbly face with the bleary red eyes. Or feel the burning hot shock of his father's belt.

*It's all right,* Kaitlyn said. *I mean, I won't look at anything you don't want me to, but you don't have to worry about me . . . and I won't ever tell anyone, and I'm so sorry. Oh, Gabriel, I'm so sorry. And . . .*

She wanted to tell him that she understood him now, in a way she'd never understood anyone before. Because she was *with* him. It wasn't even like being in the web; it was much closer than that, much deeper. He'd torn down all the barriers and put his soul into her hands.

*I love you,* she told him.

"I love you, Kaitlyn. From the very beginning."

She got a sense then, of how he saw her. Bits and pieces from his memories of her. Her eyes, smoky blue, with the strange dark rings in them, framed by heavy black lashes. Her skin tasting like peaches. Her hair crackling when she brushed it, flame-colored, silky but full of electricity.

She could sense, too, scraps of what he'd thought about her over the weeks. Lines from their lives together. *That kind of girl might be too interesting, might tempt you to get involved . . . A girl who challenged him, who could be his equal . . . Her mind was a place of blue pools and blazing meteors . . . She stood slim and proud as some medieval witch princess against the dawn.*

"And then I thought you'd betrayed me," he said. "But you really came to protect me, didn't you?"

With that, Kaitlyn realized that he'd seen as deeply into her mind as she'd seen into his. She had thought he was the one giving, while she had only received . . . but of course, he'd had to join with her completely in order to share his life with her.

He knew everything, now.

And then he came on something that sent shock waves through Kaitlyn.

"Jackal Mac said—*what?*"

Kaitlyn could feel the memory he was looking at. *He said you told him to check me out.*

Gabriel's cold anger filled the universe.

"I never said that. I never talked to him about you at all."

*I know, Gabriel.* She did know, she was certain.

"But Lydia knew how you gave me energy on the trip to Canada. She must have told him—"

*Gabriel, forget about it.* His fury was hurting her, filling her with images of death, of Jackal Mac spitting up bone splinters. *Please think me something nice.*

So he did. All that night, he thought her beautiful music and hillsides of wild mustard flowers and the smell of fresh pencil shavings and the taste of banana marshmallow candies. And the touch of his hands, the way he would do it if she ever got back in the world again.

Rob stared at the edges of the afghan that served Tony's friend for a window curtain. He didn't move, because he didn't want to disturb the others; Anna and Lewis and Tamsin on the floor. Even the black kitten Tony had given Anna was lying curled and still. But Rob couldn't sleep.

Light was showing around the blanket edges. Morning. And Kaitlyn hadn't called last night.

He had a very bad feeling.

There was no good reason for it. Kaitlyn had told them she might have to wait and watch for her chance. That was probably what she was doing.

But Rob was empty and sick with fear.

*Rob?*

He turned to see Anna looking up at him. There was no sign of drowsiness in her face or her dark eyes.

*I couldn't sleep, either.* She put a hand on his arm and he put his hand over it. Just the feel of her warmth gave him some comfort.

*You want to go and look for her now, don't you?*

Rob turned from the window again. Her steady gaze, her calm face, and her gentle presence in the web all strengthened him.

"Yes," he whispered.

*Then we'll go. I think we should, too. Let's wake up Lewis and Tamsin.*

Kaitlyn knew it was morning because Gabriel said so.

"I think they're going to take you out soon. Mr. Zetes drove up a little while ago, and now Joyce is knocking on all the doors upstairs."

*Another circus, huh?* Kaitlyn asked. She didn't know how she felt about the outside world anymore, but the thought of everyone staring at her was definitely appalling.

"I'll be with you," Gabriel said.

As the night had gone on, she'd gotten more and more of an odd sense from him. A feeling that ran beneath the thoughts they were sharing, that he was keeping away from her. Although it was tightly controlled, she recognized it as pain.

*Gabriel, are you all right? I feel—are you hurt, somehow?*

"I have a sort of headache. It's no problem. Do you feel it now?"

Once again, she had the sense that he was concealing something. But concealing it better.

"Okay, Joyce is telling us to come downstairs." After a moment, he said, "We're in the lab."

*Yeah, time for the unveiling.* Kaitlyn laughed silently, nervously. *I wonder what they're going to think. I suppose I should act crazy.*

"I think it's your best chance. Kait—I don't know how I can save you right now. The others don't like what the old man is doing—I think Joyce asked him to take you out this soon—but they're afraid of him. And I can only fight one of them at a time."

Kaitlyn knew. Gabriel's destructive power operated most strongly when he could touch his victim, and it took time. He couldn't hold off Jackal Mac and Renny while killing Mr. Z, for instance.

*And you're weak,* she told him. *From helping me, I know. I'm sorry. But we'll manage somehow—maybe they'll just put me back in the tank.*

Then she realized something that made the blood start beating in her ears. *Gabriel, wait, wait! Rob is coming. I forgot.* She'd forgotten about the outside world. *All you need to do is wait until he gets here, then he can help.*

"It depends on what Mr. Z is going to do to you, whether we can wait. He's giving a speech now. On and on."

*I don't want to hear it. Gabriel, you do know that Rob didn't mean the things he said at Marisol's house. He was mad at you. Hurt. And he felt betrayed. But that's because he really cares about you. You* know *that, don't you?*

Even now, Gabriel refused to say it. But Kaitlyn had seen inside him too deeply to be fooled. Her question was rhetorical. Gabriel *did* know. His feelings for Rob were all mixed up with guilt and jealousy and resentment of Rob's effortless ability to do good and be good, and to go through life being loved. But Kaitlyn thought that Rob would be pleased with the feeling Gabriel had under that. He admired Rob. Respected him. Would have liked to be somebody Rob could like.

*But he does like you,* Kaitlyn said again, and then she realized they were opening the door of the tank.

The clang was a different sort of sound than Gabriel's mental voice, and she thought that if she had really been in silence all yesterday afternoon and night—maybe fifteen hours at a guess—she wouldn't have recognized what sound was anymore, and screamed in fear. She was spared having to fake that because they couldn't hear her.

Hands pulled at her, the touch as shriekingly dissonant as the door clang. Everything was so *harsh.* Her skin was so sensitized that even the gentlest pressure would have hurt, and these hands weren't gentle.

Then light struck her eyes. It both hurt and dazzled, confusing her. She couldn't really see anything, only the whiteness, with occasional shapes blocking it. Squinting helped a little, but tears still ran down her face.

It didn't matter; she was soaking wet everywhere. She could feel the harsh hands taking off the strait-jacket and weights, removing the mouthpiece. Then, just as she began to really see, she was turned around to face Mr. Zetes.

She was white and wrinkled. Her mouth hurt, she had cramps in her arms and shoulders, and her legs wouldn't support her. She was dripping all over the floor.

"She can't stand up," Joyce said crisply. "Bri, get a chair."

They put her in the chair. Mr. Z looked at her.

*Now, what?* Kaitlyn asked Gabriel. *I don't think I can scream. Should I just sort of look vacant?*

*Try it,* he commanded. Now that she could hear real voices, his telepathic voice seemed different. She knew it wasn't sound.

"Can you understand me, Kaitlyn?" Mr. Zetes was asking. "Do you know where you are?"

His expression was avid and eager. Like a connoisseur just about to take the first sip of wine, stopping to inhale the bouquet. If he thought she was crazy enough, he'd say, "Ahhh."

Kaitlyn tried to look mad. She gazed at him, doing her version of the human pupa stare. She wondered if she should try to say, "Muh-muh-muh"—but she was afraid she would do it wrong. Instead, she tried to smile the way Sasha had.

She saw in an instant that it wasn't any good. Mr. Z was an

expert on insane people—he collected them. His piercing eyes widened and then narrowed as he looked at her. Kaitlyn would have sworn she could see a red spark somewhere in their depths.

Then his white brows drew together over his aquiline nose and his mouth made a bitter, scornful line. He planted his gold-headed cane on the ground and stood tall, like some patriarch from the Bible. Except that he looked instead like *El Diablo, El Gato,* Satan.

"It's failed," he said. He looked at Joyce. "Why?"

"I don't know. I have no idea." Even Kaitlyn could hear the relief in the shaky voice. Joyce's hand on Kaitlyn's back pressed gently, out of Mr. Z's sight.

"This girl tried to destroy us. Not once. Time and agai" Mr. Z's voice was shaking, too—with repressed anger.

Joyce straightened. "I had nothing to do with it. uel. I don't know how she came through like this. F she has—"

Mr. Z's face had been undergoing a str molded by satanic fury, the next smoothi Almost like Claymation, Kaitlyn thou self under control. His lips curved

"Now that she has, we'll tion," he told Joyce. "The

Kaitlyn felt a falling who was standing wi a row behind Mr. Z. An

*Kaitlyn? Kaitlyn, this is Rob. Am I in range yet?*

*Rob! Oh, thank God, Rob, you're early, thank God.*

She felt the flash of Gabriel's response as well. Desperate relief.

*Rob, where are you?* Kaitlyn demanded.

*At the end of the block. We were worried you might be in trouble.*

*We are! Rob, you'd better hurry.*

At the same time Gabriel was saying, *If you can make a distraction, I can try to get Kait out.*

Then Kaitlyn snapped to the real world. Frost had darted forward and grabbed her hand, wrapping her silver-nailed fingers around it.

"Mr. Zetes, I know how she did it!" Frost shrieked, her voice thin and sharp with spite. "She's talking to them! She was talking to them just now, and she's scared they'll get caught because they're coming right here!"

Kaitlyn jerked her hand away as if she'd touched a live coal.

fury exploded inside her and she kept pulling her hand
to get distance, and then she slapped Frost's cheek as hard
could.

Gabriel kept his head. She could hear him yelling a
to Rob. *Stay where you are! They just found out about
come near the house!*

," Mr. Z said, and his smile was more delighted
rolled the words in his mouth as if enjoying them.

"John, Laurie, Paul—help Kaitlyn downstairs, please. Everyone else follow. Hurry now. This should be very interesting."

Kaitlyn tried to fight Mac and Frost and Renny, but her limbs were too weak. She was more of a hindrance by just being limp.

Gabriel didn't fight, either—probably too many of them, Kaitlyn thought. But she didn't understand why he seemed to be hanging back, the last one down the stairs to the hidden room. She tried to get a look at him as they carried her down, but she couldn't see.

"I want to kill him myself!" Gabriel shouted from the floor above. Kaitlyn felt the pang of a new terror. What if the crystal had driven Gabriel crazy like the others? And it was just showing up now?

*Gabriel—*

He wouldn't answer her. Because Frost was touching her? She didn't know.

"Come down!" Mr. Zetes shouted as he punched in the combination to the office.

Kaitlyn didn't want to go in there. Did not. She struggled with fresh strength as they carried her through the door.

Then the smell and the psychic feel of the human pupae struck her and she went limp.

They carried her past the crystal to the only piece of furniture in the room, a chair. Everyone else was crowding in. Mr. Z was herding them, gesturing them to pack themselves more tightly. Like somebody trying to fit more people into an elevator. Gabriel was the last. He stepped back to join the others who were lining the walls.

Then Mr. Zetes backed up. He stood, leaning both hands on his cane, looking at the doorway with anticipation.

"They won't come," Kaitlyn told him. Her voice was earnest; she just wished it was steady. "I warned them and they're too smart to come when they know you're waiting."

Mr. Zetes smiled. "Do you hear that, my dear? The kitchen door breaking."

*Rob? Are you in the house? Rob, listen to me—don't do it. Stay away! Stay away!*

But the imperious tone that had worked with him in the gym did nothing now.

*This is my choice, Kaitlyn,* Rob said. And Kaitlyn heard footsteps on the stairs.

# CHAPTER 15

"Rob, go back!" Kaitlyn screamed aloud.

Rob came in. He was flushed and windblown, his hair a golden lion's mane, his eyes full of all the light of the sky. He had run down the stairs, but he took the step into the room calmly, face alert and purposeful, assessing his chances. Looking for Kaitlyn and the way to get her out.

"Leave," Kaitlyn whispered.

Anna and Lewis were right behind Rob. Stepping over the threshold and into the trap. Behind them was a girl Kaitlyn recognized vaguely . . . yellow curls and tilted eyes . . . of course, it was Tamsin.

"A visitor from the Fellowship!" Mr. Zetes said. "We are greatly honored." He actually bowed over his cane.

He didn't move to shut the door. He didn't have to. Once they were all in, he nudged Parté King with his foot, not quite a kick.

Kaitlyn felt power swelling out to hold the new arrivals in the room. As if a fence had been stretched across the open doorway. Rob stared at the lolling creatures on the floor, his face going pale under his tan, the light in his eyes fading with shock.

And even as he stared, he was caught, his movements dragged into slow motion. So were the others. Like flies in flypaper, Kaitlyn thought. Gnats in a web.

"What did you do to them?" Rob whispered, looking slowly from Sasha to Mr. Zetes.

"The unfortunate pilot study," Mr. Zetes said blandly. "Don't look so alarmed. You'll find it isn't so bad after a while."

"Muhhh," said Sasha.

Rob tried to move toward Mr. Zetes—Kaitlyn saw the determination in his face, saw his muscles cord as he strained. But Sasha and Parté King were watching him. Their power surged up to hold Rob tighter. Kaitlyn could *feel* it happening as well as see it. Rob stopped fighting and stood panting.

"You should have stayed away, Rob," Joyce said, in a voice that seemed on the edge of tears. "I wish you had; I really do."

Rob didn't glance at her. He looked at Kaitlyn.

*I'm sorry, Kait. I blew it.*

Kaitlyn felt wetness spill from her eyes. *I'm the one who's sorry. It's my fault we're all here.* She looked at Tamsin, wondering if there was any hope. The people of the Fellowship were born to a psychic race, they had all sorts of ancient knowledge. Was there some weapon . . . ?

But Tamsin's face undeceived her. Tamsin was gazing mutely at the two creatures on the floor, her lips parted with pity and helpless sorrow. She didn't even seem to recognize the possibility of fighting.

Aspect, Kaitlyn thought. The philosophy of the Fellowship. Nonviolence, passive resistance.

It wasn't going to get Tamsin very far here.

"I didn't realize that this morning would be so productive," Mr. Zetes said happily. He was doing everything but rubbing his hands, gloating. "These last two days have been splendid—just splendid. And now we'll finish up."

He took a step toward Rob, unaffected by the dragging power of the human pupae.

"I'm going to leave you down here to get acquainted with my former students," he said. "I think in a short time you'll all be on the same level of communication—especially if I tie you in actual contact with the crystal. Contact is quite painful, especially in large doses in the beginning. But of course you know that already."

"We can't just disappear," Anna said. "Our parents will come looking. My parents know about you already. They'll find out what you've done and then they'll kill you."

"In other words, I won't get away with it," Mr. Zetes translated, still bland. "Go on, say it, my dear, I don't mind the cliché.

But the fact is that I *will* get away with it. Literally, you see. I have many different residences across the country; even abroad. And the crystal isn't as much of an encumbrance as you might think. I've already brought it to the United States from a very far place." He looked at Tamsin as if this were a shared joke.

She didn't respond. He shrugged very slightly and went on. "So, you see, I can take my crystal and my students wherever I go—and that's all I need. I'll leave you here, of course. In your parents' care."

He gave his terrible smile.

Kaitlyn was proud of her mind-mates. They stood in the doorway, snarled with invisible thread, but none of them broke down or showed any fear. Anna's head was high on her slim neck, her dark eyes proud and self-contained. Lewis stood squarely, fists clenched, his round face stern and unreadable. Rob looked like a young and angry angel.

*I love you,* Kaitlyn told them. *I love you and I'm so proud of you.*

A voice broke into her admiration.

"I won't go with you! I'll stay here with them," Lydia said passionately.

Mr. Zetes frowned just a little. "Don't be ridiculous."

"I won't go! I hate what you're doing. I hate *you!*" Lydia's elbows were at her sides, fists held shaking near her shoulders. "I don't care if you win this time; I don't care what happens to me; I don't care, I don't *care*—"

"Be quiet!" Mr. Zetes said brutally. Lydia was quiet. But she shook her head, dark hair flying from side to side.

"You'll do as you're told," Mr. Zetes said. "Or you *will* be left here, and I don't think you'll like that." He looked at Joyce, his pleasure in the morning obviously spoiled. "All right," he said abruptly. "Let's finish, so we can get to breakfast. Take those chains off the boys and bring them over here."

Kaitlyn's eyes went to the chains on Parté King and Sasha. They had one on each ankle. Which meant one for her, Rob, Anna, and Lewis each. Tamsin probably wouldn't try to fight.

Then Kaitlyn looked up, because something was wrong. Joyce wasn't moving to obey Mr. Zetes. She was shaking her head.

"I'm not asking you to do it, I'm telling you. Joyce!"

Joyce shook her head again, slowly and decisively, her aquamarine eyes on Mr. Z's face.

"Good for you, Joyce," Kaitlyn said. To Mr. Zetes, she said, "Can't you see? They're all turning against you. It's going to keep happening, too. You can't win."

Mr. Zetes had gone purple.

"Disobedience! Disobedience and insubordination!" he shouted. "Is there anyone here who still understands loyalty?" The piercing eyes flashed around the room. Bri and Renny looked away from him: Bri glowering, Renny with his shoulders angrily hunched. They were both shaking their heads slowly.

Mr. Z's gaze settled on Jackal Mac. "John! Take the key from Joyce and remove those chains immediately!"

Jackal Mac obeyed. He started to feel all over Joyce's pockets for the key, but she slapped his hand away and pulled it out, slowly, staring at Mr. Zetes all the while.

Shambling to the center of the room, Mac unlocked the chains from Sasha.

"Give them to me," Mr. Zetes said impatiently. "Then remove the others."

When Mac did, Mr. Z looked at Rob. Kaitlyn could see that he was fighting to regain his smiling malevolence. But he couldn't do it. He was an angry old man taking revenge.

"Go ahead and struggle," he told Rob. "You won't be able to move. And when I have you chained, these boys on the floor will move you step by step until you touch the crystal. The great crystal, the last of the ancient firestones. Go ahead, take a look at it."

He gestured at the obscene thing towering in the middle of the floor, the crystal that shone with its own milky impure light. The machine of death waiting for them all.

"The moment you touch it, your mind will start to burn," Mr. Zetes went on with some of his old fervor. "In a matter of hours it will burn *out*. Like a gutted house. Your powers will remain, but *you* will not." Kneeling, he brought the chain to Rob's ankle. "And now . . ."

"I don't think so," Gabriel said.

While Mr. Zetes had been talking to Rob, while the human pupae were busy keeping Rob tightly controlled for the chaining, while Jackal Mac was unlocking the other chains, Gabriel had been inching forward. Kaitlyn had seen it, but hadn't known what he could do. He was empty-handed. The pupae would stop any kind of a fight.

But as Gabriel spoke, she heard a swishing *snick*. The sound she'd heard in Marisol's room and on Ivy Street, when his spring-loaded knife snapped out of his sleeve.

Only this time it wasn't a knife.

He was holding the crystal shard by its thick end, holding it underhanded, like a sword ready to thrust up. Its tip was only a foot or so from the giant crystal in the center of the room.

Now Kaitlyn understood why he had been the last one downstairs. He'd been in Joyce's room, getting the shard.

"Don't close that chain," Gabriel said. "Or I'll put it on the crystal."

Kaitlyn heard a metallic click and knew that Mr. Z had done it anyway. He straightened up to look at Gabriel. He was alarmed but not panicked, Kaitlyn thought.

"Now, Gabriel," he said, and moved a little toward him.

Just a little. Gabriel stiffened. The tip of the shard quivered. Kaitlyn could see it reaching for one of the outgrowths of the crystal, like a stalactite and a stalagmite trying to kiss.

"Stay there!"

Mr. Z stopped.

"Now," Gabriel said. "Everyone who doesn't want to die, step back."

At the same time, Mr. Z was kicking the human pupae. "Stop him! Push him back against the wall."

Parté King, the cricketlike one, rolled over on his side to look at Gabriel. Sasha turned his swollen white head. They were both smiling their face-splitting grins.

Kaitlyn felt the power surge up again, sweeping around Gabriel like sticky running tree sap around a fly, turning to amber to hold him. She saw Gabriel start to lunge forward, then freeze in place, the tip of the shard only inches from a jagged outgrowth.

Her throat swelled, and then she was shouting. "Come on! Everybody! If we all move at once—maybe they can't hold us."

She stood, heard Mr. Z yell, and felt the drag of air. She fought it, shouting, "Get to the shard! Somebody get to the shard!"

Then it seemed everyone was either trying to move, or trying to stop someone from moving. Bri was trying to move. Her glower had turned to a look of grim resolve, and Kaitlyn realized she'd finally decided which side she was on. Frost was stopping her, blocking her like a basketball guard. Renny was trying to move. Jackal Mac had abandoned the chains and was grappling with him in slow motion.

Rob and Anna and Lewis were all struggling to get to Gabriel, mostly with their feet stuck to the floor, but occasionally managing a step. Even Tamsin was trying. Mr. Z was turning round and round among them, raising his cane, shouting. He couldn't deal with them all at once.

Then Kaitlyn saw that Lydia was free and moving—slowly but steadily—toward Gabriel and the shard.

"Joyce!" Mr. Zetes shouted. "Stop her! She's right beside you! Stop her!"

But Joyce shook her head. "It's time it was over, Emmanuel," she said. In an instant, she and Lydia were caught in the sticky air, too. Lydia still struggled on desperately.

"Hold them!" Mr. Zetes shouted, and began beating Sasha and Parté King with his cane. "Hold them all! Hold them all!"

Kaitlyn heard the savage swishing sound of the cane, and the dull thud of the blows. She saw Gabriel's face tighten, saw it go grim with purpose. The shard quivered, moved an inch toward the crystal.

"Gabriel," Mr. Zetes said. "Think of all your ambitions. You wanted to go to the top. Have everything good. Money, power, position—all the things in life you deserve."

Gabriel was panting, sweat trickling down his temples.

"Recognition of your superiority—you'll never have any of it without me," Mr. Z went on frantically. "What about all that, Gabriel? Everything you always wanted?"

Gabriel lifted his head just enough to look Mr. Z in the eye. "The hell with it."

Then he gritted his teeth and the shard moved again.

Mr. Zetes lost control.

He began to scream, shrill and piercing, and to beat Sasha again. "Stop him! Stop him! Stop him!"

Sasha's voice rose, too, for the first time since Kaitlyn had seen him. "Muh-muh! *Muhhhh! Muhhhh! Moooooootheeerrrr!*"

Kaitlyn screamed herself then. She was crying wildly, fighting the air.

Then suddenly the drag disappeared. The air was air again. Everything that happened next happened in an instant, so that Kaitlyn's mind took it in like a still photograph, receiving the impressions before she could really process them.

She was moving freely. Sasha had turned to look at Mr. Zetes. She could see Sasha's face, not white anymore, but red with the fury of a squalling infant. And then Mr. Zetes was flying toward the crystal, *flying*, as if a giant hand had thrown him. He smashed into it, into its heavy solidity and sword-sharp outcrops at the same instant that Gabriel thrust the shard forward like a rapier.

It all happened at once. Although Kaitlyn's body was free there was no time to *do* anything, only time for one thought, sent out to her mind-mates as she saw the shard stab toward the crystal. With Gabriel still holding it—

*Protect Gabriel! Put your thoughts—around him—*

The words weren't very clear, but her intent was. She felt everyone in the web, Rob, Lewis, and Anna, joining with her to help shield Gabriel's mind from the destruction.

Mr. Z's high, keening wail came at the same instant, just as the shard made contact with one translucent facet of the crystal.

And then—

There were all sorts of sounds woven together in the great crashing that came next. There was the sound of an axe crashing through glass, and the sound of a sonic boom that rattled the windows. There was the rushing sound of a freight train passing by very close. There was a metallic sound like all the pots and pans in a kitchen falling to a tile floor at once. There was the rumble of thunder and the cracking of ice on a lake. There was a high, thin sound like the screaming of gulls—or maybe that was Mr. Zetes.

And through all the other sounds, underneath them, Kaitlyn thought she could hear music—the kind of music you think you hear when water is crashing through copper pipes.

There was light, too. The kind of light you expect to see just before a mushroom-shaped cloud. Kaitlyn's eyes squeezed shut automatically, and her hand flew up to protect her face, but she saw it through her eyelids.

Colors that her pastels and ink bottles had never prepared her for. Aureolin yellow with a brightness off the scales. Dragon's blood crimson spreading into tongues of lava pink fire. Ultraviolet silvery blue.

They burst like fireworks, sweeping to the edges of her vision, overlapping each other, bright explosion after bright explosion.

And then they stopped. Kaitlyn saw rainbow afterimages, beautiful fiery lattices printed on her eyelids.

Very cautiously she opened her eyes, lifting her hand away from her face.

A cobalt green stain still colored her vision, but she could see again. The great milky crystal was dust on the ground, glassy dust in the shape of a giant stone plant, or a Christmas tree ornament. The largest bits left were pebble size.

Mr. Zetes, who had been touching the crystal at the moment it shattered, was gone. Just gone. Nothing left but the gold-topped cane that had fallen from his hand.

Sasha and Parté King were lying still. Their faces were frozen into a look of empty astonishment—not peaceful, but not anguished, either. In her heart, Kaitlyn was sorry she'd called them the human pupae. They had been human beings.

Everyone else was standing pretty much where they had been before the crash. They were all lifting their heads or lowering their hands, staring.

"It's over," Lewis whispered finally. "We did it. It's over."

Kaitlyn was beginning to realize the same thing. Bri and Renny were gazing around them like sleepwalkers who'd just woken up. Free of the influence of the crystal at last, Kait thought. She looked at Gabriel. He was looking at his hand which had held the shard. The palm was pink, as if he'd been lightly burned.

"Did the shard go, too?" Kaitlyn asked.

He turned his gray eyes on her, as if startled to hear a voice. Then he looked back at his hand again.

"Yes," he said, blinking. "When the crystal did. It felt— I can't explain it. It was like lightning in my hand. I felt the power go *through* it. And the power—it felt like Timon. Like Timon and Mereniang and LeShan—all of them. It was as if they were in there, rushing out." He looked up again, almost furtively. "I guess that sounds crazy."

"No, it doesn't," Rob said, his voice strong. "It sounds right. I believe you."

Gabriel looked at him, just a look. But after that he held his head up, and the startled, furtive expression was gone.

Kaitlyn felt something like carbonated water begin to bubble in her veins. "We did it," she said. She looked at each of her mind-mates, and at Lydia, and suddenly she needed to shout. "You guys, we did it!"

"I said that already," Lewis said with force.

And then it was like a roller coaster gathering speed. Everybody seemed to feel the need to say it, and then to yell it, and then to yell louder to be heard over the other yells. People began to tell one another and then to hug one another or pound one another on the back to drive the point home. Kaitlyn found herself shaking Lydia and kissing Gabriel. Rob, somehow unchained, was wringing Anna's long braids.

Bri and Renny were part of the celebration, punching each other and whooping with gathering intensity. Joyce was crying, clutching with one hand at Kaitlyn's back and whispering something Kait couldn't hear. Lydia was a full member of the winning team, being socked in the arm over and over by Lewis.

But three people weren't. Tamsin knelt by the two dead boys on the floor. Her tilted eyes were wet as she gently closed their eyelids.

And Frost and Jackal Mac were stiff as statues, watching the wild release of energy around them with frightened, hostile eyes. Kaitlyn saw them and raised her arms to Frost.

"Come on," she said. "Don't worry; be happy. Let's all try to deal with each other, okay?"

It wasn't the warmest invitation, maybe, but Kaitlyn thought that under the circumstances it was pretty generous. But Frost's pale blue eyes flashed. Jackal Mac's face turned ugly.

They looked at each other, then with one accord they rushed for the door.

Kaitlyn was too surprised to try to stop them, and by the time she recovered, she wasn't sure she wanted to. The yelling and cheering had died out, and she looked at Rob, who had taken half a step toward the door.

"I think we should just let them go," she said.

He glanced back, then nodded slowly. Gabriel and Lewis settled back reluctantly. Kaitlyn could hear running footsteps up above, then the bang of a door.

Then, silence. In the stillness, Joyce's whispering could be heard.

"I'm so sorry. I'm so sorry for everything."

Kaitlyn turned.

Joyce's aquamarine eyes were red-rimmed. Her face was shiny with tears and perspiration, her normally sleek blond hair ruffled like a baby chick's. Her pink sweat clothes looked damp and bedraggled.

She also looked like a sleepwalker who has just woken up.

"I'm so sorry," she whispered. "The things I've done. The terrible things. I . . . I . . ."

Kaitlyn looked at her helplessly. Then she said, "Tamsin!"

The head with the clustered yellow curls lifted. Tamsin saw Joyce and got up. She looked into Joyce's face, then she took Joyce by the elbow and led her toward the open door.

"The firestones can cast a powerful spell," Kait heard her saying softly. "Their influence can be very strong—and recovery can take a long time. . . ."

Kaitlyn was satisfied. Although Tamsin looked younger than Joyce, there was a sort of ageless wisdom and understanding about her. Joyce was listening as they disappeared.

Kait turned back to find her mind-mates grinning at her.

*Good job,* Lewis said, and Anna said, *I hope she's okay.*

Bri and Renny were smiling, too. The atmosphere of wild jubilation had quieted, but a kind of dizzy glow remained.

"Let's go upstairs," Rob said, taking Kaitlyn's hand.

"Yes, I'd better change." Kaitlyn glanced down at the bathing suit and grinned wryly. "And I'm sure there are things to take care of—God, the police, I guess. We're going to have to explain all this somehow."

"I wanna get out of here before *that*," Bri said.

Kaitlyn looked behind her, held out her free hand to Gabriel. "Come on, you . . . *hero*. I want to tell you what I think of you."

"So do I," Rob said, golden eyes warm.

Gabriel looked at Kaitlyn's fingers intertwined with Rob's. He smiled, but Kaitlyn couldn't feel his happiness in the web anymore.

"I'm glad you have her back safe again," he said to Rob. He was saying two things with that, Kaitlyn realized.

Suddenly, some of the dizzy glow faded. "Please come up with us," she said to Gabriel, and he nodded, smiling politely, like a stranger.

# CHAPTER 16

"So you're not a psychic vampire anymore," Lewis said to Gabriel as they reached the dining room. "I mean, nobody is anymore, right? The Fellowship said if the crystal was destroyed, you'd be cured."

Kaitlyn realized that he was chattering deliberately, filling the silence, trying to help in the only way he could. Gabriel smiled at him, wanly grateful, but Kaitlyn could see the pain behind those gray eyes.

She herself knew that she should be going upstairs, but she couldn't seem to make herself leave. She had never imagined that a person could go from feeling so gloriously happy to so wretchedly miserable in such an appallingly short time.

Wretched, and frightened, and sick with pain. I'm being torn in two, she thought, standing in the sunlit dining room and holding Rob's hand even tighter. I'll never be whole again; I'll never be all right. Oh, God, *please,* please tell me what to do.

She pulled her hand away from Rob, because even her shields couldn't contain the pain. She didn't want him to know.

Anna slipped a jacket over her shoulders and gave Kaitlyn's hand a squeeze. Kaitlyn looked at her gratefully, unable to speak.

Rob was looking a bit lost. "Well—is anybody hurt?" he said, glancing around. "Kaitlyn—?"

"I'm fine. Gabriel's hand, though . . ."

Gabriel, who had just sat down, looked up sharply. "It's all right. Just a little burn." He had been pushing his sweater sleeve off his forearm, scratching under it absently, but now he pulled it down again.

"Let me see. No, I said, *let me see.*" Rob clamped Gabriel's left arm with an unbreakable grip.

"No, leave it alone. It's the other hand!" Gabriel's tone was almost as harsh as it had been in the old days, but Kaitlyn detected a note almost of panic underneath.

"But I feel something here. Stop fighting and hold still!" Rob's voice was equally annoyed. He wrestled the sleeve up by main force—and then stared.

Gabriel's pale forearm was covered with ghastly marks. Angry red cuts, their lips curling open and beginning to bleed again with the rough handling. Burns that were turning brown at the edges and still blistered in the middle. They ran all the way from wrist to elbow.

Kaitlyn felt giddy.

"What happened?" Rob said, with terrible quietness. "Who did this to you?" He lifted clear golden eyes to Gabriel's face, waiting.

"Nobody." Gabriel looked angry, but somehow relieved, too. "It just—happened. It happened when the crystal broke."

There was a silence, a heaviness in the web. Lewis frowned, Anna's lips pulled in at the corners. Bri and Renny had backed off, as if recognizing somehow this wasn't their business. Rob was looking at Gabriel hard.

Kaitlyn was trying to blink dancing spots away. She felt she should know what had happened to Gabriel. She should know, if she could only *think*. . . .

"Well, relax," Rob said finally, evenly. "I can make it stop hurting so much. Make it heal faster."

He put one hand on Gabriel's arm above the elbow and held Gabriel's palm with the other. Kaitlyn could see him feeling with his fingers for transfer points. Gabriel sat, uncharacteristically docile and obedient.

Rob's thumb pressed into Gabriel's palm and he shut his eyes. Through the web, Kaitlyn could feel what he was doing. Sending healing energy through the wounded limb, stimulating Gabriel's own energy to flow, as well. Golden sparks traveling down Gabriel's veins, golden mist enveloping the forearm. Kaitlyn felt warmth, and felt Gabriel relaxing as the pain eased, his muscles unclenching.

With relaxation, barriers go down. Kaitlyn knew that, and

she knew that Rob's healing brought him closer to people. In a minute, she knew that he was doing something else to Gabriel. Probing his mind, looking for something.

*Hey!* Gabriel tried to jerk his arm out of the steely grip, head lifting, face furious. But it was too late.

They stared at each other a long moment, gray eyes and gold locked as they always had been when the two of them did battle. Locked for endless, time-stretching seconds.

Then Rob's face changed and he settled back on his heels.

Gabriel held his hurt arm to his chest protectively, his own expression defensive and defiant.

"You did those to your own self," Rob said flatly, calmly. Still looking Gabriel in the eyes. "To . . . stay in contact with Kaitlyn." He said the words as if he weren't exactly sure of their meaning. "They were doing something to her and you had to talk to her over a long range. So you thought pain would help you call louder."

Gabriel said nothing, but Kaitlyn felt the truth of it. That was what he'd been concealing when he talked to her in the isolation tank. When he gave her his best memories. She'd felt fatigue and some kind of pain, but he'd shielded most of it from her.

"You used somebody's cigar and a piece of broken glass," Rob said, with growing confidence. "And then later you poked at the sores some more to keep awake."

Yes, Kaitlyn thought, feeling it with Rob in the web. She

could tell he didn't exactly understand what the situation was, but that he was sure about one thing.

"You love her, don't you?" he said to Gabriel.

Gabriel finally seemed able to break their locked stare. He looked away, at the carpet. His face was bleak.

"Yes," he said.

"More than anything," Rob persisted. "You'd crawl on your belly over broken glass for her. Easy."

"Yes, damn you," Gabriel said. "Happy now?"

Rob looked at Kaitlyn.

Kaitlyn's head was swimming, her body racked in so many different directions that she stood still. She couldn't seem to put a coherent thought together. But on top of everything else, holding her precariously in one piece, was the thought that she mustn't hurt Rob. She loved him too much to hurt him. And she knew that Gabriel's eyes on her were saying the same thing.

She now knew that it *was* possible to love two people at once—because you could love them in different ways. The love she felt for Rob now was a burning tenderness, a knowledge that he was the one who'd taught her it was *possible* to love, who had melted the ice of her heart. It was strong and gentle and steady, full of admiration and the intimacy of shared likes and dislikes. It was golden and warm like a summer afternoon.

And if it wasn't the passion and desperate depth of feeling she had for Gabriel, she never wanted Rob to know.

But as Rob looked at her, gazing with those clear eyes full

of light, she realized that her shields were in tatters around her. She had been awake for two days and in agony or terror for nearly as long. She didn't have anything *left* to shield with.

And she could see, she could feel, that he was seeing right inside her. Rob knew.

"Why didn't you tell me?" he asked her after a small eternity.

"I didn't—I didn't feel that way—until—so many things have happened . . ." Kaitlyn faltered. Of all things, she wanted to make Rob all right. Although now she saw that her love for him must have been changing for a long time, gradually, she didn't know how to explain that. "It's probably just—I'll get over it. In a little while . . ."

"Not that, you won't," Rob said. "Neither of you. I mean, I sure hope you don't." He sounded as incoherent as Kaitlyn felt, and he kept swallowing. But he went on doggedly, "Kait, I love you. You know I do. But this isn't something I can compete with." He stepped back. "I'm not blind. You two belong together."

He looked . . . distressed, Kaitlyn realized vaguely. Distressed, but not devastated. Not ruined for life. There was so much more to Rob.

And, as she watched, Anna moved up and put her hand on his back from behind. Kaitlyn looked at her over Rob's shoulder.

Anna smiled tremulously. Her dark eyes were wet but glowing somewhere down inside.

Suddenly a vast, rushing lightness filled Kaitlyn. As if a huge and heavy weight had been taken off her chest. She stared at Anna, and at the way Rob unconsciously was leaning back against Anna's arm. And the effervescent bubbles lifted her skyward.

*I just had a precognition,* she told Anna silently, a stream of unspoken love and joy. *You will be very happy. Your best friend says to go for it.*

Anna's face was bright, as if someone had set a candle behind it. *You're giving me permission?*

*I'm giving you an order!*

Lewis laughed out loud. Then he said, "Didn't somebody say something about cleaning up? And how about some food?"

Bri and Renny and Lydia seemed to recognize that as a signal. They followed him as he started for the kitchen. Anna tugged at Rob's arm, gently, to bring him, too.

Rob looked back, once.

*I'm glad,* he told Gabriel, and Kaitlyn could hear the truth in it. *I mean, it hurts, but I'm glad for you. Take care of her.*

Then he was gone.

Slowly, Kaitlyn turned to Gabriel.

It had occurred to her at the last minute that nobody had really asked him. Maybe, even if he loved her, he'd prefer that the feeling go away. Maybe he didn't want her now that everybody had had a hand in the procedure.

But Gabriel was looking at her now, and she could see his eyes.

She had seen those eyes dark with brooding anger and cold as ice, she'd seen his gaze veiled like a spiderweb and shattering like agate under pressure. But she'd never seen them as they were now. Full of wondering joy and disbelief, and an almost frightened awe.

Gabriel was trying to smile, but the expression kept breaking apart. He was looking at her as if he hadn't seen her for years and years of searching, and had just now walked into a room and come upon her unexpectedly. As if he wanted to look at every part of her, now that he could do it honestly.

Kaitlyn remembered the things he'd given her, the sun-flooded afternoons, and the cool healing ocean waves, and the music he'd written. He'd given her everything that was best in him, everything he was.

She wanted to give him the same back again.

*I don't know how you can love me.* The words came softly, as if he were thinking them to himself. *You've seen what I am.*

*That's why I do love you,* Kaitlyn told him. *I hope you'll still love me when you see what I am.*

"I know what you are, Kait. Everything beautiful and brave and gallant and . . ." He stopped as if his throat had closed. "Everything that makes me want to be better for you. That makes me sorry I'm such a stupid mess. . . ."

726

*You looked like a knight with the shard,* Kaitlyn said, moving toward him.

"Really?" He laughed shakily.

*My knight. And I never said thank you.*

She was almost touching him, now. Looking up into his eyes. What she could feel in him was something she'd only felt before when she gave him her life energy. Childlike, marveling joy. Trust and vulnerability. And such love . . .

Then she was in his arms and they weren't separate beings any longer. Their minds were together, sharing thoughts, sharing a happiness beyond thought. Sharing everything.

She never even knew whether he kissed her.


It seemed a very long time later, but the sunbeams falling across the dining room had hardly moved. Kaitlyn had her head on Gabriel's shoulder. She was so full of peace—peace and light and hope for everything. Even the nagging hole in the universe where LeShan had been was filled with light. She hoped that, somehow, he knew what had happened today and was satisfied.

"God make me worthy of you. Fast," Gabriel said. It was something like a command.

Kaitlyn smiled. His arms were tight around her, a feeling she never wanted to lose. But they were no longer outside time, and she could hear banging and shouting laughter from upstairs.

"I guess we'd better see what's going on," she said.

Very slowly, most reluctantly, he let her go, only keeping her hand in his. They walked around the corner to the stairs.

Lydia, though, was just coming down. Bri and Renny were behind her. They'd obviously been going through closets; each had a full cardboard box and at least one bag or suitcase.

"We don't know exactly what we'll need there," Lydia told Kaitlyn. Her green eyes looked out almost shyly from behind her heavy shock of dark hair.

"Go where?" Kaitlyn asked.

"You didn't hear? Oh, I guess not." Lydia headed for the front lab, with Bri and Renny following. Kaitlyn and Gabriel followed *them*.

"Joyce is going with Tamsin back to the Fellowship," Lydia said, dumping her box on a desk. "Ouch. That was heavy."

"Going back with Tamsin?"

"Yup," Bri said. "And we're going with her."

Kaitlyn stared. Renny was nodding, pushing up his glasses with an index finger.

"Tamsin says it'll help Joyce heal from the influence of the crystal," Lydia said. "And Bri and Renny, too. Oh, here they are."

Joyce and Tamsin came in from the kitchen. Joyce's hair was smoothed again, and her lips had stopped trembling. She seemed to be hanging on Tamsin's every word.

"We'd be glad to have you," Tamsin was saying. "And we

can help the children develop and control their powers. Even Lydia . . ."

"I don't have any powers," Lydia said.

Tamsin smiled at her. "You're of the old race. We'll see."

Kaitlyn noticed the sunlight change and realized that Rob was in the kitchen doorway. Lewis and Anna were right behind him, but Anna was closer.

Rob smiled at her, and it was a real smile, with his own gladness and optimism behind it. "Tamsin's been telling us about their place on the new island," he said. "They've got it pretty rough, but they're working on it. It's been hard with Mereniang gone, and now that LeShan is dead . . ." He shook his head, but his eyes were gleaming as if he saw a challenge.

"Rob! Are you telling me—do you want to go, too?"

"Well, I was thinking about it. They're going to need help."

"And leadership," Tamsin said, quietly, without sounding ashamed. "Innovation, new ideas—they don't come easily to us."

Rob nodded. "You help us and we help you. A fair exchange."

And the great task Rob's been looking for, Kaitlyn thought, somewhat giddy with the suddenness of it. Not saving the world, maybe, but fixing a little part of it.

She didn't know what to say. She was remembering Canada, the lush beauty of the rain forest, the open vastness of the sky. The wild blue ocean.

"Of course, the rest of you children can stay here," Joyce was saying. "Not at the Institute—that will be closed for good.

But I think I could arrange for you to have your scholarships after all. Mr. Zetes had the money put aside in a special account; he had to, for the lawyers."

Yes, that was the sensible thing to do. School and then college. Her father would want that. And Gabriel was a city boy. Kaitlyn's fingers tightened on his—and then she felt his thought.

*Well, we could just take a vacation, couldn't we?* he asked. His gray eyes were sparkling.

Happiness flooded Kaitlyn to her fingertips.

*We could—yes, we could,* she told Rob and Anna and Lewis. *We could make up the time at school next year. And meanwhile, it would be very educational. . . .*

*And we wouldn't break the web,* Rob said, and she could feel his joy, too. He and Gabriel were smiling at each other.

*Of course, we'll* have *to break it someday,* Lewis said quickly. *I mean, we can't go around this way forever.*

*Of course not,* Anna agreed solemnly, her owl eyes crinkling at the edges.

*But just for now . . .* Lewis said.

*Just for now,* they all agreed, together.

Talk was going on around them. Joyce was moving toward the front door, saying, "What's that?" Lydia was rummaging through her box.

"I forgot to show you. Look what I found!" she said to

Lewis. She was holding two things: an alarm clock shaped like a cow—and his camera.

"Hey, where did you get that? That's precious!" Lewis said, taking the cow.

"I know. I want you to show me what it does." Lydia smiled at him, her new shy smile, and Lewis beamed back. He reached out and squeezed her arm, just once.

"As soon as we get alone," he said wickedly, "I will."

"Kaitlyn! Rob!" Joyce was calling from the front door in a voice wavering between laughter and tears. "There's someone here to see you, and I don't think you should keep her waiting!"

They all went, Kaitlyn and Gabriel and Rob and Anna, with Lewis and Lydia following, and Tamsin bringing up the rear with Bri and Renny. When Kaitlyn got to the porch she stopped in astonishment.

"*Oh . . .*" was all she could say. Then she said, "Oh, *Marisol.*"

It was Marisol, thin and rather wobbly on her legs, supported on Tony's arm. She was pale, but her tumbled mahogany hair was the same as Kaitlyn remembered, and a smile was trembling on her full lips.

"I came to see the guy who healed me," she said. "And all of you."

"All of them were in it," Tony said proudly. He had a shirt on today, Kaitlyn noticed, and he looked as if someone had just willed him a million dollars.

Kaitlyn hugged Marisol, and then she had to stand back so Rob could do it. And then Lydia was coming forward, and Bri, looking as if they thought Marisol might hate them. But she smiled at them instead, and there were more hugs. Those who couldn't hug Marisol hugged one another.

And Joyce, with her aquamarine eyes on Marisol's face, looked as if healing had already begun.

"We brought you your kitten, too," Tony said to Anna.

"So now everybody's here," Anna said, pressing the kitten to her cheek, then to Rob's.

"Hey, yeah—everybody's here! Wait a minute!" Lewis was running. He was back in a moment. "Everybody, scrunch together by the door. Some of you get down. The rest lean in! Get closer!"

*I think we're already about as close as we can get,* Gabriel said, and Kaitlyn was surrounded by silent laughter.

"That's it! Hold that smile!" Lewis shouted, and snapped their picture.

AND COMING SOON,
THE DRAMATIC CONCLUSION TO
THE NIGHT WORLD SERIES
BY L.J. SMITH

\* \* \*

# STRANGE FATE

The girl was Kierlan's soulmate. There was no doubt of that now, just as there'd been no doubt since they were children.

Kierlan should have, by everything he knew of the Night World laws, been comforted by this. He should have felt unassailable.

Instead, he felt very assailable indeed.

But *why?* They'd woven the eternal, unbreakable thread between them. He'd kissed her, and it was a kiss he was still dizzy from. Sarah had melted in his arms. And he'd *seen* the silver cord.

They were soulmates. Even if they were parted, the cord would connect them. Nothing could sever that cord . . .

. . . except Sarah herself.

Kierlan had a chill of premonition. Maybe it was best to impress upon Sarah, and especially upon her subconscious, that once the cord was woven, she had sealed her fate. Sarah's kiss and what it had called forth had determined her destiny.

But first he needed to get Mal, his soul's brother, out of the way.

He glanced out Sarah's window, the one that looked down on the front lawn. Mal was gazing down at Sarah, who lay on her still unmade bed, as if the sight of her had turned him to stone. Maybe it had. Who knew what Mal had done to keep himself from coveting Sarah?

Kierlan was probably the only person in the world who knew that Mal loved her. And Mal was no poacher. From the beginning Mal had acknowledged that Kierlan had a prior claim, and given his solemn word not to infringe on that. He'd given his word that Sarah would be Kierlan's and that he would never interfere.

Until recently only one person had known that Mal had broken his word. Had lied.

And that person wasn't Mal. It was Kierlan.

Kierlan had used his powers, ruthlessly and without concern for Mal's mental well-being, to cut through Mal's elaborate defenses and show him the truth.

Not that Kierlan didn't see the reasons for Mal's treachery. After all, if there were no reasons to love Sarah, then Kierlan wouldn't have loved her since he had met her; although, at six, he hadn't really known it was love. He'd simply known that the fragile fairy-child with the windblown hair was his, sworn his and sealed his with their kiss shared under the oleander bush. Kierlan hadn't understood his powers then, but he had known that Sarah, with her heart-shaped face and aquamarine eyes, was part of him.

Bringing himself to the present with a jolt, Kierlan glanced out the window again. "You'd better get your car," he said. "We're going to have to get her and all her stuff out of here fast."

"You mean kidnap her? Where?"

"Circle Daybreak, of course. Hurry up."

But Mal, who usually took orders immediately, stared at him with those cloud-gray eyes. The chiseled features under his shock of dark hair expressed no emotion. "What about her stepfamily?"

Kierlan swore. "I'll send them a freaking telegram!"

"No, I mean what if somebody sees us taking her, and—"

"You worry too much. And that *wasn't* a suggestion!" Kierlan didn't like using the whiplash voice on Mal. But he had to get him away from Sarah before she woke.

Mal stood absolutely still for just a moment, then saluted Kierlan and departed silently.

Alone with Sarah at last, Kierlan sat by her on the bed and gently called her name. Her lashes were fluttering; she was deep in a nightmare-dream.

How did Mal do it? Mal always said that he just spoke to her softly. But Kierlan didn't have either the dispassionate voice or the time; he'd used a lot of Power already, and he knew how he wanted to use the rest of it.

There was no choice then but to control her mind directly.

He slipped in unnoticed, leaving her the privacy of her dreams, and told her to wake up. *Wake up, Sarah. Now.*

*Kierlan?* Sarah blinked and opened her eyes.

"It's all right," he said immediately, "you're safe." But Sarah was looking around the room in bewilderment.

"I've never dreamed *this* before," she said. "I mean, me being in my room again while I was still in the middle of the other dream."

"You're not dreaming."

The problem was that she was. He could tell that Sarah's mind was still in REM sleep, her breathing rapid and irregular, and her eyelashes quivering every few moments as if she were trying to focus on something in the distance and couldn't.

One of the secrets of Kierlan's success was his ability to adapt. "All right, you *are* dreaming," he said, cupping a hand around Sarah's chin to turn her to face him. "You're dreaming about *me*."

Sarah's blush, which came up from her collarbones and never failed to arouse Kierlan's wonder, was just as adorable when she was asleep as awake.

"Again?" she faltered. "I used to dream about you all the time, until . . . until the new dreams came."

Kierlan's heart melted. He could feel, amazingly, his own cheeks heat with blood. He hadn't thought there was anything that could make him blush, not anymore.

"You dreamed about me?"

"Oh, *all* the time."

It occurred to Kierlan that what he was doing was probably

not quite fair. In fact, it was completely and distinctly unfair. In this dreamlike state Sarah was at his mercy; she would tell him the absolute truth about anything.

It was something he definitely had to take advantage of.

"Who do you love?" he whispered, taking her chin in his fingers and using his most intense gaze to hold those aquamarine eyes with the trembling, starry black lashes.

Sarah's face went even softer, as if she could see glorious things behind Kierlan's tawny eyes, as if she could see inside him and everything that she saw made her want to melt in his arms.

"Who do you love, Mal or me?" he repeated.

And the answer came back instantly, infuriatingly. "Both."

Kierlan's breath came out in a little explosion. "Look at this. See this?" He had to tip her head down to look at the silver cord that was taut between them. "Do you know what that means? It means that we're soulmates. It means I'm yours and you're mine. Mal hasn't got anything to do with it. I'm your other half. You're sworn mine, sealed mine, *bound* mine."

The effect was not what he'd anticipated. Sarah was looking helplessly down, but then she seemed to forget the silver cord, and her gaze wandered out the window. Looking for what? Mal?

Frustrated, almost frantic, Kierlan took Sarah by the shoulders. "You *have* to love me. You *have* to."

And then he did something he knew he should be ashamed of.

He kissed her.

Helpless as she was, dreaming as she was, he kissed her.

And it was warm and sweet and long, and Sarah didn't wake. She wound her arms around his neck and cuddled to him, little shivers going through her. In Kierlan's mind, in Kierlan's heart, in Kierlan's soul, there was total anarchy, but overall there was only the thought of Sarah. His Sarah, sealed and bound to him forever.

Whatever might happen, whatever he might have to do, Kierlan had to keep Sarah.

I have no conscience or morality about this, he thought, holding Sarah, cradling her so that her soft, fine, freshly washed hair was against his cheek. He was thinking terrible things. Sarah had changed in the last few years. Her face was still waifish, her body still fragile, but there were changes. New curves under her simple T-shirts. Now, with her quiescent and seemingly happy, he was tempted to go farther—just a little. . . .

No! Sarah had given him a kiss from her heart, even if he'd had to exercise all his powers of seduction to get it. The waking Sarah would never allow . . . she would beat him away . . . she would never speak to him, if he tried something like that. And even if *she* never found out, Kierlan would always imagine the beating hands, the shrieking. Even though they were soulmates, Sarah wasn't ready to give him more.

But I still have no conscience, he told himself defiantly. I'm restraining myself for Sarah's sake, and that's all.

The thought of beating, thrashing hands and shrieking brought another scene to his mind, however. It made him remember vividly the very first time that Sarah had kissed him.

And suddenly Kierlan knew how to make Sarah his forever, without the possibility of interference by Mal, however tall and handsome and perfect Mal might be.

"Sarah?"

"Yes?" She was still asleep, with her great jewel-like eyes wide open in that gamine face.

"Sarah, can you remember when we first met? Do you remember that first day?"

Sarah's features changed. Her eyelids went heavy, half-closed in bliss. Her mouth went so soft with adoration that Kierlan had to clench his fists to keep from stealing another kiss. Her whole face—glowed.

"I want to take you back to that day," Kierlan whispered. "I want you to dream about that."

He knew he was being hideously cruel and unfair. Those kisses had been won at a heavy, heavy cost. But just now he needed Sarah to remember how she'd felt about him before Mal had come into the picture. Kierlan needed her to remember how they had already been sworn together, so young.

"Go back," Kierlan was whispering now, hypnotically. "I'll go back with you. We'll share our thoughts, our feelings. Go back to the first day. . . ."

Unconsciously, Kierlan was swaying, and Sarah was swaying with him. Grasped in his arms, her mind dissolving in with his mind, Sarah was going back, and he was following.

## ABOUT THE AUTHOR

L.J. Smith is the *New York Times* bestselling author of *The Vampire Diaries* and has written more than twenty-five books for young adults. She lives in the Bay Area of California, where she enjoys reading, hiking, traveling, and communing with her cat Suzie. Her favorite place is a cabin in Point Reyes National Seashore. Come visit her at www.ljanesmith.net, where she has lots of free stories for downloading.

The Old Powers are rising.
The apocalypse is drawing near.

The new Night People are determined to
destroy the human world.

But four children have been born, four
Wild Powers who can stop the darkness. . . .

# THE NIGHT WORLD...
Love has never been so dangerous.

Spellbinding. Enchanting. Captivating.

From Simon Pulse
Published by Simon & Schuster

# check your PULSE

Simon & Schuster's **Check Your Pulse** e-newsletter delivers current updates on the hottest titles, exciting sweepstakes, and exclusive content from your favorite authors.

Visit **TEEN.SimonandSchuster.com** to sign up, post your thoughts, and find out what every avid reader is talking about!